NIAGARA

By Robert Lewis Taylor

Vessel of Wrath: The Life and Times of Carry Nation
Two Roads to Guadalupé
A Journey to Matecumbe
The Travels of Jaimie McPheeters
Center Ring
The Bright Sands
Winston Churchill
Professor Fordorski
The Running Pianist
W. C. Fields: His Follies and Fortunes
Doctor, Lawyer, Merchant, Chief
Adrift in a Boneyard
A Roaring in the Wind

NIAGARA

by
Robert Lewis Taylor

m

F

9/80

G. P. Putnam's Sons
New York

Library of Congress Cataloging in Publication Data

Taylor, Robert Lewis.
  Niagara.

  1. Niagara Co., N.Y.—History—Fiction. I. Title.
PZ3.T21783Ni 1980   [PS3539.A9654]   813'.5'4   79-21620
ISBN 0-399-12432-2

Printed in the United States of America

Second Impression

NIAGARA

Chapter I

"Red Gill—any of ye, up the house! Turn out like a true Scot, though Canada born. A bad thing's happened tonight. Move quick, man!"

His horse was lathered, for he'd pounded the wet, faint river road in a manner not safe for man or beast. A torch of the kind today known as a burglar's lantern—that is, it shone forward, the other shutters clanged down—hung at his pommel, and a white tow sack dangled from the Indian-mount side to complete the burden.

"I creen help, and if a musket's needed to rouse this pile of logs and tin, I'll—"

There was the sound of a window opening, and a male voice bawled, "So it's muskets ye want? We can match ten of that. No stranger bristles my house at three in the morning and daffs to tell the tale."

"It's Rattlesnake Charley, Red, and it's many a potion I've mixed for you and the bairns . . . Bridget's gone over; that's the long and short of it."

A light now shone in the door, and there were noises of people getting up and throwing on rough shirts and other coverings.

"So it's come to that, has it? A man of fifty and a lass of seventeen—though a limmer known."

The owner framed in the doorway seemed as broad as a barn, rough-countenanced, with a wild shock of red-gray hair. He was dressed in the rags of his calling—a river rat, or wharf rat. A slattern with long greasy hair—coal black—stood behind him, huddling a blanket over her shoulders, and others began to appear.

"Step in, Charley, and leave your snake-bag behind, whatever it holds. It won't be said we've turned away a friend in trouble."

She spoke without the Scottish accent, having come like so many from farms below to settle in these fertile river lands.

"Friend, is it?" muttered Gill, giving way. "I have no friends that pluck a poor lass from the cradle then comes to rest on my doorstep. Where'd she plunge, and what pushed her to it?"

"It was none of my doing, Red, and I'll put my hand in the fire for it. She was cook to me only, though busked by the snakes, and she slept in the shed, on husks. Snake people canna be shunned off so easy. On the Holy Bible, God bless—"

"Ye can drop the Scots, Charley. Scottish ye may be, or not, but your tongue has been soopled these twenty years."

"I'll speak Scots in the house of Red Gill, and why not? Calm yourself, man!"

"*Me* fashed! . . . Went over where?"

The visitor appeared slightly uneasy for the first time.

"Well, since you're so precious about detail, we had a bit of a tiff—over 'crepitalculum'—a good word and De Witt Clinton's own. Then she left in the skiff and got all tumbled in the current. It's no fit there for aught but river rats."

"Did ye follow?"

"That I did, and bellowed like a clipped bull, but she dropped an oar and it spun like a whirligig, out of reach."

"Then what struck ye from catching her up?"

"*Me*, with two fresh bites last week, one on a thumb? And the other, well, there's lady-folk present—"

Gill said, "Humph," or something like, and then, "There's nought we can do till dawn." Suddenly he caught the visitor by the collar. "I must tell ye, ye snake-gatherin' humberg, that I believe no more than half your story." Then he looked foxy and keen. "The moon was up, Charlie; which channel did the bairn's boat take—the Horseshoe or the American?"

"Why, it comes to me that I was noways aware of channels, trying to scull with a bitten hand, but now you mention it, she headed toward Canada—"

"At dawn," said Gill, his face full of suspicion, "the boys and me will search the Three Sisters and Goat Island and all the willow

10

clumps below. But only because you may have saved a wee toddler of mine, which I very much doubt indeed. Snake oil! If it's the Canadian side, she's dead, and four days to pass before the body rises to view in Whirlpool. Hear it down there? Many a pretty man, and woman and child, have laid on the bottom, waiting to rise up, and then Up." He pointed to the sky.

By now Charley was blubbering, and said again, "By the Good Book, I swear—"

"I hope so," said Gill, releasing him. "I'd not stand in your shoes tonight. The *town* will hope so. Now mount your rump-sprung nag and gang off. There's a ripe smell here; you and me must twine—"

"Now hold on, Red Gill," said the woman. "We'll not turn away a known man without coffee and a rest. Besides, the lightnin's squirting, and another drencher's due, if you ask my advice, or don't ask it."

"I can get her with grapple and rope," grumbled Gill, giving in further, with reluctance. "And me with two boys gone by so doing. A hundred and ninety-nine in Whirlpool altogether." His face seemed triumphant regardless of the sons.

Faintly, in the lull, from four miles upriver, came the muted roar of the Falls, 23,000,000 gallons of green-and-silver water plunging over every hour in the day and night, gushing its way from Lake Erie to Lake Ontario, the greatest beckoning lure in the world, a hypnotic and inexplicable siren to both tourists and the strange people who lived alongside, flirting with its fatal draw every day of their lives. And none could come close to tell you why.

Chapter II

On the day of this suicide (as I learned later) I'd enjoyed the
punctual fracas with my uncle, James Gordon Bennett, proprietor of
the squalling New York *Herald*. He was a peppery little man, whose
life and career seemed devoted to stirring up rows. Now seated, flush
of face, wiry gray hair on end, behind a stingy desk cluttered with
"stories" he hoped would be libelous (he had twenty-three suits
outstanding at the moment)—he was achoke with rage that a
"streepling" of twenty should have been planted on his staff, and
himself powerless except to rant and scream. (At this time, my father
secretly owned a slice of *Herald* stock and had, in effect, put the
bombastic Scot in business.)

(It's odd how Scotsmen seem to begin this book while basically
having little to do with it.)

My graduation from college had been accomplished without
honors (and with some feeble attempts at recovery for damage and
debts) and my father savored the prospect of Bennett and me locked
in a common cage, so to speak. It was the great era of elaborate
practical jokes, there being no suitable outlet for high spirits among
the gentry. It was my father who helped contrive the massive plan to
saw off Manhattan Island (the lower end was "sinking"), tow it out

to sea and turn it around. The work is now history, though not greatly stressed. Several 300-foot saws were actually made, surveyors and swarms of workmen hired (the mayor being drunk), and then, when the great day came, the entrepreneurs failed to show up. They were, indeed, on an ocean steamer headed for Europe, where they stayed for several months, hoping, one assumes, for further inspiration. They needn't have worried; Barnum would step in with other diversions, and they could sit back and watch. Any man, who with his American Museum could tack up a sign saying "This way to the EGRESS," steering suckers to the street, where they indignantly paid 25 cents to get back in—that man, I say, defies competition in mischief.

"Well, I've found the right spot for ye, laddie. It happens to be a place I dislike very much." ·

"I'm glad of that, Uncle James," I replied. "You're a good and generous man, as everybody knows."

He was not, properly speaking, my uncle, but I enjoyed using the name he despised, as being, he thought, English. He greatly preferred the middle name "Gordon," for he was proud of his Scottish background, his tutelage in Romanism at Aberdeen, his youthful employment as teacher, his lectures on political economy (in Scottish Canada) about which he knew nothing. The fact that he liked Gordon was the reason acquaintances called him James.

James Gordon Bennett was at this time the most detested man in New York, and had twice been thrashed in the streets for personal attacks in his fast-growing *Herald*. It was a paper that began in a cellar (where it belonged) on a loan of $500. On the masthead of his scandal rag was emblazoned the admirable slogan: "We aim not to instruct but to startle." In this he was so successful that all other journals in town insulted him daily, in language commonly reserved for the saloon.

But it must not be said that he hadn't a pious side. In a windy first-page piece he said, "We will back no candidate, no party, no bloc; we will yield to no pressures, but will strive for decency, honesty, independence, and the welfare of people as a whole." So saying (typically), he then joined Tammany Hall and Boss Tweed.

The paper sold for a penny, and was worth a little less.

Bennett's arrival with the *Herald* followed a resounding series of flops, in Scotland, Canada, Philadelphia, Washington and elsewhere. But he had the drive of a deranged gorilla and opportunism not likely to rise again soon. The *Herald* postdated his New York *Globe,* into which he stepped (leaped) when the owner was shot down in a duel. Bennett and his all-embracing hates managed to kill the paper without delay.

People generally enjoy reading libel about their neighbors and the *Herald* at last was prospering on its venom. It had ascended from the cellar, where the editor's desk was two planks laid across chairs, and so we sat tête-à-tête, the proprietor eyeing me with distaste, myself amused though facially sober.

"The spot I have in mind is Niagara Falls, a damp, unwholesome place [not true], and where, by chance, I wedded an Irish lady of noble aspects. And it was from there," he cried, both his anger and himself rising, "that I dispatched an eloquent bridal euology, only to have a New York paper describe it as 'an astoundingly vulgar description of her virtues!'"

"Was that the time you were horsewhipped on Broadway after the argument?" I inquired.

"It was not, for your impertinence, and *that* snarl is by no means mended. The people of this city canna bear to hear the truth, and it was the truth I wrote about Mr. Park Benjamin, so-called editor, and supporter of brothels, gaming dens and hangouts for thieves." (None of these last was true, either.)

"He wrote a front-page editorial about you, Uncle James—"

"GORDON!"

"—but I've forgotten how it went."

"The hound had the brazen gall to call me 'an obscure foreign vagabond, a pestilential scoundrel, an ass, rogue, habitual liar, loathsome and leprous slanderer and libelist.' Now what do you think of *that?*"

"Aside from the content, which may be strong, it seems well composed. I—"

He turned a bright purple. "Oh ye do, do ye, ye supercargo whelp? He'll choke a dozen times on every word he wrote, and atop that, I'll see him ridden out of New York on a rail!

"As for you, the fevers of Niagara should clear your tongue and improve your manners, if you survive. Draw on the treasurer—no more than subsistence—and be gone by tomorrow."

I said, "I don't want to risk annoying you, Uncle James, for your calm has become a legend. But is there anything particular I might *do* up there? I'm a fair swimmer, but I doubt I could make my way *up* the—"

"*Do*, you blithering idiot! Can ye tell me you don't read the papers?"

"Only the *Herald*," I said meekly.

"Well, for reasons I can't fathom, Niagara's the chief tourist place in the world. Don't ask me why. But I can add this for a mind that appears to totter at age twenty—there's said to be 150 resort hotels clustered in that swamp" —here he looked cunning. "And who, ask you, occupies these of the summers? *Southerners* in the main. I hear their blood's too frail for heat, and so they go cool beside the tumbling of the waters."

"I know," I said, with a look of inspiration, "I can inquire why they went. That's *it!* Why do they like Niagara Falls? If that isn't news, I'm—"

"I believe you're the dunderheadedest fool I ever met. What you *will* do is this, if indeed you're able to find the hotels. Dig out their corruptions, raise the slime kept secret. I can see it well—innocent chambermaids, abortions, slaves whipped, boozling, gambling, julep-drinking, dancings, illicit fornications by the wives, as like as not. I want scandals to close that place and rid the North of a nest of traitors. If Southerners connive with Canada, find it out. Don't hesitate to broach them in the streets. Duel—you'd look grand with an extra hole or two."

"But, Uncle James," I said, pointing to his desk, "your sympathies in these spats have been with the *slave* states." I pointed to a half-finished cartoon of one Abraham Lincoln, a political aspirant (and abolitionist) from the West. It was both grotesque and insulting, making him look like an ape.

"I keep an open mind about all matters—"

I said, "I thought it very fair of you, when you went over to Mr. Tweed, maligned as he was and all."

(I couldn't help it, and, as I'd imagined, it won me an immediate exit, very nearly by force.)

Mr. Bennett was hardly a fool, unpopular or not, and I hope I haven't presented him so. He was derided on so many grounds that people marveled at his success. His slight Scottish accent, using occasional "Scots" words, or imperfect English, wore off in time, but not in the minds of his enemies, who mocked him in a kind of bastardese.

If a newspaper's function is to sell papers and make money, he was a genius. Moreover, his innovations in the field changed journalistic forms. He was the first to telegraph news; he had the first financial column; he sent out the first foreign correspondents; he launched massive crusades; he printed news—real news, aside from scandal— that other papers shied off from. His *Herald,* in short, came to bristle with excitement and, to be sure, vulgarity. But it changed the profession, and, probably for the better. Still, it was a hopeless task for me, as with so many others, not to rag him when convenient.

And sure enough, when I went to the treasurer, my traveling money was subsistence, and subsistence only. It made little difference; I was prepared for a rough journey, and I had, besides, funds of my own (as Uncle James knew and used to his advantage).

The fact that I lived in a (small) room in the Fifth Avenue Hotel played on his nerves, and it was useless to point out that I could easily have stayed in my parents' "fine home" (as one paper called it) on Washington Square.

New York then lay largely below Fourteenth Street, and it was pleasant on weekends to take a horse-cab up the unpaved roads to visit the fertile farms in what would become the sixties and seventies. Some time before, the Aldermen had voted to call the north-and-south streets "avenues" and the ones that crossed them "streets."

After a quick conference with my parents, I worked out the best (the most interesting) route to Niagara—by New York Central Railway to Albany, thence by the Erie Canal to Lockport, and the last leg by stage.

I'd never been in the Central's station, which looked like a barn in need of repairs. The sight of dozens of Irish families, squatting on their belongings, headed north to seek work and avoid the regular New York plagues, slightly dashed my spirits. At this time, New York's immigrant Irish appeared to have declared war on the world.

And any Irish drunk who managed to start a riot—over anything: the polluted wells, yellow fever, slums, low wages—was promptly declared a hero and carried on people's shoulders. If they spotted and lynched a Negro as they progressed, they'd had a grand day. (They ignorantly blamed Negroes for unrest developing in the South.) I once heard my father say later, in the era of draft riots, that "more Negroes have been lynched in New York, by low-grade Irish, than in all the South together."

Here at the depot they were trying to start a quarrel, but collections of Irish were heavily policed for years, and nothing much developed but curses and catcalls. One bruiser knocked his wife down and another kicked a child sprawling, but this was considered routine.

Nevertheless, a man carrying a pig in one hand and a shillelaghlike stick in the other lurched up and said, trying to seize my lapel, "See here, hold my pig awhile. I'm tired and have business in that pub yonder." He pointed across the street. "Don't balk, for it's Terry McGurn you're facing." He was dressed in the costume they affected:

16

green corduroy knickers, a short jacket and a high green cap that tilted saucily over one eye.

The day had been warm, the place stank to heaven, as all of New York did, and I replied rudely, "Hold your own pig, and as to the pub it would be the better without you."

"So that's your toon, is it, you with the fancy gripsacks? See here" —and I could smell his horrible breath—"you prepared to die?"

"Not at your hands," I said, amazed at my boldness. But I'd been a fair athlete in college and stood perhaps two inches over this symbol of what people then took to be the chief problem of New York.

But I was relieved to hear the familiar police, or "copper" (for the copper buttons they wore): "Here now, move along, move along. We'll have no trouble."

My antagonist put his pig down, tucked the shillelagh under an arm, spat on one hand and smacked the two hands together.

"All right, then. Since ye've backed off from a fight" (I hadn't), "I'm placing a curse on ye. From this day forward come high winds, rains and floods, explosions, earthquakes or storms at sea, you'll wear Terry McGurn's curse. It's the fourth I've placed today, and this is the worst of the lot. God help ye"—he made a gesture—"for you're that near the end of your tether."

I watched him walk, or wobble, away; then I entered a car of the best class they had. (The worst, for people like my friend, were little better than cattle cars, and indeed were half filled with pigs, fowl and the like.) From front to caboose, the train was black with soot, inside and out, and the straw seats were so worn that broken springs stuck up here and there, presenting a strong chance of punctures.

We were scheduled to leave in late evening, ride overnight and arrive in Albany at eight in the morning, meaning some time or other. It was most infernally hot, waiting; and after two hours, word came down, via a combination conductor, porter and hawker of sandwiches and tea (to kill New York's water taste) that "Old 77 dropped her boiler, and we're a-waiting for a run-in."

I looked stricken and asked that my regards be conveyed to Commodore Vanderbilt. But I was told he hadn't come aboard yet; the conductor would let me know. His impudence being refreshing, I bought a "lettuce-and-bean" sandwich from him—fifteen cents— then slid it under an empty seat. I'd paid $3.45 earlier for my passage; and the Fifth Avenue Hotel had prepared me food and drinkable water.

Shortly after nine, a grinding wrench started the train (one of New York Central's worst), but it stopped pretty promptly.

The conductor had taken a liking to me, or perhaps to my leather grips, for he came back to tell me the engineer had spent the entire day in a pub and that this—the breaking of a coupling—was the way most trips started.

"He's as bad as ever I seen him—supported by the fireman, and him little better. I'd be shook up and surprised if they didn't jump a curve and kill every man jack on this train."

I'd begun to wish I'd taken the Hudson River steamer, but I gritted my teeth, and in an hour or so we began to roll, more slowly. I had no seatmate, but a handsomely dressed man stopped by to inquire if I'd care to "while away some time playing three-card monte." Despite the clothes, his face had a sharp look, though not of high intelligence, and I replied that any spare change I had I planned to throw in the Harlem River.

Some time later I heard that he'd sat down beside a vacuous-appearing rustic (the man literally had straws sticking in his hair and a gunnysack for luggage) and talked him into playing (for fun) not three-card monte, by which the gambler made his living, but a harmless game of two-handed whist. The farmer was allowed to win nearly twenty dollars in a few minutes and then, the cards being sanded, the tide turned and he wound up losing $70, or, as he claimed, all he had. "I don't know what I and Mother'll do for seed," he said, almost crying. "Times are that hard; we're scraped to the bone, honed down like a rusted-out ax."

There being angry mutterings nearby, the gambler took his name and address and promised to send him a check at planting time. All agreed that this seemed fair, and two or three treated each other from bottles; and when the gambler came to check up, back in his car, he was missing a gold hunter-watch, his wallet, a diamond stickpin and two black-pearl shirt studs—about $1500 worth altogether. He came flying back in a rage, but the farmer had got off at a way stop.

Small-time swindlers roamed these trains in shoals, and the Hudson River boats as well. Their game of the moment was three-card monte, which resembles the three-shells-find-the-peanut game, and most made a tolerable living, with setbacks such as I've described. Once in a while a better crook came along and cleaned them out. Now I'd never suggest that these railroad dandies were in a class with three magnates yet to tangle—Vanderbilt, Jay Gould and Jim Fisk, who later were thieves on a grander scale. At one point, for example, when Vanderbilt was trying to corner Erie, Fisk and Gould were in a basement, with a handpress they'd bought, and were running off Erie stock like confetti. Vanderbilt lost seven million dollars in fifteen minutes, and the Stock Exchange was thrown into chaos. It was Vanderbilt, a former truck-garden hawker from Staten

Island, who once said, "The hell with the law! I got the power, ain't I?"

Fisk had made his start toward millions as a dishonest circus barker, and his end came (in a plush hotel) at the bark of a pistol held by one of his rivals for the monopoly of a tart. These malignancies, with the descendants of the one-time German butcher boy, John Jacob Astor, whose specialty was cheating the federal and municipal governments, formed the nucleus of what would become New York's *Social Register*, a book in which my father declined to be listed, saying it should be called, instead, *The Money-Changers' Gazette*.

In any event, while Vanderbilt's travesty of a train bumped and grumbled toward Albany, I took my bags from the overhead shelf and put them under my feet. Then, knowing my money was safe in my belt, I had a surprisingly good night's sleep.

Chapter III

We arrived in Albany at noon, having suffered thirteen break-downs altogether. The figure was supplied by the conductor, with a certain satisfaction, for he said it fell short of the record twenty-three but was "respectable" nevertheless. I, of course, was unable to count those that happened when I was asleep. I was dimly conscious that we'd hit a cow and that a free-for-all had erupted in the cattle car, with a trifling fire that stopped the train until the hay could be damped.

In Albany, looking about, one could see no special points of beauty, unless the square, forbidding public buildings could be praised. I was fortunate to engage passage on an Erie Canal "packet boat," just as it was leaving—a single barge drawn by three horses. I paid more than ten dollars for the ride to Lockport, but when I observed that the sum seemed excessive, the driver merely squinted and said it included "the finest fodder a man can get twixt here and Frisker, regular gourmey dining; swaller my word to start off on."

Speed limit on the Canal was six miles an hour, but they might have omitted this. When it suited him, our driver pulled up to chat with acquaintances, who seemed to be everybody on both banks. We had aboard perhaps fifteen passengers, including a youngish woman of caste, and as the driver talked, and the horses stumbled along, we made representations that resulted in a single "Giddyap!" It had no effect. The horses ambled on at the same leisurely pace, not having much to look forward to, as I saw it, trying to be fair. A handful of oats at the end of a trip does not really class as a fiesta.

The Canal company ran two species of boats in this period—"line" boats that hauled mostly freight (and were cheaper), and packet boats of the kind on which I found myself trapped. These latter were curiosities, being nearly sixty feet long and having a poor excuse of cabins, fore and aft and very low, where both men and women slept. These were loosely divided by a curtain and along the boat's sides were benches that made up into cots that had about the same degree of comfort as an India bed of spikes. Our female bore it all with a kind of bright, cheery fortitude, until we reached the worst nuisance of Erie travel.

Any number of ramshackle bridges crossed the Canal, of course, and the boats, without exception, cleared them by a few inches at the most. It was the driver's job to sing out "Low bridge ahead!" to alert those persons standing. Well, our driver may have done his duty here, though I, for one, failed to hear him, and the consequences were that both the lady and I were knocked flat. Neither of us was badly hurt, but when she arose, her face was scarlet. She walked forward to say, "You there—driver; what was your name?"

"Giddings, ma'am. Otis P. Giddings."

She said, "In England, we call the Queen 'ma'am'—"

"Why, this ain't England, leastways unless we've got off the course." He held one hand to his eyes and squinted back and forth. "No, by jings, I was right. That there chimbley"—he pointed—"belongs to Murphy's Tavern. We're still on the Erie, ma'am, and praise God for it!"

"You've just caused this young man and me to be rudely knocked down. The Packet literature says it's your duty to protect us by calling out every bridge—"

"Why, I hollered as loud as—as loud as church bells, ma'am. I can get affadavits if it comes to court."

"From whom?"

"Not from *these* passengers," I said, stepping up beside her. "They're fed up in general. I'm told that a woman was recently killed, bowled over and her head crushed against a gunwhale. But perhaps you misunderstood. Another person knocked down, through your fault, and you'll be dumped in the water—by me."

My shoulders were bruised, and I shared our common annoyances. My manners had gone to pieces twice in twenty-four hours and had, possibly, sunk below those of the immigrant Irish. I was appalled but stood resolute.

21

The man looked at me keenly for several seconds, as if weighing the situation. Then he slapped one knee and cried, "Now I call that fair. Nothing could be squarer—packet boat, steamer, wheelbarrer or balloon."

And then, to my embarrassment, he took a course that the tiff had made us special friends—now clapping me on the shoulder, again fetching a cushion for the rock-hard benches, offering me a filthy bottle (which I refused), confiding, "To be candid and frank, I prefer dealing with gentry; they're that fair." It was evident, as his monkeyshines advanced, that he regarded him and me to be in a single class, elevated from that of the others.

All this derived, I found, from a brand of humor native to the place, but I could easily have done without it. Also, for the next six or seven bridges, he made a point of overdoing things, wrapping his harness around a cleat and walking back and forth with a cardboard megaphone and yelling his lungs out. It was almost, not quite, as bad as his negligence.

The Canal, from the start of our journey, was busy in curious ways. I've forgotten how many locks—hydraulic lifting and lowering of water to match the various levels—we patiently waited out, but there was enlivenment to amuse us. Several private boats were fitted out as circuses, natural history museums and other cultural amenities. And a number of these had remained rooted at especially slow "basins." There were two or three library boats as well, the principal one being the Encyclopedia of Albany.

The system was the most casual I'd run across to date. The borrower was never asked to pay on the spot but was instructed to settle his account when the book was turned in—at offices along the way. Most works were religious or poetic. I had a try at both, but the religion was so fierce that I despaired of getting to Heaven and tossed that book aside.

The poetry all appeared to start with "Whither," and since I never found where the object was headed, I dropped that, too. These last were written largely by women: "Whither, yes whither, O crane in thy flight," etc. I worked hard on this number, but the crane could have wound up in Greenland for all I knew. I don't believe it wound up anywhere except in a maze of metaphors and other tortured figures.

Traffic was brisk, going both directions, and set-tos were frequent. Two locks were so narrow we had to get out and disassemble gunwhales and boards to make it. While the Canal was finished in theory, work still progressed to widen it (it was forty feet wide at present) and deepen it—by the same sort of Irish who'd built it from

22

the start. Their exertions were obstreperous, as in New York, and on two occasions, at least, the state militia was summoned to quiet them. One militiaman was killed by a thrown rock, and three others were injured; and the Irish expressed themselves as satisfied, briefly.

Things might have moved more smoothly without whiskey. Believing it prodded the Irish to work, contractors bought whiskey amazingly cheap—$4.50 by the barrel—and ladled it out on demand. We saw several work crews, red of face, stentorian of voice, waddling in the muck with pick and shovel. Despite the privations of their dirt-floor barracks, they seemed immune, someone said, to the agues and fevers of those swampy regions (that soon would be drained). Here and there among the throngs passed foremen recognizable by the absurd high hats they affected.

The Erie was costly and built by New York State, which had merry rows over the taxes laid on for payment. Without exception, the most ridiculous was suggested, and finally backed, by a Mr. Joseph Ellicott, married, and tumultuously so. He wanted a stiffish tax slapped on all bachelors in the state. But he was hooted down, by bachelors in the Assembly, and others who hoped to become bachelors soon. So—the levy fizzled out. Instead, the representatives, like politicians everywhere, commenced striking right and left, minus thought or sense, and settled on salt, auctions, lotteries, steamship passengers and all land within twenty-five miles of the Canal. In short, they taxed about everything they could find except the people who profited from the ditch.

As to the ones who owned adjacent lands, they wisely (after their first anger) started commercial enterprises along the banks, hoping to recover their money. In this, they were not uniformly successful. Our driver (or captain, as he preferred to be called) made a wide swerve to avoid a pile of debris near the right shore and then identified it as a former "grocery store." His explanation was that a friend of his, a Captain Moses, badly needing a drink, had hitched his barge to one of the grocery's stanchions and later started his horses without removing the line. Result was that the grocery, jerry-built, had followed him into the water; that is, most of it did, including the grocer and his wife. Since the Canal was then four feet deep, they floundered out in fair shape. There was a lawsuit about it, but when Captain Moses established that the drink was required to offset his ague, the jury assessed slight damages, saying, "Why, naturally. Of course. He might have died without he hitched up."

These packet boats would generally be improved in the next few years, with captains of gentility, but I doubt if the food was ever the same.

At three in the afternoon, the captain's wife appeared from the aft cabin, and dexterously set up a table that ran nearly the length of the boat—excepting only the fore and aft cabins.

She seemed an affable person, and even truthful, unlike her husband. He was explaining to the female passenger—a Miss Frances Barclay—the terrible trouble here with rattlesnakes. He was unable to accept the fact that she was English, and went to some lengths to shock her. He said the Irish, aside from being immune to fevers, could absorb rattlesnake bites "as easy as fleas," with no aftereffects. He said they gave snakes to their children to play with— "for the rattles, you apprehend."

"I really don't think we stand in great danger of rattlesnakes, *Captain*," said Miss Barclay. "From my reading, those vermin are confined largely to Florida and to the West."

"Why, ma'am," he said, growing excited, "you take in the beginning we used a rattlesnake *dredge*, they were that pestiferous."

"How very interesting. I was aware of your ice-dredges only."

Then he turned his attention to me, using the mock deference I'd noted since I threatened him. His line was that (at twenty) I was a very important person, rich, "possibly even a politician."

"Now fess up—there's scarcely any use hiding your light 'neath a bushel. You're accustomed and adjusted to gourmey dining." He winked and poked me in the ribs.

I said, "Not necessarily. I hadn't given the matter much thought."

He slapped one shank and said, "I knowed it! Modest to the marrowbone. But I cain't be fooled with Gentry—true Gentry was the nature of my allusion. Well, sir, gourmey is what we aim to pelt you with right now. Resume your pew and we'll—LOW BRIDGE! Down!—she's a bad 'un."

After this crisis, I, and the others, were astounded at the quality of our meal, which was whisked like lightning onto the long table (with a cloth). We had salt beef delightfully spiced, fresh fish, johnnycakes, pork and beans with molasses, mush, all manner of pickles, preserves and relishes, and then pies and cakes. It may not, by New York standards, have been strictly gourmet, but it was a fine, strengthening meal nevertheless.

In the midst of this repast, the captain cried, "Hold! Throttle your stomicks—I seggest we haul up, rope, and picnic. Would that flat rock to starboard suit you, ma'am?" —addressing himself to Miss Barclay again.

We looked, and sunning on the rock were perhaps two dozen rattlesnakes, in a perfect tangle.

She flushed and said, "I believe I owe you an apology."

"Scrag it; I can shoo them off as easy as sneezing. It's part of the service, ma'am—picnics when the passengers prefer it. HOLD UP THERE, YOU CRITTERS! WHOA!"

"Never mind," I said. "We're comfortable here, and our compliments to your wife."

Where all this food had been stored, I have no idea—in a smallish hold beneath the aft cabin, I supposed. Packet boats carried no cargo, but the endless strings of line boats carried produce, fruit, lumber and such toward New York City, and returned with things like coffee, tea and the heavy machinery they could get no other way.

At the moment, I was told, the trafficking down was in oak lumber that came back in barrel staves of two kinds—"slack" and "tight." The former (not watertight) were for storing commodities like dried apples; the latter to hold (for aging) whiskey and used, too, as casks for molasses, snuff, flour and sugar. "Dry Houses," or "Evaporators," had been built from Lockport to Niagara.

Changing horses pretty often, we passed Utica and finally Rochester, which seemed bustling enough. All of us, including Miss Barclay, ate the wholesome food and slept mainly on the benches, which ingeniously made up, with the insertion of poles and burlap sacking, into travesties of two-tiered beds. We reached Lockport at last, alive by courtesy of the food, and here existed the worst barriers in Erie's construction. The land rose sharply, more than sixty feet, and it was necessary to build five double locks, partly through solid rock that finally gave way to a drill devised by a youngster of eighteen.

Lockport, after a poor start of log cabins, tree-cutting, stump-grubbing, and the deafening sound of rock-drilling, had improved, I was told. There were still too many saloons and speculators, worker riots and similar nuisances of a construction site, but a respectable population was growing fast. The town had several austere frame hotels and a few rather grand stone residences, these owned by men who won out in land deals.

Even so, an air of honky-tonk continued to prevail. The steep locks were being dealt with, and near the basin, above, a "Circus Giganticus" was going full blast. Beside this, "The World's Colossus Historical Museum Animalicus, Presenting all Indigenous Fauna" had *its* barker, with a megaphone, reeling off lies. More or less standing beside him (propped up) was a poor, patchy taxidermist's excuse of a polar bear. If polar bears were "indigenous" to the area, it had escaped my education.

A main trouble here was that the attractions were too close together, so that the barkers, as often as not, were hurling insults at each other, ignoring the public. At one point, after a reference to the smaller man's mother, the victim straightened up and whistled a rock past the other's ear. It would have brained him, if accurate, for he was too bulky for fast motion.

"Ah, would yer, now?" he cried, and whipped out a wicked-looking case knife which he ostentatiously began sharpening on a whetstone, darting little glances at his rival as he worked. These occurrences were continuous, someone said, and it was expected that one man or another would be killed soon. The fact drew crowds, and was encouraged by the owners.

My plan had been to take the stage from this town to Niagara Falls, but a stage had just left and another was not expected for two or three hours, so they said. Besides, my attention was fixed on a strange contrivance, a machine, parked near the packet-wharf in the lower basin, where much of the town lay then. Of all the nightmares of invention, this was the chief for ugliness. It appeared to be, and was, a kind of miniature steam engine. The tiny boiler and its few other works were exposed, and attached behind were two small, rickety cars, no larger than our New York horsecars.

"In God's name, what's that?" I exclaimed to a man beside me leaning against a rail. Like most other Lockport men he was wearing pantaloons tucked into boots, against the mud. Despite my outburst, he spat calmly into the gorge and said, "That there's the Tea Kettle on Wheels. Board it; you ain't lived till you've give it a try."

"Try it how? It's pointed in this direction. Do you mean—"

"That there locomotive—"

"Locomotive! The boiler's no bigger than our hot-water tank at home."

He said, "Well, if your water tank's up to climbing 110 feet in less than a mile, then take my advice—don't sell it. Hang on like a leech."

"Where does it run?"

"Right smack to Niagry—turntable's direct in front of the Cataract House."

"That's where I'm headed." I'd written to reserve a room in Niagara's largest and most popular resort hotel, partly as an annoyance to Mr. Bennett who, some years before, had stayed with his bride in a place less pretentious.

"Now lookee here, for I can see you're wabling" (he meant wavering), said my companion, "my name's Emory Sikes, and I disclaim the responsibility. I don't want you coming at me litigious. *I in no wise recommend it!* Hold it in mind."

"Why, people are climbing aboard both cars. What's wrong with it?" I asked more firmly.

He eyed me carefully, maintaining, I thought, a modest balance between recommending and damning, entirely legal.

"Well, a person might say, if pushed to the wall, that she has—accydents. There, now: *I* didn't say it, and will so state in court."

Exasperated, I said, "Look here, my good fellow, I have no plans to sue you, no matter if the contraption takes off through the swamps and climbs Mt. Everest. Do you understand?"

His answer was only, "You got any idee how many lawyers swarmed in here since the money commenced to flow? Watch 'em, dodge 'em—they'll grab you by the tail. My brother-in-law—"

I left him reciting his legal woes, said goodbye to Miss Barclay, who still looked bravely cheerful (though slightly subdued since our start) and climbed down to the Tea Kettle on Wheels. It had another name, of course, the formal one of Lockport and Niagara Falls Railway, but was most popularly known as the "strap road." This was due to the fact that it ran on oak rails with a thin strap of iron on top. A diarist of the time described it as a "little machine belching smoke and wood sparks and hissing steam, amounting to a tiny boiler mounted on four spoked wheels and graced by the name locomotive." Altogether it weighed less than nine tons and was a mechanical marvel, in its way.

A brisk, wiry engineer ran the whole works, and his self-confident pomposity would have adorned the finest flyer in the land. One paid six cents a mile (in advance) for the twenty-five-mile trip to Niagara, and perhaps the experience was worth it. Curiosity overcoming discretion, I abandoned the stage.

When the last passenger was seated, that banty rooster of an engineer-conductor-brakeman bawled out (needlessly) *"Board!"* Then, whistling like a mogul, he climbed to his perch at the throttle, slapped a brick on the steam valve, and we started up an incline like one at an amusement park. The fact is, the "locomotive" heaved and jerked and belched and screamed more than it climbed. But astonishingly it continued to ascend this impossible slope. I had the explanation later that its boiler was super-strong and the overall apparatus light, producing a kind of modern miracle. I have the impression, now, that this strap engine could have climbed the Statue of Liberty.

By a passenger's calculation—he recognized a farm—we got a little farther than eight miles. Eight was enough. The first of several "accydents" happened almost immediately after the climb. The engineer having removed his brick from the valve, we proceeded through swampland at the strap's best pace—fifteen miles an hour—

lurching, heaving, bumping. Then, slewing around a curve, the rear wheels of car #2 became derailed. The curve, with our top speed, had acted as a kind of whip. There followed a hullabaloo of bumping and grinding, and we climbed down to survey the damage.

"All out to lift!" the engineer called, and I wondered if he planned to refund our money.

But it proved surprisingly simple. The cars were, in effect, weightless, and the second being filled with Irishmen hoping for work on a new Hydraulic Canal to bypass the Falls (and provide mill power) we solved the derailment in a few minutes.

Five minutes later we ran out of wood. Our host had the decency to look chagrined, briefly, and his message this time was "Ablebodied men—and women—to wield axes!"

By now I was faintly annoyed, and figured my chance of getting to Niagara Falls before winter was less than even. The engineer had on one of those high, long-billed caps worthy of a better road, and since he made no motion to pick up an ax, I said, "How about doing some cutting yourself?"

His aplomb undisturbed, he picked up a long-spouted oilcan, and said, "Time to ile up."

I said, "I could *walk* to Niagara Falls faster than this."

He took out a pocket compass, shook it (it was stuck on S.E.), looked keenly at the sun, and pointed. "She lies approximate in that direction, keep right of the single oak. Mind the swamps—there's quickmud nigh about. You won't have no trouble with snakes; they sound warning."

I heard some titters, and gave up, as the engineer looked for something to oil. "You wouldn't be entertained by a hotbox, would you?" he said as if in explanation. I shook my head, defeated, and took an ax from several tools lying before the tender.

Some months previously, a Mrs. Storrs, of Lockport, had made one trip on the strap road (coming back by stage) and offered to bet *she* could walk to Niagara faster than the train time. She knew roads and trails through the swamps, and meant her proposal seriously. To quote a homespun book of the period, "I tell you the train folks was kind of surprised when they got to the end of the twenty-four-mile run and see her settin' on the hotel steps waitin' as cool as a cucumber."

There was nothing but scrub pine and aspen here—no tall trees of hardwood—but we "wooded up" to the engineer's satisfaction in about ten minutes. Then we took off again.

Two miles down the tracks the oak scantlings had sunk beneath the swamp (the season had been moist) so we fell to without demur, pulled up the ties, and shoveled clay underneath till things were firm. By this point, I'd decided to apply for a permanent job on the road. The work was outdoors and reliable, and the countryside was pleasant if different.

It had not been long, I learned, since President Martin Van Buren, deciding on the route I'd taken, was spilled onto the ground when the rails spread and both cars went over on their sides. He crawled out "without a scratch," as a paper put it, "and was a downright good sport about it." He helped make repairs, climbed back in, and proceeded, with the others, on his dubious course.

"Those old rails made us a good deal of trouble," said a former official of the road, reminiscing for a local paper. "They (the iron straps) were forever pulling loose at the ends and running up over the car wheels." The article failed to say whether he was interviewed in jail.

At the eight-mile point, there was a terrible racket behind my car, and we had a sample of what the official meant. A length of iron broke free of the oak and whipped through the rear car floor. This, I gathered, was the worst thing that could happen among several hundred "accydents," and everybody tumbled out in a hurry, as the engineer slammed on the brakes, which took hold in fifty yards or so.

Several angry men and women came running forward, and the engineer, I thought, looked interested for the first time.

"Anybody hurt?" I heard a passenger from our car say.

"No. Irishman broke a leg."

"Well, it's a very good thing," a woman said. "A boy was crippled in this exact same way only last summer. It's a disgrace and a scandal."

But a well-dressed man of our car addressed the engineer. "Here, you—"

"*Me?*" replied the engineer, shocked.

"Yes, you. That man won't work all summer. What do you plan to do *for* him and *about* him?" The fellow stood about six-feet-four and looked tough in proportion.

The engineer, not blinking an eye, withdrew a book of Rules and Regulations from his overalls pocket, flipped a few pages and said, "Medical attention, including splints, amputations or burials, and forty dollars compensation, if alive. Standard: Make it or break it."

"The leg's already broken, you jackass" —here the engineer sat down and commenced loading a corncob pipe. "Is he in much pain?" the man asked some rear-car passengers.

"If swilling whiskey and cursing the bark off trees means pain, he's seen the hind end of *this* life."

It was the woman with the offhand manner about the injury. Apparently she shared the popular view of Irish, one that would wear off in time, but not soon. And typically enough, she and her husband had immigrated from Canada within the month. Comparatively the maimed Irishman was an old resident.

At several places, the strap road and the stage line nearly converged, making it convenient for the drivers to exchange profanity, rocks, and, often, bets. I now saw some curious stage passengers scampering across dry clumps of land toward us; and taking down my bags I headed for *their* carrier. A three-legged donkey would have been preferable to ours, as I saw it. I was determined to buy a spot on the stage, if I had to sit on the roof. But it was not filled, and I found myself next to Miss Barclay, who blushed furiously, as was her custom on most occasions. Then we settled back in genial nostalgia about the Erie, which looked better and better.

The stage driver was a weathered old crab, diminutive in size and wearing a high hat that I figured some Irish foreman had discarded, for it was far gone in its career. He insisted on charging me the full fare—one dollar—and said it should be more, what with the inconvenience.

To complain about *all* the transportation to Niagara is perhaps the act of a weakling, or "dude," as the locals viewed any city-bred man. Nobody *made* me travel to Niagara Falls, especially by the route I chose, but I'll sink below the level of the sporting Van Buren and confess that the stage had points of frailty. For long spaces, the road ran smoothly, considering the vehicle's lack of springs, but through swampy areas we traversed what the driver called, with some pride, "corduroy" roads, which were simply trees cut and pared from the splendid high timber along the Niagara River, then laid side by side. These provided a spinal adventure not unlike being flogged on the back with a crowbar. I saw Miss Barclay biting her handkerchief, grimly determined to make nothing of her femininity. As for me, I supported myself, my rear slightly above the seat, by my hands at my sides.

Miss Barclay lost her *sang froid* only once, and that having to do with the mails. Beside the driver, who was within view through an opened trapdoor, lay several sacks of mail, each marked according to locality. Through these, as he drove, he sifted leisurely, and when we reached a farmer's drive, he pulled up and halloa-ed. For the most part, the housewife or one of her brats strolled out to receive the driver's postal gift—newspapers as often as not.

In the matter of letters, Miss Barclay took exception. When a yell or two or three failed to produce humanity, the driver tossed his bundle onto the ground and cried, "'Ap there!" to the six bored horses that dragged this conveyance. I say dragged because, after a heavy rain, the corduroy was apt to go floating off and the coach struggled hub-deep in the bogs.

And now it began to sprinkle. Evidently from long use, the driver shifted into his No. 2 plan. If he yelled repeatedly, and no one came, he tossed the mail back into the sack, whipped up, and we moved on.

After he'd re-stowed one bundle that contained letters as well as papers, Miss Barclay, horrified, tapped on the roof. The bewhiskered face came into view, and she said, "I believe I'm correct that you don't return by this route?"

"Correct as pie, ma'am. You got it right the first time."

"Then what on earth will happen to that poor farmer's post?"

"Them letters, by custom, will make their way to Washington and come back in a year or two at most. There's no hurry about a *letter*, mum."

"How outrageous!" She thereupon sat back to block her face from his view. But he thrust his head down farther, to survey her, as if she were sick, or (as he said later) drunk. Then he straightened back up to bawl a few obscenities at the strap engineer, who was under way again, and, now, paralleling our road at perhaps a hundred yards (out of throwing distance).

Chapter IV

We hauled up at Cataract House at about four in the afternoon, and the driver, hoping for tips, spryly removed our luggage from the roof and handed it to three or four flunkies who came out to receive us.

This hotel, the chief in Niagara, backed onto Main Street, with a small veranda, while facing the river and the Falls. It was a huge L-shaped structure, arranged so that nearly all rooms had a part-view of the local phenomenon. Miss Barclay's baggage, as well as my own, having been seized up and whisked off, I strolled through the enormous Brussels-carpeted hallway to the veranda facing Niagara Falls and stood, hypnotized. For several miles our stage road had neared the river, and the vegetation (especially as we approached the Falls) had changed entirely. The runt growth had given way to tall trees—pines, oak, beech, hickory, maple and others I'd learn soon. Through these played numerous coal-black squirrels, of a sort I never knew existed. We'd quite abruptly entered a different world, one I consider unique to this day, and richly blessed.

My hypnotic state (which would worsen soon, and remain forever fixed) came partly from great plumes of spray that extended from slightly west of Cataract House across the river to Canada. They rose perhaps a hundred feet in the air, sparkling like diamonds in the day's last sun. Because of the tall trees, I could not see the Falls themselves, either the American or Canadian side. But I could *feel* them, despite the warmth of the day, and southward toward Buffalo I had a dazzling view of the river; broad, clear, its current rushing at what could have been twenty miles an hour.

I realize, now, that the sound of that massive deluge was one of soul-stirring elements. It was not loud, from where I stood, but it conveyed a heavy, ominous undercurrent of warning, a kind of pulse of life, like a low pounding of the heart.

Suddenly I shuddered, shaking off a desire to rush down and place a hand, at least, into some spot where the currents began their final 150-foot plunge. I was here in the interest of Mr. Bennett, and the first order of business was to be established in a suitable room.

At the desk, a gloomy-looking man in a plum-colored jacket said, "Yes, sir" (fighting to look genial), "and what may Cataract House do for you today?" He gave a disdainful glance at my traveling costume, which stood in need of repairs. "Perhaps you were looking for the Eagle Tavern?"

This was a comparatively rough, much older nearby hostelry under the same ownership, that of General Parkhurst Whitney, who built Cataract House to accommodate overflowing visitors of caste from all over the world.

"I have a reservation," I said evenly, having watched my father deal with luminaries of this breed. "I'll need a bedroom facing the river, a sitting room, and whatever bathroom arrangements you have in this hamlet. And I'll require valet service this evening. Mr. Bennett—Mr. James Gordon Bennett of the New York *Herald*— would dislike his representative to have anything short of the best." (This lie was so monstrous that I had trouble getting it out.)

The nose came down from its elevated perch and was no longer aimed at my chin. "Yes, *sir!* I believe General Whitney is a friend, or acquaintance, of Mr. Bennett. But I beg you to be patient, sir. The hotel is barely opened, and most rooms will remain unfit to use for a week."

"Indeed? This telegram"—I withdrew the New York Central ticket from my wallet—"makes things plain enough for *me:* 'Delighted your crack correspondent to describe and exalt Cataract House. Be assured he will receive every courtesy. Regards—General Parkhurst Whitney.'"

"Yes, sir—I understand completely. But at the moment we have five sets of adjoining suites—all divided by the necessary, if you apprehend me—and I insist that the porter show you each. The best will be none too good, believe me, sir. FRONT!" he cried, banging a button, producing no special activity. The bellboys were attending to other duties, I surmised. (Two, as it turned out, were at the Eagle Tavern, drinking Monongahela whiskey. In their minds, the season had not yet started.)

For the first time, I noticed that Miss Barclay was standing beside me, looking forlorn and a little frightened.

She touched my elbow and said, in a low voice, "I wonder if I could speak to you privately—"

I replied, "Of course, Miss Barclay," and led her some distance from the thoroughly subdued figurehead behind the desk.

"This is very improper"—(crimson again)—"I don't even know your name."

"Well, it's nothing very special. Fact is, it's William—Bill. If you'd like the whole string, it's William T. Morrison, III. If that suits you."

She seemed to pull herself together, and even smiled.

"This is dreadful of me, but I have an awfully cheeky favor to ask, and I simply don't know how to do it."

"There's any number of sofas in this palace. I suggest the roaring red plush behind the pillar. Then you can work on your speech. I'm not very formidable."

"No," she said when we sat down, "but everything seems much more—well, rough and impersonal than I'd thought when I left." She'd changed again and was on the point of tears, a condition I tried not to notice. "I've become a little nervy. It's odd. I thought I'd take this—this Grand Tour—just as men did, and like it. But I've become strung up—so much has happened. It's not at all the way friends I knew described it."

"Women friends?"

She managed a rueful smile and said, "Yes, well, I was not quite involved in the *Damen über alles* stirrings, but I was almost convinced there were no differences. That is, important differences [blush] between male and female. I've learned better—"

"This is a new, raw land of inconvenience and bullyboy manners, and I'm afraid they don't make allowances for a lady of your station. Not what you're used to, at least. These things will come, but it's a poor time for a single woman to tour the American frontier."

I had little notion what I was talking about, but I thought the words might soothe her. Besides, I rather fancied them.

She said, very meekly, "I've found that out in the past few weeks, even in New York. Let me hasten to say I don't mean this *critically*. I love all the—"

"New York? A pesthole. Believe it or not, shallow wells for

34

drinking water draw from old graveyards and the seepage of privies; and the sewage runs in the gutters. The Irish fight and thieve and burn all over town. No one walks abroad at night. Yellow fever, plague and typhus sweep the whole dungheap, killing thousands. People of any means, like my father, buy water carted in from farms above the Fifties. They talk, now, of building aqueducts from the Croton River.

"Why? Well, New York water is too filthy to make beer of! Good beer is imported from Philadelphia! So—we may have water from Croton, if the politicians agree on how to steal enough to make it worthwhile.

"Sorry about the rampage, but it's in the minds of all New Yorkers. In any case," I continued, swiveling around to face her, "I have a feeling you wanted to talk about something else."

She sat twisting and knotting her handkerchief. "I think I have courage enough now to ask the favor. This place, this hotel—nearly empty—is suddenly crushing. That awful man at the desk! Oh, it's huge and beautiful, and I'm certain it will be bright and gay when the Southern and other guests come."

Then, quite abruptly, "—Would you consent, for now, to take a room adjoining mine?" (A blush to make the others seem a mild discoloration.) "I have no right to ask and it sounds—fast. But you're a gentleman, no matter how young, and I'd feel ever so much more secure. There—I got it out at last."

I studied her for a second. I'd be twenty-one this week, and found it hard to guess her age. (She was in fact thirty.) So—her motive could or could not be what she stated. I imagined how chilling it must be for a delicate maiden lady, a foreigner, to be alone in such an alien and heedless place.

I arose and helped her up. For a moment, as our hands touched, I fancied a thin cry of starved femininity, but I dismissed it as ego.

"Come along. What William T. Morrison, III, can't do, Mr. James Gordon Bennett should manage very nicely.

"You there, behind the desk," I said when we'd walked back across the red carpet. "I'll take the best of your adjoining rooms, and this English lady, Miss Frances Barclay, a traveling representative of Her Majesty, will have the one next to me. Now strike that bell and get someone here for the luggage."

The man's face was a sunburst of triumph.

"I can't do that, sir."

"What the devil do you mean?"

"You haven't signed the register yet!"

"Spin the book around, and be brisk about it."

Once again he seemed to wither into his clothes, doing as he was told.

When she had signed, and I'd noted the "Hon." before her name, I made a great show and flourish of "William T. Morrison, III, Esq.," with a bold line curling around and underneath, with a loop. I was tempted to give myself a high Harvard degree, but I couldn't think of one right off.

Still, I was wrong to underestimate the venom of a subdesk clerk.

We hadn't traversed twenty yards before he sang out and said, "Will you be needing the adjoining room keys, sir?"

I turned around slowly and said, "I'll be interviewing General Whitney tomorrow."

The man turned pale. Even his gorgeous yellow mustaches appeared to lose color. When he recovered, he said, "That's why I gave them to the bellhop, sir. You can check and see. I hope you'll put in a good word for me."

The bellhop observed, in a low voice, "I was hoping you'd go back and sponge his face, sir." I made some response, then noticed that this servant must be upward of seventy. Moreover he had, aside from his monkey suit with rows of brass buttons, a scraggly gray beard about a foot long. He was, besides, around five-foot-five, scrawny and slightly stooped. Altogether he was the most outrageous-looking porter I'd seen outside a comic theatrical.

I said, "Here, give me two of those; they're too much for one man, young, old, large or small."

"I'd die in harness first," he replied in a tone of mild offense. Then the wiry little rooster tossed the bags up to some position that I could not possibly have managed, and we climbed the grandiose carpeted staircase.

Miss Barclay being installed in her room, and I in mine, with the window opened and each with the necessary keys, I gave the septuagenerian two dollar bills.

He examined them, taken aback.

"Why, that's too much, sir."

"Not for the gymnastic I've witnessed."

"If word leaks out, you'll be a target for every swindler, thief and bruiser in town—a clear majority."

"But it won't leak out, will it?" I said, smiling.

"They could take a funnel, drive it down with a sledge, run a drill in the other direction, and never a whisper."

"Good," I said, and as he left by the outside door, I called to ask, "What might your name be?"

"Name of Pete, sir; Biblical—from Simon called Peter, in the fishing way. I'm pushed back to the kitchen when the fancies arrive—eyesore, they say. But you send out word if you need help."

I figured, from the look of him he might last a week or more, but it was nice to have a friend in Niagara Falls.

I went to a window and stared out toward the Falls. Lights were turning on in Canada, across the way, and the soaring mist could still be faintly seen. And always there was the sound.

Chapter V

Sluices, or "raceways," from the river would soon be running under the resort hotels, thus providing some rooms with toilets. At the moment we had the usual chamberpots ("thundermugs") and the space between our large, comfortable, connecting rooms was, in effect, a dressing room, with mirrors, closets for clothes, commodes, and so on. Out behind stood the row of privies.

In high summer, nearly all connecting rooms were taken by Southerners with large families. For the convenience of these, there were grottoes in the cellar, with wall spancels and straw on the floors, in case they brought an "unreliable" slave or two.

This information I gained in the Eagle Tavern, next door, from a rough-dressed man—a river rat—who stood at the bar and tried to make himself heard above the din. He threw in various uninspired lies, and told me that hardly a week passed when "one of them nigries—little more than apes, absorb it"—didn't "bust loose and strangle somebody asleeping in their beds. Best thing you can do, sonny," he said in confidence, leaning over, "is keep a loaded musket on the floor and rig a wire trip near the doors. 'Less'n you've got a protection dog . . . Or a bear." (This last was clearly an after-thought.) "Them nigries ain't too long on tripes, and a bear seems to put them off, mostly."

I nodded, thanked him, sniffed in a marked way, and observed—he failed to hear—that he, personally, had little to fear from the meanest bear within a hundred miles. He really did have a most individualistic stink.

The Cataract had most of its dining room roped off, out of service, and I'd decided not to embarrass Miss Barclay by suggesting we dine together. Besides, the room was so huge and empty it had a kind of accusing look. And lastly I had no wish to strengthen the clerk's suspicions.

So—at a corner table of the Eagle, I was served a surprisingly good whitefish and a mutton chop and drank two pints of Canadian ale to wash it all down. The price came to something like forty cents. When I finished, I was so tired, after the journey, that I sat, half-asleep. Then I realized what Miss Barclay might be feeling.

Planning to walk about the town, and see the hotels, I figured that if I could make it back to my room, take a sponge bath, and fall into bed without breaking a leg, I'd be lucky.

She was not in the dining room, and I paused outside her door, wondering whether to enquire if she was all right. But I decided that an audible bustle in my own suite might be more heartening.

To my amazement, a spray of flowers now rested on my table, and I thanked Mr. Bennett's influence. Then I stood in a large washbasin and, with a pitcher, a wet towel and a dry one, removed the interesting variety of road grime. I supposed Miss Barclay was doing approximately the same. I hoped she'd had a dinner sent up.

I'd put on my pyjamas and was sprawled in one of the deep-cushioned chairs, mentally trying to sort out my first dispatch to the *Herald*, when there came a faint tapping at the adjoining door. At first I thought I'd dreamed it, but after a few seconds it was repeated, with more insistence. Astonished, I called "Come in," then got up and went forward to meet Miss Barclay.

"This is unforgivable—I'm in your debt already—but if I could chat a few minutes before retiring, my Grand Tour might not seem such a failure. Would you mind awfully? I promise not to disturb you again."

By now I had exceeded astonishment, in surveying her costume. Miss Frances Barclay clothed bore little resemblance to Miss Barclay half-clothed. She had on a respectable nightdress, which yet left an impressive cleft, slippers, and an expensive-looking robe that covered the nightgown but left the cleft partially exposed.

I gulped. (I've noticed that novelists find it convenient to have a character "gulp," though till now I had no idea what it meant; but I unmistakably gulped. There was no other word for it.) I could feel the blood pounding in my neck, and for once I had trouble speaking.

"Of course, Miss Barclay," I blurted out, and, "Why don't you sit down?" Then I had a sublime, a lifesaving idea.

"My father," I said, "gave me a bottle of French brandy, and added some advice. 'Son,' he said, 'if you're feeling peaked, take a long pull of brandy. If that fails to hold, try another. *Go to a doctor only as a last resort!* That's my suggestion for travel and I've done a good deal of it.'

"Perhaps you could be persuaded, Miss Barclay, to have a small glass of brandy, just this once. It has something to do with Napoleon," I said, taking it from my bag and holding it up, "or so it says on the label. I'm not an expert. Nearly all brandy mentions Napoleon, I've noticed. No wonder he came a cropper at Waterloo."

"Are you"—the voice quavered—"having one, too?"

"Certainly. I may drink half a bottle." I got two glasses from the bureau. "I've been feeling a little down myself lately."

"Oh, dear."

My confidence was returned. I'd made the usual pilgrimages around Cambridge, of which the suburb had the least reason to be vain, but the quality of companionship fell far short of the Miss Barclays of this world. In any case, I said to myself, those beauties were not whimsically put on display.

After she'd taken a sip, and then another, her color subsided. She sighed and said, "That's ever so much better."

"Drink it all; you'll feel even better soon."

"We English always have wine at parties during the season, and I know several, well, noble ladies who drink brandy quite privately. I'm told that's the *worst* thing you can do?"

"Me? I can beat that by a country mile. You'd be surprised."

"I meant anyone." Despite the brandy, she had a tinge of color again.

I refilled her glass, as she made a half-gesture of protest. Then she sat silently for a space. It had struck me that tomorrow was my birthday, and tomorrow was nearly here. It was a time for gifts.

She spoke up with a look of decision about her mouth, a tribute to Napoleon, I supposed.

"I wonder if I could be fully candid? Again, I have no right, of course, but for some reason I should like you to know the whole truth—"

"Fire away," I said, much relaxed by the brandy, my own robe carelessly parting.

Looking at the floor, she said, "I'm not making the Grand Tour to prove any silly equality with men." She paused a second; then pressed on: "First, you know, I could never show this much bad taste without the drink. But I had a very—unhappy experience. With a man, of course. He was a Canadian of high birth, a cousin or something of the governor-general. I believed it; *everybody* believed it. He was handsome, and dashing and witty, and society took him up. He was lionized, asked everywhere—and, finally, London's most popular extra man. He seemed to have plenty of money, and even the penny papers began to view him with pride.

"We met in the country home of a peer, and he paid me flattering attention. I'd always considered myself rather plain, and my family encouraged the view, since I had—have—a sister of great beauty. But he assured me, during a memorable walk in the Kent Weald, that I was anything but plain; he said he had the faculty of seeing beneath my clothing.

"It was there I should have stopped, to be sure. But without considering, I found myself meeting him in town for tea, and in other places, and very shortly visiting his flat. I was twenty-nine then; I'm thirty now. He spoke often of marriage, but told me the truth, with one hand solemnly on his breast: He had a vixenish wife, in Victoria, who was in process of getting a divorce.

"By now I was so besotted, perhaps with new experiences, that it made no difference. Then there was another little flat, in a not very fashionable quarter—near Kensington. A secret meeting place; and having thrown away all caution, I was sublimely, rapturously, happy.

"Then came the bombshell. You seem a rather traveled young man, so that you probably know the one thing certain for expulsion from English society is cheating at cards. If that sounds cynical, it comes close to being true.

"Well, *my* friend was exposed, at one of the clubs—White's, Boodles, I've forgotten—and then his background was thoroughly probed. He was an absolute fraud, and gained his living at the clubs which so foolishly had rushed to make him a member. He quietly disappeared from England, or at least from London, and I have no doubt he's now someplace in your country, set up with a new mistress and following his regular habits.

"Then I was astounded to learn that our rendezvous, and conduct, were known by everyone who counted. For some reason, that sort of thing always creeps into the open, at least in London. 'Poor Frances, she's had a most regrettable experience' was on the tongues of my closest friends, and I was relieved when my family, to shun embarrassment, suggested I leave England for a while. I took their advice, and here I am."

She leaned far back, further ignoring the robe. "And very happy about it at this moment. Do you think another splash would affect me? I'm quite sober, you know."

"And your—infatuation isn't worn off?"

"I *despise* the blackguard!" she said with passion, and looking me up and down slowly, then shamelessly in the face, "Periodically when I'm tired or lonely or tense I miss the flat."

For what followed I like to blame the late emperor of France. Not only for Miss Barclay's sake, but my own. After a look at my sprawl, she said, "Never mind; the Mountain will come to Mahomet; I'll get my own drink."

I have the impression she poured some brandy in her glass; then, as she stood with her legs astride mine, there was a rustle of falling silk and she presented herself as the Canadian had seen her.

I, too, was tired, but I remember thinking that Praxiteles could have done the breasts and the round, close-fitting thighs, and I clasped her on both sides, behind, then ran my hands up and over the uniquely fine bosom. Her skin was glossy, with only a wisp of down showing within a few inches of my face.

Then (I believe) the delicate Miss Barclay sank to her knees and pulled my pyjama pants to the floor. From far off, as in a play when one has a poor rear seat, I heard her say, "Ah, how lovely!" Then she amused herself as it was difficult to be amused in Scollay Square. At a point when I thought she might be warned, I tried to lift her face, but her hunger was too demanding. I subsided, and she rested her head against my leg. No matter how great a fraud, the Canadian had been a wonderfully adroit tutor in abandon.

Then I picked her up, as her mouth clung to mine, and placed her in the center of the bed. The thighs parted, and I had no further need of knowledge, twenty notwithstanding. I was guided, and fondled almost painfully as she locked her legs around and reached beneath. Then the back spontaneously arched, and I was drawn into Miss Barclay's world before the thrusts that, in a few seconds, were marked by a cry and a clinging to my neck, her head risen from the pillow. It was reasonable, I expected, that a long suppressed tension had eased.

Dimly I recall that dawn had pushed its first streaks beyond the window when I felt her get up, bend over and kiss me lightly on the cheek.

"After all, the clerk was right wasn't he?" she whispered—and left for the safety of her adjoining room.

42

Chapter VI

Next morning, not feeling too brash (after all, it *was* my brandy) I slipped past the dining room where Miss Barclay was having breakfast alone. She saw me, I think, but looked steadily at her plate. I nodded and continued through to the long, broad veranda—called here a piazza. I'd planned to reach General Whitney after breakfast, but knew what I had to do first. The sound beckoned, the sun rose, and the high plumes of mist rose to diffuse into a kind of pink cloud.

I walked the short distance to Prospect Point, on the mainland. This gave a chilling view of the Canadian, or Horseshoe Falls— hundreds of thousands of emerald tons taking their final plunge to the roaring green caldron below. Then I hurried back to the Eagle Tavern for a breakfast that a party of four might have digested, and, emerging, headed for the bridge to Goat Island, a beautiful, wooded expanse three miles in circumference, on the American side.

It had become routine to refer to America's Falls as "Belonging to the Porters"—two brothers, a general and a judge. They were large landowners and had further interests, and I'm satisfied they obtained the land bordering the river and the Falls honorably—from Seneca Indians or various parties between. But it does seem that nearly everything falls into the hands of politicians, one way or another. In any case, they had their exhibit fenced and charged tourists twenty-five cents to traverse two bridges they'd built, one to a grassy-rocky clump called Bath Island and another on to Goat Island.

Thither I made my way, paying my quarter to a Bath Island collector, who bit it to test it genuine and then explained, in a kind of apology, that "We've had a mort of coiner specimens, sir; they take if it's rubbed and place it in a potater overnight. The Guvment mint couldn't locate the difference.

"All clear here"—tossing the coin into a box. "Pass on and rim round the Goat. *But don't jump!* It's proved onhealthy in the past." He gave a hoarse laugh to emphasize his excellent joke, and I thanked him effusively.

They had a souvenir shop here that the newspaper rather impudently said sold "walking sticks, 'homegrown' Indian curios and geological specimens of doubtful value." Also, a bathhouse lay beneath the toll booth. To this the public was encouraged (at an extra fee) to descend, remove their clothes in dressing rooms and sport around. The sexes were segregated, to the lamentations of numerous wags. Needless to say, the Falls end was blocked by stone; and the toll house and both bridges were constructed of the same material. In winter, masses of ice tumbled grindingly down and had already swept away two wooden bridges.

Before leaving the bridges, I was accosted by a cadaverous apparition wearing a top hat and tailcoat, with a greasy shirt and no tie. He asked if I wanted a "professional guide." Unimpressed, I declined, but I learned that this gusher of information (for his father, before him, had been a Goat Island fixture for years) was indeed a worthwhile mentor, and I would hire him often in the future, not only for his knowledge of Niagara history but to identify flora, fauna and the like. Moreover, he was a genial companion, self-taught in the liberal arts. He did not, he told me, actually charge a fee for his work—such greed was not "genteel"—but he could be persuaded to accept "presents." At the moment, he was missing an upper incisor, and with the costume plus what I mistakenly took for a revolver butt peeping from his coat (it was in fact a walking stick) he could have passed for an unsuccessful pirate.

But now, on this first visit, I wanted to see the wonders by myself.

Once over the second bridge, I scrambled up a gravel path to level ground and stood gazing toward the thunders. All but the river, churning in high white rapids here, was obscured by a strange variety of both tall and shrubby trees. I recognized several species of maples; white, post, red and pin oaks, and chestnuts; and my tall-hatted friend later pointed out black walnut, hairy and pignut hickory, butternut, beech and sassafras, this last smaller in stature and much used each spring by housewives. These brewed tea from the bark and convinced the less acute of their progeny that it "thinned the blood." Why it was better to totter around on thin blood, I was not able to determine.

There were varieties of fruit trees that did not properly belong in these latitudes, and flowering plants that I learned bit by bit. My surprise grew until I realized, at last, that Goat Island, the whole Niagara region, had a climate so affected by Lakes Erie and Ontario, and by the Falls themselves, that it was perhaps unique in the world. It was sufficiently bland and soft—in a far north land—even to raise peaches of tolerable quality.

Hoping to give tourists their money's worth, the Porters had built a gravel road round the island, and a bridge to Luna Island, the eminence that divides the American Falls. Also they'd provided many footpaths to points of interest. To identify these they had erected signs pointing the way. The quickest walk to the cascade was to my right, but a shrinking, uneasy delay turned me left toward the island's head. Since the tall trees grew mainly near the shore, the interior of this misted sanctuary resembled a deer park, with beautiful lush grasses and blooms.

Because of the hour, I was the man of the island, and I felt like Robinson Crusoe, parted from his fellows. The Porters had once brought many deer here, but tourists, in their playful style, had chased them all into the rapids, whence they were swept down and over the crest.

My walk to the left-hand tip required about fifteen minutes, and I stood looking across the broad Niagara—it seemed two miles or more—as it rushed toward the drop, perhaps a mile to my right. The river here was much whiter than green as it entered the tumult before the Falls.

Black squirells (somehow lending an eery note) scampered in the high limbs of trees and among the wild profusion of low growth along the bank. The water was nevertheless so pure that one could see the naked stone bottom at depths of five and six feet. I say "naked" because eons of force had torn away trivia like pebbles and much larger stones. The bottom was rock—solid and even smooth in spots. It looked uncommonly odd with the stream flying past on top.

I had learned, from someone or other, that a certain John Stedman, wagonmaster and farmer, had herded his sheep, and one goat, onto the island in the 1700s, to protect them from wolves. Wolves then and later were so numerous and filled with appetite that they often stood upright looking into farmers' windows, weighing the chance of a second-rate meal. Many persons reported such occurrences, but no casualties were recorded. The people were all armed, and wolves, as well as bears and big cats, had a strong bias against guns.

In any case, Stedman lost his sheep, not to wolves but to weather. During a terrible winter, the sheep all froze to death, leaving the goat unperturbed. It was thus that the island gained its name. A feeble attempt was made to rename it Iris Island, by traffickers in tourism, but it died early. And Judge Porter, when he bought Goat Island, had intended to use it for a sheepfold, presumably having learned nothing from Stedman. Anyhow, he found tourism to be more lucrative.

And the Porters had run all manner of things—a grist mill, a shoe factory, a paper factory, a cabinet works, a planing and saw mill, and built a portage. In short, the judge's energy and foresight had pretty well established Niagara Falls. And yes, he had not forgotten to have it incorporated, in 1806. Eventually, the family would sell their holding to the state, in a spirit of wishing to share the treasure with others.

I walked the gravel path along shore, watching the crystal rapids leap up and curl over backward. Then I had an urge to take my shoes off and wade, but a little warning bell sounded. I think it was caused by the speed of the water and the nude rock surface below. Together they had a sinister look. But there was a challenge here; and I would come to know it better. It persisted past the Three Sisters—small clumps of elevated grass, rocks and exposed tree roots gnarled like old knuckles.

Judge Porter's guide-signs were artistically clear, leaving little chance of getting lost, as large as the island was. But I stuck to the encircling path, near the water.

A popular anecdote had to do with the late judge's daughter, who was traveling in Europe. Some ignoramus of a dignitary asked the young lady if she'd heard of Niagara Falls. "Heard of them!" she exclaimed. "Sir, I *own* them!" When the exchange leaked back to Niagara, the town was jubilant; Europe had finally been put in its place. The War of 1812 had seen the British cross from Canada and temporarily chase the Americans—soldiers and civilians alike—a considerable way inland, but Miss Porter's retort, people thought, had made it all up, and more.

Within half an hour, stopping to examine strange plants that turned out to be aloes, columbine, bloodroot, Dutchman's breeches and the like, I began descending a slope, and the sound grew deafening; the spray shot up from a giant's firehose. Then, at a jutting-out point, (with guardrail), Canada's Horseshoe Falls burst into view, near at hand now. The American Falls, divided, lay largely behind me, and I stared down, no more than four feet from the curving flood that dove to a dark lagoon 150 feet below. This last looked deep, and *was* deep, as deep as the Falls were high.

One's first sensation (I heard) is usually to think the silent mass falling away cannot be seriously dangerous. With fierce rapids above and fiercer ones below, the placid drop itself is curiously reassuring. Its quietness against the larger sounds removes the feeling of hazard; and the glassy race actually does draw one like the Lorelei.

There being nobody near, I leaned down, lowered a hand and felt the cold, friendly pressure. But due to the speed, my hand only skipped on the surface. Even so, like many another, I felt like wading out on the rim, while clinging to roots and branches. The feeling was strong, lasting a minute or more; then I drew back, shivering. Death lay in that curve, and I had nearly been tricked.

A few weeks before, as the season started, a Mr. and Mrs. de Forest and their young daughter, Anna, of Buffalo, were visiting the Falls with a friend, a Mr. Addington. Crossing the short Luna Bridge, Addington playfully grabbed Anna, as if to lift her over the rail. She panicked, screamed and wriggled into the water. "Without a moment's hesitation," as the local paper said, "Addington leaped in after her and both were instantly swept to their deaths."

I'd suddenly seen enough for a day, and I walked back to Bath Island, crossed the bridges, and headed toward Cataract House. Oddly, I felt both depressed and exhilarated. It was too much; Nature had lost her head. I was caught, in thrall to the good and wicked witch, one with the bemused hundreds up and down the watery mecca.

I'd planned to call on General Whitney after lunch, but the big topic of the day was Rattlesnake Charley and a coroner's inquest on his protégé. This was to be held at one o'clock, in a back room of De Veaux's emporium, the leading gossip mill of the town.

I wiggled into a front seat on a bench, one of several that faced a rickety table with a gavel, some papers and an inkstand. There was a cuspidor close by. The jury—six men placidly chewing—filled chairs with a view of the coroner and the audience. They were bewhiskered, mostly, and made free, inaccurate use of the spittoon, which lay at the edge of their range.

The coroner arrived, causing no great stir—a tall, sober man wearing a frayed frock coat, a medium-white shirt and a string tie. Despite this interesting arrangement, he was somehow imposing, and looked as if he meant to flog out the truth.

Niagara was fortunate in its coroner, I learned. He was a former engineer on the strap railroad and had a fine record, aside from an occasion when, upset by domestic woe, he'd drunk Monongahela steadily from Lockport and, filled with bliss and whiskey, had run off the turntable and into a ditch, breaking a leg in three places. This he now favored, using a cane. The only other casualty was buried with full ceremony, and a handsome purse was made up for the family, which lived near the swamps. Consensus was that the coroner, a Mr. Smithers, was not to blame for his mistake; his wife was to blame. She had no right to burn up their barn in a fit of rage, disposing of three heifers, several chickens and Mr. Smithers' horse. Niagara was indeed lucky to obtain such a man, especially since his salary was fifteen dollars a month. Moreover, he had education, not only in Buffalo but from an itinerant teacher, a drunk, who would linger anywhere for lodging.

The girl Bridget's body had not risen in the Whirlpool for six days, hence the delay. First witness was Red Gill, who refused to face his old friend. The truth is he appeared in a marvelously peevish humor.

"You are, that is to say, your name is Red Gill?"

"Do I favor the king of Belgium?"

The coroner, unruffled, duly made the entry that Gill was *not* the king of Belgium, and the nonsense resumed.

"You and your sons recovered the body of Bridget O'Brien, with a grapple, as it revolved in the Whirlpool on Saturday last; is this office correct?"

"Well, we couldn't dreel it up by whistling, could we?"

The coroner took note that such a procedure was unlikely.

"Did you notice anything about the body indicative, or suggestive, of foul play?"

"Listen," said Gill more calmly, swiveling around, "you gae over them Falls and you'll have indicatives from here to the Isle of Mull. Her skull was cracked like a walnut, her tubes dangled from her wame, one leg was missing, every bone was broke and her chest was whished down flat. Now what do you say to that?"

"And her boat?"

"Found smashed on the Canajian side—near Great Gorge. Don't tell me you ain't *heard* it yet?"

"For the record," said the coroner, writing.

"And an oar nearby, likewise kennt by all outside this room."

This struck me as advantageous to Charley. Plainly enough, he hadn't pushed her into the river without means of propulsion, and I suddenly realized that, despite snakes, and the gathering of snakes, Gill's ill-humor sprang from the opposite of what I'd thought. He'd been annoyed at Charley the night of the tragedy, but on thinking it over, he knew his old friend unable to murder. And he clearly resented other people suspecting it.

There was a bustle and bending of heads among the jurors, all of whom, curiously, were either apothecaries or grocers. One after another, they asked to testify as "character witnesses." I was dumbfounded, until I found that all—without exception—depended on Charley's snakes for their nostrums.

The foreman, a Mr. Applegate, said Rattlesnake Charley's Good Works, administering to the sick, causing menses to resume flowing, strengthening seminal force, curing consumption, leprosy, cancer, blue balls and pneumonia, aside from ailments less pressing, should see him cast in bronze rather than pilloried in public. He, Mr. Applegate, would go out of business if Charley's collections were diminished, and he'd been assured by the "cognoscenti" that the girl Bridget "served as assistant snake handler only.

"This is an absurd proceeding," he said, "and if I were Mr. MacTavish" (Charley's last name) "I'd sue. I've polled my fellow jurors and they've agreed to stand legal fees."

At this, the coroner looked startled, if not frightened. Then he permitted another juror, a druggist named Baynes, to list some of the vital medications whose base depended on Charley's snakeoils.

The man rose with a copy of the Niagara Falls *Iris* and said, "Well, you take right here on Page One (there ain't scarcely any other news) and we have—"

At this point I'm bound to step in and interrupt, giving a few remedies myself, with explanatory notes, as they appeared in the *Iris*. Nearly all ads started at the top of Page One, with several subheads like news stories, and pretty dramatic ones at that. But a closer examination revealed that "Hunnerwell's Celebrated Gum Anodyne" was an absolute specific for Delirium Tremens, and its great virtue (aside from the cure) was that it contained *"No Opium Whatever!* —unlike some rivals we can name." This went on for a column, and as nearly as I could determine, it meant doom for all ailments excepting, perhaps, some Far Eastern distempers that hadn't made their way here yet. Delirium tremens was stressed, but the generality of our homegrown diseases were not neglected.

Oddly enough, the adjacent column announced "Notice to the Public!" and I assumed that a civic innovation was in the works. But no, a tavern at Commercial Wharf had just received a heavy shipment of "Brandies, Rums, Gin, Kentucky Bourbon, Old Rye and Monongahela Common Whiskey—all to be dispensed at competition prices, wholesale or retail." Naturally, I supposed one was encouraged to swill until symptoms occurred and then hike up the street for a bottle of Hunnerwell's.

I'd hoped that Column Three might present news, and was relieved by the head in giant type: "GREAT DISCOVERY!" Now, I said to myself, somebody's gone a little farther than the New York Central and Steam, thank God, and I settled down to be enlightened. "Dr. Wallace," I found, "with offices below the Falls, has a sure preventive for Broken Breasts" and, without too much effort or expense, "can subdue inflammation and soften those most painfully disturbed, so that they may easily be drawn, or their contents pressed out."

Column Four was usurped by a Professor Degrath, who'd developed a commodity called "Electric Oil" (it leaned entirely on Charley's snakes) that was guaranteed, in the professor's local phrase, "to kick the daylights out of piles." His column explained with specifics, but I decided to pass it up. *I* hadn't got piles, and concluded to wait till I had.

By now, pelted by the deluge of disease, I'd taken the notion that Niagara Falls was either the unhealthiest place on earth, or the one best fortified against mortality. I finally inclined to the latter, especially when I saw emblazoned "Dr. Johnson's Balsam of Fir Paste," which slammed the door on wobbly legs; and Ayer's Cherry Pectoral, a "Phthisic," which hinted that old age was nothing but a bad dream. If, that is, Ayers were "swizzled" each morning after breakfast.

I tried to think up an infirmity not covered in the *Iris,* and decided I'd found a loophole—mumps—but sure enough, Dr. Sweets' Horse Linament ("good for man or beast, internal or external") smashed mumps flat while deriding the very notion of "saddle galls, mange, hernia, fistula," and additional nuisances. Even more puzzling than this was "The Great English Remedy" prepared by Sir James Clarke, "physician extraordinary to the queen," whose single achievement had been the invention of his "Celebrated Female Pills." Up to then, I hadn't realized the queen was in trouble.

Dr. Reynolds' "Hospice" at Rochester (half-page ad) was the court of last appeal, medically, and the implication was strong that a body could be carried in, presumably dead for hours, and emerge skipping a rope in about thirty minutes. (The ad was written lightly, hence my mild exaggeration.)

Reynolds had everything; and was said to be cleaning up, in a monetary way. "Ladies and Gents Private Rooms . . . pills for monthly complaints . . . pills against pregnancy . . . young men who by indulging in secret habits have contracted soul-subduing, mind-prostrating, body-destroying vice should apply at once . . . the Doctor's Patent French safe, warranted sure preventative [sic] . . . (sent by mail anywhere) . . . perfect control in all conjugal encounters . . . nurses not disagreeable to the eye"—and other sly comments on this last.

It was hard to tell whether Dr. Reynolds was in the hospital business, concentrating on reproduction, or was running an unusual kind of whorehouse.

But when I asked an elderly whiskerando at the Eagle, he bridled instantly. "Reynolds' *hospital?* Now there ain't no finer in New York. And I ort to know," he said, his nose nearly touching mine; "he cured me clean of gonorrhea four separate times." Then he more or less ruined his argument by adding, after tossing down some sour-smelling rum, "I got shut of every case but the first."

Still, others supported Dr. Reynolds' Rochester mint as being a medical wonder, with the outer room filled by women, "from dawn to midnight." "I've got six children," a man told me. "How many do you reckon I'd have without my old woman took his Stop-gut Lozenges? Being as you don't know, and couldn't, I'd make it twenty-seven. How does that suit you?"

The sole brief item of news on Page One involved a "Madam James," who was arrested on complaint of a man who "visited her rooms" and was careless in disposing his trousers; he was robbed, he said, of fifty dollars.

I should say that the Madam, released, set up a "millinery shop" —with handy rooms above for entertainment. Everything went smoothly, according to report. Mrs. James actually sold a hat now and then, and there were no more howls about theft, upstairs or down.

Meanwhile, in the coroner's court, some startling events had taken place. First off, the jury had summarily rendered a verdict of "death by an accident well knowed by all hereabouts." (The foreman being too grand for such cases, this was composed and read by a merchant specializing in "snake-oil cures" and "copper-toed shoes," both of which he recommended after delivering the verdict.)

Then Red Gill rose to announce, "There was a thing I durst to say, and didn't, the more shame for it. But the verdict gimped out catwise; quickest verdict ever *I* seen. Bridget was expecting; what's more, she'd ganged regular with my oldest son, Appin. They had wedlock in mind, could he pull her free of snakes. There ain't a connection ween that and the death, except roundabout, because Appin was home that night. But I should have said it, and hope Charley will eye it lenient. We been good friends."

51

Charley now got up. No man knew his origins; he was a mystery. Somewhere, he'd been given education (though his speech was violently affected by long river living) and he had, moreover, an air of sophistication that hinted of larger centers, a different life. It was rumored—to his discredit—that he read poetry on the sly.

"I have further to say, beyond my first round, which I should have said it then. I think you know me for an honest man, 'apart from professions.' That last requires probing, and involves Bridget. To begin at the start I'll say that there exist—well, snake people; that is, their lure to snakes weighs out other desires in life. So it's been with me. And Bridget, when she dropped by, curious, one day, was seized the same way.

"In this case I've an idee she fell to the draw of the Falls, born and raised to see others so. Likely it had laid there all along, and I didn't spot it immejit. Snake people are wide-spread odd; I own it up. Most have eyes of a faint shade of blue, verging on grayish. They have a look about them—a kind of faraway, out of the earth thought, if I may put it so.

"On her first visit, I was letting rattlesnakes run free in my back room—snakes need exercise, like humans—and I was watching to see one didn't bite another. In a temper fit, they'll strike and kill among their own; yes, it's so. And they'll strike a copperhead or a blacksnake as quick as winking—any other snake that carries venom, down to the wee bit lodged in a blacksnake. You didn't apprise that, did you?

"But when I told Bridget, she pushed past into the sod-floor room, and the rattlesnakes hushed their clickety-clacking like a steam engine gone dead. They sat waiting. And before I could grab her, she'd leaned and stroked one behind the head. It's God's truth; they declined to bite her. And odder yet, they'll bite *me*"—he held up a shrunken thumb whose cells were still breaking down.

"Bridget? Well, she commenced dropping by regular—orphan girl employed in the hotels in summer and a mean little room and job in winter. No life at all, besides. She asked to board in my back room. Now a rattlesnake man's a lonely life, special in the winter, and she talked me into it, me fully knowing how it'd look.

"I was careful to cage up the bad snakes at night, and I made her a shakedown of corn shucks at the rear, with an ash frame all around. (Snakes don't take to ash.) She more than paid by cooking, cleaning and the purchase of food, for person and reptile. Likewise she tended snakes I kept from going to earth in winter, same as I sell to the stores, after extraction. She was so mesmerizing, my rattlers commenced to breed in the cold weather, so we always had ile for commercial use.

"One day along shore we captured a beautiful big striped water snake, and you could say she fell in love with it, first sight. Even a purty little garter snake's got *some* sting, and I kept warning her not to get bit. But she handled that rascal as if he was her long-lost child, and on the night of her plunge—God rest her soul"—he crossed himself—"she made a plea to let the striper sleep along her, on the shucks, right in the bed. Also there was 'crepitalculum,' as told Red Gill. I felt I'd been more'n lax up to now, but I finally put my foot down.

"To make questions short, she fell into a tantrum, ran out of the house and jumped in the skiff. But her heat was so high, she let an oar slip in the water, not forty feet from shore. I ran alongside shouting to paddle with one oar, but she couldn't, or wouldn't, understand, and a wind was blowing, over that. I stood, the tears a-streaming down my face, watching the boat spin round and round toward the rapids. But there was awareness, too, that she didn't much mind. What did the poet write—'half in love with easeful death'? Bridget was not, strictly saying—ordinary on any level.

"That's the story, gents, and viewed from one compass pint—one only—you could lay matters squarely on me. But I want to urge this to Red Gill: Appin'll forget, and maybe he was lucky, on top. Bridget had no mind for ought but snakes, and trouble would have brewed in the end. In sum and summatum, that's all I had to say."

He sat down, staring ahead into some private snake world of his own, Red Gill stepped over to grasp his hand, and the coroner's inquest was over.

Chapter VII

"I'd be happy to show you Cataract House," said General Whitney when I called at his home, on the river bank not far up from the Porters'. Both places were large, square stone buildings that would stand as eye-catching anywhere in New York.

"I'd meant to send a formal note, sir," and in a burst of truth added, "but the fact is I got caught up yesterday in the inquest on Bridget O'Brien."

He snorted and said, "Those charades. Who knows why anyone decides to go over the Falls? And what can an 'inquest' do to bring the victim back? Well, they've had their fun, the coroner made a few dollars in tips, the apothecaries will continue to get Charley's oil (it's astonishing, sir, how much worthless oil may be extracted from a snake; no doubt you've seen the grease spots where a rattler's sunned on a rock?).

"And Charley? There's no more meanness in him than there is in an angleworm." He looked at me sharply—a tall, well-dressed, consequential man with a slight limp and a cane. "I can say no more, but never play Charley down as a fool. Or even as a normally immoral man. His life is snakes, that and something I could only divulge to a confidant of long standing. Now, will you have a glass of sherry before we walk across the Green?"

It was early, not long past nine, and I declined on the ground I had promised my father not to drink spirits before midday.

"An excellent rule!" said my host with vigor. "For myself I have a toss of rum each morning on arising and drink other alcohol moderately throughout the day. One has that privilege at the age of sixty-five, or five years short of my Biblical span. Strong drink? *Chacun à son goût*, as some neighbors across the river might put it, more or less. Have you heard Canadians speak French, my friend?"

"That's a delight for the future," I told him, knowing from my father what he meant.

He laughed out loud. "Prepare your ears for a bastardized tongue entirely alien to the Continent. The French are in the minority, of course—trouble for the future. By the way, I should have said I have a good acquaintance with your employer, Mr. Bennett. I found him, well, outspoken. A man with two sound legs might have taken umbrage at his remarks. He's interesting, *but he did not like Niagara Falls.* I believe it had something to do with the prices charged him at another hotel."

He studied me, gray eyes twinkling. "You're a very young man, and I think we'll become good friends. I'll inquire then how you persuaded James Gordon Bennett to lodge you at Cataract House, the costliest resort in this region?"

"Well, you see, sir, I have certain funds of my own. My father—"

"Of *course;* his family practically financed the Revolution." Then he burst into laughter again. "I can see Bennett's face when he hears where you are. My boy, could you harbor a slight streak of mischief? Thank God! —it gets dull around here." He frowned, looking off in the distance. "I predict that all of America will grow very serious eventually. But let's get on with your first assignment; we'll try to make it as lively as possible."

We stopped before the 260-foot piazza of his hotel, and he explained that the staff was, now, placing the dozens of rockers, settees, swings and tables where his clientele—Canadians as well as Southerners in this era—sat and chatted and viewed the river and the rising spray.

"I built the Eagle Tavern next door, as you've heard. But when the Falls caught on with the tourists as Saratoga once did, I added Cataract House as an annex. Now, you might call the Eagle the annex, with a lower degree of custom, and Cataract House a showpiece. I bought a parcel of land just up the river—there"—he pointed with his cane, "and walled off a place to swim, with dressing rooms and the like. Very popular in the hotter weather.

"Our most dedicated swimmer to date has been Jenny Lind,

Barnum's 'Swedish nightingale.' She splashed about every day, in the briefest of costumes. As headstrong, she was in a class alone. You've read of her remarkable bosom? Well, people used to flock down and watch her, for, more often than not, it was entirely exposed. She was a seductive creature without being absolutely beautiful. Frankly," he said, "I think Phineas contracted her as much for the bosom as the voice; however, I leave no innuendoes, though others, I believe, have. But she was wild and notiony. Sometimes she sang for us, to amuse herself. Asked, she might go off and sulk, or swim half-nude in the river. It attracted her strangely, but that's not new in these parts."

He said, "Porter recently died, you know, as your present guide is slowing down in his age." Then he told a story I resolved to work in for my boss, as being the kind of scandal he enjoyed. Better yet, I knew how he hated the clan in question, on grounds that "the old man robbed New York blind."

"Some years ago," the general continued, "John Jacob Astor came through here, and the judge, aware of his growing empire, asked him to stay at his home. Well, sir, you'd scarcely believe it, but the old fellow was so smelly and rank that, on some pretext, they moved him to a corner room farthest from the central living quarters. I believe Mrs. Porter, and others of the family, had threatened to leave for an extended trip to Europe. One of the family, a female, kept a diary, I've forgotten which. And the judge afterward told me that, as he figured it from the stink, his guest probably hadn't bathed for two or three years, and maybe more. An effort was made, in a picnic spirit, to get him to join in a plunge in some backwater, where people bathed then, and he left the next day. He seemed badly shaken, according to Porter."

A wooden pavilion stood between the hotel and the river, and the general described the brass-band concerts, dancing on the piazza, and other gaiety that went on when the musicians were "in good lip" (meaning sober). Cataract House itself was made of stone two feet thick, and covered with plaster, leaving it cool during the hottest summer months. This four-story colossus was painted white, with green trim, and had a mansard roof and a cupola—an impressive edifice by any standards. In the lobby was the Brussels carpet I mentioned at the time of Miss Barclay's distress, and this also covered the great staircase that allowed Southern belles to make their proper descent.

We walked about inside, the general pointing out furnishings that he'd bought in Europe or received from guests. Of these last the chief was an enormous crystal chandelier hanging in the main salon, a gift of Lafayette. The piece was so overwhelming, and had so many hundreds of little icicles, that I estimated it weighed at least about half a ton, and I maneuvered around to keep out from under. I noticed that it swayed slightly—from the Falls, no doubt.

I recalled that the marquis, after the war, had taken a liking for this country and had returned for some years. He visited around, mostly prominent people, till he became something of a nuisance. The years in France, after our War, were romantic enough. He was seized by the usual politicians (for helping us) but escaped to Spain from a prison ship. Then he made his way to North Carolina. Rich, he was lavish with gifts, the larger the better, it seemed.

In all, this hotel was so vast that I began to suspect its success depended partly on daily separations of husband and wife; they were bound to have trouble finding each other. There were card rooms, billiard salons, ballrooms, several barrooms that excluded ladies, no matter how thirsty, and a dining room the size of a soccer field. Here there were tables for two, four and six, with bigger for larger groups. Louvered French doors permitted fresh breezes to blow through on hot days; and upstairs the hotel offered everything from single rooms to kick-proof suites for families that brought children and servants. And yes, said the general, the basement included spancels and pallets for blacks that appeared (to the owners) to waltz the line of behavior.

Offsetting this flaw in his hotel, Whitney was digging a chute off the "raceway," a sluice of water that, mostly to provide power for mills, had been built along the river. The general's—nearly finished—would offer running water in all rooms and replace the line of privies outside. "I mean to maneuver it for the poor spanceled devils, too," he said. "In former years, their privies were disgusting; I admit it. Now I plan to make it up, as far as I can.

"It's monstrous!" he exploded, back again on slavery, "but at this point in history such arrangements (the spancels) are legal and we have to fall in line with other hotels and the wishes of our guests. However, it will end, this owning of people by people, here and in Africa where it started and continues. But it may take a fratricidal war to accomplish it."

He thumped his cane on the floor—we were back in Lafayette country, and the icicles jingled to his wrath, causing me another retreat from the firing line. He said, "If I had two sound legs, sir, I'd join that war at the outbreak. Meanwhile we try to make the wretches down below comfortable without causing some Southern jackass to explode.

"But here in Niagara we have a hopeful factor." He lowered his voice and stepped closer. "I dislike probing a stranger's politics, but I can trust, knowing your father, that your sympathies lie against this institution—I speak of slavery."

"They do indeed, sir," I replied, telling the truth.

"Then I'll pass on an item of news. It's not for Bennett; he seems to blow hot and cold on this thing. We have in Niagara and in points nearby, terminals for the Underground Railroad. You've heard of it? I beg pardon. We smuggle runaways across to Queenston, on the other side, and the Canadians either find them jobs or move them on. A center here is Lockport; another's Lewiston.

"You'd hardly believe that owners employ 'slave-catchers,' as their impudence terms it, and post them at points along the river, in the summertime, and sometimes in winter.

"Now, young man, I can tell you in privacy, and with satisfaction, that more than one of those—*scum!*"—he spat the word out—"have gone tumbling down the bank into the river, and over Nee-a-gah-ra, as the Indians first called our showpiece. With luck, and a shrewd prod or so, we may see a deal more. I hope so."

(I've gone into detail here, for Niagara's place in the Underground Railway is important to what I have to tell later.)

Furniture both downstairs and up was chiefly of inlaid mahogany or rosewood, almost priceless. Framing the louvered windows and doors downstairs were heavy plush drapes, and the great mirrors and other adornments (on all floors) were mainly Venetian in origin, gilded, ornate with delicate carvings—cupids and such—that might have been showy in a hostelry less grand.

Fireplaces stood in the white walls in all bedrooms and sitting rooms and were scattered through the social rooms of the first floor. The great piazza facing the Falls was, as suggested, comfortable with rockers, sofas, swings, loveseats (for honeymooners) and awnings. I should add that Cataract House had a piano in the Grand Salon, the first in Niagara. It had been brought in by sleighs years before, and the Senecas stared at it through the windows so often that General Whitney invited them in to hear his daughter play. They were interested but not crushed; one went so far as to say he preferred the eagle-bone whistle.

Taken in sum, this Cataract House was a grandiose credit to, now, the world's foremost tourist attraction. I was shown registers that contained names of (leading) European royalty, as well as our own homegrown celebrities, both South and North. I was impressed and said so.

Shaking my hand to leave, the general thereupon invited me—and Miss Barclay!—to dinner. I stood staring, shocked to find that he suspected an acquaintance between us, but I was to learn that all gossip fanned through the hotel like a monsoon. Little passed of which the staff were unaware. Then I remembered that I'd carelessly left the two brandy glasses unwashed on my table.

No matter what he knew, or divined, I accepted for both of us, then went to search for my friend of the adjoining suite.

Chapter VIII

Dinner in the hotels, and generally in the region, began at two P.M. and ran along like the Mexican *comida,* probably the best system yet devised. In that relaxed country (which I'd visited once with my parents) one may dine when he chooses, from eleven A.M. on until midnight or beyond. The chefs, cooks, waiters, busboys enjoy their work. They see no reason not to be on the job rather than loaf in the streets. Also they take pride in producing fine food, and in the praise it draws.

Cataract House (and General Whitney's home) served the day's main meal at two, but he said that to arrive punctually meant we'd have more time to "become fortified for digestion."

So—with time on my hands, I wandered through the hotel, into the town, and finally (coughing up another quarter) onto Goat Island. I had about as much knowledge of Miss Barclay as she had of me, and I speculated whether, in a fit of remorse, she'd flung herself over the Falls. And sure enough, at the same point where I'd been tempted to wade out, I saw her leaning against the rail, looking thoughtful.

"Well, Miss Barclay," I said, moving up and summoning what bogus-cheerful poise I could muster, "planning to take a dive?"

"Hardly," she said, turning around, her face happy and excited. "But isn't it just too grand for *words?*"

"Hope not. That's why I'm here. The place has been blown up to be the world's foremost resort, and I'm supposed to put it all down on paper."

"I wondered. Why you were here, I mean. You work for—"

"Mr. James Gordon Bennett, the curse and boon of New York . . . And journalistic genius, too, I suppose."

"Work! You know, I feel altogether different here, away from home. I'm not even ashamed of night before last. It's somehow erased my stupidity—before, you know."

"I can't think of anything you have to be ashamed of, Miss Barclay. Nature works in—in"— I made a feeble attempt to disgorge some high philosophical balm, but it broke down in the middle.

"See here," said my companion briskly, "we English recoil at the first-name basis, but I no longer feel, well, so very English. I saw the register, of course; would you be frightfully upset if I called you William?"

"Bill."

"You must realize that you're the first real confidant I've ever had—"

"Bill it is, and while I too saw the register, and the 'Honorable,' I'll try slipping into the habit of 'Frances.' That's not a vulgar play on words, by the way."

Smiling faintly, she took one of my hands and said, "You're my good friend and counselor. Really, you know, I feel altogether changed. I'm sorry; I said that before."

"Say it all day if you like. *Sing* it. I'm here to help even if I have to suffer for it."

"I'm losing all my Englishism. Isn't that glorious?"

She was happier than she'd ever been, and the fact is, so was I. The presence of females had often made me shy, but I felt at ease with Miss Barclay.

"And since you're to tell me what to do, or maybe what not, I have something to say."

"Say on."

"I plan to *stay* here. I *like* it. And I hated my position back home. 'Honorable,' to me, meant being the pitied sister of a beauty, yelling at hounds, snobbery, and boring, boring parties. Would it interest you to know that I *loathe* horses?"

"Any particular horse?"

"Do you realize that the upper-class Englishman spends his whole adult life comparing himself socially to those about him? Which belongs to the better club, who's the richest, whose title is the longest" —she paused here to blush, but she regained command and said, "That's American, American foolishness. I'm American now, or as soon as possible, and I hope you'll help me *get a job of work!* I mean to make myself useful. What do you think?"

"What do *I* think? For now, I think—I know—we're invited to General Whitney's for dinner, at two o'clock."

"But how on earth did he pair us?"

"He didn't; we did. That's English, or, rather, universal. Come along. Let's consider your problem with the presiding genii of the cascade. If I know that hobbling old rooster, he'll have ideas enough for you, and more."

"Don't you take anything seriously? Is that American? It's not that I don't like it, you understand."

"I take everything seriously in a nonserious way. That is *very* American."

We walked back across the bridge and up the greensward toward the general's home, which was set back from the river; here it was safe from the grinding, tumbled ice of winter. Miss Barclay (I continued to think of her thus for a while) observed that the time was a few minutes shy of one, so that on coming to General Whitney's baths, with their stone dressing rooms, I said, "It's a hot day, and the water's no more than cool—I tested it. Let's go swimming."

She tried (I thought) to look American, and said, "I have no bathing costume."

"We can study the place for later, at least."

The premises were empty, and would be for a week or more. The bathhouses were clean, and the white water outside looked inviting.

The bath area was screened by leafed-out beeches and hickories, and I took off most of my clothes and slipped into the water, swimming with what I hoped was nonchalance to where Miss Barclay was bending over a wall, letting one hand dangle in the river.

"Really!" she said, seeing me mostly unclothed, chugging along at my best breaststroke. "You *are* incorrigible."

"It's not cold at all. You could go in the dressing place and join me in your—shift? Is that correct garment?"

"It isn't, but I suspect we're badly enough off in the hotel. I *like* swimming," she said with emphasis. "It's one of my few *sportifs.*"

I said, "I leased these baths for our private use until the Fourth of July."

"Liar."

"Swimming. I can't think of a more American thing to do."

For a second, she appeared like the former Miss Barclay. Then she got up with resolution, and when she came back walked out onto the wall wearing a scrap above and below. Her lips were pursed in a whistle, as if this were a commonplace. Then she slipped off the wall to join me.

Despite the female notables (Jenny Lind) who had bathed scantily clad here before, I can only guess what it cost Miss Frances Barclay to perform this about-face from her background. But she had easily the best figure to cross my path, before or since, and it must have bolstered her courage.

"Well, how was the water?" cried General Whitney. He limped his way down the green, after we'd combed and tidied up and started toward his house. The former Miss Barclay put both hands to her face, her Americanization, or whatever, being less complete than she'd hoped. But I sang out, with faked boldness, "Splendid. I hope you don't mind our pushing the season a trifle."

"Not at all, not at all, my boy. I have a spot from my piazza where I can watch the baths through my telescope. I've never seen a couple—even honeymooners—enjoy my little gift to Cataract guests with as much gusto. Ah, swimming! I wish I were in condition for what I've just enjoyed vicariously."

I wasn't quite certain what, precisely, he'd enjoyed, but I determined to brazen it out. "Sir, Miss Barclay feels she should change into more formal attire before dinner. I've told her I thought—"

He took Miss Barclay's hand. "Dear girl, you look superb. Any improvement and the Whitneys would be forced into their Sunday best. Come along. I'm afraid we have only an everyday fare, but it seems better after a libation or two. I hope you take a little sherry or other light refreshment." he said, turning to the girl, his face innocent as a babe's.

"Well, not usually, but today's very special for me."

"Your birthday?" he asked in surprise.

"No, it's the beginning of my being an American."

"In that case, it's special for Niagara Falls. We might have to break out a Napoleon—just a sip, you understand, just a sip."

The glib old customer was so wily you never quite knew where you stood.

As we walked in, I replied that my father had given me a bottle of Napoleon for the trip, and that I'd not only opened it, being exhausted, but had forced a swallow on the bellhop. I said I was afraid he might have a heart attack after carrying all our bags.

"Very worthy of you, too. But he's stronger and younger than he looks. I'm surprised he took it, being a lifelong teetotaler. But here we are; I'll introduce you to the family."

Mrs. Whitney was at least twenty years younger than her husband, quiet and serene, and I surmised that our host had lost one wife and married another. For the rest, there was somebody's sister, I believe, and a female cousin, neither of whom made themselves felt above the general. They were very polite but I had trouble next day remembering what they looked like. His daughter (the piano player) was married and living in Albany.

All the furnishings were dark, heavy, obviously costly, and when General Whitney led us two into his office, I was taken aback. It was the kind of den, or library, that one might expect in the more affluent sections of Boston. There were rows of Morocco-bound books, a faded brown globe that appeared to have South America slightly north of Greenland, a mahogany desk covered in calf, and a couple of black-leather chairs. On the wall, behind his desk, a pair of sabers contended for dominance but did not prevail over a polished brass telescope that lay on a mantel above a now crackling fireplace.

"Yes, the pages are cut; the books are read. In certain cases, over and over," he said, seeing me eye the uniform volumes of Shakespeare, Milton, Spencer. There were poetic and philosophic works, but I saw no single sample of the religious insipidity that clogged libraries in those days. I concluded that his tastes (and common sense) were not unlike my father's.

He yanked a tasseled bellpull, and there appeared a tall, muscular Negro, in a kind of livery, who, holding the doorknob, said something to the effect of "Yassuh, yassuh." I thought he glanced at the sabers.

"Bring us three brandy glasses, Scipio," said our host. "Mrs. Whitney can pick them out. And be lively!"

"Yass, suh," said the servant and vanished.

"I've never known why all large slaves must be named Scipio or Cato. Oh, I'm aware of Scipio Africanus. And Cato, of course, suggests bogus erudition in some julep-swilling ignoramus.

"Yes, the fellow's a runaway. We'll get him across to Canada soon. My 'Step lively!' was not to stress his status but to stave off homesickness. You'd be surprised to know that many from the Underground wish they'd never left. Often they run on impulse, after an unpleasant incident. As immoral as the condition is, most slaves are treated kindly. They have no responsibilities, are well fed, and many remain content with their condition, which often exceeds the superstitious violence in Africa. The ones with force enough to break loose are, of course, quick by nature, potentially dangerous, as the owners see it. Hence the Cataract's spancels.

"The story's not entirely dark against the Southerners, much I deplore the institution. These people—the owners—are accustomed to a way of life, and appear puzzled by the hostility they've aroused. Perhaps," he said, musing, "the real fault lies with the greedy parents and grandparents—the original buyers—more than with this generation, which merely remains loyal to a tradition."

By now, the slave had brought the glasses, holding all three between the fingers of one hand (to show off) though with an uneasy look at the owner. Then, not bawled out, he skipped through the door.

"I'm really not a drinker of brandy," murmured Miss Barclay.

"Oh, come, come. On a day when our young nation has acquired such a handsome addition, a certain laxity must be urged. There—you see?—only a ceremonial sip."

"One could easily lead to another," she observed, looking happy.

"I've asked myself," said General Whitney, "what will your father say when he hears the news?"

Miss Barclay smiled. "I'll be lucky if he remembers my name. He's busy with his awful pigs and hothouses, sherry and, of course, some horse-faced women of similar tastes."

The general had apparently taken too large a swallow as she spoke. He was embarrassed.

"It's a gala day, and I only regret we can't give you a suitable banquet. Just plain fare, plain fare, not better than Cataract—"

He was rescued from floundering by Mrs. Whitney, who came in to announce that dinner was "set."

It was hardly plain fare that she, the dim relations, and two colored women placed before us. It was in fact one of the hotel daily menus that would appear there next day.

Whitefish or salmon hors d'oeuvre
Pickled buffalo tongues
Ox hearts smothered in onions
Mutton Cutlets
Stewed turkey wings
Vegetables variés (fresh green peas; potatoes au gratin; cauliflower in vinagrette sauce; green onions in sugar and vinegar, carrots suprèmes)
Charlotte Russe
Melon
Blanc Mange
Marble Cake

As we ate, General Whitney fired mild volleys of belittlement at the meagerness of the meal, until one of the family finally caught his eye and he quieted down.

These courses, you understand, were brought in *as courses*. The meal was not spread on the table "family style," as on the barge. One could not, of course, eat a Charlotte Russe, a melon, Blanc Mange *and* Marble Cake, but your choice was politely asked; and the melon I ate was the best I'd had anywhere. And when I suggested it had ripened early, the general laid this to the unusual warm and sunny spell the previous month.

The slave Scipio refilled our wineglasses until Miss Barclay and I demurred. Then the general stepped up his part, to offset our "breakdown," he said.

If the mutton chops were slightly tough, like all mutton chops, and the idea of ox hearts and buffalo tongues repelled, the local whitefish and turkey wings made it all up.

For reasons unclear, our host had brought in the telescope and laid it beside his chair. I'd begun to wonder if, foxy or not, he wasn't a sort of harmless lunatic who was allowed to wander freely, when suddenly, with first twilight, he leaped up, grabbed the spyglass and ran out on the piazza, ignoring his cane. On the way, he collected a double-barreled gun from a corner.

He set off down the lawn at a brisk pace for a man with a bad leg, shouting as he went: "All right, you skulking Turners! I've been waiting for this. I know what goes on in the livery stables around this town. Not from *my* river bank. No siree!"

Most of us followed, and saw two men rowing up the quiet eddy in a skiff. One was peculiarly trussed up, and behind them was a barrel-shaped object, bobbing up and down where it hit a swirl of current.

"Why, General, we didn't in no-wise think you'd mind, and besides, the water's free, ain't it?"

"Not by a damned sight! I own to the middle of the river and the Falls, and so do the Porters. You want to kill yourselves?—put your contraption on a wagon and haul it up to where you can cross to Canada. I thought you had a *grain* of sense, Ab Turner. You ever hear, considering you weren't drunk, that there's nothing but rocks below American Falls? The chance of busting your skull from my place don't exist. Now row in here and be spry about it, hear?"

"Dog if you ain't put up so many nigger-owning Southerners you're beginning to talk like one, Generl. 'Hear?' Well, if *that* don't come across rich! Turn her head around, Verge, and put in. He's got a shotgun, and if we push farther out we'll get caught in the rapids sure."

66

When their boat touched the bank, General Whitney and I helped pull it up.

"You know, Generl, it wouldn't inconvenienced you to look another direction. We wan't doing *you* no harm, and I recollect mending your surrey oncet, and never charged you for it, neither—"

"Very surprising, when you owed me two hundred dollars on a loan for horse stalls."

The boat, once beached, proved full of various equipment, and we had a look at it and at the would-be occupant (who seemed about to cry).

"Scipio, go fetch a lantern."

While the time was no later than five-thirty, the sky was overcast, the spray was unusually dense, and altogether we had trouble making out details.

The boy ticketed to ride the Falls had contrived (with the others' aid) to wrap himself round with bandages and pads and he had on, besides, a leather headgear (from Senecas who played lacrosse).

But the barrel was outstanding. It was encircled two or three dozen times by cables and had a top, with air holes, that screwed on. Inside was a steel frame built around a wooden seat, and taped here and there were emerging augers, punches, a saw, tubes (to thrust up through air holes, I assumed, if the vehicle came to rest upside down). This last appeared unlikely, for the barrel's bottom had a fastened-down sheet of lead, for ballast, so that in theory everything should have gone well, barring the rocks.

"Well, Ab," said General Whitney, as we looked it all over, "I see you're trying to get rid of Verge. You got something against him? Did he steal a horse? Why'd you want to murder your wedded legal offspring? You're aware there's feeling growing against these dumb-fool stunts."

"Now, Generl, you've knowed me for thirty year, give or take. Would I auspiciously and out in the open harm a hair of my boy's head?"

"No, because the head wouldn't likely rise in the Whirlpool. To tell the truth, I'm flummoxed. To go further, I never gave you Turners credit for brains to fill a thimble—with room left over for a thumb—but this!

"How many boys you lost altogether? Four? Five?"

Turner seemed outraged. "By Jesus and the Twelve Apostles, you know it weren't more'n three, Generl! I ain't the one to overtake chances with the family. The boys wanted to go, and I ain't a father to stand in the way. If they wished to better themselves, don't it appear their business?"

"No. Now fetch some draft horses and get this junk off my property. Hopscotch out of here, Ab. You, Verge, stay behind as hostage. You're trespassing, and it may come to court," and our host whipped up his gun.

"Lawdy, lawdy, 'em men goin to get shot," moaned Scipio.

"Why, Generl, you wouldn't kill me in cold blood," inquired Ab, his eyes crinkling up. "The war's been over a pretty long time." He evidently knew his man better than we did.

"Be out of here in twenty minutes," said General Whitney. "Go up and row to Canada, as stated. If you're hell-bent on filicide, he might defeat you in the Horseshoe."

"Filicide! Now ain't that a dandy? Lookee here, Generl, I'm a thirty-eight-degree mason" (leaving me bewildered to the present), "but we're obleeged and will foller suit. Filicide! But hold up here. I recollect Sam Patch went over the American, and him without a barrel . . . Durned old humbug," we heard him say when we turned toward the house.

General Whitney chuckled, back on the piazza. "'Durned old humbug' himself. Do you suppose my people haven't watched that coffin grow, up in his stable? And disabuse me if I wasn't told the attempt was set for tonight. Then tomorrow, if alive, *wouldn't* they have crowed the place down! Collections, lectures, paid-out pieces for the newspapers, and so on. *But not from my land!*"

Chapter IX

In a few days the tally-hos, horns blowing, bells ringing, horses prancing, began arriving, and Southerners, in the main, seemed to fill the lounge rooms pretty fast. Their route had been by railroad to Buffalo and then by boat to a safe wharf upriver, where the tally-hos gathered. Oddly enough, most men wore tall hats, which appeared to equate them with the Irish foremen, as I saw it, gaudy waistcoats which didn't, and frilled shirts. Acquaintances greeted old favorites and nodded at others, according to how things had gone in the past.

Oddly enough, nearly all the men signed the register and added their political affiliation: *"Southern* Democrat"; "Former Whig"; and, occasionally, "Unionist!", if the man was big enough to defend his view. One Southerner wrote, "With two niggers spanceled in basement," but I noticed the desk clerk later scratched this out.

There were numbers of Canadians, from Ontario, mostly, and why they chose to bypass their excellent Clifton House, across the river, I have no idea.

General Whitney had placed me, by request, in a bed-sitting room on a second-floor corner, with a desk for my dispatches, which I thought might commence soon.

After I'd settled in, there came a timid knock and a girl of seventeen or so came in to say, deferentially, "I'm your chambermaid, sir. Can I get you anything?"

She was dressed in a gray uniform, was slim and yet full-bodied, and—chambermaid or not—looked me unashamed and clear-eyed in the face.

"Why—why, no," I said, confused. "The fact is, I hadn't thought of a chambermaid."

"You can always use the bellpull, sir. Until eleven at night. There's one in every room."

"What do I call you?"

"My name is Betsy, sir."

"See here," I blurted on impulse. "This is a devil's hard job you've got—second floor and all. How much do you get paid? You don't mind my asking?"

"No one ever asked before. I make twelve and a half cents an hour, sir."

"That's outrageous! What time do you come to work?"

"Seven in the morning. General Whitney pays more than other hotel owners."

I said, "We'll have to come to an understanding. When you clean up, I'll leave. I've got some important work to do; and please don't disturb the papers on the desk."

"What papers, sir?"

I gave her a sharp look, but her face was entirely guileless.

"There'll be papers; don't worry about it."

"Of course there will. I'll leave if you're starting now."

"Well, I don't choose to start now. What do you think of that?"

"Nothing, sir. I bring tea at seven-thirty. It's a specialty of Cataract House."

"Well, don't bring me any. I hate the stuff. We drink it in New York to kill the water stink. Let the tea go."

"What time shall I come, sir?"

I thought a minute. "When do they serve breakfast downstairs?"

"From eight o'clock until noon."

"What kind of breakfast? Mutton chops?"

"Mutton chops, ham, bacon, eggs, porridge, bread, rolls and biscuits, pancakes, fruits, preserves, fried potatoes, and something called hominy for the Southern folk.

"Usually I bring breakfast to the room for private gentlemen, sir."

"Another outrage. We'll make an arrangement. You bring my breakfast between eight-thirty and nine, when you're not too busy, and I'll pay exactly your hourly wage in addition—twelve and a half cents. Leave out the mutton chops; give them to some animal with good strong teeth—a wolf, or large dog."

"I couldn't take more, sir. It's my job."

"Look here—Betsy? I'm the boss and it's for me to decide. I've decided it's proper to pay twelve and a half cents more."

She looked up from her clear blue eyes. "I'm the chambermaid, assigned to look after you. More money would be a poor start."

"Are you a chambermaid or some kind of wardress?"

"I hope I suit, sir." She curtsied, but at the door said, "Tea is very good for warding off the vapors."

"Bring it," I said, my voice rising, "and I'll throw it out of the window. And we'll see who wins about the money. I'm used to having my way in these matters."

"I thought perhaps you were, sir," she said and left.

Down the hall, a commotion broke out that sounded like a full riot. From natural curiosity I poked my head through the door and beheld an obviously Southern family moving in. I thanked God they were several doorways down. At the moment, however, all, or most (including a darky woman) were standing in the corridor talking. My father once observed that traveling English seldom stay in their rooms but stand chatting in hallways, going over details of their trip. He said, "Southerners aren't much quieter; they make the devil of a row."

Dominant, as bellboys struggled with their trunks, was a blond-gray man in his sixties, portly, ruddy face wreathed in good humor. The rest were females, with parasols, vanity cases, and smelling salts being passed freely (and unnecessarily).

In one hand, the man was holding the predictable julep, and he called out, "Ah, our neighbor, Mr. Morrison, I presume. Come join us, sir, join us." (He said in fact, 'suh,' but I'll give up trying to ape these accents.) For a second, I had in mind to duck back to my room and slide down the waterspout. But I was too shy to refuse.

"I want you to meet my wife, Edith" (a woman heavily powdered, to look younger), "her sister Hester, my two little darlings, Deborah and Nancy-Jo; and, finally, Atlanta's belle, Samantha."

As an afterthought he added: "Colonel Amos Rutledge, sir"—he thrust out his hand—"at your service."

Well, the girl could have been the belle of anything—an ash-blond girl with an appraising gaze that told how useless compliments were in her case. She took my hand, then dismissed me, as if in a receiving line.

Rebuffed, I regained a measure of poise and said, "Forgive me, but how did you know my name, sir?"

"I always check the clientele, especially those near us. General Whitney was good enough to tell us of your family. No offense

71

intended. But come in, come in; have a toddy. It'll give you strength to look directly at Samantha; she'll look right through you—brazen hussy."

"It's early for me, sir; besides, I have a dispatch to write. But I thank you."

"Oh, never mind that; sharpen your invention, give Mr. Bennett something to think about, eh?"

Addled, I allowed myself to be jammed, in effect, into the main sitting room. The suite had three bedrooms, a large sitting room and a playroom. A male darky inside, directing the placement of luggage, leaped to the door as the owner said, "Fix our guest a julep, Mose. Do it on the hop, and don't stint the whiskey."

"Yes, sah, Colonel!"

It occurred to me that, if I ever left Cataract House, I'd likely leave on a litter, a new-made drunk.

"We bring our own mint leaves, Mr. Morrison. The locals aren't ripe yet, and lack flavor from the pale sun and mist."

The drink he handed me—I watched it made—was purely powdered sugar, crushed ice from the ice house, and raw whiskey, with an absurd gesture of mint leaf rubbed around the rim.

"Drink it down, my boy. You'll write a dispatch to set New York afire. Not a bad idea, if you'll excuse it."

Gingerly I tasted the drink, which was molten fire, and shortly felt better, commotion and all. After another sip, I felt sufficiently better to approach the girl Samantha, who was staring out of a window toward the Falls.

The truth is, I was slightly irritated at what seemed a naked, if genial, kidnapping. Moreover, I suspected that my privacy was gone forever.

"Do *you* drink these things?" I held up the julep.

"Hardly!" She looked around, then took my drink and poured it into a potted plant, courtesy of the management.

Relieved, I said, "You too seem to have a mind of your own. That's the end of *that* blossom, by the way. It'll turn up its heels in about ten minutes."

"Good. It was hideous. Daddy'll ring down for another; wait and see. He always gets his way. Look how he shoved you in here—a complete stranger."

"And with you?"

"Oh," she said vaguely, "I have systems. Disappearing's the best."

"Well," I said, braced for another rebuff, "let's get out and walk around Goat Island. It won't mean anything."

"No," she said shortly, "it won't. I hate those awful Falls, but I'll go, no matter."

To my surprise, she left to change into snug male riding pants. In this period, ladies wore skirts for riding in public, but she said, contemptuously, that in a place like Niagara Falls she wore what she pleased. With her disposition, I wondered why she bothered to explain. And at the toll booth, she insisted on paying her own way.

"I prefer not to owe people. They expect something."

"As you wish. Pay mine if you like."

She gave me a withering look, and we went on.

"We turn to the right here," she said. "In the carriages, of course, with a driver bawling out lies."

I said, "I go left, around the head of the island."

She turned, dumbfounded, and I steeled myself against her beauty. "Coming?"

"This one time."

When we reached the head, looking across to Canada, she pointed. "What's that?"

In midstream, a deer, blood flowing from its neck, was trying to swim ahead of two pursuing dogs, or wolves. But they'd all misjudged their course. The deer hit the midstream rapids, and began futilely struggling. The dogs, or wolves, mistook this for weakness, and closed in, or tried to. All three went spinning down toward the curling white rapids, and then went over, out of our sight.

We stood a moment in awe, depressed by the power of our "attraction." My companion held both hands to her face.

"It's monstrous! Why don't they stop it?"

"Who?"

"Well, whoever's in charge of animals around this butchery."

"Nobody's in charge of animals, and how do you keep a deer from going down to drink?"

"Were they dogs?"

"Wolves, likely—wolves here, too. Plenty."

"On this *island?*"

"Yes," I said, lying. "A Mr. Stedman once stocked the place with sheep and a few goats, and wolves came in and ate them all up. One goat, was left, I believe."

She slapped a tree with a silver-handled quirt. "I'm not afraid of wolves."

"Of course you aren't, but don't handle them too rough. You'll break their spirit."

She turned the sleek, blond head to face me. "There aren't any wolves out here. What an inspired liar you are. *You* get to be a

73

correspondent? You couldn't stick to the facts for two sentences in a row."

I said calmly, "Animals, mainly from Canada, try to swim this river every day. It's a common occurrence ... such as the second deer out there now." —This time I myself pointed at the lone, doomed swimmer.

"I don't want to see it—let's go on."

Animals tried regularly to cross, and none made it except those far upstream. I wondered why they did, and it struck me they might be like the families dwelling here. Drawn to the challenge. It sounded far-fetched, but so did a great many other truths.

At the Three Sisters, we climbed over the clumps to the gnarled trees. She leaned down, with one hand in the water. Her face had an odd look.

"It's *beautiful*," she said at last, staring at the polished rock bottom. "It's the first time I ever really saw it. Oh, I took a ride on one of those scows down below—they had two then, I believe—and got a good soaking, besides coming back half-deaf. Let's wade out a few feet."

"This place is not for wading. And what about your boots and costume?"

"Water dries; hadn't you heard?"

"Not riding boots; they'll be wrecked."

"Get more boots, get a dozen more. Who cares?"

I said, "I'll be along down the path. You can catch up if you like."

I thought she might strike me with the quirt. Then she shrugged, and followed after, but she didn't look happy about it.

From a few feet behind, she said, "I wonder why I'd listen to you. I don't listen to anybody."

"Masterful. Born masterful. If you'll quit trying to be a man for a while, I'll show you some things. I know this place from one tip to another," I said, lying again.

I pointed out some coal-black squirrels, strange trees and shrubs she hadn't noticed before; and when a perfectly recognizable wolf trotted in front of us, anxious to clear off, her face at last shone with excitement.

"Was it?"

"Yes, it was. It probably got caught swimming farther up, and landed here last night. I'll inform the proprietors."

"What'll *they* do—make it pay a toll?"

"Shoot it, of course. There haven't been wolves here in numbers for years."

"They wouldn't dare!" she said, her eyes blazing. "I've seen enough water for now, and I'm not ready for those Falls. Let's strike inland, explore and all that."

"I'm not positive about the grounds. And if one wolf landed, what about ten others?"

"How very masterful. You said you knew everything. I'm off in that direction" —she pointed toward the woods. "You can catch up if you like."

I stood in a dilemma. I'd been in Niagara less than a week, and without trying had become embroiled with three strong-headed females. Miss Barclay, in her way, had ideas of her own; my chambermaid could easily have been town constable; and Miss Rutledge had declared war on the world, with me, at the moment.

However, it was my turn to shrug, and we followed a faint path that climbed slightly upward through the trees.

"This is the most fun I ever had at Niagara Falls," she said firmly. "Some time ago I decided not to like it at all."

We came to an eminence that contained a kind of cave dwelling. Some laundry, if it could be called that, for it came close to being rags, fluttered between two saplings. And inside all was orderly and neat.

"Have you brought me here for some foul purpose?"

"You were in the lead. And don't worry about the purpose."

"Well, there's another path, going off there; let's follow it."

In a zigzag sort of way, it led to a spot of the river where various small, hidden islands held out against a tearing current. They lay closer to the Falls, below the Three Sisters. The place was very secluded, closed from view by thick willows and high weeds. But the chief item of interest was a fair-haired young man hanging by his knees from a willow limb extending over the water. His face looked peaceful as he rocked gently (and suicidally) back and forth. It was my first glimpse—a shocking one—of the Hermit of Goat Island, as the townsfolk called him.

Once again, my companion put her hands to her face. "Get him! Bring him back at once!"

"Get him yourself. I can't figure out how he got there. The rapids are *roaring* between that clump and the bank. Anyhow, it's his business."

She wanted to talk about him, and maybe join him, but I was badly shaken, and anxious to move. I'd ask General Whitney about him later.

I took her arm and marched us back to the path and on down the bank. She made an ineffectual pass at me with the quirt, but seizing it I put it in my hip pocket.

"You bully! You're hurting me."

"Then calm down, and I'll show you my favorite overlook at the Falls."

"I won't! Nothing can get me nearer that trap. I know its ways. You go on. This time you aren't masterful, unless you drag me."

"You really are in a pet."

"And this is where I take over." Her blue eyes blazed. *"You* go down to your overlook. Nothing can get me there, nothing!"

And she wheeled round, a most enigmatic girl, and strode off through the woods toward the bridge.

I stood confounded. We'd come to Goat Island to see the Falls, I thought, and we hadn't been near them yet, or within a thousand yards of them. For a second, I wondered if it wouldn't be healthful to follow the girl, plop her over my knee, and give her a spanking. But she was too pretty, and I had no wish to lose even a half-friend.

I wandered on disconsolate, still puzzled, and finally went back myself, determined to quiz General Whitney about the family, and the girl in particular. After all, they'd come here for three years, and if there was anything he didn't know about them, it was probably trivial. Wondering why she'd joined me, I decided it was simply to get away from her kinfolk.

Chapter X

That afternoon I attended the funeral for Verge Turner, which was held in the Unitarian Church. The place was packed with river people, townsfolk, mourners of all degrees, including some from the Canadian side. I noticed General Whitney (wearing a frazzled armband) seated in the rear; despite himself, he had a faint "I told you so" expression.

"Mourners" is not quite accurate. The river element were talking, in very slightly lowered voices, about the mechanics of Verge's barrel, and occasional arguments arose. I heard a man near me say, "If a Falls man ain't got sense enough to anchor his ballast with spikes, or nails, then he throwed off addled along the way, no disrespect to the diseased. And I think Ab Turner"—in the seat ahead—"will back me up on that."

Turner, unoffended, nodded gravely. He said, "When we contrive De Witt's vehicle, we'll bear it in mind, making allowance for him being younger. And I've got some further and forward ideas besides. But I'm dogged if I ain't running out of sons. I may drop the whole idea."

There were murmurs of mixed sympathy and protest. "Now Ab, you done what you could ... Nobody's a-blaming you, not in *my* earshot" ... "Your family's a credit to the town, and, yes, to

Canader, too" ... "To give up at this point wouldn't be like you" ... and, "We got a power of faith in DeWitt Clinton; that boy'll make your mark, set it down."

The coffin, hastily contrived (as such grisly constructions were in this age lacking refrigeration) sat on a couple of two-by-fours beneath the pulpit. The top half was open, if you cared to walk up and survey the blue, bloated resident. But a glancing look convinced me against it.

What happened, I gathered, was that the father and De Witt had towed the barrel to Canada and released it, calling encouragements. Then they landed and made their way to a Canadian point below the Falls, where a crew waited. As to the barrel, the lead ballast loosened and the whole thing turned upside down, not giving the occupant time to drill new breathing holes. The barrel began to fill, and the crew—too late—grappled it before it sank. Verge was removed, his rubber trappings stripped away and (for future reference) examinations made for bodily injury.

"Ignoring the water, he was in prime shape, barring a dent in his skull where the lead hit him; I'll take an affy-davy on that," I heard a man say, with another backing him up: "That'll be Ab Turner for you. There's nothing parsimonious about him. Bottom lead ain't nothing, if it comes to safety. I've knowed him since childhood."

As I saw it, they'd missed the whole point. Turner's son lay dead before us, and the discussion centered not on that, but on what went wrong. If I'd been Verge, wherever he was, I'd have been peeved. And the Reverend Owen, when he entered, causing the crowd to hush—well, I'm a baboon if *he* didn't go into the fittings of the barrel, giving details and praising the Turners as being "another of our River Pioneers." I glanced around to look at General Whitney, but he chose to gaze out of the window.

From start to finish, no single reference was made to the corpse.

I fell in beside Whitney as he walked off toward the hotel, after a singing (a rousing one) of "Shall We Gather at the RIV-er?" I said, "General, you were right. A sad event, and a pity."

"Oh, it happens regular, and will continue so. *They* don't consider it sad. Now this old armband here, it's about to give up. I'll have to get a new one. The fools! One thing sure," he went on, "they didn't launch that body crusher from *my* land!"

He was still harping on the point, but I had other things in mind. "That seems a nice family you've moved in near me. The father— Colonel Rutledge?—pressed a julep on me on this morning."

"He's not *really* a drinker. He does that to annoy his wife and her

78

sister. They're Temperance, mighty Temperance—worst I ever struck."

"And the girl Samantha—an interesting case. She's not the usual southern 'belle,' as her father called her. You might stretch a point and call her a pretty strong-headed cynic. I got her to walk over Goat Island with me, or part of it."

"YOU WHAT? Excuse my shouting, but I'd better make some facts known. Don't *ever* get that girl near the river, or the Falls. It's hard to explain, but half the residents here have a compulsion to play ducks and drakes with the rapids, and even the Falls themselves. They can't explain it, and won't try. And Samantha caught the fever, long ago.

"She knows her situation and, for the most part, stays off Goat Island without her family. Now, write that down, son, and remember it. She's already tried twice! In talks with her father and me, she's admitted the urge doesn't always come on. My notion is that it has to do with the menses, or some such. I got it from a professor. But if you find yourself on Goat with her again, watch every second. Barring a picnic group, I wouldn't take her.

"Tell me," he said, "did you ever hear a circus term called 'casting'? A performer-guest once described it. Now and again, a trapeze artist is overcome by a desire to let go. No reason. Circus folk look like hawks for the type, and sell them to another outfit, cheap.

"Samantha's similar. Unpleasant as the figure is, the Falls, or the idea of the Falls, reacts on her like water on a rabid dog. She shuns them. But make no mistake; out of the midnight blue, she's apt to head for that sweep. Especially so if someone's watching. Odd? It's different from the alongshore natives. *They* want to defy it; *she* wants to embrace and love it. So her doctor said. All of them suicidal, in my view. You'd be shocked to know how many suicides go over those Falls every year and never get in the papers. And it won't end. All the fences in the world couldn't stop it. They tell me the Hungarian bridge at Budapest is the only rival we have.

"Colonel Rutledge," he said, "and his doctor, think she can be cured. Of that and a something I won't name. Otherwise he wouldn't come here. Did the girl, at any point, want to wade?"

"At the Three Sisters."

"You fetched her out? Then did she lose her temper and leave the island? That runs true to form—the single urge and then a drawing off, as if horrified, full sanity restored. She's practically admitted it.

"Be careful, boy. She likes you, no matter if she pretends not to. And if she likes anybody else, I don't know it—another of her quirks."

"Her 'liking' takes a strange form," I said bitterly.

"I expect so. But now you have the story, and responsibility goes with it. I dislike to load up a guest with problems, in particular one with a job like yours, but Miss Rutledge now feels in the circle of your concerns. She has consistently been one of mine."

Well, I said to myself, instead of covering Niagara, I could have rowed the Atlantic and produced better results. I wondered briefly if the Hermit would sublet a corner of his cave, considering I was a deaf-mute under treatment.

Chapter XI

Enough people now were assembled at Cataract for General Whitney to commence organized fun. It made a gay sight, women and pretty girls roaming the huge downstairs, male finery in the billiard rooms (there were two); the men playing cards in the club rooms; and the piazza murmurous with gossip, silk print and compliments.

Up to now, from shyness, I'd ducked out of Cataract meals, including breakfast, and dined, or bolted, at the Eagle Tavern. I figured I could afford it, since lodging, including all meals, was $1.50 a day at the big hotel in this era. Besides, at Cataract House everyone seemed to know everyone else, and I felt out of things. But General Whitney, sensing my discomfort, arranged me a table for one at a window, removed from the boisterous, wandering groups.

So—I finally headed for the dining room, was seated by a (runaway) darky waiter in a plum-colored jacket and was surprised when Miss Frances Barclay, one-time devotee of Napoleon, approached my table carrying menus. She was dressed in an unmenial costume; rather, it employed to the full her advantages.

"You see? I said I would get a job of work and I love every minute of it! General Whitney—what a good and generous man! Everybody's so nice to me!"

"Especially the men, no doubt." I hadn't seen her for several days and felt the usual jealous twinge.

"The men *are* lovely—so polite. And they all seem to stop me, wanting to talk."

"I don't doubt it, after you've leaned over to hand them a menu."

"That was unkind of you, William. I'll call you William when nobody can hear."

"I've been demoted from Bill?"

"Under the circumstances, probably best."

"Well," I said, happy inside, she looked so radiant, "I'm a grouch, and I'm sorry. And I'll tell you this, Miss Honorable Frances, nobody could do the job half as well."

"You're sweet. This time of year the bluefish gather where the Erie Canal meets Buffalo, or so I was told. Anyhow, we have beautiful bluefish, all you can eat."

"Do you take all this seriously?"

"I hope it never ends. You understand that other things come with bluefish. Would you like to finish on a mutton chop?"

"That *would* be the finish—of me. From now on, hand out my mutton chops to the underprivileged. Is there a competent dentist in town?"

"You won't change, will you, sweet William? I'll see you get *masses* of bluefish."

I watched her sift in her queenly way among the tables, often stopping for a chat. Her face was a sunburst of contentment. At no time in her life, I decided, had her loving personableness been permitted to express itself. And now, at last, hitched on to business, her flower was unfolding. This was her social life, and her enjoyment was replete. I wondered what her people might say if she went back to England, but somehow I felt she never would.

Later.

General Whitney told me he'd tried to round up musicians, without uniform success. The weather was bland, and he'd hoped to have a concert in the pavilion. What happened was, the tuba player kept his incomprehensible device hanging in a barn, where he could work the valves now and then. But his two boys (described as "incorrigible") had along the way filled the bell with water, and rather inferior water at that. When the musician went out to practice for General Whitney's concert, he pressed a valve, placed his mouth to the unused horn for a mighty suck of air, and nearly drowned. It was, in truth, a dangerously close call. They called a doctor, or an apothecary, and pumped him out, then rolled him over a barrel till he finally came around.

Oddly, the victim was not put out. He told onlookers that "to a tuba artist" water was an occupational hazard. Then he remembered a Fourth of July parade that produced a cloudburst, so that all three tuba players (two now deceased) were administered to in the street. One, he said, remained "peaked" to his death.

It was Ab Turner who, relieved at the current outcome, suggested, "Why don't you tuber-players weld on a little shed, say a foot above the apiture? Thataway, nothing could get in whilst marching, not even a sparrer." He added with emphasis, "Me, I wouldn't blow one of them things for a manufactory barrel; choking ain't my specialty." (I had a brief thought about Verge, but kept it to myself.)

The artist explained that such an addition would "diffuse and puncture the tone, which might come out"—excusing himself to the ladies—"like a horse overdosed with apples."

People had hastened to this commotion. The tuba player had some reputation as town wag. But me, I left. I didn't believe very much of it. The event had been blown out of proportion.

General Whitney later told me he'd rung in a substitute, a "fully ordained Reverend lecturer," and advised me to be on hand at eight in the main lounge. Then, brows contracted, as if searching where his duty lay, he said, "To be candid, he's got about as much sense as a half-witted billy goat. But I've used him before, and there's a clamor to trot him out again. He's entertaining; I'll go that far."

In the afternoon, the sun gone under and a wind sprung up, I tackled my first dispatch to Mr. Bennett. I described Cataract House, told of the many other resort hotels, and added some compliments to General Whitney. I'd concluded to use Turner's barrel for my next piece. I worked hard for three hours, giving a brief history back to the Seneca-Iroquois (the original owners here), and finally arrived at John Jacob Astor. At this point, I let myself go, having previously run on a tight rein. I was proud of my transitions— the hotel to Whitney to his late friend Porter, and winding up with Astor.

At the Eagle Tavern, I'd heard so many versions of everything that I felt a license to embroider. And the stories came so fast, I hadn't much work to do, really. I told how Astor (only they called him a "furbearing animal" at the Eagle) had wandered in, his repute and fortune made, and how, after Mr. Porter embraced him, the Porters' prize spaniel lit out down the road and was never seen again. I described how the scalawag had sat in the living room and the paper had begun to crack and peel at the walls (source, again: Eagle Tavern).

As to his bedroom, well (from diaries), it was the Porters' prize spare-room and later required fumigation. Astor, under some pretext, was placed at the end of an ell, and even so, as stated, Mrs. Porter and her daughters had started packing for Europe. During the three meals he ate in the dining room, only three members present made it through all the courses.

When they nudged him toward the baths, he lost color and acted, as a tavern man said, "As if he'd onexpected heard the call of the wild." A day later, he set forth, figuring he'd had a near thing. Nobody knew where he went, but most thought he took up with an Indian tribe that favored rancid bear grease for mosquitoes. "You apprehend he was comfortable thataway," I was told.

As to the Porters, they had two rooms repapered and left all windows open for about a week. As said, the dog never came back; he'd had enough, and wasn't planning to take more chances with a family as unreliable as the Porters.

Looking this over, I decided I had two pieces, and would send in the one about the hotel first, to fortify my position. It was *all* compliments. But I added a memo to my employer about the Astor piece, giving him enough clues to whet his vulture appetite and force him, as it were, to run the piece about Cataract. Then I telegraphed the dispatch in, using a code someone had invented to cut down words and save money. Telegrams were expensive. I figured even the code system would get me in hot water, and it did. I received back instructions to "Confine yourself to U.S. mails. New York not panting for news from smartaleck cub."

But I preened myself that I'd done a square day's work, all the same.

In the late afternoon, for exercise, I walked back to Goat Island, chatted a few moments with the collector and the guide, then strolled on around the head, past the Sisters, and on to my favorite point. As explained, the flying river lay two feet below me here, as it silently glided over the lip. Everyplace you looked, the place was ablaze with flowering shrubs and trees. The lilacs and myrtle looked almost unreal, like a stage set. It was gorgeous, and I expect the Senecas would have liked it back.

But the main attraction now was Miss Rutledge, alone, leaning against the rail. The day was too far advanced for tourists, so that no one was looking—the point made by General Whitney.

Taking a deep breath, I strolled up casually, and stood at the rail about twenty feet distant. If my presence altered things, I planned to leap aside and seize her. But I assumed an innocence of all her former conduct. She saw me, made no move, and said, looking at Canada and its Horseshoe, "Isn't it glorious!"

"Well," I said to myself, "she's past the crisis, whether people are watching or not."

"It's my favorite place," I said, carefully offhand. "A person could reach down and touch the water, exactly where it dives over."

"It's magnificent. I usually stay away from here—probably you've heard the story."

"Yep—part of growing up; all children want to touch the water. It's natural."

"Was that it?"

"Try not to think about it."

"I won't. Funny, I don't resent so many things now. For example—you, personally. You don't seem as bad as you did."

I said with inevitable sarcasm, "That's what I call real progress. Well," I went on, glancing up at the gathering dark, "it's getting on for supper. Do you want to walk back?"

She said in a level voice, "Don't come any closer." She placed one foot on the lower rail. "Don't try to grab me; don't do anything."

"Clifton House," I said, pointing to the Canadian side's hotel; "just lighting up. Aren't you hungry?"

She climbed up the rail to sit astride. "Change the subject, take no notice, be transparent."

Heart thumping, I turned away and said, "See you later. Pity. It's a grand walk for two, what with all the flowers."

I put my hands in my pockets, made a poor essay at whistling, and—listened for the splash. At the least, I thought, I now know how a murderer feels. And I noticed that I was covered with sweat.

After I'd gone twenty paces or so, she strode up beside me, laughing.

"Go on—admit you were scared."

"Of what? I came to see the flowers and the Falls. There's nothing scary about that."

"You were afraid I'd do it, with someone looking on. Confess the truth."

"I didn't notice you, particularly. But I'll say this: You—you, personally—are about twice as awful as I thought."

It was the second time I'd dodged her quirt. Then, out of nervousness and anger, I picked her up, plopped her down over one knee, and gave a thorough spanking to that jodphur-covered behind. At first she kicked and struggled, then, gradually, she calmed down and finally rose slowly to her feet. Her face seemed different; she was startled.

85

"You've done something."

"I spank troublesome females. That's *my* quirk."

"I liked it for a second or two, but I'm not sure it was—right."

"Every little bit helps," I said cheerfully.

"You think—"

"I don't visit this place to think."

But the day's wonders were not yet finished. She burst into tears, probably (I guessed) for the first time since babyhood.

She clung to my arm and said, seriously, "Something important happened. I'm not sure—"

"Maybe you've torn your riding costume. I'll buy a new one, not quite so snug." I examined her. "This one's slightly damaged; it might mend."

"Bill," she said (it was the first time she'd used my name), "I want you to be serious. Why do I suddenly feel all relaxed, and no longer terrified of having, well—"

I knew (and felt guilty) but decided her battle was not yet won.

I said, "It's complicated, over my head. But I'm glad you're happy for now."

"Believe this: I was fooling back there—to scare you, just what I said."

"Back where?"

"At the rail."

"Oh. Well, it never entered my head. We haven't pretty girls enough to lose one."

"Don't call me pretty! I've heard words like that all my life. They don't mean anything; it's just—Southern." She thought a moment. *"You* can call me pretty—now and then."

"I'll try to remember."

She slapped my cheek lightly. Then she said, wondering, "I'm famished; isn't that strange? Let's hurry. I'll have to change, especially now."

Chapter XII

A few evenings later, General Whitney presented his entertainment. It took the form of a tall, angular man with his collar turned around, wearing a frock coat that his grandfather likely bought, with trousers stuffed into boots. He had the wildest deep-set eyes I'd ever seen.

Cataract House's main lecture room was packed with hotel guests and a strong deputation from Eagle Tavern and the town. Most of these viewed the speaker with contained gravity—so far.

General Whitney delivered a graceful little introduction, saying that the Reverend Karp was a "nationwide" lecturer on many subjects, and we were fortunate to obtain him tonight, etc., etc.—the usual.

Standing accusing and sorrowful, though silent, the reverend provoked titters from the rear, but these were hushed. He might have provoked more, except he was the only living human who'd gone over the Falls tied between mattresses. He'd performed the feat from the American side, too, and had nothing to show for it except a slightly misshapen forehead. That and the eyes.

I'm blessed if he didn't have, in a chair beside him, that same tuba player whom the general had turned down as "sounding a little moist."

"My friends," boomed Rev. Karp, the voice sounding as if it came from somewhere down in his bowels, "my subject this evening is— yes, you've hearn it before—Temperance!" He practically shouted the last word, while raising his arms on high. In one hand he held a frayed Bible, with a number of paper markers in it, and I figured we were in for two hours at least.

Holding forth the book, he said, "What got the world off to its pore start? Well, I'll tell you," his voice rising. "It was when Eve shinnied up an apple tree, shook down a load, and beguiled—yes beguiled, or tempted—her lawfully wedded spouse—"

"Who married 'em, Reverend?" a voice sang out from the back.

"Don't tell us the snake joined them in bedlock!"

Despite the shushes, this last struck the deputation so forcibly that one man got down and rolled on the carpet.

"It was a marriage made in Heaven," another suggested, and then order was restored. General Whitney sent four uniformed men down the aisle, but their look was not severe. I couldn't be sure where their sympathies lay, or the general's, either.

"I ain't apt to forget that, Luke Threadway," said the reverend to the offender; then he added, with a humble look, "It's my fate, the load of we sanctified, to be a butt of jibes and the target of stones—so be it."

Here an elderly Southerner rose and faced the mischief-makers. "I know you mean well, gentlemen, but I think it only fair to let Reverend Karp continue his account of Adam, Eve, the serpent and their (new to me) connection with spirituous liquors."

"Colonel Pickens is right. Let the old possum dig hisself in a mite deeper."

"—having shook down the tree, egged on by a snake that's sunk in history—they advanced on to forment [he meant ferment] hard cider or applejack. The Bible fails to distinguish, and precious little difference to you or me. But the pint is this: They hogwallered round in booze till the Lord stepped in and slapped them all with Original Sin. And by Jesus and by Glory, we're still a-paying for it today—"

"Emory, could you tell a feller just how much that stuff went for— by the keg, say?" He got the words out as one of Whitney's bouncers made a feeble gesture.

"What you heerd is how liquor will take a man. Blaspheming his way to Hades."

"*And* a snake. You needn't forget the snake, you know."

"Did our Blessed Saviour beg for Monongahela, or worse, if there *is* worse, whilst he was struggling with the Cross? No, by Jings! I don't say he couldn't have used a pull, probably wanted it; but *he asked for water!*

"Now—I've been knowed to most here—the rascality group included, but not a-purpose—for forty year and upward. You're apprised of my climb and recall my pappy. *He* was a case to gall a drinker. When I was a toddler, no finer man lived in Niagry. Work? Well, he slaved from dawn to dusk, often employing a lantern to rig a barrel that a child could negotiate. And his ideas was advanced over what you see today. His cork ball filled with shotgun wadding—the one that took brother Ervin—had theories that ain't apt to be seen again soon. To sum up and be short, such setbacks drove him to— *Rum!* The truth—and I tell it humbly, like our Lord Jesus—*the truth is he never again constructed another barrel worth a fig!*

"Tragedy? Well, I hope so—for the whole town.

"I needn't say it, you know the story, but he died in delirium tremens whilst at work on a rubber chair with a parachute. But rum had slid him downhill. You couldn't strapped me in at gunpoint, and me a Falls man myself."

Here his brows contracted, as if aware he'd strayed off the path.

The Southerners (who had heard him before) chuckled but shook their heads, grieved at this decay of a highly talented man, and the reverend looked restored. He consulted his Bible, then snapped it shut. I started to rise, grateful, but he suddenly shouted: *"Israelites!* That is what I was a-working around to. Did they repay Providence for freedom from Egyptian bondage? If you've forgot, I'll repeat, for it's the primest sample on record of the subject we're at here tonight. Did they strike up the highway toward Canaan, dropping to their knees now and then in thanks? Well, hardly! What they done was find a secluded Wilderness and ripped and snorted and fornicated and—above all—*drunk up everything in sight!*

"Things become so tough that their leader, Moses—last name disremembered—who was scratching down some sensible rules on a tablet, cracked a man over the head with it—broke it right down the middle. And did that faze them? Why, it only stepped up their bellering and prancing and cavorting around, drunk as fiddlers. And people say you could hear them to Jericho. A number of families moved out of the neighborhood; said things had got too thick for *them*. (Leviticus 15:47).

"Well, sir, the Lord stepped in here. He halted that expedition, and done it with *style!* He couldn't string a few up for examples—they wasn't any trees—and the community hadn't got round to building jails yet. So—what did he do? *He said they could sit there and rot for the next forty year!*

"Absorb the picture, and recall, drink was the foundation of it all. The Good Book makes no mention of birthing or dying, so join me in viewing these felons straggling into Canaan at last. Take a woman, say, who'd been eighty. She'd be a hundred and twenty, and probably looked more. An infant would pan out middle-aged, without a occupation or two pence to rub together. But the one I grieve for is Moses, a young man in his prime. *He* hadn't earned punishment! But he stuck to the herd, and arrived forty years behind schedule with a gray beard two foot long! You've likely seen the paintings. He said he'd spent the time knocking water out of rocks. Bored? Well, I expect so.

"And it was a husky long time—upwards of a decade—before the Canaanites regarded them as saved and upright. Meanwhile they took the lowest-down jobs in the region—working in laundry tubs, shoveling up after sheep, night watchmen in the Temple. But they made it at last, and let's give Hallelujahs for it. As to drink, this bunch was *cured!* Camel's milk was sufficient for *them.*

"You, sir," he said to a florid Southerner in front. "*You* don't look like a drinking man. Am I right?"

"Never touched a drop in my life," was the reply, and his wife gave him a mean look.

"And, sir, you look it—the picture of blooming health at your age. And yes, sir, on the strength of that, I'll ask Ethelbert Givens here, lately recalled from Eternity and made a vow for it, to play Niagry's foremost selection, the town's loyalty song, as you might say."

He sat down and Givens gave a kind of croupy rendition of "Asleep in the Deep." I could see annoyance in General Whitney's face; then figured this was a new tack of Reverend Karp's, and considered short of good taste. I also doubted it was "Niagry's loyalty song" and wondered if a dozen in the place had heard it before. What's more, the general was right; besides croupy, the tone had a bubbly sound, and I imagined, at least, that I saw vapor rise from the bell now and then. That horn was not dried out yet.

"Right there," said the reverend when Givens was finished, "we'll wind up Temperance for this evening. Nought remains but the signing of the Pledge, that and contributions you care to divulge for our Blessed Lord Jesus."

"Excuse me, Reverend," a guest interrupted, "but I wonder if we could sign in the bar? I'll confess that your discourse has roused me to a powerful thirst. You might even say I'm parched."

"Not at all," said Reverend Karp, his face lighting up, "with the tables to sit at and all. Unless I'm mistook, it's where we done it last year. It seemed to bring out enthusiasm for the righteous, so to speak."

He took his book—a kind of ledger (the Bible had disappeared into a pocket)—and a tin saucepan (for the contributions) and followed the stream of penitents into the spacious room. Most seemed to be in a hurry.

"Easy, men, easy," cried the reverend, fighting off the eager. "Everybody'll get his chance. The Lord don't take note of priorities."

"Well," said a riverman, "Dink Thrumbull signed first last year, and it don't seem fair to horn him in again."

"I was only aiming to uphold tradition," said Thrumbull. "But let it go, let it go. I'll fetch some Monongahela and be back."

I watched carefully, and everyone signed the pledge, most holding a drink at the time. No matter who signed first, the Eagle group dominated, mainly because they rotated in a circle, some signing three or four times. They'd sign, then head for the bar, and return, many making idiot statements (while brushing away tears), like "I should have did this years ago—I see it now. When I think what my old woman and offsprings have tooken!"

Toward the end, because business was booming, a barman brought over a mahogany-looking julep for the reverend! He thanked him gravely and observed, "No man here heerd me maintain that *one* drink would cripple him down. Even two ain't risky. 'Temperance,'" he said, "means '*moderation,*' and that's the viewpoint of my lecture."

"What about the Pledge, Reverend?" somebody sang out.

"A *Pledge,* in the Almighty's eyes, means knowing when to haul in. Don't go and get an idee that the Lord's a bluenose. Why, Paul and them swilled wine till it run out their ears. But there wasn't a *drunk* amongst them."

Well, so many expressed gratification at this, congratulating him and buying him drinks, that he had to be carted home in a wagon, after all.

But these people, though enjoying fun, were entirely fair. That saucepan was filled to overflowing; and it was placed in his hands the very next day. The charade was an annual Cataract amusement, so I learned. I also learned that Mr. Karp was a reformed souse, and that's the worst kind, but not wholly reliable, either. He was regarded as being a trifle woozy in the head, though harmless. This was from his trip over the Falls. Anyhow, for the rest of the year, he stayed practically sober all the time.

Chapter XIII

The evening's absurdity had been frazzling, and I decided to take a moonlight walk. I alone had failed to sign the pledge, feeling that fun's one thing and complete dishonesty's another. I'd lined up, of course, not to be considered stuffy, and signed "Henry IV," with a flourish, but nobody noticed, and I drifted on out to the main salon, where the ladies, in groups, were expressing their disgust.

As I stepped off the piazza and down to the grass, Samantha emerged from behind a big oak.

She'd startled me. I said peevishly, "Why hide behind a tree? Have you got some new surprise?"

"I'm a dryad. I'm the spirit of this tree."

"Well, you'd better blaze it because you'll forget tomorrow. Then its branches will droop, the sap ooze out, et cetera. I'll tell General Whitney; he'll make you pay."

"Piffle. My daddy could buy General Whitney, and his hotel with him."

"I doubt it. How are you feeling tonight? —full moon and all?"

"If you're headed for Goat Island, I'd like to come . . . *please?*"

Despite what had happened, I was unconvinced, and I said, "I need solitude—without complications. I'm thinking up something for Mr. Bennett." (I'd wearied a little of my role as warden to all; still, the girl *was* pretty sick, or had been, so I said, "Well, come along. I won't be gone long."

The toll gate was closed at this hour, but it was easy to walk up to where the fence tapered and climb over.

"Best not to talk loud. They tell me this is against the law. Somebody's law. Trespass, I suppose."

"I'm silenter than the grave."

"Graves aren't always silent over here."

I looked down at her face, pale and serious in the moonlight, and we walked toward the island's head—without protest this time. At some point, she slipped her hand into mine. When I glanced down again, curious, her face shone with excitement. "Wolves—I *hope.*"

"You may have noticed this stick, or bludgeon."

"Don't worry, I'll protect you," she whispered, and I detached my hand to slap her on a buttock. It was evident that she had on nothing but a thin silk dress, and when she said, close to my ear, "Now the other one!" I firmly took her hand again.

Nobody would ever find peace around this girl, I thought, but I felt vaguely atingle all the same. I tried to compare her to Miss Barclay, and failed.

And then, beside us in the shrubs, it seemed, a voice spoke up to say, "I can see 'em, Otey—there! That's the boat come to pick them up. By God, we got here just on time!"

"Rattlesnake Charley—I can tell by the way he lays to his oars. That and choosing the only narrow course here. Nigger-loving bastard."

"Him and three other rowers. Don't think, by Jesus, we won't settle with 'em all afore we're done. Come along, easy now, and hold that scattergun up; you'll blow the whole works."

"Them dummies likely got the niggers crouching on the bank. This is *one* bunch ain't going to make it!"

The girl and I froze, not making a sound. We were perhaps fifty feet from the river, in tall trees. Then there arose (causing me to shake) a howl followed by several short yips. It was done very well for a girl, though it sounded more like an upset coyote than a wolf. She yanked my hand, and I joined in, doing a little better, if I say so myself.

"*Wolves*, by Godfrey, and more than one, no matter what they claim. It could be a whole pack!"

"We've got guns," replied another in an uncertain voice.

"Well, they ain't worth a puke. Yourn's got a gap at the breech you could throw a dog through."

"And where's the light to shoot by?" inquired the third. (I thought it a good point, for cottony clouds sailed across the moon every few minutes.) "Me, I'm rousting out of here. I ain't fixing to be no wolf-bait."

Meanwhile, we heard a boat scrape the bank, the sound of oars, and a voice urging, "Hop in, hop in, dammit! You there, Scipio, Cato, Ajax—*move!*"

So General Whitney was giving up his house servant!

I recognized Scipio's voice. "I ain't yearning to be drownded, massa. That boat sink, with all them people in. Water take and swaller it up."

"Then"—Charley—"we'll troop in to the authorities, and back to the fetters."

"Lordy, lordy! I most wish I'd stayed in bondage, I do."

A rattle of clambering in, and someone cried, "Shove off!" I faintly saw the boat turned bow upstream, and shortly heard the regular rhythmic sweep of men rowing. Whoever they were, they knew their trade.

But was the wolf-girl appeased? Not at all. Together we resumed our poor imitation of wolves baying, and one of the slave-catchers cried, "Boys, they're closing in! Let's make for the Three Sisters and hole up. They won't jump from clump to clump. Leastways, I hope they try. We lost the niggers, but it would pleasure me to blow the balls off a wolf a-trying to swim *that* current!"

I thought the language might give her pause, but I was caught in the game and let her pull me on a parallel course through the trees, howling as we went. Briefly, I thought it the stupidest position I'd been in; then I saw it as the only thing to do.

In a few minutes, they'd obviously turned from the path and were jumping (and one splashing) to the three small, wooded islets.

"Now we've got them," said my companion.

"Got them how? Them with guns and me with a stick, half rotten at that. More likely, they've got *us.*"

"I'll think of something. Tiptoe along, and try not to trip," she advised in a loud whisper. I thought, "This girl's incurable."

We tiptoed to the last big oak on the mainland (that is, Goat Island)—perhaps ten feet from the first islet. A river chute ran fast and silent at our feet.

"By Godalmighty, Abe, there's a white one amongst them! I seen it clear as moonshine."

"That's laurel, you fool. And get your voice down; maybe they'll skedaddle."

"Not if I know wolves. My *daddy* knew wolves, and *his* daddy—yes, sir, there's that friggin white rascal again—"

His gun must have been double-barreled, and he surely pulled both triggers, for the blast sounded like a powder-factory lit. Then there came a scream of "She backfired! I'm blinded!" followed by three distinct, heavy splashes. The other two had been standing behind him, carrying pistols, I divined.

"Abe! Help! Grab me—I can't keep a-holt on the sprigs! God's teeth, if I still had eyes!"

But the other two had been knocked backward off their knoll, and now there was no sound at all.

I felt sick. My chest was hollow, and I was covered with sweat. The girl leaned her face against our tree, hands pressing her cheeks.

"They're dead—all three, and it's my fault. You'll have to believe me—I didn't mean to go this far. I'm—I'm sick to my stomach."

"Well, I don't feel so well myself. Just hang on till it goes away."

"Maybe one's crouching there, or wounded. I'm going over and see." She looked brighter.

"But you're not. Not this time." I took her wrist in a grip that brought her to her knees.

"Let me go!"

"Back to the hotel," I said, and began the job of dragging her through the brush. She scrambled up and, at length, said, "You were wrong. I only meant to help."

"You've forgotten what they are—were? 'Nigger-catchers,' they're called. And in your case, partly as a Southerner, I don't consider you reliable; not yet. I agreed not to say that, but I'll break my promise."

"You remember the other afternoon, and something wonderful? I'm not the way I used to be."

"Maybe. A lot of people hope so."

We were in a clearing, and the moon stared down from its white rills. The girl turned to face me.

"Maybe I need more punishment. Of that same kind, I mean."

"Not from me."

"I'm all scratched up. How do I explain?"

"Tell them you went to Goat Island and ate a wolf. Tell 'em you do it every full moon. They'll believe you; take my word."

Then, by coincidence, an animal unmistakably wolfish trotted across the clearing before us. It was lean, its coat was patchy; altogether it looked like needing help.

"It's starving! If I wasn't scared, I'd come here first thing tomorrow and bring it food."

"No reason to be scared. In all history, there's been no record of a wolf attacking a human. I read that in a science and nature journal."

"It's gone for now." She shivered. "My dress is unbuttoned in back. You can do the top buttons if you don't mind."

I ran my hands over her satiny skin, and then did the buttons. When I'd finished, she whirled and fastened her arms around my waist, leaning back against a tree.

"You don't really like me?"

"I don't know."

"You needn't like me to give me punishments."

The transparency of her dress was all too evident, and no normal male could have pushed her away. She kissed me lightly, then savagely, and let her legs relax. There was nothing to do but respond and I did so, pressing her against the tree. But she did the work. At one point, I wondered if she might be bruising her pelvis, making me responsible for two small crises. But in about three minutes, or less, she lay limp, her silvery hair resting against my neck.

I was not limp, and uncomfortable besides. But there was no sense pursuing it. She had finished her second lesson.

She said, "I know nothing of men. Are you happy and feel like falling asleep?"

"No, but it'll wear off. Let's go back to the hotel."

"I want to tell you something important. I've transferred trees. I'm still a dryad, but not of that oak on the lawn. I'm the spirit of this tree right here where we stand.

"But there was more. I've hated and feared the things my mother said men did. But I don't hate you; just the opposite. It came on me suddenly. You belong to me now, so be careful."

"You might spancel me in the cellar. But while I'm still more or less free, I'll ask permission to slip over there for a few minutes."

"Please go, and I'll go the other way. I want you to go, and be happy about it. My mother," she said, "was wrong, for all these years. I wonder why."

When I came back, she was gone. I called several times, searched the area over, and began to feel chilly inside. I ran back to the Three Sisters and made my way out to the edge, waiting for the moon each time before leaping. There was no sign of the three men nor of the girl.

I sprinted down to my point, continued to Luna Island, and on to American Falls. Then I gave up, exhausted, and my mind was only half functioning. I said over and over to myself, She's gone, and nobody will know quite why. But I'm sure it was my fault. The treatment failed to work, and I had to find help.

At the hotel, I climbed an outside fire-escape stairway, having deliriously decided to rest a minute. In my heart I knew that no amount of battle, wailing, accusation, anger, turning out of rescue squads, could bring her back. But this tragedy *was* my fault, and both shock and grief had deranged me briefly.

I threw myself on my bed, more depressed than I could remember. It was my intention to hurry downstairs, when I felt a little stronger, and explain it all to General Whitney. Then I had the inspiration that Napoleon might ease the pain. Taking the bottle out of a drawer, I found the taste somehow offensive.

After this, I ran downstairs and saw Miss Rutledge dancing happily with her father.

Chapter XIV

Dimly I heard a faint tapping, then the soft tread of feet and, "Your tea, sir."

I sat up and watched my self-effacing chambermaid place a tray on my stand. Then I realized that I myself was in bed, wearing pajamas, not the way I'd drifted off to sleep.

"I can't stand that stuff. I told you."

"You'll find it helpful on gray mornings, sir."

I said, "I wonder if you'd drop calling me 'sir.' I'm twenty-one, or about three years older than you."

"It's not age, sir. It's a difference in stations."

"Poppycock! Now tell me. How do I find myself in clean pajamas, and in bed, when I remember coming up annoyed, having drunk a brandy or two, and throwing myself down dressed? I remember it clearly."

"My job, sir, is to take care of the guests, whatever they need. I came in, as usual, to turn down your bed."

"And then?"

She blushed. All the females I knew blushed, and I concluded it had something to do with me.

She merely pushed the tray a trifle closer, and since I'd run out of words, I sipped the tea. It went down well, and I took some more.

"Do you have *any* embarrassments?"

"I worked as nurse at Dr. Redfern's Clinic in Lockport, sir. Until my father decided it was a center for charlatans and worse. I've seen men undressed before."

"Have you, during your career, worked as warden of a penitentiary?"

"If you'll drink the rest of your tea, sir, I think you'll feel less angry."

"Who said I was angry?" I yelled. I drank off the tea to cover any possible anger, and the girl was right; I felt better.

"Shall I bring your breakfast, sir?"

"No. I'll eat in the dining room, and—is it Betsy?"

"Sir?"

"Still at it, are you? What I wanted to say was, I'm sorry about being cranky. You're not the usual sort of girl."

"How is that, sir?"

"Well, in your way, you're not bad-looking, dammit."

"I wouldn't curse; it doesn't become you. And when you say 'not bad-looking,' you mean it differently for different stations. With me, it's 'in my way,' as you say, sir."

"Why the devil do you twist everything? I meant *good*-looking. Now twist *that*."

"You're quite right, sir. I overstepped myself." She picked up the tray and started for the door.

I called and caused her to turn. "You're *really* not bad-looking at all."

She smiled a kind of Mona Lisa smile, in which there was no servility or impudence. It was something indefinable. When she'd gone, I decided that part of it came simply from having a good heart.

I strolled into the dining room, past chattering families, and saw Samantha. Seated with the family, she was in the best of spirits. Her father started to call a greeting, then seemed puzzled at my curt nod. I passed on by, grateful for my hidden window table.

But my isolation was not complete. Miss Barclay stopped by with an armful of breakfast menus.

I said, "Well, I see you have a suitor. I watched you dance every dance with him evening before last."

"He's a wonderful man, not really young. He's five inches taller than me. What do you think of that? A widower from Savannah. Such beautiful golden mustaches. You may have noticed, well liked. One has only to hear him talk to admire him."

"Does he know about you—the Honorable, rich, et cetera?"

"I really don't know. Why?"

"What does he do?"

"He's in finance and knows a great deal about investments, that sort of thing. I don't know why you're asking me all these questions."

"He cuts quite a figure; I'm glad to see you so happy."

"Why don't you meet him, judge for yourself? Tonight, say. And why don't you join in the dancing? Are you too shy?"

"I dislike dancing. And, yes, I'm abnormally shy. It's always held me back."

Another blush; I might have known it. Then she gave me a withering sort of look and left.

But she was only one intrusion into my breakfast of eggs and bacon, grits and biscuits. (I'd declined nine or ten other offerings, including mutton chops.)

When the Rutledges rose, the father—Amos—stopped by my table.

"My boy, I wonder if we could have a few words?"

My esteem of that family not being high at the moment, I said, "Here?"

"No, no. I'll be on the piazza. Take your time, take your time, son. Digestion, and all that."

"I'd planned to," I replied rudely.

I took a little more time than I needed, then found him seated in a white wicker chair. One of two chairs at a small table—apart from the others.

"I sense you're annoyed at our family, and I have no doubt it's to do with my daughter Samantha. After all, the rest of us hardly know you. Now be a good fellow and tell me all."

"You'd like the whole story?"

"Without a single suppression."

"Where I come from, there's a thing called chivalry. Real, not mint-julep bogus."

He turned pink, but for some reason he was not to be insulted. This matter was important.

"From past experience, I expect you have reason to be angry. I'll ignore the 'mint-julep bogus.' If you feel like helping a very pretty and troubled girl, tell me your experiences thus far with Samantha."

Softening, I said, "I'm not convinced you'd like them."

He leaned forward with a determined look and said, "Check my sincerity with Whitney, if you like. He knows this family's problems. It's the reason we go on coming here."

I measured him a minute, then said, "I apologize for my clod's manners. I still don't think you'll like it, but the story goes as follows," and I told him all details of my acquaintance with Miss Rutledge. I omitted, I believe, nothing. "I promise you," I concluded, "I made no assault on her virtue. It was not easy but I made none. And her antics of last night made me damned angry, just for the record."

He laid a hand on my knee and said, "You needn't promise; kindly don't say it again. In her way, she took you up the moment you entered our room. It's never happened before; she's—perverse."

"For a stunning girl, she is a little out of the ordinary."

"But don't you see? No matter who did what, you've helped her over some fear, and a real hatred of men? She got those from her goddamnable mother and aunt. Oh, they have good features, I suppose. It's religion's done them in. Once they were decent, fun-loving people. And Samantha, now, may be over the suicide urge that Whitney and I, and others, have watched like hawks.

"From being a very sick girl, she's possibly on the mend." (I noticed his eyes were first moist, then ablaze.) "At one point, Whitney and I took her overnight to Redfern's Sewer for Female Ailments, and she came back in tatters, on a horse she stole. An assistant 'doctor' had tucked her nude into bed, then made a spirited attempt to rape her. I called at the clinic next day with a horsewhip, but the swine had left and never came back. I thrashed Redfern instead. Look it up in the local journal, if you like."

Appraising the breadth of chest and shoulder, age aside, I took his word.

"I'm in no position to ask you a favor," he went on, "but I beg you not to drop my daughter. General Whitney, with his instinct of a fox, joins me in asking your indulgence. We know you have professional duties, but this Samaritanism would never be forgotten. I don't hurl Samantha at you matrimonially. I plead only that you assist her back to normalcy."

His eyes suddenly twinkled. "It makes no difference what's necessary to do, and she *isn't* hard to look at."

"What's her whim for today?" —warily.

"She'd like to stroll about town; she's seen it only from a carriage."

"Any way to keep her from bolting down the street, or climbing a tree and pelting the citizens with acorns?"

"Rope her."

"You're serious?"

"Absolutely."

"Mr. Rutledge, your daughter is, we'll concede, eccentric, but she might balk at being hauled through town on a rope. She'd look like a dancing bear."

"My dear boy, this was her idea. It was over my head at the time, but she said you were mad at her. Then one thing led to another—and the rope."

"It's occurred to you I might be accused of cruelty to, well, delicate young girls, and publicly assaulted?"

"You can walk side by side, and no one may notice. Just for an hour or two? I've secured a clothesline from the laundry, and you can pass it round her waist, then make a loop for your wrist. If she elects to jerk free, and does"—he spread his hands—"you've done what you could."

"All right," I said reluctantly. "This one time."

"This *is* fun! I've never been towed on a rope before."

"Yes, it may catch on nationally, as a hobby."

"Don't be angry, William. See—I spoke your name again, without any trouble. In books, I hate people addressing each other by name in every sentence, first word usually. Now try to enjoy yourself. You're showing me the town. With any footnotes you care to add, of course."

I'd had a dread of passing the Eagle Tavern, with its roughnecks inside and out. But nobody hurled a derision, and I think it was a hat I'd bought that helped.

Some evenings before, in the Tavern, I watched four men play Seven-up, and admired the heavy loser's hat. It was a cross between a cowboy's and a gambler's, or gunman's, a kind of darkish brown and having a flat brim with a spotted-animal band around the bottom and a rawhide thong beneath. I took the band to be jaguar, from the Southwest, and was envious.

And when the runty little fellow finally lost all his money, a pair of silver spurs, a canteen and a gold toothpick, plus his watch and a fob that looked like twisted human hair, he slapped his hat on the table and cried, "Now there's a headpiece to bolster a king! I taken it from a dunce contracted lead poisoning down around Arizony—Mexico. Inspect it over, gents—solid beaver with genuine *tigre* strips all round, and hardly wore at all. Situation I'm in, she'll go for ten dollars. And if that hat cost less than a hundert, I'll chew a hole through the table."

When a player suggested, mildly (for the loser was wearing two crossed pistols), that a single gun or his horse would fetch more, he swore that if the "day comes when I slip a gun that's plugged twenty-two greasers and a horse to skedaddle, you can shoot me, hang me, dose me with pizen, saw off my shanks and heave me in the river."

I thought this excessive, as well as generally exaggerated, but I picked up the hat, a perfect fit, plunked down ten dollars and prepared to leave in a hurry. But not without his advice: "Considering your elongation, together with dark-complected and them shoulders and arms, I'm a sidewinder's uncle if you ain't the meanest-looking hound twixt here and Nogales! No offense."

I didn't care for the compliment, but I thanked him and left, to dead silence. I think most present figured I'd get a bullet in the back, and so did I. But I liked that hat.

You must remember that this was Buffalo, near-about, and farther-West types drifted through often, generally on the run.

Thus, today, Miss Rutledge and I passed the Eagle without comment, and on up Main Street, avoiding the mud.

"You're expected to tell me things."

I had a *Guide and Anthology* someone had written about Niagara Falls, and had boned up briefly.

"Well, to start off, an early census showed that the town had exactly a hundred people and a hundred dogs. How's that?"

"It's wonderful," she said in her sane, or normal voice. "Where'd the dogs come from?"

"I never bothered to ask. Probably some were tamed wolves, captured in cubhood, and others were crossbreeds. The three-story building on Fall Street is the Frontier Mart. Inside you'll find Mr. Neilson, with his wines and spirits; Dr. Slater, a dentist— Do you need any work done? I'm told he's dirt cheap."

"No doctors or dentists for me, thanks," and I remembered her time at the Lockport "Clinic."

"We also have a Variety Store, with a Mr. Barber, merchant, who makes copper-toed shoes.

"For kicking dogs?"

"For longevity. And a Grocery and Provision shop, plus a Flour and Feed Store. So much for the Frontier Mart. You'll note that the named streets, such as Fall, Niagara and Main run perpendicular to the river, and so, in a general way, do the numbered streets, at a slightly different angle. Odd but true, because of a bend where the river turns west."

"You're doing very well, Bill. Keep it up."

"I expect you care, all right," but I was wrong. She acted like a different girl.

"Now—you'll observe various churches—five or six, though they

103

seem like fifty. But mainly the hotels—Clarendon, Spencer, Cascade, International House, and others—dozens of others for resorters like you, in theory. At this moment, Niagara Falls is, numerically, the world's leading attraction."

"What's so different about me?"

"We have only a few hours. There was a school, but it burned and is probably not operating. In spite of the Mart, most persons trade at Judge Samuel de Veaux's store. He's extremely honest for a judge . . . I made that last up. Apparently, everybody in town's a judge; it's obligatory, or out you go . . . Made that up, too."

"What's the book tucked under your arm? Are you cheating?"

"Yes. It's called *Beeker's Guide and Anthology of Niagara Falls,* and I hope to crib as I send dispatches to Mr. Bennett. All about mills and other eyesores. They want to ruin the Falls' beauty. You can't see them from the piazza of Cataract House, so don't worry."

"It's monstrous!" she cried, tugging at the rope. "They ought to be horsewhipped out of town!"

"Horsewhipping seems to run through your family like a fever. That includes you, with your quirt."

"I put it away. It's part of my past."

I said, "I'd like to show you a big, deserted house—will, someday, if you behave—that's pretty famous in its way. Up the river. General Whitney drove me there. Hustler House."

"One of *those?*"

"I believe not, but you can't be sure. It was a hotel and burned, or scorched, leaving its tavern intact. The tavern's still going, for all I know."

"What's so great about it?"

"James Fenimore Cooper lived and worked there, in 1821. While on the premises, he wrote *The Spy,* in which all Indians talk like Oxonians—"

"What's that? Somebody that drives an oxcart?"

"An Englishman who's been to a great university to learn about estates, to write poetry, smell flowers, and squeal about French wine."

"Is J. F. Cooper all the place has to offer?"

"Not at all. Mrs. Hustler, late wife of the owner, reared back and invented *The Gin Cocktail!* Cooper described it as 'a libation to warm both soul and body, fit for a vessel of diamonds.' Locally, that's considered to have been his best writing.

"Chances are, he wrote *The Spy* while standing at the bar. Sounds like it. I remember one of his Indians making a speech that started off, 'To be or not to be; that is the question. Whether—'"

"You can drop that. I'm not *completely* ignorant."

As we did Main Street and Fall Street, I showed her how most old houses were constructed of "batten and board," which meant horizontal boards with more boards covering the cracks. The hotels, of course, were mainly of stone covered with white-painted plaster, like Cataract House. There were many taverns, more than enough to go around. "Somebody told me there were five taverns for every church—there's the best—Simpson's—in the square building across the street."

"What goes on in the rooms above?"

"I'll tell you when you grow up. For the public, a Mrs. James runs a millinery or sewing shop up there. Oddly, the seamstresses are all very young and comely. The madam—Mrs. James—was run out of town last year, something about a man losing fifty dollars from a trouser pocket. He was having his pants pressed, no doubt. But she drifted back, from Buffalo, and nothing's been done."

"Let's go in and peek. Maybe upstairs."

I tightened the rope.

"You haven't made much use of the precious *Guide and Anthology*. Have you memorized it?"

"Since you're interested, I'll read some verse from the 'G. and A.'

" 'Beauteous Queen of Cataracts:
Cruel as love and wild as love's first kiss.
    Ah God, the Abyss.
Nymph of Niagara! Sprite of the Mist!
With a wild magic my brow thou has kissed;
I am thy slave, and my mistress art thou,
For thy wild kiss of magic is still on my brow.
Ye massive rocks! Ye rapids in your rush!
Ye trembling cataracts! Thou boiling surge!' "

I said, "How does it hit you?"

Crushed, I noticed her color had gone, then it quickly returned. It was too soon; I'd been lulled into a mistake.

"It's all right. It was just at first. I'm all right now . . . I liked the part about kissing. That sort of thing's been on my mind lately. Could we step behind that building and kiss? I'd be awfully obliged."

"No."

Persons who saw the rope were never discourteous nor did they seem puzzled. One whiskerando lifted his hat, then addressed his companion, "Now, if that ain't an idee for ye? I'll truss up my old woman next we come to shop and browse. High and low, best plan I've struck to keep females from off the rampage in stores."

I showed her where they proposed a "Hydraulic Canal" to run

105

diagonally through the town, or maybe behind the town. It would eliminate the ugly raceways and mills near the river and the Falls, starting above and ending down below. As planned it could provide power for everything. (But the canal was never successful, and the present mills eventually moved up to make way for tourists. These last provided a larger income. And the raceways were filled when proper plumbing arrived.)

"Well," I said at last, "I think you've seen it, for this trip. There's a ferry here, and one at Lewiston, seven miles north, that runs over to Queenston; and I'm told a photographer is planning to set up in Prospect Park. He hopes to take daguerreotypes of the tourists— dollar and a half a throw.

"But on our next trip—the Falls, both sides, *Maid of the Mist,* the cavern, et cetera. Right now it's getting on for dinner."

"There's one thing," she said, "and I haven't minded the rope. The truth is, I thought I might know what a slave feels like, but there's a comfort in this one—it binds our union." She looked up and smiled.

I'd briefly considered searching her for a derringer, but I let it slide.

"The one more thing?"

"I want a pair of copper-toed shoes, from that three-story eyesore right down the street."

"Don't be an ass. Those are for men, and they're handmade besides. It takes awhile."

"Could we look?"

The proprietor was lunching at Eagle Tavern, and his clerk estimated that he'd be back around five, either walking or carried. But he said brightly, "It happens we have a new pair returned by the Reverend Hayward, as being too small. Would the lady like to try them? STOCK BOY!" he cried to a sullen youth stretched out on a table. "The Hayward return, No. 7 shelf, and be quick about it, or I'll knock your head off." (I figured he was showing off before the girl.)

"They're grand!" she said, when the clerk slipped them on. (He'd turned rosy, on his stool, as he manipulated her ankles and feet.) "I've never had anything like them before."

I agreed that, in their way, they had a special hideousness. She paid, and we left. The first of my guided tours had ended without mishap. Only a lunatic could have called it normal, but it would do for now.

Chapter XV

The time had come—after three angry (short) telegrams—for another dispatch to Bennett. There being no vicious scandal just now at Cataract, I decided to pay a visit to Rattlesnake Charley. His abode was upriver two or three miles, a shanty built into a cave. Hiring a buggy, I started off before dawn, lest he leave early for his daily search. The Hermit was on my list, but it might take all day to find him, and, if I did, I might have to take notes from a tree limb over the current. I'd save him for later, when I found out more about his habits.

I drove in the half-dark up the river road, barely able to make out the marks told me by Whitney. At an oddly twisted tree, I turned left on a dirt lane and presently made out a rickety structure built partly into a cliff-face. Enclosing the front yard was a stone wall that leaned slightly inward, with a tight-fitting wooden gate. A dim light showed in back, and I opened the enclosure door.

But when I'd taken a few steps, I heard—on all sides, even behind me—at least a dozen angry dry rattles that a local child could spot.

The shack door opened a few inches.

"Don't move. Stand petrified and harmless. We've got a chance if you stay froze, but don't ignore infants—they're as pizenous as adults. And a dead rattler can kill you if you scratch a fang. So—best freeze."

Well, that was easy enough. My blood was already frozen, and I could feel the symptoms spreading out. It was full dawn now, and I could see rattlesnakes coiled every few feet—fifteen or more.

"Hold tight—only two within socking distance; they're able to two-thirds their length. *Stop that leg shake!* Cleopatra durn near let fly."

Charley slipped professionally through the door crack, sack in one hand and a rod with an L at the bottom. He wore, he said, special boots, to his knees, almost.

With monkeylike quickness, he pinned first one and then another lightly behind the arrow-shaped head with the L. Then he seized the varmint and dropped it into his sack. In a few minutes he had them all except Cleopatra, who seemed eager to improve our acquaintance.

"She's special," whispered my host. "Meanest snake ever I dealt with. She's getting even for that history ruckus with the asp. WATCH IT!" (I'd stumbled slightly.)

"I'll have to balloon her; hold steady, like Lot's wife."

I failed to see turning to salt when I was already jelly, but I didn't argue.

He disappeared, but came back shortly with an inflated child's balloon. Slithering round, he shoved the toy between me and my friend, and the snake struck. There was a loud pop, and Charley held it wriggling behind the headbones. Motioning for me to follow, he carried it inside, to be shoved into the sack with the others.

"I'll reckon to lose one or two; they bite each other, like I said at the inquest." Seeing my face fall, he added, "You aren't in nowise to blame. I can catch more, and it's catching that glories the occupation. I wouldn't care to get rich selling ile—it might interrupt my habitational style." He looked stricken. "They might force me to take and join the Church!"

I told him who I was, why I was here, and said General Whitney had sent me. Then I asked, "You do sell the oil?"

"Sell it and chuckle. As therapotic, I doubt if it's worth a puke. But it *might* be, mixed proper, and my conscience is thataway soothed."

"You mean belly oil; not venom."

"Odd you ast that. A man come here last month—scientific, belonging to a institute—and said they was working on venom to be used somehow medicinal. You see them tubes?" —he pointed to a rack. "Well, he showed me how to 'milk' a rattlesnake. Hang the fangs on the rim and sure enough out come ten or twelve drops, from baby snakes as well. He poured it down a hole, claimed it had to be cold to maintain force.

"He's coming back when they get a little farther along. If he won't tell the Niagry people, I'll sell him all the venom he wants. Get me a three-legged stool and milk like a house afire."

The sack was emptied into a screen-wire cage about eight feet long; across the room he had a cage for harmless snakes. The place, at least on one side, sounded like a cricket farm at full blast.

I said, "What were the rattlesnakes doing out?"

"Exercise, top of which I cleansed cages."

He took his lantern and pushed open a rough rear door. "I've got garter snakes and such back here, where Bridget slept—GREAT JUMPING JEHOSOPHAT! I'd forgot!"

There was a moan from one of two darkies seated against the back stone wall, comfortably removed from the cages. The larger said, "They's a rattling snake loose in here, Mr. Charley; I heered him, plainer than mud."

The proprietor now turned sharply on me. "Maybe you better confess how you stand on slave-against-free. I hope to Jesus it's the right answer."

"I don't take to threats," I replied pleasantly, "but the more runaways you get across, the happier I am. And if it comes to help, I'm ready—except for threats."

He laid a hand on my shoulder. "Now I apologize from the shoes up. I knowed the truth when first I seen your face. I can smell decent easy; I ain't sunk that low."

"'At snake fixin to bite me, Mr. Charley. 'Nen where's de freedom and glory?"

It was my big waiter, Plato. I'd missed him at dinner. The other was a boy in his teens, and could have been his son. (It was in fact his stepson; "Plato" was a kind of crude joke. I once heard a guest say, "His juice ain't lively; it won't produce, and him resembling a jackass.")

The two planned to find work in Canada, then buy the rest of the family out of bondage. The system was regularly followed.

"Tonight I'm shifting them to Lewiston," said Charley. "I'd be proud to have you along. My partner's down sick, and it's a job aimed for two, one to ride shotgun, as they say. Tell me true—does that put you off?"

I said, "No," uncertain whether or not I lied. I *was* straying pretty far afield from my employment. But I asked, "What time do you want me?" (The challenge had proved too strong.)

"Why, now, that plagued me right along. Suppose you drove back to return in the evening, when they search. Suspicious? Well, I reckon. But why'd you come? they ask. To write a piece for your paper, we'll say. The generl apprised me. How's that for a bull's-eye?"

I was confused, but said, "It *was* the reason I came, of course."

"Then I'll count you as amongst us for tonight. You can make a

109

piece, leaving out names, methods and places. If that don't fetch old Bennett—such is the name, you say?—then I've lost holt on the human race."

He went in to lay out food and water for the darkies. (All Negroes were known as "darkies" in those days.) Then he brought back a sackful of rattlesnakes and scattered them in the enclosure. He gave them advice, meanwhile. "Adam, you keep near that gutter, being sun-sickly; Medusa *needs* sun—stretch out in the middle. Theseus, you stay clear of Jason, hear? *He* ain't got the Fleece, I warrant. WHOA THERE, HERCULES! You would, would you?"

The largest snake had struck from behind, hitting Charley's right boot about an inch from the top. The fangs, I noticed, had broken off, remaining stuck in the leather.

"Lost your piercers, did you? Good—that ort to hold you awhile. Lay around and mope till they grow back. Play the fool with Charley, and you'll pay the price!"

"Why put them out at all?" I said.

"Why? Well, they's usually a reason for all, and, yes, unless my ears is playing false, you'll find out pronto."

I heard a pounding of hooves from the direction of town, and in a moment three bearded, unpleasant-looking men drew up at a skid. I'd seen them at the Tavern, but nobody spoke to them, I noticed.

"Morning," cried Charley with good cheer. "That's a lickety-split pace for so early. Relative die?"

"Looky here. Two niggers made off last night and rumor's got it they aimed thisaway. I'll tell you open, Charley, you're on our possible list. Be they crouched in that hovel of yourn?"

"Why, gents, searching houses calls for warrants, or so it come to me."

"Here's our warrant," said one, drawing a pistol.

"Put that up!" snapped the oldest of the three. "You fixing to get us jailed? We ain't too popular as it is."

"Yes," said Charley, still unruffled. "I'm compelled to report this to Constable; it's my legal dooty. But I'd be the last to hide a man's bolted property. Light, gents, and peer inside. The door's unlocked—kept so by an honest man."

The three climbed down and swung open the enclosure. Then followed a scramble back with a howl of "Jump, boys! On the double! The old fool's got the yard full of rattlesnakes!"

Then the bulkiest came back and said to Charley, "We ain't apt to forget this, you know. Speaking personal, I'm not above picking a fight at the Tavern, claiming self-defense."

"Another threat for Constable, before witness, as proper as punch.

But I'd be obliged for the fight. I get rusty lacking a scrape from big-mouthed skunks now and then. I get meaner, too" —and he whipped a pygmy rattler out of his shirt and held it in the man's face.

The intruder backed off, white as chalk, and the oldest said, "Let's get back on the road. There ain't no niggers here. I've knowed niggers since infanthood, and I never met one crazy enough to crawl into that old piss-ant's den.

"*I hope that varmint chaws your stomick out!*" he shouted over his shoulder when they rode off.

Charley chuckled in good humor. He stroked the snake's back, as if petting a dog.

"Don't be misled. This rascal don't crave friendly relations. He lost his fangs. I brought him along to place near ground-squirrel holes, as a lure for eviction rattlers. But hop alive; you'll see all."

We went on foot, first keeping to the shore, while Charley kept up a gabble to provide me with material for a dispatch twice over. Apparently, he felt he owed me.

From among some emerald green rushes at the water, he leaned down to lift up a squirming, twisting thin snake the same shade as the rushes. "Called a green snake. Purty, ain't he? Harmless, too." He slid him into one of three sacks he'd brought, and soon after, we grabbed a pretty, yellow-striped garter snake, also half in the water.

"People generly don't know a garter snake's mainly aqueous; me, I don't favor them, aside from ile. They have glands that give off a downright puky stink. Look sharp, now!"

The advice was wasted. *I* hadn't spotted any snakes, and wasn't apt to. But I was wrong. At a time when Charley was a dozen yards distant, an ugly dark snake with markings darted suddenly out of the reeds, making for the river.

"Water moccasin!" I yelled, drawing on my meager museum lore.

Charley ambled back, not very excited, and when I turned the creature with my rod, taking care to be gentle, for snakes are easily killed (I'd learned), he said, "Water snake; nice size to him. Moccasins don't frequent northern parts. But don't you fret; she's big, and should go for forty or fifty cents."

"How do you get out the oil?" (I'd been wanting to ask.)

"Them apothecaries, or quacks, buy the whole snake and mash him up. They got oily bodies and provide a good measure. I mean the snakes, not the apothecaries. Them, too, maybe. The oil is mixed with perfumeries, and called specific for this and that. Wonder to me the entire population ain't been killed before now. External or internal; you've seen them ads in the *Iris?*"

In the next hour we caught nine more garter snakes, another green one and a thick, ugly specimen called a hog-nosed snake, with a ridge atop his head.

"Now there's a curiosity. You'd think he was king of the snake world, way he acts. Catched, he'll hiss, spread, shake his tail like a rattler and strike. But it's purely bluff. St. Patrick couldn't induce him to bite. If all threats fail, he'll roll over and play dead. They make a nice pet; Bridget taken to them after I taught her."

We picked up a dozen or more bullfrogs, because Charley said he'd told the apothecaries that the creatures, as oily as snakes, were death on leprosy. And since there was no leprosy around, there wasn't any way to check. He put them in a separate sack.

"Them lazy buyers'll likely mix the ile together, snakes *and* frogs, add some peppermint, sassafras juice, and God knows what—and claim to cure broken legs. Tar and feathers would heal *their* woes, with no snakes involved."

At noon, one sack filled, we sat on a rock and ate lunch—several appetizing sandwiches from a packet, and a small flask of brandy.

"If you need water to top off on, the river's pure. Cold, too, at this season."

The sandwiches had meat as white as snow, and good, coarse bread that Charley had made himself, grinding his own flour. He had theories about refined flour, and sugar, and other foodstuffs.

"Sandwiches suit you? Tasty, ain't they?"

"I was hungry," I said, downing the last bite, "and never ate tenderer chicken."

"That was rattlesnake meat. It's mighty nutritious, the main staple hub of my diet. Particular if I spot a snake afore he's dead too long."

I felt a wave of nausea, fought it down, told myself that what we all ate was habit, failed to convince myself—and lay back to take a nap, or die.

"You was up early, and unaccustomed to reptile-grabbing," I heard him say from way off. "I'll scout around and come when the sun's right for rattlers."

When he returned, I felt refreshed, from the meat or the nap, with the odds (I thought) on the latter. But Charley was joyous, for he'd caught two corn snakes and—the prize of them all—a big, red-splotched king snake.

"He's handy, for a rattlesnake can bite him till Doomsday, and only make him bilious. Far as I'm concerned, they're the lord of the roost. In a fight with a rattler, the king wins—constricts him. Custom, when my rattlers get hard to handle, I place a king in a cage next door, and they calm right down. This is the first I've seed this season."

He'd let me sleep till midafternoon, and now we left for boulders Charley knew about and where, he said, he got his main supply. This came as mixed news. I disliked to say so, but I could have settled for what we had.

He hauled out a pair of boots like his, excepting mine were loose and floppy.

Within a mile, the ground became stone-strewn and rough. Charley had a right-hand glove made of leather and covered with asbestos. Twice we found squirrel holes, where he slowly thrust his gloved hand in, producing only the dead and legal occupants.

Charley said, "Them critters are sunning, after working their mischief. They're downright contrary. If you spot one in the open, don't hurry. Most figure a rattler—any kind—proceeds by wriggling. Well, it ain't true. A big snake's got about three hundred what they call 'ventral shields,' so I read—lateral, on his belly and attached to his ribs. These move back and forth, aiming for something to grab and then push him. You place a snake on smooth glass or ice and he can't budge. A hundert percent helpless."

I had no idea what he knew, but his "reading" sounded genuine. He said a rattlesnake could see pretty well, though unable to close his eyes. A transparent lid protected the cornea. He had some more about pit vipers sensing heat, and striking at it, but I didn't follow it.

"They can't hear, the way humans do, because they lack a outside eardrum. What do they do? Why, a drum inside picks up ground vibrations. So watch out!"

I was watching out at the moment, wishing I were home, and made no reply.

"They can smell all right, but here's a mystery. All the scientists betwixt here and Patagonier ain't yet figured out that forked tongue. It flips in and out, tasting the air, but the reason ain't tested exact. Some think it's a smeller, some not. And they argue about skin-shedding, likewise. But old Charley could tell them—it's because the hide's wore out from crawling on their belly, where the Lord set them, they having taunted Eve to eat an apple."

"If you're struck? what then?"

"Why, you tie above the bite, easing it when convenient, cut a slit in the wound and let her bleed. You'll note that a straw-colored juice comes out with the blood. The book says it's hooked up with salivary glands. I wouldn't know, them neither, likely. I do know that, aside from hissing, no snake but the rattler makes a noise—they got no vocal cords.

"Whiskey? A glut aggravates matters, but if the victim shows signs of collapse, *sips* ain't ruled out, not by present methods. But the best device invented, says the book, is silver nitrate or potassium permanganate poured in the bites. Recommended you wash out first with bleaching powder, if handy, which it commonly ain't."

"What about your thumb?"

"Out of everything, from getting frisky careless—WATCH IT! There goes one headed for a hole!"

The ground being bare, the snake was making slow progress; but it slithered into a hole before we got there. Charley slipped on his glove, and I noted an excited glow in his eyes. This was what he lived for.

"Don't take a notion that rascal cain't outwit me. This home-struck glove—constructed by Bridget—comes nigh to the elbow, but if he lets fly above, I'm in trouble. Here's a knife and a ligatoor, along with above-mentioned bottles. If I let out a howl, you'll know what to do."

He got down on his knees to peer, while I thought about a suitable tombstone.

"I'd use the rod, but the hole takes off at an angle, like."

I felt my heart thump as he probed cautiously down, down, down. Then he cried, "Yippee!" and came out with, perhaps, a four-foot rattlesnake held behind the ugly arrow head that marks most venomous snakes.

"STAND! DON'T MOVE!" —and he dexterously pinned a smaller, no less frightening snake crawling between my feet.

"That scamp had a mate, and she hiked over, domestic, headed for the hole." He sacked the male and asked me, with what I took to be humor, if I'd like to pick up the female— "for your piece in the New York paper."

I'd sooner have wrestled a gorilla, but I remembered that, as boys, we were called sissy when declining a dare. I said, "How?"

"Seize her where I've got the L, behind the head bones. Easy, else you'll kill her." I figured the odds in the opposite direction, but he said, "You'll enjoy it once you've did it four or five times."

He really was a remarkably comic man.

However, seeing this as the last time I'd call on a maniac, I leaned over, approaching from the rear, and, taking a deep breath, grasped the snake, as advised. The rattles were, approximately, keeping time with my knees. It had a dry, scaly, cold feeling.

"Ease up a mite. That specimen ain't a crowbar, you know, and you ain't a grizzly." He removed the rod, and I lifted the snake up with, I'll confess, a feeling of elation.

"Recreational, ain't it? You'll come to wonder why you haven't did it before. It stirs up the blood and whets an appetite. Now dump her in the sack. These here are Massaguas, not Pygmies; them's our two main kinds. But you never know. I catched a copperhead here oncet."

I said, "Charley, you'd better understand that the chance of my becoming a snake person is less than one in a million. As to blood, this species breaks down blood cells, along with other organs. Right?"

"Right as rain. A cobry acts on the nerves. Odd how reputations get made. Book says few cobry bites are fatal. If a person pulls through a few minutes' troublous breathing, he makes recovery, with naught but a scar to show. The only nerve snake we've got's in Floridy, mostly—coral snake, small as a pencil. I was there once."

I was tempted to probe his origins, and other details, but something about him, some personal oddity, said this was not the time. Besides, the hunt was not quite finished.

We struck back toward some big rocks, and he said to look for grease spots. I promised, while promising myself to give them a wide berth. Then we approached a long cave, and Charley said, "Look lively, now—yes, that yonder's what I meant." There was an oily spot on a rock by the entrance.

I'd been up a long time, tense for most of it, and I was tired.

"I see the spot. Where's the snake?"

Charley gave me a quizzical look. "I forgot you're only a younker, meaning no disrespect. Even Bridget fell raspy on the long days. But I don't propose to send you back without a story."

"I'm sorry it sounded that way. Especially when you're doing this for me. But I'll tell you the truth, Charley, I need some conditioning for this work."

He clapped me on the shoulder. "That respect, I got a twenty-year jump on you. Now here's a curiosity for Mr. Bennett: I don't need to *see* that snake laying up there. I can *smell* 'em."

"What do they smell like, so I can head in the other direction?"

He chuckled. "I don't apprehend you'd pick it up, just off. It's kind of a wet-coppery smell, faint, not strong, and takes a nose fine-tuned. If I ain't mistook, he's under them bushes—likely saw us coming."

When he headed toward the brush, I heard the familiar rattle, and he came back with a beauty (so to speak)—nearly five feet long.

"Now, son, I'm going to share a secret. You see that cave?"

"Plainly."

"Well, sir, back in that cave's so full of rattlesnakes you could scoop them up with a shovel. I read about such from De Witt Clinton's Journal, and located it, after some trouble. Vexation is that the grotto's dangersome. It were there I got my thumb bit. Meanest snakes ever I struck.

"But the sun's falling low, there's further work tonight, and I think you've had a bait of snakes. Truth to tell, they ain't overpopular with many."

Touched, I said, "You came out to make a living, partly, and I'll stick on if it kills me."

"Spoke like a true snake man, but we've got a representational number. And the season only started. Let's hike back and tend to other duties, if you're a mind. Kindly don't mention the cave, barring newspaper procedure."

"No cave," I said. "Forget it."

When we neared his home, he said, "I'm moving the darkies tonight, but don't consider it, son, if your spirit's flagged from this flummery."

By now, recalling his coolness with the thugs, I might have tried the Falls in a barrel. I said, "I was hoping you'd ask." I'd strayed from Niagara Falls, as I said, but I'd decided to try and make a book out of the region, the dispatches aside.

"Then we'll use your two-seater, by consent. They'll note my horse and trap in the shed, and be throwed off. Further, we can put runaways behind and cover them with blankets."

Once back at his shack, as twilight fell, he collected the enclosure's snakes and dumped them, with his pygmy, in the cage; the frogs went in one with water trickling beneath.

"Plato? Icarus?" —opening the back-room door. "You all right there? No visitors?" (The boy Icarus had undergone a name change after his mother upset a pot of boiling water on him, leaving a scar on his lower right face and jaw; the name being conceived by a highly whimsical planter.)

"Naw, sir, Mr. Charley, but we mighty stiff setting agin this rock. And with a rattling-snake loose in the room! Hongry, too."

"There's no snake, and we'll feed you up proper—all you can eat."

Thinking of lunch, I didn't envy them, but he cooked us pancakes, and bacon, and ham slices, and made biscuits; and we all felt better, and me relieved.

Chapter XVI

In half an hour Charley said, "Time's about ready. Them polecats'll be draped over the Eagle bar; you'll find them there daily, working up spunk for the night's prowl. We can match two of that; the moon ain't up, no matter what, and we'll rattle out of here safe."

He left a lantern burning low and hustled the runaways into my buggy's back seat and covered them, after telling Plato to hush up complaining. The boy Icarus had never spoken from the moment I saw him. Poor burned creature, what were his promises of life?

"It's nine mile to Tryon's Folley, give or take. We'll trot along like honest folk and have a nice ride."

But when he reached down and placed a double shotgun in my hands, the ride somehow lost its luster. A wind was up, the pines soughed and swayed, and I could hear the river gurgling off to our left now. The genii of the Falls was abroad, and I shivered in the leather jacket I'd bought at De Veaux's.

"You ain't expected to do murder," Charley said, sensing my mood. "But if you hear pounding behind, let loose a blazer over their cones. Do so, and you'll be trouble-free from *them*, I hold warrant. A slave-catcher's an ornery swab, not too long on tripes. Besides, the law ain't clear on their legals. There's been talk of rounding up the whole caboodle and adorning some trees. WHOA THERE!"

I saw a placard on a big oak, and Charley jumped out to rip it down. By the light of a match (held low) it announced the evasion of a "six-foot runner considered dangerous"; there was a smeared, unrecognizable drawing and a sketch that claimed he had a "scythe-shaped" scar on his left heel. A reward of a hundred dollars was offered, the notice mentioning a plantation near Selma, Alabama. The outrage wound up by stating, "He harkens to the name of Junius" —as if he'd been a pet dog.

"It come to me it might be Plato, but I was mistook," said Charley, as he tossed it into the bushes at his left.

"Look here," I said. "There's a lot I don't understand. Plato was my waiter at Cataract for more than a week. Why not take him there?"

Charley chuckled. "You ain't called into account Generl Whitney. He may look overgenial, but no slave-catcher's aiming to fool with *him;* it don't pay. It's been tried three or four times. Over the Falls? I couldn't say, for I don't know. You draw conclusions. Betwixt the dining room and the basement don't offer much chance, do it? No, best for them filth is wait till one makes a break for Canader. Does the generl help? You'll oblige me by avoiding speculation. If agreeable."

I said it was agreeable, and we rode on. The drive could have been pleasant, under the murmurous pines and hickories, but the shotgun was an alien thing. I knew most weapons, and once, with my father, shot pheasant on preserves owned by kinsmen in England. But I had no desire, as representing the choleric Mr. Bennett, to fall into a fight over runaways. And I'd forgotten, now, how I became involved.

Nearing Lewiston, Charley said, "I know an around loop we'll take and not be seed."

North of town, he said to keep a lookout (almost jet dark now) for a great house with many chimneys, property of a Judge (another judge!) Horatio Stow, a Buffalo lawyer. But our target was a larger house beyond, called Tryon's Folly. The reason for this oddity was that Mr. Tryon's head had been turned by the judge's place, causing him to build a stone house so big his wife declined to live in it. It had stood stark and upright, with high chimneys—vacant for years.

We drove around behind, into sheltering trees that Charley knew; then he advised our cargo to run, one at a time, onto the back porch, and wait. When they were gone, we did the same, me still carrying the shotgun, Charley guarding the rear. He'd tied the horses' muzzles so they couldn't whinny. He opened a door softly. Inside, the darkness was so intense I could only conjecture that a very large room was empty of furnishings. But my companion uncovered, without trouble, a door leading down to a cellar; found there another that opened to a second, and then, incredibly down rickety stairs to a third. No matter how many, or whatever Tryon's purpose, we were pretty far down, and the lowest cellar was lighted.

Even here, the floor was stone, and benches lined the damp walls. On one sat two forlorn-looking slaves; their faces (I thought) showed nostalgia for cotton. Four burly strangers filled another bench. And on the last was Amos Rutledge, with a woman strange to me.

"Well, William," boomed the planter, "it's good to know you've joined us." He chuckled. "You look confused. I freed my people two years ago. Nobody knows that; not my wife, not Samantha. But they chose to stay and I pay them well. They're handy as go-betweens for manipulations like these. Sit down, my boy; sit down—"

"There's no time for chatter," the woman interrupted. "The boat's ready, the rowers are ready, and we'd best hustle."

Under such conditions, one might expect a hard-faced kind of wardress, but her features were soft, if resolute. She was even handsome in a middle-aged way. At her waist dangled a bunch of keys, and I suddenly remembered the young wife who'd refused the dwelling years ago. From what I'd witnessed, mainly in the dark, one could scarcely blame her. The building was stark and forbidding, and barring a miracle, it could never have seemed like home.

As for Tryon, he'd claimed his "old woman" (twenty-two) had found the place cramped and he was planning to build another three times bigger. But he didn't; she put her foot down, hard. Tryon avoided complaints about it, but he was never the same. He seemed to pine away, and died a year or two later.

The house was built so that a lower cellar opened aslant the river. So—led by Charley, who apparently saw as well at night as ever, we crept out single file, after the rowers opened a massive door, admitting the cheery sounds of summer—locusts droning, winds high in the trees, and here, clearly, the river swishing not far below.

"Moon up in an hour," said the woman, "and we have a boat to carry out of the scrub."

Charley found the spot, and everybody, including me, Mr. Rutledge, Charley, the rowers and even the woman tugged at the craft, which was long and slender and very heavy, with high freeboard—a typical upper Niagara boat. As for the slaves, they were useless, half-paralyzed with fear.

"Easy, boys," said Charley at the water's rocky edge. "No sound if convenient. Slide her down, nose upstream . . . *Hold it!*—not a whisper," and sure enough, here came the familiar pounding of horses, half a dozen or more this time.

Strangely enough, my own fears vanished and my eyes blazed in the dark. I clicked back both gun hammers, prepared for anything. But they pounded past the house and round a bend in the river, their thunder fading till it was gone.

"Well, ain't that fine! They can ride to Californy, far as I'm concerned, the snatching bastards. So, ho, runaways, hop in and lay on the bottom; thereafter, don't move."

One groaned, Plato clasped my hand, nearly crushing it, and another whimpered, "I know we's goin drowned, but we give you thanks, we all."

Samantha's father paid the rowers (each person here had his niche) and together we gave the boat a lusty heave, upstream. With the oarlocks muffled by rags, they made little if any noise. But when the gap widened, Charley's belt (he was waist-deep in the water) caught on a cleat at the stern. No one noticed except me, and I suddenly realized he'd die rather than yell. At about forty yards out in the river, he wrenched loose. Then, to my amazement, he began silently to thrash, not to swim. He was drowning.

Dropping my gun in the grass and tossing my watch in my hat, I shot off the bank like a frog, hoping not to crack my skull. I made a slapping-loud splash, but couldn't help it. If there were persons nearby, they could tell their grandchildren about the giant bullfrogs that haunted this spot.

But Charley was making no progress; he'd disappeared. I would have seen that quickly in full light, and, thank God, there *was* light, now, a luminous moonglow across the tumbled surface. Then an arm came up, its fist clasped, and I heard a gurgling sound. I was there in seconds but had to dive twice to find him. He still struggled, but less strongly now. My first-aid lessons went out of my head, and I grabbed his collar, hauling him to the surface. Unlike most accounts I'd heard, he made no attempt to fight, to save himself, but lay limp and let me tow him in. It took a long time; we landed maybe half a mile downstream. But the woman and Mr. Rutledge were there, and we jerked him out by degrees.

"He's dead."

Half-dead from exhaustion myself, I helped drag him, unconscious, back to that gloomy failure of a house. Against the sky, now, I could see its great chimneys rearing far above the peaked slate roof. The woman, for whom it was built, was nearly as strong as me, but Rutledge was puffing and wheezing.

It required desperate exertion to convey this dead weight to the bottom cellar, where the lantern still burned, thanks to goodness. A rough deal table stood in the middle of the room, and onto this we laid the unhappy snake-catcher.

There being no sign of life, we rolled him facedown and started a rhythmic pressing against his lungs. We pried open his mouth to search for obstructions; the face was a fish-belly white. Nothing. No response after minutes of pushing, and even pounding.

"People don't know how little it takes to drown," said the woman, wringing her competent-looking hands. (It had never occurred to me she might have an emotional structure.) "Sometimes it happens in less than a minute. He's gone . . . Charley!"

But I said, "I'm *damned* if I'll give up," and I gave a mighty upward heave from the rib cage. A thin trickle ran out of his mouth, he groaned faintly, and Rutledge cried out, in a voice I thought strangely feeble, "I think I've found a pulse; try his neck. Snatch off that scarf!"

General Whitney once told me (without elaboration) that Charley was never seen without a cotton scarf wrapped to his chin. Now we all gasped. All but Samantha's father, who said, "The pulse, confound it, never mind the scar."

A broad, ugly weal nearly circled his neck. Its worst part—truly frightful—lay beneath the left ear. It was possibly the loss of his scarf that brought the victim to consciousness. Some color returned, he raised his head and said, "What's doing here? I'm flubbered."

"Well, you came within an inch of adding to the Whirlpool," the woman said, half angry. "We almost lost you, you old fool! No, lie back; get your strength—for the *snakes!*" Her eyes glistened, and I wondered at the quality of her concern for my companion.

"Yes, ma'am, Matilda. I allus done what you wanted."

"Not always."

But now another crisis developed. With a sigh, Rutledge collapsed in a chair, then slid to the floor. His face turned purple as he fought for breath, his hands grabbing at the air.

"It's a condition," said Charley weakly, under the watchful eye of the woman. "Around his neck, but be quick."

The woman placed a shawl beneath Rutledge's head, where it had hit the floor, and I opened his shirt. From a slender gold necklace depended a small, round gold box that, as I wrenched it open, contained several tiny pellets.

"Two," said Charley. "Maybe three—with brandy!"

For the first time his voice sounded stronger.

The woman burst into tears but scampered up the ladder to return with a flask of water and a quart bottle of brandy, half consumed.

121

"He'll never pull out of this one," said Charley with conviction. "Them's doctor's own words—one more and he's gone."

"Be quiet, you great gibbering *bag toter!*"

I forced open the dying man's jaws, jammed in three pellets and tried to wash them down with, first, water. But the liquid only dribbled out the corners of his mouth, choking him.

"I told you true—brandy. Amos ain't accustomed to water—it pizens him."

There must have been some truth in it, for with brandy the pellets went down after three or four tries (aided by my finger). The purple slowly receding, he retained more brandy. His labored breathing eased bit by bit, and after an interval, we sat him back in the chair, where he smiled weakly.

Charley got up, tottering, and said, "We'd best be going, when Amos feels sprightly."

"No!" the woman said with passion. "You're sick men both and a buggy ride'll finish the two of you."

Here Charley held a hand to his mouth and rushed outdoors. When he returned, he looked improved. And now he noticed the scarf was missing. He sat down.

"Well, you've seed it. I'm marked now, but I lack strength for explanations. Amos is aware."

"And nobody cares," said the woman. "A person would see you a flibberty girl, concerned with looks at your age."

"'Fess up, Matilda, it ain't ordinary mis-looks. It raises doubts, and kept me from follering wishes."

She burst into tears again. She said, "I'm obliged for your trust and low opinion," but he gazed forlornly at the floor.

By now, Rutledge had virtually finished the brandy, taking slow sips, and seemed improved. But he was still a sick man, and I thought how awful to look forward to the final spasm around any corner.

"Moon's ready to round the crest, all sails set, and we'll hike, Amos able, as stated. Them hogs will root their way back afore midnight. Truth to tell," he went on, "I'm feeling underconditioned myself, and would welcome home."

"Well," the woman snapped, "kill yourselves if you choose, but it strikes me you might say a grateful word to this young man, the pair of you."

Charley gave me an enigmatic look. "I expect we'll forget, but don't count on it."

With the horse tied behind, we talked Charley (re-scarfed) into lying in the rear, covered by a blanket. Rutledge refused to lie down, saying he had doubts about getting back up. He needed air, besides. But he agreed to wrap a blanket over his shoulders, as Charley and the woman exchanged a few low words, and I wheeled us back on the road. In a few miles, my seatmate took three more pills, and his voice grew stronger.

He turned to find Charley asleep, and said, "The scar? —I'll make it brief. There's more than meets the eye. Charley was born of a good South family—I can't mention names. But there was a scandal and his father left, taking Charley. The mother had died long before. I gather that, for years, father and son lived like mountain men, roaming the Dakotas, even farther. One evening, they and a companion were set on by thieves and robbed of pelts—in Montana, I believe. All three were then strung up, as not to identify. Charley somehow freed his hands, before the finish of choking, got his feet over the limb, and tried to save his father and friend—too late. That's *his* story, for me and Whitney. But there's more to it than that.

"He's got the scar, and he's always alerted for a man named Plummer, who's supposed to have relatives in New York. Charley plans to return to 'them two scenes,' so he says. God help Plummer if their paths cross. As I say, there's more, involving the snakes, the speech picked up, and so on—but I'll save it. Charley's rich—by 'inheritance'—and that's all you need to know for now, young fellow."

We had no further incidents this night, praise Heaven, and I delivered my cargo, turned in my rig, after some grumbling by the stableman. This shifted to outright fawning when I gave him ten dollars (extra).

Chapter XVII

Next morning a different news raced around town. Negotiations to build a "suspension bridge" had proceeded for two years, by land development companies. The International Suspension Bridge Company had finally come out winner. Efforts to interest New York capitalists were made, but these gentry had visited, looked at the deluge and gone home pretty fast. They refused to ante up fifty cents, and one remarked—to the public press—that "it would be easier to span the Atlantic Ocean." (It should be said they had points in their favor. To avoid the mists, the bridge must be two miles below the Falls, where rapids made a transportation of building goods unlikely.)

Many drawings had been made, the usual meetings were held, at which several persons practiced their oratory, while nothing had been accomplished, in the fashion of most meetings. Then a local ironmonger named Hulett came forward with a plan so simple the Company seemed stunned.

"If you'll run a cable across there," he said, pointing, "I'll build a light iron basket to run on it; then a few men can build a carriage bridge on cables strung above."

After his pronouncement, the Company exhibited a marvelous lack of foresight. Typically so. On resolving legal problems with the

Canadians, then selecting the precise site, officials announced that "the carriage bridge will be of a single lane, eight feet wide, with a bell-ringer stationed at each end to admit traffic in succession." Hulett protested that it would be very little harder to make a two-way bridge. But he was howled down, of course, with the result that, on completion of his project, lines of vehicles strung out for miles on both sides. Moreover, in a strong wind one bell-ringer seldom heard the other, and, as often as not, carriages found themselves face to face in the middle and not much to do about it.

Hulett, disgusted, accurately remarked that he supposed "bridge and road builders would go on underbuilding then adding further lanes at twenty times the original cost." When he added that "Moneymen generally can't see beyond their noses," a Company official bridled, suggesting a duel. And he generously gave the ironmonger a choice of weapons. But when Hulett selected ballpeen hammers, the matter was dropped. (Duels—that is, threatened duels—were a daily commonplace here; the antagonists were fast friends again soon.)

But those problems lay in the future. Now the town officials hit on a means of publicizing the venture. To string the cableleader, all boys in Niagara were invited to compete wtih kites. The first to land a kite across, carrying a light line, would receive a prize of ten dollars. In that era, ten dollars would buy a bushel of candy, mounds of marbles, cigars, a good secondhand pistol, or enough fireworks to blow up most of the town. It was a princely offer, and all turned out to watch what became a fine entertainment.

Any boys not dangerously ill were headed for the site by nine the following morning. They had a variety of flying objects, being descendants of men who'd spent their lives building unsinkable barrels. There were the usual tail kites, box kites, variations of both, and some that could not be identified.

Hotel guests watched from the Cataract piazza, then straggled down to see the hopefuls strung along the river. The atmosphere was competitive with jockeying for position, scuffling and a regrettable incident with a slingshot that sent one boy home with an abrasion requiring unguents. He was back in twenty minutes, carrying a bow and some arrows, and had no further trouble.

Seeing Colonel Rutledge seated in a rocker, looking tired, I asked him how he felt.

"The recuperative powers, my boy, diminish at this age, especially after a seizure. I'll be in top shape by tonight. At the moment, I don't feel up to joining the throngs, and so—once again—will you shepherd my sprightly daughter? I'll find some means of making this up, and by the way, she's coming along, coming along. I see signs of it every day."

But with his disposition, he couldn't leave it alone, and he added, "The fact that she has not to date burned Cataract House is an omen, a good one. Both the general and I," he went on in a serious vein, "have hopes of a full recovery. And it's all due to you. Oh, she has a muscular mammy with carte blanche to apply physical restraints. But it's not the same thing. You'd be surprised how clever that girl is at evasion—"

"In point of fact, I wouldn't. Nothing about her would surprise me."

He chuckled. "We used to look at her as sick. Now, thanks to you, Whitney and I see her as eccentric, growing less so daily. You've taken her that far. One means to reciprocate, even a little, is to invite you to Ravenswood—our home near Atlanta—and press you to stay forever. We have riding, shooting, good neighbors and maybe the best chef in the South— Ah, here she comes now!"

"My dear friend William, or Bill, has urged me to let him escort you to the kites. How's that for good news?"

I hadn't, but the old fox had me cornered.

"On a rope?"

"Hardly, hardly. I think your rope period's passed."

She was normally shod, and I figured the copper-toed shoe period was over as well. I hoped so. Altogether she looked lovely.

Moreover, her eyes shone. "Bill, let's get a kite! I'll hold it; you show me how."

She hadn't progressed as far as her father hoped, and I studied her. Blond hair sleeked back, the full figure, and enigmatic gray eyes. My doubts gave way and I thought of roaming the woods again. "The contest's for *boys*. No kite for you and me, if I'm going along."

Out of the corner of an eye, I saw the colonel relax at hearing someone address her firmly.

"Oh, well, you're a blue-nosed Yankee anyway. Come along."

We drove a gig—it was all the stables had left—down two miles below the Falls, where the action was. She said, "Why don't we sit up stiff, eyes closed, so people will think we're dead?"

"Stand on your head if you like. I'm sure you'll have to do *some-thing*. But if you do, I'll take you home."

"Not me. I'm not the same. I told you."

"Copper-toed shoes?"

"That was only to tease."

I tied up to a tree, high on the bank, and we walked and scrambled down. More rigs were tied here and there, and I counted two dozen

126

boys trying to launch kites from open spaces. Others were strung along the edge.

The contest was interesting but not an absolute success. Commonly in the morning, the wind blew from Canada, so that any number of kites blew back in the owners' faces. A good many became tangled in trees. There were so many of these, in fact, that the limbs literally dripped boys; the prospect was remindful of an African glade full of monkeys. The ground, too, was littered with boys trying to repair torn candidates.

Then, toward noon, the wind shifted, and the frenzy was complete. A platform had hastily been built, and the town band made efforts to perform in a sprightly breeze. But what with the noisy rapids, wind and music sheets blowing off the racks, and a wild melee of competitors running back and forth, the conductor became confused. In the end hardly any two men were blowing the same tune. It was an opinion only, but I was convinced nobody knew the difference. Instead, the conductor was praised by several who stepped up.

"I'll acknowledge," said one man, "that 'Drink to Me Only with Thine Eyes' ain't normally one of my favorites, but I enjoyed it alonger the rest."

"But I don't remember—that is, I'm positive we didn't—"

"Yes, sir, Mr. Miggs, you've got a thumper there," and, raising his voice, "What is spoke for one is spoke for all."

The mayor was on hand, fist full of notes for a speech and only mildly drunk, but he went to sleep under a tree and added little to the fête. Once or twice he started to get up, looking for his notes; they'd been abstracted to patch a kite, so he finally drifted off for good.

The trees blocking progress for a while, Samantha and I stood at the water's edge. A skinny youth a head taller than the others had a box kite that, to me, looked professionally made. After four or five runs landed him on his chin, a puff picked up his contraption, and him with it, and he headed for Canada. But a bearded man and I grabbed his legs, just short of the rapids. Then the boy's father appeared.

"I knowed that kite would fly," he said with satisfaction. "I constructed it myself, after drawings gained from a book."

"What about the boy?" demanded the stranger. "What if he'd dropped in the rapids? Then what?"

The father only stared, as if a person might be demented to pass up a chance like this.

Some highlights: Henry T. Higgins, Jr., aged nine, was pulled by a tail kite through a nasty patch of brambles and removed on a litter, with some chance of restoring his face. De Witt ("Bugs") Whelan, aged seven, flying a similar kite with a tail nine feet long, and rags sewed on, started from the ridge, shot up swiftly and dropped from a high rock to one far below, was rendered unconscious and, in two or three opinions, dead. But he came to, was helped to his feet, and a general agreement made that any possible fractures were probably minor. He re-entered the contest, dragging his left leg. James, or John, McIver became stuck in the high crotch of a bank oak and had to be lowered by the Volunteer Fire Department. Andrew ("Pig Nose") Crisp (a popular favorite) ran through and scattered a picnic, arousing a near-feud that was settled after two hours and the production of bottles.

These trifles were out of the ordinary. Gaily colored kites in numbers rose gracefully toward the sun, but most fell short of the opposite bank, half a mile distant.

An accident uplifting to me happened when a towheaded child stumbled headfirst into the water, in front of Samantha. To appreciate the occurrence, a person should see those white, angry rapids here that raced toward the hungry Whirlpool. They were so violent that the tops flung upward, curling back on themselves, three feet high or more.

There were shouts from those who saw the fall, and men started running. I was helpless, thirty yards upstream. But Samantha, without a moment's hesitation, dove gracefully toward the youngster.

I thought (with some preliminary profanity), "She's found an excuse at last! And it's my fault for getting so damned smug!"

But she popped up, only her head showing. She grabbed the boy's shirt and slowly, very slowly, dragged him back toward shore, slanting down with the current. The first shrubs she seized tore out by the roots, spraying dirt. Then a sapling held, and several men leaped forward to help pull them out. During this near-fatal mishap, the boy had clung like glue to his kite string and twineball. He grinned and said, "I thankee, ma'am." And was back in contention within minutes.

"That water's *cold!*" said Samantha. Her frock was plastered indecently to her body, and a woman wrapped her shoulders in a shawl, saying, "You poor thing! It was a noble act, noble."

Samantha surveyed me with a gloating expression. "Well?"

I gave her wet cheek a peck, and, after that, things passed out of our hands. There existed a mild division between the Niagara locals and the summerites, but it disappeared this day. Several women took Samantha into a grove and dried her, removing her wet clothes, and one produced a light coat to cover her. It covered her mostly, if she kept it tightly closed. Probably we should have gone home, but everybody insisted we join one picnic after another till I believe we'd visited forty at least, and tried to return us to the gig, after effusive thanks to all.

For the future, I hoped never to cram down so much fried chicken, cold meats, sandwiches, salads, puddings, pies, cakes and the like. I doubt whether I could have run the gauntlet if some men—river rats (and good fellows) —hadn't taken me behind a tree and produced Monongahela. They coaxed me to "drink it, then you can swaller, and wash down grub." They seemed curiously alerted to my plight.

As for Samantha, she was petted and complimented and called "as much a river rat as any man present" (the highest honor available) and it struck her all as normal. She was a tough nut. Her movements in and out of the coat, to choose this slice of cake or pie, interested the men. It was obvious, but the women made allowances, and never again, in that town, did the girl want for friends. By the act of saving a boy's life, she'd gained membership in an exclusive club. No one presumed on it, but she was one of them.

At three forty-five, a freckled but otherwise obscure child named Thomas Honan coolly sailed his kite across the chasm, where it was grabbed up and tied to a tree. After, at last, a garbled speech by the mayor, the boy was enriched by ten silver dollars, which he plopped into a pocket, a reflective look in his eye.

(His light string later was attached to a heavier one, and so on until a cable was stretched between towers on opposite banks.)

After varied congratulations, which the boy took in stride, people gathered their picnic tools and headed upriver for town. The last words I heard were from the owner of Samantha's near-garment. She said, "Honey, you can get that coat back any old time. Don't let it fret you."

We got in our gig and started for home, but about halfway there, the girl said, "It's been a gorgeous day! Let's follow those tracks and see where they go in the woods."

"They go nowhere, to a deserted shanty. I've explored here."

"With a fireplace? I'm cold."

"After what you ate? I doubt it."

"I ate loads, and it's funny because I usually eat nothing at all."

"Possibly explained by the new psychology."

Detouring round fallen limbs and an uprooted pine, we found the shack, which was beyond repair in its essentials. But it still had a fireplace, and she leaped out, probably displaying more public Rutledge than any forebear within memory. I tried not to look, but I caught a pretty dazzling show, all the same.

"Now what?"

"Make a fire, dunce. You seem to forget—I was the girl in the river."

I said, "Frankly, I don't think you're that cold."

But we went in, looking at the still-bright sky through holes in the roof, and I routed three porcupines crouched in a corner. I piled dry sticks on the hearth and shoved a bundle of twigs beneath.

"Well, light it."

I did so, after several failures, and said, "I'm not clear about this. The day strikes me as warm as matters stand. You're acting like your old self."

"Turn around. I'll slip out of the coat."

"You have two minutes to bake, one on each side. I'm in charge, remember?"

"You won't peek, Bill?" her eyes saying she hoped I'd peek.

"Are you deliberately trying to upset me?"

"Maybe. Anyhow, it doesn't matter now. I had a talk with Mammy."

"That woman can be replaced," I said firmly. Then I turned around and waited.

Someone has observed that the human male has limits, and when I felt her arms around me, I turned to respond, all thoughts of wardenhood gone. I've forgotten the rest, but the desperate thrusts were hers—I had that much control left—until she limply sighed as before and rested her face on my neck. But this time she was not alone, and I was finally glad we'd come to the shanty. Besides, I now had a different feeling toward the girl, a new and confused one.

"You aren't at *all* the way my mother described men. You're supposed to do, well, other things. I've been chaperoned, you see, and I always refused to go places."

"For today," I said, with reason for embarrassment, "I've technically retained my innocence. After this, we'll stay within sight of others."

But I was by no means sure that I meant it.

A note should be added about the route of Thomas Honan, winner of the kite race. He somehow eluded his family—near De Veaux's store, as persons later backtracked him. There he bought a pound and a half of horehound, a pickle and a can of sardines. He ate these thoughtfully as he wandered up Main Street.

At a Ladies' Aid benefit he bought a candied apple on a stick and a double slice of fruitcake. Then, it was believed, he crossed to Fall Street, where he came upon a bonanza. A new store selling "Super Fancy Gourmet Groceries" had opened. Here he bought a pint of salted oysters from a barrel, and soon thereafter, his throat tasting (as he said on the medical couch) "coppery," he washed these down with two glasses of buttermilk.

From this point, it was observed by witnesses, his gait appeared unsteady. But his mouth tasting no better, he bought a frosted mug of cider that helped, he said, for nearly fifteen minutes. During this brief euphoria, he saw a tobacconist's with a mock twist hanging in front, and he decided to branch out.

Shortly afterward, near the raceway, his groans attracted strollers who found him wrapped around a tree, his face a dull blue. He was rushed to a doctor—a real doctor—and the uphill work began.

"We approached the problem from both ends, begging your pardon, ma'am," the doctor told the mother. "The case had singular points; in fact, I consider it the worse case of acute indigestion this office has treated to date. I could wish that he hadn't swallowed the tobacco. I thank God they invented the stomach pump! For a while it was touch-and-go, but the crisis, and other objects, were passed before dawn."

The man looking prostrate after the night-long fight, he indulged a mild sarcasm. "If I were you, I wouldn't permit him to eat much soon—say for two or three months."

Chapter XVIII

That evening the hotel was dressed in full ball rig. The bridge to link the neighbor countries had actually been started, this event being the most important in Niagara history. I wandered around, looking over the guests. The ladies were gaily dressed; tables filled, the piazza not neglected; and the minor breakage by children was dismissed as trivial.

For the moment, I stayed beyond dancing range of Samantha, whose face bore a restive look. I danced once with Frances Barclay, who nodded toward her new escort, an impressive and jovial addition to the roster. In truth, he appeared to dominate the function. Within a short time, certainly, he'd become the most popular male present, and without seeming to work at it. Miss Barclay, of course, remained the real gem of the crowd; everybody loved her; her new *joie de vivre* was contagious.

Tonight her beau first enlivened the main billiard room. With great good humor, he lost several games by narrow margins, but he won others, richer. He sportingly deprecated these last as being the luck of one who hadn't played in years. And the men who lost seemed happy for him. Gambling for money was against Cataract rules, but these, for the most part, were unobserved. (Chips were used and accounts settled later.)

As I entered the large card room, the new guest stopped me, apologetically, and introduced himself as Jefferson Bulow, from Savannah. He said, "Miss Barclay tells me of your friendship during her trip. I hope we can be friends, too."

I mumbled, and he said some other things I've forgotten. But he had such an aura of good fellowship that I felt warmly captivated. Frances, I thought, showed taste; he had charm, and magnetism, and a way of putting people at their ease.

"We must have a talk soon," he said, patting my shoulder as he strolled through the entranceway.

With nothing better to do, I looked on for more than an hour. Eventually my new friend's play took shape like his play at billiards. While losing, here, some near-disastrous pots, he continued his genial banter, and it was evident that fun, among his hobbies, ranked first and money nowhere.

Then, gradually, the tide began to turn. The men had imposed no limit, and those circling the baize, seeing a chance to acquire idle cash, raised stakes until they struck me as dangerous. Miss Barclay's escort now won, perhaps, a third of these hands while folding up early in the others. Little by little the chips piled up before him, until he'd won almost everything on the table.

Then, glancing down, he reddened, half angry. He cried, "Whoa! See here, boys, this was a game for *fun!* But I appear to have held such good cards that I've cornered the market. My suggestion is this: Let's *call* it fun, and return all amounts lost. Please don't be insulted; I intend no offense, and I'll say this—I've never played with a finer group of sportsmen. You'll have to indulge me just once," and he began a reckoning that nullified his evening's play.

And to be sure, the planters and a few Northerners who'd sifted in and out *were* good sports. Their protests came close to being vigorous. The action was "against all tradition." Then their resistance weakened, and they finally took back their cash, saying things like "Well, this floors *me.*" "I've gambled a lifetime, and seen no resemblance." "This beats *my* experience!" And, strongest of all, "I'm not going to feel right about this—not for a long, long time. It's not often you strike a purentee *gentleman!*"

Only one man, tanned, lean-faced, made a sensible protest. He said, "Colonel Bulow" (yes, this was another "colonel," as the Northerners were principally "judges") —"Colonel Bulow, I'll knuckle under with one demurrer. In future, let the cards fall as they may, and the winner keeps his winnings. Charity stops right here."

Colonel Bulow only said, in his same jovial vein, "I agree completely, and apologize for my conduct. But this," waving at the table, "this was too much."

As the players left, he took my elbow and said, "Oblige me, Mr. Morrison; let me stand you a julep. There's a table for two over there. You know," he went on, "I've got to—it's a compulsion—talk to somebody, a friend, I hope, about Miss Barclay—"

"A fine attractive woman," I said, guardedly. As open as he was, I thought him a little premature in his sentiment. Or perhaps I suffered a trifle from jealousy.

"Girl. And right there lies a problem. I'm more than twenty years her senior—as confused as a schoolboy. Do you believe in love at first sight? You're not sure? Well, you may be, someday.

"Now, I want your advice, as being the lady's confidant. First of all, I've been married before. I never mention that, but the light of my life left me, a victim of consumption, fifteen years ago.

"Since that day, I've never properly *seen* another female. The idea seemed abhorrent. But the moment my eyes rested on that graceful, winning, beauteous Miss Barclay, something turned over inside me— a sensation I thought I'd forgotten. Can you understand that?"

I said (my reserve fading at this candor), "I think I do, Colonel. Probably I'm too young to comprehend fully, but I can imagine you've been lonely these past years."

He sat musing for a space. Then he said slowly, "I doubt if many persons have the maturity shown by those words. Loneliness," he went on, "real loneliness, with nobody to talk to, share with, take care of, make happy with gifts and devotion—that kind of loneliness is the worst estate God has planted in the human breast. It corrodes you, withers you, ages you in a terrible way. I'm convinced, having met Miss Barclay, that she must see me as fifty-five. But each time she consents to dance as my partner, I feel at least a year younger."

He gripped my arm like iron, his eyes moist.

"Forgive it, young fellow, but I wish I could convey this more clearly." He released my arm. "What I want, more than anything else, is for someone—you, for you are longheaded beyond your years—to caution me about the pace of my approach to this reincarnation of my lost darling. In God's name" (gripping again) "tell me what to do!"

All doubts gone, I said, "She likes you, Colonel Bulow. She told me so. And"—I hesitated—"you're making her happier than she's ever been before—"

"But I've become a clumsy ass around women! Oh, I try to revive a kind of boisterous charm, if I ever had any. And to stave off depression, I play the gabby, jovial fool around men. You've noticed?"

I said, "That's not precisely the way I'd put it."

"Well, something of the sort. You don't mind then if I'm modestly attentive to Miss Barclay? Am I overly so already? I'll be entirely guided by your answer. I've known her a paltry few days, and yet it seems I've known her forever. Be as frank as you like; I somehow trust your judgment."

I smiled. "Why don't you go ahead and keep her happy? I know her this well—she'd be crushed if you didn't."

He took my hand in such an emotional excess that I was embarrassed.

"I thank the benevolent Lord for your support! And—I won't fuss you again. I can see your discomfort at the older man's floundering.

"Now, *here*, I'm courting *your* friendship and taking a chance. First, I advise against that julep. The drink's too strong for a healthy young athlete like you: Oh, I've noticed the shoulders! The julep was a device to draw you in private. Instead, what do you say to a constitutional, along the river, before we turn in?"

I agreed, and was astonished at his conversational range. The night was clear, and he pointed out the main stars and constellations, and knew an embarrassing lot about them. Then he identified, by their Latin names, most of the plants and trees so strange to me when I arrived. He described his youthful attempt to join the 1812 war, and the regrettable restraint by his family. But he'd memorized the battles and commanders, and as he rambled on, frequently apologizing for talking so much, I began to sense a contemporaneous bond here. It was almost uncanny. He *did* have charm, and the gift of companionship, and I felt grateful for the new acquaintance. Your average man, as he said, meets only a few lasting companions in a lifetime. Then he said, "Do you ride?"

"Badly."

He laughed. "It's strange you said that. In spite of hearty exertions of experts, I've never become a horseman. It's perhaps been my father's worst disappointment. But for exercise, I'd planned to try these back roads on convenient early mornings. Now, I don't mean to press our friendship, but would you join me some daybreak soon?"

From the look of him, and his modest tone, I doubted his inadequacy with horses, but I said, "Gladly."

"Good!" And at the piazza door, he said, "Well, good night—is 'Bill' all right? I think you know what the evening's meant to me, and since I promised, I'll say no more."

"Good night, Colonel," I replied, and went to bed feeling a little richer. Of all the men I'd met, excepting my father, at his best, Colonel Bulow was in a class apart for charm. New England or no, I finally felt that, indeed, I'd made a worthwhile new friend.

On the next evening, and the next, I was again a spectator of cardplay. Colonel Bulow lost small amounts both times. During the rest of the week, though, he regained his happy-go-lucky fortune, winning unimportant sums and paying scant heed to the amounts. Then these amounts began to grow, and while there were further winners, Bulow never suffered a setback. He had a comradely way of downgrading his luck, as if he'd actually lost; but I reckoned the sums he took to be substantial. The others, to be sure, were always eager to play. No matter how affluent, they wanted their money back.

Bulow's hands began to worry me. His chatter was so continuous that nobody noticed the dexterity of those flying fingers. One finger, by the way, was ornate with what he called a "brilliant." But I happened to know the name was generally applied to a diamond cut with many facets, to enhance its sparkle.

I'd once had explained the "mechanic's grip," the dealing of "seconds," "middles" and "bottoms." And I knew about waxing aces so that a break would fall where one pleased, and had heard of methods called "edge work" and "line work" and "trimming." The "sand-tell," in fact, had caused the expulsion of a college acquaintance. Besides these, there was a favorite called "belly stripping," or shaving a pack's sides, to leave a microscopic bulge on key cards; this last was considered infallible if done by an expert. However, with confused emotions, I could spot nothing amiss from where I sat at the bar.

I saw General Whitney stroll in from time to time, smoking an Havana; his greetings were dealt out, so to speak, with equal cordiality, his expression impassive. On several occasions, I wondered how my new friend could cause me concern; and I decided, with heavy heart, that he was possibly too good, too affable, too generous, too much in general. He always led anything organized by the ladies, and his purse was quickly available. Then, maybe, to my Eastern eye, he was too gorgeously garbed. By degrees he had become the apotheosis of the rich Southern planter.

Tiring of my perch one night, I walked behind him and had an accidental close look at his "brilliant," which seemed, at table level, cut about as follows:

Artful gamblers, my father once said, eventually make a mistake. The colonel's was to clasp his hands behind his head when not dealing. As I say, on an angular plane, the facets showed clearly.

What I saw, in perpendicular, was a smooth surface in which my face was magnified. I recalled that Bulow always won when he dealt and that his habit, then, was to toy with the ring, twisting it this way and that. His way of holding the deck was also unusual; and he shuffled, while at his heartiest, with a slow, showy riffle at the end.

Even so, his advantage could scarcely lie in such small deceits, no matter how skillful, and I left, anger growing but still compelled in his favor. General Whitney sat on the piazza, rocking, and I sank down beside him, not really knowing what to say. We sat in silence; then the general shocked me.

"Wondering how he does it?"

With great reluctance, I said, "Yes," and I told him about the ring.

"Oh, we've had mirror-users before, but none exactly like this. We had one beauty with glass in a pipe bowl."

"What happened?"

"Oh, we eased him out," and I wondered if a thrashing, off in the woods, had helped the man on his way. Cataract House looked as quiet as a cathedral, but Mr. Whitney had four or five employees—"odd-job boys"—who might have looked comfortable in an arena.

"Every three years or so, we unhappily descend to the punitive. I commonly wink at malefactions short of grand theft and murder."

"And Colonel Bulow?"

"I've held off because I'm not sure. And because of Miss Barclay."

"She'd be badly broken up."

"Well, we must spare her if we can. By the way, she's off duty. Taking a walk in Prospect Park."

"Good," I said, getting up. "There's something I wanted to ask her."

"My boy, you ask instead of me. You can do it better."

"Well, Frances, do you wish to be alone, after your hectic day?"

"Not at all. These have been my most beautiful nights; the moon's only just rising above the mists, and from there"—she pointed—"you can see the Clifton House lights, off in another country. Isn't it grand?"

I said carefully, "I'm glad you're so happy, Frances." Then, "It's too bad your suitor's so absorbed in cards."

There was a perceptible pause in her step.

"He wins a great deal. I'm not a fool, William. Does he win too much?"

"I don't know. Probably not. A run of luck can go on for a long time. Look at you—everything's fallen into place."

She took my arm. "He's a *good* man! I know it, despite an occasional blasphemy of Negroes. He appears to think we have similar views on the subject. Possibly it's the English accent. He told me they were lower than apes. He said if he had, by magic, to turn black, he'd commit suicide. Was he joking?"

"He may have had a few troubles on his plantation. That's all."

"He's talked loads about himself, and I gather he's talked to you. Did he tell you about the orphanage he's sponsoring in Savannah? All by himself—blueprints, written tributes from citizens, a glorious piece in Savannah's papers—"

"Donations?"

Another pause, and, "Why, of *course*, donations! A charity like that is expensive! The colonel himself has dedicated much of his own fortune to the project. He has no heirs, you see."

I said abruptly, "How much have you given him, Frances?"

The moon made it possible to see her blanch.

"You have no right to ask. But I've donated three thousand pounds. How much is that in dollars?"

"Fifteen thousand—a lot. Now once more, and I'll stop prying. Can you afford to lose the sum?"

"My people have masses of money. But you're suggesting something horrible . . . I'm upset."

"I'm thinking of your welfare—the kind of question your father might ask. It's routine in any family. Make me a promise, as a traveling companion. Refuse or delay any more donations for two weeks. Just that long."

"But what if he asks? He's terribly winning."

"He wins at cards," I said, and we returned in silence. She was piqued, or worried, or depressed, but I'd done my duty, as both the general and I saw it. All the same, I was as downcast as she was.

Any sense of celebration gone, I climbed the fire escape again. I worked hard writing the kite story, then made up a public shotgun wedding to please my boss, and went to bed.

Matters developed the next evening. It was Bingo night. This exercise was downright gambling, as I saw it, but since it got off to a start in churches, it couldn't be bad. In fact, said one preacher, it was "sanctified" by the Lord, who he hinted was a crafty and expert player, though he failed to say where. This same gasbag was the most down on racing, cards and betting of anybody in town.

In any case, midway through this pursuit of sanctification, Colonel Bulow tapped on his lemonade glass (though devoted to juleps, he drank lemonade with Miss Barclay), arose in full plumage and begged to make an announcement. I don't recall his wording, exactly, but it went about as follows:

"Ladies and gentlemen, fellow guests of Cataract House, I'd like to try your mettle—if you'll forgive me for phrasing it so—on my most favorite venture, and I apologize for interrupting our game. I'll only be a minute.

"The Honorable Miss Frances Barclay"—he laid an affectionate hand on her arm—"will tell you of my project in Savannah, toward which I've directed much of a bachelor's fortune. It is, in short, an orphanage, and I have several testimonials here, including a heart-warming account in the Savannah *Journal*.

"It's occurred to me that to launch a like institution in this, our favorite town, would lift Niagara to new heights over the civilized world. Especially" (and he made his little joke, as all speakers must) "when described for the New York *Herald* by our talented young friend, William Morrison." (Applause.)

William Morrison smiled with self-effacement and began counting reservations. I was tempted to rise and ask to study his "brilliant," but General Whitney had said the time had not yet come.

"—yes, we must free these homeless strays from starving and sleeping in alleys, doorsteps, sheds, barns and, in one pathetic case, in a cave."

This last, I assumed, referred to the Hermit of Goat Island, who, people said, was an affable and otherwise normal and attractive young man. He bothered no one, was occasionally seen in town, and when shopping had plenty of money. He simply preferred his life to others, and people came to understand it. I wondered how he'd view being yanked out of his niche and handed to an orphanage warden, especially at his age, which was about twenty-nine.

"—to start this project will require funding. I have pinched my personal purse by a donation of twenty thousand dollars" —he held up a check. "I think that," he said smiling, "will get the much-needed enterprise started." (Louder applause, exceeding that accorded William Morrison, III.)

"For the rest, I suggest a lottery, which should provide entertainment as well as help the Lord's work. I'll have built a large wire wheel which we'll hope to fill soon with numbered and purchased tickets. Then a trusted citizen will withdraw a ticket to see which of our guests finds a windfall. And, I hope, oversees the building details. I suggest an ample—shall we say three hundred dollars?—reward for his time thus spent. With General Whitney's consent, we'll lodge the ticket money in his safe as it grows. And it *will* grow; I promise you."

139

His eruption was so brazen and abrupt, I was stunned. But I was to gain a deeper knowledge of people soon.

"Now, what do you say, you openhanded folk of Cataract House? Express yourselves!"

An ovation exploded, and several boneheads started forward to show their gratitude. But he held both hands aloft in protest, while wearing his widest smile. He said, "Wait, wait till after the Bingo. Then come up, all of you, and study the Savannah documents, especially my blueprints. And yes," he went on, beaming, "I could foretell your reaction. I know what kind of people come to Cataract House!"

A man rose to propose they make the lottery citywide, and the colonel said, with satisfaction, "I *knew* someone would bring that up! It's to be a city institution, not mine—I'm not that high and mighty *yet.*" (Laughter.)

And he finished with that entire parcel of fools in his hand. He concluded by saying that private donations, on the side, would of course be accepted, and the meeting soon broke up.

Chapter XIX

The whole concept confused me. If the colonel was crooked, how did he plan to abstract funds lying in a safe? What's more, *I* hadn't noticed any "waifs or strays" around here, not in any numbers. There were unruly boys, a majority in any town, and others too ornery for everyday use, but nothing out of the ordinary.

A few persons presently recovered enough to say a lottery wasn't needed. What kept the colonel from gathering the donations himself? Handle the whole thing? But at this, he refused absolutely.

"No matter how honorable a person, or how wide his past charities, such risk is too great. Besides," he said, winking, "the lottery's an advertisement, a publicity stunt. Who can resist showing up for the drawing? It'll pull the town together, and that's what we require."

Well, this had a certain degree of sense, but not much. So I broke off to catch up on my dispatches.

Meanwhile, a big wire wheel was made, and tickets were sold, for a dollar each, which took people slightly aback. But donations came in even from nearby towns, which *might* have had orphans, and the wheel climbed up to three-quarters full.

As I say, it seemed overcomplicated. Did Niagara need this kind of institution? I doubted it, but I was on hand, of course, when the drawing was made before a big throng between the hotel and the river. Whitney's brass band was on its stand, and was making things pretty anxious for the birds and squirrels. The jays seemed to resent it most.

Colonel Bulow presided. He was dressed in finery that would have made an enemy out of Solomon, the full exhibit topped by a white beaver hat. The general stood on the edge, watching, and so, I noticed, did Frances Barclay.

Bulow called out, broadly grinning, to say, "If no one objects, I'll now step forward and produce the magic number! The ticketholder will collect his reward and we'll proceed with arrangements. It goes without saying that I've discussed all this with General Whitney. We both stand ready to devote our full time until the groundbreaking is actually under way and a construction boss hired.

"All right, good folk of Niagara Falls; hold your breath!" and he dug deep into the wheel.

The beauty of the thing was this: I could see no possible way how he could steal more than a pittance. The heavy sum was locked in Whitney's safe.

"What do I see? Well, it looks uncommonly like Number 79." He held the ticket up, then showed it to three or four locals near him. "Now, who among us holds that historic figure? Not me," he said with mock ruefulness, tearing up his ticket. "I got stuck with 231, a pretty far cry from the winner.

"What's that?" he said to an inept-looking fellow who timorously stepped forward. "You say you have the number?"

Bulow inspected the ticket with great care, then cried, "We have our orphanage leader, folks! My heartiest felicitations, sir."

"*Me?* I don't know nothing about finance, Mr. Buler. I'm a hawker in register stoves, lately moved to town. It don't seem right that some distinguished cit—" (His occupation, to me, sounded uncomfortable, but I gathered he meant "of" stoves.)

"The perfect choice!" cried Bulow, overriding the protests. "A new resident who wishes, one assumes, to rise in the town. Frankly, I see you—in the distance—as our possible mayor."

(This appeared likely, since the specimen we had fell short of possible and was, in fact, usually drunk in one degree or another. I'd seen the "stove hawker" in the Eagle a time or two, and assumed he was one of the many transients through here.)

But Bulow hadn't made any jokes yet, so he said, "Friend, if I may now call you friend, I hope you have no objection to taking the reward?"

"I don't need a reward," said the young man meekly. "I'll do my best, and hope I don't stumble too bad along the way."

142

"Quiet your fears, sir—you'll have help, as promised. Now, could we ask you to identify yourself, since you're new in town?"

"I'm Elroy Spooner. Elroy *Norbert* Spooner, I should say. I have a wife and three children."

"And you come from—"

"We were in Buffler, and doing poorly, so—"

"Well, from what I hear," cried the pride of Savannah, "Buffalo's red-hot already, so I assume they don't *need* stoves!"

This was regarded as a capital hit, the number of Buffalo's brothels and saloons being pretty widely known. And on that hilarious note, the meeting broke up.

Me, I remained uneasy. The scheme was too crazy. And for some reason, that winner's three names bothered me. They bordered on the comic, and besides, his sudden diffidence struck me as false.

But events now moved more swiftly. That same night, a man going home late from the Eagle thought he saw Bulow and the ticket-winner under some trees; and he, the observer, stood silent behind a hickory to hear their talk. The "stove hawker" was peeling off two of the hundred-dollar bills, which Bulow pocketed. Then the colonel said, "I'll make my play tomorrow night. I'd do it tonight, but some donators might come in tomorrow, after that whopping big turnout on the lawn—"

The stove man said, "As usual you're trying to hog too much in a hurry. I didn't care for the look in old Whitney's eye. He's a substantial man, and no fool. I can rent a room, get in a few stoves and play it safe. What's the rush?"

"Dunces! Sapheads! If I tried to auction off Jonah and the Whale, they'd scramble over each other, and take delivery on trust. I know these hick towns, especially resorts where the guests all show off. You can swindle them this year and come back and do it identically the next. It's well known, outside jerkwater hamlets.

"Why the rush, you say? Well, for one thing, I'm drawing suspicion with the cards. Confound my hands! I can't seem to control them. That sprig reporter's not as dumb as he looks—couldn't be— and if I cashed that Barclay woman's check right now—" He thought a second. "I'd take it to Buffalo, of course, and no trouble. By rights," he said, looking reflective, "I ought to work that simpleton further. She's a gold mine!"

"All right. I'll go along. But I still favor dallying awhile."

"Tomorrow night. Have a buggy at Commercial Wharf. By dawn we'll be clear. We can sell the horse and buggy—"

"There's where I balk. They don't take to horse-thieving in these parts. They got the system from farther West. They'd string us up in a jiffy. By God, if you aren't the worst octopus I ever struck!"

*   *   *

Next day the man relayed this, and rumors ran over town. You'd see persons standing in groups, quietly talking in the streets. As quick as they'd embraced Bulow as savior, they now spoke of lynching, mainly, and looked tolerably happy about it, as if he'd done them a favor. I've noticed that people are generally as eager to lynch somebody as praise him, and the notion spread fast. In a sense, Niagara's temper ran higher than the Falls. But cooler heads prevailed for the moment, and a deputation called secretly on the general. That canny old fox promised matters were firmly in hand.

"Lynching gives the town a bad name," he told them. "Bulow will get his deserts; depend on it."

"All right, General, we know you're upright and able. But we'll stake out the wharf just for luck."

"Excellent idea, keep you out of mischief. For now, act innocent as lambs. Speak politely if you see him; otherwise you'll upset my plans."

In the afternoon, Whitney stopped me on the piazza, to confer for ten minutes. I agreed to a request he made, and at about midnight, when the guests had all retired, we seated ourselves in dark chairs looking toward the bar. This dark was so intense I was unable to make out Lafayette's icy cloudburst, though I tried hard. The bar was outlined by piazza lamps that burned all night.

"Shouldn't be long," the general whispered cheerily. "Not if I know this glutton. —Ah, quiet now, here's our bird, promptly on schedule."

At the bar, now, I made out a figure carrying two large bags—one bulging, the other empty, or nearly so. From this last he apparently took out a burglar's lantern, for when he crouched at the safe, there was a soft clang of metal then a smell of oil smoke, then a faint glow. He worked for perhaps five minutes before the heavy door swung creaking open.

I heard a faint whistle, and at this moment, all the downstairs lights seemed to go on. Big John, the colored head barman, stood at the bar's far end, and General Whitney, I now saw, held a pistol in his lap.

"Empty, Colonel? Well, the best-laid plans," said Whitney, chuckling. "You never can tell about 'hick' resorts."

Bulow had sprung up, chalk white.

"Now dump out the money in your bag. It must be returned to my guests. Did I smell out the operation correctly, John?" (You had to forgive him for this one crow of triumph.)

144

"Yes, sir. He cropt down every night late 'en open all 'em cards with sanded little bulges. He use the ring, too, and what you said about the not-seen inkspots, 'lessen you wearin' spectacles."

"Well, well. Now, what to do with him? Return him to Savannah? That means the penitentiary, I've learned. But it's a tedious process, costly, too. Maybe best hold him here until—would you fetter his hands behind, John? Let's hold him till morning, then take him over to the Tavern. I understand some gentlemen there have plans."

Bulow finally found his voice. "You wouldn't let them lynch me?" he croaked.

"I've given it thought," said General Whitney, musing again. "Lynching's usually a solution where constituted law is absent; it might be resented by some. Though I confess" (chuckling again), "the sight of those dandy's feathers swinging in the breeze is attractive; people would turn out. It's tempting, sir, tempting."

Bulow, still deathly white, said, "Look here, General, I've got nearly fifty thousand dollars stashed in banks. It's yours if you'll let me cut and run."

"Of course you have, and a deed to the Taj Mahal."

Our thief was now far from the dazzling fop of the recent past, darling of the ladies, the hope of Frances Barclay. I thought of her with sinking heart. The rogue that hurt her before was a card-cheat, too. A certain dark uniformity plagued the disasters that befell her.

Of all Bulow's malefactions, his callousness toward a great-hearted, gullible girl angered me the worst. At the moment, I could have choked him to death with pleasure, and saved the town a lynching.

"No," said General Whitney, arising to lock his pistol in the safe. "I've devised a solution, Bulow. What bothers me is this: You're getting off too easy. By the way, the stove man's let you down— there's no buggy at the wharf. The rascal appears to have struck inland on foot. Let's trust he avoids the quicksands."

He frowned. "But you. Well, Mr. Morrison here's going to drive you to Rattlesnake Charley's. I talked to Charley today. He knows the plan."

"God bless you, General! I won't forget this. But you aren't going to have me snake-bit?" He turned white again.

One more chuckle, and, "No, but I expect you'll remember it for some little time."

Bulow lay tied and gagged in the back, and we made good progress. We saw no prowling slave-catchers, and Charley was waiting. By lanternlight, he wore a broad grin on his ageless face.

145

"Well, now, I sure do welcome you, and what's meant for young friend is meant for both."

We uncovered the gem of Cataract House, where he lay complaining, until I booted him in the ribs, as between new friends. He'd recovered some of his spunk, and Charley propelled him into the house, not gently. No snakes visible except those in cages.

"These are scarcely the kind of accommodations I'm accustomed to," said Bulow with a sniff.

"Tidy, ain't she?" replied Charley. "Peer through them winders. Not a bar to mar the view."

Our prize subsided briefly.

"Between the generl and I, preparations hewed out and planed. Now, sir, if you'll step out of them clothes. You'll likely need help, what with spancels."

"Wait a minute! What's going on here?"

"Billy boy, just yank off that frocker and weskit. *Ain't* it pretty! There she comes— Whoa—we ripped her. But it don't signify, as matters stand. Now the britches—"

"Hold up!" screamed Bulow. "Stop this outrage—I know my rights!"

"Billy, we'll step out in the yard, and take this beauty with us." He grasped the "colonel" by what remained of the vest, and we stopped under an oak. A rope dangled from a pulley on the lowest limb. "You'll note the crackerbox, in place and stout. All set? If your worship will step up on the box. Generl Whitney said the slightest hitch—"

Bulow was blubbering. "I apologize. I beg you to accept my apology. I—I'd forgotten my situation."

"Probably I didn't make out lucid and clear. You prefer *against* stringing? It's vexatious. I can so testify."

We trooped back in, and Charley stripped him clean, including an elastic to hold his stomach in. Though seeming once hearty and trim, he was flabby and so white it made my flesh crawl. His face had now turned a kind of greenish white, and he kept glancing at the cages. Every specimen was setting up a clickety-clack like castanets; I figured they were trying to welcome one of their own. This scene in the low lanternlight was sufficiently eerie for your average man.

"Now then," stated Charley professionally, "there's only one way to convert a white toad to darky, Senecas have affirmed me. And that's with black-walnut juice; leastways it's permanent for a bothersome long while. It'll stick like stain on a fence—their very words, mighty near."

He dipped his fingers in a bowl of black fluid.

"Stop!" screamed Bulow. "You can't make any nigger out of *me!* I'd ruther be lynched!" (I noticed the speech was reverting.) "Walnut juice! You crazy old bastard!"

Charley looked stricken, but in a kind of resigned way, he caught Bulow's neck in a clothesline loop, and we marched him back to the oak.

"If it wouldn't discommode you," he told me, "hold that line taut. Thataway we can re-coax him to the box. I'll aid at the end. We can put drawers on after; it wouldn't show seemly to have a nekkid man dangling public, particular one as pussy as this."

I said courteously, "Get up on the box, Colonel Bulow. As between new friends."

Louder howling and begging, now, and we filed back to no further problems. Charley covered him head to foot with walnut stain—which, as he said, has to *wear* off. Then he put on three additional coats. As to hair, Pygmalion had a mixture of shoeblack and berry juice. He said these would hold for two or three months, unless they ate out his hair altogether. He'd cropped the head some, as well as other hair; and the golden mustaches went next, to groveling lamentations from our guest. The hair was then frizzled with an iron that slipped now and then, leaving a scorched spot. Before we stuffed him up with a rag, you could have heard the yowls for half a mile.

"Now throw on them denims," tossing him some clothes well briskened up with fauna. "We're aiming to row you to freedom," Charley told him. "If I was consulted, which I weren't, I'd let disposal occur at the Eagle."

Bulow worked the rag loose. "Damn your blasted hide! —These are niggers' clothes, and rotten at that!"

"Darkies have to wear such and make no complaints. Cheer up, Colonel. You'll get accustomed, and wonder how you done without."

"I'm to consort with niggers across there? Me, a gentleman born?"

"They'll treat you noble. According to reports, you been the meanest to darkies in the hotel, calling your waiter nigger, cussing him and the like. The word travels around. The darkies there'll be happy to receive you; likely they're crouched on the Pint now—waiting.

"Now listen," said Charley, changing his tone and moving to the man's face, "I'm drained with caterwauling. You're being throwed *free,* you weasel, when you ort to see prison for twenty or thirty year.

"Ah, shucks, Billy boy, let's take him out and hoist him. I'll explain to the generl," and he gave a wrench to the line that sent Bulow sprawling.

Charley was angry—something I thought impossible. He said, "It

147

ain't a weak feat for two to cross this close to the rapids and Falls. Toting blubber meanwhile. I've had my fill. Give him the old Strangulation Jig, Billy, and let it go."

"There'll be no more trouble," said Bulow sullenly, distastefully donning his fragrant new livery.

We pulled Charley's boat free of the bushes, we each took an oar, and the ladies' darling sat perched in the stern. When we whirled out of a ripple, the boat lurching, Bulow screamed, "I'm spanceled! What if she goes over?"

"Turn her around, Billy," cried Charley with better cheer than before. "The buzzard ain't worth the risk."

I, myself, was uneasy about that river. And, thinking of Miss Barclay, was happy at the change of plan. The lynching bothered me, though, of even a bounder like this.

"There's two hundred and some dollars in my coat pocket. Keep it, and get me over. I've spoke my last word."

But when we were half across, he cried, "There's a dark shape there. What's that?"

"Grand Island, likely. We'll drop below. As to money, the generl told me to regard it as pay; he left it a-purpose. Now, bend to your oar, Billy—this here's tricky."

But the dark shape turned out to be a small, steam-driven ship, and shortly we heard a hail.

"Boat ahoy! Come alongside. We got a gatling gun aimed right down your throat."

"I'm Rattlesnake Charley, trim and adjusted to plan. We got your cargo, if you'll kindly help him up. He ain't too spry right now."

"A Southern slave-catcher!" screamed Bulow. "I'll get you for this, both you and that devil Whitney. *I ain't no nigger!*" he yelled at his handlers.

"Goes by the name of Slothy," Charley called up. "Possible, you can flog that out of him."

"I said I ain't no nigger," his grammar slipping again. "I'm whiter than you are!" There came heavy sounds of a thwack and a fall.

"Well, you surely to Jesus don't look it, and there's a pretty for nigger impudence."

Chapter XX

Next day, I avoided Miss Barclay, for it was plain that her escort had vanished. Indeed, the hotel was filled with rumors that something strange had happened. And since my part was substantial, I felt reluctant to look her in the face.

In a resort the size of Cataract, cliques form, of course, and groups now sat whispering—inside, on the piazza, even strolling in Prospect Park.

General Whitney had restored the approximate sums lost by players and donors. But for this moment, all air of summer fun was gone; the drone of locusts and cicadas and the whispered hum seemed inseparable.

By the following day, I'd caught up my dispatches, keeping strictly to the truth. In Charley's case, it was hard to prevent an anaconda from rising in the swamps; and I managed (by changing names and places) to depict a typical hotel swindler who got his comeuppance. To my surprise, I got back a five-dollar bonus from New York, Mr. Bennett now lining up against slavery. Like one of Charley's snakes, he was shedding the old skin and taking on the new, without apology or explanation. A possibly beneficial result—according to letters from home—was that fewer people offered to horsewhip him in the streets. (My employer, during his career, was unpopular, then medium popular, then unpopular again—back and forth—but he was never ignored.)

Tripping across the piazza, I noticed Amos Rutledge seated alone in a swing. His appearance startled me. He was pale and weak-looking. The brief, illusory rehabilitation had disappeared. I walked over, took off my aggressive hat and sat beside him. He smiled faintly.

"You needn't say it. I look sick, and I *am* sick. A doctor that Whitney dragged in said the cellar attack should have finished me. Now I've had four altogether."

"Shouldn't you be in bed?"

"With those fool women admonishing, praying, implying 'I told you so'? That *would* finish me."

As if reading my mind, he said, "You needn't worry. I had the attack at Charley's, looking at snakes. All's safe on the Underground—as far as I know." He sat thinking a moment. "All right, I'll say it: Charley's getting too bold. Maybe it's the nature of his trade."

"Dear me, my radiant daughter Samantha!"

She *was* radiant, in a kind of mannish hiking costume. I said, "Bound where, rigged up like that?"

"I've worked out a grand day. For you and me, I mean."

"Maybe you didn't notice. Your father's not feeling well."

"Mama and Aunt Hester are coming to take him upstairs. Papa," she said severely, "you behave, hear?"

I studied her manner, not quite convinced of a real ring of concern. But after my work and a very troubled night, I dismissed it.

"Well?"

"We go to Canada by the ferry"—she pointed at Prospect Park, where stairs led down below the Falls. "There's oodles of things to see over there, and I've never been, not once!"

"We were there last summer, and the summer before," protested Colonel Rutledge. (By now, I'd decided to call *everybody* Colonel, including the women and maybe a dog or two. However, Mr. Rutledge was authentic and had served with Scott in the Texas War.)

"Oh, well," she said carelessly, "I thought William might be sorry. He could take a day off from his *dispatches!*"

She was in a strange humor, that is, normal, and I saw her father eye me anxiously. I'd planned to go to Goat Island and find the celebrated Hermit, promising not to disturb him again. I was even prepared to let him see a piece, if I wrote it—breaking a rule of Mr. Bennett's.

But another crisis had arrived, and I decided to do my best, as before.

"I see you've gone back to your copper-toed shoes."

"They're gorgeous. Mammy shined up the copper part, but she grumbled so, it wasn't much fun. Papa," she said earnestly, "I think she needs touching up, just a little, you know?"

He chuckled. "She's equally free to touch *you* up. She used to embrocate you, head to toe—"

"To make me soft and 'pearly.' Now she won't do it anymore. How come? I *liked* it."

"You're too grown-up. She thought it no longer seemly."

"That lovely oil she rubbed on! It made me tingle to lie stretched out without a stitch," said the girl in happy remembrance. "There was one time—" she began, looking thoughtful, as if she'd just put two things together, but Colonel Rutledge interrupted.

"That was the last time. Now if you're going, you'd better move. Here come the Dragon Queens."

We stepped fast across the park to the steps going down. The day was perfect, not hot, few bugs, high fleecy clouds sailing from our neighbor's.

The steps were the gift of General Whitney. They stopped at a wharf beside the still, bottle-green lagoon formed by the deluge. This pool was 250 feet deep and a quarter of a mile wide. The surface was glassy in spots, but the total effect was dark and ominous. Within two miles, it gave way to vicious rapids that caused the terrible Whirlpool below Red Gill's.

From where we stood, the lagoon was made almost black by the high, surrounding bluffs, and, of course, by the shading avalanche itself.

At high season, forty skiffs—ferries—plied the two shores, and it grieves me to quote a local history that found snarling fault with the ferrymen: "The ferrymen and their subordinates are addicted to habits of intemperance . . . and owing to their indulgence are often unaccommodating and uncivil to passengers, being in the habit of extorting too large sums for ferriage as well." The legal fare was 25 cents one way from November to May (when blocks of ice were frequent) and 18¾ cents from May to November.

The rowers we selected—rough, bearded men—assumed a pose of sanctified goodwill. No sooner had we taken our place in the stern, and pushed out, than one reached behind for a clay jug.

"It's mighty hot work, ma'am, and I'm aware you won't mind. Specially with them copper-toed shoes."

"Just do your job and put us across," I said evenly.

But a few minutes later, the other addressed his companion: "Now, Tom, don't that hat scare your liver out? It looks like—like—well, pictures of them gunfighters we've seen, mostly hung."

Both men were smaller than me, and both had trained for years on whiskey and little else. They could row small boats; that was their best effort. The tourists they bulldozed and cheated were nearly all elderly, and few were in the mood to talk back. They simply swallowed the insolence rather than ruin an outing. (The general had told me this in discussing the drawback, while appraising me wistfully, as if hoping someone might take measures.)

The larger said, "I cain't seem to get my mind off them shoes, ma'am, them and the striped shirtwaist," and I leaned forward. "Hold up on your oars," I told him. "Yes, you, too, with the big mouth and the warts.

"Now, listen good, if you've got brains enough. Niagara—both sides—is sick of your smartaleck manners. It's time somebody—me—struck back. General Whitney summoned me from Montana, by way of New York, to do the job.

"My hat? It's a gunfighter's hat, all right, and I'm the gunfighter. Open your mouths again, or dally on the oars, and you'll learn how fast a two-slug derringer can jump out of a jacket. Understand?"

They sat mouths ajar, and when the larger recovered his breath, he said, *"Don't* take a man up like that, governor! We wuz only passing the time of—"

I said, "Shut up and row," and shifted my position ever so slightly.

On the other side, after hesitation, one said, "That'll be a dollar each, and begging your pardon for past grievance."

"Here's forty cents; it's more than you're worth. The fare's posted there"—I pointed—"as clear as any print. And now, as requested by the general, I'll talk to the owner—"

"Don't do that, governor! He don't take to it. Here—here's your forty cents. You and the little lady ride free; glad to oblige anytime."

I lit one of the slim black cigars I'd taken to—perhaps to match the hat—and tossed the forty cents onto the ground.

"When we come back, keep out of my way."

But both were scrambling up the bank toward a tavern with a ten-foot sign that said, "Monongahela! Cheap!"

I doubt if either was much frightened; in fact, both had probably been shot somewhere along the way. But they'd been drunks for years, I learned, and the condition by no means bolsters courage.

For a moment I'd forgotten Samantha. She stood hands to cheeks, stricken.

"Gunfighter? Honest to God and cross your heart?"

"I once *saw* a derringer, in a velvet-lined case. But the bluff worked well, didn't it?"

"But those—hounds—spoke to others going up. You'll be shot from behind a bush."

"I doubt it," I said cheerfully. "It might be bad for business. Besides, I actually do carry this sheath knife. It's part of my new role of badman."

She slipped an arm around my waist, causing some rowers on the slope to look away. She said, "I've finally decided you'll do very well for me. That's been established."

I noticed that the girl was not at all afraid for herself, and I figured that I had things pretty well established, too. I had no idea how it happened. But it did.

General Whitney had given me a booklet that told what to do here, and we agreed to see everything, stopping for lunch at Canada's majestic Clifton House.

As we climbed the hill, I took another booklet from my jacket and said, "One more sour note, from a very minor English writer. Name of Anthony Trollope. He says as follows: 'The walk up the hill is very steep . . . In so short a distance I have been ashamed to trust to other legs than my own, but I've observed that *Americans are always dragged up!* . . . I have observed young men . . . carried about alone in carriages over distances which would be counted as nothing by any healthy English lady of fifty.'"

"That's pretty nasty."

"He's apparently forgotten who won the Revolution and the War of 1812. English writers write that way about America. If they believed it, they wouldn't have to say it."

All along the bank, and on the rutty road above, were frippery shops so vulgar and disgusting that we left to visit Barnett's Museum, which was advertised by bills on trees, in store windows, and even by a strolling sandwich man. This lank specimen wore his burden with such melancholy that I began to wonder about Barnett's wares.

She read, "'Moose, two large Elks, Lynx, Wild Cat, Foxes, Wolves, squirrels of every color, and many more surprises.' I'd like to see the Moose, if it isn't too much trouble."

"Stuffed."

"Also says, 'A rich collection of Roman, Greek, Egyptian and Polish coins.' Why would that be?"

"Well, Caesar moved into England around 55 B.C., took over the place with a few men and his Romans left in about five hundred years, bored. They apparently considered the pure English—Picts,

Celts, Angles, Danes, Saxons and smaller tribes—little better than animals. So I read, painfully, in a Latin book. As far as I know there was no real intermarriage.

"The Romans probably lost considerable coins to theft. Don't ask me how they, and the others, wound up at Barnett's."

"I can't wait to get back to England and see the purity."

The Canadian, or Horseshoe Falls, are far more beautiful than the American. The water runs deeper, giving it an emerald tint, the whole being curved in the shape of a horseshoe.

Perhaps the prime lure of this cataract was "Table Rock," an immense flat piece of slate that jutted high over the water at one point. Pieces broke off with regularity, and there had been many casualties. (The Table finally broke off altogether; at night, fortunately.)

"Before Barnett's, I want to go out there," said Samantha, pointing to the rock.

"Why?"

"Other people are. It's a game."

"You weren't planning to jump off?"

"That's over. The truth is, it never existed. I'll explain before we get married."

"We're getting married?"

"Very soon now. Mammy and I decided, and I told my father."

"It might have been convenient to tell *me*."

The rock was slick with spray, and tourists were venturing far out, getting soaked and scampering back; the majority showing off before girls. Most were English, and I doubted whether they knew they were getting wet or not. I took a deep breath, clasped the girl's hand in a hard grip, causing her to look up, puzzled, and we inched toward the crescent.

With our weak American legs, we went closer than anyone I saw, and there was no incident, nothing to contradict the girl. But when I released her, she whirled suddenly away. And when I felt the familiar sinking, she said, peering, and then smiling at me, "A piece just broke off. I heard people cry out."

I said, "Come along. We've done Table Rock."

But we completed Mr. Barnett's attraction (various of his works were spread over the Canadian side) by taking a wet, insecure staircase down to the gorge, thence along a worse walk to a grotto behind the Falls. I waited, not anxious to have a ten-ton slate fall on

154

me, until the girl came alongside, shivering, and said, "Let's get back in the sunshine."

For this moist discomfort we received each a certificate attesting we'd thus risked our necks, and commending us for it. Samantha tucked hers into a handbag; I tossed mine aside. In fairness, I should say that the same kind of steps led down to the "Cave of the Winds" on the American side; and that trashy shops were also around in abundance.

The Museum was confusing. Three-quarters of the place was filled with exhibits having no connection with the Falls. There were numerous badly stuffed animals, including such indigenous delights as "the Virginia Deer," "The Moose," "Martins," "Sables," and "Ermine."

Barnett, a thorough man, had even gone to work and stuffed two mice, for reasons of his own. Under the bold type, "Living Rattlesnakes," was a modifying line that added, "Some Very Interesting Skeletons."

He did have the decency to classify as "foreign" his Barbary Lion, the Agouti, an Alligator, a Duck-billed Platypus, a Swordfish and his "Sea-spider." To these you could add, "a Greenland Dog," but since Greenland was covered with ice, I dismissed the dog as a lie.

On the positive side, one wall had an artistic geologic map of Niagara Falls' origins. Done by an English scholar, it presented many surprises for the neophyte. Over the eons, as the earth's crust formed, the Falls had been between Lewiston and Lockport, but the "Great Glacier" had changed the river's course, leaving a long, high ridge between these towns. It was currently known as "the Escarpment," and wasn't of much use today.

After the glacier decided to melt and go home—probably sorry for causing all the trouble—the Falls in their fresh canyon had chewed the edge at a rate of three and a half feet a year. The people in Buffalo were naturally concerned, for the deluge was expected to reach them in about 33,000 years (though I heard of a few making preparations, in the style of Noah and his singular zoo). The subject did come up now and then, with Buffalo promising to make plans, but it was generally felt that things could be put off for a while.

I'd assumed the local rock to be granite, but it was shale layers, interspersed with hard dolomite, atop sandstone and limestone. As the soft shale underneath crumbled, the harder rocks cracked off and, in short created the Fall.

It was interesting. I tried to explain it to Samantha, but she was absorbed in a scholarly looking Chippewa Indian, who in turn gazed at "a genuine Chippewa scalp," hanging on the wall. From time to time, he glanced at Mr. Barnett, with his thick, blazing-red hair, presiding at the counter. I wondered if the tourist Chippewa planned to even the score, after business had closed for the day. I considered hanging around to help out.

At noon, at the towering Clifton House, we found a pretty cool reception. I laid it not only to my hat but to Samantha's hideous shoes. A typical English of the fallen-grandeur species functioned in gay plumage as headwaiter; he hesitated, I lit a cigar, and after the proprietor rushed up to whisper in his ear, haughtily ushered us to a table behind a post. My reputation had preceded me.

"That will do," I said, pointing to the most conspicuous in the room.

He hesitated, then angrily knuckled under.

"Why don't you keep your hat on?" whispered Samantha.

"And you could put your coppery feet on the table. But that might be going too far. And I'm hungry."

An underwaiter, amused, handed us menus similar to those at Cataract House. We lunched on small, fresh trout, new asparagus, and Nova Scotia salmon, and had lemon ice and nut cake for dessert. Along the way, mention was made of mutton chops, but I slid one hand into my jacket, and the subject died.

I ordered a bottle of vintage French wine, surprising the sommelier with his chains and keys, then listened to a carrying discourse by Samantha about the fact that alcohol never affected *her*, never would, and she didn't care if everybody in Clifton House knew it.

"Look, Bill," she said. "Do you know what I'd like?"

"This isn't the place for it."

"I'd like some downright bloody old *snails!*"

"'Bloody's' a vulgar word over here—"

"Never mind. Do you see that woman with the feathers in her hat? I'd like to hit her in the eye with a snail."

"Why? These people seem pleasant enough. Besides, a good many are Americans."

"Can't tell you why. Always been crazy about snails. Ask anybody."

"I'll try your father."

"*Him!* He hates snails. He says they're nothing but worms in shells. He says if they crawl out they look like caterpillars."

"The point is to eat them before they crawl out."

She looked thoughtful. "Angus Trollope liked snails."

"Anthony."

"Listen, Bill" —she tapped with her spoon for emphasis. "In this country he preferred to be known as Angus. What he did at home was his own business."

"Maybe snails turned him into the big walker."

She sighed. "Lord, what a pair of legs that man had! He was all over the place. Now this is not general knowledge, but he climbed the Matterhorn at five."

"In the afternoon? That's a pretty late start. I'm not saying it couldn't be done," I added hastily.

"You! You know nothing about it."

"On the contrary, I was with the party. Trollope whined all the way to the halfway mark. We had to lower him in a litter."

"Look here, Bill," she said, somewhat flushed, "you're coming close to being offensive. You may be sorry. Oh, yes, I've got ways and means."

"You mustn't be annoyed. I just didn't think you knew."

"Don't get the idea that I lack education. Tutors—good tutors— came and went, with Mammy playing chaperone. They said I was 'a difficult case'—their very words. One man claimed to have cracked under the strain. My father pays his bills.

"Oh!" she continued brightly, happy with her new concern, "did I tell you? A seminary offered to pay Daddy a thousand dollars if I didn't come back. Don't tell me about education. I got it, that's all."

"Well, walking's a grand sport," I said, hoping to change the subject.

She looked off into the distance. "'She walks in beauty, like the night' —Byron, or Bryan."

I said, "Trollope did the bulk of his walking at night. You probably knew that."

"Bill" —she was almost weeping. "I don't know how to tell you this. Angus Trollope never ate a snail in his life."

"Don't worry about it. His family ate them by the tubful."

"Dearest Bill—thanks for those words. I'll treasure them the rest of my life."

I rose and led her out, after some little difficulty. (There was still wine in the bottle.) I had the impression people were glad to see us go.

Now she wanted to visit the very trashiest shops, saying she needed some "mementos of Canada's Falls." In a large and dismal emporium, she bought a monkey-on-a-stick; a long banner saying "Visit Canadian Niagara!"; a rubber horseshoe; a *papier-mâché* icicle; an ashtray bearing a garish picture of the attraction; a beanbag and an ax handle, of "rare Canadian hardwood, sledged down by Eskimo huskies." It looked like willow to me, worth about a nickel.

The afternoon wearing on, we headed down the slope to a boat with Canadian oarsmen. They were excessively polite, and, I thought, not nervous about being shot, regardless of my bluff. Indeed, being normal river rats of the period, they were unable to refrain from overdoing things, with frequent inquiries of "Is the little lady comfortable on them cushions?" and "I hope the gent don't find the sunshine a-squinting too fierce in his eyes," and the like. (The sun, by the way, *was* "a-squinting" in my face, since the river, while in general running south-to-north, took a jog here and made its way nearly due west.)

I watched the sea gulls, so curiously abundant, swooping and dipping over the dark lagoon, and hoped my consort's wine had worn off a little. But now she addressed the larger of the men.

"You ever know a writer here named Trollope? Angus *E.* Trollope?"

"Said what, ma'am?"

"It won't hurt you to admit you *know* him, you know. I haven't accused him of anything—*yet!*"

"Trolp," said the smaller, who was chewing tobacco and now spat delicately over the side. "Bowlegged gent, tall, whiskers on both cheeks and carried a pet squirrel?"

"God bless you for the description!"

"Knowed him and knowed him well. I understand he's a-coming back in late August, and bringing his mother."

The other now spoke up to say, "I didn't rightly catch the name, at first, ma'am. Well, I reckon I *should* know him, seeing what he done for I and my family."

"Then you remember what a walker he was?"

"*Walk!*" (The idiot had the indecency to chuckle.) "He didn't hardly do anything *but* walk." He looked reflective. "I've said it before, and I'll say it now—I'm convinced that Angus B. Trolp could walk up the Falls, once he got his hand in."

I lit a cigar and detached my mind. I'd pretty well run through Trollope and wished he'd stayed home, or gone to Abyssinia. There was more, but I didn't hear it.

Then we arrived on the American side; I paid, overtipping for putting Canada behind us, as fine as it was. Samantha handed her junk to the oarsmen and said, "Use this well, to the memory of you-know-who."

In Prospect Park (which seemed oddly like home) the girl glanced up, guilty.

"Are you mad? . . . Bill," she added, "I don't feel too awfully well."

"How bad?"

"Well, I could—you know—sick to the stomach and what you do."

I took her behind an oak and emptied her; then, after I cleaned her up, she felt better.

"Tell the truth, Samantha. Did you ever drink wine before?"

"Not exactly *wine*. Wine vinegar, of course, and once I took a sip of Daddy's julep on the sly."

"Why didn't you say so?"

"Well, I may have sounded like a fool. But you have to admit you don't run across Angus Trollope every day."

"Let's bury that bore. Better yet, pretend he never existed."

"I do what you say. Now or any time, and that goes for Ang—"

I put my hand to her mouth. "Don't say it."

She looked up and smiled with more loveliness than one girl ought to own.

Chapter XXI

As we neared Cataract House, I sensed that all was not well among the frolickers. A hush seemed to lie over the hotel. And then, when we saw the piazza emptied of people, I began to suspect the truth. At the same time, the girl turned pale and put her hands to her cheeks again.

"What is it?" she whispered. "What's wrong?"

"I don't know. There's probably a simple explanation."

General Whitney came out to meet us on the porch.

"We did what we could," he said, taking the girl's hands. "The best doctors, every means of revival. But he was gone before he left the swing. I can't tell you how sorry I am, Samantha. Amos and I have been friends, close friends, for years."

"Daddy!"

I thought back to the night when he overstrained himself at Tryon's and felt guilty.

The great room downstairs was filled with guests looking grieved, a few groups talking in low tones, women touching the corners of their eyes with handkerchiefs. Colonel Rutledge had been popular, and his sudden slump to the floor had shocked people badly.

General Whitney led, half-supporting her, the girl to her family suite, and shortly afterward I made my way to the room in which the dead man lay. In my time, I had seen few corpses, and this waxen, shrunken figure was not the man I knew. But his face had smoothed out after the fatal contortion, and he looked, somehow, at ease after the years of living with a complaining shrew. Two of them, in truth, for the sister was always in evidence, with supportive views on Sin.

At the moment, no one else was here, except an ass of an undertaker. Dressed in offensive black, he was taking soundings with a measuring tape, calculating weight, etc., and humming professional jargon the while.

"Six-foot-one, in proportion broad, paunch stout. Now that would mean—"

He saw me, gave a start and buttoned his shiny coat over a pocket from which protruded a small bottle-neck and cork.

"A sad, sad day for Niagara Falls, sir," he said with the house bereavement.

I was touchy because a friend was dead, and from thinking about those two women. So the smirk and the bottle were the last straw.

"Sad, but not such a very bad day for you."

"We all have to go, sir. 'Man that is born of woman hath but a few years and is cut down—'"

"I know the lines. How much do you stand to make from this unhappy event? I ask in my position as counselor to the family."

"So young," he murmured, "so young to be counselor!" He began to count on his fingers, until I stopped him.

"Tin coffins, your worship, come high. They ain't *given* away, you know."

"Why tin?"

"The *family* prefers he be taken home to Atlanta and buried, especially now the Buffalo-Niagara railroad spur's finished. Lacking proper refrigeration, we use a tin coffin filled with alkyhol. It's specific for preserving."

"No doubt. What does it cost?"

The fingers went to work again.

"To say we could ship him for under five hundred would leave me open to perjury. I'd do it gratis 'cept for my partner. It's him keeps the books, and he's a stickler for counting the pence."

"I didn't know you had a partner."

"Mr. Spivak?" He took on a cunning look. "Why, sir, everybody knows *about* him, but there's precious few *seen* him. A thing like this cuts him to the bone. But he's stiff, mighty stiff with the books."

"Relay my condolences," I said, and left, angry at my rudeness. But to continue this drivel made no sense, so I wandered downstairs and ordered a mint julep.

It was the first I ever drank, and I did it in sympathy with a departed man whom I liked and admired. I thought he might understand.

The undertaker went ahead and ordered his tin coffin, Colonel Rutledge was deposited therein, and General Whitney held a short memorial service in his spacious lounge. Everybody attended, with that grotesque receptacle on a trolley in front; and with four black plumes at the corners. That thief of an undertaker ("mortician") undertook this display on his own, hauling it in by six men, two of them chewing tobacco. The general was beet-red, and the people revolted, for the coffin gave off gurgling noises as the six juggled it into place.

Even the service failed properly to come off. The minister Whitney normally used had gone to Buffalo (riding the rails free, as was the pious custom then and for years thereafter), and a new man, a stranger, came off the bench. He was a rather impressive fellow with an aureole of silky-white hair, and he did his level best, I'm convinced. But he had no more knowledge of the deceased than the king of the Zulus did, and so he made considerable things up.

He told of Mr. Rutledge's many charities, here and in Cincinnati, where he'd somehow got the notion the colonel lived; told of his medals from the Revolution (before the departed was born); mentioned his two trips to Africa to help "the missionaries out there"; and stressed that he "neither swore nor used spirituous liquors."

I expected the corpse to sit up in the box. When you took into account that Rutledge, when aroused, had the vocabulary of a fishwife, and that he looked incomplete when not holding a julep, people could be excused from tittering. But the minister bulled on with a tribute to the "sweetness of the deceased's family life," then supported the lies with the usual obscure Biblical quotes.

They sang two hymns at the end, and these cleared the air a bit. Most everyone had filed out, stopping to speak to the family, before the gurgling started up again.

Not long before train time, I had a chance to see Samantha alone. She sat beside me in the swing that had ushered her father to a happier, wifeless world.

"Well," she said. "That's that."

"These things happen," I said inanely. "I'm sorry. I *liked* your father."

"So did I. But you know, I don't think he believed in anything, anything at all."

"He believed in mint juleps, and don't misunderstand. He was not a drunkard, in any sense. Juleps, for him, meant keeping hope alive."

"I didn't help much, did I?"

"He was very proud of you, in his way."

"And now I've got nobody left but you—have I?"

"Just go on thinking about us," I said slowly, "and the time will pass."

"I'll send you a postcard."

"You couldn't manage a letter?"

"I'm not very good on letters. They're too long, and they wouldn't make me happy."

She had a package gaily tied in striped paper and red ribbon. She handed it over and said, "These are my copper-toed shoes. I want you to keep them, to remember."

"But you'll be back," I said, shocked.

"Oh, I suppose. But *they* will work against me. They'll try to stop everything *I* might want. And they usually win. Wait and see."

"Well, there's nothing to keep me from going to Atlanta. I doubt if they could win over *me.*"

"Goodbye, Bill." She leaned forward to kiss me on the mouth and then turned and half-ran toward the train, where her father lay defeated and pickled.

I shuddered. A shade—perhaps a dark cloud only—had moved overhead, and I somehow felt that a wild, lovely spirit, never to be tamed in this world, had flown out of my life. Then it all faded, and I silently called, "Goodbye, you sweet and tortured dream. Goodbye, if ever you existed."

In my room, I flung myself down on the bed. I'd have dinner here presently, then fix my mind on Mr. Bennett. As I drifted off, I noted vaguely that twilight was closing in on this wretched day. Then there came a-tapping (I continued Mr. Poe's poem in a kind of delirium) at my chamber door. I mumbled "Come in, whoever you are," and it was of course only the omniscient, always-present-when-needed Betsy.

She said, "You'll want a tray, sir. The oxtail soup—it's on the menu tonight—and a thick piece of rare steak. If you go to sleep now, you'll wake at two o'clock and feel worse."

"Betsy," I said. "Why do you bully me? You must know I'm not hungry."

"I do know. But tomorrow must come and you have your work."

I turned to face her. "See here, Betsy, I want you to do something for me."

"If I can, sir."

"March over to that chair"—I pointed—"and *sit down!* Oh, just for a moment. But as pretty and trim as you are, I'm tired of seeing you standing there in the middle of this room, waiting to prop me back up on my feet."

"Would that be proper, sir?" More acutely than before, I saw the Mona Lisa look, and, with male stupidity, became even testier.

"Not only proper"—I came close to shouting—"*it's necessary to my good health!*"

She crossed gracefully and sat in an upright chair (naturally not the one I meant). Then she waited for my next display of poor manners. There was neither resentment nor servility in those cool blue eyes.

"Now—are you in a rush?"

"I'm here to serve you, sir."

"You know what I mean. You have other duties, and so on. Are they pressing? Right now?"

"This is my afternoon off."

"Oh, is it? Then what in blazes are you doing *here?*"

She made no response, and I said, "Betsy, let's go to the mat, as they say in wrestling circles—"

"That might be *very* improper, sir."

"Would you let me finish? Why do you cross me all the time? Never mind. I have some questions, and you can answer or skedaddle. See what you've done to me?"

"I, sir?" But she failed to look surprised.

"Yes, you. First off, you don't ring true in the serving class. How come?"

"'Rank is but the guinea stamp' —I'm sure you know the rest of it, sir."

"No, and don't tell me. What does your father do, in this center of non-guinea stamps? Do, work at, labor over, to provide food for the family? There must be more of you, ten or fifteen usually."

"Nobody but my father and me."

"Ah, stop right there! See? Most dunces would say 'My father and *I.*' He must be some kind of emancipated preacher."

"He's the schoolmaster, sir. For a long time he had no building, so we went from place to place. Thanks to General Whitney, he has— for now—a small schoolhouse."

I sat up on the edge of the bed.

"Betsy, I'm going to speak frankly. I could use a drink."

"I thought you might. That's why I brought up the mint leaves and sugar." She half-turned in the direction of a glass on the commode. "I believe you keep a bottle in a drawer, sir."

164

"Snooping?"

She flushed. "Cleaning and tidying, sir."

"Sorry I said that, but anything to relieve the prim line of that mouth. Never mind the mint. My mint period's over."

She prepared the glass, without mint-and-sugar, and brought it without comment. I drank off about half, the girl looking neither approving nor disapproving.

"I think it's time for your tray, sir."

"Rot the tray. The tray can wait. I have something very, very important to say to you, Betsy."

"I'm happy for you, sir."

"For *me!* It was for you," and I became more vehement, finishing the drink. "It was simply this, and Betsy, I want you to attend with care— Oh, hell! I've forgotten what it was. But how about this instead? Why do you speak with an English accent? It's slight, but it's there. Now, answer me that."

"As part of my duties, sir?"

"*Pre-cisely!* As part of your duties. You've struck the nail on the head!"

"And because I grew up in England, sir. That could bear on it."

"Now that's sarcastic, Betsy. It's beneath you. I'm sorry to see that trait. It shows want of feeling."

For the first time, her expression changed—to one of reflection.

"I have no want of feeling, sir, and I regret sarcasm. But I dislike to see you suffer, and a whole glass of whiskey won't help. Especially at your age."

"Ah, so you know my age! Well, you're wrong. I'm forty-six, and been a heavy drinker since I was nine."

"You're twenty-one, sir."

"Don't bother about that. People age rapidly in these times. Do you know what the life expectancy is at this date and moment?"

"No, I don't."

"Well, neither do I. And I'm damned glad of it!" I snapped my fingers. "Good! I remembered what I wanted to know. The English accent. Go further."

"As I said, I was reared in England."

"Your father English?" I asked with a keen look.

"No, he's an American—now."

"'Now?' What does that mean?"

"He's become a citizen of this country, and very proud of it."

"Came seeking a fortune, did he? Well, he won't find it, not as a schoolteacher. And by the way, you have to be qualified for a teacher. If you were poor in England, how'd he manage *that?*"

She changed color slightly. "He was qualified enough for England, sir. And that seemed to satisfy General Whitney."

"He knows Whitney, does he? He sounds pretty unusual, this father of yours. Well, we're getting somewhere at last. Now, there's this point: It's summer—do you agree?"

"It's summer, sir."

"And no school. So—what's your father doing at—this—time? Betsy," I said, "I really don't mean to pry or be offensive. Just what's he doing?—that's all."

"He's classifying the local flora and fauna, sir. It's not important about 'prying.' I don't think he'd mind."

My head was spinning, but I had reality left to say, "I'm in business here. You know that, don't you?"

"I do, and I think a tray—"

"Jolly good, as they say in your former land. This father might make a good, short piece for my paper. Poor but honest immigrant, daughter helping budget by doing chamber work. What's your opinion?"

She hesitated. "I'm sure he'd be glad to receive you, sir."

It was the last thing I remembered for twelve hours, but I recalled that "receive" had a curious sound. It failed to fit.

When I awoke, at nine-thirty next morning, I found myself in bed, wearing pyjamas, my clothes laid neatly on a chair—all traces of the bottle gone.

There was the one answer. The girl, blast her, had undressed me again and struggled me into my nightclothes. As I sat up (painfully, as suggested) my cheeks burned with shame, and, dressed, I slipped down the fire stairs and over to the Eagle. I needed restoratives, but I recalled, all the same, the divulgence about that father.

Chapter XXII

Two days later the great news traveled around town. One "Blondin" (real name Jean François Gravelet), who described himself as a "funambulist," had left his native France and was due in Niagara Falls any moment. Purpose: "To walk a tightrope over the lethal cascade."

There was to be a fanfare of bands from nearby towns—to support the local musicians—hawkers and other thieves, "gingerbread sales-women," cake and beer stalls, "wheel of fortune" men, and further irritations. Those from the *Iris*. Tourists in the hundreds of thousands were expected, these including not only American "celebrities" (meaning mainly, politicians), but European royalty, including the Prince of Wales.

This came as wonderful news to the citizenry, especially tavern keepers, since nothing similar had taken place since Sam Patch made his foolhardy leaps some years before.

Sam was a flamboyant fellow, whose equal at brag-and-bounce had not previously been seen. (He frequently bounced two or three times before being hauled out of this river or that; he seemed to have no fear.) His motive was, frankly, enrichment (of Patch) and he advertised his intent widely. Calling himself a "wharf rat with a hobby," he jumped into water off anything high enough to be classed

167

as suicidal. On occasion, he took a pet bear with him, and shoved the animal off as well. What the bear thought of Patch's hobby has not been recorded.

Sam had already cast himself, with no protection, from yardarms; from bridges here and there; from a flagpole into a lily pond (with indifferent results), and when he was dehospitalized from this last, he realized that nothing remained but Niagara.

"The owners of Goat Island," he announced in the Buffalo *Express*, "have generously granted me the use of it for nothing, so that I may have a chance, from an equally generous public, to obtain some remuneration for my journey hither, as well as affording me an opportunity of supporting the reputation I have gained by AERO-NAUTICAL FEATS, never before attempted, either in the Old or New World.

"I shall, Ladies and Gentlemen, on Saturday night . . . LEAP at the FALLS of NIAGARA from a height of 120 to 130 feet! On my way down from Buffalo, on the morning of that day, in the steamboat NIAGARA, I shall, for the amusement of the Ladies, doff my coat and spring from the masthead into the River."

History is obscure about the steamboat ride, for no mention is made of the masthead. But he assuredly leaped into the Falls, not once but twice, fudging slightly on the first round. At one of the two Falls divisions, he built a platform at eighty feet, and stepped brazenly off in the deluge. Bobbing up from the gorge, he came ashore in such triumph that he promptly followed with another soaring spring—from the top.

These coups unquestionably went to Patch's head, for he retired, possibly as practice, to the modest falls of the nearby Genessee River. There he plunged over with a "condescending smile." But he landed on a pile of rocks, and parts of him were retrieved for some distance downriver.

Prospective Falls-jumpers took strong clues from the Patch finale, and no further gymnastics were evident for a while—excepting the ever-present builders of barrels and other "protective" devices. Many of these bore hints of lunacy. Ordinary suicides, of course, went over with dismal regularity, the remains recovered (usually) by the stouthearted Gill family, at the Great Whirlpool two miles below.

Now came trumpeting advance men for Blondin, and I checked on the funambulist's background.

I learned that that marvelous old scamp, Phineas T. Barnum, first brought Blondin to America, to stand beside the (whitewashed) white elephant; George Washington's 150-year-old nurse, who proved to be eighty; and the miraculous Feejee mermaid, who was half a monkey ingeniously joined to half a fish; and the Cardiff giant, who'd been carved from a block of gypsum and treated by experts.

Barnum or no Barnum, Blondin was an authentic wire-walker and acrobat, trained in France at five and taken to English music halls at six. Women at London's Crystal Palace fainted at his high-rope dancing, and more hullabaloo attended his climax of leaping over a file of soldiers with fixed bayonets. His stage name, in infancy, came from a thicket of yellow curls; he later announced that his father was a hero in Napoleon's *Grande Armée*. Growing up, he made much of being a gourmet and fancier of fine wines. Apparently he fancied these so much that he fancied them all day long, though the tippling never diminished his skill.

Pondering this list, in the dining room, I was approached by (the Hon.) Frances Barclay, burdened by her customary menus. I'd pretty much avoided her since her late suitor had been converted to a Negro and pointed South. But she bore no signs of grief. Indeed, her voice rang out with the best of cheer.

"William! And in the dining room, too. I expect you've been embarrassed for me."

"A little," I said truthfully. "But good riddance, and all that."

"Good riddance of *me?*"

"You know what I mean. Did you get your $15,000 back?"

"The check was never cashed. By the way, has General Whitney spoken to you?"

"Why, no," I said. "Am I evicted?"

"Hardly that. He wants me, and you, to join some sort of dinner tonight. Very mysterious. Shall we go?"

I said, "I haven't been asked yet."

"I'm asking you now. It's just occurred; I'd forgotten. Orders from the grand mogul. He's gone to Lockport for the day."

"Well, why not? I trust that old rooster. What's more, I admire him."

"Rooster is scarcely a word I would use to describe my employer. But I trust him, too. You're to collect—pick me up—here at six o'clock. I've been given the evening off."

The general was on time, and escorted us to his surrey. I'd laid aside my gunfighter costume and dressed semiformally.

"You may enjoy this," he said. "Nice people, the best. And since my family are off on a visit (as usual), this seems to be the time."

"Our hosts are alerted?"

"Of course," he replied, chuckling, "but it really wouldn't make any difference if they weren't."

We drove through unfamiliar streets beyond the edge of town, where stood a substantial white frame cottage, smartly painted, planted around with a bewildering array of flowers, shrubs and small trees.

We knocked, and the door was opened by a tall, slender, genial-looking man of about forty-five. I could guess that this was the teacher, but he had about as much pauper-humility as the king of France.

"Come in, General, come in, and bring our guests with you."

I was stunned. The décor would only be familiar to the careless-elegant. No object could be mistaken as inexpensive, from the Turkey carpet to the period furniture to English sporting prints and portraits of what had to be ancestors, most looking in need of drink.

Then Betsy came from a back room, a different Betsy. She said, "You might introduce us, General."

For the first time, General Whitney looked at a loss. But he recovered and said, "I was trying to figure out who doesn't know whom. But of course Gervais doesn't know Miss Barclay, or young William Morrison. Our host," he went on, turning to me, still mildly rattled, "is the volunteer schoolmaster of this hamlet, Gervais Lockridge—"

"The G as in J," explained our host.

"And you all know Betsy, unless I've lost my mind, which does seem the case."

For a moment, I thought he would introduce Betsy to her father, but the crisis passed. The truth is, I was not quite at ease myself.

"Sit down, sit down. I suggest we have a drink. I needn't ask you, General—the terrible raw 'whiskey'—bourbon?—you live on. Maybe you can explain," he said, addressing himself to me, "why a whiskey, as they call it, dredged out of tubs in Kentucky, should find itself confused with a royal family of France?"

"As I understand it, sir," I replied, "it comes from Bourbon *County* —in Kentucky, as you said."

"Do we have the commodity, Betsy? I should have known. Quite typical."

"I bought some today," said the girl, moving gracefully to a refectory at one wall.

"And you, young man, and Miss Barclay. I hope you'll take some moderately drinkable sherry?"

"I prefer whiskey, like the general's," I said stoutly, "unless you object."

170

"Object? Me? You can drink pond water, if it suits you. *Chacun à son goût*, if you'll excuse a pomposity. Then, Miss Barclay—sherry?" He gazed at her curiously. "I've seen you somewhere."

"That's true," she said evenly.

"Well, don't worry. I'll get it eventually. Things usually come to me later, if you know what I mean. Slow in the head. People finally notice it."

She smiled.

He studied her carefully. "I'm hanged! Five minutes and already an enigma!"

"Father."

"Oh, these are friends. I sensed it at once." But he couldn't get Frances off his mind. "You've grown up awfully well, you know."

"You may be thinking about my sister."

"Drink your sherry, and you'll be convinced of it yourself. If not, I'll mention it again."

"Father!"

"I'm finished, and submit to the usual bullying. Tell me, young man, does Betsy bully *you?* In her job as chambermaid?"

"My name is William. She—looks after me. You might call it a mild form of bullying," I said, smiling. "To be honest, she's been obliged twice to put me to bed. I was embarrassed, both times."

"Remarkable girl. We decided on her job of work because she wanted to learn about Americans. I was against it at first. One runs away from snobbery," he said musingly, "and winds up a snob someplace else."

"I enjoy my work," said Betsy, sitting down, "and I've certainly met Americans. Mr. Morrison's my only hopeless case."

"William," I said firmly, "or Bill."

Mr. Lockridge stretched his long legs out before him, in a way no American would do in a parlor.

"That brings up a point. I've noticed that members of your nationality, while annoyed at being asked what they do, or where they come from, are quickly eager to settle on a first-name basis. Why the devil's that? You see, it's my nationality too, now."

General Whitney chuckled. "The real names, and past, of many around here don't bear inspection. We're a new nation, and the drifter still outnumbers the honest man." Then he went on to say, "How are your specimens coming?"

"Aha! I'm glad you asked. Today I found a small corkscrew willow. All by itself. Replanted it, of course, and hope it survives. Come have a look." To Miss Barclay he said, "I'll work it out soon—don't fret."

I had a fancy that pink flags were flying in her cheeks.

"The 'fret' may be yours."

He led us through a library cluttered with pinned samples of leaves, twigs, bark and the like, all identified in English and most with either the Latin name—in parenthesis—or a question mark. There were reference works, with markers, most of American origin; and bottles of alcohol containing more insects, lizards and frogs than I cared to examine before dinner. Out back was a jungle of transplanted trees, shrubs and plants.

"Fine, fine," said General Whitney, obviously bored. "You're coming along splendidly. And you've been at it how long?"

"Two years here. Actually, all my life."

"And your definitive book? How far into it are you?"

His note of amusement was easy to detect.

"Three solid chapters, and picking up speed each day."

"Your three chapters are, of course, down on paper?"

"In my head. I mean to get them down next week. Accurate classification is not simple. Day before yesterday, I picked up a woman's flowered hat, where she'd removed it in a shop. I pinched a blossom, and guess what—*it was artificial!*"

"You might do the definitive work on artificial flowers."

Our host frowned, after running his hands through his graying hair, leaving some standing on end.

"You're ragging, I know. But really, Parkhurst—my God, what a name! Worse than mine—the idea has merit. Think how the consumer might be protected. An artificial orchid's worth more than an artificial pansy."

"But not before you get the three chapters on paper—"

Here Betsy took my arm and gently propelled me back to the living room.

"And now you see, William. He gets an allowance—quite a good one—from home each month, and cashes the checks in Buffalo. But he gives nearly all away to the poor."

"But—"

"You sensed something odd in this house when you and Miss Barclay came in. My father is a child, in some ways. But he's a wonderful teacher. *He likes children!* Of any kind, and he has an education hard to equal.

"So—I *need* my post as chambermaid, and General Whitney knows it. Now you know it, too."

"He seems like a wonderful man," I said at a loss for something better.

"Of course he is. And he's not crazy, or retarded, or any of those words. He's probably the only entirely natural person you ever met. And he has scientific talents. Part of him, over the years, simply clung to childhood interests. A lot of people would like that, and never admit it. On most occasions," she added defensively, "nobody would see him as different."

I privately thought it a little rough on her, but we went to the dining room, where a Seneca servant served a first course of smoked salmon strips. Our host piled some on the back of his left-hand fork, and cried, "Nefertiti! The salmon's too salty again."

"My fault, Father," said Betsy smoothly. "I meant to test it when—"

"—we arrived early," boomed General Whitney. "You'd better remember, Gervais, this is Nova Scotia salmon, saltier than the Scottish. I know; I've eaten them both."

"I've worked out a method of desalinizing local salmon without a loss of flavor. I'd explain it but it's going in the Book."

I'm not apt to forget the dinner. The conversation was a blur, partly owing to the soup, which had a taste unique in my experience. No lame pen could describe it.

"How do you like the soup?" asked Lockridge.

"It really is remarkably nasty," said Miss Barclay. "Who made it?"

"Indian soup. Nefertiti. And I thought you'd say that. It's a *strengthening* soup, with herbs and bark and mashed-up insects, and so forth. But we won't hurt Nefertiti's feelings. —Dump it out."

He took the bowls and poured them into potted plants around the room. The leaves, I noticed, began to droop before he returned to the table.

"Frankly, it's *too* nasty. I never tried it before, on the full scale. I got talked into it."

"Well," said Betsy brightly, "that's two courses failed. I should have stayed home. What's next?"

"Next" was a fine piece of fish, from Lake Erie, and then cutlets that erased all memory, but no after-results, of the strengthening soup.

"Tell us, Gervais," asked General Whitney, "do you cling to your theory that American Indians came over on rafts from Egypt?"

"My renaming Nefertiti, of course. Absolutely, though Western Indians crossed the Bering Ice Bridge during the Glacier . . . Now what the devil's this—?"

A male Indian stood in the doorway, making gestures. Nefertiti padded forward to whisper in Lockridge's ear. He jumped up and said, "Ramses came by Charley's and found dead snakes in the

173

enclosure—no signs of human life. He called, and hadn't any answer."

My chargirl whispered aside, "Ramses is Nefertiti's husband. Father has him check Charley two or three times a week."

General Whitney arose, looking serious. "If those goddamned slave-traders—" and added several remarks commonly regarded as unfit for ladies of the period. "We'd better get out there; the women can stay—"

"Not me," said Miss Barclay.

Betsy, not quite as self-effacing as usual, took a handgun from a case, twirled the cylinder and gave it to General Whitney.

She said, "There's lots of room in the buggy, and we probably oughtn't wait."

We scrambled in and were off, Miss Barclay with a pronounced "Yoicks!" look in her eye. There·was plenty of daylight left, but Ramses stuck close to the surrey on an antique paint pony. He'd been badly frightened by the remaining live snakes.

When we arrived, there was still no sign of life. General Whitney clambered down, and we followed, our dinner host in the lead.

"A light should be lit inside," he said briskly. "You others stand back, and I'll handle the snakes still alive." In the fading light, I could see a gleam of admiration in Miss Barclay's eye.

He hopped nimbly into the enclosure, with a piece of hickory stick. Then he began prodding this snake and that.

"All dead but two," he called. "They've been beaten to death, or stamped on. The two were not in condition to strike" (which he could not have known), and he picked these up, saying, "Push on in and I'll hold on till you get a cage open."

It was about here that Ramses disappeared, mumbling some tribal twaddle about "evil spirits."

My heart was knocking away, but with the general I unstuck the door and kicked it open. Inside all was confusion, the few sticks of furniture smashed, Indian hangings and pelts ripped from the walls and more mangled snakes on the floor. And then, when we lit a lantern, we saw Charley, propped against a wall behind an over-turned table. He was sitting up, though slumped to the left, and the general bent down to look.

"Dead?"

"Not quite yet, but he's taken a murderous thrashing."

Here Charley opened his blood-encrusted lips and groaned, "Coley—him and the partners."

Lockridge was busy putting away snakes and cleaning up the dead

174

remnants. I remember thinking he looked incongruous doing a job like this in his attire. But the women were no less busy.

Betsy was straightening and mopping when Miss Barclay called from outside—at the shed.

"They've cut his horse's throat. The poor beast bled to death. The *blackguards!*"

Charley groaned again, and General Whitney said, "His left leg's broken, with several ribs and his jaw. God knows what's smashed inside. I can't tell yet about the eye. The thing is, can we get him to town in time?" His face was flushed, and he added some remarks of a general nature.

But Mr. Lockridge had already left to unhitch one of the general's matched mares. Now he backed it into the shafts of Charley's trap; for lack of room in the buggy, I was to drive the injured, prostrate man. The remaining rattlesnakes were fed and watered, a store of mice drawn on in the rear.

Of that dismal ride, I recall only that it was slower, and that we stopped several times for examination.

"Pulse slowing down, respiration, too," said the general. "Can you get some whiskey down him?"

"I have none with me," said Lockridge, looking sorry about it.

"Well, this is once when *sherry's* not quite up to scratch," said the general, taking a pint bottle from his pocket. I'd never before seen him really angry, even at Miss Barclay's late charlatan. His utterance, I also reflected, might have been offensive to any but a civilized Englishman.

The new doctor—who'd saved the gourmet kite-winner—was still in his surgery. When we carried Charley to a porcelain table, all was bustle and business, and for the record (his name was Wilkins) he'd be a boon to Niagara for years.

"Low," he said, bending over, "very low. He wants stimulants, injected. You, miss"—to Miss Barclay—"kindly step to the next room and call upstairs for my wife."

"I'll wash his face and cut away the shirt and trousers," said Betsy, and, washing her hands began, as the doctor, surprised, commented, only, "Well!"

The wife, a pretty young woman, or girl, appeared slightly bizarre by the fact of her hair grotesquely curled on homemade wooden rollers. They looked to me like spools from which the thread was exhausted. But she paid us no more mind than she did the oddity of her head. Instead, after a quick glance at Charley, she went to a cabinet and began extracting utensils, medication and a coil of surgical wire. I figured that, if he pulled through, his jaw would hold its old position with props. I also figured, with relief, that this surehanded young lady would *haul* him through, if necessary, and brook no nonsense about it.

"I suggest you all go to the parlor and wait," said the doctor, not unkindly, when Betsy had finished. "We should know within the hour. I'll call if I need help with splints."

You won't need it, I said to myself. That woman will *wrench* the leg into position.

We found seats, and after General Whitney had scrutinized me three or four times, he said, "William—I'd like a word with you on the doorstep."

When we got outside, he said, "I can see in your face that you mean to take steps by yourself. In other words, you're going to make this up—singlehanded. Am I right?"

"Quite right," I replied cheerfully. "But I hope to use *both* hands."

"You can't do it. It's a matter for the police. *Police!*" he said with scorn. "Police and judges! They'll need 'proofs,' and other legal tommyrot. And, of course, nothing will happen. Unless Charley dies and there's a lynching." His face brightened, then he sighed. "I suppose that's not the way. But I can't let you get in trouble. Your father would be up here like a hive of bees. I've seen him in action."

"Me, too," I said, painfully remembering. "But on this occasion, General," I told him, "there's not a thing you can do about it, not this time." I lit a cigar—it was all I had here of my badman's trappings—and walked back into the house.

Chapter XXIII

Blondin had not yet arrived next morning, and I was relieved. No matter how things developed, I wanted the day memorable for one reason only. However, I was told that the French wonder had telegraphed ahead and a rope to his specifications was being spun at the local rope walk.

The doctor and his attractive gorgon had decreed that Charley was to lie in overnight, at least, the woman appearing briefly to say, "We'll summon you if there's a change. Good night," and she abruptly closed the surgery door.

I taped my right hand, as I'd often done in college. I took time to make it look like an injury, then strolled into the dining room, surprising Miss Barclay. But something held her to "Good morning, William," and her face was impassive when I ordered a thick steak and three eggs.

I spent the morning in Prospect Park and on Goat Island, accompanied partway by my friend in the tall hat. I've forgotten what he discussed in his duty as guide, but I believe he mentioned that, long ago, an Indian virgin was annually sacrificed to the Falls and that, to this day, they (or she) haunted the Cave of the Winds below.

But at eleven o'clock, when I started back, this concerned old beanpole, refusing my "tip," said slyly, "They's three of 'em, you know, all rough as a cob. Now I've got an old Sharp's—"

Secrecy, of any kind, was unknown in this confounded place.

I laid a hand on his arm and said, "My friend"—for he was a friend by now—"thank you. I'm grateful, but this is a job I've picked to do alone."

I left him, brows knitted, wondering what to do.

The two boisterous times at Eagle were at noon and at about seven in the evening. At noon, most clients felt scratchy from the evening before; and consequently they poured in Monongahela at a pretty brisk rate, making them scratchier.

I entered with (I hoped) a bland look, and surely enough, the villains were seated at a table alone, in the remotest corner. To say that they—or other slave-catchers—were popular would be to bend, stretch and twist the truth. They all walked a tightrope, and knew it.

I had on my vaquero's hat and my leather jacket, and got set for the usual ribbing. To my surprise, everyone was overpolite, and the bartender said, "Your usual, Mr. Morrison?" Then, seeing my expression, changed his mind.

My "usual" was a glass of beer, and these people knew it but kept silent.

The raw Monongahela worked its way down; I felt it warm my stomach. Before reaching the Tavern, I'd been stopped by an acquaintance and told that, "Charley ain't going to have but one eye left. T'other was squashed like a white grape, to dangle on his cheek."

To this day, I'm sorry he told me that; it's a picture I've never quite forgotten. It now joined hands with the Monongahela, and I turned slowly to face the three.

"Another, Mr. Morrison?" said the bartender anxiously, filling my glass before I could answer.

"See anything green, sonny?" asked the center of the three.

This was Coley; I'd seen (and heard) him before.

"Why, he's a-planning to buy you a drink, Coley. Dogged if you ain't lost your manners."

"I see a skunk—three skunks," I said pleasantly, "and I don't make a practice of drinking with—"

All three were up in an instant, guns drawn. But the bartender leaned against his counter with a double-barreled shotgun.

"My customer's unarmed, gents," he said without emotion. "Kindly lay them revolvers on the table."

Several men laughed, and the three, red-faced, and after a

whispered conference, complied, with mean looks around the room.

I said, "A skunk's a varmint that needs handling personally—deskunked, you might say. You in the middle—Coley? That the name you go by? You're the biggest by a head. Ugliest, too. Step out in the street."

"Don't do it, sir," the bartender whispered. "They're authentic and genuine bad 'uns. None other would take the jobs. They been bragging about Charley, and not a soul to take them up."

What happened next startled; it even alarmed me slightly. All three removed their hats and slapped them on the table, doubled up in laughter.

The one so far silent said, "The dude's calling you out, Coley. He's going to chaw you up proper. I wouldn't be in your shoes for a hundert million dollars."

"They tell me he's a *writer*, and that's the worst kind. My old daddy once said, he said, 'Abe, don't never mix it with a writer. They ain't got mercy in their bones. Only outright wicious type alive.'"

I was busy appraising Coley. He was about my height but more powerfully made, with a short, sinewy neck and forearms knotted like clubs.

"Charley sent me to pay respects, so to speak. He's not talking right now, but I got his message. By the way," I said, looking at Coley, "what's holding your coattails? These men'll think you've contracted the yellow-bellies."

I'll say this for him; he was confounded.

"You? You simpering dandy? *You* want a cat-fuss with *me?*"

An Indian boy scampered out of the room, yelling "Fight! Fight!" and crowds began to gather.

"Boys," said the bartender to his regulars, still hoping for peace (or maybe to save my hide), "gather up those guns." After some reluctance, two men did so. But it wasn't a job they relished, and they skedaddled back to their places.

I stripped off my hat and jacket, as Coley pulled his lumberjack shirt over his head, helped by a partner. He was awesome, with his hairy barrelchest, but I noticed that he had a paunch as well.

On my side was youth, a fair amount of skill, conditioning, and anger no longer hot but cold. I could easily have killed him if able.

In the street, people formed a wide ring and there were a good many boys in trees. The rogue said, "You had a look at old Charley, the nigger-lover?"

"I saw him, saw his horse, too."

"I'll fix you worse. How do you want to make it, bub—heel and toe, or Free?"

"Free." I hadn't any idea what it meant, but it sounded worse.

"When I'm done, Charley could act as your nurse," and he aimed a roundhouse swing which, if it had landed, might have left me on the Clifton House piazza.

But I ducked. And when he straightened up, I drove my taped right hand deep in that paunch. He grunted and tried another, and then another, but I moved backward, now, my left hand in his face.

He stopped a second, to wipe off sweat, and said, through bloody lips, "You'll pay for that, sonny. When I'm done, there ain't a hearse in town could collect you single." And here he dove suddenly forward to wrap those spars around my chest. His foul breath—whiskey, chewing tobacco, meanness—was in my nose, almost, and I was lifted off the dirt in a slow, painful squeeze.

"Your time's come, you whippersnapper bastard. If you got a prayer, spit it out."

He'd caught me by surprise. I was accustomed to gentler rules; but I forgot them faster than I was caught. I wriggled a hand down and grabbed his crotch, then gave it a mighty yank. People, later, said you could hear his scream in Lockport; I laid this to exaggeration.

And then, when he let go to grab himself, I went to work. I split his chin with a taped uppercut, hit him four or five times with left hooks and followed by a smash with my right. He was groggy, and I might have stopped, but I methodically—left and right—cut his face to shreds. When a pain started up my right arm, I switched back to the belly, and returned to his face when the arm felt better.

Probably no more than four minutes had passed when he sank to his knees, for the moment blinded by blood, and croaked, "'Nuff, don't finish on; I'm whupped. I own up."

I surveyed his position, and remembered Charley's face. Then I stepped back and kicked him in the throat with more force than I'd wasted on soccer.

"That's for Charley," I said.

I turned around to address his dumbfounded companions; "I see any of you here again, I'll shoot you, hear me?" Even in the stress, I realized I'd fallen into a Southern speech-ism.

Coley had slumped over sideways, motionless, and, as I regained sanity, I was frightened I'd killed him. Then one of the partners snatched a gun from a drover's holster and yelled, "Now, by God—"

"That's enough," said General Whitney calmly, walking forward with raised rifle. He took out a watch and checked the time.

"The three of you—if that weasel recovers—will be gone from here by sundown tomorrow. Check that—if he doesn't recover, lash him to his horse and cart him out regardless. As stated, approximately, if one of you shows your face here again, he'll be strung up, much as I might deplore it. Now whisk that trash off to a doctor."

I'd forgotten General Whitney had been a much-decorated figure of 1812, and had fought in Indian wars. He breathed authority, when needed, and the street was hastily cleared.

"You need a drink," he told me shortly. I followed him to Cataract House, where we witnessed a curious sight. Big John was on the floor, smashing three revolvers with a crowbar.

The general said, "I gathered up their rifles first, of course."

Everybody tried to buy me a drink, but John reached under for a special bottle. It had "WHITNEY" scribbled on it. I decided to stick to that, but thanked the fellow guests, and others.

"I'll confess I'm worried," said my host. "You could be turning into a common street brawler. What do you think? The man had it coming, of course, but there were other ways . . . Well, let's discuss it later. Enjoy your victory."

"I've never been a brawler," I told him, not yet cooled off. "And he had it coming, and more. My left hand's swelled up," I observed inconsequentially.

"We'll get it looked at," said General Whitney.

I was now to learn more about my fellow-men. I was the hero of the hour, but the doctor issued a report that bones in the man's throat were crushed. For a while, at least, he would wear a tin insert with a hole. If he talked at all.

This seemed to turn the tide. No single soul had liked those bounty hunters, and threats to lynch them were ever present. But the tin insert naturally turned things against *me*.

"He ortent to kick him" was the popular favorite, and the mutters swelled until the constable, drunk as usual, showed up, heavily armed but uneasy, and marched me off to "jail"—a ramshackle hut a child could have escaped without trouble. It had splits between the boards you could throw a pig through, and the constable's main weapon, a carbine, rattled between barrel and stock. I thought he would have preferred to fetter me, but disliked to come that close to such a ruffian.

I was thunderstruck, but with General Whitney gone to Buffalo overnight, I submitted, glowering. Word, I heard, had spread that I was "dangerous," and even that the town would be more comfortable with me deported. Leaders in the movement were the ones who, before the Tavern, had cried to me, "Kill him! Kill him!"

I sat moodily on a bench, gazing at a smelly chamberpot, and brooded about injustice.

The the general returned, had me released and fired the constable. He contributed, after all, most of the town's taxes, now that Judge Porter was dead. Then he led me to a niche in his largest barroom.

"My boy, you may now understand that you can't right the world's wrongs by yourself. I hinted as much before. At the moment, we have no real machinery for righting any wrong whatever, but that will improve. You may have learned, too, that the public is as fickle as the weather."

"How's Charley supposed to get his eye back?"

I was still ruffled, and not much in the humor for lectures. But I should have known better. I later found he'd gone to the Eagle and scathingly bawled out the ringleaders in my distress, calling them cowards.

Now he sighed and said, with a certain sarcasm, "Perhaps your kick will bring the eye back."

"Well," I said at length, "maybe I shouldn't have kicked him. But I saw nothing but red; I admit it."

"It was well aimed. The swine was trying to crack your spine. I suppose the truth is," he went on, chuckling, "you probably saved all three from being hanged.

"*However,* I suggest you start playing down the gunman role. All sorts drift through here, and sooner or later you'll bump into the real specimen. Or maybe a roughneck twice your size and strength. You may start to frighten my guests. They're interested, but they don't know what you are. Mix a little; they're nice people. You might even get rid of that hat." He thought this over and said, "Leave the hat alone. We'd miss the hat. I think the guests would miss it; I think they take a kind of perverse pride in it.

"But I have this word, from an old man to a youngster playing buckaroo. You remind me of myself at your age, by the way, but let injustices clear up another way for a while. It's more than a one-man job. Even Christ found it so."

Then we heard a hullabaloo, interrupting the general. Women screamed, and all the men arose, headed for the piazza. General Whitney and I rushed outside, where crowds had again begun to form.

Those three monsters were whooping through town (all except the silenced Coley) yelling curses and firing revolvers—they'd got others somewhere—and on the end of a fifty-foot line was a male Negro child of about eight, dragged through the dust. There was little left of him, and later we found that the three had stolen him from a family named Pritchard, at International House. Their idea, somebody said, was to comply with the deadline but do it with style.

We stood watching.

"You're right," I said. "I regret that kick," and I turned to go upstairs. I couldn't resist supporting my action; not quite yet.

General Whitney made no comment, but I could feel his troubled gaze boring into my back as I crossed the room.

Chapter XXIV

Next day the town started to fill up. Blondin had arrived to inspect his rope, and while he stayed at another hotel, we kept track of his movements. Far from avoiding crowds, he enjoyed talking about his favorite subject—himself—and he outlined a lot of things he planned to do. I listened a time or two, but never convinced myself he was sober. He was not drunk, but I felt that the wine kept dribbling in.

In person he was slender and graceful, of middle size, and with the "flowing pale-yellow locks." He had a look of such hauteur that I found it painful to look him in the face. This pose of superiority, moreover, seemed odd when word leaked out that he and his manager, one Harry Colcord, were too broke to pay for the 1500-foot rope. A local merchant was obliged to accept an I.O.U. for $1300.

In any case, the work went forward, the Canadian end stoutly encased in iron-and-concrete, the American end fixed to a horse-propelled winch, to encourage tautness. Despite all, the rope sagged badly and it was popularly hoped that the funambulist would take a header when starting his climb. These ambitions were chiefly harbored by professional gamblers, who arrived by every train, stage, horse and other conveyance.

Though everywhere, making book, collecting bets, quarreling, causing a general nuisance, they hardly outnumbered other notables.

Among the highest of these, the Prince of Wales was supposed to be on hand, as well as the Duke of Sutherland, and two or three kings from the Balkans. Also, the President was expected any minute, causing no great ripple, since one president or another visited Niagara Falls every summer. Unless his popularity had fallen too low.

Blondin studied his drooping path to glory and caused guy lines to be attached at intervals of twenty feet, or until the rope was over the gorge. Then the fateful afternoon arrived, and hordes headed for posts of observation. I have a photograph of that scene before me now. Spectators were so thick in bushes, covering rocks, hanging from trees and the like, that an ignoramus, seeing it, might have anticipated a Second Coming.

All hoopla of the late Sam Patch was quickly exceeded. Carts dispensing a curious lot of viands—some edible—wound among the crowds, several bands produced an inharmonious medley and souvenir hawkers were abundant. The general air of carnival was deafening. Choice seats at the water's edge, by the way, were sold by people who didn't own them, and it was among these moneyed perchers that last-minute betting was hottest. The manager, Colcord, passed among the crowds, collecting gratuities in some hats he had for the purpose.

A lesser man than Blondin might have meditated the odds. At post time, these were twelve to one that he and his rope would be divorced within two hundred yards. But on the stroke of four, the bands exploded in a rackety rendition of the "Marseillaise," recognizable to many, and the funambulist, dressed in pink tights and carrying an ashwood balancing pole, "pranced out from the American side."

A swelling "Ah-ah-ah!" arose from the crowds as he advanced a hundred feet or more, then sat down to think things over. After gazing around with "lordly arrogance" (as a writer saw it) he got up and shuffled on his way. Reaching the middle, which swayed and sagged, he showed the stuff of which he was made. Those women in London had not fainted whimsically, and now it seemed unlikely he could continue.

Down below, the first *Maid of the Mist* sightseer—a recent creation—paddle-wheeled directly beneath him, and Blondin, by prearrangement, lowered a cord to the deck, while twisting here and there in the wind. He badly needed refreshment at this stage; whether he would get it was, indeed, moot.

After several misses, causing groans from both banks (and a different sound from the gamblers), a bottle of wine was fixed to the cord, Blondin drew it up, teetering, and took six or seven heartening swigs. Then, fully revived, he tossed the bottle aside and scampered up the ascent to Canada.

The crowds screamed approval, and the bands blasted out any tune that came handy. It was, beyond doubt, a gala moment. Three women (and one man) who had fainted were treated, and the air was thick with handkerchiefs and waving hats. The unbelievable trip had taken seventeen and one-half minutes. Blondin bowed, looking more arrogant than ever, and another wail swelled when he resumed the rope—to return by the same route!

Hats flew to the ground, as I heard men cry, "Why, that rooster don't know the meaning of fear!" and "The Devil hisself couldn't walk that rope twicet in one day!" Also, a diarist heard a grinding of gamblers' teeth—their odds had proved costly. A few furtively sought exit but creditors blocked their paths. Besides, in most cases, third persons had been asked to hold stakes. Niagarans may have lacked sophistication then, but they were not fools.

The question rises: Did Blondin's triumph turn his head (which had been pretty sharply angled before)? Whatever the answer, he took to the Falls like a sea gull, and stayed on for further gymnastics. People began to lose hope. He was acting as if he might easily have hopped over on his nose. A corollary to this, of course, is that he and the manager, Colcord, collected considerable cash as the days went by. Most spectators, loyally returning, felt that *something* was bound to give soon.

Blondin's next act was to cross the cable backward. He had some narrow squeaks, but made it, whole. The tourists had barely recovered from this, when the funambulist took to the rope blindfolded. The gamblers perked up slightly from their gloom. But their euphoria was short-lived. The suicidal Frenchman made the ascent, and followed by pushing a wheelbarrow across the day after. By now there was speculation among the bookies that he might try the Falls without a pole, or, as a heavy loser said, "Hell, he don't even need a rope!"

Their attitude was forgiveable when Blondin, with moist inspiration, devised a small coal stove and carried it to the point of worst peril. Here, swaying, but "looking like a monarch," he stopped, got a fire going in his swinging cooker, then made and ate an omelet, washing it down from the *Maid of the Mist* below. A nearby gambler said, "What I got left, I'm aiming to put agin him *entirely*, for the next gyration will finish that peckerwood [sic] *sure!*"

The man was wrong. During these extraordinary feats, the manager Colcord's face shone in moneyed glory. It fell several notches when his employer announced that, on the next trip over, he would carry the manager on his back! Colcord originated in Chicago (he said) and his devious route to Blondin is lost to history. It *is* known that, upon his boss's pronouncement, he reminisced freely about his birthplace and made quick plans to return there, if he had to walk.

But Blondin, his aerial career past explaining, apparently had hypnotic powers as well, and, with the gamblers (and others) cheerfully regrouped, he stepped out on the rope carrying Colcord (all facial color gone) on his shoulders.

At the start, there was a feeble but useless struggle, as Colcord felt a revived nostalgia for Chicago (or anywhere). But Blondin firmly walked on toward Canada, cocky as ever. This was the stunt, however, that shot the gamblers' spirits aloft. Returning, near the cable's worst sag, Blondin stumbled, then fought for equilibrium. During a brief recovery, he sprinted to the first guy wire toward America. But when he grabbed this, it broke and he scrambled back, to pick up Colcord, sprawled on the rope (and, now, frozen into place).

The guy was found to have been deliberately frayed. A few years later, Colcord, after long convalescence, wrote his memoirs. "Some murderous gambler," he wrote with excusable bitterness, "had adopted this method to save his miserable stakes." He also wrote, "Just think of the situation, getting off a man's back, feeling with your feet for a vibrating rope and holding to his slippery tights, and then climbing back. And this was unsuccessfully tried *seven times!* Each attempt, to me, seemed an age," the manager concluded.

Blondin was anything but a quitter, and on the eighth try he hoisted the limp and now heedless Colcord back to his shoulders, inched past the low point, and scampered up the American ridge. "Strong men were weeping," said the local paper. "Women shed floods of tears, and only the gamblers seemed morose."

The bands, by the way, went berserk. "They tried to play," wrote an Eastern journalist, "but could evoke only discordant notes."

It was assumed that Blondin had found his permanent roost when he bought a house on Third Street and pondered new idiocies. Colcord, his nerves shattered, disappeared from the scene. A man reported having spotted him, around dawn, leaving town (and all waterfalls) on either a rented or borrowed horse. When last publicly seen, suffering a species of Saint Vitus dance, he was putting a group of small poodles through their paces.

The funambulist was partially drawn, like so many others, by the siren call of Niagara. He could have become richer elsewhere, but the cataract's challenge held him in town for years. Briefly shorn of inspiration, he began walking the rope for exercise, wheedling wine out of the *Maid* when possible. Tired of walking, he hung by his knees, by his heels, by his chin—in every way daring the Falls-and-Gorge to swallow him up. In a sense, he had joined the barrel-devising folk who lived along both banks.

The crowds, of course, thinned out gradually, the feeling being that he could have walked *on* the water without inconvenience.

Blondin's successes attracted other cranks. A competitor in the form of Enrico Farini turned up to square off at the Frenchman, and the feats grew wilder and wilder. Certainly the newcomer had an edge in labeling his art. He called himself, without batting an eye, a "pangymnastikonaerostationist."

I tried without success to break the word down; then decided to lay the blame on Harvard. And since nobody in town could pronounce it, and the *Iris* generally got it wrong, people called him, simply, Farini, a fact that put him slightly out of countenance. The "pangy——" etc. stretched his own rope; then he and Blondin performed simultaneously. The contest was dangerously, almost lethally fought.

The newcomer stood on his head, which several gamblers called unsporting; Farini's crown was slightly flat. Blondin struck back by turning somersaults, one or two leaving him precariously suspended by the crotch. He admitted the results of these were cruelly painful, but sympathetic grief caused Farini annoyance. He drew a bucketful of water from the river and laundered a lady's handkerchief. Blondin gave a disdainful laugh and went back to his cooker. This time he produced a four-course meal and served it to passengers on the *Maid of the Mist*. Most digested it pleasantly, but two were seen bent over the rail. This last could have been normal seasickness, since the waters of the gorge heaved and trembled.

Then, when Blondin chained his feet together, Farini covered his body with sacking, lay down and took a nap (or so he claimed). Niagara Falls is, and was, a fair-minded town, and besides, Blondin was its first committed daredevil. It was agreed, therefore, that Farini lacked class, and the pangymnastikonaerostationist left for less critical pastures. Years later Blondin made his way back to Europe to continue (dry) rope walking without serious mishap. At the age of seventy, he was hopping around spryly on stilts. Incredibly enough, he died peaceably in, and on, his bed. Farini, his spirit perhaps broken, drowned while leaping off London Bridge with an anvil tied to his feet. His body was never recovered.

*   *   *

Alone among the *artistes* at the Falls, Blondin finally became famous, and rich. His press spread to nearly every country. But his greatest leap forward, as it were, was of course at Niagara. Niagara Falls citizens struck off a commemorative gold medal; New York City sent up a solid-gold-headed cane; and Indians from the Tuscarora Reservation produced decorative beadwork to ornament his tights while at the cataract city.

On both sides of the river people gave him a rousing send-off when he left. All bands played the same tune, and a throng of children presented him with a pink-eared white rabbit, which he gave to the conductor of his train. (It was probably eaten without delay.)

Chapter XXV

After Blondin's last contest with Farini, I found myself walking beside a short, stout fellow of about twice my age. People then wore about what they pleased; the Northern Cataract guests, for example, leaned to dark clothes and silk hats. But my companion had on the odd combination of tweed knickers, Norfolk jacket and a cloth cap; he also wore a spade beard. He talked with verve and animation.

"Extraordinary performance," he said. "Remarkable. I'm glad I came; I wouldn't not have seen it."

My stay in the area had given me, I'm afraid, a patronizing air toward neophytes, and, clapping him on the shoulder, I said, "Well, my friend, they made it; we can rejoice for that."

He looked up with twinkling eyes. "That we can. You've struck the nail directly on the head—is that correct?"

"What?"

"The nail, and so on. I often get expressions garbled, but I'm trying to learn."

"Right on the head indeed," I replied with fatuous unconcern, my thoughts drifting to my piece of the day for Bennett. "By the way," I said, recalling the promised improvement in manners, "are you shucked down for the night? You have a look of recent arrival"—I surveyed his costume—"and the hotels have bulged. Perhaps I could help with a word or two."

"No," he said seriously. "It's kind of you, but I believe General Whitney has made me arrangements."

"Wonderful old jumping-jack," I said. "One of the best. A special chum of mine," I added, unable to resist it.

"A splendid fellow indeed. It was decent of him to put me up."

Then I saw Frances Barclay at Cataract House, talking to Gervais Lockridge, who now waved her goodbye and ambled toward his place. But when she saw us, her face changed, and she curtsied deeply.

"Your Grace," she said.

In my woolly state, I failed to decipher what she meant, and I looked with inquiry at my acquaintance of the road.

"Well, Frances. We've wondered what happened to you. You appear to be wearing a kind of livery. Do you belong to a local cricket club?"

"I am the *maîtresse d'hôtel* here, Your Grace," she replied gamely.

"Just so. A useful employment. My daughters, as you're aware, are unmanageable. Is there a position open, do you think?"

"I'll speak to the general, but it's a summer job only."

"Mr. Whitney might decide to change that, especially in view of these crowds. A good hard freeze might do my girls worlds of good."

"Your Grace, may I present my friend William Morrison, of New York? This is the Duke of Sutherland, William."

There being no handy place to hide, I bowed stiffly and said, "I'm honored, sir," but he took my hand and gave it a hearty shake. (It later struck me as an un-English thing to do.)

"Morrison? Morrison? Surely it wasn't your father's wealth that separated two nations thriving under a single Crown?"

"My grandfather's. But not that particular crown, sir, with no disrespect. And the wealth's badly diminished."

I thought he might take umbrage, but he threw back his head and laughed.

"Well spoken. Pigs' heads are not designed for crowns. The Prince is here," he said to Miss Barclay. "With an entourage."

"Yes, milord, I've seen them."

"Ah, then, perhaps you'll dine with us one night, young man."

I bowed more sincerely this time, and said I'd be honored. But I hadn't any notion of getting mixed up with *that* crowd. Royalty was over my head.

And still (the Hon.) Miss Barclay was not quite placeable, and neither was Mr. G Lockridge, in my mind. So, after excusing myself,

I headed toward his domicile. The truth was, I hadn't another place else to go, to avoid Cataract House. Excepting the Eagle Tavern, and I'd made a vow to steer around that den for a while. I wasn't quite sure I wouldn't jump some of those advocates of jail.

Both occupants were at home, the elder filled with excitement.

"My dear sir, do come in!" he cried, taking my hands. "Now you needn't deny it, I know your interest in the local soil, its composition and potential. I've made a stunning discovery!"

My absorption in Niagara's dirt (and mud) was stunning indeed. So far, my aim had been to keep as much as possible off my person, and to remove what got on. Its composition, I'd thought, was adhesive; and its potential, in the way of crossing streets after a rain, never excluded drowning.

"Father has a new hobby," said Betsy.

"Yes," said my host, plopping himself into a chair, "the plants are *catalogued*. To my satisfaction, at least. And the fauna lack stimulation. After all," he said shrewdly, "when you've seen one frog, you've pretty well seen them all—what?"

This was scarcely the vein of my last visit. But I heartily agreed, after an imploring look from Betsy.

"Frogs!" I said like an idiot. "What are they, after all? What purpose do they serve? I wouldn't give a dime for a barrelful."

"Precisely! Besides, I've really got them classified, you know. And all their cousins. You might call that book published!"

"I'll be anxious to read it," I said. I couldn't help it.

"Now, soil—and wine!" he said. "I've gone into this thing with care. After testing local grapes, I hired a rig and made my way past Buffalo, down toward the Finger Lakes . . . Testing all the way—"

The announcement was impressive. To any but an Englishman, the trip would have seemed like a backbreaker.

"Leaving Betsy alone?"

"Oh, Betsy! We have stout locks, and that girl is deadly with any kind of gun. At pigeon-shoots" —he paused. "We can explore that at another time. Besides, there's Ramses and Nefertiti."

I said, "Something puzzles me, Mr. Lockridge." (We'd gone in to dinner, and started on a nonstrengthening soup.) "Why test in this particular line? Have you had experience in winemaking?"

"I've been reading—from Buffalo's Public Library. Also"—he frowned again, trying, I thought, to make up his mind—"I have a French cousin in the business. I used to listen to him, as a lad."

"Soil, Father, and wine."

"Yes. The soil should be sandy, stony even, loose and well-drained,

protected from severe winters or summers, the area planted prefera-
bly on a slope. I'll surprise you," he said, waving a spoon. "Both
white and red wine can be made from *red grapes!* What do you think of
that?"

I said I thought a good deal of it, and drew a look from Betsy.

"—the chief difference of white wine is this: It's not fermented in a
mixture of skins and stems. That's where the wine color lies. The
ingredients in most wines are the skins, pulp, seeds and grapestems.
I, for one, find that absorbing."

Here Nefertiti brought in the main course, mutton chops, and I
had an enigmatic smile from Betsy.

"Don't worry. They're tender. I picked them out myself."

"Mutton," I said, babbling, "wonderful meat. Good for your teeth,
too."

She laughed. "Fibber!"

"—European grapes are generally lumped into a single classification—*vitis vinifera.* American wines are made largely of *vitis labrusca.* I
don't quite know what those terms mean yet. *However,* American
wines, insofar as they've gone, have a grapey flavor they call
'foxy'—"

"Maybe something to do with the fox and the grapes."

"Nothing at all, I believe. Aesop meant that as a fable only. But
can you imagine this river-lake region some day thick with vineyards?"

He was genuinely excited, and, to my surprise, so was I.

"I'm going to follow this up; make no mistake."

I said, "The main problem, as I see it, is that you'd have to buy a
lot of acres to get started. That means money."

I suddenly realized I was becoming pretty homey with this family;
New England-cautious, I wondered if I'd gone too far.

"But I have a little money, you see. Yes, the poor schoolmaster.
And I've bought twenty acres between here and Lewiston, along that
ridge. I intend to experiment there, and branch out. It has the
requirements. You'd be shocked to know that a Reverend Hilary
Fuller successfully grew wine grapes there in 1829. But he died and
his progeny lost interest. Whiskey-drinkers, most likely.

"I don't mean that last as a joke. In Pennsylvania, for example,
where wine has been produced—jolly good wine—the population still
drink twenty-four times as much whiskey as wine. I hope to change
that."

"You mean paid *down,* Father. Not bought."

"Same thing, really. I have a pittance coming from home, you
understand. I wrote the—my brother for five hundred pounds and

193

got back a rather saucy reply. I hope to take that up with him later. He's in no position to get uppity. I—" but Betsy stopped him again.

"I have some money of my own," I said, "and while I mean no offense, I'd dislike to see you lose your land."

"Decent of you, William, but there's no problem about paying." He added, dreamily, "I've wondered about having real *pots* of money, what it feels like, I mean. The truth is, I admire your Robber Barons, as they're called. Would you know how one gets to be a Robber Baron? Where you start and all that?"

I saw Betsy lay down her fork and eye him, with the gentle reproof she'd occasionally given me.

"All right—change the subject."

There was no way to foretell it, of course, but this scatterbrained talk would be the most important of my life. I remember it acutely.

During dinner also I'd noticed several family pictures, in handsome but plain silver frames, on a corner table almost hidden in darkness. The scenes were so unusual, here in Niagara, that when we left the table, I loitered and looked these over before joining the others. Most had been taken at English country houses, with the name "d'Enville" engraved at the top of the frame.

The name stuck in my mind as they insisted I be seated in a comfortable rocker before starting for Cataract.

I awoke still seated in the rocker, with a shawl tucked around me; Betsy sat across the room, studying me in what I took to be a motherly way.

"Father's in his study. He said his over-wine-talking made us all sleepy. I hope you don't mind this, but we think you need a vacation. Why not take a trip home—to New York? You haven't seen your parents in weeks."

"What brought all this on?"

She thought for a second. "Perhaps it's because you've changed slightly. And you really should *write* your parents, at least."

I made the excuse that I religiously wrote them every other day.

She arched her brows. "I mail your post."

"Once a week then."

"You must miss them, all the same. And they miss you. Wouldn't you like to tell the adventures you've crammed into such a short time? —capturing slave-traders, learning to drink whiskey, fistfighting in the streets—"

Her face was bland, but I finally broke into a smile.

"You do manage to make it sound awful."

194

"Best of all, becoming engaged to a beautiful Southern belle. What do you hear from her? If I'm not too impertinent."

"Who?"

"Miss Rutledge, of course."

"The truth is," I said, "I'd forgotten that girl for the moment." I took out my handkerchief and tied a knot in it. "I must remind myself to ask about our wedding date. Strange how these trifles slip one's mind. Too many things have happened."

"That's what Father and I meant. When you consider your work, above the recent events, you're *bound* to be tired! With a week's rest in New York, you'd come back refreshed . . . it's only because we're fond of you, and you *have* changed ever so slightly."

"If I've changed, it's temporary—to protect my friends."

I sat wondering what they were really trying to say; then I brightened and slapped one knee.

"Look here, Betsy, I'd miss you. Why don't *you* take a week off and come along? As brother and sister. I think your father trusts me, and my family would show you a grand time."

"Should I wear my uniform?"

"Rot your uniform! And quit trying to get at me. How about it?"

"I'd love to go, William—as brother and sister—but this is the busiest part of the season, and General Whitney needs me. Besides, what would Miss Rutledge say?"

"Betsy," I said severely, "that girl and I are going to be married—I've forgotten when." I searched my brain. "It's curious; I'm certain it was mentioned. It stands to reason."

"No, you go, and I'll keep your room spic and span. And there's Father. Occasionally he needs direction."

"Like me."

"Maybe."

She smiled, and the moment passed.

The next day, I left on New York Central's now finished Niagara-to-Buffalo span. Unlike the trip coming up—long ago, it seemed—we arrived a day and a half later, without event.

At home, I had a rather sedate reunion, but I believe I talked steadily for about six days, now and then interrupted by a question from my father, or by my mother. For some reason, I never got around to Samantha and decided, afterward, it must have slipped my mind.

New York had made strides—downhill—despite the new open aqueduct from Croton. As rumbles of civil war grew, the Irish had paced up their lynching of Negroes, and riots over the most trivial complaints were bloody and frequent. Walking about town, I saw two unfortunates swinging from lampposts, with children throwing rocks at the bodies. New York would at length approach anarchy; these riots were nothing to what came later. And it required generations for civilized Irish to remove the stigma.

My father said he'd kept close account of my pieces for Mr. Bennett. He said, in his dry way, that he was surprised, because he'd thought "about ninety-five percent" of the money he spent for my education had proved a "nonproducing investment." I thanked him, used to such sarcasms; then he took us all out to Brown's Chop House, best of New York's restaurants for many years.

I was minded to visit Mr. Bennett before I left, but I remained piqued about the $2.50 bonus he'd mailed for my first dispatch about Blondin; I considered it worth several times more. So, instead— reading that he was scheduled for an abolitionist speech at the Astor Place Opera House—I decided to attend.

Historians fail to acknowledge that James Gordon Bennett had first been ardently pro-slavery; then he swung over to the side of the angels. His progress reminds me of the sainted Henry Ward Beecher, who, after a very indecisive start, to find which way the wind blew, evolved as the wildest abolitionist of them all. He later had considerable trouble with choir women (in the interest of religion) but history sidesteps that as well.

Anyhow, I found the hall packed, and had to stand in the gallery, with the Irish (who'd not forgotten) and other inflammatory groups.

As usual with extremists, Bennett had swung farther in his second direction than he had in the first, and he was downright offensive. He had a curious gift, my employer, for making everything sound like a personal affront, and he was free in using names and half-accurate quotes. His arguments were often crippled, I thought, because anyone who trivially disagreed was automatically a "fiend." Prominent New Yorkers espousing a moderate withdrawal from slavery were called "hounds" and "body-peddlars" (a phrase I especially recall) and worse. My own father, whose attitude was, and had been, to recompense Southerners for their slaves, and do it with as little ill-feeling as possible, was mentioned as being a "lily-livered moneygrubber" who owned ships that carried molasses-distilled-into-rum, thus providing the second leg in the "triangle" of slave-buying.

Since I recognized this as a lie, and recalling that England and other countries took such a course without a bloody war, I relaxed and joined the hecklers. The fact that many had only a vague notion of what they were heckling made no difference. Their command of the idiom was masterly, and I joined the cries of "You swivel-jawed piss-ant!", "Swine!", "Skunk on stilts!" and the like. It is to be regretted that some epithets took the form of eggs and tomatoes long past their prime.

Resenting the slur on my father, I borrowed a tomato, and if Mr. Bennett hadn't stooped to pick up a note, he'd have received a dispatch to make journalistic history.

As the gallery warmed up, came, "Drag him out! Horsewhip him!" and, to be sure, the tiresome finale of all such frenzies: "Lynch him! Lynch him! Dance him from a lamppost!"

As stated, New York had few legal recreations at the time, and Mr. Bennett's reception was regarded as run-of-the-mill. For my part, I'll confess that for one of his correspondents to jump up and down in the gallery, shouting "Lynch him!", seemed a little out of the ordinary.

The threats were nothing but sound and fury, signifying little except that people, myself excluded, were venting pent-up but growing feelings. My own were essentially nonpolitical; I figured the bonus for Blondin should have been five dollars at the bottom.

Before time for my leave-taking, my father indicated a few words with me in his study. This room, as I grew up, had been the most compelling in the house. It was, however, inviolate, only the single maid, Mary, being allowed to enter for the purpose (I assume) of dusting and performing such other rites. In those days, men never discussed business with their wives; it was considered a sign of weakness, and "coarsening."

Trying to remember, I supposed I'd been inside a dozen times in all. No more, and those for a sardonic catechizing of my educational progress, if you wish to put it that way.

So—while the leather furniture, the coastal ship models, Morocco-bound books along one wall (with a rolling stool to reach them), the always up-to-date globes, charts framed on the opposite wall, and the teakwood desk were not strangers, they usually gave me a thrill about the outside world where ships went. My father worked hard as an importer-exporter and had risen from possible poverty when *his* father put up a fortune to help form the new Union.

He (my father) was a tall, muscular man, his head silvery now on the sides, and his face, under thick eyebrows, showing both hard and soft lines. I should say that he later gained brief unpopularity for his view that Abraham Lincoln was indecisive and impulsive, and that the Civil War should have been avoided. Most intelligent Easterners came to hold the same opinion at last, another fact omitted as the records canonized the brutally assassinated President.

"Well, William," he said when I sat down, gingerly, for *I* didn't

197

work very hard, and had been a revolving concern for years. "So you're twenty-one now. I hope you received the felicitations"—small cough here—"plus the hundred dollars your mother and I sent to commemorate that milepost."

"Didn't you get my letter?"

"Of course, and you had my postcard in return?"

My reply had been sent two weeks late, as we both knew, so I decided not to explore the subject. Besides, there was no postcard.

"Never mind. You did pretty well, all things considered. And Bennett, the nuisance, tells me your work for him prospers. You have a 'flair,' to use that troublemaker's term.

"At twenty-one, a young man is expected to foresee the future; that is, he has hints of his calling. Do you plan to become a writer?"

"Well, it's like this, Father—"

"Your Uncle Horace was a writer, for circus billboards at the end. *He* died heavily in debt."

I'd prepared myself for this lecture. But a certain doggedness had come down through the line, and I had no wish to be bulldozed, no matter how ungrateful.

"Uncle Horace was a *bad* writer," I said. "I read his unpublished memoirs. They could hardly have been worse, besides resting on lies. I also read the privately printed verse."

"You're straying from the point. I'm aware that a composer of circus puffs is not in the forefront of American art. We can put Horace aside, as a family disaster. But I'd like to explore *your* aspirations, if any exist."

He got up and walked about the room.

"These"—pointing to models of the smartly painted brigantines, barks, gaff-rigged sloops—"are doing brisk trade from Savannah to Maine. So far, you've shown no curiosity about the family business, or any part of it.

"For example," he suddenly exclaimed, "why do we use the term 'run *down* to Maine?' The state's far to the north."

"Well," I replied thoughtfully, weighing the chance of reprisals, "there'd be no reason to sail *backward*, I suppose. To tell you the truth, I'm not sure. Probably some kind of mistake, like the word 'unbend'—means just the opposite."

My father sat down and eyed me as if examining something under a microscope.

"This levity, William, is not to your credit; it has a ring of circus blurbs, though not as literate."

"Yes, sir."

He got up again. "All this"—the sweep of his hand including the models and, I thought, everything the room implied—"someday, this will be yours. But only if you work at it, something beyond your capacity, I've decided. Perhaps I've been remiss in not *forcing* your interest.

"As you know, the war nearly pauperized us. Still, I make no complaint about your grandfather's feelings. I would have done the same. What I *have* done"—waving at the models again—"is build up a fleet of smaller ships, and we buy and sell cargo for other bottoms. However"—he took me to a glass case that enclosed an impressive white square-rigger—"the *Northern Star* will be off the ways next year. The business will fully recover, I promise you. Now, what's your reaction to that?"

"Father," I said when we sat down, "I hate to disappoint you. But the truth is I don't see myself as a man of business, sitting behind a desk."

"What do you see yourself *as?* Anything at all? Speak freely. I'm not an ogre."

"You'll laugh, but I'd like to be a winegrower. A vintner they call it, in Niagara. One doesn't *grow* wine—the process comes slowly. Mr. Lockridge says—"

"Who?"

"Niagara's schoolmaster, a Mr. Gervais Lockridge. He has intelligence and education. What you might call 'poor but honest,' or fallen gentry."

I was astonished to see a smile briefly appear.

"Lockridge—an Englishman?"

"Yes, sir."

"And has a daughter?"

"He has."

"Let me see," he said, studying the ceiling. "She'd be about eighteen."

"*Just* eighteen. We became acquainted through—"

"General Whitney. The first name—Gervais, you said?"

"Gervais it is—Norman Conquest, and all that."

He laughed out loud.

"Do you know him?" I asked, piqued.

"I may have, some time ago. We're not long out of England, as time goes. And the family has made trips to the mother country, if you don't mind the term. But let's go into your plans for New York wine. I should tell you, agents of mine have walked that place over, but I've had no time to study it."

I might have known. He was into everything, like a raccoon. And here, I thought bitterly, I had a scheme of my own (hatched by Mr. Lockridge, of course).

"Don't be put off. It's your idea, if you've done real research. New York state has been considered by others who finally dropped the idea. *I* gave it up, if the truth were known."

He took a piece of paper and a pen. "Will you write down, please, some of your findings, yours and 'Mr. Lockridge's.'"

Ignoring the emphasis, I said excitedly, "Look here, Father, that region is soothed by lakes and rivers. And the soil is sandy, or gravelly, and we have protected slopes in abundance—" and I went on to convey all that I, and my pedagogue friend, knew, plus considerable things we didn't. I made it, I believe, sound perfect. (In these afteryears I've learned that my father, hardly a fool, was able to separate the wheat from the chaff, and see the picture clearly enough.)

At length he sighed, crumpled up the paper and tossed it into a wastebasket. Me, I prepared for a lacing.

"You have, I believe, a forty-thousand-dollar trust fund from your maternal grandmother? Now that you're twenty-one, you control that. Frankly, I'm anything but sanguine."

"And there's some interest," I said, hoping to change the subject. He leaned forward. "How's land priced up there?"

I told him the truth, that such worthless gravelly waste sold for only a few dollars an acre.

"Take your forty thousand and buy the best grape land you can find—from Niagara and Lewiston toward the Finger Lakes. You're young enough for risks. I'll take your Mr. Lockridge on, ah, trust.

"Better yet," he snapped, the businessman back in harness. "Go to Buffalo, get whatever mortgage you can—I'm your security, I suppose. I'll give you a letter—and buy whatever's possible. Let's say that, at the very highest figure you might manage, say, 6,000 acres. Fortunes were never made by timorous men. But that should be ample. If it's too much, sell land later at a profit." He pounded a fist on his desk, as happy as I'd seen him.

I suddenly felt contrite. He must have planned a family enterprise for years—"Morrison & Son." It had a nice ring. And I'd tossed it all away.

I said, "Father," prepared now to see things his way.

"Wire Lockridge and tell him to start. Cheer up. The time may come when Morrison ships will carry Morrison wines. I could be disappointed" (sensing my thoughts), "but I'm happier you've

200

struck this blow on your own. And it's a *good* blow; I'd tell you if it weren't. That's a thing you may depend on."

He began to busy himself, removing documents from drawers, and, after standing irresolute for a minute, I made my way toward the door, unaccountably miserable.

But when I pulled the door open, he swiveled round with a sunny look.

"Well, William," he said, "we've made some strides toward getting to know each other at last. To me, that makes up for any conceivable partnership. Your allowance will be continued. On second thoughts, I'll double it. See you at dinner."

I left, on a level of high spirits at last.

I had another, a personal mission before returning. I stepped briskly—in my mind a wine merchant already—to the Public Library. Rummaging among the reference works, I found what I wanted in about fifteen minutes. Badly shaken, I copied the paragraph carefully, not quite knowing what it all meant. Then I went back to a family dinner in which a start of respect had comfortably diminished the sarcasm.

Chapter XXVI

After leaving the family, I was tempted to repeat my old route up. In retrospect, the dingy Central train, the Erie barge, the strap railroad and the stagecoach sounded like romance; they seemed, too, a long time ago. In my present state, I was almost willing to hold an Irishman's pig if the chance offered. I also remembered the barge captain as a genial good fellow, and came close to tolerant recollection of the strap railroad. These were a normal part of the past; I had a momentary urge to bring it back.

But sanity returned, and I rolled out of troubled New York on the best train to Buffalo, with an hour to kill there before the spur ride to Niagara. I arrived at nine the next evening.

I made my way, with luggage, to my room by means of the outside stairway. I wanted to think over the events at home before greeting acquaintances. Actually, my head was in a swirl. I'd turned my back on wealth, position, command, for a pretty dubious enterprise; and this in partners with a man who was likely a lunatic, as I remembered the reference work.

Moreover, I was only twenty-one years old and had found, through my father, that there are things to be learned *after* twenty-one. Without seriously considering the business (as I thought), he saw its probable future. Experience. I belatedly began to admire it. Downcast, I wondered if I'd made a right decision.

So—I stepped to my top bureau drawer, and, slightly to my surprise, found the half-remaining bottle of spirits.

But the ever-vigilant Betsy had put on a tape to show the last level, and added an exclamation mark to show her alertness.

I swallowed a mouthful or two, sitting on the bed, hoping to regain confidence. After all, I remembered again, Darwin, too, was twenty-one when he climbed aboard the *Beagle*, and his trip ended splendidly. I ran down other persons who made their mark early, and arrived at Mendelssohn, who gave his first public concert at nine. With each dose (and recollection), I felt more and more mature, and had reached the point of wondering if, really, I wasn't too old for such an operation. There arrives a point, I was saying, as the bottle-level dropped, where we oldsters have to face the facts: Such matters should be left to younger hands—when I heard a tapping and Betsy came in, carrying a blue envelope.

She looked with cool judgment at the bottle.

"Do you feel ill?"

"No," I replied peevishly, "and look here, Betsy; this business of storming on in. You might have found me naked, taking a bath."

Her cheeks glowed pink as she said, "You might be reminded—sir—I've put you to bed, in pyjamas, twice thus far."

Glancing at the bottle, she added, "It could happen again, in a time of crisis. Who knows?" She added, "That crisis could be now" —and she gave me the envelope, which bore an Atlanta postmark.

"Should I leave while you read it? Or shall I turn down your bed? You'll have to get up, William."

"Perform your usual rites," I said, moving to a chair. "I may need your advice."

I recorked the bottle and put it away. I'd drunk perhaps three tablespoonfuls in all, and exhaustion was gone for the moment.

The envelope was smudged, and had been reinforced here and there with paste.

Dear Bill I meant to write sooner but I'm not much on writing letters and believe this is only my second or third, so you can make alowances (ha ha). What I had to say was I won't be coming back to Niagara Falls, and hope you won't be too mad with me. My mother and Aunt Hester made me see what they call my wicked ways, and really I don't think I behaved very well up there. Specially you know what, though their are things I miss if you know what I mean.

I met this boy whose a step-something of Aunt Hester and he's been atentive and people think I should get married. I told them I was already engaged on marriage and this would mean begamy and probably jail but they only snorted and said we'd like to see him try!

This boy certainly isn't you, Bill, and if he kisses me, nothing happens at all. But they say hes from the South and that makes all the difference. What difference? Something ought to happen if he kisses me, and when I told them that they locked me to my room for the day. They thought it was a punishment but I fell to thinking about you so little do they know.

I want you to cordially believe that things might have worked out fine if Daddy hadn't died, and you will always be welcome to come visit (summer or winter).

Your esteemed friend,
Samantha

P.S. They wrote a letter for me to copy but I changed it some to show you I'm not a flibbertygibbet but am truly broken up in shreds all over.

Reading this, I felt first a stab of hurt, or nostalgia, then peeve, and finally I laughed out loud. Then I handed it to Betsy, primly seated on the bed.

She read it carefully, then asked, "Does it matter a great deal?"

"I haven't got it sorted out yet. Maybe, maybe not."

"She's a lovely girl, and nothing was ever her fault. You should always believe that."

"The witches twisted her out of shape. They're still at it," I added, annoyed.

"You could go to Atlanta and assert yourself."

"No," I said, feeling an extraordinary sense of peace. "I think I'll leave it alone. In view of my rejection, you might kiss me goodnight, and be on your way. By the way, why are you here at this hour, anyway?"

"I thought you might need me."

"How?"

"That was up to you."

She looked scared but determined, a fact that sailed over my head. I gave her a brotherly peck on the cheek, as she pressed against me for a second. I said, "Now be off, and don't take your duties too seriously."

In return, I had a smart slap on the cheek. It was after she'd disappeared down the hall that I became aware that she had on nothing beneath the frock.

"Well," I said to the walls, "this has been my best day so far with females."

I decided to turn in before something worse happened. But I had a pesky time getting to sleep, and Samantha was not to blame.

I hadn't much chance to brood, for the town was in an uproar again. Blondin's lucrative acrobatics had not gone unnoticed, and others charged forward with dreams of Golconda.

Some of these made the funambulist seem normal and self-effacing. First on the scene was a Professor Jenkins (the honorific obscure), who announced with handbills and ads that he meant to string a rope and then cross on a velocipede. The advice caused the usual buzz in the taverns, epitomized by a drover who said, "Well, now, the buzzard's only got one rope, and, unless I'm mistook, a velocipede's got three wheels, and they ain't in line, either."

Even the local papers scented fraud, saying, "We have been pretty reticent in regard to the proposition of Jenkins—the 'Canadian Blondin'—to cross the Niagara on a velocipede. Somehow there appears an air of humbug about the fellow, and our suspicions are aroused."

This view could have arisen from the fact that, for some days, Professor Jenkins walked about both Niagaras while wearing a sandwich sign and beating on a tin pan with a spoon. And he declined to specify his academic claim. Before the great day arrived, nearly everybody had demoted him to "Jenkins," dropping the "Professor," with a measure of derision thrown in. But he appeared to have the hide of a rhino and would only reply, "Just you wait!"

Things being generally dull, the usual throngs turned out to crowd the banks, both American and Canadian. Jenkins, of course, had his crew of helpers, including the usual hat-passers, and at four in the afternoon, a vehicle (hitherto hidden in a shed) was fixed to the Canadian end. The *Iris* remarked that "a retarded child could have worked it." The machine was built in such a way that the professor was *beneath* the wire, standing on a crossbar attached to large wheels above; moreover he was lashed to his rolling stock so that a plunge to the gorge was impossible.

How his cart could be called a "velocipede," nobody knew. But there were various comments, all adverse. The Niagara paper, for example, said, "Jenkins' performance bears about as much resemblance to Blondin's as a poor counterfeit does to the genuine. If our Canadian neighbors can't turn out better performers than this, they'd best keep them for some more useful purpose."*

Feelings ran high, the gamblers having plunged as usual, and there began the usual thoughtful scrutiny of tree limbs. In the confusion, the professor quietly disappeared. It was assumed he was pondering worse frauds elsewhere.

The next spectacular was provided by one Bellini, who circulated that he was, in essence, a suicide and that he would probably "leave my bones in the gorge." This revived interest, many gaining pleasure from unpleasantness to others, and the same sort of crowd turned out for the kill.

Bellini did indeed go far to offset Jenkins and his dishonest craft. From his rope, in the middle of the river, he dove toward the boiling green waters 150 feet below. But the canny fellow had contrived a twelve-foot rubber strand, of great strength, which he clutched as he fell, impeding his progress. Still, he indeed landed in the river, to cheers, band noises, and the like, then clambered into a small boat he had waiting for the purpose.

The take by hat-passers satisfying, he repeated his feat, and then dove a third time. On this round occurred the first hitch in Bellini's Niagara sojourn. The band pulled loose and, at the bottom, wound itself around Bellini's feet. His crew always alert, he was plucked from the water while drowning.

Then came the Falls' most bizarre chapter to date. A housepainter named Stephen Peere became overexcited watching Bellini, and, strengthened by whiskey, skipped onto Bellini's wire. To the astonishment of all, he danced, leaped and emulated most of the master's tricks—without a moment's training. Bellini, in the manner of most artists, became enraged. Whipping out a knife, he tried to cut the heavy rope (commonly called a "wire" in the trade).

Up to now, Blondin's successor had built affectionate popularity, local papers calling him "a fearless fellow" and praising his feats without restraint. Now, suddenly, in view of his attempted murder, the tide turned and threats were muttered against his life. "Downgraded to zero, he skulked out of town in disgrace."

There exists no accurate way to explain the housepainter Peere. Untutored (except for painting on scaffolds), he assumed the wire like a veteran. Regrettably, his exhibition provided him lust for higher education. Spurred on in a tavern, he wobbled several more times to the wire, as people of both nations shouted plaudits.

*It was never fully established that Jenkins was Canadian; he merely started from the Canadian side.

Then, late on an especially convivial night, he made his way, alone, "in the general direction of the wire." Next day, his remains were found scattered on the rocks at the bottom, a deceased housepainter risen above his station.

Though the suffragette plan remained in its cradle, a woman named Maria Spelterini was the next contestant to toss in her bonnet. Accounts of Niagara feats differ in trivial ways. But there exists uniformity of opinion about the physical gifts of Miss Spelterini. She was quite a woman, of Italian origin, twenty-three, weighing 152 in flesh-colored tights, and having a glare to make strong men quail. One paper mentioned her "ample, yet firm" body; another saw her as "bulging" (from her skin-tight costume); a third journalist spoke with awe of her "competent bosom."

From my perch near the American end, I imagined that, to many, she was a voluptuary's dream of heaven. Most males, indeed, were indifferent whether she wire-walked or not, as long as she continued to strut about, exercising her anatomical peaks.

For reasons never explained, Miss Spelterini attacked the rope with both feet encased in peach baskets. From a book written near the period, *Niagara, the Scene of Perilous Feats,* by Orrin E. Dunlap: "Her crossing with peach baskets on her feet was startling, and she also walked with ankles and wrists manacled. In those days Niagara was more popular with Southerners than today, and the Southern society gathered there set the pace for all pleasures and encouraged the performance of those hair-raising feats."

Miss Spelterini gave both Southerners and others their money's worth. She headed down the rope, carrying her balancing pole, with fierce determination. But the peach baskets caused her annoyance, the bottoms being slick with peach juice. She skidded around a bit, and tripped a couple of times, raising a familiar "Oh-oh-oh!" from the crowd. But she straightened up and "put the rope in its place, shaking it as a terrier does a rat."

From this point, she had no further trouble. The Niagara paper threw caution to the winds; it even described the bulging funambulist as "traveling with gossamer step." The phrase was overdrawn; "gossamer step" is not generally stressed with one of her muscle and weight. Moreover, Miss Spelterini was a study in aggressiveness. To class her as "gossamer" is to describe the elephant's gait as "mincing."

It would be pleasant to report that Maria scored heavily at the till. But the truth is that people were becoming bored with wire-walking; their purses were not freely opened. Most funambulistic devices had been successfully explored.

But the walkers continued to arrive, in waning numbers. Unquestionably, many had simply succumbed to the Falls' hypnosis that for generations caused amateurs to build barrels and commit suicide. Even casual visitors often felt the siren call.

A New York journalist, who journeyed up for Blondin, wrote later: "What motivates these awesome capers has long bemused students of human oddity. Is it the quest of fame and fortune? If so, precedent is not encouraging. Only one Niagara daredevil ever achieved them . . . The basic drive appears to have no rationale."

An elderly resident replied as follows: "They always tell you how, if they live, they'll make a pile out of vaudeville and such. Deep down, they don't hardly believe it themselves. All they have to do is look at the record! They can tell from that they'll be lucky to make anything over and above expenses. But they'll be itching to do it anyhow. You see, the Falls hits folks in queer ways. I've seen them faint dead away, gazing at the view. I've seen them laugh, cry, get hysterical, yell, even bust into poetry. It's what you might call mystical. They feel a kind of challenge that they can't resist."

The number of ordinary suicides, too, appears caused by the Falls' beckoning might. It was common knowledge that, during the tourist season, at least a person a week leaped into the chasm. The jump is made "on sudden impulse," as an acute visiting reporter said, "prey to a fatal fascination." In general, these last fatalities never got into the papers. They were somehow seen as shameful, and besides, they were bad for business.

No matter what, professional walkers, as stated, kept turning up, money or no money. One Sam Dixon, a Toronto resident en route to a business conference in American Niagara, had the incomprehensible urge to abandon his usual boat travel, for the last leg of his trip. Instead, he walked across on a wire left behind by a retired eccentric. Dixon did not explain why he chose to walk while twirling a hoop on his right leg. (He carried a briefcase in his left hand, ready for the conference.)*

A Clifford Calverley (origin unknown) then elected to set a speed record for the abridgement and sprinted across in two minutes, thirty-two and two-fifths seconds. James Hardy, a plumber, promised the dwindling crowds to "carry over two pipe wrenches and a toilet bowl." At the last moment he left these behind. (They were promptly stolen as souvenirs.) Even so, he made the crossing, after tripping twice and landing asprawl.

The last career funambulist was Oscar ("The Great Houdini")

---

*Afterward, he said it all "seemed a blur," but he carried a pole, was athletic, and probably planned his stunt.

Williams. Since he was not carrying a giraffe or hopping on one foot, his feat was accomplished to resounding apathy.

It remains hard to explain how rank amateurs crossed these left-behind wires, or ropes. Questioned, they usually admitted to being partially drunk; but there was some other draw, a successful mystique they found hard to discuss.

As hinted, many idiocies seen on the rope were inspired in taverns, and, more important, wire-walking in general was a domestic sport of the period, like swinging on a trapeze, or high-diving. Probably few persons wholly without experience ever crossed the gorge. But certainly there were those helpless against a summons by the deluge. The sole fatality was the housepainter, Stephen Peere.

In any study of Niagara Falls stunting, a line must be drawn between the wire-walkers and those who elected to "go over," in some contrivance loosely described as a "barrel." Nobody knows how many amateur barrelists made the try in homegrown vehicles. The rides were chiefly done at night, with dismal results. (It should be said that landowners on both sides at length required barrelists to buy licenses, this swindle easily circumvented after dark.)

During one fatuous funambulism, I'd seen Rattlesnake Charley seated in moody abstraction on a rock. He wore a patch over one eye and looked, I thought, sickly and weak. He'd also lost a lot of weight.

When I hailed him, he made some attempts to regain his old humor, but the rally was slight.

"I ain't up to scratch, Billy," he said, "and you can log that in your book. Them slave-catchers like to killed me, and I'm not sure they ain't."

"Recovery from a thing like that takes time," I said cautiously, in view of the way he looked. "You'll be spry as a cricket soon."

"No, I don't think so. I'm wore out. And, Billy"—he took my arm—"I've come to where I'm a-skeered of the snakes. Now, I've said it, and thought I'd cut out my tongue first."

"Scared?"

"I'm in no-wise positive I can grapple accurate. And a a-feared snake-catcher's as good as pork. They sense it, you apprehend, and it renders them freer to strike. Without income from ile, I'm apt to lay down and starve."

"Why, Charley," I said, boldly, feeling that the time had come for action, "Colonel Rutledge told me you were rich."

He looked uneasy. "They's money banked, true. And where'd it come from? Well, sir, my old daddy was hipped on—gold! It were gold with him, and snakes to me. Lord, I cain't remember where-all he went adventuring. Unless it was Ballarat it was the Klondike, thence to the Yukon, with maybe South Africa throwed in between. And he come to settle at? —Spanish California."

"And your mother?"

"Died a-birthing me, within hollering space of Sydney Harbor. Midwifery hadn't advanced to its high level today, with washing of hands and such. So—I never set eyes on her, the more to regret, for she had a good name. Legitimate daughter of a convict transported from a successful trade of garroter—"

By now, I guessed he was creating this preposterous story as he went; and General Whitney laughed out loud (without explaining) when I told him later.

But Charley's cheeks had taken on color, and I thought his health might be improved by continuing. I nudged on, gently. "Your father finally got restless in California, no doubt?"

"No, sir, he found them Spaniards disputatious, and we set out, with others, on a ship around Cape Horn—"

"For New York, you mean."

"Weevilly biscuits, spiled salt pork, and a tumped-over cask of lime juice—it was them done him in. He was took ashore in the Brazils— him and others again—but he growed feebler by the week. Well, he had gold—gold to waller in. But sea chests ain't handy to maneuver, special of that weight, so before he died he made a swap for diamonds. Likely you didn't know the Brazils was a main place for diamonds.

"On his deathbed, even, he had a nose for dealing, and he made me a sewed-up canvas belt to tote them in. Long and short, friends rigged me on a hemisphere ship after Departure. But them Eastern cities had pitfalls for a rowdy fourteen-year-old. I'd take all day to tell you how I drifted West, blowed here, blowed there, mountain man one stretch, prospector the next. I even sunk so low, in hard times, I set up as farmer, in the Dakoties. It was—"

"You still had the diamonds—?"

"What diamonds?"

"The ones your father traded the gold for."

"Oh, them. No, I sold the whole blessed lot. A few at a time, not to arouse suspicions—"

"Why, what could they suspect *you* of, Charley? An upright boy with his heritage."

"Billy, you'll apprehend later—the world's full of twisters, bribery judges, politicians, business roughnecks, thieves and such. And you'll applaud old Charley, at his age, for having sold and banked. Them's the words—sold and banked. And after that, this chile pinted West. I dislike to say it, but I left Montaner in a hurry, but that's a whole other story, and I've been windy enough a-ready—"

I let him ramble on, looking better, *feeling* better, having unloaded such a cargo of lies and half-lies, with maybe some truth here and there. I forgot most of it soon, at least the real jawbreakers, those in the majority.

Charley was interesting, and there was no chance of his starving; or so I found. *Some* of his account held up. His speech was absurdly various, ranging from the garroting grandfather's cockney (if he existed) to the local idiom, with now and then something lucid and even literate.

A few days later, I found General Whitney seated as often on the Cataract piazza, and I sat down to express concern about Charley. Then I repeated Charley's revelations. In the next few minutes, I gathered his story came close to being *all* lies, most all but the Montana part, and that "doesn't quite bear public exposure," in the general's words.

From what he almost said, I gathered that the father had been no closer to Brazil than I had, and that, in the West for years, had been little better than a common highwayman. It was after this, I divined, that Charley had money.

I left a lot of questions unasked, and called it a day. But General Whitney enjoyed himself, straightening me out, insofar as he cared to.

It was only two days after—I remember because it was August fifteenth and tourists were arriving and leaving—that I saw Charley pay his toll and take one of the paths across Goat Island. Since he seldom came in town, unless to bring oil, and could hardly be called a sight-seer, the action struck me as strange. The hour was about nine-thirty, of a clear, blue morning, only the spume giving movement to the scene. It was a grand day to be alive; the roses and wild flowers in full blossom, now, and every prospect pleasing.

I felt good. Charley's morale and health had obviously improved, to the point where he felt like an outing. For a while, he'd left the snakes to shift for themselves.

I went onto the island and followed along a way, meaning to surprise him by and by. Beyond, the river flowed toward its plunge, silvery, fast, silent. The Canadian side was screened by one of the fogs often there on a south wind.

Charley was evidently headed for Terrapin Point. This was where one could stand at the rail, within inches of the sweeping curve. Of all vantage points, I thought, this was the best for feeling the cataract's pull. A person could probe the two-railed fence and touch the falling stream, then straighten back up, shivering. For some reason I'd begun to avoid it, though it had been my favorite overlook. Maybe I'd been here too long, felt the spell myself, heard too many stories.

"Nice morning, Charley," I sang out, coming up abreast.

At first he looked sorry. Then his face assumed a resolute beam. He said, "Billy, I've made a discovery. I've come to grips with my patch, uneasy innards, snakebite slow to heal, pore estate and the like. It's contained in the Mind, Billy. I been reading books—India-Indian books. The flesh's lower than acorns when the Mind steps in."

I said, "Doctors are finding every day that a patient's mental attitude—"

"That's it! What I mean entirely! No matter how low, with odds against headway, the Mind will haul you through. I never felt better, and done it all by Thought."

"Then you're getting your strength back?"

"Strong! I could lift a bull in each hand—my *Mind* showed the way. No need to mull further over Charley. He's *cured!*"

I tried to put this all together, knowing his crazy jumble of phrases, but a warning bell sounded faintly in the background. Leaning against the rail, his face in the sun, he looked anything but cured. His skin had a greenish hue, folds hung loosely at the neck.

"I got friends in this town," he said reflectively. "*Good* people in a good town, and I misdoubt anyone enjoyed a better life. Take the snakes alone. Lord, who's had that privilege? But friends would grieve to watch old Charley rot away, recognizable more each day. So the Mind solved it, and done it quick as blinking."

His shirt was open, the scarf had been tossed away. He even seemed proud of the scar the world was welcome to see, now that his Mind had straightened things out.

"I'm saying goodbye, Billy. Young and strong, you'll have a good run. Don't fret about Charley. He'll nudge you now and then from Across"; and he was over before I could move.

In shock I could do or say nothing. I only stood there, paralyzed. Starting the last descent, he waved, then shouted something drowned in the roar below.

Ignoring his advice, I put my head to the rail and wept.

Charley's funeral was held in an obscure church he'd visited a time or two, hoping not to be noticed. He thought everything they did was comic. He said even the hymns they sang damned everybody, leaving no hope at all.

"I'm cheered," he once told me. "There's not a dog's chance of me going to Hell; the place is busting with overpopulation, to hear them tell it. Standing room only."

But he arrived there once with a beautiful green snake looped around his neck, and was not encouraged to return.

This devotional center was called The Church of God, Jesus, and the Twelve Disciples except Judas, he told me, but when I stepped round to check, the words "Except Judas" appeared to be missing. So I figured he'd made it up.

The church's main line was "Prophecies," with everything, past, present and future, laid out in the Bible. The Ice Age had been prophesied (backward, I assumed along with Steam, the Revolution, Popcorn, Hoopskirts, Emigration, Gunpowder and the King of England. I *think* all those were mentioned.) A person only had to name it, and the Bible had got in first.

The Ab Turners had been staunch supporters of the church, one son finding a Prophecy that said, "Man could even go upon the waters and over a great deluge in the right kind of barrel" *(his* quotation not mine), but the family had lost so many members that they finally soured on religion and dropped out. They cussed out the Prophecies, and offered to thrash the preacher.

Red Gill had said Charley's corpse might not come up for days, and it was best for the funeral to proceed. I noticed General Whitney on one side, not looking happy, wishing we were in a place better suited; and Mr. Lockridge and Betsy were abreast in a row before me. The former had on a sporting jacket, with slanted pockets, and I supposed he owned no black clothes at all. He was having difficulty with his legs, which he'd propped against the seat ahead, causing that occupant to turn now and then with a threat, and once to shake his fist.

All others were dressed in the gloomiest of coats and cravats, and Betsy wore her dark uniform without a ruffle at the neck. She'd cried a little when the harmonium commenced wheezing out a hymn, and people took to coughing, as they do on these occasions, when everybody's known the deceased, and liked him, and I felt a little watery myself.

I don't intend to describe this funeral further, because that crazy old preacher, when he ascended to his pulpit, eyes blazing and carrying a frazzled Bible, bawled out, "'Those that live by the Snake shall perish by the Snake!' Luke 7:18!"

I got up and left, and so did others, including the general and the Lockridges. In the street, several were crying softly, while two or three men dispatched a boy for a horsewhip. But the general stopped them. He delivered a little eulogy of his own. He said: "This is not a time for rancor, boys. Charley was a friend, a kind man, a gentle man, beloved by everyone; and I doubt if he'd like his funeral marred by violence. Let's all go home, remembering him as he was, and ignore that fool inside. Charley's gods will provide the reward he's earned."

A man spoke up to say, "The general's right, as usual," and one or two from the Tavern agreed, saying the horsewhipping should be postponed a day, or even two. They complimented General Whitney for seeing things so clearly.

At this, the general clumped off toward his hotel, and I heard him mutter something about "The damnfool incorrigibles!"

Chapter XXVII

"I've asked Miss Barclay and Betsy to come, since Saturday's their day off," said Gervais Lockridge. "If four heads are better than one, we have every advantage."

I thought it fair to say (for the fourth or fifth time) that I knew nothing yet about wine and could even take grapes or leave them alone, particularly here where melons were uniquely fine.

Then I added quickly, "But I'm in, all right, and probably as anxious as you are."

He gave me an understanding look and said, "No doubt Betsy's told you I flit among enthusiasms. But don't be misled—I've found a lifework!

"It's pretty complicated, and I'll only bore you slightly today. After that, you'll all catch fire yourselves. I hope you have no objection"—with a sidewise look—"if I throw in a highsounding word or phrase now and then? —To make an impression on Miss Barclay."

"Do you find yourself drawn to her?"

"That woman—she's only a girl of thirty—is a creature of beauty and character. I consider you family, so I'll confess to having plans for Miss Barclay. Unless, of course, she has an objection to me. What do you think? I mean, up to now?"

"On the contrary, I've seen her gaze at you like a melting dove."

"Interesting simile," he observed as we drove to get our passengers.

Both waited at the Cataract steps, looking, I thought, unusually spruce. Lockridge adroitly avoided driving, so Betsy sat in front with me and Frances found herself side by side with the fountainhead of lore.

Now and then I glanced back and saw her brightly feigning interest. She caught my eye once and winked.

On this clear morning, the Falls could be heard like thunder, and I think we all tried to close out the sound. Charley's death and funeral were too recent and shocking. But the wildly colored flowers, the skittering black squirrels, the fleecy sky, even the gurgling river made the bad memory remote. Occasionally I heard words like "spores," "marc," "pectin," "saccharometer," "*tache*," and "*teinturier*," and it was this last that caused Betsy to say, "Father, do quiet down about wine. There're so many other things. Look around; look at the trees. *'Teinturier!'* —really!"

Mr. Lockridge, feet against the back of her seat, said, "May I remind you that this is a *professional* trip? Wine, not to say grapes, must creep in. Do you"—turning to Miss Barclay—"find yourself offended by the term *'teinturier'?*"

"*Teinturier?* I was going to bring it up myself. We have a picnic hamper and can get *teinturiers* to round it out. A dozen. Two if they're small."

"*Teinturiers* are *not* included among the local fruit; I assume you knew that. I'll keep things to myself from now on."

It was early Saturday—market day—and, from the scattered houses of the river road, farmers were setting out for town. The men had on black alpaca suits and the women their best frocks and bonnets; market day was the social event of their week, unless there'd been a suicide-drowning, with Red Gill patrolling the Whirlpool.

In the back of one wagon, a boy had two bear cubs with leather collars; and a large, patchy dog trotted behind, tethered by a rope.

The farmer and his wife seeming friendly, I drew up at Miss Barclay's request, and she called out, "Good morning. We were admiring your dog."

"I could agree and deceive you, ma'am, but that there's a wolf, and he's for sale, dirt cheap."

"A *wolf!* Aren't you afraid?"

Two younger boys about six and eight regarded us stonily from behind a box of potatoes.

"Clovis, jump down and pet the critter. He's tamer 'n a sackful of kittens."

"You mean the boy?" asked Lockridge.

"My referral was to the wolf," the farmer replied with a sharp look. But the younger of the boys scrambled down, over boxes and crates, in no great hurry, and the animal jumped up and licked his face.

"That's enough, Luther," said the farmer's wife. "You know he cain't stop, the ornery feist."

The boy suddenly ripped out a wonderfully mature statement, and climbed back up, holding his hand.

"Got you again, did he?" said the farmer, chuckling. He examined the bite, which had failed to pierce the skin, and told us, "Commonly, a wolf requires handling, a club or a chain will do. This feller likes to grab a-holt a hand and hold it, affectionate. Clovis ain't broke in yet."

"What's his name?" asked Miss Barclay. I surmised she missed dogs, horses or not.

"Wolf. Call him Wolf."

"Inspired," muttered Mr. Lockridge. Then he asked, "Did you formerly have other children?" (drawing a reproachful look from Betsy).

"See here, mister, there ain't no call to run down one of the Lord's favorite pets. Noah taken in two and come up smiling. I'd ruther you moderated down."

"How much?" asked Frances Barclay, surprising us.

"For *that* wolf? That's a *show* wolf!"

"Then why sell him?"

"Well, sir, ma'am, you're well-spoken, and I'll play fair. One reason, I got sorry neighbors, and when they find their chickens et, it appears to scrape them some. One throwed a load of buckshot at my house—"

"How much?"

"Why, let's see, for the finest household wolf in the country, excusing chicken-nibbling—say ten dollars and call me robbed."

"Five and call me a fool."

I started to protest; our horse was expressing a third opinion on the animal. But Gervais Lockridge sat back, chewing on a straw that had blown his way.

"Six, take the muzzle and rope, and I'll go home in my drawers."

The unpredictable Miss Barclay hopped nimbly down, counted out coins from her purse; then, with no hesitation, pulled the wolf's ears, as it looked grateful not to be kicked about to show who was boss, and tied it to our buggy. It followed, with what I took to be a last, baleful glance at the farmer.

"Drive on, William," said the Honorable. "A mile or two will do."

I thought she was making pretty free with our time, buggy and

217

persons, but I complied without comment. Around a couple of bends, well removed, she said, "Now draw up, if you please."

The note of command gone, I stopped, just as I'd worked out a speech of mild reproof. She asked if I had a knife, and taking my sheath knife, she got down and walked heedlessly up to the wolf and cut the rope free; then she sliced it off the axle.

The animal stood indecisive, then loped off.

"The poor beast. Anyone could see he'd been beaten and abused. And one foot partly crippled. 'Club or piece of chain' indeed! Drive on, William."

I said, "My thanks," and she was instantly contrite.

"I'm *so* sorry to take a high tone, but it was my first experience in seeing animals treated cruelly."

The Lewiston houses seemed sparkling white and trim, their lawns well tended, after the shabby souvenir shops and mills of Niagara Falls. But Betsy said Niagara had struggled with portages while Lewiston had access to Lake Ontario, with its commerce of freighters. (Before the Erie Canal, the town had been a prosperous and even a cosmopolitan port.)

"They've never had to crawl up or down to get in and out, not in the same way," she said.

Mr. Lockridge now took down his feet, straightened up, adjusted his necktie and took over. He had on the usual tweed jacket, and I wondered, again, if he owned another.

"We're here," he said, "to buy land for the cultivation of native grapes. And then, of course, to make wine. That ridge off to the right"—he waved to the formation where the Falls once were—"is the area I've researched. And I'll repeat what I said before: Reverend Fuller produced a red wine here in 1829. No doubt he stressed to his faithful the close joining of the Bible and the vine. *However*, he had the misfortune to die in midcrop, so to speak. His heirs, as stated, found the operation too strenuous.

"Our first mission, of course, is to see who owns the slope of that ridge. Then we'll talk him into selling, cheap. As you can see, the land is now barren, except for thick low growth—"

"Father," said Betsy, "maybe not take such a high line yourself. After all, William's putting up part, isn't he? Or is it *all?*"

Mr. Lockridge cleared his throat. "I've made the full turn into Man of Business, together with W. Morrison, my wealthy confrère."

"Not me," I said. "Not wealthy; modest funds here and there."

"Capital plus knowledge—the elements for success in a large corporate venture. I, personally, have the knowledge. I needn't say more. Eventually, of course, capital in abundance. My remittance days should end soon."

"Remittance!" said Betsy. "You ought to be ashamed."

"Well," said Miss Barclay briskly, "if we really want to find who owns those brambles, don't we go to the Town Archives, or Hôtel de Ville, or something? I've forgotten what it's called in England; never knew, probably."

"My dear girl, you anticipate me by a fraction. You, there" —to a man probing in a surgical way with a toothpick. "Be a good fellow and tell us where the Municipal Archives dwindle, peak and pine."

"Very diplomatic," observed his daughter. (And the town was *not* in bad repair.)

"Said what?"

Miss Barclay said, "*Could* you direct us to the Town Hall, or something of the sort. Administration, and all that?"

"You speaking about the mayor?"

"The very man; the mayor in person."

"Hold on. —*There*, by geezers!" And he cleansed his instrument and restored it to his pocket. "They got a all-day social at the Baptist Church, but that ham must be a hundert year old."

"We'll avoid it. Besides, we're all Methodists here. Now, the mayor's office, you said."

"Main corner, turn right and ask somebody."

A note of asperity crept into Lockridge's voice. "My good ass, if you don't *know*, why turn right?"

"I only been here four months. Turn around in a loop, stand on your head; it won't bother me none."

Of the first rough-dressed men we met, one said the hall had floated off into the lake after a recent rain; the second said it was knocked down to build a brothel, and the third offered to "take an affy davy" that politicians dismantled it by night and sold the lumber. All were drovers, the town was in its Saturday humor, and we gave up questions.

Then we found the establishment (unpainted, in need of repairs) and walked past the unlocked door. Only an elderly man wearing an eyeshade and sleeve garters was on hand. He was poring, exasperated, over a table asprawl with account books.

No, he didn't know where the mayor was, nobody did, but he expected the constable, along with the "Council," might be interested if we had information.

"The mayor is in, ah, some momentary dilemma?"

"He's in Buffler, if you want my opinion, along with the town's petty cash and a 'Mrs.' Hooker. I'm not saying he's done a crime, but the Council asked me to straighten out these books, and if I'd knowed, I wouldn't tackled it for gold. Neither, I'll venture, would the Apostle Paul."

"Paul was not, I believe, a certified pub—" when Betsy jabbed him in the ribs.

"Businessman!"

"I'm a trifle deaf, miss. What was your truck with the mayor?"

Miss Barclay, in understandable English, asked if we could examine some old town records. "We'd like to know who owns the Ridge," she said with a winning smile. "And the land adjacent."

"The *Escarpment?* Why, ma'am, I gravely doubt *anybody* owns it. It just lays there, has since my infantalhood. As to records, the offices been burned out four times. What's left wouldn't fill a satchel."

But here we had a stroke of luck. An imposing gentleman in white, with a white beaver hat, accosted us on the porch. He addressed himself, after a second's hesitation, to Mr. Lockridge.

"You'll excuse me, sir. All of you, I hope. But I couldn't help but hear your chat with Mr. Peebles. I'm a Buffalo attorney"—he produced an ornate card—"hired to help Lewiston during its regrettable crisis.

"The Escarpment? I happen to know it's owned mainly by a familiy named Hogstetter, been theirs for generations. It's all but worthless, you know. But the family's very poor, and if you're interested in buying—"

Frances Barclay said, "We had hoped to acquire about a hundred acres to be used for an agricultural hobby."

The lawyer laughed. "You'd be throwing your money away, ma'am. But you people look substantial, if you'll excuse me, and if you're dead-set—"

"Could we see it?" she asked. "Your fee as a solicitor will be paid, of course."

The man (identified by his card as "Henry J. Higgins, L.L.D.," with an address in the Buffalo bank) looked at his watch, waved aside all notions of a fee and said, "Since my real work here can't commence till the Council reconvenes on Monday, I'll drive you out in my phaeton. Frankly, Saturday in Lewiston bores me. It's rough; I miss the gentry."

I had no positive idea what a phaeton was, but neither did he, exactly, so it was all right. He explained that the wheels beneath the front seat were smaller than those under the rear, but the vehicle looked to me like any buggy. However, it was in good repair, woodwork polished, leather soft, the horse frisky as if it hadn't visited the Escarpment for a while and maybe felt guilty about it.

All the way, our host ran the place down and hoped we wouldn't "fritter" our money away. When we came to a point where the blue-green slope ran toward the top, Mr. Higgins stopped to indicate the ridge's immensity. And it was pretty awesome, with no visible reason for its thrust up from the earth's crust—this in a region otherwise flat. The moving on of the Falls, in that time long ago, had left it a hundred feet or so high. It was miles long and, said Mr. Higgins, flattened off on the other side.

"To buy some of this," said Miss Barclay briskly, "I assume we could study a chart, or what you may call it here. Aren't there things called metes and bounds?" (She'd clearly taken over some of Lockridge's duties.)

"Dear lady, this land hasn't been surveyed for fifty years; perhaps never. I expect the Hogstetters know the general extent of their holdings. But it's not likely they could lead you to pipes or stone markers. However," he said, thinking, "an old survey's possible, of course.

"I'll say this," he added. "No more honest man exists than Merle Hogstetter. If you bought, I'm sure he'd pace off your parcel, set permanent markers and run a new survey. He's poor, as I said; you might have to pay for it."

"Then we'd like to do this," asserted Lockridge firmly (reclaiming the gage of battle): "We could use a hundred acres, as near Lewiston as convenient, sloping land and not near the top. Now, what would that cost us?"

"Let's go see Hogstetter," said Higgins. "His wife goes in, Saturdays, but he may be tending his fruit stand. It was closed earlier, but he's likely open by now. Let's hope so."

We found him easily enough, a tall, seedy, hollow-faced fellow in denims patched so often it was hard to tell the patches from the pants. His gaunt face had a scar running under the chin, but his expression came perilously close to being affable.

"Merle enjoys a celebrity here as mulish above the level of Lewiston, and that level is high," said Higgins. "If he thinks you *want* to buy, the Falls themselves couldn't move him. If, on the other hand, he thinks you dislike the land, he might sell to spite you.

"In short," said Higgins, "he's contrary. Why don't I take him aside and see what we can do?"

"What *lovely* fruit and vegetables you have, Mr. Hogsetter," called Miss Barclay sweetly, and as Lockridge corrected his name, the man said, "Think so? —The majority look withered, bug-et and crow-pecked. Worst crop ever I growed."

"How do you hope to sell them?"

"World's full of fools," he said shortly, and when Higgins drew him apart, the two vanished into the house, which had a broken window and leaned five or six degrees to starboard. The owner had corrected this, to his satisfaction, by propping three warped planks against the downside. Even so, I thought it might go at any minute.

The two were absent nearly fifteen minutes, and when they came out, Higgins' face was glowing.

He said, in a low voice, "I think we'd better move before he changes his mind. It's all right. I have his power of attorney."

"What did we pay?" inquired Miss Barclay.

"Your suggestion was three dollars an acre, but I settled for two and a half. Now, should we whisk to City Hall and do the paperwork, file and so on?" He looked dubious. "It isn't my affair, of course, but I really wish you wouldn't. Cactus might grow on that soil, but I doubt it."

Lockridge merely smiled, and waved his objections away.

Back at "City Hall," we found Mr. Peebles departed, presumably in a rage. Several account books were swept onto the floor, and the door was left wide open. After trying in several offices, Higgins led us into what looked like the Hall's stationery room.

All bustle and business, he selected some official-looking forms from drawers, signed them, stamped them profusely, fetching a half-drunk man from the street as "witness." Then he said, his forehead wrinkled, "This purchase worries me. I told you so beforehand; I repeat it now. I can't imagine your plans for it. The ground is shaly-sandy, the 'timber' is worthless, and you may have squandered $250 on nothing of value in our lifetime."

"You'd be surprised," said Gervais Lockridge with a smile.

"Forgive me, but do you mean to prospect there? It's been tried a dozen times."

"No, but we got a bargain, in my view. Others may think so later."

Mr. Higgins sighed. "There's one way you might break even on all this. I, personally, own thirty acres surrounding the business center. I speculated the town might grow. That was year before last, and nothing has happened. Now it's likely I'll remove to New York to practice, and I'll let the plot go for five dollars an acre.

"There, too, you may realize no profit for years. Still, it could help you break even all around. Hogstetter insists on cash; I'd be content with a check. In my profession, one learns people, and you're quite obviously reliable. About my parcel, by the way, if you're planning a venture at the Escarpment, you'll need an outlet near town. I include four hundred feet of riverfront—"

"We'll take it," said Mr. Lockridge. "I think the area's bound to grow, and we haven't much to lose."

Not to bore a reader to death, the papers were drawn up (we looked them over, but could make little out of them); I paid $250 in gold for the Ridge land, and was counting out gold for Mr. Higgins, but Frances Barclay gently insisted on writing a check, on a New York bank. She said we could repay her when we chose.

"The check should clear in a week," she told Higgins. "I'll send it by messenger."

For a very brief instant, he seemed disappointed. But he broke into a smile and said, "Please don't give it a thought. Cataract guests don't travel to Lewiston loaded with gold. Frankly, I'd expected payment later. Your deeds are here, signed, witnessed and stamped. There's a dollar eighty extra for the stamps, by the way. I'll absorb it. You now own part of a town that will, I hope"—brow furrowed again—"boom in time. The Escarpment? I personally wouldn't have paid ten cents an acre. But you recall I made that clear."

The parchments had indeed been "stamped." The fact is, Higgins had gone to other rooms after different stamps, and the sheets were nothing *but* stamps, some overlapping others. Most were unreadable, but I thought one said, "Cargo Invoice." I decided not to inquire; these deeds were the most authentic looking I'd ever seen. I figured the Magna Carta was drab by comparison. Besides, I knew the importance of stamps in officialdom. They brought politicians money, for one thing.

We left town jubilant, landowners and potential grape-raisers. And if Miss Barclay appeared more thoughtful than the rest, I laid it to her English outlook on everything, so evident on the trip up, with the bargeman, the stage driver and his post, etc.

We decided to picnic a mile below the Whirlpool, where there was an "overlook." From here the deeper Canadian side looked brightly emerald and the American, silver. It made, all in all, a gorgeous and awesome prospect.

Betsy spread a cloth near three towering locusts, within ten feet of the water. This cloth, out of the common run, had been woven in Scotland or thereabouts, and had a heraldic device in the center.

She and Miss Barclay opened wicker hampers to bring out delicacies—pâté, salmon, an iced container of oysters, four boiled red lobsters and (I assumed, for me, the lone Yankee) potato salad and a fried chicken.

It was apparent that Gervais Lockridge had foreseen a success. He extracted from the buggy two bottles of claret and one of iced champagne.

Frances Barclay said, "We'll all be rolling drunk," and Betsy, as usual, "Father!"

"Be calm. I'll drink it all myself—unless William helps. There's also lemonade. And water."

"I suppose the chicken's for the native with no palate."

"On the contrary," said Miss Barclay, "I've never liked lobster, or crayfish. They taste like rubber. But I've become rabid about fried chicken. For your super-sensitivity, you can't have any. Betsy and I'll eat it all."

It had rained in the night, but a bright sun had dried the turf, and we sat eating the good food and watching the river angrily churn before us.

"Frances sneaked these lobsters out of the kitchen," said Lockridge. "That would appear to make her a common thief, like Tom, the piper's son. A very sad case."

"General Whitney gave me the lobsters, as you know. And as I said, I don't like them. But I didn't tell him; it was all for you. And now the gratitude!"

"I believe Tom ran, as the rhyme has it. So you're in the clear. But I, no thief, brought glasses for wine. I'll put them back in the hamper."

"Not quite yet," said his daughter.

"I'd like frightfully to have a glass of claret," Miss Barclay told him.

"Lemonade, unless you wish to be corrupted."

"I'd like to start being corrupted with claret."

"This is all right"—he held the bottle up to the light—"but we'll produce better here later. In a hurry, I bought it at de Veaux's store, strongly advertised, with endorsements. But you'll note the *goût sauvage*, or 'racy pungency,' of American wines. Experts say it first startles and then enchants the foreign drinker. I'm not enchanted yet, but I solicit your opinions, within reason."

"It's not bad," said Miss Barclay. "That is, what little I was given. Do you plan to *save* one of the bottles?"

"I like it," Betsy told him, pouring herself more without asking. "I like the racy pungency. It tickles my nose. William, here, drinks Monongahela whiskey, brandy, any old thing."

"Only under stress. As to your American wine," I informed Lockridge, "it probably was bottled last week."

"But do you get the *goût sauvage?*"

"It's coming through. Fill me up again; I'd like to be sure."

Lockridge shrugged. "Total waste without the *goût*. Anything yet?"

"I think so. Aha! That was the strongest yet. Believe me, I'll need no more experts' advice about *goût*. I got it, and don't mind getting more."

"Bosh!" said Frances Barclay. "That wine was your own, Gervais. I recognized the bottle. *Goût sauvage* indeed! You don't sound awfully serious about a life career in the wine business. That is, if you ask me."

"That's the way it takes him," said Betsy seriously. "To make a new phrase, he's jumping with joy. Out of his head for the moment."

"Sorry about this particular wine, but I had to test you. We're all in this together, and a house divided against itself is worth a pound of cure.

"As to the chicken," he said, holding up a drumstick, "you needn't think I don't appreciate it. Quite the converse—"

"Re-verse," said Betsy.

"The chicken is, beyond any poor powers of mine, the world symbol of human-versus-starvation. It's our staple of survival. There exists no country without its fowl. At this very moment, Siamese, Belgians, Austrians, Greeks, Eskimos—all others—are wringing chickens' necks, or using the ax—"

"I suppose we could move," said Frances Barclay, "and leave him ranting."

"He'll wind down soon," said Betsy. "He's overexcited about Lewiston. Besides," she turned to her father, "Austrians eat veal, Greeks live on sheep, and Eskimos eat nothing but blubber and seal meat. They never heard of chicken. The lecture," she said, "falls apart here and there."

"Noble bird! Wantonly slaughtered each day in the millions! All needless. Does a horse eat chickens? A cow? A zebra? A goat? Hardly. They have sensibilities."

"Or a fox, a wolf, a dog, a hawk?" I asked him.

"I'm glad you brought those up. All confused—the whole lot. And by the way, I'm happy," he told me, "our companions proved corruptible."

The claret was in fact gone, and Lockridge removed the champagne from the river where he'd tied the bottle. Then we drank it with a four-layer cake pressed on Miss Barclay by her friends of the Cataract kitchens.

"A grand picnic," I said, lying back in the sun. I'd eaten two lobsters, and only one wing of chicken.

"Frances," said Lockridge with decision, "would you like to walk downriver a bit, under those trees over there?"

"Very much."

When they'd disappeared, Betsy said, "Father's gone a-courting."

"I thought you'd notice."

"What a wonderful, a sublime solution for them both. But I

wanted to ask a question. Why, in this country, is the act of going to the bathroom so furtive? No public places, and people coming from private ones always look ashamed."

"I've thought about it. But even dogs and cats scratch, you know. Some kind of atavism, I suppose."

"Atavism, my eye. We have no such inhibitions in the older civilizations."

"So I've observed, especially in France. The older civilizations lack a good deal."

"What I meant was, what with the claret and champagne, would you consider me freakish if I stepped over there?"

"Where?"

"Behind those lovely oaks."

"I asked because I'll try the locusts. Very little difference, I expect."

"Dear William, you understand everything. Back in a minute."

Seated again on the bank, skipping rocks on the water, we suddenly saw the worst thing I could remember in my twenty-one years.

As we looked on, frozen, Charley rose up as far as his waist. He was close enough to touch. He was entirely nude, his eyes were opened, though shadowed by purple, and he was grinning. His body was intact, barring some bloodless cuts on the chest and neck.

We both shouted, "CHARLEY!"

He stood suspended a moment, then disappeared, not to rise again.

"Dead, of course," I said, regaining part of my wits. "He somehow got around the Whirlpool—it happens."

"*Charley!*" The girl sat silent and motionless, then put her head down.

I said, "Don't worry about him. Nothing can ever bother him again. You saw how he was smiling."

"It was *awful,* a death grin."

Then I learned some things about the effect of shock on women—I had a great *deal* to learn. The girl put her arms around me, crying, but it wasn't only grief she felt.

For a moment, her body could have been Samantha's. She pressed into me so tight it almost hurt, and her breath came hard and quick, until it slowly subsided and she hung round my neck, limp, her eyes closed.

And something had happened to me, too. I kissed her mouth, her eyelids, cheeks, neck, the lobes of her ears. I'd never felt such a feeling before.

"Dear Bill."

"Bill's gone a-courting." I dried her tears, and kissed her again, with what I'd learned.

"I have something to say. Do you remember the night of Samantha's letter? When I came to your room late, wearing nothing but the uniform?"

"I remember, all right."

"What did I intend to do?"

"I didn't know, and don't now."

"Neither do I, and that's the point. But it was on that night that I knew the truth."

I smoothed back her hair and straightened her dress.

"The others will be coming back soon. You won't show yourself like that to another man, ever, will you?"

"I'd die first, cross my heart."

Trying to recover, I said, "That might be a little extreme. But you'd better not."

Then her father and Frances appeared. They were filled with elation, Frances looking radiant. Reluctantly, I told them what we'd seen, knowing it was the worst of all times.

"I'm sorry it had to be now," I said in apology, "but the people downriver ought to be told."

Frances dabbed at her eyes, while Gervais picked at the earth with a piece of stick.

"All right," he said, taking his companion's arm. "Rain's coming on again. We'd best go home and send word. Nothing more to do here."

We gathered up our picnic articles, stowed them away and drove home in a downpour. It seemed somehow fitting we should suffer slightly, when our old friend had come so wretchedly to his end.

Chapter XXVIII

"The Escarpment," said General Whitney, seated at Lockridge's, "is mainly government land. I'm afraid you've lost your gold for that one. Unless you can catch up with Higgins. I've known about him, off and on. He's always courting real trouble—meaning jail—but he *is* a lawyer, I believe, and slippery, and he slides out. Moreover, he looks prosperous; that helps. His 'phaeton,' I hear, was 'borrowed' from a family spending the day at a carnival below town. The man has more gall than the pope.

"Two years ago, he sold the Falls, both sides, to a Cataract guest. And roaming about somewhere—confused, no doubt—is a tourist who owns legitimate title to Ottawa.

"As to the other parcel, that interests me." The general had brought documents of his own, wrinkled and used. "As nearly as I can determine, what you've bought here is the entire commercial section of Lewiston. Neither of these parchments—I wonder where he got the paper?—is a deed, or anything approaching a deed.

"Old Hogstetter's an honest man with barely enough wit to find the way between his house and vegetable garden. A good guess would be that Higgins never mentioned land; he probably talked of buying his melon crop.

"About these seals that cover the downtown sale. If you'd looked carefully, you could have seen that none has any mention of property transfer." He peered through a magnifying glass. "Yes, we have here an invoice stamp—"

I said, "That one I noticed."

"You should have spoken up, my boy."

"It was the overall appearance that got me," I confessed.

"We have here not only the official town seal—that's the larger one—but a stamp verifying a dog license; one attesting to the sale of a barge; the operation of a barbershop; the peaceful assembly of Seneca Indians (old and valuable, perhaps); a three-day permit for an organ-grinder with a monkey; and an intricate exchange of four mules. There are others, none pertinent. The fellow went from room to room, gathering up anything loose, and slapped them on till space gave out. I've never understood why they allow him free access to offices. To lose the gold is bad enough; the second parcel was going too far."

"You can dismiss that one from your mind," said Miss Barclay.

"I'm afraid I don't understand."

"I wired to stop my check the minute we got home. I once had dealings with a rascal like Higgins. Unfortunately, I was tardy about the first sale; William had handed over his coins. But I also telegraphed the Buffalo police, with some hope of saving everything."

Lockridge sat gazing at her, stunned. Generally speaking, I thought, his look was bewilderment tinged with admiration.

"Well," I said, "it seems I'm the real dupe. However, except for Charley, the picnic was worth it, and I can afford the loss. In a way, I had only a partial loss. I suppose I can go *look* at the Escarpment now and then, having come so close to owning it."

"We *do* thank you, General," said Miss Barclay. "You've been as helpful as always."

He said, "It's fine to have the faith of one's employees. However, thinking over your command of a knotty situation, I wonder if you'd consider a partnership. I'm growing a little old."

Betsy and I laughed, and Miss Barclay, smiling, said, "I'm content with the job I have."

Then Gervais, at last, made a pronouncement.

"It's become increasingly apparent," he said (legs asprawl) "that I was educated neither for business—a gap of the English system—nor do I possess the business *instinct* that has brought Higgins to the fore.

"But make no mistake. Before my colleagues and I see wine mature; before skin, pulp, seeds and (in some cases) stems are combined for the vats—"

(I sensed that "vats" urged him to add further lore, but he resisted, as Betsy exhaled slowly.)

"—before that event, I say, I intend to explore the ins and outs of business. This by a man who was trained to *learn,* though about the wrong things, considering my present direction in life."

"He means that," said Betsy. "I know him, and he means every word."

Lockridge then permitted himself a last observation. "If reading every business manual thus far printed, histories of business, both honest and otherwise, and extracting their secrets from proprietors of chestnut-carts to railroads—then you will behold a man capable of chatting with Higgins and leaving with his watch and wallet."

Betsy and Miss Barclay smiled fondly.

"I'd better do a little boning up myself," I said. "I'm the prize ass here, as I see it."

"A swindle like this could happen to anyone but an accomplished crook," said General Whitney. "Cheer up—all is well, or nearly so. And perhaps we've learned a lesson. I should have alerted you before you left. But I didn't imagine you'd be so quick to jump."

"Those days are over," said Lockridge. "From now on, I suspect everybody, everybody."

That night I worked late to propitiate Mr. Bennett (and recoup some loss), and in the morning I found—not my cup of tea, but a stack of gold coins, $250 in all. I was puzzled. Despite my research in New York, I continued to assume that the Lockridges were near-paupers. But when I taxed Frances Barclay with the gift, she denied it, saying, "Perhaps there's something you should know, William."

"I suppose I do know. I just remembered. But it would have been like you to replace the money. Never mind—I think I understand."

She said, "Dear addled William," and resumed her way through the breakfast room.

And when I found Betsy, finishing her morning rounds, I said, "Look here, Betsy, you and your father can't do this—a distressed *schoolteacher.* What kind of glutton do you think I am?" (For mischief, I'd decided to carry on the charade of their condition.)

"Do what?"

I handed over $125 and säid, "As partners, your father and I share equally in everything. And Frances Barclay's in now too, I gather. But I'll say it again, you can't afford to lose $250. Probably your life savings!"

I enjoyed the momentary look of indignation.

"Not exactly. Father let you pay to see how serious you were. He was going to make it up."

"Poor child! I've been to England, and I know what genteel poverty's like. It's worse than being poor. Seeing your former friends doing fine things, having the best, and yourselves scraping along, patching old clothes, probably hungry—"

She said, "What a *fool* you are!" and stalked off down the hall. I wondered if I'd gone a bit far (recurring advice from Mr. Bennett) and resolved to behave a little better.

Today was another gala celebration. Once again, people were gathered along both banks, as during Blondin's arabesques. What it boiled down to was this: The original *Maid of the Mist* was crushed by mortgage, and a Canadian from *below* the Whirlpool was anxious to relieve Captain Robinson of his burden. The craft, steam propelled, was seventy-two feet long, and had a hundred horsepower, but it was now considered too small for the swelling tide of tourists. Other *Maid of the Mists* had appeared, larger, and better equipped.

Heretofore, no boat had ever attempted Red Gill's caldron; the idea was unthinkable. Now Robinson, supported by Monongahela, talked Engineer Jones and Machinist McIntyre into making the try, and they set out, clad in oilskins, with fanfare nearly like that of the wire-walkers. Those who had wind of the cruise began arriving by dawn, aboard every conveyance at hand. One could scarcely blame them. Today's refreshment almost guaranteed drownings, maimings and destruction, and these are always a strong draw, in the similar sense of a bullfight.

Most onlookers thought the first great wave would knock down the funnel; it was in fact the second. As the boat approached the Whirlpool's upper rapids, another wave tilted the *Maid* 83 degrees to starboard, and all the deck fixtures slid off into the river.

Events then took place of which we have uniform accord. While the boat lay on her side, Engineer Jones was futilely at work on the steam valves below. But he lost his grip and spun in his confinement, striking protrusions as he passed. McIntyre, in the wheelhouse, then came through a wall and joined Robinson on deck. It is to Robinson's credit that he saved Jones' life by standing on the engineer's stomach while leaning forward to hug the binnacle.

The captain's need to steer was slight. When the boat lay tilted, the rudder was six feet out of water. But yet another wave righted the craft, and Robinson managed to steer away from the Whirlpool's deepest vortex. The fact is, he gained the rim, while Jones strove to refit belowdecks, and the steamer rode round and round in numbers that were later the subject of affidavits.

At last, as the crowd cheered, Robinson broke free and, though not in prime condition, headed erratically off downstream.

An American journalist wrote: "Waterlogged, desperately seasick and bruised from crown to sole, the trio tied the *Maid* to the dock at Niagara-on-the-Lake and stumbled ashore. The Canadian guards there, who had never seen any vessel approach from that direction, stared dumbfounded at the pitiful men. But they recovered sufficiently to collect port fees."

The Canadian buyers inspected what remained of the craft rather sourly. They grumbled, in print, but grudgingly consented to keep their bargain, while retaining the right to sue. After all, the three voyagers were in a hospital with some hope of recovery; and Captain Robinson's wife later voiced an interesting comment: "This venture caused him to become aged and reverend." (Of precisely what he was before, we have conflicting accounts.)

Someone has noted that, while animal behavior is constant, human foibles are beyond explanation. Captain Robinson's pinched success eventually started a spree of imitation. It became the fashion to attack the Whirlpool—in any sort of floatable. Altogether fifteen persons made the attempt, thirteen landing downstream safely and two remaining in the pool. Of the incomprehensible group, three were women. While it was possible, but not likely, to "shoot the rapids" and avoid the Whirlpool, the rapids themselves became a prime target for sport, the idea being to see if some harebrain could cross the river a shade above the rim.

Second aspirant of the fifteen Whirlpoolers was a Carlyle T. Graham, a Philadelphia cooper. Graham declared in jest that he could build a barrel that could "probably go down the rapids and come back up." When the count was in, he was voted the least modest but most successful rapids-shooter. Another of his statements, considered feebler than the first, was in answer to a question: "How do you go about shooting the rapids, Carly?"

"First thing to do is take aim," was the reply, thus gaining him reputation as a wit. In any case, with his nearly spherical cask, he shot the rapids five times and told people (while relieving them of a quarter here, a counterfeit shilling there) that the trip was so "enjoyable" he wished he had time "to repeat it daily, free."

Painful bruises and lacerations finally weakened his view, but no one seriously questioned his boast; he was clearly drawn to this water.

Graham's beatings inspired another ("and better") cooper, George Hazlett, of New York, to build "a bicycle built for two," as he termed it. That is to say, he created a comically large barrel, and into this he climbed with his "girl" and a basket of fruit. Curiously enough, he declined to give the girl's name; questioned, he said he might think up a "*nom de shoot*," thus taking his place beside Graham as a wit.

Hazlett seemed furtive about his whole operation, and after the two had shot and won, with confessed stomachic discomfort, they disappeared from the scene, perhaps to be treated for gastritis.

During this busy span, a good many coopers were contriving a *voiture de l'eau,* the name supplied by a French Canadian. Then the idea struck, and struck hard, of *crossing* the rapids—a shade above the pool. Now there appeared on the scene a cocky fellow with the self-imposed handle of "Professor Alphonse King." No one could trace the origin of "Professor," unless, as a reporter stated, "he was the professor of all dunces." What King brought along was a water bicycle, which looked like an ordinary two-wheeler with floats tied on.

Without so much as a practice run, King placed his machine in the chop, mounted with a bound and a whoop, and was off toward Canada. He was something of a dandy, his ensemble, with a striped blazer, remindful of a music hall. He was also, appropriately, wearing a straw boater, and this he doffed as he pedaled by the Whirlpool. King was, of course, externally soaked when helped ashore, as he'd been soaked inside. But after drinking some Canadian wine, he shook hands all around, leaped on his cycle, which was more or less intact, and pedaled back, this time upsetting into the Whirlpool, to the anger of Red Gill, who like others regarded the Whirlpool more as a genii than a repository of trash.

The professor was recovered by the Gills, still pedaling furiously around the walls when grabbed. He took up a modest collection, removed the floats from his ailing bike, and zigzagged off into oblivion, a better and wetter man.

The last (known) one of these, a man named Nevins, turned up and said he was going to *skate* across. He had an old pair of snowshoes filled in with light wood, and having a species of keel on the under side. (Nevins enjoyed some acclaim around Buffalo as an ice-skater.) But when he stepped off with flourish into the river, his "skates" (and Nevin) promptly sank. He was hauled out by three wharfmen and advised to be on his way. He did so, thenceforward sticking to his wintry genius.

These feats provided a hiatus between rapid-shoots around and through the Whirlpool. Later a fast motorboat defeated the pool, and so did a man in a steel drum, whose whim it was to pound rhythmically on the sides en route. Several experts swore that the thumping spelled out "S.O.S.", but it was too late—he was already committed. Others felt he should have been committed years previously. He was lifted out near Niagara-on-the-Lake, badly damaged.

The performers, almost continuous, now, suffered a period of bad luck. A man named Flack (first name unrecorded) scathingly remarked that the Whirlpool-shooters were "making too much of a routine trip." He constructed a reinforced kayak and, after strapping himself in, stuffed the interstices with a "secret" filling. He himself proved unable to keep the "secret"—the filling, he advertised, was "excelsior and wood shavings."

But in a tumultuous row with the Vortex, neither Flack nor the shavings stood up to the job. In short, his boat overturned, and he was unable to right it. He was given a decent burial in the local necropolis.

Then a woman, Maud Willard, of Canton, Ohio, rolled off a freight train with her dog, and a barrel having a single bunghole. Rivermen tried to dissuade her from entering the lists, but she had a whim of iron, saying she had "caulked the barrel proper." So, with reluctance, the men pushed her into the froth, shaking their heads in dismay. Night fell, and bonfires were lit on both sides of the river. When the barrel, and Miss Willard, were recovered, six hours later, the hatch was pried open and the dog sprang out as spry as ever. Its owner, however, had suffocated. Amateur sleuths deduced that the dog had stuck its nose to the bunghole, breathing freely, while Miss Willard gasped for air. In this instance, at least, dog had proved not to be woman's best friend, and no more dogs were considered for cargo.

The focus was about to shift to another, more popular folly. But before it did, two further tries should be mentioned. A pair of young men with a lifeboat spent the morning in a Canadian tavern, then started down not far from the Falls. They blithely (spectators said they were inharmoniously singing) headed into the rapids. During the morning, they'd ridiculed the Whirlpool, and even called it names, each tending to lessen its reputation. The two were from someplace upriver, and neither, by the way, had ever seen the phenomenon (which had enjoyed a good name for death and destruction up to then).

But as they progressed, bouncing from wave to wave, both men assumed a look of respect. When their lifeboat reached the rim, it began the fatal descent. The rowers were seen struggling, crabbing oars, yelling, and shouting comments educational to many of the children ashore. Then, by one of those quirks for which the Whirlpool was noted, a mighty wave tossed the boat free. Its occupants, in critical need of medication, were lifted out and hailed, though it seems doubtful that either heard more than a roaring in the ears. As to the craft itself, its days as a "lifeboat" were finished. Besides filling with water and having been chewed by rocks, the boat, in the words of a diarist, was "bent kind of off to a dogleg in the middle."

The case of Captain Matthew Webb was not so lucky, but it was widely publicized. The captain was internationally renowned as having been the first man to swim the English Channel, covering the distance in twenty-one hours, forty-five minutes. Captain Webb's performance at Niagara was similarly unique. He spurned all suggestions of a conveyance and said he would *swim* the rapids, and (he indicated) the Whirlpool could look out for itself.

When, in the afternoon, he stepped out of Canada's Clifton House, he was wearing a bathrobe over what looked like red winter underwear. His hair was thinning, the rest having conceivably been left in the Channel, and he sported a gorgeous ginger mustache.

Webb seemed composed and, despite the unhappy loss of Miss Willard, supremely confident. He was cautiously rowed downstream a way, where he stood up, waved a small British flag and laughed, comparing the stripling Niagara. Then he consigned himself to the deep. The river tolerated his presence for a trifle over eleven minutes; whereupon Captain Webb sank beneath a spirited wave while entering the Whirlpool. Some hours later, his body was removed from bushes on the American side; he was buried near Miss Willard.

It is not surprising that Britain, so eager to war with the United States, then borrow money to try again, should throw the blame for Webb on America. From the *Saturday Review,* a British magazine, we have the following logic: "It is unquestionably very appropriate that Mr. Webb should have met his death in America. That country has a passion for big shows. The death of Mr. Webb is shocking, but it will not be wholly useless if it at least awakens the sight-seeing world to some sense of what it is they have been encouraging."

When I saw the *Review,* I tried to puzzle it out but failed. Webb was English, he had hied himself to this spa, and had personally planned the swim. He entered the water from Canada and, probably, drowned in the Canadian half. The Americans' sole transgression was to lift out his body and give him a decent burial.

Did the Canadians offer to give him—a son of their own—a funeral? Not at all. Funerals were even then expensive, and Canada avoided this phase of the "big show." And did England make overtures to bring the refrigerated Channel hero home and bury it with fitting fanfare?

I finally deduced that, if he'd failed with the Channel, the U.S. would somehow have been branded as guilty of that, too.

Brief mention should be made of others who played tag with the Whirlpool and its rapids. Perhaps the first really sensible man to challenge the maelstrom was a Buffalo policeman, one W. J. Kendall, who swam but wore a lifebelt. He bounced merrily along, and told an amazed audience that he'd very much enjoyed the "dip." A Miss Sadie Allen, with a male partner, had a successful ride in an oversized barrel, but their skinned-up appearance on landing eased the minds of moralists. They traveled in unique contiguity, but it was agreed, from the look of them, that they must have been fully occupied trying to survive.

Charles Percy and William Dittrick, of Niagara, built an "unsinkable boat" which sank rather promptly, tossing the men free. A Walter G. Campbell arrived with an open flatboat, which he swore was in "perfect condition, absolutely stable." People agreed he had a fortunate trip; the boat capsized before hitting any dangerous waves, and Campbell scrambled for shore. Then came an oddity named Peter Nissen, known to his friends as the "Bowser." Nissen arrived from Chicago, where "Bowser" may have been part of the local jargon.

Nissen's case had points of interest. He, too, brought a companion, a James Rich, whom Nissen strapped on deck (the boat being decked over). After a disastrous first trip, the Bowser told crowds that the boat "lacked power." Accordingly, he placed a larger steam engine in the hull, and the two set out again. Unlike the experience of Captain Robinson, the first wave removed the funnel, and Nissen dived belowdecks. There he pulled on a lid he'd brought for the purpose. The craft then entered the Whirlpool and established an all time record for circumnavigating the catch-trap.

It whirled slowly for three and a half hours, maintaining its position near the rim. At a point when currents were running in an unusual manner, Rich (strapped above) decided he was near enough shore to dive off and swim; this he did successfully. Nissen, below decks and with steam still on, was ruthlessly flung about, as he tried to turn the engine off. His was a unique problem—he was anxious not to be steamed like a clam, and he was biased against drowning. Some time after nightfall he jumped; then he was swept down to Lewiston. Only mildly dented, he emerged from the water, greeted several baffled persons and hired a horse to return. Meanwhile, the midget steamboat had disappeared into the Whirlpool.

Certainly notice should be taken of Martha E. Weganfuher, another female with awesome muscles. Mrs. Weganfuher was the wife of a Boston policeman who, obtaining leave, came along. His aplomb, friends thought, had mysteriously been waning of late; perched on a rock near the pool, he wore, with his uniform, a black eye. Whether his spirit was hopeful or anxious was not known for sure. Mrs. Weganfuher, before entering her well-caulked barrel, performed a program of exercise that a reporter described as "aggressive in the extreme"; a number of men drew back. Roughnecks expressed mockalarm that she might begin pulling up trees, but she hopped into the barrel and roared, "Push off, men!" They did so with alacrity.

Once again owing to the river's caprice, she tumbled about the rapids for an hour; then a grapple hauled her to shore. "She was first given up for dead, then resuscitated after tenacious effort," a diarist wrote. As to the policeman, his look, all agreed, was enigmatic when she began coming round. There was disgust, too, about an impudent report. Weganfuher had *not* offered his wife $200 to make the attempt. It was her own idea.

One finds it impossible to give these and other antics in exact succession. But our group saw them all, and I gained further details from crews, the performers themselves, and from local newspapers, pamphlets and acquaintances in the Eagle, few of these reliable. The accounts often diverged, but only in detail. Me, I wrote a piece on the main stunts for Bennett, and had no complaints worth mentioning.

As to the Eagle, to sift the nonsense from the real was a chore the Three Wise Men would have rejected. For example, a drover assured me (in confidence) that Jesus had practiced here before trying Galilee.

"He worked out every day, and it come out expert. He was popular around town, too. Avoid standing His share of the drinks? I guess not!"

The remark was so irreligious that I said, with emphasis, "Poppycock!" My informant seemed surprised.

Chapter XXIX

Before the next round of lunacies, there appeared at Cataract a neat, well-dressed, pleasant-looking man with an eye like a fox's; he asked for me. Since childhood, I'd always figured that when anyone was after somebody, it was usually me, so I waited on the piazza, with a certain apprehension. He shortly showed up, wearing a respectable black hat—"respectable" was the only word I could muster; in fact, it was the most respectable-appearing hat I'd ever seen, somehow. He was also carrying a respectable briefcase of the kind used by lawyers. Further, he looked familiar.

He gave a dry little cough (most of his remarks were preceded with this) and, after a quick glance, I felt somehow that he knew my entire history from the time of my birth.

(Cough) and "I am carrying, conveying, or delivering a letter from your father, William." Then he removed his glasses and said, "It's been a long while since we've seen each other."

I was addled, but I said, "I remember. And it's good of you to bring the letter all this way."

"On a mission," he said (and I recalled he was no man for unnecessary babble. This would be strengthened as time passed.)

My dear son,

This will explain the presence of Newton B. Harbison, lawyer and friend since your childhood. Doubtless you recall meeting him often, though little lately, I'm afraid. He's a remarkable man, as you'll gather soon. Oh, you may not think so at first, but you'll learn. In a business sense, you'll find him a man of few words, but those sharply to the point. Your wire about the "buying" of speculative acres has convinced me you need help. Anyone who would—oh, well, I made mistakes at your age.

About that foolish loss, you may be glad to know that the firm's insurance covers a part. Certainly *I'm* glad. You will also be surprised to hear that, for protective reasons, you've been listed as a subofficer of this company since you were eighteen.

Harbison will stay awhile. *Let him handle ALL transactions for you and Gervais Lockridge!* Your Miss Barclay sounds as if her head were square on her shoulders. As to Gervais—well, I'll go into that later. He's a fine man, a man of almost unique education. But as to practical experience, he's been pretty well confined to hollyhocks and string beans. And before that, a social life that accounts for his presence on these shores.

In parting, I say this to you; keep it in mind: *Trust Harbison as you would trust your parents!* Your mother joins me in . . . , etc.

P.S. Saw Bennett at a dinner the other night, and he grudgingly admitted you were doing a good job there. It was Harbison who then suggested you be given a substantial rise in pay. Now, does that place him in proper perspective? (Bennett, by the way, got up and left.)

"Well, Mr. Harbison," I said, my spirits slightly damped, as if I needed a warden. "It's good to have you aboard, as they say. What do you think we ought to do next?"

He looked meditative for a moment. Then he said, cautiously, "Think things over."

By now, I'd regained some self-esteem, and felt some familiar mischief creeping in.

"Wonderful idea! We can't go very far wrong that way."

"Legally—no," he replied.

And since the utterance led no further, or could, I introduced him to General Whitney, who had climbed the steps to join us. They seemed to know each other, but the general's hearty, "Well, Newton, we meet again. Welcome to Cataract House!" evoked only, "My third visit, you know."

"Of course, my boy, of course. I hope you'll enjoy this as much as the others."

"On this occasion, it's business."

"Oh, well we're having some monkeyshines around the Falls. You might as well enjoy them."

"I've heard. But business, you understand, comes first."

"By the way," said General Whitney, looking more sober, "I haven't forgotten the legal trifle you unraveled here six years ago."

Mr. Harbison took some time to consult a leather notebook. "Seven."

"Seven it was, to be sure," agreed Whitney, falling into my vein. "But see here, Newton, you never sent me a bill. Now the statute of limitations has run out. Where do we stand?"

"I was in the company of W. Morrison, II, and saw it as line of company business."

"It didn't have a damned thing to do with 'company business,' and you know it. Another lawyer would have charged me fifty dollars, at least. Now, there's bound to be reciprocity I can make. How about a pretty young Seneca girl climbing your fire stairs two or three times a week?"

Mr. Harbison blushed deeply. "Frivolous, General; as we're both aware."

"Two girls, then. I insist on *something*."

"Forceful, very forceful. If I may say so, General, I'm surprised you escaped the war without being shot in the back."

This was the longest speech I'd heard Mr. Harbison make, and wondered if he could make a longer. He looked shaken by General Whitney's Seneca girls, and I supposed he was afraid of women.

He coughed and said, "Very well, then—say a daily apple in my room." He concluded lamely, "A small apple would suffice."

"You'll have a basket of apples on your table at all times," boomed General Whitney. "What do you think of that?"

"Extravagant, foolishly so."

To explain his presence, I decided to give a dinner for Mr. Harbison, the Lockridges and Frances Barclay at Cataract House. But Mr. Lockridge thanked me and explained how awkward it would be to have Frances both as guest and attending the table—so, I agreed to go to him.

"We can talk without being overheard," he said. "I'll show you my latest triumph, and, of course, we won't have to dress."

Wondering if he had clothes for a Cataract social, I gave in. Promptly at eight o'clock, then, my new adviser and I knocked at the Lockridge door. Me, I was scraping mud off my boots and hoped to arrive at about eight-thirty, but Mr. Harbison sent up for me five minutes before the hour.

"Do come in," said Lockridge. "I assume you're Mr. Harbinger?"

"Harbison."

"This is Miss Barclay, who has an evening off" (typically he failed to say from what), "and here's my daughter Betsy, a nuisance if I ever saw one."

She was not a nuisance to *me;* we smiled across the room.

"But sit down, sit down. No use standing about. Fact is, I'm somewhat opposed to standing. You'll find that chair," he told Harbison, pointing, "rather uncomfortable, but it's all we've got—for guests, I mean. Miss Barclay gets the best, and Bill usually sits in the captain's chair, a *real* backbreaker. Nice place we've got here, don't you think?"

Mr. Harbison said, "Tasteful."

It *was* curiously tasteful, and I watched our guest seat himself without wincing, adjust the crease in his trousers, and look at first one and then the others of us present. He did so without the smallest trace of embarrassment, as if selecting a jury. Later on, I knew nothing could embarrass him this side of Hades.

"This calls for a celebration," said Gervais, slapping his knee (and I realized he was nervous, under that steely gaze). "We've got someone with commercial sense, aside from Frances here. I think we'd better have a drink before dinner. What say, Mr. Harbinger?"

"Harbison. I never take spirits."

Lockridge's face fell; he even seemed annoyed. *"Never?"*

"Unless business demands."

"Then we'll settle on sherry. Ramses!" he cried, and when the Indian appeared, the two exchanged several words in Seneca. (They might have been Ethiopian, for all I knew.) But Ramses returned with a heavy decanter and crystal glasses, and made the rounds.

"How's that for robust sherry? No offense," he said to Harbison, "but as a Yankee you should appreciate it."

(I was dumbfounded; Lockridge usually had impeccable manners.)

"Quite so." Then he said, "Pennsylvania."

Lockridge's face fell.

"Forgive me, sir, but how did you know?"

"Pennsylvania's printed plainly on the label."

"Oh, well, the wine-snob English never consider that a Yankee—

I'm one, too, now, you understand—knows one wine from another. And please excuse my pleasantry, if you will. It was only that, no more."

Mr. Harbison permitted himself a thin smile.

When Nefertiti announced dinner, Lockridge produced a bottle with a label no longer readable. He poured some into Harbison's glass first while walking around the table.

"Now there," he said to the lawyer, "is a domestic claret you *will* savor. But you won't spot it; I'll wager on that."

Mr. Harbison lifted his eyebrows at this last sentence. Recovering, as the principal guest, he *mouthed* the wine (as I saw it), squishing it around without swallowing, held it while taking three or four breaths, mouthed it again and let it trickle down. Privately, I thought him very boorish, but I caught a gleam of amusement in Frances Barclay's eye.

As to Gervais, his face was a study in shock.

"*Not* a St. Emilion," said Harbison with finality. "I thought so at first, but the tannin's a bit strong. From the general Médoc district, of course, and a first- or second-growth vineyard. Sorry—I should know! Yes, I believe I have it—it's coming. A small vineyard, but I remember. A Château, a Château—yes, by George! This is a Château Mouton-Compiègne!"

"By *God!*" said Lockridge, to which his daughter added "Father!"

"And the year?" asked Lockridge in a low voice, as if Harbison might know some individual grapes involved.

"There," said the guest, chuckling—yes, actually chuckling— "there I'm afraid you've got me. A good year, perhaps a great year, by your leave. My guess would be '34."

"Well, it's '31—" said Lockridge, "but I'm prepared to believe they labeled it wrong. Mr. Harbison," he said, leaning forward, "please dismiss my ragging from your mind. It's hard to rid oneself of all Englishism overnight."

Mr. Harbison smiled and said, "I understand perfectly."

But Lockridge insisted on fetching a quill and bottle from a desk, crossing out the "1831" and writing "1834" on the label.

"Careless fellows. I'll make representations to the Roth— to the owners."

Frances Barclay addressed Mr. Harbison with a smile of assurance. "*Combien de temps avez-vous vécu en France, Monsieur Harbison, si vous voulez bien m'excuser ma demande?*"

I figured that the addressee might get up and dive out of a window, but he replied with a shrug, "*Seulement pendant cinq ans continûment, mais*

242

notre père nous menait chaque été en Europe. A Paris il a pris une grande affinité pour Enghien-les-Bains. Il était joueur incurable."

Gervais Lockridge's face had sunk to a point where further progress might be damaging. He said, "Sir, I owe you an apology. When an Englishman, even a former Englishman, sees an impeccably dressed American, with a celluloid collar, he unfortunately puts him down as a well—what do you call it?—hick! I, for one, won't make that mistake again. Let me add, hoping to smooth things over, that *votre accent français est parfait, meilleur que le mien."*

Betsy said, "Father, you really are an ass! I haven't heard unkind sarcasm from you in years!"

Lockridge lowered his head and groaned, but he brightened up and said, "And see what it got me? *I'm* the hick."

Me, I felt a little out of things. But I said, with no confidence, "You'd be surprised to know I speak French, myself, but I can't think of the words right off. I was taken to Enghien pretty often as a child. A little town given over to gambling, a lake, frosty-looking hotels, a woods, and, I believe, about fifty trains a day back and forth to Paris."

"A hundred and twenty-three," said Mr. Harbison, *"when I was there last."* He had to make it accurate, whether disputatious or not.

"RAMSES!" roared Mr. Lockridge, "bring us another Mouton '31—make that '34." To Mr. Harbison, he said, "I hope you have no objection to another, especially of the '31–'34 vintage. I've got only two left; under different conditions I'd call this a sacrifice—"

"Merde," remarked Betsy pleasantly.

Gervais swung around and demanded, "Who taught you that?"

"One collects tidbits at school. I've got more. Would you like to hear some?"

"I've heard quite enough."

"Well, you're one of the most profane men I ever met," said his daughter. "You can't get out a sentence without a 'damn' or 'hell' in it." Her face was flushed, and I marveled; she was still angry at his rudeness to Harbison.

"Maybe," he replied cautiously, "but not words like yours."

Here, tactfully breaking in, Mr. Harbison coughed and asked Miss Barclay, "Do you still have the deed, or deeds, you signed in Lewiston?"

"They're in my handbag; I can't think why."

"May I examine them, please?"

By now, Nefertiti had cleared away dessert, and Mr. Harbison spread the papers on the table. He placed a golden pince-nez on his

243

nose, and withdrew a magnifying glass from a vest pocket.

After an interval made tolerable by wine, he said, "It's as I surmised. You would appear, in a sense (I absolve myself as an accomplice) to own downtown Lewiston. Signatures to these deeds are forged, true, but an accomplished forgery is really impossible to detect. When Higgins left your room in that deserted building, he simply gathered these up. The seals were, probably, all in one file, left there for safekeeping—"

"But I stopped payment on my check!"

The thin smile again, and then: "When Mr. Morrison, II, (who inquires about anything touching on the family) had the facts, I spoke to the president of your bank, a dear old friend. He would have stalled, as they say."

Miss Barclay spoke up, horrified. "But a forgery's *completely* dishonest! I don't *want* Lewiston, on any terms."

"I thought you'd take that line," said Harbison with a sigh. "But you see, it wouldn't be *your* dishonesty. You had no *de facto* knowledge of the forgery." And (sighing again), "It would have been a *fine* lawsuit, and one never knows about juries. In particular when a change of venue's arranged. *However*"—he braced up—"it would only have been fun. I would have seen justice done in the end."

"Didn't I tell you?" said Frances. (On our way in, she'd whispered to me, "I think he'll turn out to be one of us.")

"Dammit, we could have grown grapes in the parks!" exclaimed Lockridge.

"Now, would you like some of my tidbits, Father?"

"Oh, well," he grumbled, "I wouldn't have stolen their town, not completely. All my kinsmen steal from *me*, back home. But it was nice to think about."

Mr. Harbison, forever nailing down his position, lifted his glass, beamed and said, "It's been a rare *coup* for me to mix business and pleasure. You said you had two more of this vintage, sir?"

"RAMSES!" yelled Lockridge again.

Chapter XXX

Agog once again, Niagara now looked forward to a string of persons who'd decided to go *over* the Falls. They had one contrivance or another, the majority idiotic. Tightrope walking had run its course, the rapids had been put in their place, and little remained to flaunt the Falls except a human making the plunge of 180 feet.

The word went out, interest quickened beyond its former high peak, and for the first formalized try an estimated 50,000 spectators lined the banks.

The towns on both sides had now passed rules against flirtations with both the Falls and the rapids. But these were courteously relaxed when an impending stunt meant business. With a crowd of the above size, souvenir shops boomed, the sale from food carts proved a bonanza, betting was heavy and crowd donations were generous.

The first aspirant (excepting Patch, part of whom remained in the Genesee River) was eccentric to a degree. It was in fact a woman, her vehicle the usual dress barrel. She called herself Mrs. Anna Edson Taylor, ferociously insisting on the "Mrs.", then abruptly she had told reporters she now preferred to be described as "Queen of the Mist." She hinted that some journalistic bodies might be found lying around if they failed to comply.

Mrs. Taylor was well equipped for combat. She weighed in at 160 pounds, "most of these pretty bunchily distributed," as a writer saw it.

Mrs. Taylor—forty-two—was from Bay City, Michigan, a former schoolteacher. She announced that her visit to Niagara was for the sole purpose of "getting rich and staying that way." It might have been well if she had. As matters stood, her clothes were almost ragged, her hair frizzy, configuration squat; worse, she appeared to care nothing for her person. But like Mrs. Spelterini, she had a decidedly martial look in her eye. Certainly she had cognizance over a small, weedy consort named Russell, whom she brought along as "manager."

When police made the usual bogus effort to stop her attempt, she "growled and flexed her muscles," showing some splendid tattoos. She also suggested that she could whip any police force in the world (laughing wildly). Just how her belligerence, the hearty remarks and her tattoos jibed with the profession of schoolteaching was mysterious, unless the Bay City school board were members of a stranded carnival.

In any case, police backed away from Mrs. Taylor to leap on the quaking and inoffensive Russell. He was told that if his attraction came to a watery end, he would be booked for manslaughter. Mr. Russell obligingly turned to leave town, but the Queen seized him by the collar.

Some luster was removed from the Michigan star when leading river experts met in solemn conclave and pronounced her "demented." They had examined her barrel, which had been thrown up almost overnight by a carpenter to her specifications. It was of oak, a tall barrel with iron hoops, small at one end and large at the other, like a Jamaican drum. Chief feature of its furnishings was a hundred-pound anvil strapped in at the small end. The proprietress said this would keep the barrel upright. The rivermen tried to shout this down, claiming the anvil would burst its bonds and hit Mrs. Taylor in the head. They also said, in strong terms, that the barrel itself would "disintegrate on impact."

"All right," she replied, surprising all, "we'll give it a trial run."

She thereupon borrowed a cat, when the owner was in town shopping, had the barrel (with cat) towed into the river, and let go.

The barrel did not in truth disintegrate entirely, but the cat did. Mrs. Taylor had the carpenter make repairs, the cat being beyond repairing, and on a fine day, she was towed upstream by two men in a skiff. She climbed in, they screwed on the hatch, then pumped in air through the single bunghole. Here they gave the weird object several raps, to signal the Queen that she was free and clear.

Historians have noted that the only thing predictable about the Falls, the rapids, and the Whirlpool, is unpredictability. By any physical law, the anvil should have shot out of confinement and reduced Mrs. Taylor to shreds. Then the barrel, no matter how skilled its carpenter, should again have disintegrated, as with the cat, though completely this time. But eighteen minutes after the drum soared over, it banged onto a reef, not in great shape but not bad, either. Despite the menacing air of his client, the carpenter had done his job well. Other rivermen, fearing the worst, opened the hatch, and, taking a deep breath, peered inside.

(For reasons never fully explained, Mrs. Taylor entered the barrel without trouble, but an exit required that the hatch be sawed much wider. Probably swellings from the dive had made an even larger woman of her.)

A cry rang out, "She's alive!" —echoing from both sides of the river—and there was a noisy rush to the river-edge.

But when the Queen of the Mists, semiconscious, crawled out, with assistance, her mother, if she had one, would have wrung her hands in despair. Mrs. Taylor had a deep, three-inch cut on her forehead, a serious concussion, rubbery legs and numberless interesting bruises; part of her costume had slipped. Briefly humbled, she uttered an official critique of the venture. She said, "Nobody ought ever to do that again!" Against her advice, followers' appetites were merely whetted.

Mrs. Taylor failed in one important field: The end of her rainbow contained no pot of gold. Crowd contributions were ample, but they fell short of wealth. The Queen yanked the manager Russell out of a bar, where he'd sequestered himself, not wishing to see his associate crushed, and after she'd spent two weeks in hospital, the two left to lecture.

Mrs. Taylor, sad to tell, described her feat to bored, sparse houses. This was partly ascribed to the Queen's lack of physical charm. Accounts agree that she was, in essence, an eyesore—her face was her misfortune—and her stage delivery was far from pedagogic.

In a peevish humor, she returned to Niagara Falls, where she lived out the rest of her life. She was a familiar, if grotesque, figure, seated in the street beside a fake barrel (the original ripped 'apart by souvenir hunters), selling picture postcards of herself. As time mellowed the Queen, she became happy to tell her story, free, to anybody who would listen. At every turn, money eluded her, and she died a pauper, to be buried in potter's field.

Mrs. Taylor's bumpy trip so stimulated other hopefuls that one of them, a native Niagaran who ran a souvenir shop, began boasting (as he peddled his wares) that "anything that woman can do, I can do better."

His name was Bobby Leach, his origin cockney English, and he enjoyed high repute as a show-off. Leach's unending dribble finally brought him word (from the Eagle) to put up or shut up.

To give him credit, he was exuberant that the crisis had arrived at last. Especially so since merchants, sensing an overflow crowd, helped raise the money to build Leach an all-metal barrel. He explained (forty or fifty times) that this was superior to Mrs. Taylor's, and so, in due course, he was towed out from Canada (as said, the deepest and safest side) and cast free.

One of the rowers said he heard him playing a "Jew's harp," as the container began to bounce. This was never verified. The familiar swelling cry rose when he disappeared in the cascade, his transport tumbling over and over. When drawn from the lower rapids, having faced all dangers, including the Whirlpool, he was comparatively whole; his jaw was badly broken, both kneecaps were broken, and the rest of him was, in effect, one large bruise. He was rushed to a hospital, where he spent six months. The harmonica was found intact.

Leach had proved he was no idle braggart, though he was a painfully crippled one. His first act of convalescence (on crutches and forgivably crowing in the pubs) was to take his steel drum, which now looked like hammered silver, and, forgoing the Falls, shoot the rapids again. He also swam the meanest stretch of chop, improving the fate of poor Captain Webb.

By now, Leach was an authentic local hero, and if his brags increased in boredom, people only winced and urged him to carry on. In the high flush of his triumph, he revisited the old country, where his gushing continued unabated. But by one of those mishaps that have become vaudeville jokes, he slipped on an orange peel, in Brighton, and broke his left leg in three places. Gangrene set in, and he died. Leach was quietly buried in the hamlet where he was born, a man with a unique bagful of falls.

For some time, or since the seated Mrs. Taylor had conquered her conveyance and the anvil, one Charles Stephens, a barber, had been quietly seething with envy, as he clipped, shaved and applied lotions. So—he began building a barrel, with an anvil, that closely resembled the Queen's. With a fair crowd on hand, he was towed out and released. Stephens was a popular and generous man, and his rowers said he took along a clipper (this was a lie), in case a rescuer, or some person on shore, needed a trim when he landed.

His right arm was recovered by the Hill family (relatives of the Gills, with whom they sometimes worked in concert).

Stephens' grisly end (the rest of his body was never found) gave the most ardent of barrelites pause. But Niagara's seductions had not died. The antics continued in wilder and wilder forms, most ending unhappily. The pull toward destruction, as explained, lies ever-present in Niagara residents, and in those towns nearby. Watching George Stathakis cook short-orders in a Buffalo restaurant where he worked, one could never have guessed that the Greek-American's mind was fixed on the cascade.

Stathakis' employers had no cause for discontent with his work; he did it well. But his mind soared aloft. He had communion with the classical land from which he had sprung; Attic voices whispered in his ear. Besides hearing the Falls' siren call, Stathakis was an unpublished novelist of note. His chef d'oeuvre was called *The Mysterious Veil of Humanity through the Ages*. It was an uncommon book, being so obscure that no publisher extant could understand it, in sections or *in toto*.

Ordinarily when a writer, with particular reference to poets, produces a work of tangled obscurity, the profoundest critics promptly brand him a genius. (Many such pundits have a tendency to recant later, when they've gained control of themselves.) As for the metaphysics of Stathakis, he had gone so far that a professor, giving the *Veil* a reading, said he doubted if the restaurateur himself understood it.

Perhaps as an upshot of duels with publishers, Stathakis turned to the river. He caused to be constructed a wooden barrel which he stocked with diverse objects: a mattress, his trusty notebook and pencil (lest he receive cosmic ideas), an oxygen tank and his discuss-sized turtle, Sonny, which the writer claimed was 150 years old. Asked how he knew, he replied, "I can see through many veils closed to the average man." (The turtle was not, of course, asked if it wished to make the trip.)

Following custom, rivermen studied the Greek-American's barrel and pronounced it "unfit in every way." When they found him obdurate, they hired two physicians and an undertaker to sit on the bank in what was considered a likely spot.

This might have damped a lesser man, but Stathakis advertised himself ready for the ordeal. He submitted to the usual towing, was released, and then had bad luck. The Falls' caprice had reappeared. A vagrant current swept Stathakis' barrel *behind* the Falls, where it was pinned for fourteen hours. When a playful eddy shot the conveyance out, its owner was found to be suffocated and his foolscap blank. Ambition had mocked his useful toil, but he emerged a martyr all the same.

Sonny, the possibly elderly turtle, was alive and cheerful. It might well, as someone observed, live on to be three or four hundred, having passed this test.

"Well, that foolishness is over for a while," said General Whitney when I joined him on the piazza. He had not gone to watch Mrs. Taylor, saying he'd seen far too many of these antics over the years. "I never felt the 'pull,' you know. Perhaps it's there in only a spectator sense. The hotel will be closed soon; then I'll stroll around Goat Island, visit friends in Canada and enjoy the show in my way. But all *this*"—waving toward the rising spume—"this is different now. It's turned commercial, for one thing, and when Big Money's involved, the fun—and often the honesty—goes out of Sport.

"Frankly, I'm glad the summer's nearly over. We've had good and bad frolics and can settle back now and wait for next year's lunacies. What I *am* glad of is this: The really monstrous deviltry here is behind us."

I'd been reading back files of the *Iris,* in line with my duties for Bennett, and I knew what he meant. The fact was I'd planned to get around to it.

"You mean the ship *Michigan,* that they stocked with animals and sent over?"

He turned a dark red.

"It's hard to understand perverted humor, and the cruelty and greed of men at their worst. You're familiar with the story, then?"

"I've read a couple of accounts and seen the handbills," I said cautiously, for I hoped to get a good eyewitness account. There had been criticism of the stunt and General Whitney's was the loudest.

"I'm not certain of the year. But it was not so long ago and I remember the prefix those hounds added to the tub. They renamed it *The Pirate, Michigan*—clever?"

He rambled on, becoming increasingly irate as he recalled details, to the point where he banged his cane angrily on the floor, startling some ladies who'd been running down the new hat of a friend who had left for dinner.

I could put all this story in the general's words, but I might find myself back in jail.

Anyhow, what happened was, the *Michigan*—a vessel of the largest Lake Erie class—had been condemned, no longer fit to voyage. The owners were aggrieved, though the ship had only flakes of paint, the pumps went continuously and the hull contained more rust than iron.

But they rallied when one of their number leaped up and declared, "Boys, we'll fill her with animals, like old Noah, and send her over the Falls!" He improved this inspiration by adding, "There's a fortune in it! We can start the promotion right away."

At first the "promotion" consisted of printing some windy handbills that were tacked up on trees, and storefronts, and wagons; they were also in newspapers from Buffalo down.

The bills were woefully ignorant. They led off (under very black headlines) with, "The first passage of a vessel of the largest class which sails on Lake Erie and the Upper Lakes, through the Great Rapids, and over the stupendous precipice at Niagara Falls, it is proposed to effect on the Eighth of September next."

I got that sorted out, after sweating a little, and went on to further brags and lies. Not only the owners but "publick spirited men" would assist in this important voyage, and "the greatests exertions are making to procure Animals of the most ferocious kind, such as Panthers, Wild Cats, Bears, and Wolves; but in lieu of some, which it may be impossible to obtain, a few vicious or worthless Dogs, such as may possess considerable strength and activity, and a few of the toughest lesser Animals, will be added to, and compose, cargo."

Studying the sentences, such as "The greatest exertions are making," I concluded that the owners had hired an immigrant Chinese to write the bill, and wondered why.

"I believe they actually captured a small bear," said General Whitney, "but the likelihood of those rogues grabbing a panther or a wolf was nonexistent; the bear was probably sick. One of the hardiest foragers snatched a rooster out of a farmer's backyard, and I had several friends who lost small dogs."

There were, in fact, two bears; the larger of these ambled aboard at night, understandably curious. But this one became bored while the ship lay at Navy Island, dove off, and headed toward upper Canada. To do the promoters justice, they stole a full-sized, wing-clipped goose, caught a baby raccoon, and made overtures to a half-grown buffalo, which were rejected. The entire ship, or that part above water, was then staffed with inept effigies of a pirate crew; these were hung from all the yardarms and crossties.

The handbill further announced that, before the voyage, spectators would be allowed aboard "at a trifling expense" and that, for a dollar a head, they could ride from Navy Island to the Ferry Landing near Niagara. Arrangements had been made for special trains to bring people here from Buffalo.

An enterprising restaurateur set up tables on Goat Island and declared he would "splendidly cater a dinner" for fifty cents. A crowd

251

of about 30,000 turned out, and the Goat Island caterer found his tables filled to bursting. But when the shout went up, "Here she comes!" all the diners ran toward the water's edge and never came back. This was a blow to the caterer, who advised that he was "ruined." He acknowledged, however, that knowing his fellow-townsmen, he "should have collected in advance."

Reports diverge on the *Michigan*'s final disposal, said General Whitney. Most sources shy off from saying it went over intact. There is uniformity only that it struck some reefs above the Falls and that the worst-flawed parts of the vessel broke off and tumbled down. The rest followed at leisure. As to the "Ferocious Animals," they were seen leaving the ship like rats, long before the "precipice," and it was surmised that none actually dropped into the gorge. Even the vicious rooster and the goose made it to shore, in good health though in a very poor humor.

The piratical effigies, loosely fixed to their perches, began dropping into the water before the *Michigan* reached the ferry landing. They could be seen—perhaps the feeblest pirate crew on record—floating behind like an elongated kite-tail. Several of the passengers who chose to ride from Navy Island threatened to sue, and one man jumped off to swim for it. (He was picked up by wharfmen.)

The craft was listing badly, it was down at the stern, and it shook from bowsprit to rudder. There had been drunken talk of teaching the larger animals to pump, but nothing came of it except that the second mate was rather severely bitten by a dog.

The ship somehow managed to make Ferry Island, where the passengers, brushing aside the crew, put down a gangplank themselves and swarmed ashore, shaking their fists and calling out curses. The crew itself got off pretty fast, to wonderfully varied complaints by the animals, and the *Michigan*'s lines were cast loose. As stated, it bumped on toward reefs, noisily shedding parts as it sank.

So far as is known, no domestic animals that escaped returned to their former owners. They retired to the opposite side of the river and took up a new, and quieter, life.

General Whitney told me that Mr. Harbison had left a note that he was off for several days, looking over promising land. I heard this as "the promised land," and pressed him for specifics, but he studied me shrewdly and asked, "You say you get along with old Bennett?"

The question reminded me that I now owed the *Herald* two stories, one doing the floating zoo and another dealing with the Hermit of Goat Island. A few weeks before, a man at the Eagle told me the

252

Hermit still lived there, had for thirty years or more, and said he knew him well.

"He's a roarer," the fellow stated. "I don't advise you to get too close." He stared musingly into his beer. "You got to feel sorry for a critter like that—a shade over eight foot high, face like a baboon, and lives entirely off raw deer meat. It ain't his fault, he was born so."

"I had no idea he was a freak," I said suspiciously. "You saw him last, when?"

"Who?"

"The Goat Island Hermit."

"Never heard of him. Look here, son, you'd better have a polisher and scoot. It don't do a young man good to overindulge in intemperance. Take my word; it's what done *me* in, got me throwed out of the church, Masonic hat tooken, drawed out of the mayor's race. No sir, take my advice—shun it!"

I should have known better. But I'd done some research on the Hermit, talking to Whitney and others, and reading him up at the *Iris*.

Thirty years indeed! The Hermit's story was strange enough and needed no embroidery. He'd begun his life on Goat Island when the place was not developed and seldom visited. The island being large and uncleared, it offered sanctuary for anyone bent on hermitcy. But this young man had no physical aberration; he was polite and gentlemanly, and had indeed come from a good English family. Nobody said so. Like so many others, he must have been *drawn* to the Falls.

He was written about, and treated with respect. His name was Francis Abbott, and he first took up residence in a hut near the head of the island. "The unusual young man is not shy," a recent booklet said, "and he often appears in town, wearing a cloak of rough brown material . . . No one seeing his first arrival ever forgets this tall, handsome, melancholy youth, wrapped in his chocolate colored cape, carrying blankets, books, a portfolio and a flute—ready for any emergency.

"Though well supplied with money, Abbott refused to stay at a hotel. He visited the local library, paid a three dollar fee for an unlimited use of books, purchased a violin and music, and proceeded to arrange his mode of living."

The mode might be regarded as erratic by any standards. Abbott's principal diet appeared to consist of flour thinned with water. The truth is that his interest in food fell far below his wooing of the Falls. He waded, swam in dangerous currents above, hung from tree limbs (as on the day Samantha and I saw him) and, to everybody's dismay, trod a balk of timber projecting over the American crest.

"Why bother to cook?" it was written by a discerning *Iris* reporter. "With the cataract and falls to feed your soul, why coddle your stomach?"

Though gentle and smiling, Abbott had days when he refused to talk. On these occasions—perhaps in town to buy flour—he carried a slate and made his wishes known. "In his rarely talkative moments," records a diary, "he shows himself a gentleman, a good musician, well traveled and educated. He writes, then tears up, page after page of Latin."

Niagara Falls was proud of Abbott, and his presence on Goat Island became known to the civilized world. He often took in and fed stray dogs or cats. But this saintly fellow should not be idealized as a hermit without a flaw. Opinions were divided, for example, about his skill with the violin, and even with the flute. To buy a violin is not *per se* to play one.

In strolls about his squatter acres, Abbott generally carried one instrument or the other, and sawed away or blew as he walked. Experts have remarked that a fiddle carelessly played can wreak havoc to a nearby ear, and there were those who thought his tone comparable "to the mating cry of a male hoot-owl." (Eagle Tavern.) Certainly it is known that he lost three separate cats under musical conditions.

As to the flute, when Abbott was *intonato,* his native woodnotes wild "were pleasant to hear above the constant muted thunder of the Falls."

But music, like good and Latin verses, was not vital to Abbott's well-being. He lived for the daily bracing of the cascade. General Whitney told me he bathed every day, both summer and winter, and that his gymnastics grew more and more daring. It was as though he invited the Falls to take him.

The Hermit also liked to walk a path to the foot of American Falls and splash about in the lagoon, near the Ferry Landing. But if a rowboat, say, moved in, he ducked under water and swam deeply away, till the invasion of privacy passed.

To a ferryman, and his regular passengers, a little pile of clothes on a rock meant Abbott was swimming the lagoon that day. But his antics above, in swinging from overhanging limbs, and venturing too close to the rim, at last accomplished what he presumably set out to do: He disappeared from his favorite spots, and his body was found days later at Fort Niagara.

"His dog, his cat, his cabin, his poor broken mind became objects of sentiment. For years no guidebook was issued without including its tale of the Hermit of Niagara Falls."

Thus I was not to manage an interview, because of procrastination—a fact I've deplored in the years since then.

Chapter XXXI

I dined downstairs at two o'clock, then I went up to write my two articles. But when I opened the door I found—seated in my one good rocker—Samantha.

I sank down on the bed, mind awhirl. I figured myself strapped for a suitable greeting, so what came out (I believe) was something inane, like, *"Well,* Samantha, how'd you get in *here?* The door was locked . . ." and then, "Why'd you come back? I thought you were—"

"That girl—Betsy? She let me in. She's lovely."

"Yes. But you wrote me a letter—"

"They made me, Mother and Aunt Hester. They told me what to say, and made me write it in my words. I didn't, exactly."

"And now you've run away?"

"I took some gold—all I could carry—out of a vase where they keep it. And I'm not going there again. Don't worry about the gold; they've got loads more. Would that be stealing? From your own family?"

"I don't know. But I've got a lawyer who does. He knows everything. How old are you? Don't fib."

"Eighteen. It's written down in the Courthouse. But what difference does that make? I'm what's called developed more than most girls twenty-one, or even twenty-five and thirty. Our doctor told me so. He had me take off all my clothes, and I won't tell you what he tried to do— 'tests,' he said. Then he unbuttoned and asked me to test *him*—so I'd know about the 'birds and bees,' he called it. I could have told Daddy and he'd have been horsewhipped out of the county."

"I'm afraid you'll run into that sort of thing for years. Poor Samantha. The question is, what do we do now?"

"Oh, I know about the little chambermaid. But she's not a chambermaid, really. General Whitney told me a lot."

"Would you trust her, as a friend?"

"Yes, and don't quite know why. There's something honest about her eyes."

"Then I suggest we three walk to Goat Island and talk everything out. It's a grand place for making plans. Things seem to clear up in your head when you look at the Falls; you realize they're bigger than we are."

"You mean right now?"

"No. Later on, when Betsy's through work. I'll give back your copper-toed shoes," I told her, smiling.

I paid our toll, spoke to my guide-friend, and we took a path beneath the thickest oaks and hickories. When we came to a clearing, the river danced as usual, the sun catching the tossed-up crystals. In this breeze, I thought they looked like soap bubbles.

"Samantha's told you," I said to Betsy, "that she found her homecoming less than stirring. And the young man selected to help tread life's path proved a dud. In a word, she's cast aside the land of her birth and ventured into the world—"

"You might put things a little less flippantly." Betsy gave me a glance of mild reproof. "After all, this is serious for—her."

"Samantha."

"If Samantha's absolutely not going home—"

"Never! I won't spend another day there, ever. It's nothing but meanness, and religious babbling and daily threats of Hell. Hell sounds fine; I wish I was there . . . Mammy kept me alive, and I had to leave her behind."

"Then we'd better find you something to do. The hotel season's ending," said Betsy, "and the winters here are mild but dull—maybe duller than what you left."

"If Daddy hadn't died," said the girl, bursting into tears.

I was surprised; I hadn't thought her capable of crying. But I was stupid about her in most ways.

Betsy put an arm around her waist. "You live with us for a while. It's awful in some ways, but my father's too erratic to be dull. I think you'd like him."

Samantha looked perplexed. "You'd do that for *me*? *I'm* erratic. I might kidnap William."

Betsy smiled. "If he let you, he'd no longer be a William I knew."

"You really *are* lovely," said Samantha. "I don't blame Will—"

"Bill."

"—for an instant. I'm the family freak, you know. I've been told so since I was five, and I finally came to believe it. It was only here—in Niagara Falls—that I began to wonder. William helped; I suppose you know that."

"I'm glad."

"Excuse me," I said, clearing my throat like Harbison, "but I wonder if *I* have any rights here. Nobody's asked my opinion, you know, and I'm no candidate yet for anything. I'm not a beauty, or had you noticed? I'm lazy, feel sarcastic about people, swill Monongahela, and dislike the social life. Moreover, if you hadn't heard, I mean to become a wine merchant. Writing has begun to pall; there's been too much written already. It ought to be stopped, before people begin to believe it.

"Now, if those qualifications suit you, either one, kindly put your detailed answer on paper, notarized. I'd like Mr. Harbison to look it over."

"We were talking about Samantha coming to us till she's settled." (I hadn't made much impression.)

Samantha thought the offer over. "Wait a minute!" —addressing Betsy, and the voice sounded familiar. "Would you or your father object if we three went to Utah and became Mormons? That might solve *everything!*"

I said, "Your 'change' has worked wonders, Samantha."

At the Three Sisters, we climbed again about the gnarled tree roots and waded in the shallows. I'd given up; the day was too fine, the river too inviting, for solving problems.

"It's against the rules to do this," I called to Betsy. "But everybody does. It's not dangerous unless you go beyond the outboard tree."

Samantha was seated on a tree limb, letting her toes dig in the sand, her face wearing a frown I didn't notice till too late. I'd just spotted the biggest pea-green bullfrog I ever saw, and determined to catch it, climbing down the slope.

Then I heard *"Bill!"* and scrambled up to see Betsy pointing at the edge, where Samantha, holding up her skirts, was standing to her knees in the naked river.

"It's glorious!" she cried when I yelled come back. "The bottom's glassy and the river's sublime—it makes you tingle."

Suddenly her feet slipped on some mossy rock, and she ducked under looking first surprised and then terrified. She was moving swiftly and her attempts to grab tree limbs were not quite strong enough.

Since I was more than fifty feet away, and Betsy less than twenty, Betsy stripped off her skirt and dove in at the point where Samantha struggled. I laid aside my grandfather's watch, ran to the lowest Sister and splashed in after them. We had, I thought, a fair chance, and would have been less frightened if things hadn't moved so fast.

Between our three islands and the rim were some willowed tufts of rocky earth, perhaps ten feet wide, and it was for one of these that Betsy steered Samantha. But they slid by it, grabbing and uprooting shrubs; and the same thing happened at the next one. Their only chance was to strike a reef head-on and scramble up toward its willows.

As the strongest swimmer, I could have made the second, but I followed after, calling out advices. I was scared enough by now, but the feeling was mixed with an odd combination of exhilaration and despair, like what I'd read of narcosis of the deep.

The third reef was to our left, out of range; there remained only a single odd rock, of dolomite, nearly flush with the rim. The formation was roughly eight feet by twelve, and both Betsy and Samantha swirled toward it in a pretty straight line. In desperation, I thrashed in line behind them and landed on top of Betsy, who had a firm hold on Samantha's arm, and I added my own. But the girl lay mainly in that tearing water. Above the roar of the Falls, I heard her scream, *"I don't want to die! Don't let me go!—PLEASE!"*

In this thunder, her cries were barely audible.

We could do nothing but cling, grimly, silently; but the river, on the edge of its descent, had too much force. Our grips slid slowly from arm down to wrist, leaving deep scratches, and then to fingers like claws.

You—as a tourist—can examine that rock, if you like. It is the only such near the American rim—perfectly barren of growth, lying about a foot above the water, leaving us no leverage whatever. We had no trees, no hollowed or projecting spots; nothing except the weight of our bodies.

I yelled in Betsy's ear, "Can you hold her with both hands?"

I thought she nodded yes, and slipped down to hook the opposite edge with my feet. But it was futile, and I started back. Samantha's flirtation with the river, after the years, was coming to a close. Whether by chance, or on purpose, she was to find out what had haunted her during the long summers.

Betsy screamed that the hands were getting away, and I saw Betsy herself sliding into the water.

I fell forward, again helping hold the hands. Then we felt the fingers slip slowly out, and Samantha's look—as she started over— was a curiously resigned smile. Or maybe I imagined it—and the blown kiss when she disappeared. Then she was gone.

Betsy flung herself facedown, crying bitterly, and I sat, hands locked across my knees, thinking about Samantha's life since I'd known her. Poor sick girl! There would be no more disappointments, but there should have been none at all.

I sat bleeding inside as the Falls moved on in their ancient impersonal way. It must have been five minutes before I heard faint shouts from shore. I looked up, not yet very interested. A crowd of men was there, most of them with ropes and other devices. Then I remembered Betsy; she and I were far from secure. A quick rainfall upriver, for example, would promptly sweep the rock clean; we were trapped, unless the crowd ashore could help.

A man was shouting instructions through a captain's bullhorn but the thunder from below drowned him out. There was a consultation, I saw a man running; then he came back with what looked like a big piece of slate. He held it up to show the words, written in chalk: "CAN YOU TIE ROPES AROUND GIRL?"

I stood up, trying not to look at the gorge, and vigorously nodded yes. Standing was hazardous, and I was numb with cold and shock, but I would see Betsy off the rock, or join Samantha.

There were nods in return; then, again on the slate: "STAND BY FOR ROCKS WITH ROPE."

I nodded and waited. The first two tries fell short, and when I leaned forward, slipping half in the water, for the second, I heard cries go up from shore.

"STAY CLEAR OF WATER. WILL GET ONE TO YOU."

It seemed like good advice. If Betsy had not grabbed an ankle, as I lay half in, half out, my rescue aids would have ended.

The third thrown rock, tied to tarred fishing line, sailed over my head, but I grabbed it when they started to draw it back. I thought: Surely they can't imagine such a thread would hold an adult against this flow. But these river rats knew what they were doing.

"PULL!" the sign said. Then, with a wave of relief, I remembered the kite contest to start the suspension bridge. So—I hauled slowly hand over hand, and, sure enough, found the line fixed to a small rope, and after that to a rope that would hobble an elephant.

Before I could arouse Betsy, the sign queried:

"DO YOU KNOW KNOTS?"

I vehemently indicated no, though I had an acquaintance with knots on my father's ships.

Up went the slate again—with a clear drawing of how an unbreakable knot could be made fast to a woman's waist.

I lifted Betsy, telling her, "Do exactly as I say. You aren't expendable here, not to anybody, certainly not to me."

Then I had to shake her out of a half-trance. When I pointed out the shore, and the rope, and explained it all, she finally nodded, the face still tear-streaked and grieved.

I thought we were ready, but were the men ashore satisfied? No—they knew these Falls from lifetimes of experience.

"WAIT. TWO ROPES BETTER."

We crouched on the rock and waited, and on the first try I caught the second rock thrown—a bigger one. Then, after close study of the knots, which had reappeared on the slate, I tied both ropes to the girl, as the men moved up shore, prepared to draw her in without the dangerous angle.

"ALL READY NOW?"

I nodded, heart thumping against my ribs. Then I kissed Betsy's cheek and slapped her sharply. She seemed to me listless, not much caring what happened. But there were more than fifty men on that rope, and she never had a chance to fail; it sounds unpleasant, but she skipped on the surface like a trolled bait. Shaking with cold, I watched them pull her up the bank and wrap her quickly in blankets.

After that, my own return was routine, except that my hands were almost too stiff to catch the rocks. Had it not been for the specter of Samantha, I might have enjoyed it.

Looking round at the faces, both men and women, I saw only friends, and I choked up at last. I had trouble recovering to tell people thanks. And later, when a boy and his father came to Cataract with my watch, I resolved never to have another mean thought about my fellows. Thus we deceive ourselves in the good times.

Betsy, taken home in a buggy, was attended by a doctor who sternly ordered her to bed for a week. He acted as if he might hold Lockridge responsible. As for me, I received more admiring claps than ever before in my life, and I was embarrassed. *I* hadn't done anything; nothing good, I thought, remembering Samantha, and only

261

felt more downcast. As I saw it then, I could be blamed for it all. It was my idea to take the walk, to begin with.

With someone's blanket over my shoulders, I made my way slowly toward Cataract House.

"Have a medical dose, partner," a man near me said, but I thanked him and refused. "You got nothing to blame yourself for," he told me, with a shrewd glance and recorking his bottle. "Truth to tell, you done heroic, no matter how it turned out," and I heard a murmured assent from others.

Miserable, I could only nod silent, half-aware gratitude. For the moment, I'd lost the power of speech, but Providence in the form of General Whitney came up to take my arm and lead me to the piazza.

"Are you cold? Do you want more blankets? Or maybe to go to bed?"

When I shook my head no, he said, "I've alerted the Gills, and when she's recovered, I'll take her home myself. Start putting it out of your mind. I know these people; they have the usual good and bad traits, but they'll never hold you at fault."

"I caused it," I said dully. "Knowing the girl, I should have avoided the river. It's something I have to live with."

"I don't think it was purposeful," said the general, musing. "It was accidental. Two couples saw it; their accounts agree absolutely. The girl was born to play with the Falls; it was her nature."

"*I* should be the one to escort the body," I told him. "I was there, no matter how charitable the people."

The general looked almost cheerful.

"My boy, you would *not* receive a cordial welcome in Atlanta; take my word. You might instead find yourself subject to bodily harm. No, it's my job. Amos Rutledge was a dear friend, and his friends and neighbors trust me.

"You'd better nip up, now, have a scalding hot bath, and change. If you don't mind, come back down after a rest. I have an unpleasant duty to perform, and I'd like you—my best witness—on hand."

He was a fine man, and must have been an expert field commander. *I* had no idea of what to do next, but he saw each detail in its place, and was ready with decisions.

When I came back down, the Catholic priest was with him.

"Father Lonergan feels consecrated ground unsuitable for burial. The Church" (here I thought Mr. Whitney gagged slightly) "holds to the probable chance of suicide. It's always strong on these matters."

"I was there!" I said hotly. "Miss Rutledge's foot slipped, and she fought like a tigress to get back. Suicide! And what about the inquest?"

"The Church holds its own inquests, in such cases. I'm afraid it leans, well, let's say away from possible mistakes." His tone struck me as oily and unctuous.

"You were discussing a new stone church with me," said General Whitney with mild distaste. "Last May, I think it was. At the moment, I believe, you're using a borrowed frame building?"

Lonergan's face changed slightly.

"Yes, I remember our chance meeting in the street."

"'Chance' the devil! You came here to beg a favor. I have leanings myself on that." He spread his hands. "I see it as capacious but symmetrical, white, of course, and with numerous gold gewgaws pasted up behind the apse."

His attitude modified, the priest said, "It's true I don't know the tragedy's exact progression." Turning to me, he added, "I understand you had a companion on the rock?"

In a very poor temper, I replied, "I'm honored by your interest," and was planning to say more—but the general rose abruptly, sensing trouble.

"Pity about the church. However, there are always other years—unless I die in the meantime."

"Just a moment, sir. Please try to see it my way. I'm merely a humble servant of the Lord. His wishes and forms are mine. We walk hand in hand—"

"Where?" I asked. "I don't believe I've ever seen you together."

The general said, "William!", in a mildly restraining voice.

"In a case like this, where such doubt exists, I hope we can recommend hallowed burial—"

"Alongside those the Lord killed by custom?" I couldn't help it.

The priest gave me a malevolent look. "I'll write the Rutledge family priest tonight. Without fail."

"Strange how I begin to see that church again," General Whitney told him. "The gold gewgaws behind the altar, people barely able to eat, but ready to contribute their all. You won't forget to give me a copy of your letter, will you? Better yet, bring the original to me; I'll mail it."

Mr. Lonergan left in something of a peeve, I thought. The general chuckled. "Well, William, you weren't much help. You're marvelously quick on the trigger, my boy. But I think we accomplished our task, all the same.

"It's not Catholics alone I dislike. It's the whole precious bagful. I've always doubted the divisibility of God, and the fact that He lives in buildings."

263

Chapter XXXII

I dropped into Lockridge's next evening to inquire about Betsy and generally get my mind off troubles. Gervais greeted me, and for the first time, shook hands, smiling but searching my face, concerned. In a way, I'd saved his daughter's life, after putting it in a position to be saved, and his gesture was somehow eloquent.

I said, "How's Betsy?"

"She's tough. I expect she'll hear us talking and come down."

"For a while, I considered myself tough," I said, "but that period's ended."

"A terrible pity about the Rutledge girl! It might have happened to somebody else; I can think of several."

I nodded, and finally said, "She had no real friends but Mammy. I think that began the 'wild, free spirit' that people speak of now. The truth is, it was the inexhaustible source of her charm."

"You aren't going to Atlanta?"

"General Whitney talked me out of it. He has friends there and expects trouble if someone else went. Especially me."

"As I see it," said Lockridge, "it was no more your fault than mine or Ramses', if you like. The girl had a great heart, but it was a little over life-size, and bound for disaster. Frankly," he went on, "if it hadn't been this, it might have taken an even odder turn.

"One thing I know," he said, leaning forward to pat me on the knee, "you're momentarily the town hero. I've heard it everywhere."

"Betsy was in the water first; she's the admired figure here. Certainly she is to me. I thrashed along later."

"She told me the details. You'll find it hard to be modest in this house."

There was a brisk, businesslike rap at the door, and we found Mr. Harbison and Frances Barclay standing side by side. Mr. Harbison's hat, I thought, looked less respectable, though it was holding up well in this land of unexpected showers.

He said, "May we come in?" but Miss Barclay said, "With these people?" and brushed on by. To me, she said, "We're awfully, awfully sorry. I suppose you know that."

Mr. Harbison coughed, gave Miss Barclay a reproving look, and observed, "My custom, when not invited, has often been to rely on warrants. It's a habit hard to break. No such instrument, of course, is suggested in this case."

"But absolutely!" cried Lockridge. "I'll get you a warrant in perpetuity here, stamped and everything. Drop in day or night."

"My suggestion, Mr. Harbison," said Miss Barclay, "is to get you back to the French-speaking wine taster of before. We should *all* try to forget, now, and behave normally. It's healthier that way, and you'd make more sense. Try to relax," she told the lawyer. "Why don't you take off your trousers?"

He smiled at last, still badly subdued (I imagined) by the unhappy day before.

"The action you mention would not come easy, madam. I've spent my life among such dull creatures as Torts—"

"Tarts? I expect William, here, could get you any number. How *are* you fixed for tarts, William?"

Betsy now came down in her robe. Her face was very pale, and she looked thinner, making me uneasy. I helped her into one of the (now) three good chairs.

"I got that at a rummage sale," said Lockridge, pointing to the new acquisition. It seemed to have three or four springs leaking out the bottom, though the top, or upholstered section, was in fair shape. He, too, was quite evidently bent on restoring light-heartedness here, especially after he'd noticed his daughter's pallor.

"That's probably the finest chair I ever saw for three dollars. We have a social group, now, and can't have guests injured. The other chairs are not reliable." He thought this over and said, "Particularly for Mr. Harbison. As a lawyer, he'd be morally bound to sue if, for instance, he chipped a hipbone."

Betsy said, "You must know that William and I feel horrible. Or have you forgotten?"

"You'll feel better soon," he replied firmly. "Why not now rather than later?"

Then Frances embraced me and put her cheek to Betsy's. "Nobody's forgotten. You poor children! But you mustn't dwell on it. Dear me, I see Mr. Harbison's wiping off his glasses. As to your father, he was trying to guide us into greener pastures. And so, for that matter, was I. The difference, of course, is that he was doing it wrong, as usual.

"Mr. Harbison," she said, "you can change the subject for us. Everyone's in a frightful tangle. You've been doing research on grapes and wine. Do you have anything to tell us?"

The lawyer removed some notes from an inside pocket. "In point of fact I do. I've been pursuing my trade with concentration, and that's why I find relaxation with friends difficult. For me there exist two worlds, that of the attorney and that of the man. Until now, I've lived largely in the former."

He wiped his glasses agin, this time with purpose.

"I have taken various actions, with money down. I assume responsibility and will so sign a document—"

"Sign a document by all means," said Lockridge. "On second thought, sign four, or one for each of us, and Ramses would like one, too."

"Gervais," said Frances Barclay. "You're rattling Mr. Harbison badly. This *is* business."

"Well, you see, I'm nervous."

"Try being un-nervous and we can be on with it."

"These transactions are not chronologically perfect, but I'll list each briefly: First, I did the research needed to know good wine-land from worthless. There's a good deal to know. That meant a trip to Buffalo, causing an expenditure of twenty-eight dollars and eighty-two cents. If business is conducted, it should be done without emotion."

"Why?"

Mr. Harbison seemed embarrassed. Then, assuming a kind of courtroom manner, he said, "I have no wish to offend, but a part-time schoolteacher does, or should, watch pennies." Then, turning to Miss Barclay, "And a headwaitress in a summer hotel must rely, I assume, largely on, well—" (He was unable to get the word out.)

"Tips!" cried Miss Barclay. "And they've been splendid! I've become crazy about tips!"

Mr. Harbison now surveyed me. "William by now has money from a grandmother—*minus*" (reprovingly) "$250 tossed away in Lewiston. He'll be comfortably off some day, but that day is not now. So—as your attorney, and emissary of William's father, I propose to keep a careful schedule of expenses."

"Oh, rot that. What was the eighty-two cents for?"

Mr. Harbison seemed badly fussed, but, after consulting notes, he said, "In Buffalo, after working all night, I found myself fatigued to the point of requiring a Turkish bath run by women. I charged *only* for the bath."

Miss Barclay's peal of laughter rang out musically.

"What did you do after the tarts?"

"I referred briefly to *torts,*" he said stiffly. "But on duty I believe in no suppression, as between attorney and client. Now, if you'll permit me, we can get to the corpus of my research.

"Item: Wine-grape land lies between here and the section known as Finger Lakes. By one means or another, I covered the area, looking into the smaller Lewiston grounds as well. I might say" (the following point indicated a small deprecatory cough) "that I resolved certain matters in experienced style—"

"How was that, Mr. Harbison?" asked Miss Barclay, who seemed to find him a riot of fun.

"In Lewiston, I found wild, virtually intestate, land claimed by a sick widow with a dubious mortgage. There were four other claimants—all akin as usual, likewise with tardy mortgages called, as you know, 'involuntary alienation,' or bankruptcy. I bought all defunct mortgages and persuaded the parties to part with their brambles, without litigation. Frankly, it was that or chance living in the street."

"Mr. Harbison, we'll be *so* popular in Lewiston!"

"Toward the nearest Finger Lake, a huge tract, or *habendum,* had lain fallow for fifty years and would likely have stayed so for fifty years more. Access here was by a leased easement on which no payments had been made"—he consulted his notes—"since 1839. The easement was acquired for a song; that is, I bought it outright, and gave the lessor fifty dollars to cool his wrath. Then, since he'd considered moving to Pennsylvania, I bought his place as well.

"Of significance to us, some of the *best* wine prospects lie near at hand—between Lake Erie and Lake Ontario. That would take in Lewiston, of course, then on past Niagara to Buffalo—inland. Needless to say, I bought much of this land, both cleared and wild.

"Altogether"—the notes again—"I took options on 1000 acres of grape land, bought 900 in fee simple, and am going to court for 500 more—a matter of *incorporeal hereditaments*. *No disseizes were committed!* And the figures are approximate.

"Very well, since I won't be here steadily, I'll remind you (no doubt without need) that a Purchase Deed contains: One, the date and parties; Two, the recitals; Three, the *testatum*, or witnessing part (price and operating words); Four, description of property; and, to be sure, Five, the *habendum*, which is showing the estate or interest to be taken by the purchaser; and, Six, other provisos or covenants."

"Mr. Harbison," said Frances Barclay, "you're a wizard. I'll repeat that—wizard. Fancy knowing what *testatum* meant! It sounds, well, almost improper. Did *you* know, Gervais?"

"I knew it when I was ten," said our host, looking exhausted, as if he knew nothing, after Harbison's recital. He looked, in fact, as if he'd like to buy a small grocery of the better type.

"I must have your attention," said the lawyer. ("Business," I gathered, was not quite finished.)

"The classic and dominant grape, called *Vitis Vinifera*, the wine-base of France, *will not grow* in this part of the United States. California, yes. Here, no. Oddly, it will not mature in Normandy, Holland, Belgium and along the English Channel." (He looked smug, as if we'd get even with *those* parts.)

"In our Northeast, we have four principal white-wine choices, since red wines are not successful here. The 'Catawba' grape, mother of Eastern wine species, originating in North Carolina and used for white wines; the 'Isabella,' a blue grape mainly good for eating; the 'Diana' grape, also a white-wine grape, blander than the Catawba; and—of special interest to us—the 'Delaware,' a native grape that makes an *excellent* and even subtle white wine, truly remarkable. The grape is pink, and its skin is thin and tender; it ripens early and grows in limited amounts. It will grow in the lands of my work here—and *it has been sought after in the picayune winemaking tried thus far!* And now I quote: 'The Delaware is the first domestic grape to give us a true idea of purity, delicacy and refinement.'

"There's more—a great deal more—but I'm convinced I have started without fear of eventual legal complications." He replaced his notes and took on his Number Two identity.

"I repeat—don't forget the Delaware. It's where your fortune must prosper or vanish."

"I have a cellarful, thriving like mad," said the languid Lockridge.

"I misunderstand you, sir."

"I, too, have been doing research, in a nonlegal way. I found it positively stated that local, or native, grapes could subsist in one's cellar. I bought a hundred plants, and, following instructions, placed them in the dirt. Have no fear; they are under continuous scrutiny."

Mr. Harbison permitted himself a thin smile. "I conceive, sir, that you and your group will not want enterprise. My congratulations!"

He thought a second; then he said, "There remains the matter of paying for these purchases. Cleared land is of course more costly than legally classed 'wild land.' Some of the latter has sizable trees—that means work."

"Mr. Harbison?" asked Frances Barclay sweetly. "Did you buy cleared land and force them to reclassify it?"

He shot her a keen glance.

"Madam," he said, "I hope you elect for the front office of this business . . . I indeed had perhaps half of our holding—in needy cases—altered to the lower figure."

He took out a gold-edged notebook. "Except for William, I understand your probable anxiety about raising funds. I mean no offense, but wealth is not a staple of village school—"

It was here that the bomb exploded, Frances having set the fuse.

"I'm afraid we've deceived you, Mr. Harbison. But not on purpose."

I thought I heard Gervais Lockridge mutter.

"You see," she said, sweetly but reluctantly, now, "I erred in placing 'Honorable' before my name—a matter of habit. My family are not at all impoverished in England. That's no credit to the present generation; they're a set of parasites. Generations back, preferments were given by the Crown for skill in shooting their fellows here and there. Monarchs, you know, become restless without a war going. My father (an ass) is presently skirmishing against pests that attack petunias. We can expect no further preferments from *him*.

"But of interest to you, various relatives left me lots of money. I'm embarrassed about it, but it's true. I have solicitors, of course, for management and advice, but I happen to be fully in charge. Would a check for fifty thousand pounds ease your worry, after I write home? Or what used to be home?"

Mr. Harbison merely gazed in her direction, mouth ajar. He might have been struck on the head with a heavy stick. It required several minutes for him to recover a semblance of poise.

"Madam," he croaked at last, "you have my profoundest apologies. But I can't help ask, Why do you choose a menial position in a hotel?"

"I wanted something of my own. I was bored with functions, that and the beastly weather, greedy kinsmen and other reasons I shan't go into. If only you could *hear* the conversations of functions; at best, it sounds like a low, offhand humming."

Here Lockridge turned his head slowly to study her. She saw the gesture and said, "Well, Gervais, I think it's time *you* unmasked yourself."

"Not more?" pleaded Mr. Harbison.

Lockridge, seeming stricken, said, "I assure you I have little to unmask, so to speak. Let's say I settled for a living remittance for now, declining something more important; but I can change my mind. Now *please*, Frances, if you regard me at all! . . . Further than that, only this: Betsy and I saw Niagara and were enchanted enough to stay."

As for Betsy, she simply stared at the floor.

I told him, "I did some research in the New York Public Library—reporter curiosity. I would never have mentioned it."

He grasped my arm in a rare show of emotion.

"I'm convinced you wouldn't. And Mr. Harbison, if—"

But Mr. Harbison became badly rattled. "Business" on this mysterious level had proved too much.

The lawyer recovering his poise, he tried to resume his usual manner.

"I really beg—"

"Don't talk," said Miss Barclay. "Gervais, fetch cognac. Surely you've got something besides your precious wines. Anyhow," she said, "they—the wines, I mean—wouldn't hold a candle to Delaware."

Mr. Harbison said, "I've always been aware that I'm a bore, a dull, literal-minded fellow. But I cannot, I simply cannot, see why anyone would wish to hold a candle to a bottle of wine. That speechism has always eluded me. Unless"—he now had strength to tap on a table with his gold pencil—"we thus cause such a wine to gain flavor. I make that reservation." He was still half-delirious.

But under cognac's genial balm, he straightened his tie, checked the trousers crease, and straightened his hair. Also, he'd somehow broken his pince-nez.

"It's nothing at all," he said, still fussed. "I have five other pairs—"

"Business expense?" inquired Lockridge.

"Precisely." He sighed. "I wish you to believe that Business has never affected me so before. I offer my apologies."

"Oh, hush up; enjoy the cognac," said Miss Barclay. "I have a feeling we'll see lots of you now. Try throwing off your official manner, entirely. Be limp."

"Miss Barclay," said Harbison, "I've been crucified on a cross of Business. It is, I imagine, something like the horns of a dilemma. Which brings me to say"—becoming limper—"that I have never known what this dilemma species is. Nor have I seen a colleague impaled on one's horns. Perhaps you speak metaphorically."

"First cousin to a unicorn," she told him. "Trouble, too. Horns or no horns, they poached them on my father's place."

Mr. Harbison laughed; he actually laughed out loud. Then he helped himself to more cognac.

"Please forgive the vulgarity, but just for the minute, the hell with Business!"

Miss Barclay slapped him on the back. She said, "Harbie, you're coming on. If you weren't so tense, you'd make a first-rate dilemma poacher."

Lockridge, still brooding about the near revelation of his state, created a divergence by bringing up the last of his vintage wine.

The Business chat had been varied and illuminating.

Chapter XXXIII

It was my father's suggestion I go to France and gather material about grape-growing and winemaking. The operation had had no real success thus far in America; besides, our aim was to produce a wine of finesse, more delicate than those getting a start in California.

"We were once in the trans-Atlantic wine business, you know, and I still have friends. I expect you'll end those unions." (I might have known.)

With his help, I arranged an indefinite leave of absence from Mr. Bennett, who was glad to shed the expense. I got a discount on the passage, and Gervais Lockridge wrote letters of introduction to people he knew in the wine area; Miss Barclay, on the other hand, said she preferred I not meet her friends, and especially her family.

"They'll win you over to their side. They're good at that."

So—after goodbyes, reception of gifts, and general ado, including advices from General Whitney, I set out for New York and home. Nearly all the way, I read wine books that Lockridge had gathered together.

I have no intention of boring a reader with details of the voyage. I'll only hit a few high spots, and handle them as I think they deserve.

My passage (on purpose, for fun) was on a Canadian tub called the

East Eldora, that took ten passengers, besides a cargo of timber, sugar and cotton. At the pier, my parents gave me baskets of food, lest the cuisine prove intolerable, which they assured me it would. We had a Dutch family of four, who spoke broken English; two Germans of Heidelberg caste (both with facial scars, and offensively loud); a pipe-smoking English journalist named Jackson, who wanted to see the old country "for the last time"; a college student of impudent persuasion, taking a year off for a Grand Tour; and myself. Thus one "state-room" (it had upper and lower bunks and was otherwise a labyrinth of iron pipes) lacked a passenger, and my father naturally preempted it for me.

Mr. Harbison was there as we cast off, and the last words I heard were his: "Keep one hand on your purse!"

The voyage was uneventful but had points of interest. The captain, a beefy, red-faced man, had a white-haired friend along (at no charge) with whom he played chess, below, coming up only once. Both offset any physical effects of inertia with whiskey.

Everyone appeared for dinner the first evening out, despite a lumpy sea, and this included the captain. He was polite as a half-drunken man could be, but his role at the table was feeding a wretched small dog, which climbed to his lap to make things easier. The fare was spaghetti disguised by curry (most sea-fare then), and we found this dreary preservative at every meal thereafter. The captain was not sober enough to prevent the spaghetti from slipping from both sides of his mouth, and it was on these strands that the dog fed.

I could feel rising an epic urge to laugh—one of those semihysterical convulsions—and Jackson, sympathetically catching my eye, failed to help. And neither did the Dutch, who tried unsuccessfully to discuss "smoogling."

The captain took umbrage when the meaning was explained by the student, and said, "They'll be no smoogling on *this* ship, by God!" (In his state, he'd forgotten the correct pronunciation.) "Trying to smoogle, are you? Well, we'll turn out ship tomorrow at twenty-three hundred; we'll go right through. I've got irons, you know."

When the Dutchman almost tearfully denied any thought of smoogling, my dam burst, and, mumbling an apology, I held a napkin to my mouth and made for the deck. Leaving, I noticed that Jackson, having bitten through his pipestem, got up to follow.

"Interesting chap," he said on deck. "I wonder who does his work?"

I told him the truth, that a lazy captain can get by almost entirely without working. "The first and second mates do what is needed on the bridge, and the bosun, of course, does the real running of the ship." It was, in fact, the last we saw of the captain, saving a regrettable mishap in midocean.

When the bow lookout called "Whale to starboard!" the captain scrambled deckside from his chessboard and appeared unsteadily with an elephant gun long past its prime. Then the ship took what sailors call a "sheer" (maybe contrived by the helmsman on purpose) and the captain fired in the general direction of Denmark. The gun fell apart, and its owner tumbled head over heels down a companionway.

The accident could have been serious; I, among others, had scrambled for cover. As it was, the captain suffered a broken left arm, beyond doubt set crooked by a "pharmacist's mate" who functioned better as scullion.

The captain did not appear again above decks, but we once heard him roar that he could beat "old Cotton-top with both arms broke and a fractured skull afore breakfast!"

A note or so more, and I'll let the voyage go.

The Germans were steadily offensive, aiming their barbs at Jackson. The Englishman never appeared to see them, which made the Germans worse. The Dutch family, crippled by language, failed to make the friends they sought; the first and second mates were uniformly nasty, offset by the collegian, who wore a beguiling and false air of innocence. He addressed the first mate:

"Sir, are all the pumps going?"

"Meaning what pumps?"

"I noticed we were ten or fifteen feet down by the stern, and knew you'd do the right thing."

"Lookee here, sonny, you get much smarter on this trip and I'll report you to the captain—hear me?"

"I wish you would, sir. I've made numerous trips to the bridge, and can't find him. Did he die? My father, New York's ship inspector, would insist on questions."

The mate turned away; I suppose he could think of nothing better to do.

The student (I found) lived in St. Louis, where his father was a railroad official. But things came to a point where the mates all but ran when they saw him coming. By then, he'd checked the number (and age) of life preservers (all were rotten); given an adverse opinion on the lifeboats; commented on rust; and otherwise expressed himself about the ship, taking careful notes.

On another occasion, he cornered the second mate and asked, "Sir, will it take long to fix the compass?"

"*What* compass?"

"According to the North Star, we're heading south-south-east. But maybe there's a ship in distress, or the captain's changed his mind about our port."

Well, the compass *had* broken down, stuck by rust, and the only person on the bridge, a boy of seventeen, had fallen asleep. We were nearly a hundred miles off course.

"No, don't thank me," the collegian told the mate. "We passengers feel the same responsibilities you do, probably more."

He made another entry in his notebook, and added, "Awfully sorry about the captain, sir. This would never have happened if *he'd* been on the bridge!"

Much of this sparring I missed, because I spent my time in my bunk, reading about wine. But I heard enough from the Germans to annoy me daily.

Finally they confronted Jackson, to ask some insolent questions.

"So—you go back to England, hey?" the taller said, as we lounged on the forward hatch, watching a school of dolphins.

Jackson removed his pipe, deliberately knocked out the dead contents, and, finally glancing up, said pleasantly, "Yes."

The German muttered a few gutterals to his friend, who called himself Young. They both laughed.

"I am wondering, and so is Dietrich—why?" (This in a thick accent that I can't imitate.)

"That's a pleasant occupation."

Young, or Dietrich, was arranging a chess set, and now he stopped, watching.

"What is you mean—'pleasant occupation?'"

The taller's name, I assumed from the register, was von Kessler, the "von" possibly being sham. He may have had a first name; I've forgotten.

As said, I'd kept out of these sessions, and was left strictly alone, standing two inches taller than von Kessler, whose careful line was bullying. To be fair, I'm sure his mood was unimproved by the collegian, who insisted on thinking him Belgian, and addressing him in pidgin French.

The Dutch, overflowing with goodwill, had taken anything thrown their way as complimentary.

Jackson smiled and refilled his pipe, but the collegian explained,

"'Pleasant occupation' means on the order of putting sticks into pigs, swilling beer, marching—that sort of thing."

"My remarks were to Herr Jackson."

"Sorry! Let me know if I can help."

"How help?"

"Translation."

Wishing to avoid real trouble, Jackson spoke up. "I go back, of course, to enjoy the civilized beauty of the land I came from."

"What beauty? Do you haff music, art? You show skill at losing wars; not much more." (As he became angrier, the accent thickened and the scar grew more pronounced.)

"Some say we write pleasant verses."

"I always wonder why. Is not much, we agree."

Young appeared nervous. He said, "The chess, Kessler. Better than arguments."

Kessler broke into a wide smile.

"Herr Jackson has acknowledged to show me English chess. Along with verses, is it, Jackson?"

The journalist had returned to his pipe, unruffled. "I haven't played of late."

"You are afraid, yes? —is a man's game."

Jackson thought it over.

"No, I was really quite a decent player once."

I know little about chess, but I later asked questions enough to absorb what happened.

Puffing away, as Kessler rubbed his hands together, Jackson sat down, the game began, and was over in a shade under two minutes.

Whatever minimum moves are needed to win quickly at this puzzle were made by the journalist, and the German sprang up and hissed, his face without color, "You make fool of me, and I reckon account. Depend on it!"

"Hey, Kessler," called our incorrigible, "why don't you duck in and write some verses? You won't feel like such an ass."

The boy was about five-foot-six, and the German started to deal with him, the veins throbbing in his forehead. But I stepped across his path. I said, "See here, friend, you aren't going to square accounts with anybody—nobody at all. We're sick of your unpleasantness, all of us. If there's one more case, just one on this ship, I'll turn you over my knee, nursery scar and all. Now, *scat!*"

He stood weighing his chances, then turned on his heel and headed down the well deck. I could almost hear his teeth grinding.

My manners had slipped again, but the voyage thereafter was far more agreeable. The Germans pretty much stuck to themselves.

We arrived in the frenzied port of Marseilles at nine in the morning, on a high tide. We dropped anchor, and the passengers were ferried ashore to Customs. The captain, I assumed, was in the midst of a chess game. In any case, he failed to appear for the usual (then) "Farewell and Godspeed!"

His omission was not made up by raucous cries from the two mates as they looked down at our small boat. But the collegian had the last word; I judged he would on through life.

Jumping up, rocking our boat, he cried, "Fire! Fire! Smoke coming out of a starboard porthole!"

His manner was so sincere that the mates broke off their insults to rush toward thick black smoke that *was* gushing from the area. When we veered off toward shore, the collegian took full credit, saying it was the best Fourth of July smoke bomb he ever bought, and he wished he'd got more.

Of our boatload, Jackson remained serene; the Germans sulked; the collegian was in high spirits from his prank, and Dutch continued unaware of bad feeling. For myself, my mind was on chores in the wine country, and it may have been by chance that I neglected to say goodbye to the Germans.

My father and French merchants he knew in New York had written to the Grand Hôtel du Louvre et de la Paix, and to friends in the wine districts. People everywhere were courteous, all over the city. To this day I'm baffled why France became stigmatized for rudeness to strangers. From first to last, I had no single disagreement with the average Frenchman.

Most male adults were bearded, clean, neatly dressed; the streets (of asphalt) were in excellent repair, and the bordering commercial houses were attractive in cream-colored stone.

I was tired from a voyage of seventeen days, with the constant malice, the unvarying diet of curry, and Canadian officers that presided over the meals like clods. I ranged the Quai for half an hour, hoping to tell one so, but the ship was moving to a dock to unload. With a cheerful porter carrying my bags, I went to the hotel, took a bath down the hall from my cavernous, rather bare room, then I improved the time till dinner (two o'clock on) by sight-seeing the town.

I strolled the Cannebière, the splendid chief boulevard, lined with mansions and noble shade trees; then I dropped into the Casino. This came as a shock, because it had no gambling at all. This place was sufficiently large, by the way, to house our late-regrettable ship. People came here to sit at marble-topped tables and eat ice cream confections from enormous glasses; to drink wine and talk in continuous prattle.

Then, later, customers could eat what the management described as "fancy oyster suppers." All the while, afternoon and night, a troupe of comic singers, acrobats and costumed actors went through their routines, with dismal response. Nobody took the smallest notice, no laughter, no applause, no break in the gesticulated talk. The players were presumably used to performing in a vacuum, for they seemed to have as much fun as the five hundred gobbling sweets.

Emerging, I was approached by an urchin who spoke surprisingly good English. He said, "Gentleman wish guide for behind streets?"

The harbor sparkled in the sun, the city was exciting; the scores of craft avoiding collision at the last second—all these were stimulating, and I said:

"Is good in behind streets?"

The boy made a curving motion with his hands and said, "No find best behind streets without guide."

"*Combien—pour vous?*" (I thought it time to practice my pathetic French.)

"Waits till come back. Then what gentleman happens."

(I abandoned my French here, feeling as if I'd been spanked.)

Then he led us into a maze of narrow, twisted streets where I saw my first signs of poverty. But if it was poverty, it had an individual difference. Street vendors—selling cheap hats, not souvenirs—squatted here and there. I heard, "Gentleman no has hat?"

"Why hat?"

"Is custom, for more fun."

I said, "I didn't bring any; nuisance." But the urchin insisted I stop and try on cheap straw hats till one fitted; then he paid a franc for it himself.

He looked me over, grinning. "Much more better. Only to wait."

We rounded a corner, and I understood about the hats. Leaning from nearly every window, close to the cobbles, was a girl—often two—in flimsy attire or none at all. The first of these, on one side, snatched at my hat, to laughter from her sisterhood. I ducked and mentally agreed that the game had merit. The fact was that this gymnastic was an old, fixed feature of Marseilles here; the theory (inside) being that if an affluent tourist lost a hat, he'd go in and get it. After that, he must deal with a persuasive sales force. For me, I later realized that the casino wine made the game seem better than it was.

The street presented a distracting variety. Here a wiggling rear exposure greeted one; there a naked pretty girl, thighs parted, framed a window. I ducked three or four times. Then I came to a house where a stunning girl of about sixteen rested her breasts on a windowsill. I stopped for the usual hat grab, but she merely shrugged. She had a body like a statue, honey-colored skin, and was, I surmised, a colonial of mixed blood. Later, I found that many of her age were sold into business by poverty-ridden parents.

"She new," said the urchin. "Not know much. But first—come."

When he insisted, I let myself be led around a corner and down a crooked street to a house with tightly shut windows. He knocked in a codelike way, the door was opened by a huge laughing woman with unlikely hair, and there followed a whispered discussion of price. It ended by my handing over three francs, the woman having held out briefly for five. During the parlay, my guide looked out for my interests.

The fee allowed access to a red-carpeted parlor, where other persons waited, and then to witness a local back-street attraction.

I was shown to a chair after buying a carafe of watered wine (for another franc). The urchin thereupon vanished, and the entertainment commenced. A kind of basket chair, with most of the bottom cut out, was lowered from the ceiling, and a busty octaroon (approximately) came in, to a round of applause. She discarded a hideous robe and seated herself in the harness, wearing crimson lip and cheek rouge, and nothing else. But the great ovation was reserved for a big Negro male who entered by the same door, in a startling state of readiness

We had perhaps twenty spectators, male and female, of a respectable caste, if one could gauge by their dress. All greeted this embarrassing sight as though the man had been an imported rhino.

"Comme il est robuste! exclaimed a woman; another added, *"Et si dur!"* while a third pleased him with a favorable comparison to a horse. The men kept their hats on, and several chatted, paying little attention. The only demurrer was entered by a youngish, pale housewife (I thought) who said, *"Ce n'est que drôle, ça."*

The Negro gave her a pitying look, as though an amateur critic had impugned a great work of art.

Two handmaidens now materialized to start the show moving. As the Negro lay back on a pallet, they pulled the chair on down, to make the required adjustment. It was not easy, but the basketeer at last was snugly impaled

Then the girls began slowly to rotate the chair until it spun briskly. When there was visibly no longer reason for motion, the conveyance was stopped, somewhat to its occupant's relief, I thought; she disengaged herself rather gingerly. Her partner lay, eyes closed, done in for the moment. Then Madame distributed towels, and the act was ended.

Cries of "Bravo!", "*Sacré Bleu!*" and *"Merveilleux!"* rang out, and coins were tossed onto the floor. But at least half a dozen men, sequestered in a corner, had continued a commercial talk throughout.

I made my way outside, mostly perplexed by the French. To me, the exhibit had been curiously sexless. It was as if a troupe of acrobats had performed a feat in which they took more pride than they'd earned.

My urchin was seated on the stone steps, smoking a cigar, or rather, the battered remnant of a green Brazilian that someone had tossed aside. By now, I would hardly have been surprised if the boy had been smoking a Roman candle. But I took the cigar from his mouth and dropped it into a sewer.

"Hey, boss, that one damn good cigar!"

"If you have to smoke," I said, "raise your sights a little." So to help out, I bought him a coal-black Havana at the next kiosk. I figured it would make him sick, and possibly cure the problem.

"You like show? Is better with night."

"No."

"Where wanting go now? Aha! I thinking maybe, boss. I can tell."

Chapter XXXIV

The girl still filled her window with, I thought, the richest allure in Marseilles. But she made no move to grab hats; she was almost overtly discouraging. And the furtive men who went to brothels preferred feigned personal interest to exalt their masculinity. I stood looking at her, as she gazed down at me, neither friendly nor unfriendly. Then I sailed my hat past her into the room.

When she let me in, I could see in the dim pink light that she was Eurasian, almost as white as I was (of, I thought, a superior hue), and faultlessly made. She also looked bored but determined to go through with whatever I had in mind. She had slipped on something transparent—and now there came a hiss from outside.

"Boss, she no good, new, not liking fak."

I drew the curtains, after leaning out to say, "Just go on smoking; that's where your real future lies."

I've noticed that novelists generally skirt round the business of healthy males and the physical. It resembles those books (which I discard) that have men and women adrift in a lifeboat and never mention the functional. It is as if those needs ceased, from embarrassment, for five or six weeks.

I insist on knowing how things work, out of simple curiosity.

I was normal, and this was a chance to soothe the tensions of an unpleasant sea voyage. It would have no more meaning than a dog borrowing a tree. The dog, of course, paid no fee.

Examining these absurdities, I'll say from experience that, usually in brothels, girls on day shifts have ambitions beyond their craft. While their response is perfunctory, the fewer demands leave them less marred. As a rule they marry soon and make good but severely chaste wives.

In Marseilles, girls take day shifts to avoid, for some reason, the Senegalese and their brothers. And why censure them, in a free country, because they select whom they please? The entrepreneurs permit it, so long as the weekly stipend holds up.

I removed the garment and looked her over; she appraised me coolly, with neither pride nor shame. As perfectly developed as she was, it was her gray eyes that caught my notice. The Near East produced black eyes, and at the lightest, brown.

"Your father—white?"

"He was a missionary, one of those swine. He left my mother and eleven children without money or farewell."

She had a slight accent, but her speech was English, with a few French words. I cannot reproduce it, or perhaps even suggest it.

As to the missionary, I was not much taken aback. "He taught you English?"

"He had little time for a half-hidden family. I, and two elder sisters, go to the English school, a school of the *première classe*. My mother sewed *longyis*—frocks—to pay the money."

I said, "You sound pretty bitter. How'd you get here?"

"I would wish to be certain. I think my father, when he saw what I resembled, sold me to Arabs. Arabs remain, *partout,* the filth of white-slave traffic—is that the word?" She pinched an arm. "You see? I am *en effet* white. I prefer to be brown, even black," she flashed out in anger.

"I'm sorry; I'd like to help. I sailed in the hat for a purpose, you know."

"Yes. Let's have it done and over."

She took my hand and led me to a small bedroom, with a crucifix above and a calendar Madonna on one wall. The counterpane was red, as always, but there were no vulgar, tasseled pillows at the top. However, many Catholic ikons were placed here and there.

"I change my religion to spite my father."

She sank back, with a look of resignation.

Then came my most embarrassing moment. I undressed, but was

surprised to find myself in a pessimistic condition. Or maybe less, shrunk with nerves, or shame at her youth. It came to me suddenly that I never should have conversed.

Lying here was as exotic a creature as I'd seen, and (with hope) I cupped a full breast in my hand. But when I lay beside her, I felt her stiffen in distaste. I smelled sandalwood and other heady spices in her black, shiny hair.

I kissed her, as one might kiss a statue. The residents of brothels are reluctant to kiss their visitors, having a trade notion that this, rather than the other, brings disease. (Girls on daring but mostly eventless college outings had told me this, and much besides.)

My efforts to do what I came for were futile. In seconds I lost interest, having not gained malehood, and lay helpless, cheeks burning. In my mind, other girls had come between, confusing me.

"Don't scold yourself," said this strange creature, when I lifted myself aside. "I am of no help, and I see that you have worries, too. Maybe another day. It might be pleasing. You are of a type."

"I could explain," I said, "but I won't."

"We might drink a bottle of wine," she suggested. "They urge the sale of wine. Not many of your type come," she observed in a kind of apology.

Doing her job, she seemed pathetic, like a child, and I said, "Why don't you leave?"

"I'm owned; they tell me over and over. The Arabs sell me to three bad French men."

"Does the law permit that here?"

"No, the law is against it. But I should be found and beaten, maybe mutilationed. They think I will someday be popular, and make a large *gagne*. They come each week to be fierce: 'Get men, or it will be the worse!'

"And the law might deport me. I have no papers. There is one law for the Cannebière, and another here. Both are very stern. I have nothing; I hope for nothing more."

Sitting on the bed, she put her hands to her head and rocked back and forth. I felt she had long since lost the gift of tears.

I said, "Get your clothes on, clothes for the street. But there's one thing I have to know. You *are* telling the truth? You like none of this? You wouldn't get a decent job, then leave and come back?"

We stood about a foot apart, nude and intense.

"I despise everything! All the horrors they make me do. Free me out of this and I will serve to be your slave; *I do not lie, ever!* I have nothing left to lie about."

She looked up with (for her) something near to affection. Then she said, "What sympathy" (she meant pity) "that we could not—"

I ran my hands over the mature curves—all admiration. But there was no excitement, and nothing happened. I was simply appraising a masterwork.

"It's a shame. But the moment is gone."

She said, without sorrow, "I have never become good, even at this."

"Put what things you have in the wicker bag and we leave. Your life here is finished."

She looked up at me, afraid. "They will find and beat you, too. I cannot let it." Then she said a strange thing: "My mother would never permit it."

I lifted her chin and said, "Do you *genuinely* wish to leave? Tell the truth."

Now she did dissolve in tears, and slipped down to embrace my knees. For an awful moment, I thought she would make the full Eastern *shiko* of self-abasement, so I lifted her up and said, "That's enough. Now, move! Or I'll beat you myself."

She dressed quickly in a schoolgirl's blue uniform, and tied her raven hair back with a ribbon. Her shoes were not the telltale high pumps of the trade but were some kind of embroidered Eastern sandals. Her meager belongings scarcely filled the bag, but I'd only just picked it up when a hiss came from outside. I pulled a curtain an inch aside.

"Boss—two men watch window; very wicked. You spend too much long. They suspicious."

"I see them. Saunter off and meet me at the Casino's front door."

Even so, the girl no longer looked frightened of anything. She came from a back room with a Penang lawyer—a heavy thorn stick, whose knob was filled with lead. It once belonged to that badly beset missionary, I surmised.

But no, she said, "A man leave it and too shame to come back." She giggled; it was the first time I'd seen her face relaxed. "I fight, too," and she showed me a curved dirk resting against that extravagant bosom.

My look was almost our undoing. I was feeling strong again.

"There won't be a need," I said, not at all certain.

We stepped out of the front door, me carrying the bag, the girl a small respectable reticule.

"Hey, gentleman, what you do with *puta* of ours?"

"Come get her," I said, and shifted the stick to my right hand.

"We get you, all right. Both, *en crapaudine,* hey?"

There was a click of a spring knife, the weapon of these streets.

I dropped the case, spat on my hands like an Irishman, and swung the club a time or two, testing. The two, even the one with the knife, seemed loath to wade into that arc. In stature, both were small, or average Frenchmen.

So—the half-comic march proceeded toward the Cannebière, we on one side, the *maquereaux* on the other. They kept up an obscene stream of threats, in the idiom, that drew awed silence (and fear) from the flesh-filled windows. It might have drawn comment from me, if the odds had been better.

Then I heard a clatter of hooves behind us, and a fiacre half filled with roisterers came round a corner, hurling endearments toward the windows.

I stepped before the driver, with a menacing lift of my club, and he pulled to a halt, protesting. But I opened a side door and pushed the girl in. The driver opened his trap to add some oaths he'd forgotten, and apologized for it, but the roisterers were in such moist good humor that they took us to their bosoms, as it were. Above the din, I tried to explain the attempted kidnap of my baby sister—pointing back at the running, half-mad *fripons,* and then, around a curve or two, we were free of capture.

At the Casino, I backed us out, thanking our hosts, who seemed crushed to lose us, and tossed a golden sovereign to the driver, whose personality changed in an instant. He climbed down and attempted to carry the wicker case. All bows and smiles, he said, "One can tell a gentleman. My former words were spoken in jest. M'sieur must weigh that carefully."

They drove off, with the driver's last assurance of my quality and compliments for my sister: *"Qu'elle est mignonne, la petite!"* and *"Une enfant ravissante, et à son age, tellement formée!"* He was an authentic friend.

The urchin was waiting and now, at my order, we scrambled into a different hack. Altogether we changed seven times, then alighted four squares from the Grand Hôtel du Louvre et de la Paix. Here I gave the boy two sovereigns and some advice: "Listen, *amigo,* if you don't leave the *Marché de viande"* ("Meat Market"—the district was called that then) "and go to school, you'll grow up worse than those we left behind. Understand?"

"I not Catholic, I not anything, and school no take me, boss."

I wrote some sentences on notepaper, signed my father's name, and said, "You've been a good friend. Take this to Father du Bois at the Ecole de la Sainte Vierge, on the Boulevard des Anglais. Tell him if he has costs, I'll pay them."

He stood blinking. "I rather go with you, boss."

"You're going to Father du Bois." Then I took him to one side and asked a favor. "Find a similar picture; usually none is recognizable in any case. Leave the papers with the Casino concierge." Then I gave him two more sovereigns, and said, "Be off. I'll check later."

He still stood blinking, probably unused to kindness. Then he darted off in a new direction. "You not do good without me, boss. Much problems. Wait to see!"

"Will he go to school?" I asked her.

"No."

"No."

"Still, one can never tell about people."

"I'll know in a few weeks."

Then, trusting few people, apart from those back home, I had us take three more hackneys, even then getting down several squares from the hotel.

The proprietor, M. Fallon, looked at the girl and said, "I thought your sister died, Monsieur Morrison."

"She was the older. This is my baby sister. The one in school in Paris."

"And her papers?"

"They were lost. A duplication is being sent today."

"To be sure. What is a formality, after all?" and he struck his bell, then placed us in adjoining rooms overlooking the harbor. My bags were transferred from the first room.

Before I could produce another sovereign, the girl tipped the *"très avide porteur"* a sum that seemed to please him, and we were alone. Despite ·the eventful nightmare (which now struck me as pretty distant from my mission, though fun) it was still only two-thirty o'clock.

Before going to her room, she said, "One can be too generous. You toss money away."

"How?"

"Do you know what gold pieces can buy? . . . One could start a small enterprise."

"You? . . . You're leaving with me for Montpellier tomorrow. Strange, isn't it? When my father first sent ships to this place, with timber, and carried back wine, I almost went to school here— Montpellier, I mean. I was to learn French. But neither happened. Cholera came to New York, and my sister died. After that, my mother pleaded seasickness, and my father brought me, alone, on business vacations. Until he built his coastal trade."

* * *

286

The Grand Hôtel du Louvre et de la Paix had a large central court, with a circle of vines and flowers. It was not for dining; mostly men sat at tables smoking cigars and reading papers. It was considered bold for women to sit there, then, in public view.

We shunned the dining hall and ate in a room of sports motif—overwhelming heads on the walls, a fireplace, blurred photographs of athletes, and a lone plated-silver cup near which a yellowed leaning news clip effusively told that M. Fallon (twenty-seven years before) had swum to the Château d'If and back, despite "proliferant sharks and refuse."

For me, this removed some of the shine, but my companion, reading, only said, *"Formidable!"* and we sat down to fish soup, then fish (loup), a piece of beef that could have been harness leather, peas, lentils, snails *en croûte* (!), roast chicken, salad, and a strawberry tarte. When a bowl of green figs, pears, oranges and mints appeared, a Belgian family left to empty a boy of five, and only the wife came back—to pay the bill and to collect some fruit from their bowl for breakfast.

The orgy required two hours and cost a dollar each. I also had a bottle of claret from the Haut Médoc, and this was thirty cents more.

I figured that, with the exchange and the cost of Marseilles, I could set up shop at the Grand Hôtel du Louvre et de la Paix, and live out my life in luxury.

My companion said, "Don't think me to be ungrateful, but I could not eat that much again, ever," and I confessed to an unsettled feeling in *my* stomach. I wondered if a slightly impoverished hotel might have been better.

The waiter, a thin man excessively polite, with several strands of hair unsuccessfully arranged to conceal baldness, beamed at his tip, for which I was not responsible. Had I tipped him, she said, he might have retired.

The Médoc reminded me why I'd come, and I resolved not to stray again. The fact is, I was so stupefied with food and wine (and a need for sleep) that I was not quite sure what had happened. I think my baby sister (M. Fallon, passing now and then, usually winked) felt about the same, and we climbed the uncarpeted stairs to take a nap, each in his own bed.

We awoke in an hour (the excitements had been too varied for deep sleep) and I wondered if there was time for the Château d'If, to be guided through the gloomy laments scratched in the damp stone cells. But the girl shrank from such an outing, convinced that, in her case, the wardens would never let her out.

To make things up, I said, "Schoolgirls here wear the saucer-shaped straw hats. We'll visit the shops and get one. Then, if you assume a childlike air of innocence, you should look about twelve."

"If they knew *how* innocent!" she said, hurt, and I was sorry I'd spoken.

So I bought her their best such hat, and, as expected, there was admiring comment when, hand in hand, we strolled the courtyard. Women were not discouraged from sitting with their men at this hour, presumably on the typical French theory that the light was too soft for sharp appraisal.

"Comme elle est charmante!" and *"Une enfant, oui, et très belle, mais pas enfant longtemps!"*—wagging a finger back and forth, happy to imagine corruptions to come.

"You see, you're a great hit."

"Hit?"

"Popular, especially now with the hat."

She smiled and exhaled a long breath.

I asked, "Why the held breath?"

"To make myself flat in front."

"Forget it; it's a battle you can't win."

"And I walk with the rear drawn in. I feel very glad. The bad seven months have begun to fade back."

"You feel like a schoolgirl again?"

"It's a sensation to enjoy. But I am not like the others, clearly. I cannot take that from my mind."

"Nonsense!" I said in a voice so carrying that nearby persons were startled.

"I wish to say you something, but I am embarrass." She straightened her shoulders, letting the front take care of itself. "You believe me?"

"Probably."

"You must believe or not. In the seven dreadful months, I have not one pleasuring from the few brutes who come and leave angry. Never once. There's a word—"

"Yes, there is. But you must have had normal wishes from time to time. Not with a client?"

"Never!" she flashed out fiercely. "I did, alone, but not often, what persons do in that way—"

I glanced aside and noted with wonder that she could blush.

"—and I could tell of bad, strange things from my school of before. There were wicked attempts on me—no better than Marseilles. They are very loose, these schools."

I suddenly understood that she was, aside from a few meaningless rapes, as decent as the girls presently shopping in the store.

288

(Marseilles, like other French towns then, closed from four-thirty to seven, for supper and a siesta.)

I gripped her hard, and said, "You're the nicest schoolgirl here. Try not to forget that."

"I saw your name on the hotel sheet. For me, it was unpronounceable. And you leave Marseilles?"

"We're going together, to Montpellier."

"I have heard; it is very chic. Nobody will look, there."

"They'll always look."

Here in September, darkness fell at around nine; so we ended our stroll and went back to our rooms.

There was a knocking at the door and the girl looked startled. But it was the hall porter, holding an envelope. I tipped him, and said, "I should have known the little devil would find us. I told him plainly— leave these *at the Casino.* I hope he remains friendly.

"Here are your papers; hang on to them."

The passport photo was interesting, taken in the art's infancy. It was of a child in a confirmation dress. Still, there was a vague likeness. But what of the dress and Monseigneur Rey, in Montpellier? I asked if she had a picture of herself, and her face lit up.

"You must give it back. It is my best possession."

I promised; and after she'd dug into the wicker came up with a surprisingly clear picture of an unclothed baby lying on its stomach.

"Excellent. We'll stick to confirmation. I'll tell the monseigneur it belonged to your sister. I expect a certain amount of *gêne* in any event."

Most surprising, the envelope further contained three francs and a note: "Good by, boss. I am in the school for tomorrow. You have give me too much moneys. But the papers were très cher. I'm saying again—good by for now time."

"He's a friend, all right, but who wrote the English?"

"Oh well, these *gamin* of the street. They learn things rapid, too much. He knows a lot, that one."

"Monsieur Fallon has reserved us two seats on the *diligence,* for Montpellier. It leaves promptly at seven. Like Spain and its bullfights, public conveyances alone are punctual in France. In other words, we might turn in. It's a long trip."

"Turn in?"

"Go to bed. Sleep."

Lighting the candle, I saw that she looked frightened again.

"These chambers, they are very large, maybe dangerous. I will be seized again."

"There's a connecting door. I'll leave it open. Which room do you want? Take your chance."

"I prefer to sleep at the bottom of your bed. I do not stir, even if I never go to sleep. You must know, I have never seen a place like this. My father took us nowhere: he could not recognize us on the street, he explain."

"I'd kick you black and blue. I'm a rough sleeper," I said, lying.

"Very well, I do what you say."

I thought: "This girl's had a complete change of demeanor in a remarkably short time." And (ever alerted) I put my purse (with several hundred francs), my gold hunter-watch, and some additional baits on the white wicker table beside me. Then I fixed the watch chain to the bellpull.

From the other room: "Good night . . . Willum, I think."

I realized that I'd never asked her name. I did so now.

She said primly, too primly: "My name is Germaine Durr."

"Sleep well."

I was half convinced, as I'd been with the urchin, that she'd be gone when I woke; together with my wallet, gewgaws and watch, if she could untangle the chain.

I was awakened, at some late hour, by a loud banging. When my head cleared, I figured it was my consort, leaving. But my things were intact, and the adjoining room was quiet. The racket was a routine domestic row, the words unclear through the double doors that the French intelligently place in many hotels. A door now slammed somewhere down the hall; and the ruckus ended. Anyway, that sound is somehow impersonal.

Before drifting back into sleep, I looked out at the moon, bright on the terraces and the harbor, quiet now. A figure moved, and I wondered if the ghost of Romulus walked abroad in such a full Marseilles moon. Legend had him here, and made no mention of his leaving. Like me, he may have liked Marseilles, and had plans for further construction.

The sun shone in my face, and promptly thereafter my bell rang, to signalize six o'clock, when I'd asked to be called. Then the import of responsibility seeped in slowly. I had trouble turning to look at the table, but all was there. And beside me, rolled up in a quilt, was the schoolgirl, her face as smooth as a light copper coin. For some reason, I felt a vast relief.

She stirred, and I said, "Up," not overly genial in the mornings, and maybe a little piqued at this *crise* caused by too much Casino wine. "Coffee's coming, and we have a rough trip ahead. Now hop along and dress."

She rose to her knees, holding the quilt before her, but she'd forgotten: The quilt was in front, leaving nothing behind. Still, she got up obediently and for some reason tiptoed to her room. But I'd once before seen her unclothed, and more. Now, however, that was different, though I had no idea how different.

The black, sweet coffee, brioche and apricot preserves arrived, with the extra pot I'd ordered, and before I could touch it, the girl ran in to make the waiter happy.

We took our leave of Fallon, who said, "Your, ah, young sister is the talk of the hotel, M'sieur Morrison. No one has seen anything so lovely. What a pity she's *related!*" And before we turned away, he gave a discreet cough and said, "Which of you, m'sieur, would prefer to correct the register?"

I looked and she'd written her correct name, after I—confused dolt—had simply inscribed my own. But before the child could improve the page, I said, "My sister's married, Monsieur Fallon. Her husband was killed in the war."

"My condolences, madame. That would have been the Napoleonic wars, of course."

"No," I said, "it was a Latin-American revolution. He was secreted in a palm tree with a bomb, awaiting a royal procession, and a monkey hit the bomb with a stick."

"*Tant pis!* The things that happen!"

We shook hands and he gave me a tiny bottle containing a full-rigged ship for my father. My admired (and widowed) sister curtsied, and the porter arrived for our bags, as the *diligence* driver waited, impatient like all his countrymen before the noontime wine.

There were three other passengers, mail sacks piled on top, and, besides luggage, other articles to be delivered along the route.

The French countryside rolled by, with olive trees in crooked files beside small clear streams and the Rhône that burst often into view. Here and there farmers, male and female, were at work, in attitudes I resolved to remember, unless they caught some artist's fancy.

I'd thought about a detour to the Camargue, an alluvial lowland southeast of Arles. It was the uninhabited delta of the Rhône, a terrain unique in France. White stallions and black bulls ran wild there, both often in the surf—a sight I'd seen once as a child. But I felt behind schedule, for no valid reason, and gave it up.

An impediment to action was the fact that Miss Durr clung to my hand most of the way. At Arles, our overnight stop, we stayed at the Hotel Jules César, on the Boulevard des Lices. This was once a

Carmelite convent, a municipal landmark. The restless Julius Caesar had called the town Arelate, and Constantine made it his chief residence on the coast. He must have been fond of wind, I thought, for the *mistral* had begun to blow. Still, we walked half bent over to see his collapsed palace, the Roman thermal baths, and the Cathedral of St. Trophine; and after a few blown minutes along the Rhône and the canal, decided that the Visigoths, in whose hands Arles had finally lodged, were welcome to it all. But unless my memory was incorrect, they passed it on pretty fast.

Chapter XXXV

Off for Montpellier, with my companion increasingly subdued. I wondered if, taken by surprise, she hadn't lied a little and now missed the old life. I asked some such question, in a roundabout way, and her eyes filled with tears.

"I go to school," she said, "and am happy, but I prefer to stay with you."

"You're not a bad sort," I said lightly, "but I've got work to do. Besides, I'll come back soon."

"How soon?"

"A few weeks. Tell me once more—no regrets, about all this?"

She looked half-angry. "If you please, don't ask again. Everything since you is exquisite. That should be well comprehended."

The *diligence* today fell somewhat below the other, but the French roads, as always, were *en entretien complet,* as the phrase went, and we rolled on toward my favorite large French city, after Paris and Nice. (The aggressive resorts soon bored me, and my family felt the same.) Maybe Montpellier's placement, outside the tourist surge, had much to do with it. Our distance was forty-odd miles, and it passed quickly. And when we climbed that fruitful plain, with the River Lez on our left, my heart seemed to turn over.

After all, I'd been here before, once for a month, and might have entered school. In his searching way, my father had decided that one could get here a fine French education, and he saw me as the company's agent in France one day. I was to learn the tongue, and visit Bordeaux.

That was eleven years ago. Now I was once more immersed in education, though under different conditions.

We stayed at the Grand Hôtel du Midi, on the Place de la Comédie, shunning the Metropole, which bulged with businessmen. As in Marseilles, the hotel people were polite, without raised eyebrows, and we had the usual adjoining rooms.

"It's only eleven-thirty," I told my innocent, "and while we have two bowls and pitchers in the *cabinet* between us, there's a bath down the hall. You need a bath, I need a bath, all God's creatures need baths. They charge extra, but bathing is a sacred rite, with huge towels and, unless you object, a chambermaid to scrub."

She looked frightened. "I'm not positive I know these baths. Back home, a can of sprinkling, yes. And lately a rub with cloth in, in—"

"The Meat Market. If you face it down, you'll forget it. Do you have clean underthings? Or any at all?"

She blushed. "Not for a school, to be sure."

"Show me."

From her bag she took two pairs of red silk briefs, with bows sewed on and an open crease in the middle below. There were further offenses, but I scooped them up and put them on the coal grate.

I said, "Lock your door; we're going shopping."

Nearby was a typical shop of the second class, with clothes tossed helter-skelter on the counters. They were conducting what we call a sale, with everything *"bon marché."* But after studying the proprietor, I figured the sale was probably going in Caesar's time. Continuing the conceit, I thought it gave one an odd sensation to tread where the Caesars had long ago trod, looking for bargains.

For a few francs, I replaced her underseductions and added some suitable night clothes and two pairs of schoolgirlish shoes.

Back, on the brink of a bath, my fugitive froze with fear.

"Is it veritably safe? There is much water here."

The maid I'd summoned tested the water temperature, and said, to me, *"Votre soeur doit se déshabiller maintenant. Le bain est presque préparé."*

Well, I was ready, too, disliking these needless foreign charades.

And here the girl made a slip. Before I could leave, she pulled her schooldress over her head and stood naked, with me in the room. I'd seen her thus several times, and she'd lost all coquetry about it.

The maid gave an unconvincing shriek and hustled me out, closing the door. It was half an hour before the two arrived at my room.

Miss Durr was glowing. "In the end I find it sympathetic," she said. "I should have had baths previously; I see it now. Certainly I should have another this evening?"

"In the morning, before we go to Monseigneur Rey. Warm yourself near the fire. I'll scrub up in five minutes, with no frills."

But the maid, protesting she'd be dismissed, insisted on scraping some skin off my back and chest, or so I felt. Farther than that, I refused to let her go. She was pretty, in her short skirt and black silk stockings, and a year ago I might have gone on to see where it led. In ninety-nine cases out of a hundred (I learned) it led nowhere at all. But I gave her a decent tip, and she left, happiness restored.

Before we left to walk, there came a knock at the door, and a man from the desk, with every apology, asked if this part of the building was on fire.

"Oh," I replied (first thinking I had a dangerous lunatic on my hands), "you mean the fireplace. I lit it. My sister recovers from the lung fever."

"*Dommage!*—the manager thought he smelled curtains burning."

"It's possibly my cigar. I import these from Peru." (It was, in fact, Brazilian, and pretty rank.)

Before leaving (with a tip) the man muttered a comment: "This Peru, she is not a land I could care to visit!"

Montpellier's a grand town for walking. It has very broad streets, and many campuses, and from places one can see the deep-blue Mediterranean. And within view, always, are the Alps and the Pyrenees.

We passed the buildings where I was to go next day, and a line of schoolgirls filed past. They eyed Germaine shyly, but all said, "*B'jour!*"—studying her face.

"How amiable!" All the way, she'd clung to my hand, but now that her self was established, by a few simple greetings, she felt able to proceed on her own.

"The girl's story interests me," said Monseigneur Rey, speaking in English. "She's had a hard time, orphaned early, came with an uncle to Marseilles, only to see him fall off a water taxi and drown, leaving her destitute. She found work in a milliner's, you say?"

I was talking to a man, as well as a priest, and was slightly disconcerted. The fact is, my invention was about to dry up. By nearly any standards, Rey was a striking figure, and though his expression remained severe, there was merriment behind his eyes.

For a Frenchman, he was tall and broad, with competent-looking hands. But his gaze was so acute that I began to get more and more rattled.

"Please remember," I said, groping for courage, "that the girl—she's sixteen—has seen such unpleasantness—"

"Her wages as a millinery clerk supported her?"

"Well, no. To send money to her mother and eleven sisters, she constructed a cart—made it with her own hands—and sold candied apples on the side."

"Exceptional!"

"She's certainly out of the common run. But my father directed me to you if I had troubles. He remembers you from functions when he was often here."

Monseigneur Rey leaned back and said, "Your father is a man to remember. What is your interest in this girl? Did you help with the apples?"

"I admire her spirit, of course, and then, truthfully, I may be swayed by her good looks. I noticed them when I first went in the shop. I have a quixotic streak; it strikes on impulse. This girl, sir, has undergone starvation. It doesn't show, exactly—"

"A person of that stripe, if she has beauty as you say, usually takes to the streets in that city. She even runs the risk of being impressed into the life."

And here he looked at me keenly from his gray, intelligent eyes.

The words and look undid everything. I once again fell prey to my childish quirk of blushing.

He waited a minute, then he said, "Suppose you start over, Mr. Morrison. God, you know, has compassion for penitents."

I took a deep breath and launched forth, with some pain. During the account, the monseigneur never changed expression. I finished with a plea that her male parent, also a clergyman, had brought these troubles on her.

When I finished, there was a silence, followed by, "The girl resisted the life? And is ready for the world? Above all—does she regret the past 'forced' on her? Forgive me, but how did you find yourself in the *Marché de Viande?*"

This was harder than I expected, and I was tempted to reply, "By watching the street signs." But I didn't.

I only reddened again and said, "An urchin dragged me in to see the 'sights.' I was there from curiosity." (I was trying to remember the late case of each fallen sparrow, but couldn't remember how it went.)

No answer; still without a clue to progress.

"You say the girl is waiting in the outer room?"

When I agreed, he said, "Bring her in, please."

I fetched my friend of the road, and she curtsied, as I'd taught her to do.

"You may sit down," said the priest. "You wish to enroll in our school; is that correct?"

"Yes, Monseigneur, with all my heart."

(I'd coached her, and so far she was doing splendidly. But I never knew when the bomb might burst.)

"And you feel contrition for all you've done?"

She turned to me. "This contrition, what can it be?"

When I told her, she got up to lean toward the monseigneur's face. "I have no contrition. Nothing was done on purpose. I am sorry to be abused. That is all. I have nothing till I meet Willum."

"Did you have a good, a proper relationship with Guillaume?"

I half-rose from my chair, but he waved me down, smiling.

"The questions are routine; some I regret. And now the decisive inquiry: Do you think you could be happy here, child?"

"Yes. I saw schoolgirls yesterday. Each greeted me as a person. I can be very happy with such arrangement."

"Do you love God?"

"I know nothing of Him," she said stubbornly. "But I bought holy objects for my room. Not to please God, but to spite my father."

Monseigneur Rey rose abruptly, and I saw that the cause was lost. Mlle. Durr had a failing; she told the truth.

The priest told her to wait outside, and I awaited my order to go. But when she'd shut the door, he put both feet on his desk and burst into laughter.

I got up and said, "I expect it *was* a stupid idea. We'll be leaving."

"If you do, you'll cost us a valuable young lady."

He produced a bottle of wine and two glasses from a drawer. "The Church needs persons of spirit. I'll tell you now, that the waxen-faced, overholy nuns and priests—the frightened ones glad to retreat from life—often get on my nerves."

"Then to enroll in school means she must take holy orders later?"

"Not at all. We'll only hope to keep her as long as possible. *Quelqu'une!* When can she start? The term is beginning now." He filled the glasses.

I took out my purse, but he waved me aside. "Uniforms and allowance only. There will be no tuition."

The monseigneur then delivered a valedictory: "The Church is in the business, as it were, of *saving* souls, not turning them away. Your family would be proud of you this day."

"They also might think me a damned fool. I *like* that girl!"

"So I suspected. All the more credit for giving her up. And the same thing, I think, goes for her. Yes, we will find that we need her, if I know people."

Leaving the wicker bag, we walked across the lawn and back, in silence. I could think of nothing to say, and she merely stared at the ground.

"Can you not enroll?" she finally said.

"In an all-girl Catholic school? I expect there'd be no trouble."

"One could always become a priest."

"I don't feel the call. It may come, of course."

"But you will return soon?"

Three girls crossed before us, and again their greeting changed things. At the door, I said, "When I come back, you'll be an honored scholar. You *will* try hard, won't you?"

"I'll try for you. That has been promised."

"Try for yourself."

She looked puzzled, then she smiled and said, "I'll try for both of us."

I bent to touch her cheek to mine, and she clung for a second. Then she disappeared into the building, head and shoulders erect, front and rear, I assumed, fighting to achieve the impossible.

Walking toward the hotel, I felt depressed, wondering about my troubles with females. But the Grand Hôtel du Midi had a known gourmet dining room, and I decided it might improve my mood. There, after a slow start with mussels, I acquired interest with a bottle of Graves, and awaited the *fruits de mer,* specialty of the house. They stressed the usual coquilles St. Jacques, lobster, prawns, sea urchins, and cockles (considered better here than oysters); and there were *haricots verts à la Provençal,* with tomatoes, flavored by garlic and herbs; Arlesian sausage (mystifying me; I'd never seen sea sausage before); and a dessert of *soufflé au chocolat.* I concluded that, to wash this down, and lift my mood further, I needed another bottle of Graves; which the waiter said was suitably "flinty," the best white wine of Bordeaux.

"Would M'sieur, a man of formidable size, like myself, wish a second portion of each?"

I said, "I've eaten all I can eat for two or three days."

"But you will agree that the cockles are outstanding? Say more cockles." He looked disappointed, so I said, "Nothing whatever. I'm fasting for my patron saint."

298

I saw I risked hurting his feelings, so I continued (helped on by the wine), "On reconsideration, I'm allowed cockles. Let the cockles appear, on condition you help me finish the wine."

"Strictly forbidden!"

"Bring 'em on anyhow."

As soon as they arrived, he tossed off a quick glass of wine, glancing about in defiance.

"*Admirable!* M'sieur is a gentleman."

"The gentleman wishes a bill, for he has an urgency for the room."

"I remind you, sir—the second serving of cockles will *not* appear on the *addition*. One also has one's pride!"

I overtipped him and shook his hand when I left. He seemed surprised, but recovered to say, "We of large stature" (he might have been five-foot four) "should eat formidably. The sea urchins—"

On that note I left and hiked for my room. The occasional French was beginning to sound even more familiar. After all, I'd lived nearly a year in this country, and had made several voyages. And there were four years of combat with irregular verbs in college. So—much of what I say here, conversations with others, were occasionally in French and sometimes in English. And from here, I intend to identify neither, only a suggestion or local idiom now and then.

I lay down, tired from my loss and my dinner, and read a badly printed newspaper. But the French lighting defeated me, and I drifted off to sleep. Why the race insisted on fixing a wall lamp eight feet above one's head was beyond comprehension. It still is; the system remains static after all these years.

Chapter XXXVI

When I awoke, I was tempted to call the chambermaid and have a bath, a full one, but I resisted. Betsy did not discourage me. In fact, I felt she sympathized, but a kind of loyalty interfered, as it had with Miss Durr.

I got up and walked the city over, then took a carriage to *la Tour des Pins* (the oldest fortifications) and finally back to the Promenade and my hotel. I'd booked my room for two days, and I made arrangements to rent a bicycle tomorrow. I now meant to visit the *small* town I liked best in France.

Sète—eighteen miles distant. Unknown to tourists, crisscrossed with canals like Venice, the main port for Spanish commerce, and a prime love of all my family, who knew it as a peaceful rest near the wine country.

I was off before dawn, after coffee and the croissant I'd asked for, not long out of the oven. Pedaling the white road past a sign saying "Sète—30 km," I saw men, and women, already out on bicycles, the men going to work, the women hoping to seize the best offered in the market.

The bicycle provided by the hotel proved defective in all essentials. (The invention being a recent one, I expected breakdowns.) The chain slipped, the seat had no spring, and the brake succumbed with a sigh. Had it not been for the strong *mistral* at my back, I might not have made it.

Dawn suddenly flamed like a red rose opening, the countryside was green, the nearly purple sea lay to my left, and I thought what a fine world it was. No one alive knew where I was, a universally soothing feeling. Still, it had small effect on the occasional persons I passed. Frenchmen have politeness, certainly, but it swings with the time of day. Before dinner (lunch) the "B'jour" is given grudgingly; after lunch (with a carafe of wine) they'd lend you their wives. But both men and women work, and work hard.

I rolled into Sète, the bicycle sending up alarms, and headed for an old friend. It had been five years, and I was dubious about recognition. He was alone in the back of his mechanics shop. But he dropped a wrench (and a bicycle with it) and stared.

"William! My God, how you've grown!"

"How goes it, Marcel?" We embraced in the style that always embarrassed me.

"Where is your family, *amigo?*"

"I'm alone, and need help."

He promptly pulled down his iron shutter, hung out *"Fermé,"* and said, "Will we need guns?"

"It's not that kind of trouble. This cycle"—I indicated the tangle of wire I'd been riding—"is ripe for a junkheap, but it belongs to a Montpellier hotel. I'd like to rent another, if possible. Now what do you say?"

He thought a minute, then asked where I was going. When I answered, causing him wonder, though he didn't pursue it, he said, "You will require an Ajax, the newest and best of a bad lot so far. I myself"—pointing a finger at the sky—"am producing a bicycle to bring pride to France! Veritably!"

Then he knocked most of this down by saying it ought to be ready in two or three years.

He wheeled a bicycle out of a rack.

"Secondhand?"

"It belongs to *le maire,* who takes himself and family a journey to Paris. To study the sewers." He changed color. "On my money, taxes money. *I* should see the sewers of Paris, is it not?"

"I can think of better recreations."

"Recreation!—the *canaille!*" Marcel had a touchy temper reserved for fellow townsmen. All foreigners, to him, were superior.

"Won't he come back and raise the devil?"

"He goes for three weeks, the crooked— *All* politicians!"

"This bike has a basket. Perfect! I'll take it. Now, begging another favor, but could you mend my atrocity, in some degree?"

He bent over to inspect, "The brake I think, yes." He got a wrench and new bearing, and in two or three minutes it worked perfectly, or as well as it could.

"*SolutiON!* As to the rest"—he waggled his head from side to side —"*comme çi, comme ça.* Plainly it needs a new seat—"

"Put it on, if you have time. The chain slips, too. I know you're busy, but do what you can. I'll pay, of course, and pass the bill on to the hotel. Pad it as much as you can."

He walked me to the door. "You go to the open market?"

"I need a picnic, and time to think."

He waggled his head again. "These 'thinkings'—I have never understood. If I stopped to *think*, I'd lodge a bullet in my head."

"I hope not, my friend."

As I started off, only a little bumpily, he cried, "I forget! We have a bad incoming of the swine called gypsies. Priests and professors tell me there is good in all. There is none in gypsies. They are wicked, and have not a desire to change. Also, they are dangerous. No, I cannot permit you to traverse that lonely, desolate road, this time of year."

"I must go; it is necessary. I have much thinking—"

"The police push them on, after the search for weapons. They have no guns, but they find other tools to use on alone persons. All are cowards! . . . *SolutiON!*" he cried again. He darted into the shop and came back with a good, stout, ordinary slingshot.

"I make it for my son—legitimate! Take a pocketful of steel bearings," filling my hands. "In this way, you can defy *groups* of gypsies."

"I'll be back in three hours."

Sète is built on silt, as much a water as a land domain, Thau being the principal harbor area. I passed the Grand Hôtel (if there's a town in France without its Grand Hôtel, I have yet to find it. There's even one, as a joke, in the Marseilles Meat Market). The Grand Hôtel Sète is where my family stayed, before my mother pleaded off voyaging.

Nothing had changed. "The food," Marcel later told me with a shrug, "is conceivably improved, but—" he was unable to think of a suitable adjective to cover the rest."

I pushed the Ajax up St. Clair Hill to the Sailors' Cemetery for the view across the Mediterranean that I fancied in my youth. But now it was only a low-lying bank of clouds.

Then I fixed my mind on the reason I came—nostalgia. The

market was now abustle with housewives, and there were many quarrels. Almost every vegetable and fruit—lentils, cauliflower, onions, garlic, African oranges, melons, and, in particular, grapes— were on display. These, to the owners' protests, were being squeezed, held to the ear and weighed with suspicion. But I knew what I wanted and bought a two-foot new loaf of bread, still warm, apricot jam, half a foot of sausage *(très piquant)*, a Camembert that I pressed for softness (having my hand slapped), a melon, a paper of sweet butter, *pâté*, and, while this was enough and more, I was unable to resist a large wedge of Brie, ripe and fragrant. One seldom saw this cheese at home. I added two bottles of table wine whose color I liked (thirty centimes) and was ready to go.

Between Sète and Agde, beside an old Roman road, stretches one of the finest beaches in the world, eight miles long, bordered by low dunes, with reedy, defiant marshes on my right. To this day, I had never seen a human on either the beach or the road, a new highway cutting it off.

Pedaling along slowly on this miracle of privacy, I thought I'd seldom been so happy before. Halfway to Agde—*"La Ville Noire,"* from the dark basalt from which it is built—I found a cut through the dunes and wheeled my Ajax in to lean it against the sand. Then I sat down, the sea thirty yards distant and the bright sun overhead, and opened a bottle of wine with my Swiss knife.

Rosé is the least esteemed of the French wines, but this seemed easily the best. Suddenly I was starving. I covered each piece of torn-off bread with *pâté*, butter and jam; ate the *piquant*, ate half the Camembert and all the Brie, holding each bite as long as possible, for the almost-forgotten flavor; then I cut into the melon.

Besides feeling full, now, I'd forgotten I was supposed to continue thinking. Seeing Mr. Bennett's trade as unsuitable, I tried to assay my skills, if any. In those years, I recall, twenty-one was a mature age, and women were old at forty. It occurred to me that I'd clung too long to childhood.

At one time or another, my male parent had arranged my instruction in boxing, wrestling, celestial navigation (a failure), and horsemanship by a man who gave up in two weeks, saying, "The boy not only dislikes horses individually but in groups." Then came a famous marksman (who only shrugged) and, supremely above all, an authentically famous Italian fencing master, who taught foil, épée and saber.

I liked this sport, but when the protective button fell off and I ran him through the shoulder, he threatened to sue. He was pacified with money and returned to his native land, wearing a small new hole. It's immodest, but I became so skilled in épée that I won the New England championship, provoking only a sardonic and rather hurtful look from my father, who'd paid the bills.

When my food was finished (or all I could eat), I stripped off and, disregarding the old warning about swimming after meals, crept into the sea. It was bitterly cold, but it was a champion way to remove melon juice.

I pushed out waist-deep, dove in three or four times, freezing, and was surprised at the absence of stomach cramps. I put the old saw in a class like tossing spilled salt over one's shoulder.

After wading back to my clothes, a warm glow returning, I heard, "*Hombre,* have you got a few francs? We need them badly."

He was black-haired and ugly, and spoke in the most offensive accent I ever heard.

Two gypsy caravans stood in the road, and this man approached from my right; another walked up from the left. Both carried long, heavy whips. Several women, and girls, were climbing across the dunes, dressed in flamboyant and filthy clothes, with bandannas around their heads.

My slingshot was in my clothes, and one pocket was filled with bearings the size of marbles. Loading up, I viewed the encounter as amusing. From childhood, a hobby had been making and shooting slingshots, having been denied a B.B. gun after removing a stained glass window from the Methodist Church. (I could have done a better job with a slingshot but didn't say so.)

"What's the whip for?" I asked the nearest, and ugliest, of the clan.

"*Hombre,* we will need some francs. Don't make trouble."

I said, "Toss your identification onto the sand. My charities are for a purpose."

"To goddamn hell with your stinking identifications! *Y ching' su madre!* Turn over three francs!"

I said, "Here comes the first one," and hit him in the pit of the stomach. He looked stupified, and sat down, rocking back and forth, clutching his middle. He really had been hit very hard.

Then I heard the crack of a twelve-foot whip behind me, and wheeled to see the other coming on fast. By now, my temper had risen, and I aimed for his forehead. I missed, I believe, for he dropped his whip and put both hands to his face. I had reason to believe I'd struck his right cheekbone. Since he sank down, groaning, I turned my attention again to the chieftain, or, as he was known, the king. He was struggling to get up, helped by a stream of obscenity.

Drawing more lightly, for I had no real wish to kill him, I said,

"Cochon, here's another," and hit him in the throat. Startled, I thought I *had* killed him here, for he lay prone, with horrid gasps for air.

With two down, I had a quick look at the women. The fattest, and dirtiest, was wheeling my bicycle toward the caravans; and this round gave me more satisfaction than the others combined. Selecting an enormous right buttock, as being nearest, I hit her as hard as Marcel's "legitimate" weapon could manage. She dropped the wheel, grabbed the injured member, and turning, made the men's speech sound like children reciting their A.B.C.'s.

The other women and girls headed slanting down the dunes, so I got between them and the caravans. Unhitching the horses, I gave each a whack with a stick. They broke into a grudging shamble, one kicking at me first, and after saying to myself, "Like master, like horse," I sped them on with a few well-placed pellets. I continued till they were nearly out of sight.

Then, thoroughly vengeful, for I'd ridden down here for peace, I searched the marsh for a stouter club and knocked out the spokes of all rear wheels. I opened the rear caravan, stirred some debris, and found a big new bronze propeller. Carefully covering it, I rejoiced that the police had something to go on, now.

The band had gathered on a dune, watching. When I reached for a bearing, all dropped in an instant. But these people—everywhere despised, and with reason, called by English reference books "the lowest breed on the Continent"—these people had chosen a rough life, and the king (partially recovered) got up, holding a handkerchief high.

He said, *"Señor"*—I was *"Señor,"* now, not *"hombre"*—"I have a most shapeful daughter; she make *chingue* with you—five francs."

He said something in a low voice, and a girl of twelve or thirteen stepped forward and slipped out of her single garment. She *was* "shapeful," and filthy as the rest.

"Tell her to take soap, wade into the water, and scrub till she shines."

"Señor, we nearly winter; this water kill my Angelica to death!"

I fitted a bearing into the leather, there was a babble of protests, and the girl walked wailing into the shallows. She could scarcely have had any soap, and had possibly never known soap since she was born.

"All over!" I yelled, proceeding forward. Hereupon the king waded out in his clothes, dunked the girl several times, and the women rubbed her with sand and grass.

305

"Once more for the hair."

They sanded her hair, the miserable creature, then rinsed it several times.

"She ready now, *señor*. Throw up the moneys."

"First send down the girl. *Ven acá!*"

After a consultation, she walked toward me, angry and sullen.

I said, *"Sonría, por favor,"* and she made a poor effort to smile. When I waved her to stop, about ten feet away, I looked her over. Everything was there, all right, in ample proportion.

"Now, go back and tell the others to scrub up, too."

She spat in my face, and when she turned to run, the sun glinted on a knife she'd held behind her. Doubtless she would have gone through her familiar act if I'd thrown the money down first.

The band retreated down the beach. Then I finished dressing, facing them, and relieved myself as an impudent gesture (with some difficulty) provoking a few "ohs!" and "ahs!"

Now, mounting Ajax, I called, *"Adiós, cabrones y ladrones!* A pleasant journey! You have more need of horses and spokes than francs!"

Their orchestration of oaths, threats and permanent curses was almost pleasant, like a bad symphony tuning up. I waved and left, but I remembered that, in a sense, they'd won a small triumph. My second bottle of wine had been left behind.

I reflected that, over the generations, nothing had changed about the scum. My mother, being softhearted, would consent to watch them mend pots and pans in front, while others were stealing pies and cakes from the rear windows. But I thought about the girl, too, as I pedaled back toward Sète.

"The caravans are immobile?" said Marcel, "and they hide a new propeller? I know where it comes from. Now the police can move— wait here. The station is around the corner."

When he got back, he said, "Five horse police are on the way. *Amigo,* you have performed a service for Sète!"

"What will happen?"

"They will be taken on to Agde and put to work on the road. And do they care? No. They are fed, they will put their women to use, and in the end mend the caravans."

I thought again of the girl.

"Isn't there one—just one—with a spot of decency?"

"Not one," he said cheerfully. "And here's your bike, fully mended. Behold the new seat."

"And I," I replied, "hand over the mayor's Ajax, a trifle sandy. How much do I owe?"

"Not a sou. No, I refuse. The town will take up a collection."

"You will always be a friend, Marcel," and we again embraced in the way I disliked. "I'm off, then. Back in a few weeks, I hope."

"*Adiós, mon ami.* You have made the day bright. As to the collection—"

"Adiós," I called over my shoulder.

The Montpellier hotel bought me a train ticket for Bordeaux, first class—uncommon in Europe—and I left, with exchanges of felicity, at eight-thirty in the morning.

Sète had a canal—the Canal du Midi—that ran to Bordeaux, but transportation was slow and, besides, I'd had enough barge life on the Erie.

Our route to was to Béziers to Narbonne to Carcassonne and Toulouse; there to change trains, and on to Bordeaux, a total of about 300 miles. A wine festival was under way in either Béziers or Narbonne, and the train was crowded; I had my ticket stamped five times. Usually, my first-class compartment would have assured some privacy, but shortly after we rolled out, it filled—four facing four— with people I felt had neither first-class tickets nor any means for buying them. The wine festival, a uniformed guard said, made a shifting of classes "acceptable, and *pourboires* more moral." (I stupidly gave him one, though I was being deprived.) "After all, m'sieur," he said, "the passengers must sit somewhere."

The trip was generally an ordeal, if one discounted the clean French countryside, with its rows of poplars, faultless highways, streams, and (unlike rural America) front yards free of old bed-springs, broken crockery, retired mattresses, and busted-out harrows.

Our seats were well padded, and starting at about noon, my group began producing wine bottles in anticipation of the large meal at two or two-thirty.

The train had neither dining car nor sleepers, but it stopped for a thirty-minute meal, which was excellent, varied, and cooked as only the French know how.

Sleeping provisions were less satisfactory. For motives known only to the railroad heads, the conductor locked all compartments at nine P.M. And since the cars had no water or toilets, I began to feel more genial toward Commodore Vanderbilt. A man told me compartments in other classes were not locked and that ours could be, and were, easily pried open.

"It is expected," he said. "A ride like that. People are not horses, you know."

I was tempted to except railroad officials, but ours were so

307

courteous, on this level, that I laid the nuisance down to everyday French red tape, inspired from the top. It may clear up someday, this paper chase of the French, but I doubt it.

We passed through Béziers, where the annual wine festival was booming, besides three fairs. Striped tents were visible in the distance, along the Orb, and the streets, lined with chestnuts, looked washed and trim. I thought it a strange amusement, these wine festivals, and wondered who paid the bills, the French being notably penurious.

We lost passengers here, including three from our compartment, but it made no difference. All families had been sedate, polite, and generous with wine and food, and while I had fewer seatmates, now, I was sorry, for I'd been practicing my French on anyone willing to chat.

The only other large town I remember (for I slept off and on) was Carcassonne—founded by the Romans in the first century B.C. I climbed down to the platform from which the crumbling Old Town could be seen, and wished I had time to explore. But it was looked on with small attention then. Later it was restored in sympathy with its medieval form. Our stop was near the Aude (which would have been called a creek back home) at the Hôtel Terminus, and I was privileged to watch an extraordinary feat of water transport.

A small, low bridge stood here, and down came one of those barges that house a family, cruising Europe's river-and-canal network. The boat's stern cabin was several feet higher than the bridge, and the housewife had, besides, two stakes erected, fore and aft. Here her laundry whipped and snapped in the breeze.

"All right," I said to myself, "this is where we smash up a barge and a bridge together; it should be interesting to watch."

But as the barge neared its obstacle, two boys ran out with poles, stopping the craft, and young and old went to work. Each cabin component—sides, roof, even the wheel and other units—were fixed on brass hinges, and within five minutes this barge was as flat as a raft, and the laundry not neglected. All slid smoothly under the bridge, with six inches clearance. Then, on the other side, it was reassembled in three or four minutes (and the laundry went back up). The barge looked like a barge again; the family thereupon varnished everything removed (a trademark of caste) and it proceeded on its way.

I boarded the train, realizing I'd seen something rare. Then I further learned that my night train, much superior, would be at Toulouse, and that first-class passage was respected. Moreover, the door was not locked, and one was at liberty to smoke.

Between trains, I had time (at twilight) to walk and peer at the famous pink houses of Toulouse, the stone having come from a pink quarry now forgotten; and, back on my train, had a single gentleman in the compartment. He wore a tall hat and other black garments.

We sat avoiding each other's glances until I began a conversation in which he announced himself as a mortician "of the first class"—on an assignment. From then I had a whim of suspecting an odor of formaldehyde, and I lit a cigar.

He leaned forward to say, "M'sieur, I must beg you not to smoke. I suffer from quinzy throat."

Either I didn't like him or his profession; certainly I cared little for his protest, for I said, *"Mon ami,* you'll understand that these are medical cigars. I have a heart laboring on one valve. Deprived of the cigars it would stop abruptly. It will fail soon notwithstanding."

"Your state is fatal?" the vulture replied, measuring with his eyes. Doubtless he took account of an expensive suit I wore, anticipating high-flown, alerted friends.

"I hope to get through the night. Each day is thus depressing."

His demeanor changed on the instant, he said, "M'sieur will kindly accept my card, but allow me to express the highest hopes."

I was baffled how to take this, whether for him or for me. But I bowed, looking morbidly grateful. And in the morning, when I awoke in Bordeaux, he was gone. I think my robust snores diminished his "hopes," together with the fact that, needing exercise (before he went to sleep), I chinned myself ten times on the luggage rack.

Chapter XXXVII

Arrived in Bordeaux, settled at the Grand Hôtel Médoc, I dug in and applied myself for ten days to the purpose of my trip. I spent hours at the *Syndicat d'Initiative* (Chamber of Commerce), discussing with the serious, learned men there all aspects of wine and viniculture. They were courteous, even mentioning local vineyards of peculiar interest. For not *all* of Bordeaux has perfect soil, and a sun angle that makes the region famous.

I visited outstanding vineyards, notebook in hand, and acquired a variety of advice.

In a "wine library," I studied most everything printed on the subject. And at last, I felt (rather shyly) ready to visit the first of my father's friends. I sent a note to the Vicomte de Brionne-Bouscard introducing myself, and asked permission to call. Two hours later, the hall porter informed me a gentleman awaited me in the foyer. He looked impressed.

A man remindful of Gervais Lockridge approached, apologizing for his "informality," and identified himself as the vicomte.

I confess to a certain sinking of spirit. He was wearing well-used boots, shiny corduroy riding pants, and a Norfolk jacket, whose best days, I figured, were at Oxford or Cambridge, for many upper-class

French then went to those universities. Also, I noticed, he carried a stick to offset a slight limp of the right leg.

But he looked cheerful, like Lockridge, and said, "I received your father's letter and yours as well. Frankly," he went on, "I came because I wanted a talk before the Château Brionne-Bouscard rose emptily into view."

His words were certainly puzzling, but his manner was so charming that I shook his hand with warmth.

"My trap is tied outside. We can put your luggage in ourselves."

I was anxious to bring matters to a head, and said, smiling, "The hotel has *porteurs*," and I waved one toward the two heavy bags.

My host's face clouded over, and he said, ruefully, "I'm afraid our credit at the Grand Hôtel is depleted, and I didn't think to bring money."

"I have money," I said shortly, and, outside, tossed the porter two coins.

The trap and horse were a counterpart of their owner, if he was the owner, and I shared the late mortician's optimism that the horse would not fall in its shafts during the eight miles south.

"I can see you're disappointed," he said when we had gone a mile or so. "And I understand. This is not the sort of story one tells strangers, but your father, when he bought wine here, performed such services for this vineyard, and its owners then, that I feel we can be friends—"

"We're friends. What shall I call you?"

"My name is Gérard. Call me by that, if you can."

"Technically, William. Bill's clumsy and stuffy; it sounds like a circus performer. But make it 'Bill'; it's the best I can offer."

"Well, then, our plight is this. But above all, be assured that our grapes produce great white wines. We, alone in Graves, won the government seal of 'Grand Cru' last year. Graves, as you know, is the Bordeaux district for white wine; the word means 'gravel' in your tongue. It has to do with the soil, of course. The rest of Bordeaux's wine country, mainly north from the city, raises red-claret grapes that Frace thinks incomparable."

"And your trouble, if you don't mind going on?" I said, determined to know why a château's great vineyard left its people destitute.

"Yes, I strayed from the subject. The trouble, I'm afraid, started with my father, an—ingrained, in—?"

"Inveterate?"

"Odd, I went to school in England, but much slips back. Inveterate, to be sure. I remember now. An inveterate gambler. But

311

'diseased' would be better. He lost most of our money; then he began to mortgage the château, little by little, to a man—a neighbor—named Gruner. He calls himself a baron. I suspect he consistently cheated, but we had no real proof and wished to avoid an open scandal. I was not much more than a boy, then, and my mother and sisters and I sadly watched Brionne-Bouscard in effect pass from our hands."

"You no longer own it?"

"Oh, yes, and its income is ample in good wine years, but part of the money's for keeping my father on the Riviera, and nearly all the rest goes for mortgage payments. To the odious Gruner. He's a thief and blackguard, whose place lies just out of sight. He fleeced some of my father's friends as well."

For a moment, his eyes flashed fire. Subsiding, he said, "We do what we can; our share is bare subsistence by now. My wife sells off objects of art, piece by piece, so that we keep up appearances and have friends—sympathetic friends—in occasionally."

I asked carefully, "How large is your mortgage by now?"

He flushed; then he named a considerable sum by French standards, but, with the exchange, far less by American.

The country was covered with staked-up grapevines, with poplars and fruit trees in the background. Then we came at last, the horse stumbling, to a lane that ran between planted grapes until there burst into view—"burst" was the only word—a château typically French—huge, more cheerful than most, asymmetrical as succeeding generations had added wings. There were the usual battlements, turrets, gargoyles, mullioned windows and many entrances. In short, everything in accord, so far as my experience went.

"Hideous, isn't it?" remarked my host as we entered an area of rolling lawns, nonreligious statuary and, thank God, no sign of topiary foliage. As if reading my thoughts, he said, "My father, a man of uniquely bad taste, once had five meter boxwoods representing all pieces of a chessboard. When he left, we trimmed them to miniatures, and one day we dug them up altogether. They made a grand picnic fire, the only occasion when we enjoyed them."

I murmured something about the place's imposing look, and he said, "To be sure, French châteaux are eye-catching, but one gets bored merely staring at the size. Not to speak of the upkeep."

Then I noticed that a clear stream wound its way out of a little wood and passed between two wings of the house. The effect, closer, was charming, and I exclaimed.

"Oh, yes. The dividing stream makes it worthwhile, somehow. One can sit on the stream bank under a skylit roof. I've never been certain why that's desirable."

"It reminds one, of course, of Chenonceaux—"

"Then you've seen the Orléans exhibits? Now I'd like the truth: have you ever come across anything so grotesquely awful as Chambord?"

I protested, "Half the architecture was added slapdash—from native French to Greek to Roman to Gothic to Byzantine and on to the onion domes of Russia. And probably some in between. No, I find it fascinating; to answer you truthfully."

The vicomte sighed. "I thought you might see it that way. I've never been in agreement on this matter; I've had some lively arguments here and there."

"And Chenonceaux?" I asked gently.

He shrugged. "The water goes *round* it, ours comes *through* the house. Chenonceaux has a certain something. I only hope Diane de Poitiers was worth it."

I smiled to myself, finally understanding.

"Monsieur de Brionne—"

"Gérard."

"It's not easy to ask, on this acquaintance. But would you be willing to sell, let someone else pay the mortgage, and move, say, to Paris?"

He nearly exploded with French idioms unknown to me, a fact that I regretted. "I would die first. My family have held the Château Brionne-Bouscard since the fifteenth century." He stopped, looked at me and laughed. "I see. You saw through me easily, didn't you?"

"Well—"

He continued. "Like all French châteaux, it was originally built for defense. Now these big houses are divided into two species—the *château fort* and the *château de plaisance*, the latter meaning it's been converted to be a residence. The former is merely an object of curiosity. One which the tourist pays to see."

During the explanation, he'd driven round and round the great oval that passed the doorsteps, while a footman in frayed livery stood patiently in the entrance, prepared for anything, I thought. I was surprised to see that he was colored, and learned that the elder de Brionne had hired him in New Orleans.

As to the horse, it took the extended route badly, with a baleful look over its shoulder, then some gratuitous stumbles, and, at last, a display no one could misinterpret.

"—In your Orléans country of châteaux, only one—Langeais—is still preserved as a perfect example of the *château fort*, with its tenth-century keep, and thirteenth-century walls. But I see we're holding things up, especially the horse. He's ready for the knacker, poor fellow, but I have nothing with which to replace him.

"Where's everybody, Alphonse?" he asked the footman, who stepped forward with alacrity, despite his age.

"In the fields, suh, lookin' over them women pickin'."

(I should say that the grapes of Bordeaux were picked by women of the villages. It was, mainly, a fiesta, with laughter and chattering. The system was to slice off grapes in bunches and throw them in a basket. The women wore skirts pulled up and pinned by the back for freer movement, and they wore, too, *fichus* against the broiling sun here. There were women of seventy-five and young ones given to rough-and-tumble. Even the small children were encouraged to pick. The baskets were dumped into containers—*gerles* [I know of no English translation] and transferred by men into wagons drawn by red oxen, ready to head for the press. Unlike the women, these men were serious; though tolerant of the chattering women, they seldom spoke a word.)

"I'm glad the family's out," said de Brionne. "I can show you the house without contradiction. For one generally unopinionated, I come in for a lot of criticism. Would you believe that?"

I said, "No!", incredulous.

We entered a gigantic hall with a single table but no carpets on the floor.

"Fake," said de Brionne, tapping the table with his crop. "Sold to pay bills. Imitation all the way through."

The table, heavy, inlaid with mother-of-pearl, was so obviously a piece from one of the early Louis that I prepared myself for a bizarre tour of inspection.

"See those tapestries?" —pointing to the wall. "Got them for a song. Originals gone long ago. There's not a figure that has the smallest connection with our family."

On the contrary, I thought, no single figure lacked a resemblance to my host.

The place was certainly bone-bare, but the pieces that remained would, I thought, have come close to the amount due Mr. Gruner.

De Brionne did his best work in the portrait gallery. We strolled down the line of family likenesses while he explained.

"See this?—the local postmaster. My daughter Jeannette did him; cost me five francs for the frame. My great-great-great grandfather once hung in that space, and I believe he actually *was* hung, during a Spanish war.

"After such a historic past, I naturally persuaded the girl to replace each painting sold, doing the best she could." And then, walking on: "Garbage hauler; chimney sweep's son—I like that one; Madame Fous, proprietress of a Bordeaux whorehouse; deathmask of a rapist—Jeannette had only fifteen minutes after the guillotine, but she sketched what was left in charcoal, then managed to paint the eyes open—"

The main trouble with these, again, was that all were facially similar to de Brionne, even to the madame. But he was having a wonderful time, probably his first in weeks, and I let him ramble on.

"This last one," he said, "I consider the only perfectly executed head in the lot—Charles the First. Now, I suggest we go past the minstrels' gallery and on to other rooms."

These last, to my sorrow, were entirely denuded of enrichments— eight reception rooms altogether. I began to wonder whether de Brionne was a lunatic, himself responsible for the château's low estate. But as if he'd read my mind, again, he said, "I was only a boy, but I recall your father's visits well. We played practical jokes on each other, and sometimes my father joined. That was before the gambling."

He looked at me shyly to see if I was offended by his fun; then he said, "Let's visit my *retraite particulière*. It at least gives the illusion of life."

It was a beautiful room with very old furniture—but a man's antiques—and the floor-to-ceiling bookshelves, with ladder to reach, were crowded with classics in red leather. Here his gravity revived, and he stopped at Voltaire and said, "All front; you can buy these in any *atelier;* rows of spines, as I believe they call them."

I went over and pulled out *Candide*.

I said, "An interesting spine. It looks almost like a book."

"You remind me of your father," he said, sitting down at his desk and waving me to a seat with cracked leather cushions. "You'll have to forgive me, but I couldn't resist testing you out. Besides having some sport. Things are not frolicsome here anymore. But you are a family son, I find. I'll try to make it up before the others come."

He pulled a bellcord, and the footman-butler-porter answered smartly.

"Monsieur de Brionne, I heered you talking foolery with this young gen'lman, a guest in your house, too. Now Miss Rachel, she put her foot down about that; you know the truth."

"Alphonse, you're a bore. You've also developed into something of a sneak—"

"Sneak or not, Miss Rachel keep Château Brionne-Bouscard serious, like others. I'm obliged to tell her on you. *Charles the First!* That there's your great-uncle Jacques. I got me some pride even if you ain't."

De Brionne languidly waved him away. "Bring us, properly chilled, a bottle of the '41. And don't waste time about it."

"That's serious, more like for company. But I ain't movin' till you promise to quit skylarkin' Mr. Morripson. And his father been here, too! Shame!"

"You have five minutes, Alphonse, and then I turn loose the wolfhounds."

The darky chuckled, but he made a leap for the door, and was back almost immediately. He was twirling briskly a bottle in a silver bucket. It was astonishing wine.

"Do you get the flintiness that good white wines must have?"

I'd heard this so often, I had trouble keeping my face straight. "I get it all right."

There was a bustle outside, and de Brionne said, "The tribe's arrived. Let's get this down fast." He sighed. "Pity to do it that way, but there's no avoiding it, I suppose. In any case, the wine should help."

Despite our refreshment, I began to feel depressed, expecting (with him) that the female contingent of the Château Brionne-Bouscard was a collection of gorgons. Some garments were added to ours on the hallway table, I noticed. We passed through several empty rooms, and at a door done in red-and-green Chinese laquer—the effect was superb—de Brionne stopped, straightened his clothes, and pushed on in.

It was a small, nearly normal-sized drawing room, handsomely done in every detail. Madame de Brionne, it was clear, had fought for one bright sanctuary as the cold castle gave up its treasures. A fire crackled on the hearth, and before I could emerge from my stupor, an exceedingly chic woman of about thirty-five came forward and gave me her hand.

"Since Gérard seems stricken dumb, I'll introduce our daughters."

Jeannette, the portrait-painter, including the guillotined head, was about eight; two others were younger, and the remaining two, of perhaps fifteen and seventeen, were striking. The eldest had a singular kind of beauty, almost blue-black hair, deep blue eyes, skin tanned, and a slim, full figure. The tan had come from riding (hatless)—her principal interest—but her real oddity lay in the fact that as she appraised one, she made me, for instance, feel like a schoolboy. I was irked. I felt she had studied me, found me of no account, and dismissed me. I, on the other hand, thought her one of the most stunning persons—girl or woman—I'd ever seen.

I was told their names, of course, and forgot them promptly—except for the critic, who was called Renée. All of these people were brunet, but the equestrienne was by several shades the darkest.

Something was wrong in the room; it was palpable in the air, and while Madame de Brionne made herself agreeable, Gérard, for his part, sprawled on a brocade sofa, watching her. Then suddenly

Renée's nearest sister burst into tears. I was painfully fussed.

My hostess frowned, as if at a loss. Then she said, briskly, "I'm told others of your family have visited here, and have been of help to the de Brionnes. That, monsieur, enfolds you into our family, by custom. I see you are bewildered."

"I told him all, or nearly all," said de Brionne from the sofa.

"Did you tell him," she said sharply, "that the lawn figures, by famous sculptors of history, are going tomorrow?"

"Gruner insists on that Friday payment. What else could I do? Sell one of the children?"

"There's that possibility," she snapped. "We'll go into it later. The truth is, Gérard," she said, approaching the sofa, "that you've gone soft as flan. A *man* would have made a stand, figured a solution, long before now, scandal or no scandal. The Château Brionne-Bouscard will leave us forever unless something is done." She turned to me. "You have seen this vacant shell? You've wondered, no doubt."

"Your room is beautiful, madame," I told her lamely.

"And we produce the finest white wines in France. But the income goes to the cad, Gruner. And, of course, to support the donkey de Brionne on the Riviera."

"Others have lost châteaux, Rachel, and for similar reasons. But it won't be lost. Take my word—murder will be done first. I've thought it out; the charge will be manslaughter."

"Yes, you can resolve the dilemma by sitting in a French prison. Where do we sit in the meantime? On the curbstone? A mortgage is legal, not so easily disposed of. Gruner, by the way, has invited himself to dinner Friday week. He has what he calls a 'proposition.' This is Monday; that leaves nearly two weeks. I'm sure you will have solved things by then." (But her face belied her words.)

"It's quite possible, madame," I told her, struggling for a silver lining. "People sometimes turn compliant. I'm anxious to meet Baron Gruner. Perhaps *I* can persuade him, somehow."

The old story—an eccentric girl, a challenge, a faint hint of violence—and none of it my affair. I furtively glanced at the girl, ready but not eager for her contempt. To my surprise, the deep blue eyes had turned almost to violet; I wondered what it meant.

"You're a good young man," said my hostess, taking my hands. "You are like your father, ever ready to help, I suspect. Well, you must put it out of your mind, and take our apologies for this breach of good manners."

I smiled. "You have forgotten, madame. I'm now a member of the family. In such an arrangement, your problems have become my problems."

She put both hands to her face and turned away; and a servant came in to announce that dinner was served.

"So few people know about wine, and so many pose as if they do," said de Brionne, as we walked down the rows of vineyards. "To start off, Bordeaux includes about half a million acres, surrounding the city, which is sixty miles from the sea, separated by the Garonne. Once, believe it or not, Bordeaux belonged to England, when King Henry II married Eleanor of Aquitaine, in 1152. She gave it to him as a dowry. Silly thing to do—she could have used money instead; God knows she had plenty. Anyhow, we eventually got the land back; that's the important thing."

I looked around. Between all the rows were women pickers from the villages, bent over, skirts (and other garments) pinned up behind, with no thought of modesty. It made an odd sight, as if a clinic had arrived for medical inspection. I tried, without success, to look elsewhere.

"They're known as *vendangeuses*," said de Brionne. "The *vignerons*, the men, load the grapes and tend them at the *pressoir*. As you note, the women are boisterous, the men solemn. They take the full *gerles*, pass a wood rod through the handles and gently rock them into the wagons. The *vignerons* are directed by André, with the gray beard and the hawk's eye. He stands on the front wagon—the *chef de culture*.

"I, of course, am the *Maître*, and in any decision, my word is law. Also, I pay the pickers each day. At the moment, we have twenty women and have kept most for years. I know the name of each. We approach," he went on, "a ritual time of day. The chattering ceases, I gather the pickers atop that little hill. By custom, I plant my cane in the earth, and they circle around. All noise stops, and I confess I enjoy my little moment of triumph. Usually the château's windows and slate roof reflect the setting sun, and I feel, indeed, proprietor of my *domaine*.

"I call each by name—*tutoy*ing them. Should I see one on the street, she would be '*Vous*,' of course. Again, I say, everything is done by a custom of generations. As to the women, I'm apt to chaff a bit with ones who have been lazy that day.

"Each recipient, handed her pay, says '*Merci, M'sieur le Vicomte,*' and always I throw an affectionate handful of sous to children too small to work. Also, I enjoy causing an occasional embarrassment. Only yesterday, to a beautiful young girl, I said, '*Sois bien sage, petite; vertu passe beauté.*'

"But she's a bright spirit, and replies, '*Oui, m'sieur, mais il vaudrait mieux les deux!*'

"Then, when everyone's paid, I ask, *'Tout le monde est content?'* There's a heartwarming chorus of thanks, and the day's picking is done.

"What makes great wine? Well, it's a combination of factors. Gravelly soil, which reflects the sun's warmth by day and holds it during the night; the sun itself; bland weather, and, of course, the way the grapes are grown and handled. If we climbed that higher hill, we could see the Garonne. The people of Bordeaux, all Frenchmen, think the soil near a river is finest for wine. Or, as they say, 'If the grapes can see the river, they are good.'

"We live in the district of Graves, which is suited for white grapes, especially. The components to be crushed—by many feet in a huge vat—are the skin, the pulp, the stems and the seeds. To a stranger it appears odd that white wine can be made from red grapes, while the reverse is not true. A wine's color is produced by the skin, and if we used red grapes, we could take care to remove the skins quickly; otherwise a white wine is said to have *'tache,'* meaning 'stain'—it has a brownish color.

"Then the juice goes into oak casks to await fermentation—about two months in the case of white wine—and the 'young' or 'free-run' wine is afterward put in smaller casks to age. Once, all of Bordeaux's red wines were aged for fifteen years; now, well, maybe a little less. Whether we've done a good job, or had a good year, depends mostly on weather and hard work.

"Enough for one day, *mon ami?*"

I said, "I'm here to learn about the art of making fine wine, and I'll take notes till your patience wears out."

De Brionne, with a pooh-poohing motion of his hands, said he could talk happily about wine all day and, by now, would rather talk about it than make it.

"Still, I'd rather drink it than either, you know. We'll resume soon, if that's agreeable" —he looked at his watch. "But the time has arrived to give the pickers their *paie.*"

I watched him limp up a hill, using his ivory stick in a way not to attract notice, and wondered in which of Europe's blundering wars he'd been wounded.

He assumed his stance, and the setting sun *did* strike the leaded windows and varied roofs of the château splendidly, firing rich glints in every direction. I began to grasp his affection for both his home and his calling. The giggling *vendangeuses* clustered round him, he began calling out names and permitted himself a two-way bantering with the women. (The *vignerons* worked at the château all year, and were paid weekly.)

As each woman received her due, she withdrew leftward, by custom, making way for the next; the vicomte tossed handfuls of sous to the children, and there was a merry, curiously unavaricious scuffle. I noticed one boy with two coins give one to a smaller child with none.

"Tout le monde est content?"

And the chorus of *"Merci, M'sieur le Vicomte!"* and other forms of thanks, sometimes more formal, occasionally less, depending on the picker's age, ended the rite. Everything was left in its place, and the *vendangeuses*, the female pickers, headed off toward the village. Passing me, each gave a polite *"M'sieur,"* but a few pretty young girls added a kind of acquiescent smile, with a bold look of appraisal as well. I smiled back, pleased at their happiness.

By now, I realized that these people, called peasants, of course, held in low esteem by the ignorant, had great pride in their work, and a family feeling about the Château Brionne-Bouscard.

"So," said my host, coming down at last, looking satisfied. "I think I did rather well today," and I was struck again by his resemblance to Gervais Lockridge. "I contrived several memorable *mots;* unfortunately, I've forgotten what they were. But it's a grand way to make a living."

His face clouded over. "What a pity it's in jeopardy. And there's another, kindred matter that I must bring up. We'd like to have a fête for you, but you see, Gruner has frightened off many of our friends. How? Well, we've had 'below average' vintages—*Syndicat*'s judgment—and since none know Gruner's worth, they fear he might strike at them too. And because he's announced his intent to foreclose us, we are, for the moment at least, pariah dogs, *en effet*. I'm not sure they have mortgages, but *we*, you understand, enjoy the near-ruin caused by my father's folly."

"Tell me, de Brionne, is this bounder really in a position to take your *domaine* next week?"

"Oh, probably not. That is, he could by legal right, but he's stated that, for now, he covets only our priceless statuary—fixtures here for more than two hundred years—Grecian and Roman.

"And most of this," he said, with such bitterness as he could muster, "because my gullible weakling of a father allowed himself to be cheated at cards over a period of years. Oh, it's true. After I came to age, Alphonse told me over and over what occurred. He knew exactly how and when it was done; it's amazing how omniscient that old bully is! But he comes from New Orleans, and I suppose that explains everything."

(I didn't quite follow, but said nothing.)

"Yes, there were neighbors who lost here, too, some giving up small mortgages, but they had sense enough to stop before disaster. Now, they're reluctant to recall Gruner's attention by coming here. All write me apology and explanation, and I understand. And yet a few still come. But the house seems bare of *joie de vivre*, what?"

"Couldn't these friends have helped you with a loan?"

"My young friend," said de Brionne, "you must understand that we've *all* suffered from our ancestors' debts. No, my mortgage is too much for their purses just now.

"I mentioned that the government (meaning the *Syndicat d'Initiative*) following as a dog under a cart, has pronounced our last few years as, let me see: yes—''42, average'; no crop in '43; ''44, average'; ''47, average.' Both '48 and '49 were 'Excellent,' but they hardly made up for the disastrous ones before.

"Last year was again 'Average,' but on one joyous occasion we were rated 'Superb'—the highest possible.

"But you must recognize the *noblesse oblige* (as they think it), the compulsion of our former gentry to spend money. House in Paris, winters in Italy, mistress or two, and gambling, gambling, gambling. There are more casinos for high-stake play in France than in the rest of Europe combined.

"But, as to Château Brionne-Bouscard, it was my father, bathed in wine, who caused our collapse—one can scarcely blame Rachel for bitterness."

I said, "But he lives on the Riviera still. In some style, I suppose?"

"He was never a man to face trouble. When things became thick, he found it convenient to leave. But I was fully grown, then, and with our solicitors I insisted on conditions. He would make over to me the château and lands; he, in turn, would receive a remittance each quarter in Nice, at the Negrette, of course. And that, my esteemed William—you don't mind?—is how matters stand. In a sense—I disclaim this as any comparison of virtue—your grandfather and my father ended the fortunes of two families.

"The difference, of course, is that your grandfather stepped forward like a hero, to finance a war; my father's actions have been contemptible from the start.

"Can you forgive these revelations? It's that I need a sturdy, levelheaded friend to talk to. I need him most awfully badly."

I said, with even more than my frequent pomp, "Forget your problems, Monsieur de Brionne. I've taken them under advisement."

He looked at me, amused. But he said only, "They are not your problems, *mon ami*, and never will be—you must believe me. You need only listen; that is all. And that, rated by the Bordeaux *Syndicat d'Initiative*, is 'Sublime.'"

Chapter XXXVIII

Several days passed in this tension-filled home, with everyone busy harvesting grapes. De Brionne continued to enlighten me about wine, and, occupied as we were, all had an unspoken agreement after the first day to avoid discussing Gruner.

The family did have friends—exceptional people—in to meet me, and I was taken to visit their homes. In brief, I was treated like royalty, and nearly forgot I was an American.

Then, quite suddenly, it seemed, it was Monday again and I'd finally worked out a possible plan. It was so tricky, it was worth Mr. Harbison at his best, or worst. But my plans were to be radically changed.

I was strolling the lawns that afternoon when I heard a hoarse "Suh!" from behind a shrub, and it was Alphonse. He stepped out, and I said, "What is it, Alphonse?"

"*You* don't mind open scandals, as I reckon you up."

"Why no," I replied, "but the vicomte mentioned scandal as applying to *his* place; nothing to do with me."

"'Scuse me, suh, but I calculate that's wrong. It's *time* for a scandal, and got to be done before Friday, else that polecat coming here to take over."

322

"Baron Gruner?"

"Baron! He ain't no more baron than one of them pigs back behind. I know all his people, and they tell me things. They hates him proper, Mr. Morripson."

"What do you want *me* to do?"

"Dat Gruner, he no more own this place than I do. I know three genlemen hereabouts what played some cards here once, a while ago, and then quit. They knowed the polecat was cheating, and so do I—ways, means, tricks—all de rest.

"I didn't work in a N'Orleans gambling house for nothing, rec'lect." (I detected a flash of pride, which struck me as based on pretty thin material.)

"Well, then what?"

"He ain't *foreclosing* this château; he thieving it! An I got notes from them three genlemen saying they'll testify if it heps. They know how sharp Mister Brionne feels about public ruckus and the fambly. 'Sides, they already talked to him and got nowheres.

"And dere's more—Mister Brionne and his friends got *influence,* and Bordeaux hates that weasel's guts. They might even collect a offering to see him git what's coming."

"How do I figure here?"

"You like this fambly, Mr. Morripson?"

"Most assuredly."

"When you gets a chance, then, rattle into town and see Mister Brionne's lawyers. I got their names right here"—(he gave me an envelope of papers)—"and show the letters. They good men, and they hep, wait and see.

"And they's one more thing. Ol Gruner's got another idea, and that with the château and Mr. Brionne shorely shoot him; I knows my boss. Matter of that, he shoot him for *either* reason, and maybe get in a powerful lot of trouble. Don't get an idea Mr. Brionne's any kinda coward; de Brionnes don't breed genlemen of dat *kind.*"

He was going on, but Madame and her daughters were arriving from the fields, and we agreed to confer later.

Supper that night, in the hall bare of everything but a long table, chairs and a sideboard, and lit by candles (there being a hole above, where a chandelier had been removed)—supper, I say, was silent and dismal, despite de Brionne's attempts to cheer up his family and guest.

"This is Monday," he said, "and we have until Friday. William, here, feels that our luck may turn, and all troubles with it."

As guest, I sat at Madame de Brionne's right and was glad of it. I admired her in every way. She put one hand over mine and said, "Monsieur Morrison is the worthiest of young men, but it would require a Merlin to solve the dilemma left by your precious father, Gérard. No, we've lost Château Brionne-Bouscard. Then what to do? We shall go to my sister in Paris; she, at least, does not gamble."

I said, "Madame de Brionne, there are four or five days between now and your Friday deadline. Try to be optimistic, I beg you. I must leave tomorrow on business. I'll be back by Friday, and who knows what might happen in the meantime?"

We were served by Alphonse and a helper, and Alphonse kept up a low, indefinable rumbling. I was probably wrong in some details, but it sounded like, "I done tol' you, Vicomte, dat de only way to handle old Gruner's with a shotgun. You turn him over to me, we take and bury him so deep ain't no well-crew on earth find him lessen fifty years. More'n 'at, you give me leave and I pull the trigger. 'At man don't deserve to live; lowdown skunk and I said it!"

"Dry up, Alphonse," said de Brionne at last. "I've never been a murderer, and hope not to become one."

The Negro continued to mumble, and soon after dessert and *bonbons variés*, I excused myself, saying I had to pack.

Instead, I went through a French door in the drawing room, then stepped onto a terrace and down to the lawn. I needed time to think things out.

Nearing a statue of Apollo, I heard a hiss, and pulled up, curious. It was the girl Renée.

"Well, miss," I said. "What brings you out?"

Her face pale, her riding clothes stained with grapejuice, she said, "I'm not sure—something about your face; it can be very *hard*."

"Well, that would scarcely attract a pretty girl."

"My father's wonderful, kind, considerate, tolerant, and courageous: but he lacks that now-and-then rocklike look. He might have delivered us from"—she spat the name out—"Gruner, if he'd chosen to fight, even in the courts."

"And as you see it, .the result is to lose your home of three centuries?"

"There's more." She'd moved up to within inches of my face, a very troubled beauty. "I happen to know, from the large-eared Alphonse, what Gruner's plan is for Friday. Nobody else knows, but Alphonse sees the Baron's servants in the village. *Gruner will tear up the mortgage if Papa gives me to him in marriage!*"

"That's a joke, of course. You couldn't, you simply couldn't think that ill of your father."

"Oh, no. He'll shoot Gruner, and go to prison, or worse. You seem, well—actionable. Tell us what to do?" Her eyes, filled with tears, looked like stars glistening in the moonlight.

"See here." I lifted her shapely chin, so that the startling blue eyes looked tearfully up at mine. "I told your father I'd taken on the case, for better or worse. That sounds absurd, at my age, but I mean it."

"Somehow I trust you, and while I shouldn't say it, you interest me as well. Undeniably, you are a species."

I heard an echo that I failed to recognize.

"If you weren't so *hard,* that is."

"Well, that's the way I am. Hard as nails. Suppose you trot back in—canter, if you like—and try to trust me. How's that?"

She threw her arms around my neck and held me a moment. I kissed her on the cheek, and pushed her back gently.

"You won't marry Baron Gruner; depend on it. First, your father would rather lose the château—"

"That is not without complication. Shootings, yes—but you don't understand this family's traditions."

"Go to bed like a good girl. We'll see what happens."

"Alone?"

I sighed. Was it the same old trouble? I finally figured out the answer. French females liked a sober, sincere man. If I'd played the jester, I might never have attracted a glance.

"Of course, alone—"

"I meant not with Deirdre. I don't want her to hear talk in her sleep, and be upset. What did you think I meant?"

I was far from sure. So I said, "Deirdre, of course. We mustn't start a panic."

I watched her half-walk, half-skip toward the house. Once she looked over her shoulder, possibly piqued at the stupid Yankee.

Before turning in, I left Alphonse instructions to get me a buggy and fast mare in the village. I also wrote a note to Gruner:

My Esteemed Neighbor:

We look forward to your presence Friday at dinner. Might I ask a favor? Will you please bring the original mortgage? My copy is lost, and I've forgotten the exact amount owed. Your document might help expedite whatever you propose. Perhaps we can get things settled at once. Another point—please don't mention your ultimatum till after dinner. My wife is nervous to the point of infirmity, and is being cared for by my daughter

325

Renée, whom possibly you remember? With every protestation of felicity, your obd. servant,

DE BRIONNE

And here I ran into a snag. Alphonse had taken to me, it seemed, and thought I meant to help, but he refused "absolute" to deliver the message.

He could speak and read tolerable French by now, but with me he reverted to New Orleans.

"I ain't fixin to go on that man's propity! I been a man of God, Mister Morripson, but I got me a han'-size pistol. One whiff of dat skunk, I take an blow his chin off. No, suh. We got to make furder plans."

I'd verified the solicitors' names and by coincidence they were good friends of my father's, giving me my first real feeling of hope.

The stableboy, aided by a coin (which astonished him), agreed to deliver the letter; then he got the rig, and I was off, very early (and softly) for Bordeaux.

The time was around six-thirty, and I don't believe I even glanced down at the Garonne, the inevitable Roman structures, or the lighthouses. I was in a hurry, so that I arrived on the Esplanade prematurely, of course, and spent two impatient hours wandering among the characteristic low white dwellings.

Then, I found a neat sign: "Roquevillard, De Villefort and Carreau, Attorneys at Law," and even here I had to pace the corridor for an hour. France in general goes to work early, and works until late in the evening, if one excepts the siesta. But the practice does not apply to solicitors, bankers and a few others.

At last, what I took to be a secretary arrived and unlocked the door. He was a typical Frenchman of his class. He had broad facial bones and was neither agreeable nor patient-looking. Also, he took an instant dislike to me, as a foreigner, I assumed. He reminded me, waspishly pointing to the sign, that the office opened at nine o'clock; further, that I needn't expect the trio to turn up before ten or eleven.

"They may not come at all," he said with satisfaction. "Lawyers are not navvies, you know."

"You won't mind if I wait."

"And your appointment?"

"I have none."

"Then go home and write for one. It should require about two days."

Typically middle-class French underling as he was, I rather enjoyed him. Especially with a bomb to burst.

I said, "Your honor will under—"

"M'sieur!"

"I started to say" (this time humbly): "I have a letter to Monsieur Carreau from my father, W. Morrison, II; Monsieur Carreau is the senior member, I believe, and what a merry row he'll raise that I was turned from his door." I looked down and shook my head.

"Now, wait, my friend. You are an explosive type! Let us see thees letter that claims my employer's time. It is no great thing of cleanliness."

It was true that, in travel, the envelope, with its impressive letterhead, had acquired a measure of French soil. Not necessarily the gravelly earth of wine culture.

I sat on the bench, trying to look demure, while he tapped the letter against his cheek. Here three well-dressed gentlemen came in, he greeted them—using the names on the door—and helped remove their garments, slowly, giving me an apprehensive glance.

The elder member saw me looking on, unperturbed, glanced away a second, then came over to scrutinize me carefully.

"Sacred God!" he exclaimed at last. "It can't be the ten-year-old boy I once called Willy!"

I arose and shook his hand. "B'jour, Monsieur Carreau. I'm surprised you recognized me; I've changed."

"Changed! Mon Dieu, you have grown into a giant! De Villefort, Roquevillard—come! You have often heard me speak of William Morrison, a client for years. This, I assure you, is his son, and heir, and, one hopes, in no need of an *avocat.*"

I shook hands around. All were genial, and from a fragrance, I divined that they met at an outside table each morning, for a glass of wine and a discussion of the day's problems. It was a common practice. I thought how much more civilized, and fun, than the solemn bores of our "conference room" meetings.

"*Alors!* I will now capture you," exclaimed M. Carreau. "I wish to hear news of your family."

"If your secretary will permit it, sir," I said.

"Permit it! *Nom d'un nom, d'un sacré nom!* What's Gaston got to do with it?"

"I had the impression, Monsieur Carreau, that he wished me turned out of the office." (I realized this was unsporting, certainly beneath me, but the secretary happened to be a breed I disliked— petty authority—some of these in our shipping office.)

"Gaston! Apologize instantly!"

"Yes, sir, I do. I failed to understand—"

"I think you are not a type for these offices!"

"Oh, he was doing his job, as he saw it," I said. "One must overlook stupidity." I smiled tolerantly at the secretary, as he gave me a false servile glance.

"We shall see," said M. Carreau. "But it goes against custom to begin business meetings without a glass of wine."

He poured two glasses of a château red. "Especially in Bordeaux," he added. "Eighteen thirty-four—with a rating of 'Excellent' by the government and, of course, the Bordeaux *Syndicat d'Initiative.*"

The wine was wonderful, soft and mellow, even to a nonexpert; but I'm afraid I broke the rules by gulping rather than sipping.

"A Château Lafite Rothschild," he said, "from the commune of Pauillac, the best of our five *premiers crus.* You must help yourself, when it suits you. Now tell me your mission, if any, in Bordeaux. I guess," he said roguishly, "that it has to do with your parent. It is our foremost hope that he will resume trade here, now that steam comes to make it easier."

"Monsieur Carreau," I said, pulling my chair up, "I have a story to tell you, about friends of yours. I solicit your advice, and—worst of all—beg a possibly unethical favor. It has to do with my hosts, Monsieur and Madame de Brionne—"

"The most charming of people, but alas!—"

"And Baron Gruner."

"Fils d'un chameau!" he spat, his color deepening. "A dog of an intruder. A veritable *allemand,* you understand. These rich Germans—what trouble they cause! But continue—I shan't interrupt again."

Trying to marshal my knowledge of the all-but-ruined family, and using Alphonse as a reference, I established that Gruner had cheated the elder de Brionne in every way a gambler can cheat. Then I showed him the darky's three notes, which the lawyer studied carefully.

"These are men of substance," he finally pronounced, "and what they depose cannot be taken lightly. Gruner's dishonesty is well known, but he's a formidable figure, an expert swordsman, and people—even the police—have been loath to act."

But when I reached the point of the baron's proposed marriage to Renée, the attorney leaped to his feet, livid, and shouted, "My godchild! No, I shall not see this happen!

"Unethical?—I don't care a tinker's damn what you propose. (Oh, yes, I attended an English school for three years, and know many idioms. Would you care to hear more, as they apply to this Gruner? No, I shall control myself.) Pray, what is your plan of action?"

"Well, first, does Gruner keep de Brionne's mortgage document here? I'm inclined to doubt it. Second, is his, Gruner's, estate in sound condition? He plans to foreclose the Château Brionne-Bouscard on Friday, you know—"

M. Carreau leaped to his feet again. "We shall seek a postponement of foreclosure! And we will then explore the chance of a trial. Yes, this is the time! There's also the matter of a killing—a 'duel'—of which you could have no knowledge. But there were no attendants, and an elderly pair of his *vignerons* know the whole truth, I'm convinced. It was no duel; it was *murder!* And I think we can act upon it now. With these three letters, Gruner's word is no longer of any account."

"Then," I said, "we can leave it at this: should your postponement fail, I stand ready to buy the de Brionne mortgage, if possible. The vicomte is, after all, a very dear friend of my family, and I hope to see him through this crisis.

"And now we come to Gruner. His place—"

"Pardon, un moment, mon ami." M. Carreau called in his partners, apologizing for the interruption, and told them my story, wholly, in concise detail. It was odd; I'd wondered before if he was fully listening, but he missed no single point. "And now you ask about Gruner," he concluded, with a second apology.

Roquevillard stepped forward. "This is a matter which I have had the dishonor to handle. Gruner's château and vineyards are mortgaged to the top, and he has five arrear payments. I rejoice at it . . . No, no, I make no apology.

"The mortgagee, an elderly resident of this city, is now sick, and himself in financial distress. *Eh bien,* he asks me to find a buyer for this mortgage, which he sells very reasonably. It is in my possession now!"

I said, "I wish to buy Gruner's mortgage—at the bargain you mention."

Now M. Carreau coughed in embarrassment and said, "Forgive me, Willy—William—but I must ask the embarrassing question: Are you in a position to afford all this?"

I stood up and emptied the contents of my money belt (a considerable heap of gold, almost unknown in rural France this year); then I showed them certification of my trust fund; and finally I waved my father's letter of credit in front of their faces.

"Parbleu!" exclaimed de Villefort. "We have enough here to buy Bordeaux. The outcome is foregone. I see it."

Roquevillard burst into tears, while de Villefort collapsed on a couch, and Gaston dashed at his forehead with cologne.

Then, after an interval, we agreed to reassemble for Thursday lunch, and see how far forward we had gone. With this vow, I was off (with the usual embraces) for the few miles northeast into the red wine country—the Haut-Médoc, of Bordeaux. The country of the clarets. (The word "claret," by the way, being an English abstraction of France's "clear"—this at a time when England had begun ruling the sea-trade.)

The most important Bordeaux red vineyards were the Châteaux Margaux, Latour, Haut-Brion and Lafite Rothschild. These had the permanent class of *Premier Grand Cru,* or First Growth. In Bordeaux's district of half a million acres, the white wines are grown, as said, in Graves, south of the city, and our Brionne-Bouscard is the single *Premier Cru* of the area.

To a foreigner, it can be confusing. Burgundy, unlike the Bordeaux château wines, comes from small vineyards, and the wine is made in a central press. The area north of Bordeaux breaks down into Médoc (also known as Bas-Médoc) and Haut-Médoc, where the best red vineyards are. East and north of all this is Burgundy country. All agree that Burgundy wines are richer, stronger, better in every way except lightness and clarity. And then, to be sure, other white wines are grown north of Burgundy, notably Chablis—drier, sharper (or "flintier," again)—than the Graves, which most Frenchmen prefer. Champagne is a different category, and comes from a different area.

The bulk of the Bordeaux wine trade is done in the red clarets, since (from what I learned) one can drink more Bordeaux than Burgundy without effect. It is morally permissible for ladies, for example, to sip Haut-Médoc and suffer no loss of repute, while a female swilling Burgundy might be regarded as a pretty tough proposition.

I was royally treated in the best châteaux, and no single *Maître* was too busy to show me his *domaine* and explain how things were done. The Baron Rothschild, for one, walked me stoutly, as I was stumbling like de Brionne's horse, over his unusually broad expanse, far larger than the average vineyard. This banking family (so I gathered) were buying another château and vineyard, to be known as Mouton Rothschild. Various family members were said to be wealthier than the normal French businessman.

The baron, gruff in manner, warm in spirit, rattled off a lot of statistics that I failed to grasp; but the important majority stuck, I believe. On everything said, I took readable notes.

The Haut-Médoc, supplying the world with the finest Bordeaux grown, is only thirty miles long, and includes twenty-six *communes*, or townships, foremost of these being Pauillac. I gathered from what the baron didn't say that there was a good deal of scuffle among these *communes* to have this or that vineyard recognized, or others promoted or demoted. This onrushing competition sometimes extended to the personal. He also mentioned that communes near Haut-Médoc, like St. Emilion and St. Julienne are of such merit as to clamor incessantly to be upgraded.

I was also told what de Brionne did not tell me, that the best sweet white wines of France—Barsac and Sauterne—lie at the southern tip of Graves.

"How is de Brionne? How's his health, I mean? I know that bastard Gruner—calls himself—has got his hooks in him, but how's de Brionne holding up? Fellow's got an artificial leg, you know. He won't tell you that, unless you ask him bluntly. Had it made in Switzerland—devilish ingenious."

I was happy in this man's company, happier yet to say, "De Brionne's no weakling, and besides, his troubles with Gruner are over."

Rothschild pulled up—a tall, mustachioed man wearing a cloth cap—and looked me fiercely in the eye.

"Over? What do you imply? His ass of a father got him into the mess, you know. But 'over.' Speak up. A sworn secret is held sacred on this estate!"

When I told him details of what I'd done—the whole story—he clapped me on the back like a thunderbolt, and said, "I've heard of your father, never met him, but I expect he can handle this without trouble. Now here's a secret for *you*, young feller: if a hitch develops, any kind, depend on me for a loan. Hear? No interest charged. We'll run this 'baron' out of the country, what? Gives the place a bad name.

"Besides being no good, he has rotten workers. At least, they won't work for *him*. *Premier cru* there! One has to *work* for it. Tell you what— to help along, I'll send down a dozen good *vignerons* for a while. Till you get on your feet."

He talked as if his life had been largely spent in England, and though his French was perfect, he chose English for me. He drew off again to look me over.

"Pickin's on, but I've got good men—women, too—and I want you back at the château to visit us—oh, say, for six months. Stay a year, get the real hang of the business. Your father'll understand, if he's what they say he is . . . By the way, I've got five good-looking girls. Should have said so at the start. All right. We'll consider it done."

I explained that I only had a few days here. And then back to de Brionne's for a showdown with Gruner on Friday.

"All right, deal with him. After that, back here. Put your right hand over your heart."

Too feeble to resist, I did so. Then he insisted I come meet his family, which I did. I dislike to sound fulsome, but all were charming. And he'd underrated the girls, as if he'd underrated the *premier grand cru* of his wine.

After promising Madame Rothschild "A year, not a day less"— after promising her to come back, that is—I took my leave with reluctance.

Chapter XXXIX

Today—Thursday, and I left, thinking over the helpful guides given me by the baron. They were more than I expect to write down here; I'll save all notes on wine*making* from the vats on, for example. But I should mention the year-to-year ratings of vintages.

The Bordeaux Chamber of Commerce in solemn council—a ritual like none on earth—tasted, washed the wine in their mouths, smelled the bouquet, and even smelled their own breaths and each others'. Finally, after discussion, argument and mild quarreling—they arrived at the traditional judgment of that year. From top to bottom these were: Superb (very, very rare), Excellent, Very Good, Good, Above Average, Average, Acceptable, Mediocre and Passable. Below these, in a bad year, the wine was not rated at all. But as I said, certain châteaux of pronounced excellence, had won special permanent designations—*premier cru, deuxième cru, troisième cru,* and the like.

In any season, with all differences resolved, a generic rating was applied to the crop, and it covered all vineyards. It was a judgment of the *year*, you see. The vintage stamp was the result of that year's sunshine, storms, rainfall, temperature, and other elements of weather.

* * *

It being one o'clock, I encouraged my mare to scamper along, so as to make my lunch with the lawyers. The truth is, my heart was in my mouth. On reflection, I was convinced *anything* could go wrong.

We were to meet at the Café de Petits Joueurs, and all were there, at an outside table, looking (I thought) like a bereaved family at a funeral.

The local sense of humor usually escapes me entirely. Its subtleties are too many to explore here. When I approached the table, the three shook their heads.

I was crushed. I said, "Nothing worked, I suppose. Well, the plan was too good, too pat."

At this low moment, all sprang to their feet, tried to embrace me at once, and shouted—literally shouted—*"Quel génie!" "Un miracle! Un miracle véritable!"* and then, "Bordeaux shall not forget this day!"

I was assured that the mayor wished to present me the keys to the city, and take up a purse besides. They were just that happy to rid the town of Gruner. I hadn't much notion what the keys unlocked, but said I'd take them anyhow. I resisted the purse. It was unnecessary (if indeed it or the keys existed at all; the French in high excitement being capable of grand extravagance).

Messieurs Carreau, Roquevillard and de Villefort all talked at the same time.

The de Brionne mortgage extension had not gone through, but was promised for this evening. Also, Gruner's sick mortgageholder had borrowed some money and was traveling in South America. He was expected back when he became tired of the bribery, or *mordita* system of living—that is, soon. He had, however, left a power of attorney; thus I was able to buy the mortgage without trouble at a price I could afford from my own funds. And the lawyers promised to keep the sale a secret until after Friday.

Gruner's château, however, was now officially mine; that is, I had the right to foreclose when I pleased.

The sole failure (of the extension) no longer made any difference; my plans had changed slightly, though I didn't say so.

Holding hands (to my great embarrassment) we danced, actually danced around the table, while people at other tables ignored us completely. A quirk I've noticed about the French is that they're too polite to stare. While the Spanish, Mexicans and others always pester a lone girl, say, by walking close beside her, gushing compliments and suggestions, the French seldom bother even the handsomest. As a rule, the antics of foreigners go unnoticed.

After lunch, declining numerous invitations, pleading urgent business and the need to write letters, I was accompanied to the

Crédit Foncier to establish an account. Then, shaking hands around once more, I returned to my hotel—the Royal Médoc, off the Allées de Tourny, which was near town center. The hostelry had stabling, and I paid a groom three francs to work down my horse.

Feeling committed, I wrote letters to Betsy, Gervais Lockridge and Frances Barclay, and sent a postcard featuring grapes and wine to General Whitney. I'd already written my father, with some mild apprehension. By this time, it seemed to me, I'd been involved with half of France, and expended my trust fund, over which I now had control. So long as I kept up payments on the former Gruner château, I was financially comfortable. And the mortgage, in my view, on this rundown property, was piddling; I even thought I might make a profit on it, if the holding was put in shape.

So—I decided to take a nap and decide the de Brionne issue all in good time. My correspondence finished, I fell into a deep sleep, like the rest of Bordeaux at this hour.

Before eating an early dinner, I walked outside, and a pestiferous guide finally overcame my defenses. I engaged him for an hour.

I said, "An hour only; no more!"

"*Entendido*, m'sieur. And may I ask where the gentleman is staying?"

When I told him, he clucked and thought La Réserve was more suited to a visitor of my class, but I told him I was happy enough.

"I hope the gentleman is on the side where the fire exit is, to absorb the breezes from the sea?"

(I thought the question curious, and made no answer.)

I studied him in the twilight; and thought he looked like a gypsy. But he snapped "Ser*vice!*" and went into a long explanation about Bordeaux being a product of the Bronze Age. Liar! I said to myself, but it turned out to be true. The Romans had developed it during their heyday, and I concluded that, if I bought a dog team and sled and mushed to the North Pole, I'd find a handful of Romans either building a road or drawing up laws to fleece the Eskimos clean. *Never* was there such a race for poking their noses outside their own backyards.

After an hour, I paid the gypsy, if he was a gypsy, his five-franc *prix fixe* (his word) and he looked more gypsylike when I handed it over.

"The *prix fixe* was seven francs, gentleman."

"Here's eight." I felt like putting him in his beggar's place. "That's all you get." But, being in a generally bad humor, I felt I'd come off rather poorly, so I said, "Why didn't you take me to the Cathedral of St. André? You ever hear of it?"

"It's closed at this hour, gentleman. Also not very good."

"Well," I said, letting down a little, "how about the Roman Elk's Club? And the famous Roman Fire Department?"

"Roman Fi— I do not know these thing, maybe twelve century ago, I am not sure."

At last comprehending, he gave me a typical gypsy look, and I handed him another franc with a lecture.

"Take a couple of days off. Collect up some facts. I warn you, as American agent for the *Syndicat*, don't hit these streets again till you've picked up some information. What I've had so far's what my country calls 'a gyp.' Come to think it over—'gyp,' possibly from 'gypsy.' I'll—"

But he was gone, and it was half an hour before I spotted his voice for sure.

After dinner, I found Hugo's *Hernani*, and, piling up four cushions to sit on, was able to read awhile in reasonable comfort. But I was sleepy, and gave up; I could have done better suspended from the ceiling. I opened a window, did feel grateful for the breeze, and drifted off.

Sometime around midnight, I woke up, wondering why, then made out a dark shape going through my trousers. Moving slowly, I silently found a match, and struck it, leaping out of bed. It was my gypsy king from Sète, all right, and he hadn't time to straighten up before I rammed his smelly head into a corner. There was a feeble flash of a knife, but I stamped on his wrist to grab it.

Lifting the rogue by his collar, I marched him down to the desk. Assuming all the anger I could, I told what happened, and demanded they call the gendarmes.

The manager, routed out, pleaded, "Please, m'sieur, such a thing can ruin the Hotel Médoc! The police—ah, you have no idea! The questions, the forms and filing, the wait in jail for court! Does M'sieur lack any belongings?"

All was intact but a cheap watch—I'd put my grandfather's gold hunter in the canvas belt while driving—and since I'd come off *this* well, at least (barring inconvenience), I'd begun to enjoy myself. In fact, I found the gypsy's plight more valuable than a single cheap watch.

Downstairs, again, the manager suggested as follows: "Sir, the Médoc is very ancient. Besides locked cellars for wine, we have others for long-ago prisoners. I beg you to let us place him in lockage until morning and M'sieur has departed. Then the police shall be informed; you have my word, on the sacred head of my mother!"

(I could think of other things she might prefer on her head.)

"Naturally, M'sieur will consider his *addition* paid—in full, including the tax."

"Very well," I said, with reluctance. "But I feel I am not doing my civic duty to Bordeaux. *En effet*, I am placing myself in the role of aiding criminals. I think I'd better—"

"I *beg* you, m'sieur. All is made legal in the morning."

"Send up a man with a hammer and nails," I advised him. "The windows will be fixed not to admit further *ladrones*. This will be under my supervision, a registered architect with certificate from the *Instituto Marché de Viande*, in Marseilles. And now, where is your cellar door?"

At its entrance, on second thought, I recovered my watch. "An error, I see. One assumes you have a police whistle—"

"M'sieur! see incidents sympathetically!"

To the gypsy, I said, "Bend over, that I may recognize you later." When he'd stooped down, looking apprehensive, I planted a heavy boot against his fat rump, as I'd once used that leg in Niagara. This, of course, was different, but not greatly so. The thief tumbled higgledy-piggledy down the stairs, with an inspired improvement on his idiom at Sète.

"I'll be leaving early."

"A forwarding address, sir?"

"Château Lafite-Rothschild."

"Mon Dieu! We could be destroyed!"

"My passport?"

"The law is very strict—"

I went to the door to shout a muted, "Police!" but the manager gave way, crushed.

When the windows were nailed a foot high, arousing picturesque comment from guests down the hall, I turned in at last. This, too, had been an interesting day.

Chapter XL

The mare and I were in rare spirits as the former (filled with oats) pulled the latter (filled with coffee) out of the hotel's stable. We were away from town in minutes, coming out as usual between the rows of poplars lining the Graves road. A breeze was blowing, and the leaves, whipped about, showed pale as often as green. Breasting rises, one could see châteaux off in the distance; white, a few miles apart, with no high trees to block the view and the sun glinting off a thousand panes (or so it seemed).

It was a grand day for living, and I was hopeful of ending it that way. Over a shaly hill the towers and turrets of Château Brionne-Bouscard shone in the climbing sun. I remembered a man saying that this autumn there'd been little or no rain; he worried about the wine and vintage rating if the weather failed.

Then I heard a dull thud of hoofbeats, and reined in slowly, to let the daughter Renée canter abreast me. She was carelessly clad for riding astride; only her hair (with tortoise combs) was in place.

"Well," I said, stopping, "you're out early."

"On purpose. I wanted to see you. An impetuous type of your sort is certain to be early on the road, and I'm to tell you that today we dine at two."

"Impetuous? Tie on your horse and come up to the seat."

She said, "This is Friday, and, you know—"

"I like Fridays," I said with a slap of the reins. "Good things happen on Friday."

"But not for me. This is my day for Herr Gruner."

"Still, it's I who have you now. We can hide out all day in the bushes."

"You must try to be serious," she said, looking genuinely forlorn.

"I told you before I'd take up these matters, and I've done so. I can't tell you all. But to make your Friday gayer, I'll say this: You have nothing to fear. Understand? You're as free as—as that lark singing on the signpost."

"Is this true?" The fathomless blue eyes looked through me again. "There's no lark on the signpost, by the way."

"Well, there could be. And I cross my heart."

"Signifying what?"

"It's a saying we have. It means I'd rather die than lie about this subject."

She threw her arms around me, giving me the benefit of her half-buttoned blouse, but she held on a second too long, and I sensed the tick-tock in that alert, exquisite head. She drew back and said, "You are trying to say, easily, that we've lost the château. There will be trouble. I *assure* you—my father will shoot that *animal!*"

"Is your father a good shot?" I asked playfully.

"No. Nor a good swordsman, or any of those things. His leg was injured in the wars. He went because it was expected. He dislikes violence, and was never tutored."

"Oh, well," I said, still optimistic, "it'll probably work out all right."

"What will?"

"Everything."

But she had a curious, stubborn streak. "Why should I believe you?"

"You have nothing else to believe in."

She reflected. "It's true you are of formidable physique and have comic *confiance* for one so young. Yet you have a way. When we met, I was not inclined to think so . . . but I have decide to drop worrying," she said after some thought. "I also feel I might like you. Unless you prove false, of course."

"That certainly follows. Now, on toward a solution."

"Much too early. The family are in the fields."

"Why not you?"

"For the reasons that I said. I could possibly believe—it is a specialty you have. Doubtless it is no great thing."

"Then drive to the village. Or let's go to a fair. Or buy some wine for your father. I'm told one finds decent white wines here."

"I have choose another, and you are not to be—yes, shock. I am not perfect, you know, though I may look so." (!)

"You choose—what?"

"We have warmth, now, to bathe in the Garonne. The horses and buggy can hide in the willows; we will not be seen. My special place is within a kilometer, or less."

"And what do you propose to wear?"

"I have a bathing costume; also towels. You may wear what you please. Men are nothing to be seen—fat statues, little more."

Stung, I started to demur, then decided to find out. I had no bathing costume, or any plans to contrive one.

But I felt misgivings; the girl, indeed, had certain points in common with Samantha. She undressed in the shrubs and came out with no self-consciousness wearing a scrap that would have seen her jailed in New York. Then I recalled that, in Nice, years ago, I saw people undress on the beach, or shingle, and often swim nude.

For me, I had underdrawers of conceivable use for swimming, but they had a fair chance of coming off.

"I've been much complimented on my figure," she told me, as if she were speaking of someone else.

"So have I," I said, and waded leisurely in. (The water struck me as icy, but I didn't flinch or say so.)

Surprisingly enough, she'd actually come to swim, and she did so beautifully, with professional-looking strokes.

After a space, she wriggled out of her loin-scrap and tossed it onto the bank. "It impedes my *vitesse*," she said, her English far from her mind, and as if she might be explaining to a nurse.

Sporting about, so to speak, she dove and came up before me, and pressed the much-complimented body hard against me. I started to dive aside when she pushed me away as if I'd been the aggressor, confound her.

She said, "No, we cannot even play with innocence until I see what you so boastfully mean to do later."

My ego was bruised, and I said, "Suits me. I'm busy swimming anyhow."

In twenty minutes or so, she said, "I'm cold, now, and go to dress. You may watch me leaving or not; such things, to me, are not disturbing. People make too much of seeing each other without clothes. What are clothes, if one is warm?"

I began to have doubts about my overwhelming effect on girls, but I was in no condition to climb up at the moment. Annoyed, I decided

340

to even the score. Removing my garment, I strolled up casually behind her. She looked back quickly, then dressed without comment. There was no more talk about statues.

For the next two miles or so, she said nothing. Then she burst into laughter.

"It's what I deserved. *Voyez,* it never before occurred that men, young men, might have vanity, too. I grew up among girls."

The day still being young, we drove into Pessac, and, walking around, ate ices. The peasants curtsied her, and we went hand-in-hand into the rather imposing but always gorily decorated church. And before we left for home, I bought her a small yellow parasol against the sun; a length of silk ribbon; and a black velvet band for her hair. And she, reminding me of Samantha (and giving me a stab in the chest), a monkey-on-a-stick.

Then we drove home as the sun passed the meridian. Thinking defensively of Betsy, with her pale beauty, I felt that under these conditions she would have swum with equal candor.

Rounding the oval drive before the château, we stepped down as Alphonse came out to scold about her complexion and the sun. But he quieted down when she showed him the new parasol.

She pushed him away. "We don't want you here, Alphonse. Your spying exhausts me. Go someplace."

He turned, grumbling that he preferred to know what transpired in the "chat-toe," because the place was worthless without him.

She replied, "You seem to think you're king here; you just wait!"

The threat was empty, and he knew it; nevertheless he left.

In half an hour Madame de Brionne arrived from the fields, looking anxious. Then her cordial self emerged, and she extended both hands, saying, "Welcome back, Monsieur Morrison. I do hope you had a good and successful trip."

"I'm sure you'll be pleased, Madame de Brionne. But you must wait awhile yet. No longer than dinner, I hope."

Renée left, her face filled with wonder, and I asked when Gruner might appear on the scene.

"Perhaps two o'clock, but it could be later. He enjoys being late."

"Why don't you go rest, madame? You look tired."

"No. Only sick with worry. This dinner—"

Here we heard the sound of a carriage, and she paled. She whispered, "That evil man comes. I believe I could bring *myself* to shoot him!"

As I saw her toward her dressing room, I said, cheerfully, "I hope to enjoy this. You must promise a dinner that seems perfectly normal,

341

with light conversation. Then leave the rest to me, and to your husband. The point's important."

"But I'd so like to see it *all!* I'd feel as if I were doing my part."

"Then begin by humoring me."

She gave me one of her winning smiles. "And why would I not? You to whom I suspect we owe so much. I'll dress quickly, and be down straightaway."

I reminded her, "You really must understand that I look forward to the drawing room, this afternoon especially."

"Yes, the large drawing room being the only one left intact, that must be where we meet. Otherwise, one would sit on the floor, would it not?"

I climbed up to my same cold stone chamber, containing a bed, a travesty of a fireplace, a bureau, and no chair.

Dressed, I told myself that the great moment had come. I descended and was admitted by a very friendly de Brionne. Madame—a pale Madame—was seated on a satin lounge, a fireplace fire had been lit, and the girls all sat on the rug around it. Despite the fire, the room was cold.

All the girls, I should have said, except Renée, who leaned against a table, gazing without fright at our odious exhibit. (I thought her capable of putting a dagger in his back if my plans went astray.)

A man with thick black hair, of medium height, bulky, not ill-made but with a face that seemed to have a deep, permanent look of disdain. On the surface, he was suave and, I suppose, polite. Being biased, I only supposed.

As de Brionne led me across the room Gruner looked up, surprised. But my amused tolerance (half-feigned) alerted him all the same. It was the expression I strove for, and it was helped by his dandified dress.

"So, we have a guest?"

"Baron, may I present William Morrison, a young American whose very popular parent once bought and shipped wines from Bordeaux?"

Gruner got up slowly, to show a certain offensive reluctance.

"We have a Yankee with us. How refreshing."

I ignored his half-outthrust hand, nodded briefly and said, "An *American.* The word 'Yankee' carries opprobrium in some areas, Herr Baron."

He flushed. "Yes, I am German; my father was German, my mother Alsatian." He looked me up and down, and said, graciously enough, "Young American, if you like, but exceedingly well grown."

342

By now no one but a fool could have failed to sense the atmospheric change, and an immediate showdown was avoided, I think, by Alphonse announcing dinner.

The baron escorted Madame de Brionne into the vacant hall, Renée having avoided his arm, and I (behind) noted the angry red at his neck.

Once seated, and perhaps on this account, he resumed what was clearly banter meant to annoy. Thus far, however, it was not Baron Gruner's night.

"Well, de Brionne, will you have a fat purse left this year? I see you grow a healthy crop."

I said, "I think I can assure you, Baron, that the purse will be sufficient. I should have told you, I've been appointed temporary *Maître*. Our host's leg has caused trouble of late."

De Brionne started to protest, but I ambled happily on. "Yes, I've taken matters in hand."

Gruner burst into laughter, nearly choking. "A Yankee! As an expert on wine? De Brionne, my friend," he said, turning, "you must surely have a touch of brain fever."

Our host (helpless) began a feeble reminder of my family's years in wine trade here, but I interrupted. I thought it only fair to let Madame and the girls have some fun.

With an ingenuous smile, I said, "I believe I objected to 'Yankee,' Herr—well, Baron. An onlooker might think you deliberately offensive."

He studied me carefully, and said, with a note of sarcasm, "My apologies. I hadn't realized the term was seriously insulting."

"Very serious, Herr—ah, Baron."

He laid down his knife and fork. "Why, may one ask, do you my title give at the end?"

(Rattled at last, I congratulated myself.) I'd never really known a better dinner.

"I find the *Almanach de Gotha* pleasant reading. Is it not so, Mr. Gruner?"

He leaped to his feet, having trouble with his trembling hands. "Do *you* mean to insult *me*? Speak out!"

"Baron, Baron," I said soothingly. "You will recognize a slip of the tongue. On the order of 'Yankee.' Pray be seated. You are upsetting our hostess."

(He was, by the way, doing nothing of the sort; she covered a smile with a crested napkin. In the look there was an unmistakable degree of reprisal.)

This once, I gloried in my rudeness. For a very long time, this family had suffered terrible hardship from a cardcheat, thief, possibly a murderer as well—the most unpopular figure Bordeaux had ever known. He was received in few houses by now, and those of unimpressive vintage, to coin a phrase.

Standing there, the only one present to lose his composure, he must have realized what a fool he looked, and he sat down, with a snort of laughter.

"These Americans, they are sensitive," he observed. "The word 'Yankee' shall not appear again, sir." (No mention of the *Almanach de Gotha.*) He figured, one could assume, that his time of triumph was about to arrive.

Madame de Brionne at length said, "And now, girls, I think we must leave these gentlemen to their brandy."

She arose in improved spirits, I noticed, and let her brood out. But the irrepressible Renée's tinkle of amusement was clearly heard, and our guest once more turned a dark red.

Regaining control, he said in a bullying voice, "I find a change of atmosphere here. I fail to understand, de Brionne. Today is Friday. You realize I take possession, if I wish."

I marveled at his bluff; everyone's hand was set against him, and he must have heard rumors. Three splendid lawyers, a pair of elderly *vignerons*, and three important letters had altered his position.

In the blandest manner, I said, "Kindly address your remarks to me, Gruner. You may have forgotten—I'm acting as *Maître.*"

He leaped up a second time, shouting, "Who is the *Nasweis?* Already several insults I overlook. Have a care, de Brionne."

From the start, as much as I liked him, I'd wondered about de Brionne's traditional gentleness, and I looked on curiously.

He said curtly, "Sit down, Gruner. You're making an ass of yourself," and I sighed in relief.

"An ass, you say? You pusillanimous hobbler from a wound probably self-inflicted. Your château's going, and you still play high-caste with *me?*"

I reminded him to address the new *Maître.* "Frankly, Gruner, I'm on the verge of becoming annoyed."

De Brionne, still seated, said slowly, "Yes, it's possible I shall lose Château Brionne-Bouscard soon. Until then, you will treat my American guest with courtesy. If we go, we shall do so without complaint as my ancestors would have done. You, I find at last— even worse than a grip on my home—are a *bore!*"

Gruner made a hissing sound. He actually sounded like an angry snake hissing. "I would throw wine in your face, you weakling, except that I have a proposal. It will solve all problems except your drunken fool of a father—"

De Brionne smiled. "I beg you to throw the wine. It will help solve a great deal, despite the new law." He rose.

"With your leg and timidity?" Gruner laughed in his rasping way again. "And I the best swordsman in France?"

"Let me correct that," I said, smoking an Havana, now, from a box on the table. "You mean the best swordsman at the Salle d' Armes in Munich."

For an alarmed second, I thought he might seize me by the throat; he was, after all, conspicuously muscled. But he breathed heavily and finally spat out, his face inches from mine, "Your insults will be atoned for presently, *Yankee! You* a *Maître!* Can you tell white wine from red? I'd be surprised."

"Yes," I said, thinking it over, "I really believe I can. I can also tell trimming from honest dealing. Many other devices for one so young."

This time, the first in my life, I had a glass of wine thrown in *my* face. Continuing to smile, for I had plans for Gruner, I wiped my face and brushed the wine from my clothes. (Luckily it was white, not red.) As I did so, I noticed Alphonse, just out of the light. He appeared disappointed but ready.

"A coward like all Yanks, are you? Some day we'll have to whip you in war, no doubt. But you will pay for your innuendos; I make an oath."

Gruner still stood, and now he pushed de Brionne back down, holding a glove. "Listen well, my spineless friend. I have this proposal: I tear up the mortgage if you will give your daughter Renée's hand in marriage, tomorrow. I've watched her ripen, with those plump buttocks and high breasts" —he was slobbering. "Frankly, I now have an obsession for those things named. I make no apology. Your financial woes will end, cripple, and your daughter will know delights only dreamed of in her case—"

It was an ugly scene played out in that bare dining room. And the surprise now came quickly. At Gruner's words, de Brionne said, "A daughter of *mine?* Married to a slippery, thieving, ill-favored cur from the wrong side of the blanket? Married? To a *dog?*" He laughed, leaning back in his chair. "You wish your answer now?" and he drenched Gruner from a full glass.

Then de Brionne, according to custom, half-stood to take the age-old slap across the face.

Startling everyone (to stop this for now), I applauded loudly, crying, "Bravo! Bravo! Alphonse, will you step here a minute?"

"Yes, suh!"

"You remember our talk of some days ago?"

"I remembers *all.*"

"Will you tell us, you from a New Orleans gambling house, what you observed about Baron Gruner's cardplay here? Just list things, without the usual moralizing."

"Well, suh, as follers: use of Seconds, Middles and Bottoms; waxing of Aces; Edge Work and Line Work; Sleeve-feeder—and, mostly, Shiners, on the deal—the things all cardsharps do."

I knocked the pistol out of Gruner's hand, to keep Alphonse from being shot. Weaponless, Gruner told our host, in a finally composed voice, "You first, de Brionne. You have a choice of weapons." Then he turned to me. "Afterward, I recall, you have a choice, too."

"I've decided to choose pistols at the usual paces, whatever they are," said de Brionne. "I never bothered to ask. Where and when?"

Gruner was back in his own country, his own milieu. He said with professional style, calmly calculating, "The great entrance hall, with its furniture gone, appears ideal. Especially since you *poseurs* of a family are too lazy to wax the floor. The nigger either, it seems. It's far enough removed so the ladies won't hear your screams."

We all rose, and, as I saw Alphonse take an antiquated revolver out of his coat, I shook my head. We walked in solemn file, de Brionne limping, to the front of the building.

Three sets of weapons were produced: a beautiful pair of dueling pistols, a pair of foils and a pair of épées—these last, of course, with the one sharpened edge. The swords all had buttons at the ends, as if someone past had used them for practice or tutelage.

Gruner selected a pistol, checked its load, hefted it, tested its balance and said, "Ten paces from back to back. Your Yankee can count them off, if he can count." He looked as happy (to use Alphonse's later phrase) as "a pig in swill."

But this had gone far enough, as the "greatest swordsman in Italy" once thought when he left New York with his shoulder punctured.

I stepped between them. "Unfortunately, you foulmouthed bastard, I'm familiar with the Code Duello. Any man can insist on replacing another, for cause, such as overage, underage, handicapped, and the like. The Vicomte de Brionne-Bouscard has a metal leg. You will fight *me*," and then, almost unaware (but probably from strain), I knocked him down.

He got up, holding his cheek, which was bleeding, and started to shoot me. But he was pinned from behind by Alphonse, who still, with the years, was stronger than most men.

I almost admired Gruner's struggle to command his features, and his breathing, which now came in dangerous-sounding rasps. But in a few minutes, when the import of a duel with me burst on him, he moderated his voice to his highly unpleasant shouts of laughter.

"You, a *canaille* of a Yankee, wishing to duel *me?* Your weapon, you said?"

During all this, de Brionne was vigorously (and futilely) trying to interfere. He simply lacked the strength to separate us, and Alphonse found no safe position from which to use his antique.

"Epées will do darn well, I bet!"

His bushy eyebrows shot up, but he continued to laugh.

"Do you know what an épée is? Or how you'll be carved to pieces?"

"Isn't it some kind of gun?"

Convulsed, picking out a slender reed of steel, he ran a finger over one edge.

I asked, dumbfounded, *"That's* an épée? Good gosh. I thought it might be something like hunting rabbits. Oh well, so be it."

Gruner said, "I believe you struck me," and aimed a backhanded slap at my face. But here he was out of his element. I crouched slightly, and the blow missed by half a foot. De Brionne, still protesting, tried to hold me and take his rightful place, but I shook him off a second time.

"By the way, Gruner," I said, "you may be interested in these," and I tossed the three letters from neighbors he'd swindled onto the table. "I really advise you to read them. And Alphonse has kept a careful log of all your cheating here, with specific details of how it was done."

Gruner hesitated, looking puzzled, but he finally picked up the letters and read them, one by one, and his expression at last was one of concern, even of fright.

"All lies!" he shouted, without conviction, "and to be sure, who'd believe the word of a New Orleans nigger? But there's an easy way to solve these," and he tore them into shreds, throwing them back on the table.

"Oh, those are copies, of course," I said. "We aren't such damn fools as to present the originals to a cheat of your high repute. The originals, at this moment, lie in the hands of the authorities. They seemed quite delighted to get them, and implied that the new dueling law is often overlooked."

"Then I can solve *one* problem, at least," said Gruner. "Make your peace with God, Yankee. Ignorant or not, your time has come. None in this room will move till it's finished."

De Brionne begged Gruner one more time. "I *beseech* you! Morrison knows nothing of these matters!"

"Time I learned," I said, and I froze them all by facing the villain, sword pointed upward and performing the traditional rite.

"En garde! Duel!"—the words came from Alphonse, who seemed in a hurry.

Gruner's first, premature slash with the edge was, I believe, meant to cut my throat. But with thanks to the punctured Italian, I parried the stroke. Then, being much taller and stronger, I lunged him, running *en flèche* across the room. To me, his look of stupefaction was manna from Heaven, and from the corner of my eye I could see de Brionne, mouth ajar.

Most triumphs have their conditions, the rose hides its thorn, the thistle its sting.

Gruner was a powerful man in better than average condition. He practiced at swords several times a week, and he was certainly expert. Back to the wall, he slithered out from under, and, using the attack I least expected—a cutover—sliced my right cheek.

I began to wonder if I'd plunged in over my head. I can surely be excused for that. Gruner was highly skilled, and he made me sweat, but his fiber was no longer tough enough, and, as said, I was half his age.

I felt his aggression fade slightly, and I methodically went to work on his face, having pointed him elsewhere before. Within five minutes I saw at least eight deep cuts from his forehead to his chin, and heard his rattled panting. I backed him again to the wall, roughly, and presented my point at his throat.

"Produce the mortgage, Gruner. You've nothing but an illicit claim, and you're going to prison for it. But I'll have the mortgage document, or run you through now."

Badly bleeding, he fumbled in his pocket for the paper, and tossed it onto the floor.

To Alphonse, I said, "Tear it up. The Château Brionne-Bouscard belongs to the vicomte, and has for many years."

"Kill 'im," Alphonse pleaded. "'At man won't never be no good."

"Be quiet!" I heard de Brionne say.

Taking the swine's sword, and lowering my point, I said, "There's another, more serious matter.

"A 'duel' took place on your property; it was in fact naked murder."

Here I saw de Brionne slap the pistol from Alphonse's hand.

"An elderly guest you'd swindled threatened to expose you—two of your then *vignerons* witnessed it all. The police have been alerted; probably you can expect them soon. So unless you escape, I'm afraid you'll meet"—I made a gesture across my throat—"Madame Guillotine herself. I'm told the crime is viewed as final.

"Actually, I'll ask you to *get* out, for you see, I bought your mortgage." I showed him the document. "You are presently without a home. But I'm tolerant of dogs like you and will give you twenty-four hours to vacate, not a minute more."

"It seems I owe you a good deal, my friend," he said, staring at me as if he meant to remember what I looked like.

For all his wicked ways, Gruner was no coward, and as a younger man would have beaten me. Now, sweeping his cloak off the table, a handkerchief held uselessly to his face, he gritted out, "This round you win, Yankee. But another will come, at another place."

"Not if you don't have a head," I responded with great good humor, and the utterance appeared to hasten his movements.

"Gruner," implored de Brionne, "hold a minute. In the name of humanity, let us summon a doctor from the village."

"Damn your doctor, your house, and your whores of a family. Be certain," he advised me, "our paths don't cross again." His face was, I'm afraid, slashed to mincemeat.

"Yes," I said, even more cheerfully, "you're in wonderful shape for a comeback."

I'd noticed he had a wound near the right lung and one, worse, in his sword hand. This man would never hold another sword or gun. But I said, "You really should let us get a doctor. You could bleed to death going home."

His parting curse, while he slammed the door behind, was in German, and so I had no idea what he said. But none in the district ever saw him again, and this chapter was closed.

Chapter XLI

We—the family—sat in the drawing room late after Gruner left, discussing the day. (My own face-cut had been stanched and stitched by a village doctor who borrowed crewel silks from Madame de Brionne. He refused payment, and took off and put on his hat at least a dozen times.) Alphonse was permitted to stand back from the firelight, and de Brionne now asked him, "What, pray, was your plan with the superannuated weapon?"

"I fixin to shoot 'at man, sometime along 'ere. I *ain't* fixin to let him hurt nobody in this fambly, and I does mean to include Mr. Morripson. He good as fambly now."

(Before the evening was over, I'm convinced he thought he *had* shot Gruner, and would continue to think so all his life. At the very least, he would say so.)

"Yes!" cried de Brionne, striking his chair. "I'm glad I used the word 'weapon.' It makes it easier to ask—the skilled use of an épée. Surely there's no way to explain it? I, of course, am covered with shame, but you looked like a professional duelist."

I told him about the Italian, and other butchers that had touched on my boyhood, and he said, shaking his head, "I should have known! Did he leave you *anything* untaught?"

"Yes, the enforcement of proper college learning. And even that wasn't wholly his fault. I always found other things to do."

"I must change the subject," said Madame de Brionne firmly. "I really must. How are we ever to repay you? And why step forth as our champion at all?"

"About your second question," I said, still feeling somewhat in command. "You may remember once when I came seeking help about wine. Wine, and the growing of grapes. Everyone—all the people here who knew these things—dropped important tasks to rally round, during a critical time. I'm positive," I went on, "they would have let the crop go rather than refuse aid to a stranger whose kinsman they once knew. Well, as a Yankee of modest means, I could hardly fail to reciprocate.

"Now your first question, madame. You have repaid me twice over. The fact is," I said truthfully, "I've had a great deal of *fun!*

"But there's one string hanging. Let me play *Maître* an hour or so longer—till midnight, say. It's important."

De Brionne said, "For a year, if you like."

"Only until midnight. For now, if you please, have the stableboy fetch my rig. I have an errand. Really, my friend, you must indulge me in this."

After all was ready, I drove into Pessac, taking Alphonse along for directions. There, as we enjoyed ourselves, I sent a quite rude wire to de Brionne's parent in Nice, advising him that his funds were cut off, and if he had ambitions to eat, it might be wise to come home and bear a hand.

When I returned and announced what I'd done, I detected a strong gleam of triumph in Madame's eye.

"He's the author of your misfortune," I assured de Brionne, who was looking doubtful, not yet able to cast off all traditional authority. "I dislike to speak harshly of him, but he's the malefactor, almost as much so as Gruner. And, Gérard, I hold your promise"—looking at the clock—"to be sacred until midnight. Then you can resume being *Maître.*"

De Brionne flushed, but said nothing.

(Here fate steps in to take a kindly hand. In the morning, after I left, a wire came from Nice saying that the parent had suffered a stroke, lingered a few days and died. I was not to know this till afterward.)

"As you observed, I, personally (with a debt) now own Gruner's holding. It should complement our grape-growing in Niagara. But if it makes you feel better, I'd be pleased if you looked in from time to time. And, perhaps, line out chores for the baron's *vignerons,* and find

351

an acting *Maître*. I know this is asking a lot. I would insist, of course, that we divide the crops."

"Gruner's former château will make good fruit, our young friend. Be assured of it. And I aim to send you several boxes of plants, to see how our product does in your country. I doubt if they transfer without loss."

"But you're not leaving!" cried Madame de Brionne as I rose, with another look at the clock.

"Early in the morning, before any of you get up. Please don't try to se me off; I'm very bad at that sort of thing. But I'll be back, as fast as we can organize Niagara.

"I won't deliver a speech about the Château Brionne-Bouscard and its people. You know what I'd say, and I'd only make a fool of myself. Good night, goodbye, my new and always friends."

Then I turned abruptly and left for my room. As I said, I never knew how to handle these individual goodbyes, and I probably used the wrong and embarrassing words here. (I beg the reader's indulgence.)

I harnessed my rig at dawn, and tried to roll noiselessly round the oval. But the great door opened, and all the family, including Alphonse, who was waving a towel, came out and stood lined up. Renée alone was missing. I myself stood up to wave, not stopping, and cries of farewell followed me to the poplar-lined road to Bordeaux.

My spirit was badly depressed, but it began to revive as the sun's first fingernail showed over the estuary. And then, again on this road, I heard the pounding of hooves. I stopped, and Renée came up beside me. Her horse, wishing to run, switched around.

She soothed him and came close to my seat.

"I have not settled what to do about you. I feel something quite unusual," she said matter-of-factly. "Unmistakably, but it is not fully identified."

"Maybe it's a fever." It was the only popular ailment I could recall. But she saw this as serious.

"Yes, a species of fever . . . Are you not coming back to us?"

"When I do, I'll no doubt find you married." Trying to keep things light, I stupidly went on, "Baron Gruner paid you interesting compliments last night."

"I heard them. The door was partially open, you know."

"And you were insulted?"

"From him—yes."

Then my pose fell away in shreds; I'd been under strains that cried

352

for outlets. But I had obligations, and more, at home, so I said, "Dear Renée, I have feelings, too," and I leaned down to kiss her.

As I drove off, I heard her call, "William, goodbye. And don't look back!"

She was gone, leaving an emptiness in my heart. For her, and for Betsy, and for Samantha, and for a friend in a convent school—for all the people I loved in different ways. I was so confused I could barely see the road.

It should be remembered that many new things had happened, and I was twenty-one only. Nearing Bordeaux, I know I'd never seen things that many others saw.

Quite suddenly, I badly wanted to go home.

In Bordeaux, I sent back the rig, generously tipping, and bade farewell again to my lawyer friends. Then I got off a thank-you note to the Rothschilds and boarded the night train for Toulouse and Montpellier.

I had one more obligation, as I saw it. Staying overnight in Montpellier, I walked that afternoon to the convent, not certain what to do. I'd mailed a sum for expenses, but Monsigneur Rey's benefactions had been broad, and I wondered if I owed him a visit. All things considered, I was not sure he would wish it. And I was afraid. Only a miracle, I saw now, could have made things turn out well. A known life, and habit too strong, and once more—once more, I done something almost comically absurd. Downcast, I walked the convent walk behind a five-foot wall.

Then, out of a door scampered a group of uniformed girls, laughing and chattering, their classes finished for the day. I crouched down, and, with more moral courage than I thought I had, I forced myself to look over the wall. In the midst of the group, and very much of them, was Germaine, radiant and happy. I started to call, then decided not to.

I'd receded in her memory, and to change what she'd become would be cruel. All these girls, including my ward (for that's how I viewed her) were the same light copper under that fierce sun. Yes, she was emphatically one of them.

I silently said, Goodbye, for whatever life you choose. Goodbye, my brief and unattainable fancy.

Then I dragged myself back to the hotel, to spin down into a nightmare sleep.

At Marseilles, there was a two-day delay to get a fast packet home. I spent this time strolling the Cannebière, buying gifts and trying not to think of my adventures. My head badly wanted clearing. At an outdoor exhibit of hopeful young artists, I studied the work of a man whose lines had magically caught the spirit of peasants in the fields, or so it seemed to me. His name was Millet, and I bought (despicably cheap) four paintings by him and two by a failure named Corot. One Millet for the Lockridge house, one for Frances Barclay, and two (with the Corots) I'm ashamed to say for me. (To be candid, I felt I'd earned them, and besides, they'd probably amount to nothing.)

For my father and General Whitney, I'd already shipped each a case of the finest Bordeaux claret, and for my mother (from Marseilles) I bought a bottle of expensive perfume. On second thought, I got Betsy a flask, too.

And then I checked on my urchin. The kindly, sad-faced priest said, "Monsieur, I regret to tell you. He stayed three days and then disappeared, back into his former life, one assumes. I'm sorry; we did what we could."

I thanked him and left, only half a winner.

Then the ship was ready, and we bucked equinoctial gales and cross-seas for day after day before sighting the Battery. My father and mother were there, and at dinner that night, I talked myself hoarse.

Afterward, in his study, we turned to business, myself slumped in a chair, ready for anything.

From behind his forbidding desk, he said, "You've spent a lot of money, young man; maybe more than you can afford; I haven't checked. In some ways, I'll add, you've done pretty well, possibly better than that. More than I thought likely in your case. Fortunately, our new republic matures its citizens—or most of them—early."

He leaned back and smiled.

"Thus far in history, growing up quickly is the rule. Later, when we're fat and soft, men may be children at thirty. As examples of this in general, I'll remind you that Charles Darwin, starting his voyage on the *Beagle*, was twenty-one.

"And how old," he went on, "do you think Captain Fitzroy, commanding His Majesty's *Beagle* was, to start this same voyage?"

Getting home had placed me back in my relaxed mental frame. So after deep reflection, I ventured, "Seventy-two?"

"If you have a fault, William, and a few exist, it is that you slip with no trouble into nonsense. Fitzroy was twenty-three. Now, Harbison"—I'd nearly forgotten the lawyer—"Harbison and I have contrived a means of recovering your expenditures, with a little

354

besides." Musing, he said, "Perhaps I have a little of your mischief in me.

"Our scheme is this: You've told me that even vineyards like one of the Rothschilds' are in size limited, most to 175 acres. After this, in most cases, the law of diminishing returns takes over. You know the law? I imagined not.

. "During your frenzy in Niagara, you, and your equally untutored friends, and, I'm afraid, Harbison, gobbled up 2500 acres. Enough, if worked, to place wine on every floor in China, and in India and the Dutch East Indies, as well. Now, you've surmised, no doubt, that within the next two or three hundred years, you won't be able to work land in such volume.

"Harbison, then, will go to Niagara and spread the rumor that your friends have found their acres a bonanza for the growing of grapes—among the few Eastern places to be thus blessed. Let it be known that you've come back from Bordeaux. You may trust Harbison to whip up a frenzy exceeding that of a gold rush.

"Obviously, the land value will instantly boom." He tapped on his desk with a ruler. "When it reaches treble what you paid, sell half, or 1200 acres. Now, seeing it rise, don't wait for five times your price, or ten. More fortunes have been lost trying to extract the last farthing from an investment than from overcaution.

"Our plan involves cunning, true, but it is, in every way, honest. If *you* can gamble on growing grapes, *they* can shake dice on their half. I allude, of course, to greedy buyers. After all," he said, sitting back again, "it's only business."

I shook my head. "I'm beginning to see," I said slowly, "how New York families remain so prosperous."

"Let's not forget your gyrations in France; they could make a textbook on stealth."

"Gyrations?" I started to protest, but the scheme would indeed solve any financial snags of the moment; it was honest, legally, and it might accommodate the second half of our operation—the growing, fermenting, aging and bottling.

Summoning all possible brass, I complimented him on a "thimblerig" of inspiration. He looked fierce at first, but nothing came of it.

Then we had a glass of (I thought with my new knowledge) conspicuously overfoxy wine, and turned in for the evening.

Chapter XLII

I sat in the train, depressed again. I missed France, its ways and its beauty, all my friends, Renée. In a very short time, it had seemed like home.

Perhaps one difference was that, now, I looked through a sooty window at a brown, dull countryside on this gray November day, and contrasted the sunlit cities of southern France.

But in the morning, nearing Niagara, I felt my heart begin to thump, and the prospect of reunion with those I knew best erased all else. Also, I had ample news about my trip, and could scarcely wait to share it with my partners.

I saw the mist rise first; and the Falls' roar beckoned, as usual, like an unknown keeper. Many good and bad things had crowded that summer, and I felt again the silent rim's challenge. And November Niagara Falls, I realized (as the square little dwellings now came into view) was not Niagara of lilac-rich June.

Then we came to a grinding, bumpy stop, and I was with them again; they were all lined up, patiently enjoying the smoke. Nothing had changed. Lockridge had on the same handsome but exhausted jacket; Frances Barclay glowed with good looks, and maybe a new dimension of thought, and Betsy's blue eyes appraised me calmly and (I hoped) fondly. Certainly she made a close study of my face, but it was as though, in this life, neither triumph nor disaster, would diminish her, ever.

I was fussed, and said in a too-loud voice, "Well, I hope you got all those postcards and letters."

"Two postcards and *a* letter," said Frances. (Confound the girl; she would keep count.) "You *are* a letter-writer, William. Is postage frightfully expensive in France?"

"Well—" I began, but Lockridge, with his excuse for everything, said, "Letter-writing only leads to more letter-writing," and Frances, one hand on his arm, said, "Yes, I expect you're one of the world's greatest."

"I wrote you a seven-page letter once; tell them, Betsy."

"I was at school," she said, "and you needed my allowance for an experiment."

"Frankly," he said, ignoring this, "I never cared for letters, writing or reading. Put things in notes, read 'em to people later. Better system."

Sympathetically, I sensed that they themselves were homesick, in small degree. What I'd recently seen made Niagara unbearably drab for a second, as indeed it had struck me from the train.

It was at that precise moment that it began to snow. It started falling thickly, but not as though it meant to retreat after the first arrival. The south of France was nullified on the instant, and I began to have some thoughts of miracles.

"How marvelous!" exclaimed Frances Barclay. "Pure white! I've seen only little sulphurous spits, you know." And I noticed Betsy hugging the flakes to her face.

Suddenly things were changed. We came to life, no longer trying to make artificial conversation. I threw my bags in Lockridge's luggage box (I had three more bags than when I left), hopped nimbly in, and we headed off through a snowfall clearly mounting in strength. He took a back route, to avoid a jam now developed in the street.

The downfall was so intense we had to grope our way, scraping one fellow-townsman's rig. People were vacating all thoroughfares. These Northerners knew the signs of a blizzard coming, and scrambled to prepare for it. And, as if he'd noted a real storm at last, Lockridge said, "This *is* dense! We could use a sleigh."

Betsy, more excited than I'd seen her, cried, "Father, please do! You really must. You as much as *promised!*"

"Get home first," he said, slapping the reins, producing nothing. The horse had almost fallen twice. "I think we're in for a real smasher." But he was not able to avoid adding, "One develops these senses—science."

"Really!"

The temperature had dropped, and I shivered, dressed mainly for the vineyards of Bordeaux.

The horse slipped and stumbled, and we consumed probably half an hour before approaching Lockridge's cheery white domicile. All thoughts of châteaux had gone out of my head; this was more fun. By straining, as we neared we could see the outlines from the road, and little more. The wind had dropped slightly, and the flakes were smaller; but they were still thickly together.

Ramses, peering from a window, ran out, directed a friendly species of "Ugh!" at me, and removed the luggage. Inside, he had a pine fire going. It cracked and hissed, besides being blessedly hot.

Lockridge claimed to have trained these excellent Senecas. In point of fact, he'd done nothing; Betsy was responsible for everything, as we knew. But to give him his due, he'd hired them two years before, because, on their own initiative, they'd come to his school and were extraordinarily perceptive, when one considers their different background. (Afterward, when Betsy told me what he paid them, I was shocked. His plan was for them to save and go into some business of their own.)

So—it was no great surprise when Nefertiti, smiling at me, padded in with a tray of eggnog whose central ingredient was not, praise God, Monongahela. Before tasting, I could tell by my new word of "bouquet."

"This is something like," said Lockridge, taking a cup. "Let it storm till Doomsday; we've plenty of wood and coal oil, and can always get more." He went back to look at his instruments.

"The glass is low, very low, well below twenty-eight, and I think we have a temperature inversion," he reported happily when he returned. He confided to me that he'd added this last, to make a sounding report.

Frances Barclay had been at a window, watching Ramses put the rig in Lockridge's barn. She'd rubbed a little circle.

"Let's have a temperature inversion, to be sure!" she exclaimed. "I've never properly had one; does it mean upside down? . . . I've never had a blizzard, either."

"To take a storm like this lightly," said Lockridge, slumping into a chair, "to take it lightly is to beg trouble. How are we stocked for food?" —to Betsy.

"We have food for a *long* storm, Father," she replied, and he nodded as if he'd seen this coming and himself laid in extras.

"There is," he said, "the matter of snow crushing roofs. But you will note that, when I went house-hunting—"

"Or, rather, Betsy did, I imagine," said Miss Barclay from her window.

—"as I was saying," resumed Lockridge, "when I went house-hunting, I selected both house and barn with steeply sloping roofs; also shingles from the first slice of the pine. I rather fancy myself in matters of that sort."

"Did he?" asked Frances, turning to Betsy. "I don't believe it." After a wait, they both laughed. But Miss Barclay was so absorbed in our fierce and sudden spectacle that her mind was not off it for long. "Couldn't we *do* something? Go out and throw snowballs? Or, better, make a snowman? I've read of these done."

"I'm thinking," said our host.

I glanced around the cheerful room, in this essentially humble town. I'd forgotten how it looked. The walls were papered in a colonial design, the furniture was perfect, seeming less costly than it was, and there were family pictures here, too, in heavy silver frames on shadowed corner tables. On the main table, apples and nuts filled a center bowl, the summer fruits being gone. But Niagara apples were famous and these took the others' place.

The sun-drenched towns of Provence faded from my mind; the warmth of old friends, a blizzard and rough weather moved in to round out a progression. I watched Betsy move deftly about, and was glad at last to be home.

Remembering, Frances turned from the window. "William, I'm sorry—you must be bursting to talk about your trip, and I've let a snowstorm interfere. Now tell us everything you've learned, and done, even the naughty parts."

"At lunch," I said, listening to the timbers shake and creak, wondering if they'd hold in this dangerously rising wind.

"Lunch!" she cried. "I have it absolutely! You can tell us then. Gervais, hire a sleigh and let's have a picnic!"

"Please, Father," added Betsy.

He looked startled. "In this howling tempest? I assume you haven't lost your senses."

"*Bill,*" pleaded Betsy, holding my hands.

"It's obvious," I told him, "that Science would profit. Science has been founded on risks. The late Galileo—"

I was perfectly comfortable before the fire, listening to the wind howl. But Betsy's rare beseeching drowned all objections.

"I was about to suggest," said her father, "that it's foolish not to take Time, and Science, by the forelock. There may not be another blizzard all winter. Niagara, despite its latitude, has a name for blandness, caused by the lakes."

There followed a collection of heavy clothes; Nefertiti found buffalo robes and blankets, and Lockridge produced an ax, a spade and a knife from his woodshed. Ramses followed him in, carrying an asymmetrical bundle.

"By George, the venison! Are your teeth sound?"

"Father! Ramses made us this gift."

"I'd forgotten. But I don't think he heard me, not in English. Lug it along. Worse than mutton," he confided to me.

"How on earth do you cook it?" (Frances)

"One eats it raw," Lockridge told her.

"Father!" said Betsy, angry at last. "Couldn't you try a *little* harder?"

Largely oblivious of her humor, he said, "I have a steel rod to use as a spit. Pass through, place over a hot fire, cook like the devil and—it comes out splendidly. No change at all."

"I'll ask Betsy," said Miss Barclay, and did.

"To taste best," Betsy admitted, "it should be roasted for a long time, but we can cut strips for broiling."

I felt better in a wool shirt, a wolfskin cap of Ramses' and a heavy jacket. And when everyone was faithfully outfitted against the gale, which now tore at the house, Ramses went three blocks for a sleigh. Though its runners were free from rust, Ramses greased them, while shaking his head in disapproval. Before we burrowed into our seats, the Senecas made us tell precisely where we were bound, which Lockridge did with believable authority.

Then, with horse robed, provisions and gear stowed, we were off. It really was a very bad storm, our end of the hurricane season; we were, as our host had hinted, probably being foolish.

Cataract House was, of course, closed for the season. It was my duty now to find another place to live, and there were questions I wanted to ask. But the snow took precedence today. And it *was* exciting. I guessed the wind to have reached Force 8, just below a gale; and the snow, driven horizontally, was absolutely steady—thick, if smaller flakes now, and yet greater in volume. There was no hint of sleet. It was fluffy but firm, and three or four inches had already gathered on the ground.

Lockridge, driving, peering hard ahead, took the roundabout way toward the road for Lewiston. Doing this, we passed International House, the sole hotel to stay open all winter. A hundred yards farther, a walking figure loomed up like a giant in the center of the street.

Lockridge hauled in the reins. "You, sir. I nearly hit you. Be kind enough to let us pass, if you please."

The giant seemed to be smoking a cigar. He turned slowly and menacingly back.

"Why, it's Harbie! Mr. Harbison, the landgrabber," exclaimed Frances Barclay. "What on earth are you doing, Harbie? Out on a legal crisis? Or looking for wine?"

Her spirits were so high, even in this devil's brew, that I suspected a major change in her life. There could only be one answer, of course, Lockridge—and I felt a glow of warmth. A little embarrassed, I imagined he had small idea of what grand times he was in for, and I thought, too, what an unusual girl Frances was. She was still only thirty and, I believed, Lockridge was forty-three. It seemed, then, like the perfect span.

Mr. Harbison was adequately (and respectably) outfitted for the weather, with a Russian-looking chinchilla hat, a greatcoat, mittens and galoshes. But there was no good way to wrap up his vision. From time to time, as he approached the sleigh, he removed his pince-nez and cleansed it with a silk kerchief.

He affably shook hands around, apologized for blocking the road, and explained that he had preceded me by a few days, in, then, good fall weather. But he had delayed calling until I enjoyed my reunion. It was like him, I thought.

In the middle of the street, I would normally have worried about collision, but these streets were bare. And the people were in their homes making preparations for the worst.

Lifting his voice against the storm, Mr. Harbison explained that, "It's been my custom, in fair weather or foul, to take a constitutional before my two o'clock dinner. In that way, I've kept fit, as no doubt you've noticed. But I'll say this; the day has turned worse than foul, and as you coasted up, I was thinking of cutting my constitutional short. *I seldom if ever do that,*" he said firmly.

"Harbie," cried Frances, competing with the wind, "your constitutional, with its various amendments, looks frightful. We're going on a picnic, and—"

"A picnic, madam?"

"—and you're coming with us. You see," she said, rollicking along, "we're not certain it's legal and we need our guide, counselor and friend."

Taking him by the collar, she almost literally dragged him up beside her in the back.

"Yes, a picnic, to be sure," he replied, wiping his glasses again. "A capital idea. Do you have some abandoned shack in mind or do you plan to sit in the snow? My dinner is a hearty one, I warn you."

"*Hearty!* When we get back—"

"*If* we get back," said Lockridge.

"—you'll think you've eaten a bear singlehanded. We've got what it takes, Harbie! Don't forget it."

He looked pleased, almost boyish, and called out playfully, "On, coachman! By all means, hie us to this unusual repast. But since I'm making no contribution—"

"Except your life." (Lockridge)

"—I should perhaps buy a bottle or two of wine, if the Grog Shop's not closed."

"I have wine," I said, and I did. In Bordeaux, at the last minute, I'd picked up a small straw-stuffed box containing three bottles of a *premier cru*, for a dinner of celebration.

Lockridge, feeling his way, got us out of an empty, white town beneath a dark gray sky, and, somehow, onto the road to Lewiston—the town Miss Barclay had owned briefly. Once in the open, the horse appeared to sense our festiveness, and it trotted briskly through some amazing snow-blasts. It was piling up. Nobody said much; we were too busy snuggling into our clothes.

At one point, Mr. Harbison, again compelled to clear his glasses, observed that "When I was a child, my father insisted on picnicking often; that is, at least once a week, though I'll confess that, as a conservative man (he was also a lawyer) he seemed to select days, ah, slightly less aggressive."

But he hastened to add, "I'm not saying he was right, you know. This"—and he tried vainly to look ahead—"is entirely suitable for me. *All* Harbisons," he said sternly, "have been regarded as durable. Though in comfortable circumstances, we were brought up to believe in austerity." As he and Frances Barclay necessarily pressed together, "This would appear a day of special category."

(I'd wondered before, seeing this and that, if our legal adviser hadn't some respectable hopes, or plans, for Miss Barclay, and knew he would take things respectably if they failed.)

But by now, I was far from certain about the day. This storm was building rather than subsiding. On all sides, nothing could be seen but white. And while the big trees near the gorge knocked out part of the wind, the snow beneath our runners was accumulating fast.

"Here!" sang out Lockridge at a place where the town (for six or seven years) had planned to build an "overlook." We turned aside, the runners sounding smooth, not crisp, as when the snow's about to melt. The temperature was just on 20 degrees Fahrenheit; I'd looked before we left.

"See here, Mr. Harbison, I want to speak to you very, very seriously," said Frances Barclay.

"I was trained to be serious, Miss Barclay, and can be serious even on an outing. Pray state your case; that is," he said, smiling, "take the witness."

"Sure you don't mind?"

"Positive, madam."

"Well, it's just this: Before we saw you, we all had a pretty stiff round of eggnog. And, as I'm becoming more and more of a souse, I poured out a second when we left. I'm finding it awkward to hold. Would you drink it, like a good fellow?"

I could see the counselor's features relax to satisfaction. Then he handed down a kind of summation.

"Frankly, and few know this, my custom in late years has been to imbibe a pre-dinner drink of spirits, in my room. Sometimes two. My physician is partly at fault. He says it benefits digestion, far better than wine. But are you certain, madam?"

"I do wish you'd quit calling me madam. I've never properly been in the business, you know. What can these people think?"

"Madam! Really, it never occurred—"

"There, you see—again. But it doesn't matter. My name is Frances, or Barclay (Miss)." She gave the second of these some thought. "Barclay, Miss—that has a nice ring, and it's unusual, too. But go right on with madam. You never know. It could happen to anybody."

Lockridge chose a spot on the slope, down toward the river. The Falls, for once, could neither be heard nor seen. For the moment, they'd given way to a fiercer transient.

We bent into the storm, climbing out, and Betsy and I helped Lockridge with the tools and provisions. Mr. Harbison carried the venison.

"This is a good spot," explained Lockridge. "The Canadian bank is higher, and we're surrounded by big trees. Bets and I drove here often last year."

"Tell me, Gervais," said Miss Barclay, "do you plan to go *into* the river, or stop this side? There's a river down there, you know, a particularly nasty one."

"Wait and see."

We half slid down the slope, the snow now near the tops of Harbison's galoshes, and came to a halt beneath a pine whose branches drooped almost to the ground. Unlike most of its cousins, it had limbs that grew low; three formed a pretty snow-tight roof for us all.

Nevertheless, Lockridge (surprising me) cut branches from another tree, threw them over the top, and spaded out the snow inside.

Then Betsy spread the robes. The wind, here, was all but blocked by the bank behind, the higher one across, and the trees. Still, you could hear the snow softly falling—a happy sound not easy to describe. Faintly above that there was an occasional gurgle from the river rushing along.

"Well," said Lockridge, resting from his labors, "we're about set for what loosely could be called a picnic. What have we got, Betsy— aside from the meat?"

"Nefertiti hard-boiled eggs, and I filled a basket with three tins of salmon, two very soft loaves of bread, cheeses, sweet potatoes, butter, jam, salt, pepper, knives, forks—"

"We'll take the rest on trust. Main thing's the venison. I think Ramses lifted, or poached, this deer from the tribe. Poached venison—there's nothing like it. We can rig a spit in front, and soon be slicing off steaks." He turned to Harbison. "What do you think of that, legally speaking?"

"I see no valid impediment—"

"You did drink the eggnog, Mr. Harbison?"

"I'm afraid, madam, that such is the case." After a pause, when he plainly wrestled something out, he resumed: "What I have to say is a trifle embarrassing. But I make a practice of carrying a flask of cognac, on nearly all occasions. It was a whim of my mother's, whose family judged raw spirits to be a last court of appeal, as it were, for most ills. 'In desperate emergencies, son,' she would say, 'turn to brandy, *but at no other time!*' This was begun, I believe, by her paternal grandfather, a worthy man who found so many emergencies that he died at twenty-six. I do not think," he said judiciously, producing a silver flask, "that anyone here runs a risk of overdoing.

"This brandy happens to be Spanish," he told us. "I prefer it to the best exported French."

"Harbie, promise you won't go off in delirium tremens, won't you?"

"My mother took the strictest precautions," he replied with a touch of stiffness.

"Of course she did, and don't think my family didn't. But they're all drunks, just the same. No, my cousin Jasper's a teetotaler; he's the halfwit. It was sherry, mostly, that did them in."

"You have my every sympathy, madam."

"Oh, they're not really drunks. They just drink all day, especially my father. They've got little pet names as excuses. If it isn't an 'eye-opener,' it's a 'stirrup cup,' or 'one for the road,' or a 'nightcap'— that sort of thing. The whole lot's got a faint rosy tinge."

We were snug under the boughs, but Lockridge suggested that he and I fetch the sleigh seats.

Mr. Harbison got up to help, but Miss Barclay told him, "Just go on swilling cognac, like a good man of the law. It's cold, and getting colder."

We fought up through the deepening snow, and eventually pried loose the seats. Back under the boughs, we placed them face to face, with a few feet between.

"This is something like," said Frances, sinking down. "They have backs, too; fancy that. You're awfully ingenious, Gervais, but why don't you go on with the fire?"

Lockridge (not absentminded with something to do) had brought several copies of the *Iris*, and, after we'd all foraged, he built a roaring high fire from deadfalls. It felt so good, I hadn't realized how cold I'd been; in fact, I'd failed to notice how the storm was worsening.

Betsy cut and strung meat in strips, over the steel rod, and Ramses' venison, very red-looking raw, began to sizzle and drip. She pushed forward the potatoes, and we sat back, each (except Betsy) with the bottom of a glass covered with cognac. As yet, the wine was not quite up to the cold. The temperature had dropped farther, and I felt the fiery liquid work its way down. Despite certain small discomforts, it was stimulating, though I'd begun to worry for the first time. Still no snow came through our roof, and the wind behind was arrested, but we often heard the crashing of wedges sliding off branches; and Lockridge, once, with his ax, went out to cut two poles for support.

Well, I said to myself, we may never get home, but right now I wouldn't be anywhere else on earth.

"Forgive me, sir, but you said something about wine," said Mr. Harbison when Betsy opened the salmon and handed round tin picnic forks.

"I forgot it! It must have been the brandy."

I struggled *(having* to struggle now) up to the sleigh, fastened a nosebag of oats to the horse, and lifted out my little wicker box. When Lockridge wiped off a label with his sleeve, he shook his head in disbelief.

"I can't believe it, sir!" said the lawyer. "Surely they export all such wines to *England,*" he said half-accusingly to Frances and the Lockridges.

"I was able to buy this through friends."

But it was Mr. Harbison, of course, who had a small gold knife with a corkscrew on his watchchain. Cold as it was, the wine had

Bordeaux's best mellowness, and I held the first sip on my tongue. Then I looked up to see Betsy standing by the water, on the river's extreme edge. Lockridge leaped up quickly, strolled down, took her hand and said a few words, and they came back to join us. I thought nothing of it at the time.

At last, drinking the extraordinary claret, we found that our appetites ignored both cold and snow, and we ate Betsy's eggs, cheese, and salmon, and were ready for the venison. "A blizzard's a wonderful spur to out-of-door dining," and Lockridge further explained (pedantically) that it had to do with the body giving off calories in the cold.

"Oh, pooh!" said Frances Barclay. "I'm hungry all the time, and I'm very free with my calories. Under any condition. Don't tell me about calories. Betsy, dear, I'll help remove the meat. I'm still quite hungry; shameful, isn't it? But how does one recover the potatoes?"

"Rake 'em out," said Lockridge, raking them out with a stick and leaving them near the fire to warm.

I'd never eaten venison, and had visions of the worst cut of mutton. But the strips, still dripping, were either tender or the wine had made them so. And they had excellent, if rather strong flavor. We ate them in our fingers, greasily.

It was just after Betsy had produced a plum pudding that we heard the first animal cry, not far distant.

"What was *that?*" Frances got up to peer out.

"To the best of my belief," replied Lockridge, *"Canis lupus,* or the common wolf. They're still near here, especially in Canada, in some numbers. Last year, Betsy and I saw one often, with deer and dogs ahead. They tried to swim the river and escape. Most didn't make it, poor devils."

"But we have a storm, a crazy one, and your 'poor devils' might be hungry."

Lockridge seemed uneasy; I'd never seen him so. "Animals behave peculiarly before a bad weather disturbance. I myself have watched fish—off Cape Cod—almost mad to take lures—any kind—with a hurricane coming. Animals move about before a big storm; nobody knows what they'll do."

The high, mournful sound was heard much closer at hand, and Lockridge unobtrusively slid the ax toward him with his feet.

"I'll be frank," said Frances Barclay; "I'm frightened. My experience with wolves is limited to a single purchase, and that of a cub. We are *not* full friends, not yet."

Our fire was high enough to scorch us, but Lockridge threw on several more deadfalls.

Then we heard a mighty scuffle of snow, and I shortly saw what I'll probably never see again.

The lead wolf appeared, to our right and headed left. Ignoring us, he sprinted ahead, having to leap in the snow, and was followed by a pack of fifty or more, headed for parts unknown, maybe even to them. There could easily have been a hundred. They seemed not to see us, or even our fire; flashing past us, some making growling or moaning sounds. Then they were gone.

Above this, we heard our horse neigh and stamp its feet, and Frances put a hand to her mouth.

"They won't hurt the horse," said Lockridge, awed. "They're keeping some mysterious tryst, far from here. But my word, what a sight! We've seen something."

"Not again soon, please."

"That first fellow was huge," I said. "Surely they must have smelled the meat."

"Their instinct pointed them elsewhere. Or maybe it was panic. Who knows?"

Mr. Harbison said with finality, "Our 'business' conference will obviously have to wait." He told briefly of my father's plan to inflate and then sell half our land. Then he said, "If you'll let me proceed on my own, with occasional assists from you"—he swept his arm around—"I think I can promise results that will see us through the planting and harvesting, with money left over."

All of us, but Frances (who looked curiously thoughtful) agreed, and then thanked and congratulated him. I think we'd begun to have second thoughts, and this, almost certainly, was a way past the first big hurdle.

Then, after he'd given a few more details, Betsy began putting away the utensils, and I volunteered to haul a load of robes up the incline. I was stunned. The snow was up to my thighs and still pelting down. The wind had shifted toward us, too, leaving me half-blinded. There was no way to guess the time of day, without consulting a watch. The sky had worn its steely, dark gray look from midmorning. I supposed it was about three-thirty.

We had a struggle getting things back to the sleigh. The spit still being hot, Lockridge said, "The devil with it. We can pick it up another time. I could cool it in the snow, but I think we'd better move along."

"The road's disappeared," observed Miss Barclay.

And the horse had understandably become impatient, neighing and stamping around. I doubted the wolves had improved its picnic air. With everything in, we climbed back aboard, but found that the extra weight of snow had put us down to the floorboards. Turned around (finally), the horse pulled like a Percheron, but even with us out, mushing, we moved only a few feet at a time, using Mr. Harbison's compass to find S.S.E., our calculated direction to Niagara. Every ten or fifteen minutes, we fell, exhausted, but we stopped only to shed clothing or to take a brief rest.

By good fortune, the runners told us that the sleigh still held the road. This was made easier, of course, by skirting the great trees some foresighted saint had planted fifty or sixty years before.

"You know," said Lockridge, dead-serious at last, "if night overtakes us before we reach dwellings, we could freeze. We'd better have a conference."

Mr. Harbison stated, "As I hinted, we Harbisons are durable. Perhaps I can push alone into town and find help. Of course, tents can be made by blankets and robes, if worst comes to worst. Still," he said, looking determined, "I stand ready, if you think best."

"William's long legs might do better, but I'm not sure it's possible," said Lockridge. "We can hardly sacrifice our strongest defender."

It was about here that we noticed the light was fading.

"My God!" exclaimed Lockridge, futilely peering at the sky. "Dark *would* fall more quickly, of course. What a blithering fool! This was all my idea."

I thought to myself, There's more to this fellow than a professor sprawled in a chair. He's a good partner for a wine business. Harbison's mildly boring durability was fine, but I'd forgotten several qualities of the English.

"The idea was mine," said Betsy. "And, Father, we can go back to our lean-to and keep a big fire going. We could unhitch the horse and lead *him* down."

"Good girl," said Mr. Harbison, straightened up from a blood-coursing calisthenic.

I thought, again, Here's a couple of others that won't panic, and I included the whole group when Frances Barclay cried gaily, "And we have food left over! Six eggs, pudding, and meat to feed those addled wolves, if they come back. I hope it goes right on snowing!"

Me, I saw our predicament as dangerous. No one would travel this road next day, and I said, fastening down my cap, "All wonderful. Sounds like a real lark, but I'm off" —and I took the flask Mr. Harbison held out.

Then we heard, somewhere beyond the wall of white, a kind of aboriginal *"Har-oo! Wah-hoo!"* The imitation is not precise; the sound had alien elements, as of an acquaintance losing his hair.

"To be sure," said Lockridge, rubbing his mittened hands together. "I'm ashamed not to have known."

In five minutes or so, several giant and ghostly figures took shape in the darkening white void, and it was Ramses, mounted without stirrups, dressed in skins, leading two draft horses and dragging a toboggan.

After clapping him on the back, and saying a number of welcoming things, we helped him hitch the draft horses in tandem before our now thoroughly disgusted beast, and tied the toboggan behind.

Ramses seemed in his usual good spirits, as if generations of forebears were used to weather and its crises, but he permitted himself a single mild rebuke.

"Bad thing whites to do. Not know how."

"You put your finger on the problem," said Lockridge. "We're too white for antics like this. Lead on, Macduff," he cried in his normally careless way.

Chapter XLIII

Near International House, Mr. Harbison wanted down, but Ramses came alongside to say, pointing, "No water there. Sluices freeze."

"Then come to us," said Lockridge. "We'll wait till you get what you need."

The lawyer protested but was ruled down so emphatically that he nodded, and fought his way toward the door. Seeing him struggle, Frances invited herself, without baggage, to share Betsy's room for the night.

Meanwhile, the snow continued steadily with no letup. I remembered how, as children, my sister and I thrilled at a bad snowstorm and then gloomed around the house when things began to clear. And how we hated, for that moment, the sun that blazed through and ruined it all! "Well, back to school," we said in hopeless tones.

This storm was not one of those. It was worse, and when Lockridge had barned the horse, with extra rations and a rub that set him steaming, Ramses returned the horses and rig. We rebuilt the fireplace fire and shed snowy garments now soaked. The substitutes were grotesque, but we were comfortable again, except for aches and pains that served as reminders. Only Mr. Harbison, his galoshes, greatcoat and Russian cap removed, looked his former lawyer self, the pince-nez having weathered it all.

Lockridge, since he bought his house, had dug a well that had a pump in the kitchen. After the water was lifted, with a few strokes, it fell back under the frost line, and so was immune to freezing. Many of these ornamented New England homes. He'd got the idea during his schoolteacher visits and, typically, seized on it. There was some indication he thought it was his idea. But many, many other homes brought river water from a wagon, or used cisterns, since we had more rain than we needed in unexpected seasons.

He had a kerosene stove in the kitchen, too, and this, with the fireplace and a smaller one upstairs, heated the house.

The wind still tore at the outside, and Lockridge, rubbing another hole in window-frost, said, "I wonder what's to become of this. Surely it can't go on forever. What about people who have nothing—food, fuel, water? Should we tramp around and divide up our stores?"

We talked it over, and in the end sent Ramses to make a check. In his skin garments, he seemed physically immune to the storm. On coming back he reported that both the Methodist and Baptist churches were going full blast, with soup kitchen workers, medical aids and plenty of stores. The two said (with thanks) they needed nothing. Each church, by the way, had checked our house and, finding it empty, had assumed we were in the other's. They advised us to snug down and be sparing of our supplies.

Lockridge said, "I feel guilty. We have tons of dried meats and other things in a cellar. Maybe divide up?"

"I've never quite seen that," said Frances Barclay. "It may sound terrible, but because one's been provident and farsighted is no reason to be punished by the lazy, drunken, and so on. And that goes back through history or anyway modern history."

"Well, at least we can shovel out to the road, in case a straggler comes along."

But to do so was nearly impossible. Betsy and Frances, pushing into the yard, measured the height thus far at thirty-six inches, and the fall had increased, if anything. As the *Iris* was to say, "The worst blizzard in the history of Niagara Falls, or anywhere in this region, struck Sunday almost out of a blue sky, and—" etc., etc.

But we made tolerable paths to the road, stopping frequently to pant and rest, having been warned by Lockridge about calories and heart attacks; and, when finished, cleared a narrow road to the barn.

Ramses had been sent to check our closest neighbors, most of whom had left for church. He (Ramses) left one place without delay when the proprietor leaped for a fowling piece, not recognizing the servant and thinking the Senecas had come back to reclaim their own.

The *Iris* also did a good job in listing the major roofs to have fallen in, with other damage. And it fair-mindedly included the total collapse of its new rear addition. This item was coupled to a thinly disguised threat to sue the Hawkins Brothers, Builders. The paper might have done better to sue the Eagle, which the brothers Hawkins supported with better results.

Later, we found that the storm had claimed one life, that of a drunk who'd stretched out for a nap in the doorway of a saloon whose employees had closed up and gone to the Baptist church, where they were relieved of several bottles in pockets having unseemly bulges. He (Elliot Skinner) was mourned by all, for he'd been one of the first nocturnal victors of the Falls in a barrel. He'd since worn a dent in his head, and a charitable coroner's jury laid his death to this rather than drink.

We brushed the snow off outside, and comparatively dry, this time, arranged ourselves around the hearth. Since Harbison had no further clothes on the premises, we'd insisted he stay inside and feed the fire. But I found him outside once, shoveling durably, in darkness, in his vest. With his pince-nez, a gold watchchain adangle with academic keys, and a pair of earmuffs to protect his head, he looked somewhat out of the ordinary. (I afterward found that his Russian pot of a hat was a gift, and highly prized. He was drying it slowly, to avoid shrinkage, in a small parlor off the living room.)

We restored him to the interior after a speech covering his civil rights, with three flimsy precedents.

And then, having completed the job and joined the lawyer to warm and dry out again by the fire, we found ourselves limp with the exhaustion of that day. I was so hazy about what went on that I have no clear idea how we slept, or whether we had a meal. There were several bedrooms upstairs, but I'm confident I never reached one.

The fact is, I slept near the fireplace, beneath a blanket and with a pillow Betsy must have placed under my head. Concentrating, I recalled seeing her concerned face above me, and I took one of her hands, but she slipped away.

I was conscious for a time that Nefertiti crept in and out, doing what was needed without being told. And Ramses was so crushed by the outing (having done most of the work) that he put on snowshoes, mushed down to the river and caught thirteen fair-sized trout.

"How the primitive races suffer from their 'ignorance,'" Frances Barclay observed. "This place will eventually go back to the Indians; wait and see."

In the morning, all refreshed, washed up and original clothing back on, we had a late, anecdotal breakfast, and the Indians were called in before we ate. They were polite, but I noticed that neither really touched the small portion of wine given them.

We were starving at last, and Nefertiti gave us Betsy's sugared fried apples and then platters of fried eggs, bacon, ham, sausage and round fried potatoes—and fluffy baking soda biscuits with fresh butter. These last were curious to me, being larger and higher than the common kind, as good cold as hot, and filling.

"You'd think we hadn't eaten for a week!" said Frances Barclay. "And only yesterday—or a hundred years ago—we were bolting deer strips in numbers to interest a doctor.

"American food suits me *perfectly*," she said. "Let me tell you what an ordinary breakfast, where I lived, in this Victorian age, consisted of. It was latish in the morning, after everyone had ridden horses and the like; but I never found that much of an excuse. Can you bear it?

"Well, it started off with ham and eggs, of course; and went on to a variety of hams—fried, baked, smoked—and now came venison pies, kippers, Easterhedge pudding (which was concocted of sorrel, *nettles* and barley mixed with eggs and butter); and then fresh breads, creams, curds and marmalades, always served with mead and wine and hot chocolate.

"And that was every day! It's revolting—barbaric, really. No doubt you've seen portraits of those gentry, all with a pronounced paunch. The paunch is much admired; it means success, you see.

"I'd ever so much rather have one of Nefertiti's breakfasts."

Mr. Harbison gave a little pat to his middle.

"All of the Harbisons," he stated, "have been trenchermen. Yes, the word is archaic, but let it stand, and I could add that my father—"

"Your father," said Frances Barclay firmly, "was the most gallant of all. Isn't 'gallant trencherman' the phrase? *How* that man could eat!"

For the first time, the lawyer gave a satisfied chuckle. "You needn't spell it out. I realize I'm heavy going for you young people" (he was fifty) "and I deplore it. My life has been geared to the serious, and it's hard—though thoroughly enjoyable!—to unbend with you casual British."

"We're not casual," she said, "we're just stupid. And besides, we've become Americans too, now. Frankly, I don't know how we passed the test."

The lawyer, sensing a generally complimentary vein, was much affected. And when he recovered, he said, as if addressing a jury, "Those words will not be forgotten. And I wish to say—you can take it down, if necessary—I've not had such jollity, and, yes, friendship, before in my life—"

Here he choked up, made a diversion by cleaning his glasses, and we clapped him on the back, with cries of "Harbie!" (And again) "Our guide, counselor, friend and good angel!" "A sport of the old school!" "May he never eat less than he's eaten today!"—etc.

After breakfast I was urged to make some remarks on wine. It really wasn't the time; I would do it fully later. A friendly fire crackled in the fireplace, the storm was abating, and, to save me, I couldn't describe my Bordeaux education in grape-growing and the rest, without an overpowering tug to embellish.

When I'd truthfully told all I thought the occasion demanded, I added a few harmless curlicues. I pictured again (as Lockridge watched me quietly) the people crushing grapes with their feet, and added that the more aristocratic these people were, the richer the wine turned out, and that titled persons were positive winners. I said Baron Rothschild could take one stroll around a vat and that crop was nailed down.

"Fascinating," said Frances Barclay. "And my word, what a lie!"

"One thing I forgot," I told them. "The feet have to be filthy. That is *very* essential. They have a box of mixed mud and sand, and everybody scuffles around inside before climbing the little ladder.

"As I've outlined it, the whole business produces that soft mellowness so prized when the ratings are given. Also, this same procedure evokes the unique flintiness in the white wines of Graves."

"Anything else on this round?" asked Lockridge drily.

"Well, yes, but it's a bit on the vulgar side." And I told them how the *vendangeuses* pinned up their skirts behind, while bending over to pick, leaving them fully exposed. "It's a tradition, goes back five or six hundred years." When I noticed Betsy regarding me steadily, I brightened and said, "The men have an equally strong tradition, and that is—not to look. There's no hanky-panky in those fields. I'll take an oath."

"That's a grand job, William," said Lockridge. "We'll be anxious to hear the rest sometime."

Mr. Harbison cut the end off a Havana with a gold cigar clip. "Ah, to be young again," he murmured.

The snow slowly gave way, as the sun struggled out, and we went about town to see where help was needed. Among other things, we lifted two rafters (or joists) off a pair of saddle horses trapped in a stable; hospitalized (so to speak) a woman who was momentarily expecting and helpless (her husband being in Buffalo, buying a steel drum); led some kenneled dogs to the streets (which were being cleared); and removed a man from an isolated shanty where he'd been shoveling the roof. He was all right, except for a broken leg, and hailed us, holding up a bottle.

"Come up, ye good Samaritans!" he cried. "The ladder's perched agin the backside. Now I don't know when I've had a friskier time with a snowstorm!" (The roof being frail, his left leg had plunged through a hole.)

He said heat came up through the attic door, and he was as comfortable, as he put it, as "a chimney sweep on Christmas." The man, an Eagle veteran, was harmless though simple. We got him down and took him to the doctor's, shouting greetings and waving his bottle. It was embarrassing.

The leg was splinted then plastered up, but he scraped off the plaster in a few days, and carried a limp thenceforward. The whole thing, he acknowledged, had taught him a lesson. "I should have knowed that roof was a two-bottle job," he said. "I had to ration the full three hours whilst there." What's more, the doctor had "pizened" him by forcing down enough coffee to get him sober. He planned to get the doctor's license removed if possible.

As we drooped toward home, Lockridge said, "You've been back two very busy days and may not know that General Whitney died during your absence. He had a heart attack, lingered for two days, and died, as they say, very peacefully. This is bound to hit you hard; and we'll all miss him badly. He was as large a man as his Army rank, and that's rare."

"And Cataract House?" I asked in a low voice.

"The heirs plan to carry on. Closed now, of course, together with all the big hotels except International House."

"What about Frances Barclay?"

"She's taken the top floor of Mrs. Murphy's rooming house. She has her own cooking arrangements, and all else needed. The truth is," he said, meditating, "she's a calamitous cook, but she's having a splendid time. Says she's never even touched such an experience. Actually, I think her technique's improving. We were there for dinner last week, and I slept the night through without cramps. In the beginning, things were remarkably nasty; of late, Bets has been helping. Grand girl, though; I mean Frances—Betsy, too, of course."

I said, "We're what I would call good friends by now, Gervais—and business partners, too. Maybe I can take a few small liberties . . . How do you feel about Frances, beyond her being a grand girl?"

He waited a minute, in the racial style. Then, "I may have a divulgence about that this evening. And I wanted you privately about another matter."

At home, Betsy said, "There's more than an hour of light left. The word is that ice-bridges are forming again, after this deep cold. Why don't we go look? You may not have heard of them. The temperature's dropped lower, and it was bitter before you got home. Do come, William. It's a thing to see."

"Ice-bridges? I know them well," I replied, succumbing to a lifelong weakness not to appear at a disadvantage. "Let's go, by all means."

Lockridge frowned, and when she'd left the room, said, "Watch her carefully, like a good lad. Don't let her out of your sight, please. I'll explain later."

"You needn't," I thought dismally. Samantha's pale face moved between us, as I sharply remembered the details of that nightmare at the rim.

But nothing happened. Winter ice-bridges were part of unusually cold Niagara seasons. And when we reached the ferry landing, many people, forgetting our late snowstorm, were venturing out to explore the river ice, with the caverns beginning to take shape.

Later, when the span froze over, shacks would be built from shore to shore, and the owners would go into business, selling souvenirs, edibles, and the like. Years later, in truth, these bridges would start Niagara's winter tourist season.

But now the river ran in broad, shallow rivulets, in and around the formations. The Falls were subdued; and no mists rose.

I studied Betsy carefully, depressed again. But she showed only the normal curiosity of her fellow-townsmen. Once she said, "Let's see how far we can get toward Canada," but I said evenly, "Maybe not. Twilight's coming, and you can't tell. The bridges may be weaker after today's sun," and I kicked off a greenish shard with one foot.

I added casually, "I didn't know you had a special interest in the river, Betsy."

She thought it over. "During the first year I didn't. It was an attraction for tourists. In fact, I disliked the Falls themselves. They were too overpowering. In a strange way, they could interfere with your life."

"How?" I asked gently.

She looked up, blond hair tied in a ribbon, the blue eyes always searching. I thought she probed how deeply I knew her mind; and wondered, too, if there were any uncomplicated women.

"Well"—she waved—"all these people. Some are the ones who

spend summers making barrels and talking about wire-walking. They—and I too a little now—think of the Falls as a kind of mysterious friend, who can answer questions."

I held up her face and kissed her, the cheek cold against mine. But she pulled me toward her, and I was belatedly aware, even standing on ice, with the leashed river above us, that this girl—my girl?—was more feminine than Samantha, Germaine, Renée, all the others I'd met and fancied briefly.

She even unbuttoned my coat and pulled me close against her. The demure chambermaid was gone.

"It's true about the 'pull' of the river and the Falls," she whispered. "I once thought it was a Chamber of Commerce creation; but it's not. Don't ask me to explain, not yet."

I said, as if soothing a child, "Chances are it's the excitement of the storm. There's no mystery about this overblown river and its plunge. I thought you, of all people, had that in mind."

"I do," she said, still pressed almost expertly against me, causing my mood to change. "Yes"—she smiled brightly now—"it was you, and your coming home, and the fierceness of the storm. I needed something different; maybe you can take its place. But you aren't a woman and won't understand; and I'm not the calm innocent always. Sometimes I feel a kind of empty yearning. Tomorrow I'll be sorry, but during the summer there were several mornings, as I brought your tea and you slept, when I fought off a desire to undress and slip into bed beside you . . . Now you can forget I said that."

Chapter XLIV

Mr. Harbison and Frances had been invited to help eat the trout, which Lockridge had scientifically pronounced at the peak of flavor on the second day. He took his findings seriously, whether they worked out or not.

Entering Lockridge's door, I was struck by an oversight—I had no home. Frances Barclay had new lodgings; Mr. Harbison was at International House, "comfortably" installed in a large suite, with a river view, so he said. But this house belonged to Lockridge. I'd somehow slipped into the notion that I lived here as well. Or, as my father might have put it, I hadn't bothered to give the matter any thought at all (followed by a detailed account of similar inattentions through school and college).

The rest were there, and I brought the matter up promptly, saying to Lockridge, "I'm embarrassed to admit it, but I'd forgotten I was homeless."

"I recommend International House without reservations," said Mr. Harbison, preparing a cigar. "It is not the Cataract House (which, by the way, I predict will slide downhill, now that poor Whitney's dead), but the rooms are clean, the service adequate, and the food passable."

"Without reservations?" asked Frances Barclay. "I thought you always needed a reservation."

The lawyer studied her carefully. "That was a joke, wasn't it? I was never given a chance to develop the faculty. I've often regretted it, at business luncheons and the like."

"Oh, well, not much of one. Let's see—International House—"

"Don't bother about the jokes," I said to Harbison. "I think I'll join you there for a while. But you know, I'm tempted to buy a little house, if our land campaign works out. I have money of my own left, though certainly not as much as before. Of course," I added, brightening, "I could always borrow against a great-aunt's bequest. I believe it's clearing soon. She died, you understand."

"You sound as if you'd been awfully close," said Frances.

"Matter of fact, we were," I said truthfully. "She *never* made jokes, and was beloved by all."

"Can you cook?" asked Lockridge, throwing a log on the fire. Except for the snow, we were collected much as the evening before, and I would miss this crisis when it ended. But in answer to Lockridge's question, I said, "No, but I'd like to get Betsy—all of you—to help me find a house. I've made up my mind. Then perhaps Betsy'll give me a few cooking pointers."

"Of course she will," exclaimed Frances Barclay, "and so will I. I expect you've heard," she said to me, "that I've become practically a gourmet chef. No, I'm serious. I don't mind saying that I'm *very* pleased!"

After a brief, strained silence, she turned to Lockridge. "Well?"

He measured his response carefully. "The words 'gourmet chef' embrace a variety of levels. For my part—"

"That bad, was it?" said Frances, reflecting. "The corn pudding, from Mrs. Murphy's recipe, *was* a trifle peculiar. I noticed it myself. Did any of you suffer a mild distress during the night?"

"Cramps," said Lockridge.

"Father!"

"I shouldn't have added the cream of tartar," said the chef, reflecting again. "And I do believe I stuffed the chicken with some things meant to go out. I'd hoped nobody would notice," she said briskly, in no sense disturbed.

"Maybe Betsy will give you both some pointers," said Lockridge, "and—"

"I have a grand idea," Miss Barclay interrupted. "Aside from Betsy's pointers, I think I'll stay glued to the recipes for a while."

"If you mention 'glue' metaphorically—"

This time, Betsy's "Father!" quieted him down.

Forgetting the food, Miss Barclay turned to her favorite target.

"You must tell us, Mr. Harbison, where you got that wonderful array of hardware on your weskit."

"Weskit, madam?"

"Cockney for your 'vest.'"

"I see."

"They're lovely, Harbie, and they make such a nice tinkling noise. Keys? Academic honors? Phi Beta Something, Summa cum laudanum, secret clubs and societies, with oaths, signs and signals. —But tell me, what is that gorgeous yellowed fang?"

"That, madam, is an elk's tooth," replied the lawyer, smiling broadly. "It represents, as you say, a secret and even dangerous organization. If I divulged a single oath—one only—my life would be forfeit within a week."

"My *word*, what a horror! What do you call it? Does the society have a name?"

"We call it the Elks' Club, and, madam," Mr. Harbison now said gravely. "I killed that elk with my bare hands."

She walked over and patted him on the forehead.

"I knew you had; something told me. Aren't you ever afraid you'll turn on yourself?"

He sighed. "It's something I've had to fight since childhood. You see, my special violence is throttling, and I'm always fearful of waking up having choked myself to death in the night."

In a lull that followed Frances' laughter, Lockridge shifted his feet, and said in conversational tones, "By the way, I'd meant to bring this up, but it slipped my mind."

To Frances he said, "I wonder if you'd care to get married? Sometime this week, if you have a free day. We can slip in and out of the town clerk's office; avoid fuss."

"*Me?*"

"Why not? I'm sound of wind, sound of limb, too, for that matter, and I'm easy to get on with. I can support us, and I've developed rather a fondness for you. Be a good sport."

She said, "I'm bewildered; you sweep a girl right off her feet. You can feel my heart thump, down beneath everything."

Lockridge started to get up. "I wonder if I could? I've wanted to for some time."

"Well, no. That's a privilege I reserve for my husband."

"Father!"

"Well, I'm practically your husband. You draw a pretty fine line here."

"Now, Father! *Really!*"

Miss Barclay produced a lace handkerchief and said, "In front of all these people, too. How *could* you, Gervais?"

I was unable to tell whether, behind the handkerchief, she was weeping or stifling laughter. As for our host, he seemed perplexed.

"Have you got something against me?"

"Well, *I* have," said Betsy briskly. "Wedlock is supposed to be a holy estate, or words like that. And unless it's a European-arranged marriage, there's a little matter called 'romance.'"

Lockridge stretched his feet out further.

"Well, I'm hanged; I confess it. Here I make a perfectly sane proposition, nothing underhand, certainly not bigamous, not after your money—by the way, do you *have* money? If you've got lots, the deal's off. Bets and I live simply—"

"Bets," said Betsy, "may have plans of her own."

"You've broken my heart, Gervais," Miss Barclay told him. "I'd been waiting, dreaming; orange blossoms, visions of wedding cakes dance in my head—"

"Oranges are out of season. Besides, they don't grow this far north," replied Lockridge in thought, trying fairly to see her side of the question.

"Forgive the intrusion, my dear fellow," said Mr. Harbison, badly fussed, "but as a kind of general counselor, I have this suggestion: Could you possibly get down on your knees? It's customary, and it might tip the scales."

"That's *it*," said Frances Barclay, snapping her fingers, taking down the kerchief. "The *knees!* I don't promise it'll work, but give it a try, Gervais, do!"

"My knees are pretty bony. I'm forty-three, you know. I might break something."

"Oh, rot. It was on the picnic when you turned into such a commander that I felt my first thump. As to the knees, you're not that fragile. Anyhow, you can lower yourself gently. You needn't slam around like a donkey."

"Let me put it another way." Lockridge sat up. "You're now living atop Mrs. Murphy's. By bad luck, she had a separate apartment, with a stove. Eventually, of course, you'll poison yourself; you've come within a whisk of poisoning *me*. Now—we get married, you move in here—we've plenty of room—and Betsy can teach you to cook. If the job's too touch, Nefertiti can step in. You'd be surprised; a healthy human can live indefinitely on pemmican! Now, speaking of romance, what could be fairer?"

Here, Miss Barclay could no longer contain her feelings. She was, after all, only thirty. She burst into such laughter that her rocker swung back and forth. She leaned her head back, the handkerchief disappearing completely, and laughed, her pretty, perfectly even teeth showing.

"You can't," she finally managed to gasp, "—you simply *can't* be what you seem. *Romance!*"

Her voice changed to a softer, but businesslike tone. "It isn't possible to be so unseeing! For months, now, you've been my version of St. George. Or maybe Galahad or one of those. I never could remember them all. Besides, they were too goody-goody to believe.

"But you, with your genuine life for others! And now you can spend some altruism on *me*. You *will* get down on your knees. As a schoolteacher, you'll recognize that that's absolutely required. There will also be a mention, or demonstration, of Romance. Now, I'll give you ten minutes."

"That's very fair, Father," said Betsy, with her grave look. And I noticed Mr. Harbison wiping his glasses.

Lockridge groaned. "Dammit, I'm shy. I'm not sure I can. I mentioned it in our group because I was too shy to say it alone, Frances—"

"Eight minutes."

There was such dimension to this languid fellow that I hadn't any doubt what he'd do. He would, I thought, despite his forever flippant bride, be master in his house.

He tucked in his legs, jerked suddenly to his feet, walked over and lifted her up to face him.

"What I've meant to say is that I love you and beg that you marry me. I'll make you a good husband. But—there's a small condition: *You'll learn how to cook eggs!* Just that much; I expect no more."

Then he drew her forward and kissed her like a natural man. It was a good resounding kiss, and at the end she threw her arms around him and broke into tears.

Betsy cried, too, and Harbison emitted a champion series of tentative coughs. Even I felt choked up. In my case, I was not only happy for Frances; I was proud of Lockridge.

"And now the knees," said Lockridge stoutly.

"Oh, piffle. Just kiss me again, and promise you won't be carried off by schoolgirls."

He said, looking bemused, "Funny. I thought I was through with all this sort of thing, but when I first heard you laugh and talk, well—"

"Not first, not in England. I was ten years old then and you were twenty-three. Country houses, the gay young blade, and the little girl with spots."

"I was never the gay young blade. I was shy then, too, and I disliked the overhearty types, and their hounds, and port, and talk of annexing this defenseless country or that. It's why Bets and I left after her mother died, wasn't it, Bets?"

"In a sense, that goes for me," said Frances. "But not quite. I—"

"I'm not interested in why you left," said Lockridge as if he knew. "We're in Niagara Falls, now, and you have no past. It's a marvelous way to be. You can quit crying, if you don't mind."

"I don't know whether I'm crying or just feeling warm." She held her hands to the fire. "I had no idea I'd be this happy, ever. Look at me—a husband I adore, a place to live that I'll never leave, an exciting business coming on—and friends who love me." Then she sniffed, and the kerchief came out again. "Dear Harbie, fun-loving and lawyer suppressions; my little sister, Betsy, always better than me at everything; and sweet William, to take up the gauntlet. It—it's too much for one person."

She buried her face in Lockridge's elderly jacket.

Mr. Harbison, reduced to shreds, made a noble recovery and feebly suggested what sounded like punch.

"I—I need restoratives," he managed to say, and added that, "Anyhow, it's the form on these occasions."

When Lockridge left to seek Ramses and Nefertiti, Frances whirled round and sank down to the floor.

"You'll all tell me what to do, won't you? You see, I've never been married before. Or even proposed to."

I looked at the floor, trying to make my face blank.

"Never mind, William. It's dear Gervais knows about me, and doesn't care. I'm convinced of that."

"Tut, tut," said Mr. Harbison, embarrassed, "life takes queer twists and turns. It can't be run in a perfectly straight line."

"Faithful Harbie," she said, standing again as Lockridge led his servants in, "we'll make it our business one day to see you happily married, with children running about and all the rest. Wait and see."

"No, my dear. I'll always remain an old bachelor. I say 'old' because I'm oldish in my ways. I don't mind at all, you know," his glasses blurring again. "Such a stiff, pompous fellow could never interest a woman. I'll have my enjoyment romping"—he looked round the room—"with the children of my friends, as they come along. I 'romped,' to use a term loosely, thinking back to William, and would like to, ah, improve that experience, if possible. No offense, William, but you were, well, just a bit—"

"Difficult?"

"A *good* description! A very mild word for a man with a hornet slipped down his collar, his foot caught in a raccoon trap, and varied discomforts from which I bear small scars to the moment. No, Frances"—it was the first time he'd called her by her first name—"my lot is to work hard, be lonely in my way, and, now, watch my friends' families appear."

"Wait and see! Just wait and see!" Frances insisted gaily, as he coughed with resigned finality.

Lockridge said something in low, pleased tones to Ramses and Nefertiti, and their faces lit up. Or as much as a Seneca's face is capable of lighting up. Nefertiti crossed the room with her tray and handed Frances a glass, and smiled at her in a way I thought Indians never smiled, and Ramses went so far as to shake her hand, his face now solemn as an owl's.

Miss Barclay cried all over again, and Nefertiti, serious and wishing to be helpful, wiped her face with the edge of an apron.

Thus we passed an unexpectedly emotional evening, and, at last, fell into the old bantering vein, having an overabundance of both punch and wine.

Nothing would change.

Chapter XLV

The wedding, at the Methodist Church, went off as well as could be expected. In some degree, Frances, while still emotional had slipped partly back into her rollicking role. The bustle of preparation took place at Lockridge's, after three days. I was best man, Harbison (taking his duties seriously) gave the bride away, and Betsy was maid of honor.

The time was to be eleven o'clock, and from the window I observed that the church—just up the street—was filling before ten. All of these people, even including me, had made friends in the town, and besides, people turn out for weddings and funerals as a matter of course, I've noticed. Both festivities remind a good many of how lucky they are to be in the audience.

"Surely, Gervais, you aren't planning to wear that seedy old jacket?" Frances asked her groom-to-be.

They'd waived the rule about not seeing each other before the church; the house wasn't that large.

"Why," he said, sticking his head out-of-doors, "it's quite warm enough, I think. What's more, I'm used to it; it gives me confidence."

"Well, it's terribly scratchy, and might give me hives. You can't possibly not have something else?"

"Father was going to give his dinner clothes away to an old lady making a rug," said Betsy, in a grown-up blue velvet gown, in which she looked very grown-up indeed. "But I hid them. And, Father, you do have your uniform blues, from your time in the Navy, gold stripes and all. Do wear them!"

"Take the ribbons off?"

"No," said Frances with vehemence. "Give the *Iris* fellow something to write about. What ribbons have you got?"

Lockridge was confused again. "I really don't remember. Nothing of any real account, I know that. I was only in for a year. They gave you ribbons for everything, you see. I may have had one for putting on the suit. And another for stepping on shipboard. Not much else. I'd look like a jackass at Niagara Falls."

"Father, you know they gave you two more. Splendid ones. Hardly anybody else got them. Sometimes you annoy me seriously."

Her face was flushed, and I made a bet with myself that the ribbons, or medals, would be worn.

He sighed. "I had a quite simple life here for a while. I suppose it will never be the same."

"Oh, nonsense," said Frances. "It's just for today. A girl wants something pretty to remember. I need hardly ask if you bought a ring?"

"Well, Miss Know-it-all, what do you think of that?" And he slipped on a truly startling engagement ring, then showed her the plain band, which he handed over to me.

"They don't have rings like that in Niagara Falls. Where'd you get 'em?"

"From a retired New York City burglar who has a child in my school, if you must know. He has others, if you care to swap." (I took this to be a lie, and put them down as family rings, and even Frances smiled.)

It was Betsy who insisted we say a little prayer, or observe a silence, for dear friends who wouldn't be here—General Whitney, Rattlesnake Charley, Samantha and her father. We stood awkwardly for a space, me thinking back, not to Samantha but to General Whitney, whose counsel and friendship had meant so much when I arrived in Niagara Falls. Then I tried to remember what all the others had looked like and been, but I saw the general and Rattlesnake Charley most clearly.

The observance took a few minutes to wear off. Then we fell into another mild wrangle about clothes. Betsy got out Lockridge's uniform jacket, which was well adorned with ribbons, but the trousers appeared to be missing.

"I think these will do," he said, coming downstairs in a pair of corduroys shiny at both knees.

"They're perfect," said Frances. "This is a proud day for the British Navy!"

"Well, I'm not British any longer, with documents to prove it. This combination, dear girl, happens to be what they wear at fashionable Fifth Avenue weddings."

Mr. Harbison emerged from a downstairs bedroom in formal morning costume, striped black pants and all. I wondered how the strange, formal fellow expected to use these at Niagara Falls, but we congratulated him, and he took it beaming.

"Now," he said, in his lawyer's voice, "according to this little booklet—courtesy of the public library—the father, or one who gives the bride away, bears responsibility for the bride's flowers, and I've taken the liberty of cutting these from the conservatory," and he handed Frances the bouquet.

"Harbie, how lovely." She put them to her face. "I never was much on flowers; I'm more of the cook species" (Lockridge put his head in his hands) "but I'll carry these as a knight carries his lady's emblem, jousting."

"—Then the bride tosses the bouquet to be scrambled for among the bridesmaids. The one who gets it," he said roguishly, looking at Betsy, "will be married next."

She blushed, in a routine manner.

"Booklet says further, your honor—I mean, friends—that the best man," laying a hand on my shoulder, "is responsible for the bride and groom's luggage and tickets on either the carriage or a train for the wedding trip."

"A *wedding* trip!" cried Lockridge, looking dismayed. "You want to go on a wedding trip? I can hope," he said feebly, "that you have no ambition to return to England. That'd be ruinous." Then, brightening, "How about New York, say, for forty-eight hours or so? First-class accommodations and all, of course."

She was dancing around with her flowers, and came face-to-face with the groom, wearing a demure expression.

"Don't be angry, Gervais, and for heaven's sake don't back out! But this is a terribly important time for a girl. She doesn't want to miss anything, nothing at all. I'd like, I really would like—now brace yourself and be a good boy—what good Americans do—and I'm an American now, I can do no less. I'd like to go to Niagara Falls for my honeymoon! There, it's out."

Lockridge put a finger under her chin and lifted up her face.

"You certainly are the fairest maid in the kingdom, and—"

"You mean in America?"

"A slip. It won't be repeated, but—"

"When I was a working girl, I never properly got to see the Falls. I loved the work so much, I stayed on the job seven days a week. I'd *love* to see Niagara Falls. I've heard a great deal about it, of course."

Lockridge was so relieved that he slumped down in his chair and stretched out the long legs.

"I know it's asking a lot," she said, leaning down to hug him, "but could we cross to the Canadian side? I'm told they have lovely things over there; a 'Horseshoes' Falls, a zoo and loads of naked Indians—"

"Horseshoe. The Horseshoe Falls. We'll go," said Lockridge bravely, looking like Cortez at Darien, "and we'll stay two nights at Clifton House. Or one, if it turns boring. Can't stay much longer," he said, relieved. "I still have grape-roots in the cellar, and I have to tend them. Among other plants."

"Ramses and I will tend them, Father," said Betsy, with a touch of affectionate malice.

"Then make it two nights."

Here Mr. Harbison cleared his throat and thoughtlessly addressed "Your Honor" again, correcting himself hastily. He'd taken over the wedding, all right, and it would be done correctly or he'd die in his striped trousers. However, a part of him was rattled.

"Counsel for the defense objects. —Forgive me, I do not find in the booklet where one is absolved from an authentic, meaningful wedding *trip*. The defense sees no loophole in the statutes there." He was crimson but determined. "And again, my apologies. Could you not arrange a *de jure*, if not strictly *de facto* trip, and give things a proper tone? I grieve to insist, but it says here—"

"Gervais," cried Miss Barclay, excited, "let's persuade dear William, our very best man, to hire a carriage for after the rite—with four horses because of the floods and mud—and drive to Lockport and back! The weather's grand at last, the road's smashing since they cleared it, and we can be back to Canada for a wedding supper."

"I'm off," I said, and was shortly back with the best rig in town. They cheated me on the price, but said they'd knocked things down "to bedrock" because "the little lady and the schoolmaster" were "the salt of the earth."

As I drove out, the hostler came forward sheepishly to hand me a half-wrapped bottle of Monongahela, as a wedding gift. "Me and the old lady will be at church," he said, "but I wanted to shove this in aforehand, case the groom gets a dose of rubber knees . . . And God bless you all," he added.

Somewhat affected—in fact, with a lump in my throat—I drove up to the house, the wedding party came out (wearing boots) and Mr. and Mrs. Ramses, III, waited behind in the Lockridge surrey. They were dressed in subdued Indian costumes (no feathers) and looked like moguls.

"William," said Mr. Harbison sternly before climbing aboard, "I'll ask you to produce the ring. You *have* a ring, you've attested to that ring, and I, before starting down the aisle, must even see that exhibit. If you please, sir."

Frances was wearing the diamond-encrusted engagement ring, and I went into a pocket after the other.

As a final precaution before taking up the reins, Mr. Harbison made a quick scrutiny of his booklet, but printing being what it was in those days, the next paragraph was solid "Z's," and the following type was pied beyond reading. We agreed that the text went downhill as a bottle tuned up, and were off.

As I suspected, the Eagle Tavern gang lined the sidewalk going in, and made suitable comments: "Now, I mean, Schoolmaster, you got something to hang on to there!" (I'll interpose that Frances had made the most of her impressive figure, or maybe a little more than that) and "Don't kick him out of bed, Miss Barclay, not under *them* conditions," and others, worse. A beer pal of mine cried, "Where *did* you get that suit, Billy?" And a second later, "How come you left your leather hat behind?"

But it was all in fun, and we smiled (me stiffly) and Frances blew them a kiss, whereon several whiskerandos threw down their hats and stamped on them.

"You saw that, Jim? Now don't tell *me* it warn't worth hiking two miles through mud for! Special to see them two—"

"Hold up, Hank; this is a holy event. Tone down some."

"Well, that's true. I'm downright ashamed, and should have knowed better." The speaker seemed abashed. "But you got to admit—"

"Oh, shut up!"

Buggies were tied up everywhere, and the church was bulging. I believe the entire town had turned out. When we went into the pastor's back room to wait, there was a buzz, from outside and in, and I heard one man say, in awed tones, "That schoolmaster musta bin chief admiral of their Navy, afore he come here. And ain't it like him not to let on!"

The church was packed. I said that before, but people crowded the side aisles, too, and Mrs. Shulman, wife of the town's new plumber, was playing the Bach wedding music, to my stupefaction. After the pastor, wearing a white surplice, had shaken hands with us all, including Ramses and Nefertiti, and told us the line of march, he left to appear at the rostrum.

Lockridge and I disappeared to a side room, and there was a brief hiatus. Then Mrs. Shulman struck up the happy but jangling "Here Comes the Bride," and that uniform with those medals caused a lively stir. I listened to a comment or two from down front. "I told you we had a dyed-in-the-wool celebrity in town, when first he come. Jake Motley'll bear me out on that. Ain't it so, Jake?"

"Well, I knowed it myself, for that matter," etc., etc.

Betsy, an angel with a white ribbon in her ash-blond hair, followed by Nefertiti, moved across from the other side, and then the entire church swiveled around to see the elegant Mr. Harbison walking sedately toward us, the irrepressible Frances on his left arm. More than half the congregation were women, and I doubt if there was one that Frances hadn't somehow helped in her time off.

There was the usual swelling "Oh-oh-oh!" and Frances did indeed look handsome. At the last minute, searching for a suitable dress, she'd decided to wear her evening hotel garb, which was white, well-cut and no longer recognizable as a uniform. She'd stuffed maybe two flowers in her bodice—from General Whitney's sensible décolletage days. But she looked about the same now as then.

Every man in the place, barring two nearing eighty, looked at her with admiration and hunger. But confound the girl, she was having such a jolly time that she stopped every few feet, despite little jerks by Harbison, to shake this one's hand, whisper in that one's ear, or wave to somebody down an aisle.

This pastor had a mellow, touching voice, with a face and white hair to match, and he'd no sooner started "Dearly Beloved, we are assembled here in the presence of God—" than the women were out with their handkerchiefs, and a lot of men surreptitiously wiping their eyes. There'd been so much storm trouble lately, and backbreaking work to restore the town, that people were ready for an outlet.

So when the reverend came to "comfort each other in sickness, trouble and sorrow," I'm blessed if the Eagle Tavern group didn't tune up, not making fun, either. These roughnecks were sentimental, and at heart most had crossed off their lives as failures (though preferring to die rather than admit it) and, all of a sudden, this thing struck them hard.

At the words, "Whom God hath joined together—" etc., and with spirited wrenching of the organ, the general mood changed to joy and congratulations, and the Eagle contingent shifted from boo-hooing to whoops of "Praise the Lord!" and the usual "May all their troubles be little ones."

But it was not quite over. Being too backward to bring presents to the house, these good people had set up a table in the rectory, and crowded it with gifts, in many cases (I thought) somewhat beyond their means. These were "Ooh-ed" and "Ah-ed" over, and I reckoned, watching, that Frances kissed all the women in the house, and maybe two or three men.

Gervais, on the sly, had engaged the rectory for a "reception," or binge, and had smuggled in five cases of champagne, talking the pastor into believing it was nonalcoholic.

The Eagle group were suspicious at first, sniffing and tasting, but as the hubbub swelled, they found their spirits wonderfully elevated though they behaved like soldiers. There were only three fights.

Prodded by Mr. Harbison, I managed to slip a gold piece into the pastor's hand, as he was dozing off in a rocker.

Lockridge, I gathered, had hoped to slip away in his rented (and loaded) carriage, but the guests good-naturedly took charge. The bride and groom were made to run a gauntlet of thrown rice and a scattering of old shoes. One of these, a copper-toed ruin, hit Mr. Harbison on the head, sending him reeling, but he took it like a good sport, and then, unexpectedly, a lull fell over the crowd. Lockridge had the top down, and Frances, looking out over the throng, suddenly gave way to tears. (Knowing that tough nut, I figured it was at least half champagne.) But it proved a crusher, and we had the church tears over again.

Betsy and I walked home in silence, hand in hand. It had been arranged for me to stay till I bought my house, but when I saw Mr. Harbison clumping alone, let-down, toward International House, my chest felt hollow for the first time. What did he have to go back to?— that lonely bachelor with the fun and importance snuffed out?

Late that night, as Betsy slept, in her upstairs room (chaperoned by Nefertiti), and I lay awake downstairs, the people came for an old-fashioned "shivaree," but they left quietly on hearing that the couple were staying at Clifton House.

I lay long awake, suffering for something I couldn't define. And through the rest of the night, I had nightmares about people gone, people changed, time passing, growing older and losing a little part of cherished friends and companions.

Chapter XLVI

Next day, Betsy had promised to join me, house-hunting, and we struck out after breakfast for a new addition to Niagara Falls—a real estate "agency." The firm was emblazoned as "Honest John Murchison and Wife." I thought the sign curious, for it was hard to tell if only John was honest (and his wife a crook) or whether both were in the clear.

In any case, we walked into their gleaming office (they had it fixed up to shine, some arty ornaments, besides). Descriptions of houses were stuck in the windows, and a few recognizable pictures, photography being yet in its infancy.

Before we reached the place, we ran into Mr. Harbison, who was starting his campaign to boom up half our land. He had a story he'd written for the *Iris,* and another for the Buffalo paper, and said he meant to talk very secretly to all local bankers, as being the best way to get the word out. We wished him good luck, and needn't; this kind of thing was right in his line.

Honest John was a large, corpulent man, with a pinkish complexion and a kind of nailed-on smile. (I kept looking for it to fall off.) His wife, though thin, had a similar bright air of success, as if she'd just closed a deal on Buckingham Palace. Both should have inspired confidence but didn't, quite.

The male of this novel duo stepped forward from behind his desk, hand stretched out, and cried, "Aha! Honeymooners, I'll stake a wager! And decided to settle down in our beautiful little town. Niagara Falls has got—" (Niagara had virtually nothing but the Falls at this time; it was, in fact, ugly.)

"I've been here since before you came," I said, having taken an unreasonable dislike to the fellow, "and Miss Lockridge has lived here for more than two years."

"Capital!" he cried in his foghorn voice. "Then you know approximately what you want. Why don't you sit down and tell me, as closely as you can? First off, how much do you hope to spend? — No, don't be offended; youngsters, limited income, gotta make plans. *This* office is sympathetic with those sort of things."

He leaned forward and lowered his voice. "Kids, don't be embarrassed; we've all been through it. No matter what I sell you today, I'll bet I sell you a home twice as fine in three years. What do you say?"

Because of this hogwash, because of the "kids" (I stood over him by five or six inches), I said, "We'd *hoped* to spend about a million and a half dollars, but have settled on five or ten thousand."

He laid back his bulbous head and roared. Then he said, "Did you hear that, Martha? We've got a pair of wits on our hands."

She said, "You better step proper with these youngsters, George. They don't look the usual sort."

And *she* gave us a winning smile that might have curdled milk. But my judgments of people were hasty, and apt to be wrong, and I knew it. So Betsy (knowing it as well) said sweetly, "It's true, Mr. Murchison—"

"Call me Honest John!"

"—we have limited funds to spare just now" (she just *couldn't* lie, I realized) "and William has his mind fixed on a, well, two-story smallish frame house in good condition, painted, all conveniences working and not very near neighbors."

"Martha!" roared this nuisance, "isn't that what we've got the most of, on our list? Just tell them."

Martha said, "Children, you're in luck. For some reason, that kind of house has been going begging. We have at least a dozen. Even so," she added at a look from her husband, "the market is tight right now; prices are up. People are fighting for places."

"Would prices be tight if I were selling?" I asked. I couldn't help it, and, besides, Mr. Harbison had once outlined an amusing vignette of real estate brokers.

Honest John gave me a quick, shrewd glance, but I looked so

innocent that he recovered and, consulting a box of cards, said, "Martha, how about the Robbins place?"

"Why, I believe that's stone, George."

"Sorry," he muttered, "I had the wrong card out." Then he snapped his fingers. "I've got it! The Dexter house—absolutely ideal."

"You understand," his wife said to us, "it needs a little work—nothing, really. Now, you go take them, George. And take some other cards, too."

He spent a minute extracting a dozen or so bargains (on a normal market), threw on a kind of sailor's pea jacket, appropriate to an out-of-doors realtor dealing with "kids," and said, "Do you have your buggy here?" When I said no, he looked disappointed; then he assured us we'd take his.

"A house that looks to the water would be fun," said Betsy.

"Water! Why, that's practically all the houses in town! We've got 'em, don't worry. Whoa, there" (to the horse). "Here's the Dexter house, and if it don't look to the water, I'm a monkey!"

I thought the figure well put, but we climbed out in front of a two-story house, badly wanting paint, that seemed tilted toward the left.

"Now, just let me get the keys," he said, producing a ring of about ten or twelve. "Confound it, I've brought the wrong ring. You kids walk around behind; I'll be right back."

Despite effusive pointers about this wreck, the only one to endure was a tree-hidden view of the water. The grass had not been cut that summer, and now, with the snow melted nearly to the ground, after a rain, and two hot days in a row, a splendid array of weeds, or hay, showed through the dirty white.

It was in back that the real shock lay. Some time ago, the roof had caved in over the kitchen and other rear quarters. Before Murchison returned, I'd begun to feel red creeping up the back of my neck.

"Surely," I said with sarcasm, as he came puffing round, "you didn't think you could sell me a derelict of this magnitude? With a few repairs, you might keep a dozen donkeys in there. But you certainly can't keep *me*. Or, for that matter, anyone I know." (Betsy tugged at my sleeve.)

Murchison's brows contracted as he surveyed the ruin.

"To tell you the truth," he confessed, "I haven't been down here lately."

"Lately! Honest," I said, "if I may use your professional handle, you've only been in town for two months. Niagara has high hopes for your real estate shop—we all have. So if you've got a decent house to sell, trot it out."

But he had the hide of a rhino, to use Harbison's generic view of the guild. He said, "Kids, forgive me. I should have checked this. We'll see some houses; don't worry about it."

We looked next at a place painted green, on one side only, and with a bordering neighbor who had a baying hound tied in the yard, nearby.

"Does the dog bark all night as well, or is he only a day hound?"

Honest John snapped his fingers again. "I was confused on this place; I acknowledge it. *Now* I know what you want, and at her price you'd be stealing it. Mrs. Wiggins—she's moving to her sister's in Lockport."

We drove out Lockridge's way, but stopped short, nearer town, before a house that had won its education by degrees. That is, it was a jumble of small additions, without shape. I thought it possible, by ascending to the second floor, to see a small, dull piece of the river, a half-mile or more upstream.

"Let's go in," cried Murchison, undaunted. "She's a lovely woman, Mrs. Wiggins. Sophisticated, you might say."

Betsy shook her head, but I was beginning to have fun, and pulled her down with me.

"Mrs. Wig-gins! Mrs. Wig-gins! I have some people I want you to meet. They're interested in houses."

The door opened a crack, and the muzzle of a double-barreled shotgun inched out slowly.

"I'm armed," called a shrewish voice. "I may be alone, but I've took precautions. Consider it."

"Why, Mrs. Wiggins, it's Honest John Murchison, with clients."

"Well, why didn't you say so right off?" and there followed an unbolting, unchaining, unbarring and (I thought) a heavy table slid out from behind.

We went in to behold a skinny female in her fifties, her hair tied in a knot on top, a vixenish look on her face.

"This is the fourth party you've brought, and I ain't sold yet." She shot him an accusing look.

"These things take time, dear Mrs. Wiggins. You know that. Let me introduce Mr. Morristown and Miss Lockport—"

"I'll not have nobody living here in sin," she cried in her best vixen's bark. "I may be temporary run down, but—"

"Lockridge," said Betsy, still sweetly. "Mr. Morrison's buying a house for *himself*, but this won't be the one. Excuse me, please—" as she stepped by and through the door.

"Now, hold on," the woman cried. "No offense aimed or took. I've got water from the sluices, likewise a barn. All it needs are shingles."

"Someone will be enchanted," called Betsy, and we followed her out.

But was Honest John daunted *yet?* Not in the least. He snapped his fingers again, and I weighed the chance of throttling him if he did it once more.

"The Hobson place!" He struck himself on the forehead with the flat of his hand. "Why didn't I think of it! Come along, in a hurry. A lot of other people are interested in this estate, by the way. I'm not sure we don't have a deposit on it in the office."

I took him by the lapel. "Honest," I said in a friendly way, "is there *anything* positive you know about these houses? Name one."

"What's your first name, sir, if I may ask?" ("Sir!")

"William."

"Bill," he said, "we're going to be good friends. I sensed it when you first come in. Your face looks, well, companionable. I'll bet we know people in common. It's going to be grand to have somebody of one's own class to talk to."

Betsy turned aside to stifle a sobbing giggle.

"All right," I said, releasing him. "On to the Hobson place."

And here we pretty well struck pay dirt. A trim two-story house, not unlike Lockridge's and only a few hundred yards farther up his road. It was painted smartly white, looked to the river, had a decent barn and seemed in good repair.

"And it's got *land*—five acres at least," cried our guide. "Oh, this is the primest place for sale in Niagara Falls today."

"Why for sale?"

"That's a sad story, Bill"—he turned to include the girl—"and Betty. Over the years, old Mr. Hobson saw all his sons go over in barrels, and when the last was gone, at night, he took it personal. They recovered him two mile beyond Lewiston."

"Then who's selling?"

"A Mrs. Whetling, wife of a clerk at De Veaux's."

I knew her, a nice, motherly soul from whom, thank God, I thought I might get some accurate details.

"Honest," I said, now overfriendly, "let's put all our cards on the table. Do you have the information on this place? For example, do you know where the front door is?"

He brought forth a sheaf of papers. "On *all* the houses in Niagara Falls." (He seemed proud of this tinselly collection of data.)

"Can we go in? That is to say, do you have the keys?"

"Right on the ring, Bill. Hold up, here. I've got the wrong ring again. Stroll around the estate five minutes, kids. Back in a jiffy!"

He leaped in his buggy and slithered off in a spray of mud.

We walked around, and Betsy said, "It's rather lovely in its way. Don't you think, Bill?"

"Do you honestly like it?"

"Why?" She looked innocent.

"Well, dammit, what if you had to live in it someday?"

"Are you planning to move out?. . . And profanity doesn't, well, seem to suit you, William."

"Confound it, Betsy, you know what I mean," and I drew her against the back porch.

The girl said, "Bill, let's be sprawled out, without clothes, making love on your coat when Dishonest John comes back. I'd like to see his face."

"You can find another way to ruin your reputation," I told her, half-angry, and she smiled, making a motion to slip out of her skirt. But she finally—almost too late—put it back on.

"Poor William—likes to make jokes but can't take one."

"Not where you're concerned. Not like that."

Then Murchison returned, not to see a nude exhibit after all, and this time he had the right keys. After he tried them all, as my patience began to wane, the last one worked, and we were in.

The arrangement of rooms was so similar to Lockridge's that I gave a surprised gasp. The place was shiny clean; Mrs. Whetling had seen to that. We went upstairs and down, and the only fault was it had no water. The residents, John said, must buy it from the town wagon; he said it was a recreation for them, and broke up the day.

"Daddy and Ramses can dig you a well in a day," whispered Betsy, and I held a finger to my lips. We had a bargaining point. I had no wish to shortchange Mrs. Whetling, who was a friend, but I wanted to cause John some trouble, all the same.

Downstairs again, I said, regretfully, laying a social hand on Murchison's shoulder, "Pity about the deposit, and the place being sold. It's close, very close to what I wanted."

"I checked that in the office!" he cried. "The man failed to turn up this morning. Of course," he said, still playing poker, "he'll likely be in after lunch."

"Too bad," I said, turning away.

"Again, he may not." The realtor's face, to me, was eager to the point of being revolting.

"Where are the markers?"

"Markers?"

"Metes and bounds, whatever. The pins that stake out your five acres plus. Let's look at 'em, even though it's sold."

"Five acres plus. So I was told. Well, we can probe around. A pipe, a stone, sometimes a fencepost."

"Why, John," I said soothingly, "surely you have the information on your card. Did you bring the right card? I hate to see you make another trip."

"They *must* be here," and he actually found one marker, stumbled over it by accident, bruising his instep. Then Betsy and I found another. Both put the house comfortably centered, and I resolved to ask Mrs. Whetling about the land behind the barn.

"How about a deposit, Bill?" —in almost a wheedling voice. "She won't last a week, take my word."

I looked bewildered. "A deposit against what? Against a price? .What price?" (For just a second, I caught a malevolent, a murderous look, but it was replaced by the professional syrup.)

However, there was no way to persuade him to business, here on the lawn, so to speak. He said, "Let's all go back to our nice warm office. That's the way to hammer out details."

"What kind of deed do you get? Quitclaim? Warranty? And I suppose there's a survey?"

Looking at last annoyed at this expertness (from Harbison) he riffled through his papers, and said, "All that's in the office, kids. Let's go in a hurry, before that man comes back."

"He'll take it, I'm sure," I told him. *"But* I suggest you show him the others we saw, too. He might fall in love with one. No way to tell people's tastes."

Murchison gave an uproarious laugh. "You're a card, Bill; you really are. I can see the end of this, all right."

Following Harbison's counsel, I shrank from seeming too eager, and mentioned the lack of water, reaching back to pat Betsy's knee just the same.

Honest John looked crushed, but he whipped up the horse, optimism ever on the rise. Toward the center, he asked me, in his social tone, "Where'd you go to college, Bill? You've got Yale written all over you."

"Southern Arkansas Tech," I replied. (To give him credit, I don't think he quite believed this, and I put it down to Betsy's regal look.)

"I'm a Harvard man, myself. Ah, good old Varsity! Those were the days. Osky-Wow-Wow" —he looked slyly aside.

"I've heard of it," I said. Then, to my surprise, we arrived at the first of Honest John's alternatives.

This house was near the center of town—two houses, rather, for it was, really, twins, and I said, as one collegian to another, "John, you're a wizard. I'm told most real estate people are. But do you know, it would be downright awkward to hop back and forth between two houses."

"You wouldn't have to hop," said Betsy, relaxed, now that the other was settled in her mind.

So—I rambled on. "—And furniture. Anybody with taste would of course make them identical, and I doubt if there's that much furniture in town."

"Not so, Bill," said Honest John; "we have some fine furniture-and-mortuary shops in Niagara."

"No," I said, "the duplications make it impossible—two razors, two hairbrushes, two sets of clothes—"

Mr. Murchison gazed at me with what passed for shrewdness, to see if I was joking. Then, ever resilient, he said, "If you're talking about privacy! Well, wait and see the next one!"

"Good boy, John," I cried, clapping him on the back. "When it comes to comprehension, I'll take a Harvard man first, and the rest nowhere. No offense to Southern Arkansas Tech," I added hastily.

He looked pleased and showed us another house on the outskirts, but it stood in a swamp, after the floods, and the people had moved out—by boat, I assumed.

"Hard luck!" I boomed. "That devilish blizzard! And probably not another house like it for twenty-five years."

"This next one," said John (and he sounded slightly daunted at last) "is a little larger than you described, but"—spirits bounding again—"you talk about bargains! They want five thousand, but they'd come down to four, I'm convinced! And that means furnished!" (I figured it might have been worth three.)

The house *was* large, near town center, painted and trimmed on the outside. My plans had been made, but I insisted we look inside. John had both key rings, exceeding real estate practice, and neither came through. But we found the door unlocked and pushed on in.

It was bare but decently furnished, for that day and place, and we walked up a pretty, white stairway, with John's outlook improving at each step.

"On a sluice—bathroom and all," he confided, blown sky-high with satisfaction. (I hadn't yet uttered a single critical word.) But as we opened one room after another, we entered a bathroom where a man was taking a bath.

I knew him; it was Dave ("Square-head") Johanssen, an engineer on the railroad and a weighty figure at the Tavern, with a habit of consulting an enormous watch in an important sort of way, and a vocabulary to confound the wisest man alive. Everything he said came out backward, mostly. He was also regarded as the best-natured fellow in Niagara.

"Come in, step aboard!" he cried cheerily. "I'm sorry about accommodations, but the little lady can perch on the stool. Where's your cowboy hat, Billy, and who's your friend?"

"This is Honest John Murchison, our new real estate seller," I said as we backed out.

"Mighty upset to meet you, sir," and the bather extended a soapy hand.

"Isn't this the Martin place?" inquired Mr. Murchison sourly, trying at once to remove the soap and inspect his now worthless cards.

"Next door left," cried Mr. Johanssen, in his usual high spirits. "But fetch some chairs from a bedroom. Visitors ain't something a man turns his head on, scrubbed or likewise. I set a store by friendship, as Billy there will deny."

Backing slowly out, Betsy trying to contain laughter with both hands, I said, "Awfully sorry, Mr. Johanssen, but Honest John must have made a mistake. Odd, too, for like most of his trade, he's usually dead accurate."

"Is that the schoolteacher's daughter? Betsy—right? Now if she ain't growed! Why, she's developed into an outright succulent little lady; that she has." (He meant no impudence; he scarcely knew one polysyllabic word from another; besides, I agreed.)

Betsy said, "Thank you, Mr. Hojamsen," and we called apologetic cries all down the staircase. The responses were, generally speaking, in his non-Eagle, or sensible vein, for which I was grateful.

We told Murchison we'd seen enough for one morning, and I said, "Either I or my representative will call at your office this afternoon at three. You might make a point of being there. It's around the corner from Crawford's store."

"Representative?"

"I'm a very busy man, John," I said. "Result in part of going to Arkansas Tech. Three o'clock. No, never mind," as he strove to get us in his office. "We can walk from here. Fact is, we have some errands to do. Goodbye for now, and thanks."

With his mind on three o'clock, no doubt, he whipped his disgusted mare into the mud, and we made our way home—to Lockridge's place. I begged off lunch, knowing what I wanted to do. And sure enough, I found Mr. Harbison, busily writing, in the dining room of International House. He got up and found me a chair.

400

"Sit down, William, and have a sandwich and some beer. I've spent the morning on our campaign, and am presently drawing up a paid story for the *Iris*. Is something on your mind?"

I told him about Mrs. Whetling's house, Honest John Murchison, and the fact that I hoped not pay more than I needed but wished not to skin Mrs. Whetling, too.

He said, musing, "Have no fear. I'll be there at three o'clock and deal with this bounder. There are matters to be looked into—deed, of course, encumbrances, easements, town roads—matters long familiar to me. Now—Mrs. Whetling. I think we can strike a price midway between Murchison's swindle and what Mrs. Whetling's willing to settle for."

"That's about what I'd figured," I said, "but I'd feel much more comfortable if you handled it."

We left it there, and the upshot was that I bought a tidy two-story house with, as Murchison had reluctantly confessed, everything shipshape but water. A deep area behind the barn was well fenced, and there were other extras.

When I went to see Mrs. Whetling, she said, "Now, William, I told them I'd settle this property for $3500, and you've lifted that up to $4000. You ought to be ashamed, treating me like a charity patient."

"Murchison was asking $6000," I said.

"Yes, and never sell it. I want to know something. Did he tell you there was no water?"

"Then we'd better kick it up to $4500."

"Oh, go along with you. Try to give me more than $4000, and I'll take it off the market." Then she turned red and said, "The miserable liar! He never once mentioned $6000 to *me.*"

"Just remember this, Mrs. Whetling: I figure I got a *bargain.*"

"You aren't going to step a foot in that place till I set it in order," she exclaimed.

"Why, it's perfect!" But she went on to give me a rundown of the most absurd flaws possible: there was a broken curtain rod; a blotch of paint (two inches square) spilled on a top stair; a board was missing from a barn stall; the feed trough leaked; and a section of the fence bulged where Mr. Hobson (unused to farmwork) had lodged a yearling calf, and regretted it. Aside from the fence, he'd been soundly kicked.

"Abel Hobson (rest his water-soaked soul) was a joiner, not a farmer," she said. "And while I shouldn't say it but do, he had no business throwing his family away in barrels! You take a yearling calf," she added, summing up, "and it's more trouble than a bee-stung buffalo. Strong? And frisky? Well, I'll take a voucher!"

I tried to talk her out of doing anything at all, but she was perfectly adamant. And to seal the bargain, she kissed me on the cheek when I left.

Chapter XLVII

Betsy insisted that she and I look into their barn, most of which was filled with furniture they'd brought from England. I protested, but she rampaged through, tagging a marquetry table here, a brocade chair there, beds (including a double one with cupids inlaid on the headboard) and other articles I'd never have bought myself.

Then she dragged me to some school friends of her father's, and arranged for her selections to be moved. By this time, Mr. Harbison had concluded all the deal, as they say, and I'm afraid I was a little falsely reluctant, after all. I had no idea how to furnish a house, and wouldn't know where to start. I might have gone to International House and waited to see if the house would furnish itself. It was, as they say, another flaw in my character. Watching Betsy, I thought of a line from a book I'd been reading: "She's nesting," and felt happy, but with a kind of floating anxiety, too.

Betsy, in her thorough way, had made a diagram of where the pieces were to lodge, so we finally turned our backs on the project. And I'm hanged if she didn't end by snitching a beautiful copper fire screen and firedogs before we locked up. I can't say why, but these somehow struck me as outright theft.

"See here, Bets," I said, "your father's going to raise a merry fit when he comes home to find his barn gutted and family heirlooms gone. Why don't you put the fire things back?" (The broad top rim of the screen had a handsome little crest made of brass, or some such metal; it was done artistically, by an expert in that line, I surmised.)

"Oh, pooh. He has no idea what's back here, and doesn't care; besides, I picked them out to bring. Don't be so straitlaced; in England they'd take the barn."

This was the little chambermaid I'd once thought prim and puritanical. She had, I was beginning to think, the soul of a river pirate.

"Well, that's done," she said at last. "Maybe we can play awhile. Everybody says the river is very dramatic with great floating cakes that go over like thunder crashing. Let's go see."

I had a sharp stab inside, and studied her guileless blue eyes. I said, with reluctance, "I told your father I'd help teach now and then—I've got a few bonehead things to say. But school's out for his wedding. I'll go if you hang onto my hand."

"I *want* to hang on! Your hands are so nice and rough and broad; flat, sort of."

There were numbers of onlookers at Goat Island, and more down the stairs to the foot of American Falls. We tried to get to the Three Sisters but couldn't. It was awesome. The river was roaring, and huge squares of crystal-clear ice were being tossed or piled crunching against the island's big trees. A heavy new plank approach was still intact, but only a fool would have ventured beyond the first island.

We asked several men—natives whom I knew—whether the river was rising or falling, and were pleased to get vehement replies to all questions. They did not precisely solve things, for one man would swear "She's falling fast—noted it a hour back," while another, Deke Slater, who knew everything and was on town relief, offered to bet five hundred dollars (he couldn't have raised seventy-five cents in a week) that the river would come on up and, before it was through, knock down Cataract House and everything near.

"I seed this oncet before, when I was a boy," he said. "She rizzed, shaved off all the trees, banged down houses and taken thirty or forty lives, not counting Injuns and Canucks. You take a tip from Deke, Billy—*Git!*—while the gitting's good. There's going to be hell to pay afore dawn."

"Git where, Deke?"

"High ground! If you can't find none, hike to Buffler. That may be safe, but don't hold me to it."

"Well, then, what are *you* doing here?"

"I'm a Special Safety Warden, duly swore by Constable. Now, in your case, Billy—you and the little lady—you go where you like, seeing you've bought me beer, but I'm scooting further arrivals out. Got to."

There was as much chance this old codger had been "duly swore" in by anybody, including the garbage collector, as I had of jumping the moon with a broomstick. So I said, showing off for Betsy, "When the big crash comes, what do *you* aim to do?"

(I noticed, again, that both my speech and my writing were getting pretty slangy, but I couldn't help it for talking with the Eagle bunch.)

"Me? Well, I've got a gift you couldn't guess in two hundert year. I can size up and spot the trees that withstand and them that won't. The river makes a kind of booming crack when she means to explode. I'll be up that black oak in two shakes. It's why I was duly swore."

"There's not a single low limb. The lowest is thirty feet high."

He put his face next to mine, the whiskers almost touching.

"Billy," he said, in an almost plaintive voice, "I want to ask you true. Did you ever see Deke Slater fail to come through on something he undertaken?"

The obvious answer was, "Yes," but I replied hotly, "Of course not! Don't be an ass!"

"I got ways of shinnying up that tree that a coon couldn't figure. Don't worry about Deke Slater and *trees!*"

I said, "We'll try not to worry," and we turned to go. And then something happened that was to haunt me, coming and going, for the rest of my life.

A cocker spaniel, the property of Mrs. Whetling, trotted over the plank walk to the first island. Jumping to the second, it was heavily struck by a blue shard of ice, causing it to spin like a whirligig off the island and into the rapids, with Betsy behind him like a shot.

I stood transfixed, and for just a second, I thought: "It's happening again." Once again I saw Betsy Lockridge sweeping toward Niagara Falls, in a river filled with ice-blocks—for the most foolhardy reason possible. It was like a nightmare fought twice over.

I hit the water (which could scarcely have been above 33 or 34 degrees) a few seconds after the girl, who was gaining on the dog. Below the Three Sisters, as I've said several times, were various little clumps of rock-turf with willows to hold them together. The dog and Betsy glanced off the first half-swamped islet, inside the ice-line (I thanked God) but the dog was too thoroughly panicked; it spun on down the current while Betsy snatched at roots.

I yelled above the roar, "Try for the next clump! It's bigger!"

She was whisked on, and made a determined grab at runt willows, which held. I came smashing beside her and onto her, and reached up farther for a stronger growth.

Then I was able to look at her face. I expected to see her crying, but she was laughing, and I'd seen that expression before. As for me, at this critical moment, I was too confused (and scared) to know where.

Then a voice: "I've got me a-holt of a young maple, Billy. I'll let my feet swing out and you can grab them."

Slater, shaming me, had pinned a grip to a stout little tree at the water's edge, just above us, and, at a cry of *"Now!"* he immersed his lean, stringy body in the river, swung into the current and floated down in an arc, much as primitive bridges once were made.

I grabbed his shoes and shouted in Betsy's ear, "Now, dammit, pull along us to shore!"

She looked startled but did as she was told, the silvery water dancing over us all. Slater, almost routinely, reached down and grabbed her flowing white hair; then, without further ado, he jerked her to the bank. (One hand still gripped the sapling.) The girl seemed to come to her senses and screamed "Bill!"

Well, Bill had just enough presence of mind left to scramble over that outstretched body, and flop heavily on the bank.

"Billy, my maple's giving way," said Slater in his normal voice, and I slid into the water's edge and heaved him up to safety.

He was not young, and he lay a moment, gasping in the cold. Rubbing his arms and legs, I said, "Deke, you—" It was all I could get out.

"I recall the beer, not oncet, but numerous."

For some time I'd known these Eagle loungers, though rough, could be gentlemen when the cards were down. And when I say rough, I mean tough as old leather, smoke-cured like mountain men, which many had been.

"The poor little doggie," exclaimed Betsy, shivering, hugging her knees.

"The 'poor little doggie' almost cost three lives," I said, ungently. "See if you can't behave for a while. Or go on over the Falls. There's the river—right there. Quite suddenly, I'm tired of all this balderdash about the 'pull.' You damn near got Deke and me killed. As well as yourself."

The girl stared at me wide-eyed, and even Deke managed a quizzical look. Then he said, "Company's shaking like a old hound; likewise sopping from head to toe. Foller me."

He got up, pointing, and I wrenched the girl to her feet. She studied my face, troubled and bewildered.

We trailed after him stiffly, limping, the icy water sloshing from us all. I still felt Betsy's mixed-up stare, but I never once looked aside. I'd had, at last, a stomachful of this siren humbug. And the Falls themselves. It occurred to me, in disgust, that the Victoria Falls were about three times as high, and had yet to see a barrel.

"The Hermit's cave's back here," yelled Slater. "He's a long time gone—went over like the little lady nigh done, and we'll borry his accomydations. Make a fire, to start. Then strip off and dry.

"Don't worry, ma'am, I've seed a mort, of females pelt-bare. It wouldn't be no novelty, at my age. But I recall it all, same as being there," he said. "Oncet," he went on, "I had me three Injun wives. And not a flea amongst them. Aristocratic, they were. You can measure an Injun lady by the number of fleas she's got," he explained.

"Matches?"

He looked at me pityingly. "Now, Billy, you didn't think Deke Slater was helpless without matches? You're acquainted with my accydent in Montana. I wouldn't be on town relief otherwise. But I've got a few tricks left."

Well, I did know it, but decided not to think about it now.

Kneeling down in the cave, he whirled a stick in what looked like fungus and was probably shredded dry grass, and, throwing on little sticks and then big sticks, shortly had a fire blazing to the ceiling.

"Now, little lady, just step kindly around the fire and shuck down. Yup, to the last under-frilly. Billy and I won't look, or maybe just a peek for luck; and we'll dry ourn over here."

I did have a peek for luck, and then two or three, and I might as well have never seen another specimen. It was the simple clothes she wore, I realized. But this creature was perfect, or as near so as a girl could get. And maybe a little past perfection, everywhere.

The first time she faced me, she was still confused; but by the third, with her astonishing femininity lighted by the fire, she said in a nearly controlled voice, "I jumped in after Mrs. Whetling's dog?"

"Never mind the question mark," I told her, despite the dazzling body. "You jumped in to show off, and I've had too much of this."

Slater gave me a quick, keen look and said, "It was a noble act, young lady, noble. Don't fret yourself with talks about the Falls being stronger than you. Best get it said now. I've seed this a hundert times and upward. It's all moonshine."

Like a child, I continued to brood. I was vaguely aware, as I stood there, naked, that Betsy once looked me up and down, and smiled. Her approval made no difference; I was still peeved. I concentrated on Deke's exceptional variety of tattoos. These spread mainly around an eagle whose wings were American flags. But there was a laughably voluptuous woman on his upper right arm, who did an expert shimmy when he flexed his biceps.

Our clothes dried fast, or, more properly, scorched; and we put them on slowly, hand-softening piece after piece. I looked round the cave, which had lingering scraps of poetry in corners and on ledges, and bits of sheet music for the Hermit's flute and violin.

Betsy was dressed, all surprises hidden, and even her coat was dried out. She said, in an unsure voice, "From the bottom, you can see ice-blocks as large as wagons tumbling over to smash below. I'm very warm. Could we go look? Please!" She'd addressed herself to me.

I felt Slater stiffen beside me, but he only gazed at the ground.

"We're headed for home," I said. "If the river runs like this today, it'll run like this tomorrow. And there'll be other times, and other years. You can suit yourself. Go over on a sled, if you choose."

Slater relaxed, but eyed me with a mild look of reproach, and Betsy said, "I expect you're right. Let's go home."

Coming round the fire, she kissed Slater on his leathery cheek, bringing forth a toothless smile. But he still looked disturbed, and so did I.

Angry or not, I was anxious not to have the story spread, and I called his name as he stalked off through the woods. I imagined he thought it inevitable her clothes would be off again in a minute. But he sensed what I meant, and cried, "A leetle incident, nothing furder. And it stops here. Besides," he added, "you bought me beer."

(I was fully convinced this was the cheapest beer I ever bought.)

Deke now took a deep breath. A pronouncement was coming, and knowing the code, I could guess how he hated to pry into something not his "business." But he called, kindly, "Little lady, I'd leave them Falls, the river similar, go their way, if I was you. Hallacious accydents happen, and persons lean to misinterpretations. Moreover," he added, the words almost killing him, "Niagry needs the schoolmaster."

I trotted after him, laying a hand on his arm, "Deke, you won't take this amiss, but you could favor me" (in his sort of speech) "by drinking what beer you want, on my account. I'll tell the bartender."

He looked slightly hurt. "Billy, I'd a-leapt in nowise. I thought you knowed that."

"I know it, all right, but I'll suffer under bad obligations, if you don't have the beer. You wouldn't want that!"

He thought it over and said, moving away, "I may have one, two if I feel roopy, and *warn't* it a frisky outing! That girl and all. No offense meant, but she durn near revived me. I never *see* such a female girl!"

"Me either," I said with reluctance, and went back to join Betsy. Despite my harsh words, I was frightened half out of my wits that she might be gone.

But she was there, and we started for home. I was aware she had a speech prepared, but we made the trip in silence.

Silence or no, I was thinking that if I stayed on here, it might indeed mean living with the phantom genii, never being sure, hoping, always. Had all this taken place for eons, as the deluge chewed remorselessly northward?

And then, the last sunrays glinting a rainbow over the mist, I thought: "The risk should be mine. Living means a risk, and Betsy's worth any barrier erected to test us."

In that moment on Goat Island, my mind was made up for good.

Chapter XLVIII

Meanwhile, Mr. Harbison had been busy with his campaign to sell half our land. Also, he was hiring men to clear the twenty-five acres we authentically owned near Lewiston. (Frances had decided to give up her possible claims on the town's business district.) The Lockridges staying on an extraordinary three days longer, Harbison came often after dinner—lonely, I'm sure—to report his progress to Betsy and me.

"I've got people stirred up, no question about it," he told us by the fire. "The bankers have kept their secret well. Nearly all their funded clients have tried to get in touch. The highest bid I've had is double our original amount—for a hundred-acre tract."

I thought he might in decency look tired, but he was astir with action. His pince-nez was squarely set, he seldom coughed, his face was aglow with the challenge. And his clothes had lately been sponged and pressed at International House, where I suspected his largesse was out of the usual run. Finding his hotel had stabling, he'd hired a rig and spent the whole of several days spreading the word.

But his real triumph was a "news story" he'd paid for in the *Iris*. I've said before that this splendid paper was choked with ads for worthless nostrums. Plus worse doctors and cure centers, with the result that front page news was nonexistent. Suicides went unremarked, and other unpleasant news. You'd pick the paper up (hoping) then read, "Great Discovery in Buffalo! Men of Science Confounded! Revolution in Current Procedures!" and gratefully settle down to read an important story. And by the fourth line you'd learn that Doctor Euclid T. Frisby had blended some copperhead oils to eliminate bladder trips at night.

It was depressing. If Jesus had decided to return (the time being overdue) there might be a paragraph on page three, buried between the new Male Erector and an item on restarting the menses.

It was, then, the worst paper I'd ever read, slowly sinking financially; and to come to the point here, the editors were doubtless grateful for the lucrative bombshell from Mr. Harbison. One could buy a news story in without either trouble or checking.

Mr. Harbison waved his clipping triumphantly. Through his bounty, he'd tied up Column One of the first page, too. The *Iris* was a paper of four pages, at its height, so to speak, and laid forth an average of fifteen column-long quackeries an issue, with pictures and enrichments between paragraphs. The remaining spare was given over to doctor ads and religious claptrap, much of this last in verse. The editors charged a penny a copy, and should have been sued for their impudence.

Anyhow, Mr. Harbison handed over his creation, and I read it aloud. The headline, in three blocks, was "NIAGARA AREA ON VERGE OF GREATEST BOOM IN HISTORY! GOLD RUSH PALES! STAMPEDE EXPECTED!!!"

He'd persuaded them to run the headline across two columns, nudging out "Doctor Morton's Vermifuge Expectorant for Consumption," then the story settled down to a single column.

Excitement ran high today in the Niagara Falls and Buffalo areas when an alert *Iris* reporter learned that a foreign syndicate has pronounced this section a certain bonanza for the production of wine. Much of the best land, alas, has been snatched up, at what the *Iris* now views as bargain prices.

Working in tandem with several of Niagara's foremost townsmen, including Gervais T. Lockridge, the town's whilom schoolmaster—a naturalized citizen and former official wine taster to the Court of St. James—and William T. Morrison, well-known correspondent for Mr. Gordon Bennett, of the New York *Herald*, the syndicate plans to start clearing land at once and commence the more arduous chore of planting grape vines—*already bought*—in the Spring.

All phases of the venture have been explored by the *Iris*, in line with its policy of Front Page coverage of the news, and it can be said that the discovery is genuine and the men involved of the very highest calibre.

"It has further been ferreted out by *Iris*'s sharp-eyed scribes that Mr. Morrison, in the late Summer, made a surreptitious but honorable journey to the Bordeaux, in France's Haut Médoc district, where he conferred with important Château owners, including the Baron Rothschild, on the finer points of bringing this biblical liquor to fruition. Interviewed, Mr. Morrison explained his trip and added that arrangements had been made to ship grape-roots in quantity from his Bordeaux friends to this city. He said in candor that these might not prosper, and that local grapes would possibly be used. Moreover, said the magnate, all of Bordeaux, after his speech at the Chamber of Commerce there, felt that our soil was more suited to the production of light white wine, rather than red claret or the richer Burgundy. (He did, in fact, take a vial of our soil to be analyzed by experts there, and that was their opinion.)

Pressed, Mr. Morrison politely declined to give further details, but promised to keep the *Iris* abreast of developments.

"You must understand," he said at one point, "that our purchase of local land was made at going rates and was in every way upright. Wine land, as you know (we did know, but had forgotten) is shaly, gravelly, inimical to other growth, and, up to now, has been regarded as worthless."

All this, we should inform our readers, represents a *coup* of great magnitude. Towns from Lewiston on through Niagara and Lockport to Buffalo, Canandaigua and beyond are without doubt pointed toward prosperity beyond their wildest dreams.

A Mr. Newton B. Harbison, attorney, who lately has resided at International House, is currently representing the prospective growers, and has been largely responsible for purchasing land acquired to date. Though he declined to give the full acreage, it is said by *Iris* sources to be considerable.

Chatting easily, in International's lobby, an impressive New York figure in tailored clothes and gold spectacles, he verified all the above, with no attempt at suppression. Then he added valuable kindred items.

"Young Mr. Morrison, who has made himself a favorite at Cataract House, the Eagle Tavern and throughout town this summer, is the son of none other than William T. Morrison II, perhaps the largest operator in coastal-sail freighting, specializing in wine. It is possible," said Mr. Harbison, his shrewd eyes twinkling, "that nine out of ten wine bottles consumed each

412

summer at Niagara's numerous unique summer hostelries and certainly at the grandest of all, Cataract House, have been brought our way in Morrison ships. The reason for this," added the attorney, "is that the elder Morrison, now nearing sixty, was once in transatlantic wine shipping, and became a connoisseur and devotee during his many extended visits to the Médoc (Bordeaux)."

This knowledge he passed on to his son, our own W.T. Morrison III, who, we are proud to say, intends to marry and settle permanently in Niagara Falls. (Several of his friends at Eagle Tavern, where he sometimes goes to relax from his dual labors, verified this. There were details which we'll omit as being possibly frivolous, though well meant.)

Mr. Morrison, again cornered by *Iris*'s indefatigable XYZZZ scribes, announced that Niagara had won SLUG-ENYSIPELAS-BLUE BALLS-LLLL both his heart and purse. "Except for visits home and occasionally to Bordeaux," he said solemnly, as is his wont, "I've finally found my Elysium." (Hooray! —from we editors of the *Iris*.)

In conclusion, the *Iris* gives its humble readers the very best news of all. In a sub rosy survey of lawyer Harbison's purchase, the elder Morrison has stated, for his vast knowledge of wine grape growing, that the syndicate recklessly over-bought, and pointed out that the best-known claret vineyards in the world, those of Baron Rothschild, encompass limited acreage. "To work much more," he confided to our late, grievously missed General Whitney (who, it is whispered, was to have joined the group) "would entail too complicated a process."

"HENCE," (and here the *Iris* returned to shrewd lawyer Harbison), "the prospective growers are considering the sale of up to 1200 prime, shaly, weather-protected acres, possibly risen slightly in value on today's market. *This decision has not yet been made*," said Mr. Harbison in his honorable way, "and if it comes, we will make a public announcement in due time."

More is bound to follow soon on this supremely important development for Niagara Falls. Let the town be assured that the *Iris* will follow every step to keeeeep its humble readers abreast.

Doctor Morley absolutely guarantees the strengthening of seminal fluid by a marvelous refinement of his wide-sung Seneca Kickapoo Gooser—

"Oh, sorry," I said. "They forgot to separate the pieces, naturally, and I ran over. You might advise them to put a slug in at the *end* of your next one, Harbie," I suggested.

"Yes," he said, elevated with whatever conceit he owned, "I noticed that, and recovered two dollars for the error. As to the typos, as I believe they are called, they have to engage typesetters, regrettably, and the relief man has to be dragged out of the Eagle. I let those errors and grammatical disasters go without recompense—in view of the position I managed on page one, crowding out the nostrums. I'll confess," he continued, "that I was disappointed in the type size. A man with 20-20 vision might conceivably have read it with a microscope—anything less would have blinded him." (I was both surprised and amused at his exaggeration.)

"They told me," he continued, "that it was a nice, sickly season just now, with influenza over the town and some hopes of widespread pneumonia. The quack ads were flooding in when I quietly and *firmly* —if rather expensively—bought our space."

"It's smashing, Mr. Harbison!" said Betsy, trying to choke down laughter but showing admiration, too. "I think it would sell anything; and by the way, why shouldn't we go into the real estate business on the side? Harbie" (it was her first use of his nickname) "can go on feeding fibs to the *Iris* and the rest of us can sell. Just think," she said, elated, "how awful that Honest John Murchison was, and how much better we can do!"

"Young lady—that is, my dear young friend," said Harbison a little stiffly, "I have practiced law for forty years, most of these for William's father, and I urge you to believe that there is *no single actionable fib* in the account just read. You must trust me. I know the ins and outs of the law—an admittedly deplorable trade—and a jury would beat down complaints against that story anywhere in the land."

"Oh, Harbie," cried Betsy, crushed, "I thought you were only ragging in parts, the way we do. It was a glorious story, and I really and truly don't see how you did it so *well*."

"Can Baron Rothschild sue? Is the late General Whitney to shed the integuments of the tomb? Will William, his father, your father or myself take umbrage at this mildly expanded account? Hardly. Is the *Iris* (granting they ever read it) apt to complain about clapping itself on the back? No, and a thousand times—No!"

"Harbie, you must forgive me," said Betsy, wringing her hands. "You know how we all love and admire you."

"Please calm yourself, child. I was only professionally miffed. It is the custom of opposing lawyers to throw spittoons at each other in court, and then, arm in arm, repair for the friendliest possible tête-à-tête lunch."

But I decided not to be so easily soothed.

"These 'humble' readers you speak of," I said. "Well, *I* read the *Iris*, being interested in seminal strength." (Betsy blushed.) "Now, do I strike you as 'humble'? Beyond the ordinary, I mean."

He waved the objection aside. "I am not, as you know, an accomplished writer of journalism. I tried hard to recall from recollection's vaults the style of my favorite authors. It seemed to me they occasionally referred to the 'humble reader.'"

"They describe *themselves* as humble, the humbugs," I said. "The reader's usually snuggled up to as 'gentle reader.' That's to keep a book-buyer on the job and slugging away, whether he likes what he's reading or not. Generally," I added, "in my own case, I'm far from gentle after being told so thirty or forty times. In the case of *Jane Eyre*, I suffered along, gentled every two or three pages, and when I came to that noble, lofty-browed ass of a St. John Rivers, I threw the book in the fireplace."

"Waste, waste," muttered Mr. Harbison, taking me literally. "Property, either real or portable, should be treated with respect—"

And at this point the newlyweds burst in, filled with themselves and the glorious vistas of a world seen *à deux*.

After they'd settled down, and been kissed, and made over, and praised for embarking on a honeymoon trip so elaborate; and Lockridge had unfairly blasted the Clifton House food, while Frances called it "divine," she said, "I felt like the most awful imposter. I am, as you know, a headwaitress by trade, and here I had all those little people dancing attendance on *me*. I'll never get used to the grand life, never.

"But we had the most splendid good time. Man over there, in charge of a kind of zoo, has human scalps for sale. I bought three— thought I might send them to friends. Would you like one, William?"

I said, "No," and then, when we'd brought them up to date, Lockridge checked his cellar roots, which were thriving, and Harbison (wound up, now) insisted on reading his news story all over, with flourishes. I tried to doze, but couldn't, and Frances took objection to nearly everything he said, of course.

"Why, Harbie," she cried at one point, "I didn't know William had gone to France 'surreptitiously'!"

Mr. Harbison cleaned his glasses. "He did in the *Iris*," he said, pretty well on to her by now.

"But what about me?" she said. "I'm the only member of the company left out. I'm hurt."

The lawyer leaned forward. "Let me assure you, dear Fr—, dear Mrs. Lockridge, that you figure most prominently in my second piece."

"Splendid! Describe me as 'that madly attractive headwaitress of Cataract House.' You might add, 'recently wed to the local schoolmaster.' But I wouldn't give his name; it might hurt him socially. And of course there's Betsy to think of."

I said, "Frances, I'd hoped marriage might settle you down. You're worse than ever."

"It's true!" she exclaimed. "I've been freed entirely from the formal restraints of my childhood. Isn't it wonderful?"

"Not completely," I said, as Lockridge, enjoying himself, proud of his babbling wife, lit a cigar.

"Speaking of schoolmasters," he finally said, after dropping the first ash on his corduroys, "I believe you wanted to help during the winter, Bill?"

"I have nothing else to do, except to oversee land-clearing while this weather holds."

"Never mind," cried Frances. "Harbie and I plan to do that. We talked it over."

"And then," said Mr. Harbison, "I must go back. I've been away too long as it is. But your father," he said firmly to me, "said stay as long as needed. He made that point emphatic, and signed a contract clause."

"Now you *are* fibbing," I told him. "You and my father never had a contract. He told me so, once."

Mr. Harbison sighed. "I meant, of course, the proper legal course in *case* we had one. I am, you know"—again a little stiffly—"an authentic attorney, qualified to practice where I please."

Ashamed, I said, "You know my father might have failed without you. You're the hub of the enterprise, Mr. Harbison. I heard him say so. He said, 'Without Newton's devious—'"

"Never mind, never mind," the lawyer interrupted, smiling at last. "I wouldn't have chosen another path, even to be attorney general. It's been a rewarding relationship in all ways. But I've never abused it socially; I think you know that."

"Too bad for me you didn't."

"Well, then," decided the groom, changing the subject, "let's start dispensing knowledge day after tomorrow. We've lost several days already. They gave me a log cabin when I started. It'll probably serve you for now. What do you plan to stress? I was last grappling with geography, when one Ben ('Hogwaller') Casper thought

Belgium was south of Vermont. It was a setback, but I mean to charge ahead. You were saying?"

"Grammar, and speech. The average American speaks in terms so ignorant we have a worldwide dis-reputation. Read any English book that hauls in an American character, even a senator or diplomat. Study the awful talk. It embarrasses *me*, and I'm pretty well immune."

"Excellent," said Lockridge. "We'll establish here a pocket of literacy—"

I shifted uneasily. "Hold on; don't get your hopes too high. I wasn't exactly the shining star of schools I attended. But my family used correct grammar, and it more or less stuck. I'll start off with grammar. I'd like to get the parents in, too. Could you get some kind of ordinance passed, Mr. Harbison?"

"Entirely without municipal precedent," he stated positively. So I dropped the idea.

"Day after tomorrow, then," said Lockridge. "Frances and Betsy can help by additional knicknacks, and you can probably move in the new home by the weekend. We'll all help," he said, "and have a housewarming later. Meanwhile, Betsy can prepare your lunch; take dinner here. Oh, yes, I know. Ought to by now. If you feel like contributing, pray do so. Keep happy."

So we left it.

Chapter XLIX

The porcupines and other trash had been cleaned out, two prospective students helping. Besides, a desk, chair, blackboard and benches had been provided by my fellow-townsmen. And since a workable stove was already there, I trudged optimistically up a rise toward my school on The Day. I opened the door, expecting to find no one now at eight o'clock, and found—fourteen students impatiently waiting, courtesy of threats by their parents.

I walked to the front and looked down on, as I thought, my heart pounding—the Enemy. These youngsters were of about an age—thirteen or fourteen or thereabouts—and dressed in the heavy workclothes of the region.

I found a ruler on the desk, tapped it and said, meaning to be hearty, "GOOD MORning, class—" and heard a round chorus of giggles. For the first time in my life, my voice had failed. Since a start like this would scarcely do, I boomed out, "I'm getting over laryngitis. You'll have to put up with it for a day or two."

My confidence—indeed, a measure of fun—was returning by the moment, and I thundered on. "This is a *school*. We're planning to learn some things here, and if you join me, like good youngsters, you'll be grateful later on in life. I *promise* you that!

"Now, I suppose the first thing to do is get your names."

Lockridge had no grammars but he'd provided me with copybooks, pencils, chalk, and erasers, and wished me Godspeed. The benches, from some defunct church or other, had both backs and numbers, and I instructed my brood to write their names, aisles and seat numbers each on a piece of notepaper.

"I assume all of you can write," I said.

A girl with twin braids spoke up. "Mr. Lockridge taught us, sir." (I figured they'd been prepped to address me as "sir.")

"He was a *real* schoolteacher," said an outsized boy with red hair and an expression that, to me, was a mute appeal for a slingshot.

I gave him a look that failed to daunt him, and said, "So am I. I'm six-foot-three, and can be meaner than a bobcat. That is, if I have to."

Recognizing my old failing, I added, with a smile, "But we'll get along fine. I take it you *are* here to learn, so let's learn. Our subject, as we begin, is grammar."

I searched the lists. "Reuben Hawes, what do we mean by grammar?"

"His grammar's dead," the red-haired boy spoke up.

I walked down the aisle and leaned over to look him in the face. "That joke had hoarfrost on it when I was eight years old—"

"Oh!" shrieked one of the girls. "What you said!" And the other girls all giggled and gathered briefly in a cluster, then dispersed to their seats. Searching back over my words, I picked out the offender and realized I'd made a blundering start.

I returned to my desk, my normal color slightly deepened, and explained slowly, "The word 'hoar'—H-O-A-R—means" (for a second I was stopped for a precise definition, as one often is with English words)—"well it means white, or sharp, or long frost—but over the years, it's come to mean 'old,' or 'ancient'—or, in the case of this joke—smartaleck, trouble-causing. It's a little complicated. Even so, it was wrong of me to use a word too advanced for you, or over your heads."

"Can I tell my mother about it, Mr. Morrison, sir?" asked the girl who had shrieked. She was ripely pubescent and was, I became aware, teasing the twenty-one-year-old amateur pedagogue.

"I can't see any conceivable purpose in your telling anybody"; then she said, "I wouldn't, of course."

I soon realized that these children were, aside from having fun, anxious to learn. But few had been prepared by Lockridge, and their general ignorance was appalling. In the main, the girls had more ambition than the boys, and knew more, to use the term loosely.

Of geography, history, literature, mathematics, physics, most knew next to nothing, and in a probing attempt, I decided to ask some random questions before settling down to grammar.

None had heard of Napoleon; one child (the pretty girl who took umbrage at "hoar") had been told that the earth revolved round the sun; and one boy knew—indeed was familiar with—the name George Washington. He was a railroad agent in Lockport, whose face was scarred from stirring a pot while his father, a "chemist," transformed lead into gold.

(I should say that this student was not wholly to be blamed. Using powdered sulfur and a ton of yellow flower petals, such as dandelions and marigolds, the Lockport father actually turned out two dozen "gold" [or goldish] bricks, most of which he sold in Utica—then a village—until the citizens raised a posse and ran him out of the state.)

"I thought *ever'body* knowed Mr. *Washington*," said the boy, interested in my ignorance.

"I had him confused with someone else," I said. "But that's not a story for today. Listen carefully, now; we're coming to grammar. What is it? Well, it's a foundation of the way you speak. Tomorrow we'll go into structure itself—what a sentence is made of, what are the terms, and the like. This morning, I think we'll take up a few of the commonest errors, the ones that bother *me* most, so you'll get some idea of what we're shooting at. Understood?"

"Sir," said the boy with the red hair, raising a hand. I looked down the lists. "Ebenezer McJohn?"

"People call me Eb, sir."

"Well?"

"I wondered if we were really going to shoot something, like you said. I haven't got only a single-barrel twenty-gauge that belongs to my father. Would it be all right to sneak it out, with some shells, after he's gone to bed?"

"One," I said with menace, "I think you know I was speaking figuratively; or having fun. Two, your address to me was incorrect enough to frighten an ape" —here he made a show of looking about with apprehension, searching the corners of the room.

"No," I said slowly, with increased menace, "we have no ape here. But I've ordered one; it should be here by Thursday. Again, though you're too dense to understand, I was speaking *figuratively*. I'll explain that soon."

"You were saying something not true to illustrate something else, sir."

My jaw hung ajar. I was, needless to add, dumbfounded, and yes, it was the girl who'd first been shocked by "hoar." I looked down the lists again. "Danielle Lomond?"

420

"I was in Mr. Lockridge's school for two years, sir. And my parents took the textbooks and helped."

"You're a joy to have with us," I said. "And I think you can help some others. Now, don't you answer this, Danielle; you're too bright. But, class, pay attention. Would you say, 'Let him lie there,' or 'Let him lay there'?"

The red-haired imp thrust his hand up and asked, "Who? We're all sitting down here."

"Eb, come up to the front. That's right—stand up. Now walk up here."

"You better not whop me. I'll pick up a stick."

On this note, I met him halfway, picked him up (a handful) by his collar and the seat of pants, and plopped him hard into a chair near the stove. His face looked mean, but his eyes were filled with tears of humiliation.

"Now, hear me good—" I began.

"You mean 'well,'" said my star pupil.

"Quite right. But I'll make a concession in this case. In your kind of words," I said to the boy, "I advise you to hear me good and clear—"

I waved down a "Clearly" from Danielle, who nevertheless volunteered, "Ebenezer won't pay attention. He's downright ugly, and a bully besides. I'd send him away, Mr. Morrison."

"My father made me come," he said sullenly. "I got no notions of being here," and he added to the girl, "I'll get you. Wait and see. I'll make you wish you was never born in Niagry."

She looked frightened. So—seizing his belt, I lifted him out of his chair.

"You lay a hand on that girl and I'll take the hide off your rump, hear? And don't think I'm bluffing, you troublemaking pipsqueak. *You'll* wish you'd never been born."

"I was only funnin'," he said, but with some low utterances when I plopped him back down. "Anyhow," he said, not to be quenched, "the two halves of her bottom grind back and forth when she walks away. She think's she's grown up, and full of piss and vinegar."

Up to now, I was far from happy with my first day. But I threatened Ebenezer again, for his vulgar talk, and, promising frightful mayhem, told him, "Now, you see that stove, and you see the woodpile in the corner. You won't join class today. You'll be stove-tender, and if you don't do a good job, I'll tend *you*, after school. First of all, fill up that corner with deadfalls," and I added, "You'd better believe me, sonny. Understand?"

He nodded, to avoid further manhandling, and I returned to grammar.

"The answer to my question—yes, I'm convinced you know, Danielle. We'll try you later, on something more difficult. The answer, I say, is 'Let him *lie* there,' not 'lay.'" And I had them copy down all tenses of lie, lay, lain; lay, laid, laid, etc.

Practically all of these were potentially smart and even eager children, and I was warmed by the way they tucked in, eventually understanding, and finally memorized.

"I led off with 'lie, lay, lain,' et cetera because it's probably the most common error—used by large and small—bankers, generals, newspapers and, above all, those ignorant, self-serving swine known as politicians!" (My bias, I think, came from Mr. Harbison and my father, after a dinky appointed judge's unsuccessful attempt to shake the firm down.)

"Now, Billy." (Third aisle, seat six.) "We see him *lying* there or *laying?*"

"Lying, sir." He was a bright-eyed little fellow, on Danielle's level but younger. Groping for an opposite example, he stunned me by saying, "We might see a hen laying there, sir. Or we could see somebody lay a book down."

"Billy," I said, "you're going to be an important man some day. The reason is that, unlike our stove-tender here, you take this seriously."

He said, "Both of my parents often say 'Let him lay there,' sir. But sometimes, now, they don't. Thanks to Mr. Lockridge."

I said, "They haven't had your advantages." (I reflected that the boy had had few yet himself, and that I, of all students, was getting a swelled head.)

"All right," I continued cheerfully, forgetting Ebenezer as he sullenly fed wood into the stove when needed. "Today we'll take up some of my special hates, before pinpointing grammar. Now listen, which do you prefer: 'All he needed *was* rocks,' or 'All he needed *were* rocks'?"

To my chagrin, all but Danielle voted for "were," and I explained that this was a trifle advanced, but they could learn it for my sake, and—after a few more such—we'd knock off and have some fun. Draw maps and diagrams in colored chalk.

For an hour or so, I showed them how to outline the nations in Europe. That went well, for I'd traveled several times in Europe myself.

After that, I took on South America, but I was on such shaky ground here that I saw Danielle eyeing me curiously, and I gave it up, with a lame excuse.

"They have revolutions down there, about one a month each, and the countries get swapped around. We'll finish up on Europe, then bear down on Scandinavia tomorrow."

They were all happy; the drawing with colored chalks on the blackboard had sparked their interest, and they seemed eager to learn the components of their world. Ordinarily, villagers show little interest in the Great Outside, but bray in a vehement, brass-lunged style, "Why, we've got the best (doctor, hospital, lawyer, etc.) right here in Frumbo! They ain't a particle of use searching further."

"All right," I said at last, to their great disappointment, "let's try one of my pets. This, too, is a little advanced for you, but we'll go on a hit-or-miss basis for a while.

"Do you feel 'bad,' or do you feel 'badly'? If you're a little sickly, I mean."

I had gone too far, for most of them, misunderstanding what I meant, thought there surely must be a trick in it, and replied, "'Badly,' sir."

"'Bad,' of course," said Danielle. "'Badly's an adverb, not used that way with verbs of 'being.' 'I feel bad.' You would hardly say 'I *am* badly,' would you, sir?"

I studied her in wonder, the swelling Canadian sweater, the luminous face pointing to a mind that would outstrip the others here, and hoped, prayed, she would grow up to have a happy life and share it with a good man of her mental stature.

I said, "Frankly, you amaze me."

"Mr. Lockridge said I amazed him, sir," she said without modesty. Then she made a statement that should not have surprised me but did. "I think he put Billy and me here to help get the class started, and make things easier for you."

That *was* why he put them here, and it was very like Lockridge. I should have known.

"Of course. You see, I've never been a teacher before, but I'll get better, just as all of you will. I went to a fine college, and that should help. My mother was a teacher, a good one, before she married my father, and she's a poised, erudite, still pretty woman, too."

I hadn't any notion why I put those last three in, but I was beginning to appreciate my mother, as I see it now. Also, I think I wanted to make the point that schoolteachers did not have to become old maids, as many thought, usually coupling the two phrases together.

"What does 'erudite' mean, sir?" asked the least likely towhead in the rear, and when I said, "Well—brilliant, educated, knowing-by-instinct—maybe a combination of the three," the boy wrote it carefully down, and my heart glowed. I was beginning to understand Lockridge's role.

"Let's try this," I said, "one of the most commonly used errors: Would we say 'those kind of people'? Or, 'those *kinds* of people'?"

It was inevitable that my chief luminary should speak up and put the problem in order. "It would be," said Danielle, "either 'those *kinds* of people,' or '*that kind* of people.' You can't use the plural adjective ('those') with the singular noun ('kind') and the other way around."

I said, "Fine, Danielle, but don't answer *all* the questions. Now we have another of the most-used, and I'd like you to listen carefully. Does Mary—sorry, we've got a Mary. Does Sally—Sally, too? Well, does Phoebe give a party 'for my wife and *I*' or 'for my wife and *me*'? (considering I was married). —No, not you, Danielle and Billy."

The "I" was an error most adults made, in my view, some form of it by college graduates, and even teachers. (It made my mother blush when it happened around her, I'd noticed.)

Most of my pupils settled on "I," as I'd feared, and I carefully explained about the objects of a preposition, getting nowhere. I needed textbooks, and I resolved to travel to Buffalo and buy some myself.

But the class both memorized and wrote down all the samples I offered, and that was enough for today.

I said, "Tomorrow, we'll take up 'Who' and 'Whom,' and that's pretty rough going. But not for this group. Someday you'll be the leaders of Niagara Falls, and maybe bigger cities. Wait and see."

There was a grinding of teeth, and a gritted-out "Ha, ha," from Ebenezer, and I said, "You're welcome to join us tomorrow, Ebenezer. Nobody's your enemy here, unless you've deliberately made them so."

He looked me steadily in the eye but he said nothing, and turned back to the stove.

"Now, we'll diagram some sentences," I told them, erasing the blackboard. "It can be fun, like a puzzle, almost. Seeing where the different parts fit. And later I'll get textbooks to help. Before we're through, you'll know the sentence—and sentences—as well as you know the road to Lewiston.

"Now—one mention of 'who, whom.' You can start thinking about it. Whenever you're in doubt, when you're about to say, for example, either, 'He was a man *who* or *whom* you admired,' just substitute 'him' or 'he' for the choice—if you'd say, 'admire he,' then use 'who' not 'whom.' That's a pretty poor example; the question form is better. But one last try before I leave you with, I hope, something to ponder here—"

"'Who' or 'Whom' hit me?" offered my star pupil, coming to the rescue. "'*He*' hit me, so it would be '*who*' not '*whom*.' Excuse my interrupting, Mr. Morrison."

"Thank heaven you did. We'll put all that off till later."

For the first time in my teaching career, I'd gone blank, and I flushed, turning away from Danielle. I badly wanted a kind of reverse sample of "who-whom" but was not up to "They gave it to whom?" —there were too many ramifications. It occurred to me I might have done my homework.

Then I had a half-brainstorm. "Listen closely, and which is it? 'He said *whoever* (or *whomever*) wants the apple can have it.' Think *hard!*"

There was a rousing chorus of "*Whoever!*" and I thanked Heaven I'd made even this poor start. These children had good ears.

All had been told to bring their lunches, and did, in black lunch boxes or galvanized pails. The majority consisted, I noticed, of heavy food like sausage sandwiches, pickles and the like. Betsy had prepared me, in a wicker hamper, a sandwich of chopped ham, another of lamb (not mutton), two hard-boiled eggs and, to my amazement, more than a dozen apples. I took the hint and disbursed these to students who (not whom) I thought had brought skimpy rations; then I gave Danielle and Billy each a hard-boiled egg, as "prizes" for outstanding work.

"There'll be a variety of prizes from here on, whether a student once studied under Mr. Lockridge or not."

For drink, some had brought a half-pint of cider going hard, and these, I noted, were the first asleep after lunch. But for the commonweal, we had the fruit of a pump that Lockridge had dug, of his below-the-frost kind, and he'd dug a privy equally deep. He was planning to dig both for me, and I would have intervened, but I thought it gave him pleasure.

Because of winter and our far North locale, dark came early and class was dismissed at two o'clock. All (except Ebenezer) seemed in a good humor, and a girl in front, cried, "Eb's trying to burn us down! The pipe's *red hot* and the bark inside's starting to burn!"

It was true. The scamp had deliberatly overloaded the stove, hoping, I supposed, to end this nonsense without delay.

He started to run out, but I grabbed him, then asked three boys to hold him, and the rest of the class and I poured what we could on the pipe and wall.

But the dry part near the flue burst into flame, and we had to form a pail, or bucket, line to get it into a smoldering state. And try as we might, that was the best we could do.

A boy with fireproof gloves painfully pulled log after log from the stove and hurried them outside, and in doing so produced steam enough to clog the place. As to the charred and smoking planks, we soaked them thoroughly, but they continued hot, in diminishing degree, I hoped.

The class left, after three or four girls and two boys had come up to curtsy or shake my hand and thank me. All in all, despite Ebenezer, I realized that I'd had a rewarding day. Nevertheless I resolved to stay on through the afternoon and watch the residue fire.

As to Ebenezer, I dismissed the boys holding him, and when they were gone, took him outside, found a stout hickory stick, and laying him (not lightly) over my knees, gave him a drubbing that I figured would leave welts. I was angry, and hoped he would show them to his father.

And sure enough, released, he ran off toward Lewiston and screamed, "I'll sic my Pa on you! You wait and see what's coming! You're going to be the sorriest schoolmarm in the county, you big ugly—*possum!*"

I went in, sat down, and sighed. Further violence was coming, I concluded, and wondered how Lockridge would have managed.

Perhaps an hour later I heard a crunching of dry leaves, and removed my jacket. The building had grown cold, but I supposed I'd be warm soon.

I sat inside and waited, while the tread in the leaves continued closer. Then a figure, carrying an odd gun, framed itself in the doorway. The light was none too good, but I eventually made out, to my amazement, a small, red-haired, rather wizened fellow about the size, or a little less, of Ebenezer.

He stood silent for a moment; then he said, "I've got a blunderbuss."

"So I see," said I, standing up a little stupidly, thus giving him a better target.

He whistled at my size, but not in the manner I might have suspected.

"I heerd you whupped my son. Ebenezer, with the red hair."

"I did," and I pointed to the charred (and still smoking) boards around the flue.

"He burned down my chicken-house oncet, and cost me two horny roosters."

This conversation was not going the way I expected, but I moved ahead cautiously, saying, "The boy doubtless has a lot of good in him. I was sent here to help bring it out. I don't get paid, you know."

This brought on a spasm of anger. "That's the hell and devil of it, by God! Ruint your first day, you say?"

"Well, almost. The other kids"—my speech was slipping, by college standards and under the strain—"were all fine, an attractive group. I'd still be happy to work with Eb—"

"I heerd likewise you was a tempery feller—streetfight in front of the Eagle and all."

"What's the gun for, Mr. McJohn?" the tempery feller asked. "I take it you're planning to shoot me because your bullyboy misbehaved. Am I right?" And I took out my sheath knife and balanced it on my palm. (The chances of my hitting him were slim, and of hitting him point foremost none at all.)

"Whoa! Rein in! Re-cage that knife! What they said is shorely borne out. I taken my scattergun down so's I wouldn't be whupped myself. How big do you stand, in socks?"

"I don't know," I said. "I seem to be growing still, at twenty-one. A trifle less than six-foot-three, I'd guess—in my socks."

My spirits had lifted faintly. A shotgun, or blunderbuss, makes a terrible hole in a human, and he could hardly have missed at ten yards.

"Then you ain't aiming to whup a runt like me, standing five-foot-six in his shoes?"

"Why on earth would I 'whup' you, as you say, Mr. McJohn?"

He sighed and laid the gun down on a bench.

"No misdemeanors or skulldugs if I come sit beside you?"

I sat down and said, "Come on in. We can get this thing thrashed out, and maybe do your boy good. I'm sure of it."

"I've worked hard, I hev, going on thirty year, and all I've got to show is Ebenezer. Now you're a schoolman, right bright, they say. Where could I trade that hulk of mine for a nice young grizzly, that a body could hope to train?"

"Oh, it won't come to that. We can work together with the lad. He has a fine physique—"

"By cracky, I never thought of giving him physics! I coulda kept him running all his life, and maybe he wouldn't be so hearty. You see, sir, he's in a position to give *me* orders, now, and I'm up a stump for sure."

"I assume you beat him when he was smaller?" But before he could answer, I said, "Did the boys half his size, say, tease him about outgrowing them? Did they make up nicknames and such?"

"Outside the house, Ebenezer goes by the name of the Ox, if they're out of running range, Mr. Morrit—Mr. Morse—"

"Morrison. Did they rag him half out of his mind, would you say?"

"Why I never stopped to recollect Ebenezer *had* a mind, leastways civilized. If it wasn't the chicken-house, it was chopping a hole in the roof, and if it wasn't that, it was loosing a floorboard so's I'd be injured. Now, lookee there," and he pulled up a pant leg to exhibit a six-inch scar on the shin.

"It's hard to know what to say, now that he can 'whup' you, in your words. Where's the boy's mother?" I asked.

"She done up and died afore the real trouble begun. Visited one of them medical mills in Rochester, and come out dead. They said I'd got her there too late, and promised to hunt me down if I stirred trouble."

"The bastards did, did they?"

I'd turned a bright scarlet. Nobody could have hated those frauds worse than I did—excepting Rattlesnake Charley. I don't believe I ever heard him say a decent word about one. Even when he was selling oil, he told them it was no good, and derided them for buying it. And fleetingly, as I'd done in the past, I remembered Colonel Rutledge's "Charley's rich," wondering what had become of his money.

Suddenly, I asked this forlorn father with a problem child, "Where are you from, Mr. McJohn?"

"Why, my family was split betwixt England and the coast of France, accordin' to accounts in the family Bible. Reverend Frith spelled it out."

"Brittany, Normandy—do you remember those words?"

"Seems I do, Mr. Morristown. And I know what you're getting at." (This fellow was a rough diamond, hardly used by life, but he was not stupid, else he would never have sent his boy to school.)

"I heerd it said by my grandpappy—they's a mort of redheaded folk along that north French coast. They was deposited there, mostly, by Vikings, who come in the summers and pillaged for the winter months; that's the way they lived. Them men was red-haired, in the main. And I recollect my grandpappy making mention of an Eric the Red, to suit you. More 'n' that," he said, a little sadly, "I don't know. I'm ignorant and was working while my wife studied with a teacher come through here."

"Well, we're off the track, I suppose, though what you say interests me. I've seen the red-haired people of Normandy and Brittany. As to your lack of education, Mr. McJohn, *I* didn't know the Vikings left those red-haired people in France, and I've been to college.

"But this boy of yours, this Ebenezer. Why did you come to see me?"

"'Cause I calculated you'd call on *me*, seeing other bairns had told the whole story. To speak the truth, I was downright afeard."

"Do girls tease him, Mr. McJohn?"

"Something cruel, since he growed so."

"And you can no longer whip him?"

"He's powerful. I'd dislike to undertake it. I only make threats."

"But you don't mind *my* whipping him? I used a hickory stick, you know."

"I seen the welts."

"Most parents would be sore, and stop my work. I hope you don't try to do that, now that you've decided not to shoot me."

He fumbled in a pocket. "I ain't to say rich, far from it," he said, "but I got a quarter here, and I'd take it kindly if you'd whup him every day after school. Whether it's called for or not. I'd feel satisfied he was gaining an eddication, like."

I got up and said, "I think we can beat that. Let me work on the case. Something's bound to occur. Meanwhile, you keep your quarter. The fact is," I said, an inspiration having struck me, "I think we can kill two birds with one stone, in a manner of speaking. Keep Ebenezer coming for a while at least. All right?"

"I—I—somehow I trust you," said the little man, almost in tears. "I'll shake your hand, sir, barring objections, and go home uplifted."

"Yes, I understand," I told him.

I lit a lantern and inspected the burned plank-ends. They'd subsided with the cold, and, in fact, were out, as far as I could see.

Then, as dark came on, I sat down to think for a while before heading for home.

Next day the same group assembled on time, barring little Tommy Barnes, who had a cough, and I treated Ebenezer like the rest, except to address the class as follows:

"I'm informed some of you make fun of Ebenezer McJohn here, because he's so big. That phase has ended. I dislike to threaten youngsters I'm now fond of, but if I hear—or hear of—his being called 'Ox' again, that person or persons will not return to this school. And I'll tell their parents why. Do I make myself clear?"

"But he's always roughing us up," cried Aisle 4, seat 3 (one Donald Loker, one of my outstanding clique).

"Leave that to me," I told him.

I saw the malefactor look at me with opened mouth, but I kept them busy diagramming sentences all morning, and there was no trouble.

When everyone had lunched and I finally dismissed the class, I asked Ebenezer to stay behind. "Goodbye till tomorrow, Ebenezer," called out my star and most admirable pupil, in sincere tones.

Despite this, he sat—sullen again—while I threw a chunk in the stove, nearly the last. I'd seen to that; and sat down on a desk beside him.

"We're about out of wood, Eb," I said, chattily. "It's a whopping big job for one man."

"That's your rassle."

I said, "I doubt if the other boys could wield this extra ax I brought. You're probably the only one, with those shoulders."

"You making some kind of trick?"

"Oh, no. We have a lantern, and I'll have to get us ready for tomorrow. I just thought the only other real man here might want to help, for fun."

The sullen look faded. He searched my face, and said, "I might cut one or two."

"Good fellow!" I cried, and as we walked out with the lantern and two axes (I'd given him the sharper), I said, "I'm pretty good-sized, too, Ebenezer, and glad of it. People somehow look up to a big man."

"Not me," he mumbled.

"Wait till you're a little older." I felt his right bicep. "By George, you *are* strong!"

And things abruptly changed for the first time in his life. He attacked the nearly dead trees like a boy possessed; we laid in enough wood for the whole next day, and a considerable heap over.

"Well, that's done," I said at last. "I couldn't have managed it by myself, and the regular chopper's down sick. You're husky, all right, and you swing an ax like a veteran. Where'd you learn?"

He hung his head slightly. "Chopping down fences when Pappy was in the hospital."

"There are better ways, Eb, old boy. Your father's not robust, and he could use help. It cost him money to send you here; no matter what you've done. He's lucky, though, because he's got a son that would make three of other boys hereabouts."

I heard a low "Yes, sir."

"Well, Eb," I said with good cheer when we'd stowed the utensils, "that's a job well done for today. Do you want the lantern to light you home?"

"I'm not afraid of nothing!"

"Of course you aren't. That's one of the fine things about being big. Don't you think"—and I named some small boys of my class—"don't you think they'd be scared to venture two miles in the winter dark?"

"Them! They'd lay—lie—here all night, quaking under a bench."

"You see? Count your blessings. It's not everybody that grows up to size. Look here—I have to duck under the doorway. You will, too, in a year or so. And you'll be glad."

"Good night, sir," and he struck off through the woods as if daring a family of bears to tackle him.

Next morning when I arrived, I was astonished that he'd come back later and skillfully replaced the charred planks. And you can bet that he was on hand to receive his encomiums.

"Did you do this, Ebenezer?" —leading him to the scene.

"Yes, sir," but he looked around as if to bridle at ridicule.

I said, "I believe that's the best workmanship I ever saw. Now, where'd you learn *that?*"

"My pa's a carpenter—a good one," he said with satisfaction. "And, well, before Ma died, I was taught some things."

Wonders never cease, and, looking around again, to see if we were alone, he burst into tears.

"I'd like my ma back," he said at last.

I put an arm around his bulky shoulders, squeezing.

"Of course, you would, and I've lost some friends lately, too. But they won't come back, your ma either. So the best thing to do is make new friends. Starting with your pa. He's getting older, you know, and he needs you.

"The ridicule," I told him, "won't stop right away. Children can be pretty beastly"—he smiled through his tears—"but it'll fade bit by bit, when they understand what you're like. You can become really grown-up by ignoring it till it blows over. It won't be long, and then you'll be a leader here. Wait and see."

He said, "Yes, sir," again, and I gave him a pat on the back.

Our hired chopper left town five days later, and when I came to work early, having contracted with Niagara's leading fuel supply to keep us in wood (for which they would take no charge) I found, atop my desk, a bushel of the most beautiful apples I ever saw. Niagara apples, much renowned. Pinned to a handle was a piece of paper with coarse print. "THANKS—ELLERY MCJOHN."

It was the first time I ever felt encouraged by my progress, and I sailed through the day, making maps, giving away apples (nobody would take more than one, and Ebenezer none) looking forward, now, to finishing grammar and then teaching these children to speak on their feet, the most important gift of all. It happened to be something that I myself abhorred, and I determined to erase this as a barrier in life.

431

It would be gratifying to say that Ebenezer became one of my showcase students. He was—in the sports I devised for recess. And he learned well to read and write and figure, and he taught those skills to his father (evoking another bushel of apples).

And, like a reformed drunkard, he was stern when he saw boys (or girls) picking on somebody, or tyrannizing in any form. The "Ox" was dropped, as I'd advised, and he became popular with both sexes.

But he was not interested in really high learning, and I placed him in a group that seemed headed for manual skills. (May there always be such wizards!) And he was given good jobs, and some years later, he became head of the town council, a lofty and powerful carpenter-builder, a toiler like us all.

Chapter L

Betsy and Nefertiti had hired me a cousin of the latter, a dark but kind-looking Seneca, to cook as well as look after me and the house. But somehow she couldn't get the hang of things, not like Betsy at Cataract. The fact is, she was uncommonly slow for an Indian.

So—Betsy had begun visiting in the mornings, to get my breakfast and prepare my lunch for school and generally ready me for the day. I'd been a teacher so briefly that I often started off without the proper tools.

But this morning she was late. It was dark, and I felt peevish.

"You're late," I said, when she whisked in.

She stopped momentarily, without turning her head. Then she smiled and said, "I'm awfully sorry, William. I overslept fifteen minutes or so. I'll put the coffee on promptly."

But when she brought it to the table, I said, "This is more like pondwater. Did you make it too fast?"

She looked down at me, curiously, and said, "I'll make you another cup. Go on with your bacon and eggs."

"That bottom sandwich I had yesterday. Mutton?"

Another pause, with a frown I failed to notice, and, "No, it was the last of the venison. I thought it kept well, salted in the cellar."

"Well, it *tasted* like mutton!"

433

I failed to see the hint of tears as she brought in the replacement coffee, so I continued on in the same stupid vein.

"This Isis you dug up. Isn't she a little hammerheaded?"

She said, gently as usual, "It required a year for Father to train Ramses and Nefertiti, you know."

"I didn't. I wonder if this redskin understands the important work I'm doing."

Betsy bit her lip. (I'd read about people doing that in books, but I doubted it.)

"Is it fair to call Isis a 'redskin' because God failed to make her white? What's so wonderful about white? She could deride us as 'whiteskins.' Maybe it's what you're used to, William. Frances and I will try harder to teach her the white man's ways."

I scarcely heard her, but I mumbled that both, after the summer past, should be well poised to teach domesticity.

She said, in a different but still low tone, "I was paid for that."

But I was too woollyheaded to comprehend. Or to grasp anything till it was too late.

She handed me my lunch bucket, and I thanked her by remarking that the house was in such ratty shape (a lie) that the Thanksgiving party I'd planned had better be postponed. "A good many things have been overlooked," I said.

She replied evenly, "Frances and Isis and I will get down on our knees to get it spic and span, and we'll shop madly to see you're well equipped."

"You do know, don't you, Betsy, the importance of my present contribution? I dislike to be bossy, but this is a critical time. What's more, I slept very badly last night. I kept seeing some kind of female with shiny black braids. It bothered me."

"Of course, William. And I do understand. I remember when Father—"

"Father! Couldn't you make it Pop once in a while? Or the Old Man? Or Governor—to suit your Englishism? You're too old to go on calling him Father. It makes him sound, well—holy."

"I'm eighteen, and I do believe I'll go on calling him Father. You see, Frances and I, I confess, devote a little time to him, now and then. Not, you see, that Frances hasn't worked like a slave over here."

"Well, this has been one heck of a morning. You may have fouled up my lessons. This is too bad of you, Betsy; a side I've never seen before."

"Is it, William?"—flags flying in her cheeks. "I must tie a knot in my handkerchief and try harder."

"Oh, well, you're not so bad, Bets, taken all around. I wonder if you'd mind fetching my boots, hat and sheepskin jacket from the closet?"

I was seated reading a piece in the *Iris* about a woman who'd tried suicide seven times, landing always on a tuft, then she divined that the Lord needed her for other things. She made it to shore, and was now a mainstay of the Methodist Church. (If she'd gone over, a prominent woman here, the *Iris* would have ignored her entirely.)

Betsy came back with my garments, and said, "Here they are, sir."

I was yanked back to the chambermaid phase. I looked up quickly, but her lovely face was grave. Then she broke into her customary radiance. "Have a fine day, William," and she slipped out the back door.

Walking to school, my mind cleared, and I was horrified. I had no idea what demon had pursued me. I'd treated this loyal and trusting girl like a common deckhand, assigned me to hand and serve, as the sailors say. And in all my life, I'd never used anyone meanly. Clutching my head, I wondered if I'd taken leave of my senses.

After school that day, I perched confused on a front bench and became aware, of a sudden, that someone was sitting beside me. I turned to see Danielle Lomond.

She said, "Mr. Morrison, I have a favor to ask . . . a great favor."

I was dimly conscious that, the day being warm, she was wearing a much thinner sweater and nothing beneath. A child, wanting to be a woman, hoping to attract the schoolmaster's favor.

"What is it, Danielle? You've already done *me* several favors."

"My mother, who once taught school, like yours, and my father, who owns half of De Veaux's store, think I could learn above our lessons, you might say. They think our school's fine, but—but—they wonder if you'd tutor me privately—for a fee, of course."

"But when? This shanty's already cooling off, and the kids haven't been gone half an hour. I can hardly tutor you while feeding the stove."

"At your new house. You have a Seneca housekeeper, Miss Betsy comes over often in the evenings; and besides, my parents say you're a gentleman."

"I'm not so sure of 'gentleman,'" I replied. I was thinking of how I'd whipped Ebenezer, perhaps too hard, and of my roughness to Betsy that morning.

"I'm willing to take a chance."

I sat and thought. "Tell me, Danielle, why did you choose a very thin sweater today and nothing else under? You're a young lady now, you know."

"To attract your attention," she answered frankly. "I think men would rather tutor an attractive and, well, possible girl than an ugly duckling."

I continued to brood, indecisive.

"Well," I said at last, "I'll do it, but there'll be no fee except De Veaux's skinny black cigars." (They were embarrassingly cheap, and worth less.) "But mind, Danielle, wear decent clothes. And there'll be no 'possible' in the picture. Understand?"

"Yes, sir, and *thank* you, sir. To reassure you, I'm a"—she fumbled—"a maiden, and Daddy'd shoot you otherwise."

I sighed. "This has been a grand week for people visiting me with guns. When do you want to start?"

"As soon as I can."

"All right. Let's make it two times a week, but not on weekends. Tonight at eight. Does that suit you?"

She threw her arms around me and kissed me on the cheek. "I only want to *learn*, Mr. Morrison, and my folks feel the same. I might even teach school in New York or Boston someday."

"No. You may teach for a while, but with your looks you'll get married. Just as my mother did, at a cost to education."

"If I turn out brighter than you think, truly bright—could I come three times a week?"

"Now, Danielle," I said severely, "I have things of my own to do"—I was not quite aware what they were—"and we'll have to see about that. For now, eight tonight, and leave the sweater behind." She stood up, giving me the benefit of the curves, and I wondered what I was getting into. I had rotten luck with girls, I remembered, and I thought about Betsy all the way home.

The child turned up promptly on the hour, and brought a protractor, a compass, a ruler, and some graph paper.

"Grammar for quite a while," I said firmly. "And syntax, and rhetoric, and maybe get familiar with some classic books—Shakespeare, Boswell's *Life of Johnson* and—for fun—Sir Walter Scott. That is, if you're a good girl and show talent."

We sat by Isis's fireplace, and while my visitor seemed disappointed, she gracefully submitted. She had not quite acceded to my dictum about clothes. The Canadian sweater was back on, and a plaid skirt, but I felt that neither rubbed against a material below. However, she was the soul of demureness, and that would do for now.

"To give you some idea," I said, "work this out in your head; it's elementary. 'Neither he nor they *was* or *were* at the party.'"

She looked confused for the first time since I'd known her.

"I suppose you could use either one—"

"—and be wrong. The verb—you know what a verb is?"

"Yes, sir."

"The verb agrees with the nearest pronoun—in this case, 'they.' And what's wrong with this one? 'Handsome, tall, strong, the girls all liked Harry.'"

She knitted her brows, and was about to give up when she blurted out, *"Harry* should follow 'strong.' Or one of the adjectives. Is that right?"

"Right. As I put it, it dangles; it's ungrammatical. But we'll go into that later. Now, do you need your protractor yet?"

Sheepishly, she slid what she'd brought into a school bag.

We went on for an hour, both having an exciting time, you might say. She *was* bright, and we let the hour run over to an hour and a half.

Then Betsy burst in, using her key, and stopped short, though she was not dismayed.

The girl and I got up, and I said, "Betsy, this is Danielle Lomond, whose father is a partner at De Veaux's. Her parents thought her advanced enough to be tutored personally, aside from school. I get unlimited cigars out of it. Danielle, this is my fiancée, Betsy Lockridge."

Betsy first looked astonished, but she quickly recovered and said, ignoring "fiancée," "That's splendid! I'm sure Danielle's very pleased."

She took her hand in the friendliest way, smiled guilelessly at me, and said, going out, "I won't interrupt."

"But we're finished," I called into a gathering storm. Apparently she failed to hear me.

"Well, Danielle, that's all for tonight," I told her. "You'd better scamper home before we have a cloudburst."

"I'll bring your cigars tomorrow," she said, looking up into my face. "And thanks for everything, Mr. Morrison."

"It was fun, child," I said, and slapped her on the behind. Sure enough, there was only the skirt.

For an hour or so, I stretched out on the sofa and tried to read, in French, *Manon Lescaut.* That's where Isis woke me at one o'clock, and I went to bed. It had been a dizzying kind of day.

"But I wanted to have a housewarming party Thanksgiving," I said to Frances and her husband, and to Betsy and Mr. Harbison, next evening at Lockridge's.

"William," said the lawyer, "grant me this favor. I must go back to

New York after the holiday, and I'm determined to pay a token on my social debts. My boy, you have all winter for your housewarming."

"Besides, the shape that house is in!" put in Frances, bringing a headshake of protest from Betsy.

"Well, I promise you this," I told him: "You'd dine better with me than at International House."

"But my dear fellow, I'm not taking us to International House. We're going to Rector's in Lockport, a famous center of *haute cuisine.*"

(I should say here that Rector's had got its start in Lewiston, then moved to Lockport and, later, Mr. Rector's son Charles took it to New York, where it reigned for years as a spa for the rich and famous. Its symbol was a huge, carved griffin, that hung outside. He, Charles, by the way, was earlier put in charge of the first Pullman dining car to cross the continent, and afterward he opened Rector's Oyster House in Chicago, with the original Lewiston griffin still in evidence.)

"Rector's!" cried Frances Lockridge. "What is it, some kind of homespun cooking place? This is Thanksgiving, *in my new land!*"

"No, my dear, Rector's has a certain reputation that extends as far as, say, San Francisco."

"Bosh!"

"Not at all; wait and see. And I have one or two other reasons, too. We'll go the long way, by Lewiston, and pass about twenty-five acres cleared for spring grape-planting. Another motive is that, ahem, William's father and I own a small part of the restaurant."

"Aha!" said Frances, "we get a discount!"

"On the contrary," said Mr. Harbison, "I'll insist on paying the full account, and tip the waiters holiday gratuities."

"Forgive me, Harbie," said Frances, patting his knee. "I should have known. We'd love to go, wouldn't we, Gervais? Betsy? William?"

"Since you put it that way, yes," I answered.

"Our carved and gilded sign," said Mr. Harbison, "shows an animal consisting of an eagle's head and wings on a lion's body—a 'griffin,' it's called. And that sign is now known on several continents, from which people come to visit the world's richest allurement—Niagara Falls! I'd been meaning to bring this up before."

"A griffon!" cried Frances. "A griffin as ever was! I had one as a pet, once. Look where it bit me." (A tiny white scar showed on her right index finger.)

"You mean clawed, I assume," said Mr. Harbison, comfortably. "The lion's not in a position to bite. Its head is supplanted by the eagle, you see. I believe the figure goes back to medieval times. I've vowed many times to check it."

"Well, mine didn't go back to medieval times! My uncle caught it in Park Lane. Of course, it was only a griffonette, then, or puppy. Tell me, Harbie, and this is serious, what's the statute of limitations on a griffon bite? Somebody's going to pay for that!"

"My dear, it just happens that I do know. It expired in 1436."

"Well, there's legislation for you! It could only happen under a monarchial system. You can depend on this—I'm going to write the Queen. And I'd like to see *her* face when she's slapped with a subpoena!"

(Lockridge muttered something I couldn't hear.)

"You'd probably do better to enjoy the food," said Mr. Harbison.

I found later that Mr. Rector suffered a great deal of ragging. The woodsmen and trappers continually wanted to know if the creature was furbearing, some saying, "Now, will it fly? You can let on that much, you know." And such other nonsense, until he was driven half out of his wits, or maybe to New York.

Chapter LI

So we left it that Mr. Harbison would use his rented buggy, with an extra horse, and if the weather held fine, we'd drive to Lockport, see some activity about our grapes en route, and dine at an amazing place, considering its locale.

"Wait a minute," cried the irrepressible bride once more. "It *is* Thanksgiving, and I suppose we can get in at any time of day?"

"My dear, I made our reservations by wire on October 28. A few more at my table won't matter. One makes reservations at Rector's for *any* day in the week."

The girl was taken aback, but she leaned over to say, pleadingly, "Harbie, you won't throw your weight around as an owner? Send food back, get a table near the orchestra, that sort of thing?"

"I'm sorry; there is no orchestra. People go there to eat, or gorge."

We left with blankets and buffalo robes before ten Thanksgiving morning, and I thought back to our snowbound picnic. But the day was cloudless, the Falls mist rose higher than ever, with rainbows starting from both the Canadian and American shores, and we were happy for an outing without complications. (I was a little relieved not to preside at the housewarming, too.)

I looked back at Betsy, who smiled in her warm way, and imagined that she felt firmly possessive.

Toward Lewiston, Harbison waved toward the right, away from the river, and we saw an expanse of ground from which the rocks had been rolled, runt trees and shrubs removed, and the shaly soil raked fairly even. Two men were still there, picking up bundles of branches.

"Harbie, you are a darling. How did you accomplish all this so fast?"

He beamed, slapping up his mare, but said, "I'll take the credit only for paying decent wages, or a little better. For the rest, I remind you we noted that a farmer—a minister—grew fair grapes here many years ago."

We stopped for a moment, and I think we all felt a swelling of pride. This traditional absorbing (and wealthy-making) enterprise gave us a sense of importance. Then the reins were slapped again, and we went on through pretty, white Lewiston, with its several grand houses, and clip-clopped toward Lockport, the now broad river and then lake dancing off to our left.

The horses had caught our contagion, for they were mettlesome and often needed drawing in, which Mr. Harbison did with expert, amusing flourishes. Frances sat beside him, bundled up to her ears in robes, and he looked shyly aside to note whether she was impressed by his driving. Being no fool, though troublesome, she sensed this, and asked, once, "Harbie, you drive like a professional. Are you sure you weren't a harness-racer in your young years?"

"Younger," he said, with signs of mischief in his face. "No, my dear, but I have a handsome rig-and-two in New York, and my relaxation from work is driving into the country."

"Alone?"

"No," he said soberly, "I have the horses."

She studied him, to see if he meant more. But for once she failed to score.

Lockport was jammed with people and carriages. People had come from everywhere, almost, to see the Erie Canal, its unique locks and its boats; to inspect the strap railroad and its phenomenal climb (that weasel of a conductor had suspended regular operations and was hauling people up, fifty cents a head); to "Ooh" and "Ah" over the mansions; and, if possible, to be fed at Rector's, which today was open from noon to midnight.

Special trains had run up for the holiday, and I heard that the hotels were full. The attorney stabled his horses and carriage, with a handsome bribe for preference, and we walked around for a while.

The houses of Erie and railroad profiteers were gorgeous, though not as good as my father's in New York, but I didn't say so. That Frances had a tongue like a file, and I was too slow to think of comebacks right off.

"They *are* nice," she said at last. "Boating and railroading must be very lucrative."

This was spoken seriously to Harbison, and I thought it civil of her, considering her background. The girl was not as bad as I thought.

"But Harbie," she said, "I'm starving. Do get him to take us in, Gervais."

The lawyer consulted his watch. "Precisely the moment of my reservation, lacking a minute and a half. I think we can jump the gun without argument."

"And you owning the place! Well, I should jolly well think so. Why don't you put everybody else out, if, say, we talk business. Serve 'em right, anyhow, for coming in such clusters."

Lockridge muttered something, and she subsided. As a new bride, and with friends on a holiday, she bubbled over. She locked arms with her husband and pulled his head down to kiss her.

I studied the great gilded sign of the griffin. It was indeed impressive, and I wondered if the artists who carved and painted it were still around. And if they could afford the restaurant.

This last was in a noble white-frame building, smartly painted, with a line of people strung outside for a block or more. I felt a trifle guilty when Mr. Harbison, apologizing at every breath, gently nudged us past the line and into the entrance hall, where people left their wraps on big brass hooks. I concluded that people didn't steal leaving Rector's; they were too warm and happy. And I thought, in feeble epigram, that happiness meant a good digestion.

When Mr. Rector, a large, comfortable man wearing mustaches, striped gray pants and, I believe, a swallowtail coat, saw Mr. Harbison, he rushed past the jam to greet us.

"Newton!" he cried, and the two men embraced. Then, introduced to us, the proprietor led our group to a round table in a secluded corner, where we had views of both the Canal and the strap railroad.

The table linen was thick and snowy white, with a little design; the silver was sterling (I picked up a knife to find the mark); and a bud vase in the center contained a single red rose. I wondered how they'd got it here.

By now, I was—characteristically, I suppose—growing slightly annoyed at all these frills about filling people up, and I remembered the fellow who dismissed France as a "nation of belly-culture."

"That's quite an artificial flower," I said, not wishing to skim Mr. Harbison's fun, but trying to keep things in perspective. Or maybe I was jealous.

"Son," said the lawyer, picking up the flower to hand it round for inspection, "that's a fresh Lord Canberry, shipped weekly with others from the South and kept on ice for occasions."

"Harbie!" Frances was genuinely impressed by this, and so, I'm afraid, was I.

Mr. Rector brought over the sommelier in his wine-colored jacket with the gold chains and keys round his neck. He circled the table to shake Mr. Harbison's hand.

"Newton, you don't need a wine-waiter, but he's new and wanted to meet you. For your table, I've selected a few trifling wines and, for dessert, a champagne that may surprise you."

Mr. Harbison thanked him, they shook hands again, and Rector himself handed out the menus. The regular waitresses, I noticed, wore aprons of vertical white stripes on blue. They were, I had to admit, attractive, and my jealousy gave way to warmth.

The menus were huge, embossed at the top with the identifying griffin and bound all round with gilt. And the offerings were enough to haul gourmets up from New Orleans, which took such pride in its cuisine.

We started off, of course, with iced Blue Points from Long Island, served on hammered silver plates with sauce in a middle cup; and went (slowly) from there to onion soup *au gratin* (the first I ever liked); and to a kidney omelet; thence to filet of sole Mornay; and then to the biggest, brownest turkey I ever saw, this last filled with almond, chestnut, and sausage dressing, with a tureen of giblet gravy. There was a huge brown ham to match, this with raisin sauce and spice sticks thrust in everywhere. For the rest (I think) apple fritters, wild rice with mushrooms, candied sweet potatoes with orange peel, glazed onions, Brussel sprouts *"Béchamel,"* cranberry shrub, and corn pudding New Orleans (drat it); both hot rolls and biscuits baked lighter than a thistle, with sweet and salted butter and a variety of jams, jellies and relishes. For dessert, as if we needed it, ices, plum pudding, a *"Trifle à l'Anglaise"* and pumpkin pie.

All this (and the portions were absurd, at least for this table) was followed by a decorative platter of cheeses—Camembert, Roquefort, Port Salut, Stilton, Cheddar in port wine, and others. And, of course, there was a silver platter of nuts, grapes, dried figs, with Niagara apples to cut in quarters to put the cheeses on, a practice then becoming fashionable.

With each course we had different wines, beginning with a coldish

Graves for the oysters and the soup; Chablis (from north of Burgundy) with the fish; and rich Beaujolais with the turkey and ham and "fixings," as we commonly said in New York (back in my peasant days, I thought, almost bitterly).

And Mr. Rector himself set up a larger wine bucket for a magnum of snow-white Taittinger, which was a champagne new to me.

"My word, Harbie, how you exaggerate!" said Frances. "I easily ate enough for two," and she blushed slightly. I thought of nothing of it at the time.

"Betsy," I said accusingly, "you ate least of all. Are you sick?"

"Not at all, William. Mr. Harbison will bring me back again when I'm hungrier."

For some reason, the whole business struck me as an absurd species of Roman orgy, but I pushed on through as best I could, because of Mr. Harbison. It did occur to me, once, that I was not in an especially festive humor.

With the cigars came port, and that pushy Frances insisted on having her share, like a man.

"That's not bad port," she said speculatively.

Mr. Harbison replied, "Any old port in a storm, my dear." Reflecting, he said, "I didn't make that up. I heard it in a play."

Then we sat for a while, four sipping port, Betsy pretending to taste her champagne. You might say we were digesting, as unsocial as that sounds, and then Lockridge said, "William might want to tell us some more facts about producing our own wine."

I could have done better taking a nap, but I drew a deep breath and said, "Well, we can plant in the spring and while the *vignerons*—I mean workers—are tending those grapes, keep clearing ground and plant again in the fall. But we'd better remember what de Brionne told me: Bacchus loves the hillsides."

"I thought he loved *wine*," said Frances. "What could he do with hillsides?"

"You've had too much port," I said, and went on.

"As to weather, it's about perfect; even the Bordeaux Chamber of Commerce agreed to that. We have, it seems, enough snow to protect the vines, and cold weather near the water keeps them from budding too early and being frostbitten."

After a brief altercation with Frances (which she won, with a terrible joke or two), I said, "We must avoid wet places—they give grapes a tough skin and hard flesh and make the taste too foxy, as it's called; or sharply overflavorsome, say."

"Foxy! Fancy that."

"And we need to be high enough to avoid lasting cold fogs and mildew; in general, here, look for southeastern exposures. You'd be surprised to know that in Niagara, near the Lakes, the strongest and coldest winds seek the lowest channels."

"That's all interesting, William," said Mr. Harbison, "but the land's been bought, you know. I sought southeast exposures when I first shopped, but, southeast being rare, I settled largely for southwest, and now find that probably best, locally. Southwest winds, for example, pass over the water."

I resumed my lecture. "Sometimes a shelter is needed for small plantings, in high places—a board fence or something like, to keep out especially strong, cold blasts.

"We've settled on the kind of soil, and we're pleased with that—clayey, shaly, sandy. In France, grape soil is good for nothing else whatever. Here, I believe, soil that will grow wonderful grapes might also grow a poor kind of corn."

"Corn for whiskey, grapes for wine," said the nuisance. "We've got a jump on both!"

"My dear, if you please," said Lockridge soothingly.

"Now, we can come, I hope!"—looking at Frances—"to preparing the ground for putting down plants. Several ways to prepare, but I'm convinced 'trench plowing,' with oxen, is best for us. It chews up the land and gets it ready.

"Gervais has successfully kept his roots in the cellar, and we can start with those. You dig a two-foot hole with a spade, after trenching, and place the plant in. Yesterday" (and I'd kept this for a surprise) "a boat at the landing had a big bundle of roots for me, from Gérard de Brionne in Graves. However, they were accompanied by a letter—"

"I'll bet you've written *him* loads since you got home, William."

"Listen, Miss Smarty, I've written to everybody I know in France. What do you think of that?"

"Little," she replied. "Very, very little," and Lockridge laughed.

"And what de Brionne said—"

"That's a pretty familiar address for a viscount. Are you a family member?"

"You might say so," I said, thinking of the duel and the mortgage. "But his point was this. He doubted, somehow, that Graves plants would thrive here. After, that is, I ran my soil test, and the Chamber of Commerce heard all the facts.

"About me writing letters. I know I'm not the world's greatest. I

445

should know; I've been told often enough over the years. But when the chips are down, I come through!"

"William," said Frances fondly, putting a hand on mine, "I was only ragging. You know how I love you"—and, the circumstances being what they were, she blushed furiously.

To myself, I said, "Yes, I damn well ought to know, and, Miss Rattlebrain, you'd better tread with care." (And was instantly sorry I'd had the thought.)

I took a deep breath and went on. "Anyhow, the oxen and plow go down deep—say two feet—and one manures from the roots to the stalk all the way up."

"One?"

"Really, Frances," murmured Lockridge.

"Ordinary barnyard manure is best, according to French *vignerons—*"

"Working in French again." (Frances was retuned up.) "I want you to know something, William. I knew French when I was eight years old! So don't throw any *vignerons* at *me!"*

"Keep on, Frances, and I'll turn you over my knee. I mean that literally. I think your husband would enjoy it, too. You're only costing yourself money, you know. I've decided to hand the firm an expense account—"

"What's money? I operate by the barter system. If you know what I mean."

"Now, Frances"—Betsy put her hand over the bride's mouth.

"The manure should be worked in thoroughly for a depth of about twenty inches."

"That lets me out"—this last gurgled through Betsy's fingers.

"All the way down, the soil should never be rich. I wish you could see the ground where our Graves of today came from. It looks like an old riverbed.

"And about the planting—space the plants out, and use the following method— Be quiet, Frances; this is important. Space the plantings two feet apart, take the topsoil of the second slice and cover the bottom of the first roots, then on top, here, throw the bottom soil of the first. Keep separating the plants two feet, topsoil on bottom and bottom on top, till you have the vineyard planted, and don't forget the manure.

"For Frances' sake," I went on, "and because she's so interested, I'll show you what a planted grapevine looks like. To the neophyte, it would seem to be upside down," and taking a pencil, I desecrated Mr. Rector's immaculate linen:

446

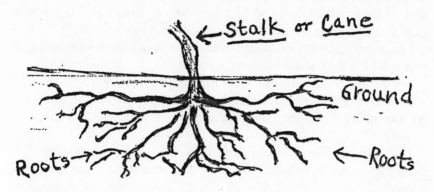

"William," said Frances, almost tearfully, "I want to buy that picture. Oh, I've got paintings, but *this!* —Well, it could easily be a Rembrandt. Done after his death, of course."

"Frances," said Betsy, "William's doing his best. Couldn't you just *shut up?*"

Mrs. Lockridge (and I) looked startled.

I said, "As for harvesting, crushing by walking barefoot in vats, the placing of juice in casks thirty to sixty days for fermentation, then filling the smaller oak casks for aging—I'll let those go for now. Maybe Frances can tell us when the time comes."

"William," she said again, her eyes filled with tears, and restrained by the groom from pouring herself more port, "I'll never be able to thank you for that speech. And I'd like you to know this"—taking my hand—"as God is my witness, I didn't understand a single damned word of it!"

"No, you were talking all the time. If you ever stopped to *listen,* your education might be improved."

"You're right," she said. "It's a lack of education that's always held me back. Tutors. All interested in the same thing, except one past seventy-five. I was interviewed in New York about a job selling hats, but when I told them about the tutors, they showed me the door."

"Frances," I said, running a (slight) chance of offending Lockridge, "don't you *ever* stop babbling?"

"Not so much on Thanksgiving. That hat store—when they wanted further information, I told them my father was a duke, and they threatened to call the police."

She gave way a little at the memory; then dabbed at her eyes with a handkerchief.

I thought I'd delivered a confusing report, and blamed it partly on

447

Frances; and then I decided to sharpen my drawing. I'd brought a stick of charcoal for this, but had forgotten it, so I said, "Bets, be a good girl and get a piece of charcoal you'll find in my coat."

I thought I saw an exchange of looks between Lockridge and our host, and felt they applauded my decision.

"Of course, William," she said, getting up.

But when she came back, Harbison said gently, "Oh, I think we get the general picture, William. No sense wrecking a tablecloth entirely."

"All right." Then I said truthfully, "Maybe it was only the champagne. Both champagne and port can cause trouble, you know."

Here, Mr. Rector came to inquire about our dinner, most others of our sitting having left long ago.

"Mr. Rector," said Frances, "in the line of—*haute cuisine, comme a dit St. Paul, Prends de la chartreuse pour l'égard de ton estomac!* That's from the Bible," she added.

He beamed, and said, "Dear lady, your dinner would hardly be complete without a sip of our special bottled gold. The finest French chartreuse—"

"*Chartreuse!* Chartreuse, by all means, if we never get out of Lockbridge, Lockport? —Correct?"

The fool rose and kissed Mr. Rector on the cheek while Lockridge and Mr. Harbison made negative gestures which he failed to see.

But the proprietor was so touched by the kiss that he left a bottle of the liqueur on our table, though by then she'd forgotten it. Mr. Harbison, at a sign from Lockridge, rose abruptly, and we filed toward the door.

There the lawyer held a brief, whispered chat with Mr. Rector, pressed a sum of money into his hand for the staff, and we left, after Frances had told him, "You lovely man, inviting us all here—virtual strangers."

In the buggy, as Mr. Harbison sent his mares into a trot, I noticed Frances (now in the back seat) asleep on her husband's shoulder.

When we reached home, and she woke up, she expressed herself as feeling a little sick. But naturally she had to add that she thought it was something she ate.

We put her to bed, muttering (I believe) something about being "burgled" of her chartreuse.

Chapter LII

The class had voted for a session on Friday, and when I awoke, my head aching, I found Betsy fixing my breakfast and lunch. She said nothing and, annoyed and casting about for a complaint, I announced, in a schoolmasterish way, "You know, Betsy, you didn't add much to the gaiety for Mr. Harbison. You neither ate nor drank enough to keep a flea alive. And you were silent, mostly, too. Like now." (Admiring my own grammar.) "I ask you again: Are you sick?"

There was a moment's hesitation, then, "No. I feel perfectly well."

"At least you could try." I said. "And my room's probably something of a mess." And I slammed out of the door.

I felt better later in the day, and when I came home, finding the house empty, I walked up to Lockridge's. He and Frances (subdued) and the lawyer (who was about to leave for New York), with what I thought was a sad look, sat at the fire, softly talking.

"Well," I cried heartily, "here we are, including Frances, all alive after Thanksgiving . . . but where's Betsy?"

"She's gone," said her father, straightening up, and I had an unreasonable premonition of the Falls.

"Gone? Where? I'll go join her."

Lockridge said very deliberately, "I'm afraid you don't understand. She's left Niagara, for good."

"Let me do the talking," said Frances. For once I decided not to interrupt.

"To begin with, William, I think you know we're all fond of you. But in some ways you aren't terribly bright; I'd like to meet your father and tell him we're in agreement. You take the easy way around everything. Do you have *any* idea how you've treated that girl lately? Did you think she was still your chambermaid? You've ordered her around, and let her break her back decorating your house, cleaning it, even polishing your boots.

"You couldn't get *me* there every day to send you to school, for more money than you possess. And have you thanked her even once? No. You brought home a scheming little tart to spend the evenings with—"

"Danielle's not a tart," I said sullenly.

"Perhaps not, but tutoring was about half of her plan, if I know the type. You fool! You took Betsy for granted until even she, the shy, confused, unhappy child finally had enough. She nearly idolized you until, I'm convinced, your precious schooling gave you the worst swelled head in my experience.

"And now you've lost her. Just what you've lost you'll find out as the days go by—"

For the first time, I began to see it more clearly, myself. The leather hat, the buckskin jacket, the roughneck. Even the duel at de Brionne's—not my affair by any rule. I was halfway showing off, like any other bully. But Betsy!

I groaned and bent my head toward my knees.

"I can't make do without her," I said, straightening up. "I can't run that house. I *need* her."

"You need certain chores done."

"But I want *her*, too. I've been so stupid and rude I can't believe it. I wasn't that way before. But right now I want Betsy back. What do I do?"

"I'm afraid you'll have to do without," said Lockridge, with no note of accusation.

"Harbie," I said, appealing, "have I really been this awful?"

He was emotionally affected. He coughed three or four times, then cleaned his pince-nez, before committing himself.

"Well, by your leave, there have lately been moments when I thought your manner more that of a man with a servant than with a prospective fiancée." Then his face looked firmer: "William, I'm sorry, but you've behaved like a jackass. There—I never thought I could say that, but I'll testify so in court, if called."

"It's true," I said, pressing my hands to my head. "I'm the blindest fool alive. I've lost the only thing I ever cared for deeply. What's left to be done? Where do I turn?"

"What would *any* real man do?" said Lockridge. "Start your search. No, I don't know where she is, and wouldn't tell you if I did. But I'll say this much: She left on the morning train.

"Now, if you aren't dramatizing, you'll prepare yourself for the kind of time you gave *her.* And if you should find her, get to work persuading her you're worth owning. As I see it, after watching you lately, it may be you'll find her, then lose her all over again."

I looked at three largely unpitying faces. I said, "I was off my head for a while; you'll have to believe that, and I can't explain it. I'll find her. I don't know how, yet. But I *will* find her, and make it up, somehow."

"Oh, William, you immature child!" cried Frances, kneeling beside me. "We could have stopped this, but we thought you needed a lesson. Go find her. It shouldn't be too hard—"

"Frances!" The voice was that of the man in the family, the father whose daughter had been treated so shabbily.

But Mr. Harbison's twinkled flash gave me some hope, a few ideas, and I hurried home to make preparations. Isis had apparently left after Betsy did, and I performed all the many small and large chores for myself and was happy doing them. Then I suddenly noticed that I was very tired, and felt even worse about Betsy.

I arranged with Lockridge to take my pupils in his class, hired a caretaker, and two days later was off on the morning New York train. But as I waited, early at depots as usual (while late for everything else), there occurred a very odd happening.

The day was dark gray, with fog, and I thought I heard my name called, several times, in the overcast. The cry grew stronger each time. And presently a grotesque sight appeared: Gervais Lockridge, half-running, hair disheveled, and wearing no outer garment on this nippy morning.

He arrived, gasping, and managed to ask how long before my train left.

"About half an hour," I said. "But they never come very close. I'm told the engineer's in a saloon at the moment."

"Thank heaven!" said my once-prospective father-in-law. He pointed to an iron bench the Commodore had disgorged, as it were, and pinned by chain to a steel upright.

"Can we sit down?"

"Of course, but what on earth—?"

He spent a brief interval getting his breath back. "No, Betsy hasn't come back, but I'm afraid we've done you a grave injustice."

"Me?" I said like a clod. "How come? Anyhow, I don't think so." For the past day or two, I'd felt much better at this time of day, and I stared with something like amusement. But I was rattled enough without this interruption, all the same.

"Just give me a minute . . . All right, now listen carefully, William, and try to remember. Betsy prepared your breakfasts and lunches for school, right?"

"Yes—during my professorial career."

"Isis has been gone two days; is that right, too?"

"Perfectly precise, Gervais. Two days, eleven hours and a few minutes."

"You seem in good spirits."

"Well, you must be trying to tell me something, but I'm a slow-witted fellow, as you all made clear, and in spite of that, I suddenly—"

"You feel—physically and mentally—improved since Isis left? Be as serious as you can."

I thought back. "I believe that to be true. What does it mean?"

"Give me time. Isis, then, prepared your supper?"

"That she did; very tasty, too."

"Did you start with soup every night?"

I thought back again. "I remember the soup."

He seemed to breathe a sigh of relief. "You'll excuse me if I feel grateful for my own memory. Now, hear me through—it's important."

I'd sobered down, and said, "Lay on. I'm getting the idea it is important, and in my favor."

"Completely . . . Well, when Ramses and Nefertiti first came to us, *we* had the soup. Betsy's idea, of course, because we'd always started any main meal with soup back home. But Bets didn't like Nefertiti's soup, and whisked hers out of the way, somehow.

"Now we get to the crux of this matter. I always drank mine, and shortly—in no more than three days—my temper turned sour for the first time, I believe, in my life. I was impatient, snappish, and critical of Betsy, and looked with disfavor on everything. But on each occasion, the feeling tapered off before evening.

"All right. Then—when Betsy said she wanted to go home, *was* going back to England, I locked myself in my study, and *scientifically* went over the evidence. I could pin the condition down to one possibility, and I came out to talk it over.

"To sum up, Betsy—without seeming to—watched Nefertiti pre-

452

pare our soup. On each occasion Nefertiti added a few drops of some villainous-looking black draught.

"Thinking Nefertiti was trying to poison us, I confronted her. I demanded an explanation—and she was innocent as a lamb. She was doing it *for* us, as Isis was for you. What she'd been adding was a familiar Seneca 'tonic' that they think makes them strong, calm, able to sleep better, and a few other things.

"But it had, and has, exactly the opposite reaction on unaccustomed whites. It makes us rude, surly, savage almost. We stopped the stuff, of course, and let Nefertiti serve her harmless 'strengthening soup' now and then, to keep her happy, It is *not* palatable, as my bride once observed in terms a little more brisk.

"Now, we forgot to instruct Isis about the potion and you. In effect, you *have* been poisoned, and you're in no sense guilty about Betsy. We're sorry as the devil, and hope you'll forgive us. That's the gist of it. I could probably guess the child's whereabouts—"

"Please don't," I said firmly. "Naturally I'm relieved about something that's baffled *me*. But I've got some further reforms in mind, and I prefer to find Betsy myself. I've been pretty much of an ass, off and on—gunfighter hat, acting the roughneck, hanging round the Eagle, poking my nose into things that don't concern me (including several you don't know), shirking my job for Mr. Bennett—who's treated me very well, all in all—and more I could name.

"No, *I'll* find Betsy. And I hope no one blames me if I tell her about Isis and the magic elixir. But I'm embarked on a cleanup, and I'll have to do it alone. Thanks. Thanks for running up to tell me. You can understand that I feel better than ever, of course.

"And now"—looking at his wet jacket—"you'd best start home. You'll catch pneumonia."

I brushed the droplets off his clothes, and for the second time since I'd met him, he shook my hand.

"I'll leave," he said. "But that drug"—over his shoulder—"I've been analyzing. I believe it's akin to the root *Rau wolfia*, which India-Indians use to control nerves, high blood pressure, and the like. This black-sheep cousin appears to have a reverse effect on us, as I said."

I waved. "You'll get it, Gervais. Don't worry."

He disappeared into the fog.

For some reason, I thought only of the city, remembering that look in Harbison's eye. Besides, I wanted badly to see my family.

In this, my first serious blow, I felt painfully homesick, for a change. In the years past, I'd been too self-absorbed to know the sensation. But now I had the notion that my father could mend anything; and my mother, I knew, would find me excuses against the world.

Seated on the Commodore's patchy cushions, I tried to open my eyes to the world around me, rather than the one in me, and found it rewarding, despite my still anxious state. I was aware that I'd turned a milestone corner.

I was seated over a flat wheel (like most others) and meditated how anybody could run a railroad so badly while piling up millions for himself. It really was a remarkably poor ride. A passenger observed that it was best to keep one's mouth shut tight, especially if he had gold fillings. I had none, but a man across the aisle, after we'd rattled through an intersection, saw his false teeth pop out and onto the floor, where the conductor, superciliously taking tickets, stepped on and crushed them. I didn't envy him. The owner was at least six-feet-five and rough in proportion.

He got up, his face fixed in wrath, and said, "You see them ruint teeth?" —pointing down.

In the manner of American train conductors, this one answered up with lofty impertinence.

"What about it? I didn't build and construct these wheels. And nobody asked you to ride, neither." But this particular bully had made a mistake. Accustomed to cowing passengers, as if they were sheep, he'd fallen into his usual address.

"That's your toon, is it?" asked the passenger, and grasping the official's belt, he lifted him off the floor. Then, with one hand, he opened a window, admitting a belch of bituminous smoke. "Now tell me frank. You'd rather pay for new teeth or go kiting out the winder?"

"I'll call the engineer and brakeman and flagman and put you under arrest!" the conductor managed to gasp.

"You think you got some kind of police heft? I never liked none of your breed, to tell the truth." (I'd often wanted to say the same myself, and others in the car applauded out loud.) "Go git your flunkies, you'll all sail out—one atter the other, head to heel."

And he swung the conductor in a quick, looping arc, stopping just short of the opening.

"Hold up! All right!" screamed the high symbol of authority; then, pale and restored to his feet, he produced a notebook and said, in his surly style, "How much did them teeth cost? They looked cheap to me."

"Twelve dollars and fifty cents—on *sale*," said the giant. "They come from Wolfe and Meisner's, in Rochester, a honest and honorable emporium. Solid baked enamel. Without I get paid in full, plus five dollars for being put to trouble, your life ain't worth a buffalo nickel. See here"—and he sailed the conductor's cap, with all its super-valuable data, tickets and other trash, to the filthy roadway outside. The official stepped back, then broke into a run toward the front.

I waited, curious. The train ground to a halt, and presently four fattish men appeared through the vestibule. Seeing their antagonist, they stopped.

Not 'completely cured, despite Betsy, I stood up. "I'm this man's brother," I said. "I'm also an attorney. And when we arrive, I'll sue the road, in his behalf, for $20,000—for public humiliation."

The four stood, bewildered. Probably no one had ever before challenged them either physically or financially, and they whispered among themselves.

"I'd like you to know something serious, alonger my brother here. I got 'complices strung along this rout from New York to Niagry. If I ain't had money delivered—Ben Tolliver, Gen'l Delivery, Size eight and a half, Albany—in forty-eight hours, I'm plannin' to release them 'complices. They know where to find you, and they enjoy tearing the limbs off railroaders, hear me? Now just write down your name, and show identification. Try and 'scape us—do please."

From this, I somehow inferred that he was an Erie Canal man, and probably an oddity even there. In any case, the conductor wrote down the information, the helpers repaired to their stations, and the train started up again.

But the flat wheels were no better, of course, and we finally arrived, bounced half to jelly, in New York. The creature across the way shook my hand, winked, grinned, and withdrew another set of false teeth from his pocket.

"Three dollar, fifty cents lower Broadway," he said. "It's a regular occyypation. But you got to work different crews."

For a while, at least, I'd been diverted from my misery. I looked for a hansom home, and got cold feet. When the humor was on him, my father had a tongue like a blacksnake whip, and I knew what he'd say.

So—lacking another idea, I went to Mr. Harbison's offices at the Battery. He'd left before me, and he was present, in his usual bland, essentially unafraid but cautious mood.

"I thought you might be along," he said, rising to shake hands.

"Do you have anything to tell me, Mr. Harbison?"

455

He sat down and drummed on his desk. At last he said, in his courtroom voice, "Along what lines? Or in pursuit of what objective? I'm afraid that, at this moment, I lack the *res gestae*."

"I need your help, Mr. Harbison. Don't shrink back into your legal clothes. We've been companions at a blizzard picnic—remember?"

He took a deep sigh. "William, you haven't given me a specific reason for your presence in this office. I can hardly prepare—"

"You know the reason," I said. "Betsy's gone, and I thought she might come here. I'm afraid I didn't quite realize, especially considering Isis' help," and I explained Gervais' dash to the train. I could see, however, that he didn't fully believe me.

"Why come to *me*, William?"

"Because you know where she is."

"I admit nothing and deny nothing," he said, trying to be firm. "Let that stand."

"Speaking of 'stand,'" I said, "it seens to me you once stood as my godfather. What's a godfather for? I'm confused."

"You place me in an awkward position. Surely you wouldn't have me betray a client's trust?"

"Betsy's your client?" I cried. "I doubt that," my ire rising higher. (What I said to myself was, goddamn and blast all lawyers, including this pompous ass of my childhood.)

"William, you shouldn't—"

"Moreover," I said, "I have a right to doubt any man who placed that mendacious story in the Niagara Falls *Iris*. Oh, I might have written one just as tricky. If I'd done it at all."

"I'm sorry you consider me 'tricky,'" he said gravely.

"So am I. But I could probably be three times as tricky; it wouldn't strain me any."

Thinking I'd been a little rough, I said, "I've looked up to you, Mr. Harbison, and my appeal was to a *godfather!*"

Then (thinking the battle lost) I heard, "Do you wish this lovely girl, of exemplary character, to be your wife? I'll say frankly that, watching you together, it hadn't occurred to me."

I said, "Yes" and waited him out.

He studied me shrewdly. "Betsy is *not* my client," he said slowly. "I have another. Do you wish me to break my legal oath?"

"Just as fast as you can, and you won't be sorry."

He sat without moving, not cleaning his glasses once. I, in the interim, twisted about impatiently.

At last he said, "I think I've hit on a very 'tricky' compromise" (with the briefest of smiles). "You see, I have only one client!"

I was up, gave his hand a wring, and out of his office without closing the door. I had no idea why I hadn't thought of it before.

I hailed the slowest hack in New York and sat sweating while it rolled to Washington Square. Before we arrived, I'd concluded that the horse, a collection of articulated bones, would drop in its traces short of our destination.

But it managed, somehow, and throwing a handful of silver beside the driver, I leaped out, sprang up our steps, and used my key to get in. I had neither the time nor the stomach for greetings from domestics, no matter how esteemed.

My mother was crossing the foyer, about to ascend the broad, white staircase, but on hearing the door slam, she turned around.

"William!" she said sweetly, kissing me on the cheek. "What a nice surprise!"

"Where's Betsy?"

"Betsy? I'm afraid I don't—"

"Betsy Lockridge. You know who I mean; don't deny it."

"*Whom*. William, your father will want to see you in his study. He has a cold, dear, and may seem a trifle curt."

I thought I detected some mild motherly malice, and learning about my father, my spirits sank. Nevertheless, I told myself, I'd face a dragon to find Betsy, and, heart thumping, banged at my father's study door.

His "Come in! Quit knocking the wall down!" was hardly reassuring, but I found him behind his desk studying a manuscript, his feet in a pan of hot water. I pulled up a chair, and he delayed looking up for a minute or so.

"So—the prodigal returns," he said at last, leaning back. "And in certain difficulties, Newton tells me."

"There's a girl named Betsy Lockridge—"

"Yes, I knew her when she was three years old."

"She's a wonderful girl. I thought we were engaged, but I conducted myself badly, and she ran away from Niagara. Her father—"

"Gervais."

"—her father and his wife—"

"Go on."

"They and Mr. Harbison have told me what a fool I acted, and yet I wasn't entirely to blame. It's a long story, and involves my Seneca cook . . . The woman and her 'tonic.'"

"Did you ask her hand, and tell her how you felt? And all the rest? . . . Damn and blast the thing!" he cried, pouring in more water from a copper kettle. "They've scalded me! . . . Well?"

"She must have known how I felt."

"By ordering her about like a servant?"

"Yes," I said, "I did. But her father came to the train to tell me about the tonic. He had the same experience from an Indian remedy once."

Newton Harbison was a bachelor, I remembered, and probably had wellsprings of emotion. This specimen was harder to crack. I reminded him: "I need your help, Father, and I believe I'm the only son you've got."

"Yes, I always wanted two sons. One to rip around and gamble at college, and another to graduate with honors, so that the business could be passed on."

I was of mixed emotions, feeling a little unfairly treated. I said abruptly, "Where's Betsy?"

"Did Newton tell you she was here?

His look was hard, and I couldn't have lied if I'd wished. "Not exactly. He told me nothing, but he left a clue."

And then came a very joyous sound; he chuckled.

"That's what he would do. Why, yes, as a matter of fact, she is—temporarily. She went to Harbison for a job, which he gave her, naturally enough. As receptionist, I believe—a beautiful and intelligent girl—"

"I didn't see her there."

"—and when I heard, I checked her out of a hotel and persuaded her to come to us. No, you didn't see her. Newton released her early today—to keep an engagement for dinner and then to the Assembly."

"Alone?" I stood up.

"Sit down! Certainly not. We had people in to meet her." He pulled a bellcord.

"Good evening, Mr. William," and then, "You wanted me, sir?"

"Yes. Whom did Miss Lockridge go out with tonight? Do you remember, Jenkins?"

"Yes, sir. He gave me his coat and hat when he came. He and Miss Lockridge and Mrs. Morrison took a glass of sherry before they left. It was Mr. Quincy Lowell, sir."

I jumped up again.

"Quincy Lowell! That fop! I could break his back over my knee. I believe I *will* do it. Where'd they dine?" I looked at my watch.

"I'm sure I don't know, Mr. William."

"That'll be all, Jenkins. Thank you," my father said.

"Yes, you could likely embarrass him physically. That appears to be what you know, more or less. But in all other ways, Quincy Lowell is your superior. And I'm not even sure that you *could* whip him. I'm told he did very well at crew, and that requires conditioning. I'm also told you keep yourself in shape at a place called the Eagle Tavern."

He had experience of the Eagle Tavern, and, moreover, was aware that I knew it.

"For God's sake, sit down! No wonder the girl fled. You seem to have turned into a savage, at Niagara Falls. Perhaps it's time you came home and forgot about the wine business. Let's see"—he mused, with his chin in his hand—"I believe we have an opening filing invoices."

I sat down and said, in low tones, "Then you aren't going to help me?"

"*Help?* How can *I* help you? I have no control over Miss Lockridge and would commend Mr. Lowell to her if I had."

I had only one shot left in my locker.

"Well, I'm awful in every way; let's agree on that. And I did pretty badly at Bordeaux, too?"

"We'll go into that later. For now, the answer is—yes and no."

"You're my father," I said, not very pleasantly. "You're supposed to give me advice."

"Tonight?"

"Yes, tonight. Right now."

"Perhaps I can. Go up to your room, take a warm bath—or maybe a cold one—have Jenkins bring you a tray, read an improving book, and get a good night's sleep."

I tossed and turned, lying on the bed in my clothes, now awake and listening, now shallowly dozing. Through my mind, asleep or awake, raced pictures of Betsy and that bounder, Lowell, and I weighed the chance of killing him for taking an innocent girl to a public restaurant at a time when such places were frequented by the demimonde.

I wished I'd brought my gunfighter hat. It seemed the life I was fit for, and, at the moment, wanted. Just now, I hated all of these people. All except Betsy.

Infrequently I arose to tiptoe out and silently stare downstairs, to find some hint whether they'd come back. If I'd been rational, I might have looked at my watch and seen that the time was only ten o'clock.

But the hours wore on, with no sound to suggest the couple had returned from whatever low den Lowell had suggested, probably with strong drink or worse. And always the hollow feeling inside, the ache of something gone, to be forever missing. And the pictures raced on in procession. I knew that silken body, tanned from summer swimming, and I could even envision obscene embraces in a hotel room. (It was much later that I realized what an offensive view of Betsy I'd taken, and was aware that these traits lay in me, if anyone.)

Once I thought I heard whispered voices, and I crept out again to find—nothing. A house empty and still, all the more ominous for lack of any sound. Like a fool, I even tried the principal guest room door, but it was locked. Could they be there? Briefly, I considered taking an ax propped in a corner against fires and smashing the door in.

Delirium came and went, and during certain hours I sat on the edge of my bed, trying hard to plan, in what passed for normalcy now.

But I wore myself out, trying to erase the ugly scenes, and toward morning fell into a heavy sleep.

I woke with creases covering a side of my face, from the depth of that sleep, and sprang up, momentarily panicked. It was broad daylight, as the saying goes, nearly midday, in fact; and I washed and shaved hurriedly, a measure of sanity returned.

I'd remembered Harbison's job, and while I thought it a long chance, I slipped downstairs, heard Jenkins' "Good morning, sir," and let myself out. It seemed three or four hours before I could hail a hackney and a couple more before it pulled up at the offices. But I'd learned (or almost) the folly of temper, and I overtipped the sluggish rogue; then, heart thumping, made my way toward Harbison's receptionist.

She was seated there, as perfect and fresh as if the orgies of the night had never touched her.

"Why, William! How jolly!" Her smile was as sweetly guileless as ever.

I sat down on a chair nearby and said, "Well, Betsy, I heard that good old Harbie had given you a job."

Her face lit up. "Two, actually. I—receive people, and I'm to stamp and mail these letters at noon. And, William, he's paying me masses of money. I never got much pay as a chambermaid, you know."

I winced, but my line of march had been fixed, and nothing could distract me again.

"Did you wish to see someone, William? You'll be my first receptee. Mr. Harbison's work is mainly for your father, I find."

"Betsy, I want you to listen carefully. You thought well of me once, did you not?"

"Why, I still do," she cried in surprise.

"We were friends?"

"I hope you aren't going to cast me aside now. We'll always be friends."

460

"Then I have a favor to ask."

"A favor? Having to do with Mr. Harbison's work? Of course."

"Having to do with you." I had to bite back what I saw as my habitual vehemence.

"Me? Whatever kind?"

"It's lunchtime. I promise to disappear from your life if you'll join me walking up the street. It's as important—as important as possible." My words were fast failing me.

"You sound solemn this morning, William. Didn't you sleep well last night?" The clear blue eyes were as curious as a child's, nothing more.

"I had no sleep whatever."

A shadow of hurt crossed her face. "You're sick, and should be in bed."

"That can wait" —I blushed. "What I mean is, I'm not sick. All I want is for you to walk out of here with me for an hour, however much time Harbison gives you at noon. Then you'll be rid of me, like a bad dream."

"But I don't want to be rid of you, William. We'll always be friends—remember?"

"Will you do it?"

She looked at the letters. "I feel I should stay in today and take care of the post. Mr. Harbison is a good man, and he's been grand to me. You used to call him Harbie," she observed.

"He's been demoted. Damn near everybody has. Please, Betsy. It'll be the last time."

"Funny. I never before heard you say 'please' to anyone."

"That's probably true, but things have changed. I say it again."

She sat thinking. "I'd be a very wicked witch to say no to an old friend who asks like that" —and again the clear, curious blue eyes.

She got her wrap, and we stepped out into the street. A light snow had begun to fall.

She asked, "Down toward the Battery, perhaps?"

"I had that in mind. Bets"—I took her arm—"no matter what, we've had good times to think back on. Or perhaps they weren't, to you. And now I have something to say about your Isis." (The "your" should have been deleted, but wasn't.)

She put her hand to her mouth. "The potion! I forgot. *William!*"

"Yes, the potion; but I haven't been exactly a paragon, anyhow. Still, I suppose you remember the picnic in the snow? And Harbie trying to be proper and stiff and legal—and enjoying himself?"

Before she could remind me of "Harbie," I said, "We—I—had fun in that blizzard. And I even had fun, though I could have spanked you when Deke Slater and I pulled you out of the river and we dried in the Hermit's cave. It was only that I was afraid for you, you know."

From the tail of my eye, I saw her color deepen, and thought I'd rushed things. "Maybe the best times I've had in my life were in your father's cozy house, him stretched out, Frances prattling her nonsense, Harbie loving it all—and you, sitting on the floor by the fireplace, looking like an angel—"

"William." Her voice was low and unsteady.

"Here's a beautiful snowy iron bench. We can see the harbor ships, and—please don't say no—I have only a little more to say."

We sat face-to-face, and no pedestrian came by in the snowfall.

"Bets," I said, taking an unresisting hand, "I remember once when you kissed me as though you meant it. That's something I'll remember always. But you've probably forgotten—"

"William—please!" Her voice was even lower, her eyes were filled with tears, and her face covered with the little quick disappearing stars of snowflakes.

"Dear Betsy—I'm not good at this, but it's customary to tell you I love you. There'll never be another girl for me. I know I've treated you badly. But I'm not like that; not really, and you know it . . . That was mainly what I wanted to say."

She put her hands to her face. "William! I had such plans to start life over and forget you. But the snowflakes have blurred them—"

"Betsy, please marry me. Right now. I know girls like big elaborate weddings, with a church, bridesmaids and the rest, but I feel—I feel if I don't marry you now, I'll lose you."

She almost whispered, looking down, "I don't like churches."

"Then come along," I cried, still hoping not to press. But I jumped up. "We can have a big church wedding later, if your family insists, but I seem to remember your father's attitude about weddings—"

"I'm all mixed up, for the first time in my life. I don't know what's right. It's odd." And then, decisively, "Maybe you'd better kiss me. I'd like to see if it makes a difference."

I did so promptly—on her lips, cheeks, hair, neck. "What a fool I've been!" But she put a hand over my mouth.

There were papers to get at windows of City Hall, some of these illegal, to be covered by gold and a mention of my father.

Then I arranged more than we needed, working in a hurry. The janitor gave the bride away; my best man was a felon in handcuffs, on his way to the Tombs; Betsy had glowing and (I thought) exquisite bridesmaids from a group of elderly women applying for municipal relief, and my ushers were, of course, the guards clinging to my best man. (Drunk, he wept quietly throughout.)

By some means, the mayor heard of the proceedings, and, back with his family from studying London Bridge, he came in ponderously to perform the ceremony. After shaking my hand, he asked only one question: "William, does your father know about this?"

I lied, and said, "Yes, it was his idea." Then I said, "How did you and your family and aides like London, Your Honor?"

He gave me only a medium-hard look, since he had a hide like sheet metal, and was politically beaming again soon.

I had a ring—my grandmother's and now mine. I'd seen to that, and for a wedding present, I had what people were calling a "guard ring," a band of both diamonds and emeralds.

Betsy cried a little, and the mayor "Harrumphed" several times and then insisted on kissing the bride. He did a bang-up job of it, getting even, and I briefly considered knocking him down. But I'd decided to put rages behind me, and did so.

Then I gave everybody money—lots of it—and the mayor said he'd condescend to keep his hundred dollar gold piece, "to remember the occasion by," the faker. (He spent it that night at Madame Fifi's.)

"Betsy, we're married!"

"Oh, William!"

We dashed out into the street, misunderstandings gone, and a tug hooted offshore—for us, I imagined.

"A wedding feast! It's absolutely necessary! Boy!" I cried to a passerby. "You got sense enough to deliver a message?"

"William!"

I'd slipped again, but not badly, and I wrote a note and handed it to him for Mr. Harbison, with five dollars to make the errand of two blocks worthwhile. Then I stopped another boy, larger, and gave him ten dollars to follow the first one.

"But William, I don't want a wedding 'feast.' I want one of those wieners, from that cart right there."

It had "Manny Scholl's Rolling Delicatessen" lettered on the side, and we both ate three wieners, with sauerkraut and mustard, in soft rolls, as the snow continued to float down.

"So you're married at City Hall a-ready?" inquired the proprietor. "Weenies on the house. No," he said severely, "no, you needn't pay. Not a cent!"

So Betsy kissed Mr. Scholl, too.

Chapter LIII

Well, I see I've run on too long here, maybe, but I've only got a few more things to tell, including how we prospered with wine. So I'll get them said, and quit.

I'd learned a few things about writing books, and I showed the first chapter or two to my father, and to Frances and Gervais Lockridge and Mr. Harbison. If I say so myself, I picked up some compliments that helped me along.

Much later, my father read all the chapters and said, "And to think I sent you to Harvard!" When I asked what he meant, he said, "Well, for one thing, you've fallen into the habit of too many contractions, such as 'I'd' and 'he's,' and the like. The fact is, here and there you've been writing the way they presumably talk in Niagara Falls. Your mother noticed it first, but she always gives reasons—"

"Well," I said, "my system was proved correct right there. In the first sentence you said 'You've.' Now, that's the way people *talk*, so why not follow the system, in some degree? Besides, it's easier to read. There's such a thing as common sense, you know, and Mother has a great deal."

He looked up sharply, and I eyed him back without flinching, for a change. I was tempted to ask him what books *he'd* written, but decided against it. I'd finally realized that he grew unpleasant in arguments like these.

Gervais Lockridge read the manuscript carefully, too, and after meditating, legs at their outermost, said, "Interesting, interesting indeed, William. You may be breaking new ground in literature. We're proud of you, my boy."

But it had to be that wiseacre Frances who gave me the finest boost. I watched her face as she read, and it grew mellower and mellower. Then she put it down and said, "It takes real courage to write a bad book. You've shown your mettle, William; you really have."

"I knew I could count on you," I said. "Anyhow, there isn't a college or school for women in all of England. I looked it up in the library. Whence cometh *your* brilliance?"

I could count on Harbie, who had to cleanse his glasses several times throughout, as well as cough, but said, "Well, it's *not* a tale told by an idiot. On the contrary, it kept me absorbed throughout. But why, William, did you bother to tell the truth anywhere? As a lawyer, that point bothers me. In any case, you're a remarkable young man."

"Maybe I am," I said fatuously. "I may just be."

But now, with a relationship that had gone through a mill, Betsy and I, newly wed at midday, comfortably filled with the excellent Mr. Scholl's "weenies," found the house empty, except for Jenkins, and sneaked out our luggage. Betsy left a letter of thanks on the foyer desk, then wrote a note of explanation and thanks to Mr. Harbison. For reasons I've forgotten, we agreed to keep the marriage secret for a while. I gave Jenkins a gold piece and shook his hand, and we were off.

We checked our bags at the Commodore's station, me figuring to lose no more than one or two, and, having hours to spare before the night train to Buffalo, I showed Betsy such sights as I could think of. New York, then being approximately an open sewer (as stated), with Irish riots still booming, lynchings and other unsavory facets, the job was not easy. As I made an apology, Besty confounded me by describing pompous Victorian England as one big debauch. Despite its prim reputation, she said, nearly every man had a mistress, and the women, lovers. And there was a great deal more.

We saw Fraunces Tavern, where George Washington told the Continental Army's officers goodbye; St. Marks in the Bowery, where

Peter Stuyvesant was buried; Trinity Church at Broadway and Wall, built in 1696; and the first bank in the city—the Bank of New York, founded by Alexander Hamilton; and one or two other places. There wasn't much. There was, for example, not one handsomely built building, and I concluded there never would be.

So—we had an oyster stew at an oyster house across from the station, and climbed aboard a few minutes before the train left.

In the morning, we arrived to find the Lockridges waiting, having been wired of our return, and we drove home for a merry breakfast. No one mentioned Betsy's leaving, or my finding her—even Frances, which was an authentic milestone.

After breakfast, Lockridge resumed work on a letter to Mr. Harbison and to my father, asking them, and my mother, up to visit for Christmas, because he (Lockridge) was dreadfully afraid of being invited down, and would have moved West rather than go. He was not an admirer of New York, so he'd resolved to get his licks in first, as they say.

Betsy had Nefertiti fetch Isis back, with some firm instructions; and we decided to announce our union at Christmas dinner, especially if my father accepted, which he did in a few days. He said he'd be "charmed to resume an old acquaintance," and went on in that vein for a while. (I could have improved his sentence structure, but considered it best to remain silent; no sense in stirring up trouble.) Mr. Harbison also said he would come, but preferred to stay at International House, thus inconveniencing nobody.

I thought, "Chances are, we'll never *really* be married until Christmas," but Betsy came in often, in the evenings, and was as warm and affectionate as anyone could be—up to a point. The instructress of her chambermaid phase had not quite disappeared, any more than I'd turned saint overnight.

On an evening soon, she said, "Isn't it time you took your pupils back from Father, William? You were having fun, then, and so were they."

"But no home tutoring," I told her. "You may not believe it, but that girl was nothing to me but a mind at work."

"Was she, William?" Always without guile.

"Well, she won't be back, I promise you that. For one thing, I hear she's getting maried."

"That *is* good news, isn't it? But you could have done what you thought best."

What was best, it seemed to me, was to come—sprinting—home after school to find Betsy waiting, busy tacking up curtains, adding furniture, even bringing family pictures in the heavy silver frames. She had her rings and our certificate, which had been liberally stamped by that old humbug, the New York mayor. All these tokens of our estate were hidden under a loose board in an upstairs closet.

My students seemed glad to see me, and Ebenezer continued reformed, and I could scarcely ask for more, I thought.

The days moved along without event. Betsy and I took walks, sometimes to look at the Falls. But for superstition's sake, I never suggested we go to Goat Island, and she never once asked.

My father and mother and Mr. Harbison arrived the day before Christmas, and my father, having considerable luggage, bossed that train around as if he owned it. I was embarrassed. It was possible, I considered, that both the Commodore and the engineer might prefer to stop the train at the point of their choosing, rather than at a spot indicated by my father. Of course he had his way; he generally did, but he was headed for a collision with me, and I think we both knew it. That burden (as I then saw it) had leaned over me too long.

He and my mother greeted the Lockridges like old friends, and Betsy as if she'd never disappeared. It was baffling. I failed to understand it.

The weather was conspicuously warm. I heard a river rat say that the "glass is acting mighty notiony, and it wouldn't surprise me if we had a typhoon." He was one of those long ago drifted over from the Pacific and since he obviously meant to be heard, I assumed he was trying to scare the tenderfeet.

My father could never let such a jackass statement stand, so he said, turning around—a massive figure of a man, "Such sea-storms are called 'hurricanes' in this hemisphere, my man, and I've ridden through more than you have fingers and toes."

Evidently he looked so overwhelming that the scamp involuntarily touched his cap; but he had to add, "I speculated you had, gov'ner; I placed you as a seagoing man when first I clapped eyes on you. If she blows up, she'll be a hurricane—right and proper, and no fuss from me."

"Let's hope for the best," and my father gave him a shilling.

"Is that you, Billy?" responded the scoundrel. "Things been mighty quiet around the Eagle since you jumped ship. Welcome home and hearty!"

It occurred to me that throwing him under the train, if the train moved, might divert my father, but I received no more than an amused look.

Since my mother was tired, we went to bed early, or after a ceiling-

467

scraping tree had been decorated with ornaments fashioned mainly by Lockridge's class. My students had given me presents, too, and these, together with all our others, were piled on the floor beneath. My parents were to stay with the Lockridges, their hosts.

It's hard to believe, but after my father had stared out of a window, he said, "That scalawaag at the train was right. It's starting to snow, and I think we're in a for a squall, or worse."

He and Lockridge went to look at Lockridge's gauges, and when they returned said the temperature was falling fast, the wind was coming up, and the bottom had dropped out of the barometer.

And it was still snowing, and piling up, the next morning, with both houses shaking and complaining all night, or "talking," as sailors say of a ship. As before in this crazy winter, it was exciting.

We were to have presents after Christmas dinner, which turned out different from the ordinary. For one thing, we were snowed in tight. Ramses and I had to use snowshoes to get articles from my house. We also picked up Isis (who was coming over for dinner, but was frightened).

But storm or no storm, it was a wonderful feast that the women had prepared. And instead of eating, of course, I sweated because of my announcement to follow.

With the dessert and champagne, I tapped on my water glass and arose, my throat dry as a bone. (I can't think of a better figure even now.)

A little silence fell, then my father spoke up. "Yes, William?"

"I—I have something to tell you, of interest, I believe, to you all—"

My voice was fading, but when I looked down at Betsy, it came back.

"As you know, I'm not much at speechmaking—"

"Singular flaw for a man teaching speech," muttered my father (and I marked it down for later); then I sang out boldly, "To come to the point, Betsy and I are married. Now, what do you think of *that?*"

Instead of the normal exclamations and embraces, Mr. Harbison passed a note to my father, who passed it along to me. It said, in my own untidy scrawl, "Dear Mr. Harbison, I must leave job as Wm. and I being married at City Hall. Your friend—Betsy."

"*I* wrote this? When?"

"I knew you might be struck by its eloquence. No doubt you recall the messenger you employed at the Battery? What, exactly," asked my father, "did you think 'Betsy' had written? And do you generally sign other persons' names to your letters?"

I was as stupefied now as then, I suppose, and said, "I thought I'd only explained that Betsy had to leave her job and go home." I felt briefly deflated, but the congratulations and the hullabaloo that followed offset my superfluous speech. All I could say, over and over again, was, "So you've known all along; you've *all* known all along!"

"We thought it only decent to respect your wishes, William—and Betsy," said Gervais Lockridge.

Mr. Harbison was at work with his glasses again, as Betsy kissed everybody but me, and Mr. Harbison twice, then finished putting on her rings, with my help, and I think she was as rattled as I was, for once.

"Gervais," said my father, "do you mind my taking about five minutes before we go to the presents?"

Lockridge replied of course not, and my father, as if he'd been at business, began.

"First off, we'll take up the two châteaux. You did some good work there, William, as I understand it this far. I was surprised, as I told you."

"Why surprised?"—and he looked startled at my tone.

"The preposterous idea of you owning a château, or its mortgage, is about as absurd as my buying Potsdam. I assume you exhausted, or nearly so, a substantial letter of credit, and—curse the luck— you've been lucky all your life. How the devil you'll ever acquire a sense of values, I'll never know."

"Maybe it wasn't luck," I said. "And I'm tired of being bawled out for succeeding."

This was the first time I'd ever talked back to him, and I went on. "I assume you didn't give me the letter of credit whimsically, and for your information I didn't even use it. I waved it around, and used my money—well enough, too."

"It happened," he went on, ignoring my impudence, "that due to a series of bad harvests, châteaux were going begging just then and, of course, Gruner's hurry to get out—"

"I knew they were cheap at that point," I said, "and I did all the research—good research—with many friends there."

"You did nothing of the kind. You were eighty percent lucky, as I said. Now, since that money was mine, or appeared to be, I've taken the liberty, through de Brionne, an old friend, of selling your château; that is, I've written him, asking. And, confound you, at a profit. Luck again. The coming Bordeaux reds and whites look at least Good, if not Very Good, or Excellent, and the market's firmed up. Tell me, you didn't think you and Betsy were going to live in a château like trillionaires, did you?"

"Probably not," I said. "We were going to use it for vacations until

469

we sold it. Besides, we have to be here, near own own vineyards."

"I don't believe you told me," murmured the practical-minded Betsy.

"Well," I said, "a man doesn't burden his wife with fine financial details. How much do you know about the shipping business, Mother?"

"We're off the track," said my father. "It's Christmas, and I'll keep things in the spirit, and make them short. As you know, I'm growing bored with coasting. Harbison and I have decided to go back into the trans-Atlantic trade. One reason is that he acquired two fair square-riggers after an indebtedness—"

Harbison nodded, and I wondered how he'd managed *that* indebtedness, but decided not to ask.

"Yes, at the age of sixty"—my father looked proud—"I'm resuming an enterprise of my youth, and that swings back to châteaux. Gruner's place will be sold. But I'm buying what's apparently a handsome cottage near Bordeaux. Quaint, more English than French, once owned by an Englishman. White plaster, thatched roof and all, and with a wing for visitors. Sits in its own grounds of about three hectares.

"In short," said my father, seeming pleased, "that's my wedding present to you and Betsy. No, you needn't thank me—"

"I wasn't going to," I said. "I would have handled things there in time, perhaps better."

"Are you questioning my decisions?"

"Yes, I am. I've done all the work, and you've tried to seize the reins, as usual. I don't take this kindly."

"You don't take it *kindly?* Are you seeking a confrontation with *me?*"

He looked around at the group, and apologized for what was taking place. "What kind of confrontation?"

"Anything you like. You've played the sneering critic of me long enough, Father. Quite suddenly I'm tired of it. I fought a duel over Gruner's château, and I have a right to do as I like with it, as long as I'm paying the bills. As for de Brionne's mortgage, it no longer exists. I took care of that in a way you probably couldn't have managed. In other words, it required finesse, and maybe a knowledge of épée, the last mostly for fun, or emphasis. And no, I don't feel like explaining it. Not now, at least."

My parent stood up, breathing heavily.

Then *I* stood, outstripping him by an inch or more.

"Don't be a fool, Father," I said. "I'm twenty-one, skilled, and in

470

rock-hard condition. Big as you are, I can pick you up with one hand. And no, you couldn't have won a duel, if indeed you know one sword from another. And while we have it out, I could have done well in both school and college, if you hadn't ridden me two or three times a week about it. I just couldn't suit you, could I? So I reacted from your damned sarcasm and laid my ears back—anyone would. You've got a good enough son—or did have. Now try and find another employee as competent. This one's out."

"William!" said Betsy, stricken.

"The truth is, you're growing old—you are, in fact, sixty-four—and you'd be a fool to make an enemy of me. I learned practically all to be learned about Bordeaux and its wine, and did a good job of it, as I said before. I can do perfectly well without you, and will if I have to. As to the château and the cottage, Betsy and I would eventually have made some such swap, of course. That was before I decided not to be your agent in Bordeaux, as I've done just now."

He sat down uncharacteristically pale, and looked off into space.

Then, shocking us all, he burst into laughter. "Most of what you say is true, I suppose. I've had to fight so hard to restore a family fortune that I failed to see your good points. I've become a bully, tyrannical no doubt, perhaps even a little coarsened.

"I beg you"—turning first to me and then to Betsy—"please do settle for my cottage, if de Brionne can get it. And, William, with all your tough grown-upness, I can't think of a better agent. A duel! My God! . . . And I'll add this—"

"Yes, sir." (He was still my father, disagreement or not.)

"I *was* rough on your schooling, I'm afraid, and I'm sorry about it. And for things lately done in my bull-like way. Especially to all of you for ruining Christmas."

I noticed that my mother was crying, and it occurred to me she'd suffered some subconscious bullying, too.

"Oh, come," said Lockridge. "You haven't ruined Christmas. I'm glad you got these things off your chests. Maybe you can be friends, now—after twenty-one years," he added drily.

Mr. Harbison wiped his eyes, then drew an envelope from his pocket.

"I have here my wedding token, if our host"—a glance at Lockridge, who was eating nuts—"will forgive me presenting it at table. But you see, it more or less goes in tandem with Morrison's."

"Morrison's wasn't quite Morrison's, as it turns out," said my father ruefully.

471

"Betsy and I choose to view it so," I told him.

Harbison then handed the envelope to Betsy. —"And my blessing on you both." (Cough, glasses cleansed.)

"Am I to open it now?" Betsy asked.

"As you please, my dear."

He plainly preferred that she did, and she took out a check (which of course was certified, and crossed, and cashiered, and I don't know what all).

"Yes," he said, when Betsy looked up, shocked, "it's for a honeymoon in your Bordeaux cottage—if we get it and William agrees."

"But, Harbie, we could go twice round the world on this! It's *much* too much!"

"Nonsense, my dear. At my age, I have my fun watching youngsters have theirs." This appeared to strike him as admirable, and he added, after some thought, "Not many elderly persons can say that, I believe. They seem to take a criticial view. Anyhow," he summed up, "I consider you my family."

Then we all got up, I thanked Mr. Harbison sincerely, and Betsy threw her arms around him and kissed him. (He got the pince-nez going again.) My father and I shook hands, just a trifle stiffly, and I half-crushed the bones of his knuckle. But he only nodded and said, "I see what you mean. I've been living in a fantasy world, myself not growing up. And, William, I hope to use civil persuasion and have a very *good* agent."

"The 'good' can work both ways," I said.

We embraced, and both, I think, felt that things would be all right.

After all this, we had Christmas and opened presents for nearly the rest of the day. But they were mixed with wedding gifts, and many, such as affectionate oddities fashioned by my students, I've nearly forgotten in the passage of years.

Gervais and Frances Lockridge gave us a pair of skittish mares and a buggy, and Ramses and Nefertiti came in to hand us a tanned deer hide that Isis had helped them buy; it had wonderfully artistic drawings of delicate deer and bison and wolves and a naked Seneca shooting a bow, and further decorations, almost professional. Whereon Frances, suddenly thoughtful, said, "William, do you remember the painting by one Monsieur Millet you gave us? Of French peasants gleaning in the fields? Well, I read a piece lifted?—copied—from a New York paper that said he might become a classical genius. I'm going to be rich at last. Isn't that grand? But your Monsieur Corot has never sold a painting yet, poor fellow."

"Give him time," I told her.

In some way, this reminded Mr. Harbison of a business transaction. He said, "Before I forget it, on this memorable day, I'll report a curious happening. Last week, an attorney unknown to me appeared at my office and bought that half of wine-land we decided to sell. All of it—1250 acres—and paid *exactly* what we had in mind—*treble!* Just like that. He bought it for a name unfamiliar to me, paid in cash, and refused to discuss it further. I placed the sum in a secure, interest-drawing account."

"What luck!" cried Frances. "Now we have funds to improve the land we have left. Cultivate 'em all—that's my view. Pile it up and buy a railroad or two."

I looked at her with a trace of suspicion. I'd never been sure how rich Frances was. But I didn't trust her, in certain ways, and she emphatically had a mind of her own. Good-hearted girl, the best, but sharp, too sharp to suit me.

And now a wild happening was about to take place, far beyond my experience.

When all the goodnights, and jokes, and other tommyrot had been shouted out of the door, Betsy and I, on snowshoes, mushed silently and self-consciously to my—now our—home. I felt nervous, and my hands were sweating in my gloves. I felt, I thought, much more at home in the Marseilles Meat Market, and I almost wished I were there. As events turned out, it would have been a terrible letdown.

We'd no sooner got inside than Betsy turned in the half-dark (Ramses had left a lamp burning) and said, clasping me around the waist, "William."

"What's wrong?" My voice was slightly trembly.

"I want us to do me a favor. Do you feel nervy, well—not, you know?"

I said yes in a hurry.

"Get a robe and a couple of woolly blankets. I want to go back to the Hermit's cave—the same as when Mr. Slater dried our clothes. It's hard to explain, exactly, but it's been in my mind all day."

It was all up with me, I decided. So far, here, I'd never met an entirely normal girl, and wondered if there was one.

She whispered, "It's something to do with the Falls. I felt that way then, badly. The roar, the river rushing, the wild, bloody history— they do things to a girl. I don't believe I could make you understand. But it's important. Please!"

The last word had a low, urgent, throaty tone, and when I thought back to that body across the firelight, my nervousness faded.

"Hurry up! Please hurry, Bill. And this time don't forget *matches!*"

I added a copy of the *Iris*, thinking of the snow, and Betsy carried my ax. It was still snowing lightly, the drifts had grown, and we had hard going to Goat Island. I was not absolutely positive where the Hermit's cave lay. But when we reached the Three Sisters, Betsy took an unerring line into the woods and on and on through the forest until the dark opening appeared.

It looked uninviting, but only briefly. The night was cold, too cold for this whim, I thought, but I was wrong. Betsy was down on her knees, furiously at work with the *Iris* and some twigs, and tossing aside the robes, I started work outside with the ax. The flame began slowly fighting the cold, then built up and up with pine and dead hardwood, and the cave was suddenly warmer than my house.

Outside, the wind still howled, but not quite drowning the roar of the Falls. This last seemed to make the earth tremble, and probably did, and I began at last to absorb some mystic hint of its power.

Betsy had spread the robe and blankets at her feet beyond the fire. She whispered, "You stay there, just as before. And, Bill"—with a strange, un-Betsy-like laugh—"do dry out your clothes."

I undressed slowly, to mimic the other time, and when the last garment was shed, my nerves were no longer a problem. I had no problem.

"You can turn around, now."

What I saw was what Deke Slater and I had seen, all right, but it was a different girl now, a long way from the prim little chambermaid.

She'd taken down her hair, and her eyes were not blue but greenish and remote. She stood barefoot on a robe, and her clothes were scattered about. She appeared almost to pulsate with the demands of the Falls, and for a second—a second only—I stood gazing at this piece of perfection.

"Now," she whispered. And in a louder voice, "Hurry —*Right now!*"

Nothing in Marseilles, nor any other female, could have interested me again. I had one delusion of being tightly swallowed, and then, scorched by the fire, she dragged me into the snow. This chambermaid turned wanton had for the moment resumed her directorship.

When, finally, we went to sleep, a part of me still hers, some rationality returned and I knew all I needed to understand the Falls. And the hundreds of honeymooners, now and especially later, would never be a mystery any longer. But there remained the Genii's immutable warning.

Chapter LIV

I disliked the look of the weather when Betsy and I started back, on snowshoes and carrying our robes, at about dawn. The snow had stopped, the temperature risen rapidly, and there was an ominous feeling in the air.

Betsy sensed it, too, and asked, "What is it? What's wrong?"

"I don't know. This must be Niagara's wildest winter—where the weather's usually mild and stable, too."

The sky, now that the snow had stopped, was cloudy dark one minute, and then, as the sun struggled up, a kind of coppery color the next. And over all, a gale paradoxically blew from the southwest, in the middle of winter. I disliked that sky. Now and then low clouds scudded before the gale almost on the ground. I'd never seen any such thing before.

I could hear ice grinding in the river, and above it, the roar of the Falls. But the roar was different, somehow. I put it all down, of course, to the gale. Since this wind was blasting our faces, as we tried to get off Goat Island, and the drifting snow smashing us in stinging sheets, I drew up behind the empty toll house for a rest, letting the phenomenon race past.

"This is the wrong time of year," I muttered to Betsy, whose face was white, not only with snow but apprehension. Still, she looked determined as well.

"I don't like it," I kept saying. "I don't like anything about it. And we've got a long way to go. Maybe we should have stayed in the cave."

"We'll make it," she said, putting an arm around me. "And the others'll think we were crazy, spending our honeymoon out there. Did *you* think we were crazy, Bill?"

A big tin sign from a gewgaw shack whipped loose and rolled end over end into the window of another place. It made a jarring sound, and seemed to clear my head.

"Crazy? Let's be crazy often. But we're never going to make it home like this. We'll be buried in a drift. The toll house door's open, and I'll throw everything—axes, robes, blankets in there. Then we'd better tuck in our chins and mush like hell for home. I hope I can find the way."

The wind was rising, and hand in hand we made our way slowly. Our legs were punished with fatigue (and honeymoon) and then, out of the flying drifts, I made out the Eagle Tavern. Two roustabouts, looking grim and sober for once, were leaving as the proprietor boarded up the windows.

One, whom I consistently beat at cards (and had been known to tell others that he'd "fix my wagon good, if he ever caught me out"— meaning nothing; he was as harmless as a mouse) called, "Is that you, Billy? And Ma'am? You'd best scoot for home, and rapid. They's things happening. I'll take you both a-horseback if the lady's tuckered."

I thanked him, said I thought we could make it, and he led his horse off toward a stable. Every building in town was rattling, and we saw a dozen or more shutters break loose and go winging away.

It was good to find our road leading out of town, away from flying objects. I heard Betsy panting, but she never complained, no matter what kind of drift we fell into.

"No good can come of this," I said once, and regretted it, for she was scared enough. But I hadn't considered her the kind to feel fear, not after the events of last night.

When at last I saw our white gate looming up, I felt a glow of relief. And after we'd checked our house over, fastening down shutters and tying doors from the inside, I saw to our new team, whose eyes were walling like marbles. They were nervous. Betsy added to my rations, giving each mare a handful of sugar and an apple. But they were too jumpy to eat, switching around instead and kicking their stalls.

Then we grabbed what food we could carry and made our way to

Lockridge's, hurried on by quick, sudden blasts of wind. Most were at windows, rubbing holes in the frost again, and acting very serious. My father and mother had been going to move to Betsy's and my place, but there was no talk of it now.

Frances—a much subdued Frances— was feeding the fireplace, Mr. Harbison and my mother peered through frost-holes, and both Lockridge and my father went to the back, to study the instruments.

Lockridge, of course, was trying to solve things mathematically, or meteorologically, while my father was saying, "I've seen this phenomenon twice before, at sea. It caused damage."

Lockridge said, "Have a look at this barometer and the wind gauge I built last year. What do you make of *that?*"

My father whistled. "I've seen the glass lower than that one time, in the Barbadoes. I lost a fine little brig."

"But the wind gauge! I don't get it at all. See that?"

"By God, it hit Force Eleven, a single notch below 'hurricane,'" said my father. "Now it's backed off the nearly zero. All we can do is batten down and wait."

Ramses came in from the barn, his face curious and grave, and said something in Lockridge's ear.

"What is it? Indians know more about these matters than we do. What are we in for?"

"I'm not quite sure. Funny," said Lockridge. "I've learned the language well enough to know he's talking about the *river*. And the Falls. But I can't make head or tail of it."

"Don't dismiss it," said my father, leaving for the front room.

All day the thermometer rose rapidly, and the snow commenced to melt, but the gales lashed harder at the house, and seemed likely to pull the place down around our ears. The room was all right for a space, then it filled with smoke. It belched out as if kicked, and scattered little red embers on the rug nearby. They were driven through the iron screen Lockridge had made. Mr. Harbison and Frances scooped these up and stood by.

Betsy and I pushed home after supper, and lay abed, alerted for mysterious noises, both upstairs and down. Half a dozen times I got up to creep down, carrying a rifle (knowing about looting from New York riots) but the storm was the sole invader. A shutter began clattering at one o'clock, and in half an hour blew away altogether. I figured I could find it later, but I never did.

My thoughts were partly on grapes. I wondered if good wine grapes could prosper in such an unpredictable climate. But what was coming had not been seen here before, and probably wouldn't again.

Next day the same—thawing, erratic high winds from the wrong direction, and ourselves sticking close to our homes. Ramses bucked the gales to hire a sleigh, for my father wanted to show Lockridge changes in Niagara over thirty years. But they were back again soon. It was hopeless—dangerous—they said. The remaining snow clogged their vision, and fences and signs were blowing down and tumbling northward all over town. The few people they saw were scurrying for home, looking frightened. The streets were all but bare.

One of Lockridge's horses had a bad cut above its left knee, and Ramses, with the two women, applied a poultice, compounded (I fancied) from bats' wings, horse dung, menstrual blood, spittle, and a handful of Grade A maggots.

Since my mother was not up to snowshoes, we supped again at Lockridge's, off our laps, by the fire. Our host was missing.

But in a minute he called from the back, "Morrison, could you come here a second?" I went back, too.

"I can't believe my eyes. The temperature, now, is dropping two degrees every ten minutes."

My father swore one of his favorite oaths (he had a rich and varied stockpile) and asked, "How much fuel do we have?"

"Coal oil for the kitchen, and Ramses is cutting firewood."

"I'll go help him," said my father, shedding his jacket. He picked up an ax and spat on his hands. I was amazed; I hadn't thought of him doing work like that for twenty years.

In an hour, we had freezing again, and Lockridge called, "Wind's swung to steady due north. Now figure *that* out!"

Betsy and I went home soon after eating. Our house was icy in front, and I built a big fire, part of whose heat sifted upstairs. I thanked the saints for Gervais' below-frost pump (we had nothing else to freeze). The horses were blanketed tight, and I carefully left a coal oil lamp in the barn. Then we went to bed early, using what covers we had left.

It was past two when I snapped fully awake, knowing something was wrong. Not waking Betsy, I tried to make it out. The wind had eased off a trifle, and the house was no longer talking. Still—some important change had taken place. I felt the gooseflesh rise on my arms.

I stole out to peer through a window toward the Falls, and was struck all of a heap, as they say.

The Falls had stopped! And the river was not flowing!

No sound whatever came from that quarter, even on a north wind.

It was unbelievable, yet we had the evidence of our ears. I called Betsy, and she came silently to stand beside me, awed by something that couldn't happen.

Now we heard people running in the streets, horses neighing, and all manner of babble and shouting. Betsy and I threw on our sheepskins and headed for Lockridge's. On our way, two wagons rattled slewed by in the refrozen slush and mud, and others seemed to be coming.

I heard a man yell, "It's the end of the world, so writ and so prophesied! God help us all!" And from the sounds swelling up behind us, the whole town appeared in a panic.

But when we got to Lockridge's, with everybody up and dressed, and looking uncertain, Lockridge had pretty well worked out matters, of course.

For two days the gales had blown from the southwest, breaking up ice on Lake Erie, and starting it to its outlet, the Niagara River. But as it ground past Buffalo, where the Niagara began, the wind untypically shifted to the north. All the ice was stopped, forming a mighty barricade.

"From there," said Lockridge, "probably only a short time was needed for the river to run out, the bed dry up, and the Falls stop entirely. I wish I could carry this simple fact to the town."

But it was too late, for any practical purpose. People were congregating in churches to pray for the Right Road, now that the world was done, and (I learned) the loudest wailers included the river rats who'd been so profane before. Clusters of people were on their knees in the churches and on the streets, and some were singing hymns of salvation.

And in the streets, when Lockridge and my father and Betsy and I reached them (Mother and Frances stayed behind, with Isis and Nefertiti—holding a bow—and Ramses went to my house, to protect it) there was such a ding-dong, wheel-screeching, blim-blamming din of an uproar, with both men and women running and wagons careening around corners, and signboards littering everything, that *I* commenced to wonder if the world had run its course. Certainly these people looked unfamiliar, or maybe humans en route to a new destination.

The night was still dark, of course, but the sky had an unearthly glow, and I finally figured that all was up. Lockridge had miscalculated. We had to step into three doorways to avoid being hit by panicked teams and rigs, and I saw at least one wagon skid round a corner onto its side. The driver got up cussing, so I assumed he

480

hadn't made the Transition yet. More order prevailed at De Veaux's, where the owners and clerks had turned out to form a ring around it, as an antilooter device. The Eagle had, to be sure, reopened for the journey, whatever it might be, and numerous men were pouring down Monongahela to grease them for the trip. And meanwhile, if one or two strangers broke off to poke into unguarded stores, that was the owner's bad luck.

We could just barely see, and wished we couldn't. This was a town gone wild. A rough-appearing man bumped into my father, and grasped him by the coat. "Hand over your purse and wallet, by God, or I'll—"

My father, who was about twice as broad, despite his age, knocked him flat, with an unhealthy cracking of bone. But these kinds of incidents were few, compared to the people turning saintly, and saying so, in public.

We passed the Baptist Church, and the entire flock was on the floor, making a noise like bees humming. Mrs. Olmstead, a friend, who worked the melodeon, was trying to play, "Oh God, Our Help in Ages Past," but she was so rattled her fingers hit the wrong keys and what came out was a medley of four or five tunes, sounding pretty eerie. The fact of church bells ringing all over town, at that time of night, added to the panic.

The constable ran out in the street, making some pretense to restore order, and was jostled so badly he swallowed his whistle. Taken to a doctor, he made it through all right, though it required "castor oil to uncork an elephant." (The doctor's words.)

Worried about the women, we went back to check, and found my mother and Frances calm by now; Ramses showed up and Mr. Harbison, rather formally dressed, but not scared. On the way from International, he'd somehow made notes on five men he saw looting, and argued the notes would be valid in court. Also, he'd been obliged (and apologized for it) to coldcock a stickup man with his umbrella.

Dawn came at last, with the town racket slightly subdued, and a deathly silence from the Falls. Nefertiti gave us a hasty but good breakfast of pancakes and a platter of ham and eggs, and some kind of Seneca dish to ward off evil spirits (*not* the potion), for we planned, all of us, to go to Goat Island when full light came.

We made an odd procession, my father helping my mother; Lockridge trying to help that impudent Frances, who now, was having a sprightly time; me with a gun strapped on, and Mr. Harbison carrying his beautiful little derringer.

By now, the town understood that the river was dry, and the Falls

481

nonexistent, though nobody knew why. A perfect stream of men, women and children and wagons jammed in traffic headed toward the scene, both above and below the Falls.

A brief attempt had been made by two wags to man the closed toll booth, but more of their general kind had assisted them into pools of water, and we went on to Goat Island without challenge.

Wearing boots, we sloshed toward the Three Sisters, ventured to the farthest, and beheld a sight that, Lockridge said, we'd probably never see again.

Everywhere you looked, the river bottom was shining bare, rocks that made the rapids showing here and there, as well as ice-bergs that had yet to break off and crash over. We tiptoed to a safe flat part of the bed, daylight come now, and the quirk I remember best was hundreds and hundreds of turtles, mainly on their backs, strewn up and down the bed. Lots of fish were either flapping or dead.

I saw two boys struggling to right a turtle the size of a washtub, with a string they'd tied round its neck, hoping, I suppose, to drag him home and feed on turtle steaks and soup the rest of the winter.

Wagons and buggies were out where the river had been, and were picking up loads of that water-soaked wood which, dried out a little, made such a roaring hot fire. But maybe the majority of people here wanted souvenirs to sell next summer.

When the winter tourists ventured out, some (showing off) even rode horses, but stepping pretty gingerly, too. The river was absolutely stopped. Only a thin trickle—maybe six inches deep—ran through crevices in the Canadian Horseshoe. You could jump over it.

Within a hundred yards, I found a long-drowned Indian tomahawk, and we found six others before we were through. We crossed from American to Canadian, each holding to another, for it was slippery in spots, and then examined what we'd never see again—the dry rimrock of that mighty cascade in Canada as well as America. It thrust out, I thought, with a sheepish look, like a person who's got his clothes ripped off before a crowd. The green lagoon below had dropped a few feet, of course, and I learned that the Great Whirlpool, on downriver, was now all but unmoving but still mysteriously deep, awaiting what impended.

By noon, the booming of ice-floes breaking upriver had audibly increased, and all but my father and Lockridge and me went home to rest.

"It's still too cold for a widespread thawing," said Lockridge, scientifically proving that many small animals had been exposed, and turned out bewildered, from their hibernation. He was collecting fossils, too.

482

Winter tourists from both sides now rode horses onto the dry bed, and I had one of my "typical" ideas (Father). While he and Lockridge "collected," speculating on the Falls' geological past—placing it at the Ridge Road between Lewiston and Lockport, which I already knew—I slipped off and came back riding my lead mare with only a halter. I had no saddle.

My father gave me an unfriendly look.

I cried, "Everybody's doing it. Look over there."

More frolickers on the Canadian side than on the American were riding to impress their girls or wives, and I joined them for a while.

Coming back, at about one o'clock, I judged—thinking they would all be hungry—I had gone a way upstream and just stepped onto the American half, when I heard a crashing that froze my insides. An ice-block the size of a church had somehow broken loose and was tumbling over and over toward us. I kicked hard at the mare, who then slipped and fell down, pinning me briefly.

I scrambled up and dove pell-mell for shore, or the head of Goat Island, but the horse had trouble regaining her feet on the rock and moss. Her front quarters rose three or four times, as I heard shouts of people running free below; and then the cake—towering over us with thousands of green diamonds sparkling—gathered the mare like a pebble and carried her on down and over.

Despite my father's and Lockridge's urgent shouts, as they ran toward me, I sat down in the river and cried. Betsy and I, so proud of our gift, had yesterday named that mare Minerva, from the way she held her head, and I didn't think I could face her.

And I felt answerable to Gervais and Frances as well. It was a wonderful, strong, shiny-black little horse, and could not be replaced.

Nobody upbraided me. The two men picked me up and walked me to the point of Goat Island. I tried to think of something handy to say, but failed. And that night, going out to the stable, as if I meant to tell Juno, I put my head on a rail, grieving. Betsy said nothing, only holding me all night, and at about two o'clock, again, we heard a terrible crashing, and presently the familiar roaring, and we crept to the window, aware that the river had bored through and the Falls were smashing down once more. But the next day, when we got up, I still felt that I'd ruined the holidays. My mother and father and Mr. Harbison were staying until New Year's, and we heard all manner of stories about lost people, animals, wagons and buggies. On that second evening, at least half the town had regathered in the churches, still hoping (I figured) for the end of the world, with things looking better the second time around.

Defeated, they were the ones that spread most of the stories. I suppose they were ashamed, and needed excuses for timidity. One brazen-faced jackass. a stranger, collared me in the street and told me, blow-by-blow, what had happened to a "young fool named Morrison," who, he said, had been dunce enough to ride a thoroughbred saddle horse halfway up an ice-berg. "Trying to show off and be king, you apprehend, and pushed the horse under to save hisself, when the cake begun to go.

"Didn't give two figs for the pore horse," he told me. "Laughed and bragged about it later. They tell me he's some kind of liquor merchant. Now don't that square with the breed?"

I lowered my face toward him, and said, "Bullshit!"

"Said what?" He backed off.

"In politer terms—humbug, tommyrot and piffle. You and your lies. Why don't you skulk back to church?"

"Now looka here. Statements like them can get a body's head uprooted. For two cents, I'd—"

He turned and skedaddled before I had my coat completely off. I surmised he was one of the many traders, high and low, caught here by the storm, and I didn't mind that I'd slipped back into violence. I felt bad enough as it was.

The Eagle reopened, of course, and was in good shape except for the back door being removed (though none of the stock was missing). Mr. Murdock had tied an Eskimo husky inside, one he kept starved down for occasions, and there was evidence of intruders, for a right trouser-leg lay on the floor, together with considerable blood.

There were stories, rumor and lies galore. A regular Eagle client told me he'd seen a Canadian man unhitch and rest his horses beside a cache of logs near Luna Falls (in the middle) and the wagon had quietly rolled over with the man unaware and stacking wood till he hit the lagoon.

"It was the absentee of noise that done it," said my informant. Then he had the gall to strike me for a chew of tobacco.

There was the rumor that the "entire fourth grade" of the Canadian school had been smashed and swept down, but this shaped up as absurd because the river (and ice) commenced reflowing at two A.M., and it was unlikely they'd be turning out for classes then.

Deke Slater was said to be missing. A man saw him chipping ice from a berg into a glass he'd taken out, with a bottle, and it was assumed he'd mooched on that berg about ten minutes too long. But he was found by and by, drunk behind the Methodist organ, so that worked out to be a lie, too.

As far as I could learn, no lives were lost during the whole jamboree, but people naturally preferred to believe that casualties were high. I talked to Red Gill, and he saw nothing of interest lodged in the Whirlpool.

The family were coming to us for New Year's Eve, and my father had got Gervais Lockridge to drive him and Mr. Harbison around town, to inspect Cataract House, boarded up and gloomy; the start of the Suspension Bridge; Lewiston; and even Rattlesnake Charley's sad, decaying old shack—and, of course, some of our acreage. The three even planned to take a ferry over below the Falls (they normally ran all winter) but big hunks of ice still fell now and then.

All day Betsy and the rest had prepared our house for a merry good time, with decorations, a backlog fire (by Ramses); and the women had broken off briefly to attend an afternoon service, to greet people Betsy knew.

But me, I wandered around lonely, and when I came back, toward evening, I remembered that Juno might be lonely, too. I went to the stable, carrying apples, my heart dull with apology, and, filling the stall beyond Juno, was Minerva, or as near a replica as a sculptor might make.

I stopped, dumbfounded, thinking I'd lost my mind, when the barn door opened and closed softly behind me, and my mother came up and stood alongside. Then my father came in to watch us both.

"No," he said, "don't look to me." He sighed. "You're an incorrigible, William—you remind me of myself at your age—let's leave it at that. And as I said, I'm not without guilt. But it was one of your perfectly typical acts, losing that horse. Still, it's the New Year, or will be soon. I suggest we forget it."

His tone mellowed. "You, too. The fact is"—and I could see it cost him dearly—"I might have done the same thing once. I *know* I would," he added, thinking he'd been too severe.

"But how—?"

My mother said, "I knew horses well as a girl. You probably never knew that. With some help this morning— Well, she *is* a beauty, isn't she? And they're as alike as twins."

"Mother, I—"

But my father interrupted. "Oh, come on. Everybody's waiting." After kissing my mother, as if I meant it, for the first time in years, I let them go on ahead.

It was a Happy New Year.

Epilogue

I'm coming closer to the end, now, but I naturally want to tell how the wine came out. In mid-spring, with our free school suspended awhile, we planted Gervais' native cellar grapes in the twenty-five acres cleared near Lewiston. He'd carefully tended them, in clean, coarse sand, moist but not wet, close together on the dirt floor. He'd worked the sand through the root tendrils, and covered each plant with little sandy mounds. Now and then he'd moistened the sand, for if the roots dried out they died. We used oxen and the trench-plowing method, and manured the soil lightly to a depth of twenty inches. (Overmanuring weakens the grape-stem.)

I don't think the crew we hired much believed in our operation, and considered us amusing amateurs. (They were not far wrong.) When the plants grew higher, they were known as canes, and these were "athallized" from time to time. What that means is pinching off buds to avoid too many canes shooting off the sides and up.

In the late winter, too, we'd cleared about a hundred acres just south of Buffalo, and to plant these involved a curious fact. As I said once before, we were after whitish grapes to make good white wine, as de Brionne and the Bordeaux *Syndicat d'Initiative* (Chamber of Commerce) thought possible; and then we were, briefly, up a stump for the proper grapes.

487

Here Mr. Harbison, looking as formal as always, came up burdened by a sufficiency of our familiar Delaware grape-plants. I don't think these were connected in any way with the state of Delaware. In fact they got their start in New Jersey; don't ask me why.

In any case, Delaware grapes somehow shifted to the town of Delaware, Ohio, New Jersey presumably not thinking very highly of grapes, or of wine, either, for that matter. In the Ohio town, these small, pink, good-eating grapes caught the attention of vintners, who probably came from an old country of white-wine growers.

In one patch, we put down the plants sent over by de Brionne (with his reservations about their success) and carefully marked the place.

In course of time, we (our employees) staked the canes, keeping them as straight as possible. In the main, we had good employees, because we paid good wages; these were made easy by the profitable sale of half our original 2500 acres.

Ordered—and to arrive in several months—were vats, large and smaller casks; I talked to my one-time difficult student, Ebenezer, and his father, and they agreed to get help and construct these during the summer growing period. (If there was a long-time Niagara native who failed to know how to make an expert barrel, I never met him. Their original motive was, of course, somewhat different, or mobile.)

A large, stout barn stood on our Buffalo property, and we had a cellar, lined with thick concrete, dug beneath this for the fermentation, aging and storage.

Needless to say, the town became interested, and we received many reliable suggestions, together with nonsense from the Eagle Tavern. All of us, Frances and Betsy included, worked hard, helping supervise, and Frances finally came to feel that, socially, she'd even eclipsed her former niche at Cataract.

In off times, Betsy and I continued to work on our house, took drives, and went often to look at the Falls, me almost having forgotten her affinity for the now rapidly booming attraction.

Any number of resort hotels were going up, and the town was crowded.

Mr. Harbison shuttled back and forth from New York, to solve small legal snarls inevitable in the ownership of all that land. I noticed that, without making enemies of anyone at Niagara, he usually maneuvered so that we came out on top, somehow. He was, by the way, not quite so fastidious at Buffalo.

An example was that the worthless farmer who'd owned the long untilled land where the barn stood brought forth a man described as "my lawyer." Then he claimed that the barn was not included in the deed—a feeble swindling attempt. Since we'd been absent from that area for more than a week, he and his sons had already ripped off part of one side.

Without emotion, Mr. Harbison filed suit for trespass, destruction of property, damages, and one or two other counts; then proved that the "lawyer" was not a lawyer at all but a defrocked evangelist. Rather than go to jail, the man packed up and left for Wyoming Territory. I believe he was wanted nearly everyplace else. So it was said at the Eagle, whose clientele had settled on the perfectly (to them) logical explanation that "Pore old Billy's gone off his head, and we'd like to help him but cain't."

But when Mr. Harbison won this victory, the river rats practically dragged him from his usual suite at International and down "to jine the club." They said, "Anybody makes Buffler look sick is a Charter Member at Eagle."

Then they allowed him to buy them all drinks, and he himself tossed down a jolt of Monongahela without batting an eye (I was there); and from then on he dropped in regularly. He was regarded as odd but "Chock to the gunnels with grit—one of the best men we got, and I'll fight the skunk that—" etc., the usual.

I should have said that Mr. Harbison, and the court, not only made that farm family restore the ripped-off side but repair other flaws, including reroofing and digging the basement clean as a whistle, ready for concrete.

Our impeccable attorney was, to be sure, only doing his job, but I began to feel guilty, as no good and shiftless as those scoundrels were, so I gave them a hundred dollars, and explained that Mr. Harbison was running for governor, and needed to make a good showing.

Well, *weren't* they satisfied! The money for their small part of our tracts was long ago spent, and most had never seen a hundred dollars before. So they became friends, and finally went to work for us.

One cool evening, after we'd come in from the fields (and me from Ebenezer's father's shop), we were sitting before a small fire, reminiscing, and Frances spoke up to say, "Isn't it fortunate? I'm to have the baby before harvest time! I don't quite know about the baby, but nothing could make me miss the harvest."

Well, she'd been growing some around the middle, but it was so gradual nobody noticed it, and I put it down to her splendid appetite. She was a tough bird and no mistake, but she managed to shed a few tears (probably concocted for the occasion) when we congratulated and kissed her, and shook Gervais' hand.

As always, he accepted the honor without emotion, as if to say, "Oh, anybody could have done it. Don't give it a thought."

At this typical display, Frances at last grew nettled, and said, "Surely, you can get up from that sprawl and show a *little* joy at becoming a father!"

"My dear," he said wearily, "I've been aware of this blessed event, as the embarrassment goes, for a month or more. *You* should have known. In any case, I hope you don't consider *me* blind. Moreover, I'm a scientist—amateur to be sure, but with a substantial following."

"Father!" cried Betsy severely.

This caused him to rise, groaning (he'd worked hard that day), kiss his bride, congratulate her (and himself) and then subside.

"Some father!" said Frances. "You'd think one of his mares was about to foal," but she looked at him fondly.

In late September, we buckled down to the harder if more delicate work. Our first grapes were about to be harvested. We were pleased that, in the Lewiston tract, the loss to hungry boys, and others, had been minimal. We wondered why, but sure enough, one of Harbison's agents (armed) had caught a man filling a pushcart from our crop. Harbison had won a change of venue, and the fellow had been fined fifty dollars by a city judge new to the job. The fellow hadn't fifty dollars of course, or a dollar-fifty, so we made him night watchman.

The judge further ruled that parents henceforth would be liable for their children's thefts. This news nearly broke the Eagle Tavern apart; Mr. Harbison came as near to getting drunk as I ever saw him.

It was human nature that anything bad happening to Lewiston came as good news to Niagara; and Harbison, it was stated, had "put them squawking buzzards in their place. Now there ain't nothing lower than a thief!"

And they clapped the lawyer on his back so hard and so often that a gold cufflink popped out in the confusion, and a loudmouth talker snatched it up and scooted.

But Mr. Murdock had seen him, and made him give it back the next day.

"That bauble got catched in my trouser-leg, and I never noted it till I sobered up this morning," the man explained without a trace of guilt.

Mr. Harbison only smiled and thanked him.

* * *

For some time, I'd been astonished at how low the great clusters grew to the ground. But there were plenty of these, all right, except in the Lewiston area. From the start, it seemed evident that the site was too damp and the soil too rich, and in the end, we opened the vines to the town, which later made the area an exceptional orchard.

We transferred our operations to Buffalo's hundred acres, hired wagons, and mainly women—housewives—to pick, and checked Ebenezer's oak casks and the barn where they were going.

We'd bought a special kind of bottles and the best corks from New York. These bottles had to be of a particular toughness, to withstand pressure while they lay on their sides, for the wine's further aging.

The Buffalo grapes were healthy, pink and delicious, and had a sturdy, wholesome look. After our two untimely blizzards, we'd had a moderate winter, with everything working in favor of growing good grapes. And now, at picking time, the weather was sunny and *dry*— an essential.

For some time, too, I'd wondered how producing wines could justify all this work and expense, but it was astonishing how quickly the big wagons filled, and their contents were carefully lifted into our two vats. And everything moved fast, now, because you couldn't dally here—the juice would sour.

Husbands of the Buffalo women were happy to have their wives bringing in money, with only the outlay of well-honed knives, and the women were relieved to be free of home. But their allure might have ripened, I thought, if they'd hitched up their skirts behind, as at de Brionne's, following the Bordeaux custom.

Ebenezer emerged as *chef de culture*. He may have been slow in his studies, but his touch with grapes could scarcely be matched.

Ten barefoot people trod the two vats, and these, I'm glad to say, included Frances. I think the chief interest from Buffalo, with the towns around, was not so much in the vats as in the size and number of the clusters. People drove out by the hundreds to watch, especially on weekends. Their general attitude could be locally phrased: "Well, if that don't beat all!"

By Lockridge's reckoning, we'd ordered a thousand of the special bottles and corks, but for once, science had missed fire, badly. As joint *Maîtres*, Gervais and I stood looking, while the wagons rolled in, and the monster clusters went into the vats, the juice far too much for our containers.

Our big mistake was ignorance that these grapes were nearly pure juice. As soon as the barefoot women crushed them (lightly, as not to mix in stems and pink skins, but to lay pulp bare) the pulp was removed to a secondhand cider press that completed the job of dejuicing. And then we siphoned the juice into Ebenezer's large casks for fermentation. This process would take from thirty to sixty days. (The casks had been soaked for a week in cold water and then in hot water to "sweeten" them.)

The fermentation casks were kept only two-thirds full, for the process here was known as "violent fermentation." The aroma of these, by the way, was agreeably pungent, so maybe some of the visitors drove out for that. The vats' empty third, on top, was to allow for rising gases and small bits of stem and skin.

As for Frances, her baby, a male, *had* been born before the harvest, and, holding him in her arms, she became another barefoot nymph of the vats. Seeing Lockridge, she called, "It's absolutely wizard, darling! What luck I washed my feet this morning!"

"Last night."

"Darling," she went on, "I believe your son is becoming intoxicated from the fumes. Will it hurt him?"

"It hasn't hurt *you*," said her husband, and turned to attend other crises.

When fermentation was complete, the wine was "racked"—transferred to smaller oak casks for aging, while care was taken not to disturb the sediment, or "lees," in the fermentation casks. (Another racking rite was gone through when the wine was removed from the aging casks.)

The aging casks, unlike the others, are filled to the top. Oddly enough, a certain evaporation takes place through the wood; Ebenezer was charged with the job of adding to and keeping all these full.

Now we must mention a sensitive step: While in the aging casks, the wine "breathes," and if the breathing leaves too much air, at any time, the wine may turn to vinegar. Ideally for aging, I should say, the temperature should be in the neighborhood of 55 degrees Fahrenheit, or slightly cooler than for red claret.

We eventually learned that, normally, the aging process for such white wine should run from six months to a year. But it can be drunk in a few weeks without pain. Good reason for the short aging process here is that white wine continues to age in the bottle.

Overanxious, of course, we began to turn cask tops and test the wine within six months. It was surprisingly good, but it seemed, to both Lockridge and me, to have a more affirmative, or "flintier," taste than the comparable Graves we knew.

So—we decided to bottle in exactly a year's time from picking. And here we learned our grievous lesson. We found ourselves flooded with a shocking superabundance of wine. As Ebenezer observed, trying to take the blame, we should have known from the number (and size) of those aging casks. In a word, we'd all miscalculated, as stated.

The thousand bottles ordered from my father were in fifths; they scarcely made a dent in our volume. He managed us four thousand more. These were promptly filled, the corks capped in sealing wax (according to my researches) and stored on their sides, in cellar racks.

Then we had to buy and cleanse gallon jugs, which made no great difference, and it was Ebenezer, at last, who solved the problem. He bought, sanded inside and out, and washed all the stout oak barrels up and down the river. And we filled *those*—with none left over, either.

Altogether, and we could hardly believe it, we'd bottled nearly thirty thousand gallons of wine from those hundred acres! (My pomp about my Bordeaux researches began appreciatively to subside.) Clearly we had far overplanted. Make that total a little less, for the five acres allotted to de Brionne's plants produced grapes inferior for processing here. This was not their kind of soil and weather; the truth is, they never grew much larger than buttons.

It was now, with both cellar and barn bulging, that we rented another, nearby, barn, to round things out. For the next year, we decided, another storehouse of our own must be built, and who knew how many more following that. After all, we still owned 1125 acres, which, if cultivated, meant big business indeed.

But we had problems enough with our hundred acres. And here my father and Mr. Harbison stepped in to lend a hand, out of their experience.

Some of those jugs—and barrels—had to be sold, and quickly. We needed the cash. The wine in the bottles was aging, and we decided to leave that alone, later to be sold for a higher price.

My father had a friend named Lyman A. Spaulding, a boat builder operating a fleet on the Erie. There were, I might say, a few steamboats now on the Canal, but Spaulding's were the old-fashioned horse-drawn boats, which he thought safer. It was "arranged" that Mr. Spaulding convey our containers to Albany, where they would be transferred to a coastal ship of my father's.

"But what then?" I asked him, on one of their trips to our vineyard. "How will the stuff be sold?"

"Don't worry about it," my father said. "We'll have it decanted and properly labeled—"

"That would be?—" began Lockridge.

"Properly, meaning attractively, suitably, in such a way as to attract buyers. I can see," he went on business-dreamily, looking over the fields (deeply interested for the first time), "that this shapes up— luck again—as a large commercial enterprise. Our expenses and time will be deducted, of course. I'm a man of commerce," he said, as if I didn't know his twists and turns, and Harbison's.

"Labels," mused Lockridge. "I'm afraid we never thought of them. What could they say?"

Mr. Harbison harrumphed and murmured, "Taken care of, all taken care of. And entirely within legal bounds!"

I wasn't so sure, or thought the labels might skip a tightrope. But I didn't say so.

What we did before starting another crop, I could scarcely say. But we seemed always to be busy. We taught school for a while, off and on, but Niagara Falls was building a school of its own, and had a regular schoolmaster. Both Lockridge and I were given town medals for our volunteer work, in a ceremony at City Hall, and while I rather enjoyed it, Lockridge squirmed and sweated.

I'd sent a case of wine (twelve fifths) to de Brionne, and now we had an answer. For the reading of this, we four assembled at Lockridge's.

"How does it shape up?"

"Well, good and bad. Or somewhere in between."

I read:

My Dear William:

Your wine arrived, and I'll try being as helpful as I can. First, I had the Bordeaux Syndicat d'Initiative test it, and they gave it an individual mark of "Passable."

I realize that this is a blow to your hopes, but when I explained your bare start at viniculture they (and I) decided that, with proper cultivation, more mature vines, and much more aging in the bottle, you will have a *fine* white wine, similar to ours here.

What I, and they, tasted was a little sharp. (I recall you mentioned "too aggressive" in your note.) And I think that comes close: slightly sharp, flintiness too pronounced, and, my dear boy, of a very faint pinkness when held up to the light.

No doubt your vignerons will learn more caution for the next crop. Now, I'm aware that my bottles from you have aged only a few months; these will be mellower and better in two years. We must thank le bon Dieu that red claret is not our concern here!

494

Only recently, I remind you, it was Bordeaux's custom to let that product age for fifteen years! (Now, I feel sure, they have shortened that span, being as avaricious as most Frenchmen.)

The baron's, and then your, château has been sold to a most agreeable count and his family, from Chantilly, I think. (The family were in the wine trade a generation or so ago, so they are not without experience.)

I have inspected—well, to tell the truth, I found it for him— the "cottage" bought by your father, and we all regard it as charming. We miss you, and will be hard to contain, until you decide to visit us again, taking the chance of losing your new bride!

Yours affectionately,

DE BRIONNE

"I don't suppose your father can get much for *that* swill," said Frances, steering her offspring from trouble with her stockinged feet.

"My dear girl," said her husband, "you forget that he's comparing our wine with the finest white wine of Bordeaux. And he does offer hope for our future. Be of good cheer."

The two had enjoyed their first spat over the naming of the child. Lockridge, taking everything into account, had fixed on the atrocity of "Bacchus," but Frances stepped in, fighting mad, to observe that, as their last link with England, she was determined on "Lancelot," the boy to be called "Lance" for short. Lockridge shrugged it off, putting his mind on other matters. He suggested "Bacchus" as a middle name, but it didn't seem to fit, somehow.

Then, on a day after the letter, Mr. Harbison arrived with some startling figures. The harvest was about to be reckoned.

"I have all the figures," he said. "We left to age, I believe, five thousand bottles, and sent the weighty rest to New York. Sold at wholesale, using the name 'Delaware White Wine, Bottled and Aged'" (aged!) "'at the Cascade Vineyards, of Northern New York,' we disposed of the remaining twenty-nine thousand gallons at the wholesale rate of fifty cents a bottle. The gross sum," he said, furiously cleaning his glasses, "is precisely seventy-two thousand, five hundred and twelve dollars and eighteen cents.

"For our first harvest, at least, there were numerous expenses— labor, plants, casks, vats, presses and incidentals. Next year, some are unneeded, but we'll still have the plants, salaries, administrative lodgings in Buffalo, and others for Ebenezer and his father, transportation and the like.

"However," he said, pleased, "your profit, even split among partners, could reasonably be called a bonanza. Wine is catching on in this country, and *good* wine will go at a premium. I foresee," he added, looking off into space, "a day when most of the hills between here and Canandaigua will be ripe with grapes, and when Delaware White Wines will be as famous as anything Bordeaux has to offer.

"And if the vineyard is to be expanded—remember the unplanted 1125 acres—things should be placed on a professional basis: offices, employees' huts, contracts for bottles and hauling, larger space for storing, other—"

Here I saw Lockridge stir uneasily.

"And now," said Harbison firmly, with a look at Frances, "I feel it my business duty, though breaking a promise, to reveal the real buyer of half our original 2500 acres."

"Harbie!" cried Frances.

"I am employed," he said firmly, "to act on the firm's behalf. I had no concept of what a successful vineyard might mean. A sum of money put at bank interest is hardly a sum invested in wine grapes. My duty, as I see it, is to protect you *all!*"

"*You* bought it?" inquired Lockridge, turning to his wife.

"I'll never forgive you, Harbie, never!"

She was close to tears, but she said, "I thought other people here might be interested, but only at today's normal price. If we could make our acreage pay, that is. That's *not* a selfish motive, you know."

"If a hundred acres brings in a gross of seventy-two thousand, five hundred dollars, then twenty-five hundred acres—well, the hell with it. Dammit!" said Lockridge, with far more than normal vehemence, "All this is what I tried to get away from."

"Darling, I'll do exactly as you please. Now I *have* it!" she said, inspired. "We'll give it to the Methodist Church! They've been ever so sweet."

"Why not the Anti-Saloon League?"

"My suggestion," said Mr. Harbison dryly, "is to think it over for six months and then," turning to Frances, "you can decide."

And so we left it.

Betsy and I planned our long-delayed honeymoon to Bordeaux for March, before the next spring planting. We were depressed by the great events arising before us. None, including my father (he told me later) and Mr. Harbison—so set in his bachelor ways—wanted to be a mighty mogul of trade.

"Bets," I said, "let's walk down toward the water."

Somehow, things had gone wrong, despite our financial success. As

496

we went toward Goat Island, she said, pleading, "William, I *like* our simple village life. I like the people, and they like me. For the first time, lately, the roar of the Falls almost seems the solution to everything. I'm afraid."

From Terrapin Point, I watched the mists wave like funeral plumes, not knowing how to reply, holding her elbow lightly. Warning voices spoke again from that deluge. I wanted badly, now, to conquer its power. But if I failed, what would the coming years bring?

How many lives had it claimed, as it slowly moved up in its good or evil way? I thought back to the first day I came here. How many friends had failed to understand? Samantha; Charley; well-remembered Hermit—won't you come to us and tell us what you know?

Betsy? The Falls?

Niagara Falls,
Bordeaux—1979

Acknowledgments

The author is greatly indebted to Donald Loker, director of local history at the Niagara Falls Public Library, who made available all his shelves of material about the area in its heyday, during the mid-1800s—early newspapers, county documents, the first histories, maps, guide books and the like.

I am equally grateful to Miss Marjorie Williams, head of the Niagara Falls Historical Society, who indefatigably produced from her vast collection memorabilia of perhaps a more personal nature. These included such treasures as old registers rescued from the great hotels of the past, letters, diaries, journals and photographs. (Among her registers from Cataract House, the signatures of "A. Lincoln and family," Edward, Prince of Wales, many of Europe's royalty and American statesmen are to be found, usually written in pretty ornate scrawls, as was the custom then.)

It should be said that Miss Williams' father had, before her, been the Historical Society head, and had thus passed along a great deal of anecdote and color from his own recollections.

(Marjorie Williams, almost uniquely popular in the region, died of a heart attack a few months ago.)

Many elderly persons, on both the American and Canadian sides of the river, generously gave up their time to reminisce about the

Falls life in pioneer days; and George Little-Fawn, a college-orea Seneca, who presently farms a few miles downriver, contributed many valuable stories (these handed down from his forebears) about the relationships that existed between the Senecas and other tribes and the whites who sifted in. Mr. Little-Fawn, by the way, does not believe in the legend of an Indian maiden annually given to the Falls in sacrifice; he feels that whites contrived this for the tourist trade.

All newspapers—the Niagara Falls *Gazette,* the Buffalo *Courier-Express* and many others—were eager to make available their sources bearing on the time and place. This was also true of the several other historical societies in the area, and of present-day residents of Niagara Falls.

Finally, the work done by my wife, Judith Martin Taylor, in helping with research, typing, copy-reading and expert editing, can only be described as immeasurable.

*

The author considers it fair to emphasize the obvious fact that certain liberties have been taken with time sequences here. All the "stunts," for example, could scarcely have taken place in a single summer, so that in some cases the most dramatic of them have been used, faithful to detail, as if they followed one another in close order.

Also, Cataract House *was* Cataract House, and General Parkhurst Whitney was its proprietor. However, he emerges in this book as a generally fictional character, with points of similarity to the original. (Other recognizable personages have been drawn with accuracy.)

For the above tailoring the author claims poetic license and makes no apology.

—R. L. T.